As part of the **Núminway Chronicles**:

* * *

I0634197

MAGIC'S HEART

by

Thomas Oliver

September 2011

*

2nd Edition January 2014

*

Cover designed and produced by

James Willis,
SpiffingCovers

*

Inspired by the artwork of
Jennifer Lea

A Beginning...

How often through the years do we listen as others, speaking sadly and, often, not a little afraid, tell that something, somehow, feels... *not quite right* with their lives? How many times, either in brief moments of doubt or through long years of uncertainty, do we each feel the same? This is not necessarily to speak merely of the myriad regular, personal, day-to-day things – those which can seem to threaten to accost us with unrelenting regularity and severity as we move or more often are moved along through the hectic passage of our lives: of being in the wrong profession; of a difficult or painful relationship with family and those we would call our friends and our loved ones; and of other such matters and problems so trivial and yet so grand, so common and yet so unique to all peoples across our wide and little world. No – rather this is to ask of the deeper questions: those whose foundations lie universal beneath us all, whether we see them or not; those which haunt the thoughts and dreams of those who are open to them; questions so profound as to be often impossible to put into words, though the feelings they bring come clear and undeniable... The feeling that something is missing; that something is wrong with the world. And the feeling that there must be more to these lives we live upon it, not simply more as defined and limited by the searching for love or adventure or wealth or other such yearnings of endless dreams, but *more* even than that. The feeling perhaps that we, either alone or as a people, simply *don't belong*. What is the meaning of all this? we ask ourselves. What is the meaning of these lives we live; the truth of them; the *point* of them?

And those who we ask would often have us believe that we will never understand these things. From our very first years they, or most of them at least, would have us *know* that these are the eternal mysteries of life, the grand unconquerable roots of philosophy and all its innumerable branches, unknown and unknowable, so grand in scale and complexity as to be worthy only of the Heavens themselves to

3

answer. Parents, ministers, teachers of all varying faiths and persuasions and backgrounds – all may phrase their replies with differing words, but most in the end say the same: These things will never be for us to know.

But these *many* are wrong. They are not for the most part bad people; their intentions – sometimes – are admirable. But they are wrong. Not *wholly* so: for there will always be some things in this world, and our place within its history and its future, which we will not and cannot ever understand. And that is as it should be. But these few great things aside, there is yet so much more to know. So much more to understand about ourselves than those parents and ministers and teachers would have us, for ignorance or other reasons, believe. And this understanding comes from knowing of our past – our *true* past: of where and when we really came from, and how we really came to be. For if we do not understand these things, *why* should we ever feel like we belong? Why *shouldn't* we feel that there is something wrong; something missing?

Recorded, written history can take us only so far. Recorded, written history as taught in schools, and in libraries – at least, those schools and libraries you will be familiar with – and passed from generation to the next as gospel can only take us to a certain age of our past. Sometimes the details of the inner chapters of the great tome of our world may be expanded or refined, but ultimately the bookmarks and the layout of what we believe we know of our way of life today remain more or less fixed and clear. And in order to move beyond this, in order to understand the deeper, truer reaches of our past, we must do what so few people now are willing – and far fewer still are truly able – to do: We must move far beyond known fact – those facts of history, and of science, and of all related branches of traditional teaching, however worthy and necessary they may elsewhere be – and headlong into the mist-shrouded records of tales, and of song, and even of faith. Those parents and ministers and teachers and great academics of today would speak of such things which lie beyond the scope of their specific field fondly and dismissively as legend, and as myth. And in this case, for the most part, they would be right to do so...

For the most part. For while many myths and stories and legends are no more than these terms suggest, there are others which are, in truth, quite different. Others which, when brought forward and pieced together onto dry land from the timeless swamp of hearsay and fiction formed over millennia, through one Age to the next, begin to paint a picture of a world distant yet linked – albeit vaguely, often hanging by a thread – to that in which we live today. The hardest part to believe about what follows here, this land of legend and of myth, into which we shall shortly delve, may well be that this world, curious and fantastical as it will seem, is not in fact as remote and removed from ourselves as you may think. Were ourselves and recorded history as we are taught it to be seen as a blinking of an eye in the great timeline of the world, this deeper past may perhaps be seen as linked through the shutting of the eyes for a brief sleep. A great many years and mysteries lie between that which we know and that which we do not. But it is there nonetheless.

Where exactly to begin in the telling of this earlier world is difficult. Telling of the rising of the first mountains, and the sinking of the first valleys; of the flowing of the first rivers and the filling of the first lakes; of the coming together of the first peoples, and of the doing of their first deeds: all form part of this great story, and all deserve to be known. But if there is to be time for such things, it will come later. If we are to begin – and only begin – within these few pages, truly to know what it was which shaped us and brought us here, what it was which created the quiet anguish passed down through the ages – that nagging thought, that restless searching for the truth of ourselves which so many of us are rightly but agonisingly never free from – we must move forward slightly from these first years. We must move forward to a time when this distant world in its infancy, and in one of its many small but vital ways, would stare ahead at a branching of the road, and be forced to choose a path.

And so it is that we do not begin at the beginning of all things. Peoples have grown and united and split apart; many – though far from all – of the mountains and the rivers and the wide swathes of land have formed and have been given names, though not those names by which we would easily know them now. And deeds great and small have been done and retold for lifetimes beyond count. But it is here nonetheless that we start. *Story*, *history*, or *myth*: the choice is there to make for all who read on. But the telling and the truth of it will be the same.

*

Welcome, now, to Azhera.
Welcome, now, to the Núminway Chronicles.

*'In life, never underestimate the importance
of a good imagination.*

It can transform the world around us…

*And sometimes, just sometimes,
it can allow us to find others
that are waiting to be discovered.'*

A passage from *Concerning Storytelling*
One of the *Lessons of Sabine*

Date unknown

Chapter One

An Ember in the Waves

Sometimes amidst the dark they seemed like the type of high, rolling clouds of dreams and paintings; at others like banks of mist drifting thick over soft green fields. This time, however, they seemed more like the currents of some deep ocean, washing softly over and under one another in an endless harmony of effortless, simple beauty. Whatever they were, Yori was deep amongst them, rising and falling as they did, drifting soft and content in whichever direction they saw fit to bear him. He could happily have stayed here for hours, drinking in the blue around him, silently savouring each fresh ebb and flow of this joyful, overpowering sense of serenity.

Indeed, he may well have already been here for hours. For suddenly he realised he had lost all track of time. This was why he so rarely let himself delve this far… He could barely recall any of what he had been doing before, just as he struggled to picture his home. Even the faces of his family were blurred and distant, a hazy memory, though somewhere deep down he knew in truth that he was scarcely more than a few feet from most of them.

But this is what he loved so much about being here, amongst the waves. Nothing else mattered. Not that he didn't love his family, and enjoy the life he had with them. It was just that here, everything was always so much easier. There was nothing to think of; no questions, or chores, or worries about the future. Just peace. The type of peace which the outside world could never offer.

Just then the whispering of a woman's voice broke gently through from outside; distant, quiet…

'Is he alright?'

'Shh! Let him be…' came the echo of a man's reply, somewhere far to the other side of him, through the waves. He turned slowly, first to one and then the other, but the sources of the voices were nowhere to be seen. He knew they wouldn't be: they were not here with him. It was just him in here, as it always was. He smiled lazily as another bank of blue swirled over him, following it as it faded slowly into the distance.

But the voices had stirred a far-off thought in his mind. He remembered now that he was here for a reason this time… There was something that one of them had asked him to do. His mind drifted as the current that held him slowed and calmed, before being picked up by another, casting him off in yet another direction. The fog around him swelled, taking his spirits with it, and once again he became lost in the eddying beauty of his world.

He couldn't say how much longer he stayed there, sometimes floating peacefully amongst the waves, at others soaring easily and swiftly through them; but after a time he began to feel that he should be starting to make his way out. He never enjoyed this, often finding reasons to stay a while longer, but with each passing minute he sensed something reaching to him from outside, as if one of several pairs of eyes were gazing at him from just beyond his sight, studying him, pulling him gently but surely out of his world and back into theirs. With a reluctant heart, though content in the knowledge that the waves would always be here for him to return to, he lifted his head and gazed vaguely towards the soft light which glowed gently in the distance far above him. He started to make his way towards it, still flowing with his surroundings, calm as they were.

The light grew slowly brighter; the waves thinner, softer. He had almost reached the surface, turning one last time to gaze down into the blue beneath him. It seemed darker from where he was now. He was within moments of the surface, so close he could almost smell the world outside… But just as he turned back to it a sudden flickering caught the corner of his eye from below. He stopped.

It had come from somewhere far beneath him. Deeper even than he had just been. *What was it?* Often he had seen shades of colour and light in the depths before, but nothing like that. He strained his eyes in search of it, but it had vanished, like the briefest of shooting stars through the black of night.

'Is he back?' came the woman's voice again. 'Yori?' She was worried. He looked above him and for a moment thought he saw the shadows of two people just above the waves, looking down into his world. But he cared little now of them. He turned away from the light

8

and began to swim once more into the blue, looking all the time for whatever it was that he had seen.

Down he fell, deeper into the darkness, this time crashing through the waves as he searched with a strange and unbidden sense of desperation for the tiny pinprick of light. The waves began to batter him from left and right, grasping at him, shaking him… but he broke free and continued. It was almost entirely black now, the waves rising to vast, thick columns through which it was all but impossible to hold a straight course. They started to pull and push at him once again, gripping tight like cold hands as they tried to lift him out from the depths. He fought to free himself – and suddenly as he did so it was there again, right in front of him: A tiny, glowing spark, like the remains of a once great star, hovering within arms reach. It burned with a dazzling silvery brightness the likes of which he had never seen, and then it sunk slowly back away from him, deeper into the black. People were shouting around him; the woman calling to him again as with all his might Yori freed one of his arms and reached out, his fingers inches from it… but then with an irresistible strength the hands grasped him one final time, tighter than ever, and he was struck by a blast of ice across his face. He heard a light, high-pitched *clink...*

*

Yori opened his eyes. His breaths were coming deep and painful, his heart thumping quick and hard against his chest, and cold water trickled slowly down his face and into his clothes. It took several seconds for his senses to return…

A woman was stood before him, loose strands of golden hair framing the green, frightened eyes which glazed like dimmed emeralds amidst her pale face. She was hunched over as she studied him intently. A large wooden pail, now empty of the water which a moment ago it had held, hung loose by her side, still dripping onto the floor of half-polished dark blue stone.

Beside his Mother, an old man with the tanned and weathered skin of a lifetime's adventures was kneeling, his grip still tight upon Yori's arms with those strong, bony fingers. He was being studied by the dark, sharp eyes of a woman of similar age who stood a step behind him; straw-like hair tied back tight from her thin cheeks, her arms folded firmly across her chest as she flicked between infuriated scowls at the old man and looks of deepest concern towards Yori. Yori couldn't help but smile back at his Grandmother: the warmth in her kind face matched, he was sure, by none other in the world, but a warmth nonetheless which could turn to frost at the snap of a leaf, and Url,

9

friend and self-appointed advisor to the family all their lives, was receiving the full chill of it now.

Yori himself was sitting in the wide, almost circular front room of his home; the washbasin and stove lining the opposite wall, the far side of a circular, heavily dented wooden table which filled most of the floor. Somehow, more than anything else it was the piles of mismatched cutlery, and fruits, and various trinkets he saw as he gazed about the room, none of which he usually noticed, which did most to clear his mind. He felt a hand upon his shoulder…

'How're you feeling?' his Father asked, walking round from out of sight behind him. His words came slowly, heavily to Yori, whether through his fear or through Yori's remaining grogginess Yori could not tell. Well-built within his calm and unassuming frame, with wide, brown eyes, and thick hair as dark as his wife's was bright, he held Yori's arm with a gentle hand roughened by long and often unforgiving years in the grain fields and spice gardens which surrounded their home.

Still hovering on the verge of dizziness, Yori simply nodded, and gave a weak smile in reply.

'You found something, didn't you?' asked Url, an excited glimmer burning in his eyes. He released Yori to pick up the shard of crystal which lay on the floor by his feet. Yori had almost forgotten it in the confusion of the past moments, but now he stared carefully at it, studying each of its countless faces as Url turned it carefully in his hands.

'*Found someth*…!' his Mother screeched, before Yori could answer. 'We could have lost him!' she bellowed at Url. 'That is the last time I let you use him for any – of – your – ridiculous – experiments!' she shouted, swinging the bucket hard and to Url's dismay not inaccurately at the old man with each vigorously growled word.

'He's fine!' cried Url through shielding arms. 'Ouch! Wait – listen! You *know* I'd never let any – Ahh! – any harm come to him!'

'I'm fine', said Yori quietly.

His Mother halted midway through another swipe; Url uttering a silent sigh of relief, his expression flashing once again with excited curiosity as he looked to Yori.

'So, um… did you?' he asked.

This time he received both a bucket to the stomach and a sharp pinch of his neck from Abetta, still standing behind him, who seemed to have been preparing for the moment…

'Urlmaeus –' she threatened with the measured, threatening snap in her voice that not a man alive could stand against for long, '– you ask that again and I'll –'

'Yes, I did', Yori interrupted quietly. They all stopped again, studying him silently.

'You...' his Mother hesitated, glancing at Url, still holding the bucket menacingly beside her. 'What do you mean, Yori? What did you see?'

Close beside Yori, Url said nothing. He crouched down quickly beside the chair once more, one eye watching the bucket nervously as he did so.

'I – I don't know what it was', said Yori. 'But... I've never seen anything like it before...'

In the warmth of the heavy afternoon light streaming through the window, it was all coming back to Yori now. This wasn't the first time that Url had asked him to study something he had found: Over the years he had brought him everything from leaves to various stones, pieces of bark, or small plants and flowers. Once he had even brought a bowl of water from a tiny, hidden rock-pool he had found nestled amongst the hilly woodlands miles to the south of here, insistent despite the rejections of the others that it contained a tiny fraction of some rock or mineral he had found. And each time it was with an excited grin and a bounce in his step of someone less than half his age, whatever that age may have been; always eager to see if Yori could sense anything in his newest discovery.

For Yori, his mind like that of a skilled, silent scribe to the world around him, had always been able to sense things which others could not. Be it the physical elements of which people, creatures and other items were formed, the emotions of those close to him, or even the very traces of Magic within something, Yori could feel and explore these things with a mastery at which the others could only wonder. Other people had particular affinities for particular parts of the physical or elemental worlds: his Mother and Father taking great delight from the forests and grasslands and other green places, while his older sister, Aliya, just turned seventeen, would spend her days around and amongst all manner of lakes, rivers, and waterfalls wherever she could find them. His older brother, Crick, birthbrother to Aliya, had developed the unnatural agility and swiftness to complement his never-ending thirst for adventure and exploration, much to their Mother's dismay. And Abetta, his Grandmother, could and often did spend days at a time drinking in the hues of a changing skyline, gazing into the risings and settings of the sun, or standing contentedly amongst anything from the gentle whisperings of a warm breeze to the power of a raging storm, taking solace or finding intrigue in all, and seeing further and keener from her old eyes than most birds of prey. Url, his Grandfather in practice if not by birth, was usually happiest amongst the rocks or the earth, often found digging his way into or out from yet another self-created underground labyrinth; though just as often he would leave to explore the foothills of the mountains to the north-east, or any number of other locations.

But Yori, eleven years old and to his despair forever the baby of the family, was quite different. While those around him would often be drawn off into their usual favourite places or pursuits, he was delighted to simply wander without purpose or destination. Aliya and Crick had taken the straight, dark hair of their Father, but to Yori had come a tangle of fine, blonde locks, brushed and tied with a weary sigh by his Mother or Grandmother most mornings; each knowing that barring some terrible accident or illness it would be hopelessly loose and knotted by the coming lunch. He would stroll through fields and up into hills, explore forests, rest and swim in the lakes and streams or perhaps ford across them to some new place, and overturn rocks and old tree-stumps in search of small creatures. He would marvel at the intricacy and splendour of everything from the smallest of flowers to the grandest of trees, gazing out over distant horizons, and delving into the darkest caves and tunnels. And much else besides. He could never understand why or how it was that the others took such fulfilment and joy from just one aspect of the world around them. He could see, perhaps more than they could themselves, why they enjoyed the things they did, but he had never understood why they immersed themselves in them alone, at the expense of all the other wonders which the lands around them had to offer.

It was not only the elemental realm to which Yori's sensitivity extended: He had also found as he grew that he could understand *people* far better than others could. Or more correctly he had found, more often than not to his confusion and frustration, that others could not understand *him*, or themselves, as well as he could. He could with little effort read and understand the briefest of movements in face and body, the hints of variation in voice and look, and even, with time, the varying sounds of their silence; all of which told him with unnerving accuracy how a person was feeling, or even sometimes what they were thinking.

This had not always been a pleasant capacity to have, however. Along with the way in which people were often wary of being around him in difficult or worrying times – even on occasion, though they tried in vain to hide it, his own family – he was also exceptionally affected by the ever-changing dispositions of those around him. His sensitivity for the feelings of others was not something which could be turned on and off at will when desired: It was forever present, flooding him day and night with waves of emotion, of all different types. When someone close to him felt joy or excitement, his spirits would be lifted and he would feel a warm surge of energy rush through his veins. But just as vividly when they were saddened or afraid he would feel these things too, even if the feelings were entirely hidden to everyone else. At these times it would seem as though a dark, cold, impenetrable cloud had descended over Yori, smothering him, draining him of all vitality and happiness, lingering as long as the other person felt that way, or until Yori was far away from them.

Yori had one final gift, however, which more than all else was what made him truly unique, and had made him the centre of Url's excitement and attention many times in the past, and once more today. It was something which none of his family could fully comprehend; something which only a small number of people across the land could ever truly claim to have experienced. Even Yori himself was unsure how to explain it. The best he could manage, when asked, was to say that it was like being able to see the flow of Magic with which things, people, and places were filled. While many others could use Magic to varying degrees, Yori could *feel* it. It was as if, while others were happily playing in the lake without knowing or caring how the water got there, he alone could see and feel the tributary which fed into it from some great source far away. Almost without trying he could delve deep into the soul of anything from a person to the rolling countryside itself, sensing the mysterious energy which gave these things life and Magic. Sometimes the current would be strong, others less so; but it was always there.

But never, in all his eleven years, had he felt or seen anything like this…

He looked down at the shard of crystal which Url was holding gingerly between the fingertips of each hand. Its colour had already begun to fade when Url had run in with it earlier, and now it had gone completely, leaving behind a simple though nonetheless pretty silver gem. Everyone was still staring at him: even his Mother behind her scowl of disapproval was intrigued now, the bucket hanging unthreateningly by her side.

'I don't know what it was,' Yori repeated at last. He wondered how long he had been silent.

'Well, I'd wager I do,' said Url, standing with the difficulty of his years, still holding the crystal out before him, a grin broadening across his cheeks as he looked from each face to the next. But his look of excitement fell unreturned into the silence of the room. Indeed, suddenly the others seemed to become positively uninterested. Yori's Grandmother rolled her eyes, sitting heavily back down to the table and a large pile of half-peeled carrots. A weary look passed between his Mother and Father.

Yori well understood their scepticism. Certainly there was a part at least within him which felt it too. So often had Url claimed to have found a clue to the fabled source of Magic, and each time it had come to nothing. None of the family save Url himself still truly believed in the old tales of the Heart, or at least the idea that it could ever be found; and with each passing *discovery* Url had received less and less interest and indulgence from the others. Yori knew he should feel the same. And yet...

The ember of light glowed bright in front of him again for an instant; vanishing just as swiftly into the depths. Even merely in memory its power and splendour seemed overpowering.

'It was... bright,' said Yori.

'I'm sure it was nothing to worr–' began his Grandmother, but Url interrupted her:

'Go on, lad.'

Yori's eyes moved wonderingly to the crystal once more, trying to recall what they had seen.

'It was like a spark... Like a small piece of fire, moving down into the crystal.' The room fell silent again; Abetta's hands halting their work. She looked at him with renewed if reluctant interest, as did his Mother and Father. 'It was only there for a moment,' he continued. 'Then it kept moving away from me, deeper than I've ever been before. I...' He frowned, not knowing how to explain... 'It was strong. It felt... *alive*.'

'We need to get back there,' Url uttered breathlessly almost before the word had left Yori's lips, his eyes now close to bursting with excitement.

'Where?' asked Yori's Mother.

'The cave! Where I found it. We need to look for more!'

Abetta let out a jaded laugh, while to one side Yori saw the bucket raise to an ominous height once again in his Mother's hand.

'Absolutely not!' she said definitively. 'Not *again*. We've wasted too many good days over the years searching for your – whatever it is you think you've found... We will *not* be dragged into another waste of time. We've dug holes for you, scoured riverbanks, walked for mile upon mile –'

'Yes, but –' Url tried, but to no avail.

'– picked through mounds of leaves, and stones, and branches... You've even had Crick stuck halfway up a Gargantree... remember?'

'Yes, I know –' Yori could have sworn that he saw the vaguest hint of a smile pass briefly across Url's face, though fortunately his Mother seemed not to have noticed, '– but –'

'But nothing. If you wish and choose to spend your days in search of your Magical fancies then that is indeed your choice. But I won't have our time wasted any more!'

Url looked about him for support, but found no encouragement save for a hidden, pitying glance from Abetta that only Yori saw. Deflated, he looked again at the crystal, sitting back despairingly at the table.

'I'd like to go,' said Yori suddenly, already prepared for the stern gaze which, sure enough, his Mother shot in his direction. 'There was something there,' he said defiantly as she opened her mouth to dismiss him. 'I don't know what it was, but there was definitely something.'

His Mother opened her mouth slightly again, but then closed it slowly, looking slightly deflated herself. Like all the others she admired and respected Yori's abilities, despite his youth and the fact that she could understand little of them. Url was quick as ever to pick up on this momentary change in the balance; the spring returning to his step as he got to his feet again. Yori's Father put an arm across his wife's shoulders, letting out his breath in a long, weary sigh.

'All right, old man,' he said to Url. 'We'll help you. Again.'

'Ha!' Url cried, bending to give Yori an enthusiastic hug.

'But this will be the last time.'

Url stopped, looking up. His face became set with the dogged determination that marked him above all else.

'It'll be the only last time I need,' he said. 'I'm *sure* of it.'

'If I'd had a Silver for every –' Abetta began.

'Don't you start, woman!' growled Url, but he was met with a look of such fierce warning that he couldn't help but recoil slightly.

'So, what are you going to need this time?' asked Yori's Mother with a small, resigned shake of her head. Url gazed up at her, a childlike excitement brightening his old eyes...

'More pairs of hands.'

15

Chapter Two

The Nothingness

Peering slowly around the rough corner of the high rock wall, damp and broken by thin tendrils of glistening moss beneath his hands, Crick could see nothing but the last section of narrow gorge running down and away from him, and far beyond it the entrance to the Grasslands, glowing in the distance with rich, dark greens and oranges in the late-afternoon light. A gentle wind blew quietly through the rocks above and around him, funnelled through the gorge with a constant, high-pitched whistle which seemed to unnerve the horses. Even Railer, his own, was shuffling uneasily and impatiently behind him.

A twelve-year-old, light brown stallion, Railer was by far the bravest and worst-humoured horse Crick had ever known. There were those who were quicker, and many who were easier to control and infinitely more pleasant to ride, but none at all who had the courage and endurance to tolerate Crick's frequent forays into the dark and dangerous places of the Heartlands as boldly as he had done over the years, since Crick had reached his tenth birthday, begging for the impetuous animal to be trained as his own. But even he was unsettled now amongst the thin, dusty air of these tight grey corridors.

It was always Crick who led the way through this final passage, but it was a task he relished. Sometimes he would take the front without being asked, while at others he would wait for Leyon or Natt to drop quietly behind or give him the small nod born from years of Crick's constant desire to be the first of the three of them to explore anything new or dangerous. Tonight for their entertainment they had decided once more to journey through the rocky foothills of the western tip of the mountains, two days' ride north of his family's home.

Crick's two companions were from the nearby village of Reiomarsh, and though their sense of adventure and risk could never quite match Crick's, they were by far and away the best he had ever been able to find. Neither of them enjoyed this part of the trail. If he was honest, even Crick found it slightly disconcerting. His eyes were wide and unblinking, his breath quiet and deep as he scanned the ground in front of him for a second time. They were past the border and into the Outerlands now. It was not by much, but that was little comfort. Never yet had they encountered anything out here. But then, neither had they ever been here this late before.

Predictably it had been Crick's idea to venture out here now, rather than earlier during the day as they usually would. It was the Guardsmen at Fellgate who had given him the idea, with their low talk of strange sightings of dark shadows across the far Grasslands, and of distant echoes of the Black Wind itself being felt throughout the hills at the height of the evening. How could he possibly ignore the lure of such wonderfully dangerous talk? So far, however, despite their many attempts, Crick and the others had seen nothing. On over a dozen days over the past months they had ventured into the rocky paths, through Fellgate and past the Guardsmen there who thought Crick a fool and the others more foolish still for following him, up and through the warren of stone corridors and high walkways, and down at length to the end of this final ravine – the desiccated remains of a once-raging river, now long since dead – to a wide platform, below which the trail ran steeply down to disappear into the Grasslands, and from which they could see for mile upon mile into the hazy distance. For the others, it was excitement enough to be outside the Heartlands. But Crick wanted more. He wanted to see these shadows for himself; these beasts of darkness sired or claimed by the Black Wind. And there was little anyone could say or do to convince him otherwise. And so it was that he found himself now again outside of the protection of the Heartlands, searching once more for some distant glimpse of something which all others did their utmost never to encounter. And this time it was nearing night. *Their* time.

'*Crick*!' whispered Natt from behind him. Crick blinked, suddenly aware that he had been staring around the corner for some time. 'What's wrong? What is it?'

'Nothing,' said Crick, standing and stretching his arms behind him, shooting a confident grin at the others. 'It's fine, there's nothing here. Come on.' He offered Railer a reassuring pat on his neck before leaving – the horse snorting quietly but indignantly to let him know that the thought was both unnecessary and unwelcome – walking with a purposeful if rather gentle step around the corner, hopping lightly down the loose bank of the ravine. The others followed awkwardly behind. Crick knew that few people had his skill and ease of movement – at least none who unlike his and so few other families of the realm were open to the old Magics – but every time they traversed this part of the trail he was reminded how particularly clumsy his two friends seemed to him. Stones clattered noisily down the slope and echoed off the rock faces above and around them, making all their attempts at a stealthy approach up to now seem quite worthless. With a weary sigh he jumped the last few feet and made his way along the bottom, the Grasslands growing wide and wider still through the gap at the end of the ravine as he approached.

The familiar but nonetheless splendid view of the apparently endless plains below greeted him as he emerged onto the ledge: Wide stretches of open ground crossed occasionally by the winding path of a river, specked with isolated trees and patches of scrubland, but otherwise flat and uninterrupted for as far as the eye could see. He took his usual seat against a large boulder at the very lip of the ledge, the others sitting quietly in theirs beside him. For a while none of them spoke. They simply watched. And waited.

'…How far do you think it is to those trees over there?' asked Crick at length, stirring the others from their uneasy trances, both staring intently out into the darkening lands ahead of them.

'Why?' asked Natt, eyeing Crick warily as he glanced over to the small cluster of low evergreens which Crick had gestured to, nestled amongst a kink in the river which swept away to their left, perhaps a quarter of the way to the horizon. The river was the Maiyen, which, from its source in the mountains just east of the Grasslands, ran west for several hundred miles, forming much of the old northern, and still a great portion of the north-western, borders of the Heartlands.

'Just wondering,' said Crick. 'Well...?'

Natt considered it a moment.

'Ten miles? Twelve, maybe…? And no, I don't.'

'Don't what? You have no idea what I'm –'

'Yes we do,' interrupted Leyon. Crick turned to face him. 'In fact we've got far more than an *idea*. We know *exactly* what you're going to say… It'll be something like,' he raised his arms and gave an overly enthusiastic mock impression of Crick, the accuracy of which Crick attempted poorly to wave away, '*Well it's not that far… why don't we go take a look at it? We could be there and back in no time!*'

Crick turned from one of them to the other and back again, wearing the most sincere look of innocence he could muster. It didn't last long.

'Well, we could!' he said, to a sigh from Natt and a wearied laugh from Leyon. 'We could get the horses down there, leave after dawn, and we'd be back by lunch! It's so flat we could see for miles around us; we'd see anything that was coming. And it'd be in bright sunshine; they wouldn't even be out! We could –'

'No,' said Leyon simply.

'But don't you want –'

'Absolutely not,' interrupted Natt. Crick opened his mouth to argue again, but he had seen that look in their eyes before. He knew it wouldn't do any good. In a moment of thoughtless impulsiveness he considered that perhaps he could go himself… But though he despised having to admit it, even to himself, he would never go down there without the others. The ledge they were sitting on now was quite far enough for three people to be, let alone just one. If but half of half of the least frightening tales of the most honest of talesmiths were to be believed, one man by himself would stand little or no chance that far into the Outerlands, daylight or no daylight. Even Crick, swift, intrigued and willing as he was, knew the difference between adventure and suicide.

'Well how about we –' he began, but he halted as he looked over to Leyon…

It wasn't Leyon's raised hand that had silenced him, nor his abrupt '*Shh!*' It was the look in his eyes… They were wide, scared; his mouth hanging open slightly as he strained his senses in sudden concentration. Leyon was always the first to notice things. And he was rarely mistaken.

'What?' asked Crick, quietly.

'Listen…' said Leyon.

Crick tried, but he heard nothing. He waited; his breath instinctively slowed and quietened. And suddenly, with a terrible leap of his heart, he realised… There was nothing. No sound, no movement at all. The whistling of the wind through the rocks behind them had been slyly replaced with a deathly silence, as if the very soul had been ripped from the air. The beating of Crick's heart suddenly seemed horribly out of place amongst this… this *nothingness*.

The Nothingness it was; Crick was certain of it. He had heard tell of it in accounts from the few Guardsmen and venturers and miners who claimed to have journeyed out of the Heartlands: Tales of the cold, sickening void which always preceded the Black Wind and the evil that came with it, in which only fear and madness thrived. Few had experienced it, and far fewer still had ever survived to tell of it. It was everything and nothing like Crick had imagined it.

With a look of purest terror Natt realised as well.

'But… there's still light left...?' whispered Leyon, frozen and gasping for breath.

There was, but only barely. The sun itself had disappeared; only a few of its rays crept back now uncertainly above the horizon. Looking away from the open sky and back into the ravine behind them, Crick realised for the first time just how dark it had become.

But surely it *couldn't* be what they all feared: One of the few aspects of the tales which was always the same throughout was that the Black Wind itself only came during the middle of the night, when darkness was at its strongest. Nobody had ever heard or seen it this early before.

'It's just a break in the wind,' said Crick, but his words were hollow and afraid despite his best effort at the unruffled nerve upon which he and the others so often relied. Doubt and fear were etched into the faces of the others. This was no mere break in the wind. This was something else entirely. 'Let's go,' he said. The others needed no convincing; all three companions were up and heading back into the ravine by their next breath.

The climb back up was significantly more difficult than their descent had been. Between darkness, loose rock, and the building of fear which was creeping steadily and inescapably into each of them as hard as they fought to force it down their steps were clumsy and awkward, making them slip and spit frightened curses under their breaths as they struggled to reach the high ground. For the first time in a long while Crick himself lost his footing, doing little to raise any of their spirits. As finally they neared the top of the slope they heard again a gentle trickle of stones being dislodged and falling. This time, however, it was none of them who had caused it. As one they stopped, motionless, staring at each other. Dread gripped them with the crippling claws of its icy fingers as they turned and looked, slowly and reluctantly, behind them…

For a moment there was nothing, and Crick dared to hope that they may have been mistaken. But then they heard it again, quiet but now more distinct: the sound of something grasping at the loose stone and earth just beyond the rim of the ledge on which they had been sitting a few short minutes ago. Somewhere inside Crick's mind a voice screamed *run*! But his body refused. He found he could not bring himself to move enough to turn away from gazing, terrified, at the opening below. Again they heard it… and again…

Then silence. Crick took in a shallow, silent breath.

But just as he started to let it out something scrambled quickly up and over the ledge: A shadow, darker than those around it, wolf-like in shape but slithering swiftly like a serpent through the ground. It reached the stone against which Crick had been sitting; circling it for a moment, studying it. And then in a violent flash of movement its head jerked upwards towards them, revealing two deep red eyes shining like distant orbs of fire against the black. Unbounded menace pulsed in thick waves from those evil, awful eyes as it stared, pawing the ground lightly and purposefully in front of it… and then with a shrill noise somewhere between a screech and a howl it flew straight towards them, jumping a clear twenty feet with its first bound.

Finally Crick found his voice:

'GO!' he screamed to the others, scurrying in a blink of one of their eyes up the final few feet of the bank. Trying desperately not to look back down the slope he turned to pull the others up to him, but from the corner of his eyes he saw the shadow leaping and sliding over and through the rocks, closing in upon them with horrifying speed. Its eyes glowed fierce and bright; a constant, terrible snarl filling the air. 'Move! Don't stop!' Crick shouted, pulling first Natt and then Leyon onto level ground and pushing them on hard into the passage. In an instant he had overtaken them, rounding the bend behind which the horses were tied. He found two of the animals as overcome with fear as he was. Railer stood frightened but firm amongst them while the other two stamped and reared; Crick pulling a short knife from its sheath along the back of his belt and slashing their reins from the dead tree which had held them. He was already mounted and on the move as the others appeared, holding the shortened reins of each of their horses either side of him as they ran and vaulted without slowing into their saddles, snatching the leather straps and crashing like lightning away through the passage.

*

Their careful journey into the hills earlier in the evening had taken nearly an hour, but it was less than a quarter of that before Crick and the others were storming back up to Fellgate, none of them having said a word since the ravine. They slowed, as they had to, for the Guardsmen to scrutinize them before waving them through; but they answered the questions that were thrown at them with little more than nods and breathless pleasantries.

'Ha! Think the young'uns went a spot further than they'd the stomach for!' Crick heard one of the Guardsmen shout loudly after them once they had passed. He didn't bother to turn back. In truth he barely even noticed him. He knew that if they did tell of what had just happened, the Guardsmen would either not believe them or would tell them furiously that it was their own fault, and that they shouldn't have been tempting the creatures of the night and the Black Wind itself so close to the border in the first place. And with a fleeting pang of embarrassment, he knew they would be right. They *had* been foolish to leave the Heartlands at this time.

Yet at the same time, now that the terror had almost subsided and they were trotting slowly into the open, down the last of the foothills and through the clear night sky and a wonderfully comforting cool breeze, he felt the familiar and entirely intoxicating sensation of warm exhilaration pounding through his chest and around his body, stronger by far than even the various liquors Url had accumulated on his travels. He turned to the others…

It took them a little longer to regain their composure, but after a few minutes, as they entered a small wooded hollow beyond which lay their hastily-constructed campsite, Crick saw a nervous smile break across Natt's face.

'You happy now?' Natt asked. Crick smiled back.

'What in the world *was* that thing?' asked Leyon.

'No idea,' said Crick. 'Did you see the way it moved? It was like it was two different beasts at once! I've never seen anything like it!'

'Doubt anyone has,' said Natt with typical but good-natured self-importance. 'At least, no-one who's lived to tell of it.'

'Well in any case this is unquestionably another addition to the long and hard-earned list of incidents which my parents do *not* need to hear of…' said Crick as they rounded a bend lined thick and high with brambles on either side.

'Indeed…' came a low voice suddenly from beside him as a sharp pain shot quickly through the side of his head. He reeled back, disorientated; Natt's horse rearing up again while Leyon nearly jumped from his saddle in fright.

'Who's there?' Crick shouted into the bushes, clutching his head and glancing with mixed anger and confusion at the branch above him, which seemed to have reached out and struck him of its own accord. 'Show yourse–'

'You can stay out for nights on end,' came the man's voice again; something moving through the brambles towards them, 'you can go off on your absurd adventures, and worry your Mother and I silly, but –'

the brambles untangled and parted softly, allowing his Father to emerge unscathed onto the track, '– you will *not* be giving me orders like that. Understood?'

Crick opened his mouth but found no words whatsoever. Fortunately, Leyon was quick to find some for him:

'Mr Orlando, sir! Umm, hello! Erm… what are you doing he–'

'I've come to collect my son,' said Crick's Father, not taking his eyes off Crick. 'I would ask where you've been, but I fear I can guess without your help.' Natt and Leyon glanced at each other uncomfortably, unsure what to say or do. Crick remembered now how different and intimidating his father's stare could be, when he wished it to be so.

'And from the looks on your faces,' Orlando continued, 'you've had quite an evening!'

'We –' Crick began, but his Father cut him off again:

'It can wait.' He turned to the others. 'You two ride on to camp, get your things, and get home. You…' he looked to Crick, 'will walk with me.'

Natt and Leyon needed no further encouragement: With a brief murmur of goodbye to Crick and a clumsy attempt at a more courteous one to his Father, they sped off hastily along the track. Crick dismounted and walked silently beside his Father.

'Url's found something again,' was all he would say at first to Crick's look of confusion. But as the others disappeared from view amongst the brambles his gaze softened, and he released a long breath; the tension easing from his shoulders and his thickly-stubbled jaw.

'So…' he said, looking sideways at Crick. 'Tell me everything.'

Crick smiled, and did.

Chapter Three

Waterfaery

If of all the types of days the world had to offer, there was one type of day which Aliya had to choose amongst all others, this would almost certainly be it. The warm sun was high amongst small scatterings of wispy cloud, the breeze was soft and cool, and she was alone, undisturbed in her own thoughts, interrupted only rarely and pleasantly by the various sounds of the wildlife around her, all she had heard all morning. And, above all, she was enjoying all of this from the western shore of Lake Iris, her favourite place in the world; gazing out over the still, blue scene broken occasionally by the joyful *plop* and ripples of a surfacing fish, or the landing of a bird. There was little else Aliya enjoyed more than resting amongst the creatures which called these places home, which is why she was rarely found anywhere very far from them.

She had been sitting here all morning; Nightwind a great shadow behind her, quiet and calm as ever save for an occasional nicker or gentle flick of his glossy black tail as he grazed on the thick waves of grass and wildflowers which covered the gently-sloping bank, tumbling lazily down to the lake. The far side of the water could just barely be made out in the distance, from where there came the occasional tiny glints of light reflected from the casting of a fishing rod; though the figure of whoever it was who was doing the casting was too small to recognize. It was probably Jacob or Merien... They alone enjoyed and appreciated the lake almost as much as Aliya, fishing or swimming amongst its northern banks most days, occasionally calling a distant indiscernible greeting across the enduring tranquillity of the water. They were the closest thing to neighbours Aliya had in this quiet, forgotten corner of the Heartlands. Not that that was a bad thing.

Aliya stood, stretching her rested legs, and made her way down to the small boulders that lined this section of the shoreline, between which the water swirled and swelled in gentle, constant rhythm, or else lay flat and still in dozens of small, oddly-shaped pools. She hopped up onto the first, skipping to another, examining the rock-pools briefly as she danced amongst them.

Several blue-eye frogs were basking by the water's edge, asleep despite their large, ever-watchful eyes which followed Aliya as she passed above them. Had she been anyone or anything else they might have made their quick well-practiced hops to the safety of the lake. But they recognised Aliya. Like everything here, they knew they had nothing to fear from her. Tiny skaters, their many legs an elegant flurry of silvered needle-tips beneath slim dark bodies, skipped lightly over the water's surface, and for a few seemingly pointless and charming seconds a flock of goldcrests emerged like a quiet squall from the woodland further north along this side of the lake, circling and singing merrily above the water before plunging swift and straight, back into the treetops.

After a few minutes Aliya glimpsed the silvery-blue scales of a baby spriggleback, its long, thin nose poking warily out from the shadows. She halted on one leg, crouching down so that her long, dark hair skimmed the surface, placing her hand slowly into the pool without even the tiniest of ripples. As her fingers felt the coolness of the water a wave of quiet, peaceful energy coursed up and through her arm, and she sensed the fish hovering inches away from her. For a moment she stayed there, unmoving, reaching out to her new aquatic friend as its curiosity prompted it forwards to drift lightly through her fingers. She wiggled them in greeting, stroking its smooth sides…

In a sudden blue flash something flew out across the surface of the pool from beneath the rock she was standing on, jumping up onto another on the opposite side. She toppled back but regained her balance in time, and as she looked across the pool she saw it hovering nimbly above the rock: A waterfaery. The shimmering blue tangle of light turned to face Aliya, and as it did so several others shot out from below her to join it. For a second the other side of the pool was alive in a bright blue glow, and then as one the spirits fell back away from her into the lake. Aliya hopped quickly across to where they had been, and in the water a few feet away she saw a dull light gliding soft but swiftly into the depths of the lake. It travelled a while longer, until the light was almost gone… and then with an explosion of blue mist a dozen bright blue sparks burst magnificently through the surface, spreading quickly out across the water. There they fluttered merrily about, over and around each other, skipping lightly across the water or diving briefly beneath it, emerging a few feet away in brief showers of tiny droplets.

Aliya had seen waterfaeries before, of course, but this didn't dampen her delight at seeing them again. Of all the creatures of the water they were possibly the most mysterious, and certainly the most charming. It was rare to be this close to them, though. Even with her affinity for such things, she had rarely seen them like this. She longed to join them in their watery games, but knew that if she tried to get any closer they would vanish faster than she could blink. So instead she sat carefully on the rock, and watched, dangling her hand loose in the water in front of her.

A while later, her neck beginning to feel hot and sticky beneath her hair and the sun now high above it, Aliya felt a soft swell of brightness brush lightly against her hand. For some reason she looked not down, but up and slightly to her left, and as she did so she saw a tiny waterfaery hovering, away from its friends, staring at her. At least, staring as much as a waterfaery could stare, not having any recognisable eyes to speak of. But Aliya could tell that its attention, in whatever form, was on her. And as Aliya returned its gaze she felt the touch again, knowing somehow that it was coming from the motionless creature. She smiled uncertainly. She felt it again, and this time she followed the swell as it turned and meandered back to the faery. It *was* looking at her… It seemed almost to be pulling at her, inviting her towards it. She wished desperately to join it. She thought she could feel the others looking at her too, but she dared not take her eyes off this one…

And then as if it had heard her wish, it started to float calmly across the water towards her. She could see its features clearly now: bright fragments of twinkling dust shaped into form by tiny limbs which resembled thin, blue twigs. Within moments it was barely more than an arm's length away from her; all the others seeming suddenly to have moved closer as well… And that was when she glanced around her, and realised: The faeries themselves had not moved at all. The water was moving *her*.

Looking down she watched, dumbstruck as the soft, rolling currents passed in smooth drifts beside and beneath her, carrying her closer still to the faeries. She was right amongst them. They hovered for a moment, just above the water, and then as though deciding suddenly and unanimously that they approved of her they continued their skipping and playing just as they had been before; Aliya merely a curious new frame to be climbed upon or swum around. Their tiny paws pressed light and quick upon her skin, fainter than those of any newborn creature. One of them flew briskly up her arm and the side of her neck, diving elegantly from her head to land without breaking the surface of the water ten feet away. She had no idea what she should do. Or perhaps she should attempt to say something...? Gingerly, still trying not to think too hard about how or why she was floating above the water, she reached out a hand to the faery which had first looked at her, now paddling contentedly down by her right knee. It flicked a mischievous splash of water up at her, and then jumped up towards her hand –

'*Aliya!*'

Instantly Aliya felt herself fall with a loud, clumsy splash through and into the cold water. She reached down with her feet and found the bottom; the water coming up to her shoulders as she stood on the tips of her toes. Frantically she wiped the water from her eyes, looking around her... but they were gone. All trace of the brilliant shimmering blues had vanished into the lake, leaving no trace whatsoever of their presence.

'Aliya?' Yori called again, now standing on the rocks and looking out at her with utmost bewilderment. Nightwind stood behind, gazing out briefly with a somewhat more steady, tempered intrigue towards Aliya, before returning to the grass.

'*What*?' she snapped back irritably, trying wholly unsuccessfully to regain some form of poise as she half-swam, half-waded back onto shore.

'You've... still got all your clothes on...'

'I know I have! It was... Didn't you see them?' she asked in frustration.

Yori raised an eyebrow amidst his scowl of confusion.

'The waterfaeries!' Aliya persevered. 'They were all around me! I was sitting over there and... I don't know, they just sort of *lifted* me over to them. I was floating! They were playing all around me like I was one of them! And then *you* –' she splashed him hard as she passed him, dragging herself and her sodden clothes out of the water, '– you came and ruined it!'

'Sorry,' said Yori simply. And Aliya knew without doubt that he meant it, probably far more than he deserved. 'I was told to come and get you,' he added, looking at her apologetically.

Aliya halted in her bedraggled attempt to shake the water from her trousers and held up her dripping arms, her shoulders and cheeks covered in a heavy tangle of hair. For Yori's benefit, and to his evident relief, she managed a laugh.

'Don't worry about it,' she said, flicking another sleeveful of water at him. 'I –'

'What do you mean *you were floating*?' Yori interrupted.

'Why were you told to come get me?' Aliya asked.

'Url's found something again. I think we're all going to go have a look.'

Aliya was able to turn the curse in her mind to a gentle sigh before it left her lips, not that it would have been hidden from her brother. Whenever Url *found something* it meant entirely too much digging, climbing, or usually anything else that would keep her away from the water for a long time.

'I think it might actually *be* something this time…' said Yori. But Aliya was no longer really listening. She was staring back out towards the spot where the waterfaeries had been, wondering if she would find them again – or if they would find her – and considering whether or not she would ever be able to repeat whatever it was she had just done. She would have given anything to be allowed to linger by the lake a while longer.

'You're not listening, are you?' said Yori.

'Oh – umm…' Aliya muttered distantly.

'Come on, let's go. I'll tell you *again*. And you can tell me all about how you've learned to…' he gave her another inquisitive glance.

But Aliya barely heard him. And for a while longer she refused to be moved, gazing out eagerly into the afternoon across the lake, silent again.

Chapter Four

The Humouring of an Old Man

The first familiar breaths of varying rich, pleasant aromas were already working their way gently out through the back window of the family's cottage as dawn broke over the eastern fields. Inside, despite being the one person who did not in fact call this his own home, it was Url alone who was already sitting at the thick, round, cracked wooden table, waiting with an impatience to rival that of a newborn child.

In front of the thick paned window, still somehow bright despite generations of spattered grease and other various foods through which the rolling fields of green and brown appeared overrun by a great but not unfriendly swarm of dark splodges, Siu was expertly juggling a large frying pan full of sausages and mushrooms, another with newly-cracked eggs, while somehow managing also to find a third hand to keep guard over a tall pot of boiling soup which sat precariously atop the cooker. With a deft flick of one hand she flipped the sausages and mushrooms onto their uncooked sides, and with the other she seemed to be stirring the soup and dividing the whites of the eggs at the same time. Not that Url noticed any of this, so lost was he in the depths of his thoughts, as usual. Nor did he notice when she asked him to get the water and cups and cutlery for the table. She sighed, not bothering to ask again.

With a creak of old, tired hinges Orlando appeared through the front door, carrying an exhausted scowl and the smooth, newly-finished saddle he had been attempting to fit to Oden, the strongest and oldest of the family's two workhorses, a mottled, dark brown gelding with patches of black across his mane and ears who was growing weary and ill-tempered with his age. Sire to Nightwind and Railer, he was becoming less like the one and more like the other with each passing day, much to Orlando's mounting frustration.

'Still not right,' he grumbled, dropping the tangled mass of sweet-smelling leather in a heap beside him. 'Not that that damned animal is helping.'

'He's served us well,' said Siu absently, still working the pots, pans and other various utensils swiftly in front of her.

'In all his years I've *never* had trouble fitting him. If he'd just keep still for a –' but he paused, seeing the look on Siu's face. 'Url!' he called sharply, gesturing to the sizzling and simmering food, snapping the old man from his daydream. 'Help with the table!'

'Oh! Right, yes – sorry, my dear,' said Url, offering Siu a repentant smile as he jumped to his feet and began digging through various draws behind him for a clumsy handful of cutlery. 'I just have… rather a lot on my mind, you see. Would rather like to get started, um, as soon as possible…?'

'And we will,' said Siu, returning his smile with one of her own. 'But not until we've eaten. Could you call them?' she added to Orlando.

But as Orlando moved to the door and reached out to it the handle turned slowly by itself; the door inched gradually away from him to reveal the yawning figure of Crick, still rubbing thick clumps of sleep from his eyes.

'Sausages…?' he asked through another cavernous yawn.

'Get some water for the table and sit down,' said Siu. 'It's almost ready.'

Crick obeyed sleepily, resting his head in both of his hands, his eyes barely open once he was sat at his place beside Url.

'What time did you two get back last night then?' asked Url.

'Not until the early hours,' said Orlando. 'My wonderful old ride out there decided to try and throw me a few miles out. Snapped half the buckles on his saddle clean away.'

'I'd told you to replace that thing months ago,' said Siu, 'It's been –'

'So…' Url whispered to Crick, having succeeded in occupying the others in their own conversation; his smile just about subtle enough to avoid Siu's detection. 'Been out searching for monsters again, have we?' Crick's eyes widened in surprise, but he managed to keep his head pointing firmly down to the table, forcing another attempt at a yawn. He looked carefully up to his Mother, then sideways to Url…

'*Finding* them,' he murmured.

'What's that?' asked Siu before Url could give voice to his look of excitement, giving Orlando enough time to reach the doorway, from where he called hurriedly up to Yori and Aliya.

'Nothing,' Crick answered, forcing a yawn and sniffing the air a little too enthusiastically. 'What is it?'

'Potato and onion,' said his Mother flatly, fixing him with an accusatory glare.

'Smells nice...' Crick mumbled, trying to smile.

'You said,' said Siu, withdrawing the ladle from the pot and resting it above the cooker, upon which it dripped a thick, dark yellow soup. Pumpkin. Crick grimaced at his mistake, though he tried not to let it show. 'You hate onion, remember? Now what's got into y-'

'Aliya!' Crick called happily, hearing her emerge into the room behind him.

'What?' said Aliya, stopping suspiciously.

'Just... saying good morning,' said Crick.

'I see...' said Aliya, looking questioningly to her Mother.

'Ignore him, he's trying to hide one of his adventures from me again. Come and sit down – I think it's all ready to serve...?' She looked back to the foods, checking and giving a satisfied nod to each in turn.

Orlando helped her ladle the soup into low, green ceramic bowls, and the rest of the food onto mostly matching plates, and quickly the kitchen was full of the homely sounds of breakfast once again. Yori was soon down with them as well, though he wore a look similarly distant to Url's; neither young boy nor old man uttering more than a few, distracted words as the others talked of the fields, and the horses, and of other everyday things.

*

Siu had barely finished her last mouthful when Url spoke up for the first time in several minutes, raising his eyes eagerly from the licked-clean surface of his plate into which he had thus far with mounting frustration and difficulty kept his gaze firmly held...

'Can we get started now?' he asked hopefully.

'When Abetta gets here,' said Orlando. 'I don't want to be having to go through everything twice.'

'I'd rather we didn't have to go everything *once*', murmured Aliya, quiet enough that only her brothers heard her.

'Where is the blasted woman?' asked Url, sitting bolt upright and aghast at this new delay, seeming not to have realised that Abetta was missing. 'The sun's full up! It's not like she hasn't seen it wake before, and it's not like she won't see it hundreds more times again!'

'Just let her enjoy –' started Siu.

'I'm going to go get her,' said Url, pushing his chair back noisily and storming from the table. 'We can't wait around here all day while she stands out there doing nothing… She's…' But his blustering was cut off as the front door drifted shut behind him.

Siu gave a weary smile after him and then turned back to Aliya, who continued with her story of the waterfaeries and what she thought she had been able to do in the lake. Somehow her enthusiasm had grown still further during the night; she spoke now in the most intricate detail and greatest excitement in what seemed like a single great breath until shortly the door was barged open again, Url all but dragging a very harassed Abetta through with him.

'…swear this is the last t–' she grumbled irritably, stumbling upon the straps which lay beside the doorway.

'Yes, yes, yes,' said Url dismissively, smiling as he helped her regain her footing. It was a largely hidden, wholly gentle smile which marked the curious bond between the two which none of the family had ever been able to work out. But it was a brief smile at that. 'Ah!' He held out his arms to the family; their responses ranging between wearied and confused, or some variation of the two. Through ignorance or determination Url was unfazed. 'There we are, then; everyone's here. Let's get started, shall we?'

Instinctively Siu opened her mouth to argue, but instead with the look of one reconciled to her fate she simply got up and motioned to the others to help clear the table. Even Url helped, enthusiastically this time, darting to and from the table with a sudden manic energy, ferrying one armload after another swiftly to the side. When everything was washed, dried, and put away in its place around the numerous nooks and concealed crannies of the kitchen, they all retook their places at the table; Url pulling out Abetta's chair for her with an open grin and the most courteous little bow he could muster, to even Siu's amusement. Abetta glowered and pulled the chair briskly in herself. Finally Url sat himself ceremoniously down beside her, looking round at each of them, studying them.

'Let's hear it, then,' said Orlando after a moment. 'What do you think you've found this time?'

A distant glimmer lit up Url's eyes. He took in a shallow breath. 'I've found… *it*.' But his wide, excited eyes and dazzling grin were met with a continued impassive silence from around the table. Through the window came the shrill call of a white-tail, as though the birds and beasts themselves had been holding their silence until realising now that he had nothing new to say. They were as accustomed as the family themselves to Url's adventures through these lands, and they must have thought him quite the strangest creature of them all. Oden could be heard to snort grumpily in the bird's direction; the white-tail itself suitably undeterred, continuing its song, echoed now in places by the rising and falling pitches of answering calls. Several heads turned towards Abetta...

'He's laughing at us,' she said, eyes closed and head cocked sideways a fraction in concentration. Whether or not she meant it the others were unsure, but it certainly seemed likely. The little creature continued its playful tune as Orlando leant forwards onto the table, staring heavily at Url.

'You've found... *it*,' he repeated, slowly.

Url nodded, resolutely oblivious to the fog of scepticism around him, his smile growing even wider.

'Urlmaeus, if you don't start putting meat to the bones of your words I swear I'll –' started Abetta. Aliya leaned quietly across to Crick as their Grandmother made her vows...

'He's talking about the Heart again, isn't he?' she whispered forlornly.

'If he is,' Crick mumbled, 'I'll kill him right here and end all our suffering.'

'That won't be easy.'

'Why not? He's old enough. And he won't be expecting it...'

'You may be fast but I'll have got there first,' said Aliya, menacingly fingering the tip of a knife which had somehow escaped notice and been left on the table. When Url spoke again, however, all she could manage was a gentle thrust in his direction...

'I believe I've found a thread of the great rootway to the Heart!'

Siu seemed to have been prepared for it as well, replying instantly:

'And what *precisely* makes you think you've found it this time? What makes it *any* different from *all* the other times?'

'Because this time I *saw* it!' The singing outside stopped abruptly; a brisk fluttering of wings preceding a grumpy neigh as Oden finally mustered the energy to do away with the tiny invader from the thyme bushes. He really was getting old. 'I saw the rest of it bury itself down into the ground when I pulled out the piece of crystal I brought back here,' Url continued. 'I've never seen anything like it before... It moved like it was *alive*! You could *feel* the power coming from it... Even *I* could feel it. But ask Yori!'

Heads turned as one to face Yori, who until now had been sitting silently, listening intently.

'We all know he can sense these things better than any of us,' Url continued, 'and he said himself he's never felt anything like it! Didn't you? Yori…?' He nodded encouragingly, motioning Yori urgently into the conversation.

'I… I don't know what it was,' said Yori. Url nodded, gesturing again and with a degree of desperation for him to continue… 'But, well, yes… it was… definitely something…'

'*Definitely something*?' echoed Crick, letting a few seconds pass in silence before adding, 'Of course it was *definitely something*! Yori can sense Magic in most of anything; and besides, it was a big piece of shining crystal that *moved* when you touched it…! *I* could have told you that it was definitely something. That doesn't mean it's something that's worth us spending another day or ten looking for!' he finished, knowing where the conversation was leading if Url was to have his way.

'It does if your brother and I say it does!' said Url, cutting off Orlando's attempt to interject. 'Apparently young man you have still to learn that there are some things which other people know or can do far better than you! If ever I am in need of a wraith of a boy to run around the house and fetch things nice and quick for me, I shall for certain come straight to you! But when it comes to the sensing of Magic, or the understanding of Magic, or the search for all things subtle and Magical, you are arguably the least qualified here! So –'

'Okay, alright... enough,' said Orlando, holding up his hands. He sighed as he looked to Url. 'I said we'd give you one more chance.' Beside him Siu buried her head faintly in her hands. 'So one more chance you'll have.' He waved away Crick's look of frustration. 'Where exactly did you find it?'

'In one of the last of the caves up in the far edge of the Eigerhills. One I'd never known about until a few days ago. A few miles west of the mines. It's not more than a half day's ride from here.' The eager glint was back in full strength in his eyes, sparking like struck flint, and even Crick could see that there was no point arguing further.

'I'll pack some sandwiches,' said Abetta after a moment, standing and making her way slowly around the table, shaking her head as she disappeared into the pantry on the far side of the room. 'Yori, help me would you –' Yori had already nodded his agreement '– while the others make ready to go. We might as well make a day of it.'

*

34

By mid-morning the horses were saddled, food had been prepared and packed, and each of the family were dressed, equipped, and nearly ready to leave; all waiting or finishing their preparations in the small, stone square which lay between the main house, Url's cottage, and the stables. Atop Crash, as he had been for the past twenty minutes, and wearing his dark green, deeply weather-worn riding cloak and a black bandana which held back his shaggy hair in a tight line, Url cut something which could almost have resembled a rather dashing figure, with more than a few of his many years stripped oddly away. For all the trouble it caused the others, there could be no doubt that this was what Url was meant for. Every inch of him burned with a timeless vitality. Seeing him like this again, they could almost forgive the nuisance of a trip to the far side of the Eigerhills. Almost.

Crash herself was just as eager: bright snow-white even without much of a sun, her sinewy frame rippling as she reared and neighed excitedly. Url had traded for her with a enture he had met in the far south of the Heartlands, a young and inexperienced man who had just returned from a brief and wholly disastrous expedition into the Long Plains. Url had given away his much-loved, orange diamond armlet, and a great deal more Silvers, tools, and even quite literally clothing off his own back than he could afford, but he had gained in return the liveliest and most loyal companion he could ever have asked for, with the energy and enthusiasm to carry him anywhere and everywhere he wished to go on his adventures around the Heartlands, and more besides, often getting the old man into as many difficulties as he was able to get himself. Which was a rare achievement indeed.

'Ready?' Url asked loudly, for the fourth time in as many minutes. Yet again nobody but Crash answered, but with a careful nudge of his ankles Yori at last pushed Cloud forward towards him; Orlando following close behind on Oden, studying the young horse and rider carefully.

An eager, three-year-old colt, Cloud's greys and whites mirrored those of the morning's skies, broken only by the smallest of black lines and rings across his shoulders and around his neck. Yori had been delighted to finally have a horse to train as his own, but though he took great enjoyment from spending time with the creature, he was – known and obvious to all but himself – far from a natural rider. Half a year on, and it still frightened the others to watch. As long as they kept to an easy pace Yori would be fine. Unfortunately, Cloud more often than not had other ideas.

Siu was riding Chestnut, a mare almost of Oden's age, the colour of her name apart from a speckling of white marks around her lower legs and through her tail, and with Oden dam to Nightwind and Railer. After helping Abetta up into the rear of Chestnut's saddle, behind Siu, Crick mounted Railer and joined them; Aliya upon Nightwind following behind as without another word they set off westwards, down the poorly-cobbled path which ran away from the square, thankful for the slightly overcast but otherwise warm and pleasant day.

They soon left the path to cut north through undulating fields and woodlands, fording the first river they came to, but later turning west again to reach a bridge which crossed the second. For much of the journey they were each distracted in their own particular ways: Aliya often riding swiftly on to the next waterway, lingering there for a while after the others passed; Abetta amused and affected as ever by the slowly-changing shades of blue, white and grey which danced softly through the sky above her, seeming almost to fade and sway gently with each in turn; Crick with a general restlessness which would see him spur Railer quickly off in no particular direction for no particular reason; and Siu and Orlando absorbed with the abundant greenery and wildlife around them, which even in the few weeks since they had last been through this way had blossomed and grown almost beyond recognition. Never were they nearly as happy or as quiet as during the height of spring, especially after winters as long and bitter as that which had just passed.

And amongst them all rode Url and Yori quietly at the front, silent and still, but more distracted by far than any of the others. They gazed ahead with near-identical expressions, each filled to bursting with the deepest of thoughts and a curious, guarded excitement.

*

Quite before any of them realised it, therefore, they looked ahead to find that they had come to the twisting line of oaks which marked the beginning of the Eigerhills. The old wooden sign, still just barely reading *Silver Mines*, pointed crookedly up along an overgrown dirt path to their right, which disappeared into the trees and around the base of the first low hill. But Url led them instead to the left, and straight into the undergrowth. They were required to bend fully down to avoid being struck by the lowest of the great, hulking branches above and around them, to the point where it became far easier to dismount and walk beside their horses. The others watched enviously as all but the thickest of foliage parted gently to one side for Orlando and Siu as they placed a careful hand to it, each walking amongst the comfort of the woodland with an ease and grace which had prompted all three of their children at some point in their lives to enquire with utmost seriousness

36

as to whether or not they had been born from the very trees and bushes themselves; one or both hands now outstretched, concentrating dreamily on their surroundings as they walked.

It was in this manner that they travelled the final few miles, slowed temporarily by Siu's insistence that they pause to examine a small plant which she spotted tucked amongst the roots of one of the enormous oaks. Neither she nor Orlando had seen anything like it before – its dark, vivid green stem with purple, waxy leaves broken by thin streaks of black running through their centre – which said much of its rarity. With every care she drew the thin knife from around her ankle, disconnecting several leaves and part of the stem, placing the cutting delicately into the small woollen pack which she carried over her shoulder for just this purpose, before again the group set off.

Half an hour later the trees around them gave way suddenly to clear sky, and they found themselves looking down across the width of a long, narrow valley which sloped softly away to their left, out into the very south-west of the Heartlands for mile after gentle mile. Only Url and Abetta had been to this particular section of the Eigerhills before, though how it had escaped the notice of the others for so long, none of them could comprehend. Crick was particularly aggrieved to learn that there was a part of his own homelands he was yet to know, making little effort to hide it; he had long assumed, with certain pride, that he had found more or less all there was to find.

'You've a way to go yet, boy,' murmured Url, grinning at Crick's irritation.

The far bank was shielded almost entirely beneath a thick swathe of trees which mirrored those from which the family had just emerged, if perhaps slightly taller still. From amongst them a tiny trickle of water wound its way delicately down into the middle of the valley, twisting chaotically from side to side like the shallowest of cracks through an old wall of green stone, before straightening and drifting into the distance. And upon a step of flat ground just beyond the stream, less than halfway up the valley's far side, a small, thatched hut sat low and inconspicuous within a circle of what looked to be miniature apple trees, the base of its wooden walls seeming to merge into or perhaps grow up from the tall drifts of mud and shortened grass around it; lines of bright grey smoke meandering high into the still air from two outward-pointing chimneys at either end of the roof.

Url made to move off again, prompting Crash along the side of the treeline to their right, but as he did so the door of the distant hut opened. From the darkness within a man peered cautiously out, gazing up at the group. He stood as tall as the doorway around him. A simple, dark green tunic over a grey robe was all they could make out from here; even Abetta's eyes struggling for some reason to pick out the detail of his face. She knew who he was, though. Crick called forwards to Url, who seemed not to have noticed him...

'Ah,' said Url, turning and frowning as he caught sight of the open doorway, within which only the man's head was now visible, the rest of him having shrunk back into the gloom. 'Aulan.'

The word meant *outsider*. It was given to those who had moved into the Heartlands from beyond its borders, escaping the Black Wind; and as such it was a word now which applied in truth to most of the realm's inhabitants. Whereas almost all outsiders – along with much of everyone else – had by now opted for or else been coerced into the vast numbers and protection of the City, however, this Aulan had chosen quite the opposite in this quiet, entirely secluded little dwelling.

'Only ever seen him twice,' said Url, his frown lifting. 'Tried saying hello, introducing myself... but he didn't seem to have a word in him. Others have said he used to live somewhere in the north. Or was it west...? Said that he lost his family to the Black Wind. Every one of them. Everyone he knew. Hasn't spoken a single word since. He's been here longer than I can remember.'

Even had not they not been quite so far away, the man's long, black hair covered his face and made it difficult to judge his age. But the stoop in his stance and the laboured manner of his movement as he turned back into his home, shutting the door gently behind him, all told of a good many years.

'Cheery fellow,' said Crick.

'About as cheery as you'd be if you'd seen your family taken like that,' said Url, softly but with a thin but purposely cutting tinge of bitterness to his words. 'Had to flee for your life from everything and everyone you used to call home...' To everyone but Orlando's surprise a look of sudden understanding passed across Crick's face, and he said no more, as with a brusque 'Come on,' Url set Crash quickly off again.

The treeline bent slowly first to the right and then back to the left, so that they came at length to the point at which the two sides of the valley joined in a grand upsurge of rock, interspersed here and there with the twisting, trailing ends of roots from the surrounding trees, which flailed out into the air and then cascaded like a strip of torn, brown rope down into the valley. The longest made the fifty feet or so to the dusty soil below, burying themselves hungrily into the ground, while the rest hung slimmer and of a slighter duller hue, swaying rigidly in the breeze, looking decidedly less impressed with their lot. A thin, overgrown path disappeared once more into the trees. This time, however, it was barely more than a few minutes before Url called them once more to a halt.

They had come to the verge of a wide clearing, into which the high sun fell like warm water into a freshly-drawn bath. Before them the flat ground was broken by a soft hillock, no more than fifty feet wide and less than half as high. As they walked around to its right, each of them studying the smooth, perfectly-formed dome of grass and thick, blue moss, Url stopped a final time, pointing proudly.

The others made little effort to hide the shared look which spoke that their worst fears had been realised. Cut into the side of the mound, fringed with numerous assorted lumps of lightly-coloured rock spilling from inside like spittle around a gaping mouth, was a narrow opening. About three feet wide and four high, it revealed none of whatever lay inside; an almost unnatural darkness shielding Url's prize from view. Url himself was hastily retying his hair behind his bandana, a sure sign of his excitement. Ignoring their reactions he quickly unpacked two torches from the pack which hung beside Crash, lighting them and disappearing without a word into the opening.

'Come on, then!' his muffled voice drifted back to the others a moment later.

'Let's get this over with,' groaned Abetta, muttering various ancient curses none too quietly under her breath as she led the way through.

The stifling air of scepticism with which the day had begun remained firmly intact once they were all inside – not that any of the family had truly dared hope for much else. The oval cave was around fifteen feet wide and perhaps thirty long; completely still and silent. The light from the torches reflected eerily off the dull white rock, and their bodies cast distinct, flickering shadows upon the walls and the low roof. Url handed one of the torches to Orlando, holding the other down to a tiny hole below his knees, less than a finger's width across with chips and a cluster of deep scratches all about it. And then from the depths of his inside cloak pocket he pulled out with great delicacy the dull slither of crystal, turning it slowly in the torchlight for a moment before lowering himself to one knee, and placing it carefully into the crack. On the wall behind him one of the shadows flinched suddenly…

'You felt something, didn't you?' said Url immediately, wheeling round to Yori.

But Yori looked uncertain, confused. The others watched him with a budding interest as Url turned back to the crystal.

39

'The tip was sticking out when I got here…' he murmured. 'When I managed to get it out, something broke off inside the wall and disappeared into the ground. I heard something cracking behind here…' He placed a palm flat against the wall in front of him, his mouth hanging open a fraction as he ran his fingers slowly over the smooth bumps in the rock. 'Something big.'

'Alright…' said Siu, standing beside Yori, rubbing the back of his neck to break him from his trance, 'but what do you want *us* to do?'

'We can start by looking for any others like this one. When I found it only the very end of it was poking out of the wall; a tiny little pinprick of light… There might be others I missed.' He clambered to his feet and turned, holding the torch into the middle of the cave.

So with Crick and Aliya beside Url, and Siu and Abetta either side of Orlando's torch, they began to scour the walls, floor and roof of the cave. Amongst them Yori stood silently, gazing absent-mindedly about him, paying no particular attention to where the torchlight and shadows were falling.

'How did you find this place, anyway?' asked Crick.

'The usual…' said Url with a youthful grin. The others all knew what was coming – his favourite of all words: '*Exploring.*'

*

But despite their best efforts, after nearly an hour they had found no trace whatsoever of anything but the light-coloured rock of the cave.

'Didn't think so…' muttered Url.

'*Didn't think so?*' answered several of the others at once.

'What do you mean?' asked Orlando, forcing a measure of patience into his voice, wiping away the beads of sweat which had started to pool above the collar-bone of the arm he was using to hold up the torch. With all seven of them and the two torches in the cramped confines of the cave it was growing far warmer than it had been, only the strongest of the occasional gusts of cool air from outside finding its way in through the opening.

'Like I said, it disappeared into the ground there.' He looked around at them all, breathing deeply. For the first time he seemed nervous as to their reaction. 'I... scared it off.'

'You –' started Orlando, hesitating.

'– scared it off, yes,' finished Url resolutely. 'If we want to get at it again, we're going to have to work for it.'

'If *we* want to get at it?' said Crick.

'Yes, *we*,' said Url. 'You're Father's already agreed to help me again,' – he turned to Orlando – '*one last time*,' – and then back to Crick – 'so help me you shall.'

'You want to dig for it, don't you,' sighed Aliya.

'Indeed I do,' said Url, showing a full set of yellowing teeth as he smiled, as though he believed he could inspire the others with them if he tried hard enough. 'It shouldn't be difficult; this rock'll come away easy enough with the right tools and a bit of muscle.' Aliya remained unconvinced. Url looked from face to face for some sign of support or enthusiasm.

'It'll take a day just to get all the tools here!' said Crick.

'Stop finding things to moan about,' said Url with a dismissive wave of his hand. 'The point is: will you all help me?' His eagerness and desire were palpable. Orlando looked to Siu, and then to Yori, still standing quietly in the centre of the cave. Yori shrugged, but then looked quickly to the hole from which the crystal had come, and at length he gave a small, decisive nod.

'We'll help,' said Orlando. Url all but jumped with excitement. 'But for ten days. After that, we're done. We won't waste any more time here. We've got our own lives to be getting on with, Url. Unless you're content to go without food next winter.'

The look on Url's face, the manner of his stance, the very brightness of the flame beside him were all infused in the blink of an eye with the strength of steely resolve. He turned his back on the others, his eyes squinting to fix firmly upon the tiny hole in the base of the wall. Between the tips of the bony fingers of his left hand, held close to his chest, the crystal revolved slowly.

'Ten days...' he said, almost to himself. 'We'd best get started, then, hadn't we.'

Chapter Five

Believer

Aliya studied the outline of the sun as it tracked slow and bright behind another of the thin, high clouds drifting directly above her, turning her gaze away at the last second as the rays burst forth once more into open sky. As the warm, still water touched her cheek, she was reminded again just how delighted she was to be here. On first sight of that black, cramped, entirely awful cave she had pictured day upon day of long, dark monotony, until Url had found what he was looking for or her parents had found the strength to call a halt to this ridiculous venture. But as it was, Url in fact had had quite a different task in mind for her, much to Crick's aggravation.

She was to keep watch over a section of the Talon, the second of the two main waterways they had crossed to reach the cave from their home, and the mark over which all travellers to these far western reaches of the Heartlands were obliged to travel. She was to watch for anyone who looked like they might be journeying into the Eigerhills – though *watch* perhaps was not the right word – and if any did come, to ride swiftly back to warn Url and the others, so that they could seal and conceal the cave and wait for whoever it may be to pass through.

And by *whoever*, it had been clear enough who Url had meant. Guardsmen. The great and ever-growing cadre of men and women from all ranks of the City, trained and armed ostensibly for the protection of the realm but also used, somehow in these recent years with even greater bitterness and efficiency, to control it. Some were eager for glory, others desperate for pay in these lands where such a thing was growing scarcer by the year; some knew and loved the purpose of the orders they followed, others spent their lives in contented ignorance of them. But within one and all alike was a common strand; a quality which could never be forgiven, not by Aliya, not by Url, and not by any other who would claim to live free still amongst the Heartlands: They served the Council with zeal, and without question.

And so it was that for the fifth day running, Nightwind chomping silently once more on the grass just behind her, Aliya was simply waiting, and listening, laying flat amongst the shallows of the western edge of the river, her feet floating lightly in front of her, the water covering all but her face. Her arms hovered weightlessly to each side; one pointing north to Orrin Bridge, which they had used to cross the river, the other reaching southwards, to Carp Bridge, nearly ten miles away. Were any patrols to reach Url and the others, from this direction at least, it would almost certainly be through one of these two crossings.

Strong and fresh-minded as she was feeling today, it would nonetheless take the utmost of her senses to feel that far downriver. But hard as she was trying to concentrate, Aliya couldn't help but briefly open her eyes every few minutes or so, eagerly scanning the water around her for the smallest sign of the wonderful little creatures she longed so desperately to see again. Waterfaeries were just as likely to be hiding somewhere along this river as they had been on the lake, and a small but nagging part of her felt that if she could just keep still and quiet enough she may be able to spot them again; perhaps even to float and play amongst them as she had done. They had been so... beautiful was the wrong word, too simple by far. She remembered their bright, sparkling, perfectly formed little bodies, and she yearned deeply to see them before her again. Being one of them, even for just that briefest of moments, had brought her closer to the spirit of the water than she had ever been before. It was, she mused, like the feeling her Grandmother had so often described when staring deep into a sunset; like the realm of being her parents on many occasions had talked of being transported to when sitting silent amongst old woodlands; that curious but unmistakable line beyond which all knowledge and enjoyment and skill were suddenly combined and then forgotten in the presence of true, ancient Magic...

Just then a soft, strange ripple brushed against the left half of her body from cheek to toe. It took a second for it to register through the pleasant haze of her thoughts; whether it had been sound or touch, Aliya couldn't tell, or perhaps couldn't remember. She opened her eyes, searching upriver, but all she could see was the constant, steady flow of the water, and all she could hear above that was the steady grazing of Nightwind. Slowly she closed her eyes, lying back into the warm, welcoming...

But immediately it was there again, distant but distinct amongst the gentle throb of the day. Water cascaded from her hair as she sat quickly upright, but still there was no sign of anything along the river. She waited a moment, breathless in concentration. Five days of uninterrupted peacefulness had slowed her mind considerably: It was several seconds before she reacted, darting quickly from the water and heaving herself up onto the high back of Nightwind, who gave a quiet snort at the unexpected interruption. Moving a short distance from the bank so they were partly shielded by a thin line of bush and the deep red of occasional maples, Aliya began to move quietly but swiftly up alongside the river, scanning the ribbon of blue and its surroundings for whatever it was that she had sensed. She rode without stopping for twenty minutes, rarely taking her eyes off the water, but in that time she saw little other than a cluster of large reed-trout, and a swan and her young passing regally downriver. It had been none of these things; Aliya still was unable to say what it *had* been... but she knew it was none of them.

There was one final bend before the bridge, sweeping long and gradually round to the right. Surely it hadn't been anything this far away? Even though it was the two bridges that she had been focusing dimly upon, she had expected at most a dull echo if anything were to have crossed there; what she had felt had seemed far closer and more defined than that. Tentatively, still trying to maintain her focus on the river, she dismounted and led Nightwind slowly around the last part of the bend. Over the top of a thick mound of sprawling, barbed gorse, the flat, wooden bridge appeared ahead of her, less than a hundred feet away...

There was nothing. No sign of anything or anyone; no unnatural ripples of movement in the water below. And then, she realised, clenching her hands in disbelief: no daisies. She had completely forgotten about them, the two tiny milk-daisy chains she had hung carefully over the side of the bridge, tied to an invisible thread which she had laid over the crossing, so that when broken would release the flowers and their distinctive scent into the water. It had been her Grandmother's idea, and one which Aliya had been in little doubt would prove unsuccessful. Yet she knew now that they had worked. It had been them which she had felt fall into the water. But if that were so...

Aliya halted. Something had broken the thread, but what that something was, and where it was now, and where it was going, she had no idea. Perhaps it could have been one of the others returning home to fetch something? Without moving she tried to see through the bushes around and ahead of her: Perhaps whatever it was had seen Aliya's trick after crossing through it, and was waiting for her up ahead...?

A childish fear, she told herself firmly, focusing on her hands and trying to let the tension ease from her palms and fingers as her Mother had taught her long ago. The thread which Abetta had given her to use had been so thin that even Aliya herself had lost sight of it the instant she had put it in place. And even had it been spotted, the most worrying creatures this far inside the Heartlands were the Guardsmen themselves – and for all their strength and cruelty, they were hardly known for their subtlety. Taking a bracing breath, and standing tall in the best she could do to resemble the manner of someone carelessly wandering the calm waterways of the Heartlands on this pleasant afternoon, she let Nightwind lead the way around the bushes in front of them, stepping out and walking serenely along the riverbank, towards the bridge.

She reached the first set of tall, wooden posts, passing between them and making her way slowly into the centre of the bridge. She gazed to the far side, then behind her, and then slowly up and back down the river. Still there was nothing. Examining the ground around her carefully, she eventually found the broken strand of one of the threads, cut midway across the bridge. She wished one of the others were here: Through water it was to her they all turned for guidance, but any one of them was easily better at tracking on land than she was. Even Yori was fast acquiring a respectable aptitude for it.

But they were not here. So with another deep breath Aliya set to work again, exploring the ground, looking for some sign of recent movement. She had seen Crick do this a hundred times before, but almost always he had done so in silence, rarely explaining his thoughts or his actions. He enjoyed the attention this silent mysteriousness brought him, she thought crossly as she searched around her, uncertain what she was supposed to be looking for. Wooden beams lined the low sides of the bridge... splatters of mud... leaves... small splinters and cracks in the old wood... the crusted droppings of some small animal... more mud... The mud. It was wet... Not slightly damp or soft like normal mud, but smooth and watery; small droplets splashed around larger clumps of it, not yet dried and hardened. They were new. And from the way they had been formed, they all seemed to point to westward movement over the bridge, back the way she had come. Towards the hills.

Abandoning all pretence of calm Aliya jumped clean onto Nightwind and spurred him back across the bridge. Just as she reached the other side, however, she paused; her eyes caught by a line of large hoof-prints in the mud. Now that she was looking for them they were perfectly obvious to her, and though she still lacked the skill to read them accurately she could tell that there were at least two separate tracks. They led again away from the bridge, towards a gap in the bushes where the narrow dirt path which she and the others were using to get to the cave disappeared westwards to meet the beginnings of the Eigerhills. Aliya spurred Nightwind again.

The path ran straight and level for a time, then for half a mile banked slightly uphill, and finally after what seemed like an eternity Aliya reached the crest of a low ridgeline from where she looked down across a rolling carpet of open fields. And there, suddenly in the distance she caught a brief glimpse of four riders, each glinting in the bright gold and white chainmail of the City, before they vanished together into the front edge of the endless, rising sea of oaks.

Aliya's thoughts twisted and turned in frantic circles, her mind racing as she tried to work out what to do. She knew what Url had told her – *Ride quickly and warn us* – but that had been on the assumption that she could get round in front of whoever it was fast enough to take the main route up to the cave. As it was now, with the riders already that far along the path, she would have to detour so far around them that she would barely get there before they did. Perhaps they were not going that way at all…? But she couldn't take that risk. She could think of nothing else but to follow behind, hoping to think of some sort of distraction along the way before they reached the cave.

Nightwind struck an incredible pace beneath her, and before long Aliya was entering the treeline into which the figures had disappeared. They had been cantering at a good but not fast pace when she had seen them, and to her silent, unspeakable relief, when she paused to listen she could hear them, not too far ahead of her. Their voices were muffled through the trees, the words stripped of meaning, but the raucous tones of their speech and laughter were easily discernable even from here. Guardsmen, without doubt. They reeked of it.

Aliya did her best to pick her way along the quietest parts of the path; Nightwind sensing her fear, moving quiet and soft as the trees themselves behind her. The dirt track twisted and weaved continuously up into the hills, but still Aliya could think of nothing. Perhaps she could ride up to them and claim to be lost, or in trouble? Appeal to their good nature – she almost laughed aloud at the idea. If she tried she knew in all likelihood they would either ignore her, or... She didn't like to think of what else they might do. New accounts of what Guardsmen had done to women and girls, men and boys alike when drunk or far enough away from the order of the City were not difficult to come by. Not that all of them were like that; there was even one Aliya had met, many years ago, who *had* helped her, when she had very nearly drowned trying to cross Lake Iris. Guardsmen such as him, though, were few and far between. She wouldn't take the risk unless and until she absolutely had to.

But what else was there...? She could make a noise somewhere in the woods, or along a different path; try and draw them away... But then they would either ignore her and carry on, or else chase her. And ignorant, arrogant, violent, and generally unpleasant as they might be, there was little doubt they knew how to ride and chase down their prey with brutal efficiency. The very thought of complimenting the Council stuck like a ragged knife in Aliya's chest, but if it was one thing they did well, it was to train those who served them with the skills to do so. It was, though she despised admitting it, one of the few reasons the borders of the Heartlands still stood after all these years.

The talking had stopped. Their heavy movement, however, was still easy to hear. Aliya glimpsed a glimmer of low sunlight through the trees ahead, and with it she realised they were nearing the point at which they would emerge to overlook the valley, with the outsider's hut on the far side. They were getting far too close. Without thinking it through Aliya suddenly found herself picking up a thin, broken branch from the ground, turning Nightwind around and pointing him back along the path, and bringing the sharp end of the branch alongside his flank. There was a good spot in the bushes behind her where she could hide and wait for them to pass; she just hoped that he would make enough noise to attract their attention. He'd be safe, she told herself... Calm as he was most of the time, Nightwind could move as swift as any other when roused to it. He would make his way back to the house; Aliya would just have to make her apologies later. She gripped the branch firmly, scowling as she patted Nightwind, drawing her hand back to thrust it at the unsuspecting animal...

Suddenly the voice of one of the Guardsmen came clearly through the trees:

'This is it,' boomed the deep, rumbling tone of what must have been an exceptionally heavily-built man. Aliya hadn't realised quite how close she had come to them. They couldn't be more than a few dozen feet from her.

'*This*?' answered a second, much younger voice. 'This is barely path enough for a rat! Why can we not just carry on up here?' He paused a moment. 'We can go take supper at old black's again – I fear he may have missed us!' His grunt of laughter was mixed with another from a third man.

'Well, it *would* suit me to see that miserable old mute again, I suppose,' said the first. From his voice alone Aliya could sense a wicked smile. 'I've not had my dues off him for near-on twenty days.'

'*We* haven't,' said the younger. The deep voice grunted some sort of agreement. 'So let's –'

'We've got our orders. Captain wants us at Eaglesreach by sundown. We'll be late as it is.'

'But can't we just –'

'No point arguing it, lad,' said the fourth and, Aliya hoped, final voice, surprisingly clear and gentle – entirely unlike any Guardsman Aliya had ever met herself or heard portrayed. 'You know how Burn here gets when he's *got his orders*... Would rather drink a horn of his own piss than upset his dear old Captain!' There was a loud, metallic *thump* and a groan of pained amusement from the fourth man.

'We're going up here,' said the first – Burn – shortly. 'It cuts out most of these bloody hills, and it'll get us there before dinner's done for the night. Get moving.'

None of the others said a word, but the sounds of their horses moving again told Aliya that the command had been followed, if unwillingly. Keeping low to the ground she crept, foot by careful foot along the path, and, poking her right eye cautiously around the side of a thick trunk, she saw the four men venturing off to the right of the path, into the undergrowth. A squat, middle-aged man with at least three rolls of neck squashed uncomfortably above his unpleasantly tight breastplate brought up the rear. What they were following was no more than a thin line through the long grass, one which Aliya on any of the several trips she had made along here had failed to notice. Her whole body felt light with relief as she watched them disappear into the grass and close trees. She smiled, on the point of turning away and back to Nightwind when one of them spoke again:

'*Why*'ve we got to come up here, anyway?' It was the youngest.

'Because I told you to come up here,' answered the one they called Burn, cursing as a low-hanging branch whipped back against him.

'But *why* did you tell us to come –'

'Because the *Captain* told *me* to come up here,' he answered wearily. 'And I go where I'm told. And *you* go where I'm told, too.'

'But –'

'For mercy's sake, Erren, drop it!' said one of the others. Aliya couldn't tell which it was; their voices growing fainter with each pace.

'It's the Black Wind, isn't it!'

Aliya's heart jumped at the words. She strained to hear them more clearly…

'Mind your tongue, boy,' said Burn, warningly. 'People who get that excited when they talk of the Wind usually end up dead or worse.' There was no reply; Aliya hoping desperately that they hadn't passed out of earshot… 'But, yes –' Burn continued, '– it is.'

Aliya fought to hear more of their conversation but they were moving too far away. They were completely lost from sight now. She and her family were safe: She could ride either to the cave or back again to the river without worry, and she knew there was little doubt that she should. And yet at the same time she couldn't help but yearn to learn more of what they were talking about. The Black Wind was rarely talked of in her household, or by any of the few others she knew. And when it was, it was always amidst the oppressive air of overwhelming fear and uncertainty. It was nothing like the way these men were talking of it. For sure the fear was still there in their voices, but alongside it they seemed to know a great deal more about the matter than she did. Trying to ignore the thoughts of what her Mother or Father would say if they knew what she was doing, she edged quietly around the tree, skipping delicately amongst the twigs and leaves along the path until she reach the narrow track the men had taken. Crouched close as a wolf-pup to the ground she peered through the grass and along the track, but they were still not in sight. It took several tortuous minutes of silent scrambling through the undergrowth before once again she was close enough behind them to hear their talk. It sounded like the youth and his portly leader were continuing with a strand of the same conversation as before…

'…but never into the *Heartlands*,' the young man was saying. 'We've got thousands of us all round the borders! *Tens* of thousands!' One of the others gave a grim laugh, but he ignored it: 'We're better protected than any land there's ever been on this world! And even if it did – which it won't – it could never reach us inside the *City*! How many walls have we got now?' He didn't pause for an answer. 'And all that and then the Haven'll as well…?'

'*The Haven!*' Burn exclaimed. One of the horses pulled to a sudden halt, the others following suit in quick succession. 'The *Haven?*' he asked again, incredulous.

The youth was silent under what was certain to be a ferocious glare. Aliya longed to be able to see what was happening, but was suddenly thankful that she was well out of sight. Their leader's anger was sure to be terrible... For anyone to talk of the Haven so was bad enough, in *their* ignorant eyes, at least. But for a Guardsman himself to do so... It was unheard of. *Surely* he couldn't have meant it...

'That palace of Magical piss-water and prayers of the ignorant? You think *that's* what'll save you?' asked Burn, his voice so thick with contempt that even from a distance it weighed dark and heavy in the air. 'You think you'll be able to run back behind the City walls and live happily behind them while that *plaything of sorcerers* protects you?' He spat.

'The boy was only joking, Sir,' spoke the gentlest voice of the four, even more soothing than before despite the sudden formality which had been forced upon it by the unexpected change in topic. But his attempt at placating the disgust of their leader passed unsuccessfully...

'Jokes are for matters that are amusing!' he bellowed. 'With words that make others laugh! I heard neither! And besides, there was a seriousness in what he said... Wasn't there, boy?'

'No, Sir,' the youth attempted, but he was cut off:

'A *believer* in our midst, indeed...' The word was sneered as though spoken by the tongue of the Council itself. In her anger Aliya tried recklessly to think of a way of striking him without being noticed or caught. If Crick was here he may have been able to get in and out without being seen... Meanwhile the youth's mounting gasps of denial were going unheeded, swept hopelessly beneath the bitter tirade being cast upon him like a vicious fall of ice...

'You *truly* think we're going to be saved by hiding behind a bit of *Magic* of our own? Don't you think the other cities had the same idea? Are your parents and tutors so ignorant of the history of our world that they have taught you *none* of it? What's become of those cites, boy?' Every word now was being shouted with a fury which seemed to have risen like a great and sudden tide to engulf the young man. 'What's become of them? All the other realms which relied upon Magic to guide and protect them – I shouldn't have to be telling you this! All the other cities – what's become of them?'

'Sir –' one of the others tried.

'Quiet!' Burn screamed with a great clatter of armour. 'Nobody's heard from any of them since long before you were born, boy! All because people like *you* thought they could hide, and wait, and outlast... Wait for the *old Magics* to return; for the old strength of witches and wizards to arise spectacularly to life from the graveyard of myth to aid us!' He spat again. 'And they were *wrong*! All of them!'

'Really, Sir, please –' the youth was utterly drained of the vigour with which he had spoken until now, '– it *was* a joke…' In the silence the leader's breathing was quick and loud through his fat nose. 'Truly… A poor one, I admit – but there was no seriousness to it. None… I'm no *believer*, Sir. I've as little patience for those fools as you do.'

After all that had been said, Aliya could not tell whether he telling the truth now, or whether his mentioning of the Haven had been an honest if careless slip of the tongue. The horses were pawing restlessly at the ground around them; Aliya suddenly thinking back to Nightwind, thanking the stars for his continued silence. She could only hope that it would last.

'Tell me of your plan, then,' said Burn; his anger turned suddenly to scorn.

'My …?'

'If you've the strength and spirits to make mock of such a subject, I trust you also have the knowledge to guide the rest of us through these dark times…? Come – tell us: What is to be done? How are we to protect ourselves? *Answer me*, boy!' he screamed when there was no reply.

'I – um – we should keep our walls strong, and –'

'*Walls* again… You talk of them as though they were assembled by the old gods themselves! I assume it is the great walls of Immelus you speak of? You wish to hide within the city – is that it?' Silence again. 'And how, if I may presume to be so bold, do you propose that the entire population of the Heartlands outlasts the Black Wind *within* those walls?'

'I'm not saying everyone could be saved… There'd have to be sacrifices, of course – but we could store enough food and drink for some of us for decades, and in that time we could find some way of –'

'*Sacrifices?*' exclaimed one of the others. Burn gave a bitter laugh…

'They'll make a Councillor of him yet,' he sighed quietly.

'I didn't mean –'

'And what will you and your special little group of survivors do once the rest of us have been *sacrificed*, then?' asked Burn.

'I – I didn't…' He was sounding less a man and more the young, unproven boy with every painful second. For a brief moment Aliya was on the verge of feeling pity for him. She snapped herself quickly out from such stupidity. 'I just thought that, if we could have more time to work out what it is, perhaps we could come up with something…?'

'*Come up with something…*' Burn echoed, and with it he let out a long, heavy sigh. When he spoke again his voice was suddenly quieter, tinged with something resembling sorrow…

'Listen to me, boy… Time won't save anyone. Neither will the Haven. There'll be no easy answer to our fate. Nobody's going to *come up with something*. The Black Wind will keep growing in power. Soon it'll be stronger than it has been since before any of us can remember. And hiding and hoping won't do us any good. There's already been reports of the Nothingness felt all round the border: some even say they've spotted gloomed beasts trying to come through the mountains at nights. No…' he sighed again, 'the only chance we've got is to keep putting more men on the Gates, keep strong, and keep fighting and pushing it back from our borders. Quite *what* it is behind the darkness that we're to fight, Gods only know. But fight it we must. What good is it being protected inside your walls when your *lands* have been overrun and you can't grow *food*, and every source of *water* around you has been spoiled and poisoned? With your plan your walls would become the great edgings of your tomb before you realised it. What we need is more young Guardsmen being born, more crops being grown, and more blades and bolts and armours being made than we've ever made before. *That's* the best and only chance we've got. Don't you ever go relying on anything else. And don't – ever – make jokes about relying on Magic like that. Not in my presence.'

For a moment none of them spoke; the whispering of the trees rising to a fleeting clamour with a brief gust of wind, reminding them all of where they were. With a grunted 'On with it,' from their leader, the horses started forwards once again.

Briefly Aliya considered whether or not to follow, but finally now she decided her luck had been pushed far enough. She waited, listening while the Guardsmen rode noisily out of earshot, before standing and releasing the breath she suddenly felt she had been holding since she'd entered the woods. Only when she was certain they were no longer close did she turn and sprint hurriedly back to the path and her waiting, curious Nightwind, mounting and tearing quickly up towards the cave; her thoughts all the way torn uncertainly between the Guardsmen behind her and the terror of whatever it was beyond the borders which could rouse even them to such indiscipline and fear. And then there had been the way they had spoken – of the City, of those who like her lived beyond its control, and most keenly of all of Magic itself… Long into the afternoon she found herself unable to put aside the overriding sense of anger and revulsion at those words. At length the bitterness did begin to diminish, but even then it was only to dissolve into a deep, painful sadness. Why did they so despise Magic and those that loved it? She had never understood. And she was sure she never would.

Chapter Six

Light from the Deep

Clink... Clink... Clink... Clink...

With each dragging minute it was growing harder and harder to block out the noise of hammer upon hard stone. Crick as ever was doing his utmost, but each time he managed to veer his mind away to thoughts of something or somewhere else a piercing, high-pitched *clink!* Would enter into his mind like outside noise infiltrating and assimilating itself violently into a dream. Either that, or he would lose concentration altogether and miss his target, more often than not resulting in injury or a frustrated shout of disapproval from an ever-watchful Url behind him. Or both.

Eight days of long, hard, dark, hot, and bone-achingly cramped work, and what little interest and enthusiasm Crick had been able to find for Url's idea had long since disappeared. The routine had been the same each day: Crick and his Father taking turns working at the rock with the great pick-hammer that Url kept for such special occasions, the pointed tip of which – despite its weight, Crick and his Father's best efforts, and Url's former assurances – was only able to nibble weakly at the hard, unrelenting rock ahead of it. When not using the hammer they would help Url to carry the loose rock back up the tunnel into the cave, within which it was piled tightly up against the sides. Not that Url had proved the greatest of help when it came to this. His time, rather, seemed largely to be spent gazing distractedly and eagerly over the shoulder of whoever was hammering, or else encouraging Yori to see if he could sense any sudden surge of Magic up ahead.

But Yori, his eyes a constant, pale glow in the gloom behind them, had felt nothing. Nothing at least beyond the steady, peaceful throb of that which he could usually feel around him. They had dug perhaps thirty feet into the rock in a slow, gentle gradient away from the cave, following the direction in which the crystal had disappeared, but in all that time, with each long day and every piercing *clink*, Yori had made no sign whatsoever of sensing anything new.

'It's getting late,' his Father called wearily down from the cave. Url gave a quick, irritable glance over his shoulder but motioned Crick to continue. Looking at him now, Crick could see more plainly than ever the growing desperation which had been spreading like mould across his hot, dusty face these past days.

'Just a few minutes,' the old man muttered. 'I think Yori's onto something...'

Yori looked despairingly at Crick, shrugging his tired shoulders. If Url noticed, he made no show of it.

'We're not having this conversation again,' said Orlando. 'I won't have us all riding back through the dark. We'll leave home by sunrise tomorrow.'

Again... thought Crick. His penchant for rising late and staying awake long into the nights was being entirely ignored, and he was becoming thoroughly jaded with the constant stirrings before even the sun had made any show of itself.

Url was looking dejectedly into the ground; Yori staring at him with an intense pity...

'I'm staying here tonight,' said the old man, exhaustion telling clearly through the determined grit of his voice.

'Don't be ridiculous, Url. Come back and –'

'I'm staying here,' he interrupted flatly. 'Leave some water and bring me back some food tomorrow. If you'd be so kind,' he added with a sigh and a brief apologetic nod to Orlando, wiping the sweat roughly from his face with the back of his grimy sleeve. 'I'll see you all in the morning.'

Crick let the hammer fall to the ground with another heavy *clink* and leant heavily upon it, studying Url. Then he spoke up to the flickering figure of his Father above him:

'I'll stay with him,' he sighed. Url's eyes softened with appreciation as he looked back at Crick. His Father considered it for a moment...

'You stay in the cave. You don't go wandering around the hills, understand?'

'I'll stay too,' said Yori, but his Father had cut him off almost before the words had left his mouth:

'*You're* coming back with us.'

'But if Crick's here I'll be –'

'Are we nearly done?' echoed Siu's voice down the tunnel.

'Just finishing,' said Orlando, turning away into the cave to answer her. 'Crick and Url are going to stay here tonight.'

'Is that a good idea?'

'Not particularly.'

'We'll be fine!' Crick called up the tunnel, still leaning on the hammer.

'They'll be okay,' said his Father. 'It's only for the night. And I'm sure Crick's spent nights in worse places,' he added with a hidden, knowing glance back down towards Crick.

'You look after my son!' said Siu after a moment, appearing in the entrance hole above them and jabbing a threatening finger towards Url.

'Can't I stay w-' Yori began imploringly.

'Absolutely not. Come on, let's be off. We'll see you first thing tomorrow!' she called down the tunnel as she left; Yori trudging crossly up the tunnel, barging past his Father with a grumpiness welcomingly amusing to all but himself.

'Don't work too hard,' said Orlando with a resigned smile, and then he too disappeared, leaving his torch wedged into the rock where he had been standing, so that it flickered lonely above them like a large, eerie star.

'What're you waiting for, then?' asked Url with an encouraging slap of Crick's shoulder; a grim resolve returning to his demeanour as he stooped to lift a thick shard of rock which lay between them. The hammer seemed welded to the ground for a moment as Crick tried to raise it, but with a great heave he managed to lift it onto his shoulders, and once more the *clink... clink... clink...* sounded through the closeness of the tunnel.

*

They worked for over an hour after the others had left, but with only the two of them it was even harder going than before. And slow. Crick was doing all the hammering now, his arms soon growing tired and weak, and despite his truly remarkable strength for his age Url quickly began to weary as well, only able to carry small fragments of rock out at a time, pausing at either end of the tunnel to wipe fresh sweat from his brow and the bridge of his nose. To his credit, though, and to Crick's admiration, he never once complained or stopped altogether – not that Crick would ever have expected him to. But this did nothing to change the fact that, given all their effort, the progress they made was nowhere close to as great as either of them had hoped for. Were it not for the fact that they were slowly transporting pieces of the rock away, it would have been all but impossible to tell whether or not they were advancing at all.

'I need a drink,' said Crick, panting heavily. He had no idea what time it was, only that there was no sign of light at all coming in from outside, and that he had now gone well past exhaustion.

'And something to eat,' admitted Url, pausing as he reached down awkwardly for another splinter of stone to add to the small bundle in his arms. After a moment's thought he cast the armful down instead at his feet, and turned away into the tunnel.

The fresh night air came as a surge of glorious relief as Crick emerged from the tunnel for the first time in what felt like days. Url set to work building a small fire just outside the entrance to the cave, beyond which their surroundings were deep black beneath a silent, starless sky. Crick took some bread and strips of dried meat from the sack which had been left behind for them, sitting opposite Url as the fire spluttered welcomingly into life from the sparks of the old man's flint. For several minutes they simply sat, without talking, letting the exhaustion drain slowly from their aching limbs. Then they tucked eagerly in to their simple but exceptionally refreshing food and drink, talking briefly between mouthfuls of the horses, the occasional rustling or call of a nearby creature, the fire itself, and other such distractions.

'So, tell me,' said Crick with a satisfied stretch once his thirst had been fully quenched, 'what is it you're hoping to find down here, really?' Url looked up and gave a weak smile, hesitating a moment. 'Do you truly think the origins of all Magic in our world are going to be buried somewhere beneath us…?' For some reason neither he nor any of the others had ever asked the question so directly before. Most likely because they were all quite confident as to the answer. Still, Crick was curious now for Url's response, and this seemed the time if ever there was to be one to ask. Url himself was watching deep into the fire.

'The truth is…' he said at length, casting down the last shred of dried lamb in front of him, seeming suddenly to lose his appetite, 'I don't know. It could be nothing.' Crick didn't need Yori's abilities to see the desperation in Url's eyes as he looked back towards the tunnel.

'But then… it could be *everything*. I don't know *what*, or *how*… I just know there's something down there. There has to be.' The last of his words were masked by a long sigh. Pity forestalled Crick from voicing the *why*? which sat inside him like a splinter needing to be pulled out. 'We should get some sleep. I want to be up and started before they all get here.'

The tiredness which Crick had briefly forgotten came back to him instantly. Sensing that he would get no more from Url tonight, he simply nodded, leaning in to douse the fire.

'Leave it,' said Url quietly. 'I think I'll rest here a while.' His eyes fell closed, still staring into the flames. Before Crick had even made it over to his blanket in the middle of the cave, the old man was snoring gently.

*

When Crick opened his eyes again it was full dark about him. The tiny, struggling embers of what remained of the fire told him he must have been asleep a good few hours. For a second he wondered what had woken him, but then in a great gulp of a snore Url's body was lit up beside the embers, still just about propped up in an ungainly fashion against the wall behind him, half in and half out of the cave.

His Mother's warning words from earlier were still fresh in his mind, yet above them the still night and the cool, fresh darkness which Crick was swiftly coming to associate with adventure were calling to him from beyond the entrance. Feeling suddenly quite awake he untangled himself from his blankets and made his way carefully through the cave, stepping light as the freshly-formed aches and pains of his body would allow around Url, and out into the night.

It was wonderful… the stars were now full out, unhindered by even the slightest sign of cloud, while a gentle, invigorating breeze blew silently from the north. *Perfect…* he thought to himself with a grin. At the edge of the clearing, still and quiet as the gnarled trunks around him, Railer was tethered to a large oak. As Crick approached he lifted his head from slumber and gave a quiet soft snort of recognition, poking at the ground restlessly with his front hoofs.

'You want to go too, don't you…?' Crick whispered into his ear. But just as he began to unfasten the reins there was a rasping call from behind him:

'I'm afraid neither of you are going anywhere!'

Crick froze, briefly startled by the loud voice which cut through the quietness of the night like a sudden thunder, but taking then a deep breath of mixed relief and frustration as he realised it was Url.

'I'll be gone a few minutes – an hour at most!' he said, turning back to see Url sitting upright, pulling his cloak tight about him, rekindling the fire.

'No, you won't,' said Url simply. 'You're staying right here.' Crick opened his mouth to argue but Url got there first: 'If you think I'm going to risk incurring the wrath of your Mother and Father – not to mention no doubt that wretched old hag –' he added with a partly serious scowl, '– then you are, I'm afraid to say, entirely mistaken, young lad. I fear I'm pushing my luck quite enough as it is, keeping you here.'

'But they don't have to know!'

'Crick, my boy,' said Url with a small chuckle, 'you still don't know your parents or Grandmother at all well enough, do you? If you think you can run around in these woods – or any other woods, for that matter,' he added with a quick glance up at Crick, 'without your parents knowing or finding out about it at some point, then you are, once again, very, *very* –'

'Mistaken,' Crick finished. 'I get it.' He looped the reins back over the branch and strolled back to the cave. He wouldn't win this one. Even Url, sympathetic as he was to Crick's adventures, was never going to go so explicitly against the wishes of Crick's parents and Grandmother. Crick could hardly blame him for it.

'But if you've got this much energy,' said Url with a broad smile, 'we might as well get started…'

'*Now*?' asked Crick, already thinking of his blanket. It would still be warm… 'It's not even –'

'Maybe it'll teach you to stay asleep a bit longer, next time.' Crick decided against informing the old man that it was his snores which had woken him: Url had little time or sympathy for those who complained about such things. 'Anyway, it won't be long until it starts to get light. Come on, help me up,' he said, reaching out his hand.

While Crick cleared his possessions and re-piled some of the bits of stone which had fallen loose into the middle of the cave, Url went to fill a large pitcher with water from the small, fast-flowing stream they had been using, which had been found, fortunately, just a few hundred feet away from the cave, winding its way deep into the soft, mossy ground. When he returned they cooked a large bowl of some type of thick, tasteless porridge of Url's – his customary foodstuff when away on such expeditions as this – which he flavoured with the last thin slices of the apples they had brought with them the previous day. They ate in silence; Crick eyeing the grey, lumpy mass suspiciously while a distracted Url seemed not to notice his at all.

By the time they had finished, the first hazy glimmer of daylight was beginning to creep up over the horizon. They used the last of the water to wash the worst of the mess from their bowls and spoons, and while Url went again to fill the pitcher for their drinks through the morning Crick clambered reluctantly back inside the cave to change into another shirt, only now realising just how dirty and sweat-stained his current one was. And once he had changed, he sat by the entrance to the tunnel, looking down into it with an expression almost as gloomy as the hole itself. But suddenly, just as he was thinking disconsolately about how long and dull the coming day was sure to be, something strange and altogether quite wonderful appeared from nowhere before his eyes... He blinked, twice, but still it was there: Where before there had been nothing but dark tunnel there was now a shimmering mass of tiny flecks of silver, quivering brilliantly as they reflected the light which Crick realised was coming in from outside the cave. Looking back once more into the tunnel to make certain of what he was seeing, he jumped up and dashed outside, seeing between the dozens of trunks of the tall trees which lined the eastern edge of the clearing the dazzling flash of the newly-risen sun. Somehow the light had found the narrowest of gaps through the thick mass of woodland and was pouring, almost wilfully, directly towards the cave.

'Url!' Crick called into the trees to his left. '*Url!*' But even as he did so the sun rose up another fraction and was lost, hidden behind the thick, vivid veil of green. Crick leapt back inside and looked down into the tunnel... seeing nothing. The lights had gone; replaced once more with the dull gloom of before. There was a crashing of loose rocks behind him as Url appeared at the entrance to the cave, panting.

'What? What is it?' he asked with quick, excited concern. 'Are you alright? What's wrong? What happened?'

'I – It's...' Crick stammered, looking back confused and frustrated into the tunnel. 'It was – *they* were like firefaeries – dozens of them, but silver, all over the walls!'

'What do you mean?' said Url, nearly falling over himself in his hurry to Crick's side, from where he stuck his head quickly in front of Crick's and into the tunnel, searching around intently. '*What* were? Where did they go?'

'I don't know... It was the sunrise. When the sun came up it shone through the trees and... and into here somehow for a few seconds. It reflected off them, or – or brought them to life or –'

'Brought them to...!' Url's words trailed off as he clambered through and disappeared inside the tunnel. 'Don't just stand there!' he called back a moment later. 'Light some torches and get down here!'

*

But by the time the others arrived, nearly two hours later, nothing
had been found. Despite his half-dozen descriptions and best guesses
as to where they had been there was no sign at all of whatever it was
that Crick had seen; Url having spent the entire time with his nose
virtually touching the walls, floor, or roof of the tunnel, scurrying
around like a demented spider searching for hidden flies as Crick held
the torches beside him. It took a long time to explain it all to the others;
Crick's uncertain attempts continually interrupted by some
unintelligible mumble of excitement or confusion from Url, whose
wide eyes never left the rock as he felt his way ceaselessly up and
down the tunnel, picking at various places and scrutinising them with
even greater care.

After a long while, as Url began what must have been his
twentieth scan of the tunnel, Crick started to feel that this waiting and
watching was even more tedious than the digging had been. And
almost as one the others too seemed to come to the same conclusion,
each wordlessly going back to their separate tasks. Siu left to keep her
watch over the woods outside, Abetta going with her to fetch water and
brew something hot to drink in the chilly morning air, while Orlando
and Crick went to the far end of the tunnel, to begin hammering away
once more at the rock. As Yori came down to join them, however, Url
took hold of his arm and pulled him to one side...

'Take a good look here,' he said, placing Yori's hand against the
wall. 'Can you feel anything?' he asked with a fanatical smile.

'He had that same look about him when he first came back with
the crystal,' sighed Crick's Father quietly beside him. He lifted the
pick to one side; the *clink... clink... clink...* beginning again, louder
and more grating than ever.

*

Midday came, and went, in another slow blur of cramped,
sweltering silence, broken only by the sounds of constant hammering
and of rock splitting piece by minute piece to being carried back to the
surface; the shards now becoming fewer and smaller; the ground
seeming increasingly reluctant to let them through. After a brief lunch
Crick took his fourth turn with the hammer; Url reluctantly letting Yori
go to help at the bottom of the tunnel. After stooping and craning for so
long to examine various parts of the walls which Url had continued
pointing out to him, Yori was thrilled to be able to move around more

freely, eagerly picking up an armful of loose stone and making his way back up to the top.

'I'll be staying here again tonight,' Url muttered distractedly.

'Is that really necessary?' Orlando asked as Crick with burning shoulders swung back the hammer for another strike. 'I think it would be good for you to –' but he never finished the sentence: The instant the pick struck the wall there was a piercing cry of pain from Yori, and as Crick turned he heard stones clattering to the floor, Yori staggering and crashing into the side of the tunnel, clutching his head in agony. His Father was at his side in the blink of an eye, faster almost than Crick could have got there.

'Yori!' he called, looking down at him and lifting his head gently off the ground. 'Son – what happened?'

And to the overwhelming relief of the faces staring down at him Yori opened his eyes, blinked away his confusion, and sat upright.

'What happened?' Orlando asked again as Yori sat, unmoving, staring distantly down to the end of the tunnel. He opened his mouth as if to say something, but couldn't seem to find the words. Instead he raised his hand, slowly, and pointed. His Father patted the side of his head and called to him again, ignoring his outstretched finger, but Crick turned and looked… And there two feet from the ground, at the spot which Crick had just struck, a thin strand of silvery crystal had been revealed, glimmering softly now in the light of the hastily discarded torch which lay flickering below it.

Crick nudged his Father in his side… and again… and finally on the third attempt Orlando turned. Url looked up as well, and as he did so he let out a wholly uncontrollable splutter of excitement.

'*There it is*!' he gasped, stepping carefully around Yori and sprinting down the tunnel, virtually picking Crick up along the way and carrying him with him. He halted abruptly a foot away from the crystal, picking up the torch and checking it carefully from all angles; a manic smile spreading wide across his face.

'This is it! We've found it!'

'Well, let's get it, then!' said Crick, reaching down to pick up the hitherto unused chisel from behind him.

'No!' shouted Url, 'That's what I did last time! Leave it!'

'But I thought –'

'Just wait…'

Crick didn't understand… Wasn't this what they'd been searching for?

'But what if it disappears again?' he asked.

'That's what I'm waiting for!' muttered Url, still grinning.

'Have you *completely* lost the last of your mind?' said Orlando, standing with such astonished indignation that he altogether forgot about the roof of the tunnel, striking his head hard against it. We are *not* spending another ten days down here searching for it if you lose it again!' he finished with a grimace, rubbing his scalp.

'You won't have to; just wait – and *don't touch it!*' he screamed at Crick, who had raised the hammer and chisel just above the crystal.

'But why don't you want –' But even as Crick spoke the crystal quivered. As all eyes watched it paused for a moment, and then slowly, smoothly, it began to withdraw into the rock. 'Url...'

'I know... just wait...'

Crick looked once more to his Father, who shrugged helplessly, and then he watched again as the crystal continued to disappear slowly out of sight. There was only an inch left... '*Url...*' now less... And then it was gone. But before Crick could say anything else Url stepped forward, gently, closer to where the crystal had been. Holding the torch up next to him he peered into the small, smooth hole... and smiled.

'Look!' he whispered excitedly, gesturing to Crick to see for himself. And as Crick bent down and looked into the hole he saw, glittering a few inches from the surface, the tip of the crystal, firm and unmoving. 'When I broke the piece off last time I hurt it – scared it away – but now we've found it again we can follow it all the way down! As long as we don't strike it, it shouldn't run too far from us.'

'*Run...?*' Orlando murmured.

'*You* think of a better word...!'

'But how did you know it would do that this time?' asked Crick. 'How did you know it wouldn't disappear completely again?'

'I, umm... well, after looking at the various –'

'You guessed,' said Yori.

'I... Well yes, I did.' He smiled. 'Right though, wasn't I...?'

*

There was an entirely different atmosphere in the tunnel now. The rock was just as hard, maybe more so, but despite it the work seemed easier somehow. Url bounced enthusiastically from place to place, helping to move the rock and peering continually into the hole down which the seemingly unending line of crystal kept disappearing. Time after time Crick and his Father would break away most of the rock around the hole, and then using the chisel would delicately chip out the remaining pieces which surrounded the crystal, the glittering tip of which would then wait secretively, quiver gently, and pull back away from them. Abetta and Siu appeared at various points through the day,

63

just as intrigued and excited by the crystal as the others. And Yori, who had recovered almost immediately after his fall, could barely take his eyes off the tiny speck of silvery light which could be seen through the rock.

Far quicker than anyone realised, therefore, the sun was beginning to sink low in the sky, and a cool wind was bringing with it the evening air. Url, of course, decided to spend the night in the cave again, as did Crick. And after some debate – and numerous assurances from Crick and Url that they would take good care of him – Yori too this time was allowed to stay. They worked long into the night, rising early the next morning to watch as the sunrise once again lit up the cave for a few brilliant seconds in which the tunnel was speckled with bright, shimmering pinpoints of light, which seemed to become more and more intense the deeper into the tunnel they went.

All through the morning and afternoon nobody mentioned the fact that this was the tenth day since they had started work on the tunnel. And to Crick's surprise – and Url's quiet, unbounded delight – as the end of the day approached there was little disagreement as to whether or not they should continue tomorrow: Against all former expectations there was now not one amongst them who didn't hold a growing curiosity as to what it was that lay at the end of this trail. Apart from all else, there was also the feeling that after so much hard work it would be absurd to stop now, when they seemed surely to be doing so well.

*

The excitement and expectations that the finding of the crystal had brought, however, gradually began to wane. They worked for another day… and another… and others still after that. Seven days from when they had originally planned to stop they were still hard at work; hammering, chiselling, hammering, chiselling, clearing away the stone, and moving inch by inch deeper into the ground. Siu had come to know the woods around them so well by now that she could sense without thought or hesitation if anyone or anything was approaching for several miles around, so Aliya was granted an unrequested leave to depart her now much-loved position along the river to come and join them. Her interest in the crystal lasted a few hours, perhaps, but quickly her mood was dragged down into the sense of frustration and dejection with which the tunnel was once more beginning to fill. Url's face flicked continually between brief shades of excitement and miserable contortions of despair, and he started snapping angrily at anyone who got in his way or strayed too close to the crystal. By the end of that evening, Orlando had finally had enough.

64

'We can't just keep digging like this, Url,' he said, apologetically but quite definitely. 'I've no idea what this thing is...' he sighed, 'but the fact is, we don't know where it ends. Or even if it ever does...?'

Url lent heavily on the side of the tunnel, breathing hard; his chin nearly touching his chest as he hung his head with exhaustion. He forced a tired nod, unable to look up.

'We'll work a few more days,' continued Orlando. 'After that, that really is it. We've got crops and animals that need far more seeing to than we've been giving them, or none of us'll eat once the whitefall starts. Url nodded again, forcing himself back to work with a great, silent effort. Orlando looked at him, pitifully, and did likewise.

For the first time in many days, Crick felt that he would have dearly loved to have gone home with the others when they left that evening. But somehow he couldn't abandon Url here by himself, no matter how bad-tempered he was becoming. He was pleased that Yori was staying as well: at least the old man's grumpiness would be divided between the two of them. Sure enough, as he stood just outside the entrance to the cave beside his brother, nodding goodbye to the others, Crick heard another loud, muffled grumble from somewhere down in the tunnel.

'Guess that's our invitation to get back to work,' he said to Yori, and together they left the orange sky and rather pleasant drizzle for the dry, dreary interior with which they were growing thoroughly fed up.

Over the last few days the path which the crystal had made through the rock had curved upwards slightly, levelling off, so that after digging slowly downhill for just over sixty feet the tunnel now ran straight for just under twelve. The end of it still looked exactly the same as it had done for the past many days, however. And it was here as ever that they found Url, scraping together some loose chippings of stone which lay scattered across the floor, ignoring as far as possible the spasms of pain which had begun to cripple his back. Crick took up the pick, his fingers finding the familiar grooves his hands had by now marked clearly upon the wood, stained dark with sweat, and began to work at a piece of rock with which his Father had been struggling before he had left. Even compared to the increasingly tough stone which they had been facing up to now, this section was particularly stubborn, and after ten minutes Crick had barely forced a scratch in it. The rock simply sat there, mocking him with its serene, unchanging stillness.

'You two know how much I appreciate you staying, don't you,' said Url, quietly and quite unexpectedly. Crick stopped and studied him: his face was drained and colourless, though with a hint of its old smile.

'Keeps me out of trouble, I suppose,' said Crick with a sympathetic grin. He started beating the rock again. 'And anyway, who'd want to be outside in the wilds, exploring, when there's a lovely, dank little hole in the ground to be playing in?'

Url laughed and swatted him round the ear – or rather he tried to: Crick dodged easily to one side; Yori catching him instead as he smiled haughtily at his victory.

'Well you two clearly still have far too much energy,' said Url. 'Back to work.' Url took up the few scraps of stone he had been clearing and carried them up to the top. The cave was now almost completely full, forcing them to start putting all the new rubble outside.

'Tell me again what happened that evening in the ravine…' he called as he started to make his way back down the tunnel.

'Url!' Crick shouted back, glancing at Yori.

'What happened?' asked Yori.

'Nothing –' said Crick, continuing resolutely with the hammering.

'You saw something!' His eyes narrowed as he studied Crick.

'No I didn't,' Crick muttered pointlessly.

'Oh come on, lad; he's old enough to hear, [] enough to pick up on it sometime soon anyway, and above all smart enough not to tell your Mother!'

'Tell them what?' asked Yori, playfully narrowing his eyes still further and grinning at Crick's disquiet.

'Nothing!'

'Well I'll just have to tell young Yori what *I* know of it, then,' said Url, appearing out from the darkness.

'I told you –' said Crick, swinging the hammer with increasing enthusiasm and inaccuracy against the wall, '– nothing – hap–' But with a sudden dull *thud* his voice was silenced… It had taken them all by surprise; nothing like the sharp *clink* they had all been subconsciously listening for – rather a low, heavy thump which lingered in the air a moment before fading slowly into the walls around them. Crick looked down, and by his knees saw that he had struck a point just a finger's width from the crystal. And then to his horror the tip of the crystal just barely visible started to quiver in an odd, new way, entirely unlike any movement it had made up to now. All three of them held their breath; the quivering growing into a soft rumbling, and then to a definite and sustained shaking. The stone around the crystal started to quake and split as a deafening tearing echoed all about them. Url took hold of Yori and Crick and braced them firmly beneath his

arms as the whole tunnel shook violently, almost throwing them off
their feet… And then in an instant everything stopped, and was
completely silent and still once again. Crick felt Url's arms relax
slowly above him, and they all let out a long, collective breath of relief.
But then as though in an afterthought by the tunnel the crystal quivered
gently once more, and then fell backwards, out of sight.

'*No!*' Crick shouted, turning away from the hole and swearing
loudly in frustration, waiting for Url to do something similar…

But Url was silent. And completely motionless.

'Don't worry,' Crick sighed, 'we'll… find it again.'

'Put out that torch…' said Url, slowly and quietly.

'Put… *What?*'

'You heard me,' Url whispered.

Crick picked up one of the large, damp rags which lay on the floor
behind him and walked over to wrap it around the torch. The old man
had surely lost the last of his senses this time, but Crick had neither the
heart nor the energy to argue. As the flame was enveloped with a
muffled sizzling the tunnel was plunged abruptly into night; Crick
sniffing gently at the thick waft of burnt oil and cloth which hovered
about him, but seeing nothing now even as he waved his hands and the
extinguished torch inches from his face.

'Well, that's wonderful, Url… Now what're we supposed –'

'*Look…!*' Url interrupted, his voice eager but quiet, barely
reaching through the darkness.

'At *what?*' asked Crick. 'I can't see *anythi*–' But as he started to
adjust to the darkness he saw then from the corner of his eye a soft,
warm glow… It was coming from the hole where the crystal had been.
He heard slow footsteps behind him as Url moved cautiously forwards
toward it; the gnarled outline of his face appearing from the shadows,
pressing itself close against the hole. Crick stepped up to one side of
him, Yori to the other, and they watched in silence as Url's wide, dark
eyes, almost overflowing with wonder, reflected a tiny, brilliant glint
from something bright on the far side of the wall. Standing utterly still,
Url halted at the words which had started to form upon his lips, as
though having waited a lifetime to say them they were now almost too
much for him. Finally, with a joy Crick had never known in the old
man, he let out a timid, breathless whisper:

'We've found it…'

Chapter Seven

The Chamber

Even before Url's words Yori had known they had found it. Whatever *it* would prove to be. There was such power behind that wall... The light streaming through into the tunnel was so full of vitality and Magic that Yori could barely consider an attempt at putting it into words. It flowed like water suddenly set free from some hidden, underground lake, pure and ancient. Though whether the others could truly see this force, this glorious wave of energy, beyond the simple if captivating light which marked only its outer presence, Yori found difficult to judge. He guessed not. The current of Magic, fathomless as it was, appeared somehow to run just barely beneath the surface of sight, veiled by a form of enchantment he had never encountered before; an enchantment born it seemed somehow of design rather than chance. For his part for now, all he could do was gaze into it. Url, however, had other ideas...

'Quickly!' he whispered hoarsely to Crick, thrusting the pick back into his hands 'Get us through!'

Still confused, Crick nonetheless worked with a newfound strength and speed the like of which was rare even for him. And whether it was this or whether the stone seemed to come away slightly more easily now it was difficult to tell, but whatever it was Crick had soon opened a hole large enough to fit a head through, which Url promptly did. An inane grin lit up every inch and wrinkle of his face when he returned a moment later, gesturing to Crick to have a look, and after Crick had reappeared he did the same to Yori. With the feel of diving head-first into warm wind Yori bent down and placed his head carefully through the gap…

Another tunnel ran away ahead of him, though much wider and tall enough for two people to stand comfortably above each other. It sloped downwards perhaps a hundred feet before curving sharply away to the left and out of sight. *Tunnel*, however, though accurate enough perhaps in simplest form of meaning, was far from grand enough to do it any level of justice. The walls, floor, and roof all dazzled with a shimmering silver light; the surfaces formed entirely by long sweeping clusters of the very crystal which Yori and the others had been chasing for the past seventeen days, interspersed here and there with brilliant streaks of every other colour imaginable, all drifting like a gently flowing stream through the jagged, undulating surface. It felt a long while before any of them could speak…

'Step back, Yori!' said Url excitedly, pulling Yori from the hole before he had had a chance to comply. Url and Crick exploded into action again, working furiously on the edges of the hole, hacking and tearing, loosening and removing small clumps of stone piece by piece away from the centre. With Crick and the suddenly much lighter pick, Url and the chisel, and Yori and what little he could do with his bare hands the hole was soon just over two feet wide. Rubble strewn around his feet, Url stood and held out his hands to halt the others. He took a step forwards, bent down, and stared again through the hole.

'Crick…' he said, suddenly resolute and serious. Crick stepped eagerly closer… 'Go and get the others.'

Crick was stunned for a moment. He tried furiously to muster some kind of retort, but as the first word of it left his mouth Url spoke again:

'Boy, this place has been here for… well, I've no idea…' Yori felt the flash of a smile within him, 'but it's certainly not going anywhere soon. The others need to see this. If you ride quickly you can catch them and be back here in the hour.'

Crick realised there was no use in arguing further, but for a moment Yori was almost overcome with the heat of anger boiling up and venting from his brother as he sprinted away up the tunnel, stealing one final quick glance through the hole as he did so. The instant he had gone, Url turned to Yori.

'Ready?' he asked, a tinge of nervousness to his voice. Yori nodded faintly, somewhat shocked at the invitation, expecting Url to have been about to command him to stay here and wait. It was rare for people to surprise him in such a manner; he hadn't realised how distracted he had become. 'You stay close behind me, understand?' Url finished. And with that he lifted one leg, then his body, then the other leg through to the far tunnel. And with a deep breath, Yori followed...

It was as though they had stepped into another world. As soon as the toe of Yori's boot touched the surprisingly silky, supple ground, all thoughts of the darkness outside were forgotten completely, as though they had never existed. Light shone around and through him from every direction, as real and illusive as thought, and it was only as he felt the firm touch of Url's hands upon his back that he realised he had been swaying sideways, his gaze having shifted straight up into the roof above him. With an effort he fought to regain his senses, focusing with difficulty on the ground ahead as it led away down the wide, crystal corridor, waiting breath by breath as slowly the tunnel became whole again.

They soon found that if they tried to walk quickly the sharp crystal would crack and splinter beneath them, doing its utmost to pierce thin tears in their boots. But as long as their steps stayed soft and slow, it would instead flatten and mould itself carefully around their feet, easing them gradually down into the ground. It forced them into a calm, graceful stride, giving them to Yori's delight ample opportunity absorb each of the many various subtleties of sense around them.

At the bottom of the corridor they veered left, expecting it to continue. But it did nothing of the kind. Instead as though a mountain had been turned on its head and hollowed, a vast cavern opened up beneath them. Its roof never rose much higher than the level at which Yori and Url were standing now, arching gently across to the far side, many hundreds of feet away. And as wide as the cavern was, this was nothing compared to its length, or its depth, both of which could only be guessed. Peering cautiously over the jagged, coloured edging before them – Url with a tightened grip on the back of his shirt – Yori saw that they were standing close to the rightmost end of this side of the cavern. Just in front of them the ground fell away in a sheer cliff to a distance perhaps slightly deeper than the cavern was wide. Looking over to the left, however, the distances were wholly immeasurable; the far end so remote that despite the spectacular fashion in which every surface was lit, it was simply beyond sight. By the furthest visible point that Yori could make out, the base of the cavern had sloped down so steeply that it appeared to be nearly three times as deep as it was here. The light was everywhere... perfect... It made Yori feel as a dirty speck of mud on an otherwise perfectly polished piece of grand furniture. He was about to ask whether this was it – whether they had come at last to the Heart... But then he realised he already knew the answer. *Not yet.* Something else lay deeper still. Yori could feel it like the sounding of a great whisper through the ground; he listened hard for some form of words amongst the strangeness of the noise, but could discern none that held any meaning.

'I… I don't know where to go…' said Url with delighted confusion, looking this way and that and then finally back to Yori.

'Down there,' said Yori without thinking, pointing across to a sharp, far-off outcrop of crystal near the bottom of the opposite side of the valley, far to the left of them, just on the edge of sight. What it was that made him choose that particular spot he could not have said, even had Url had the patience of mind to ask him. Something inside him seemed to be pulling him down there, tugging at his mind with warm, enticing strands of… *what was it…*? Blinking, he realised that Url was looking at him, questioningly. All he said, however, was:

'Hold on to me.'

Moving down through the side of the cavern was far from an easy task. Yori quickly gave up holding on to Url, who was barely more stable on his feet than Yori himself. Crick at this stage would have been invaluable, but it was impossible to be sure how long it would take him to return, and neither Yori nor Url paid a moment's thought to the idea of waiting. So together they walked, scrambled, climbed, and occasionally slid down the steep bank, painfully at times on the hard, jagged surface, in what was perhaps best described as a barely-controlled fall, bearing always as best as they could towards the distant section of the cavern that Yori had pointed out.

As they descended, however, they found to Yori's continuing enchantment and Url's lingering concern that while the ground was beginning to level off, it was also starting to produce substantial clusters of crystal which had been largely camouflaged from the height at which they had first observed the cavern, which projected out at varying angles and to ever-increasing heights around and over them. By the time they had reached the floor of the cavern they were moving through a sea of enormous boulders which towered well above their heads and also seemed to take great pleasure in barring an occasional path, forcing them time and again to turn back and find another route.

Yori couldn't even have guessed how long they wandered through this dazzling labyrinth of light. All he knew for certain was that Url was leading him through with a firm hand around his wrist, and that, sometime later, they emerged from between two exceptionally tall and imposing spikes crossing thirty feet above them, into a small clearing. In front of them, beyond the curving row of pillars at the far side, the cavern continued into its hazy vastness. Just beside them, however, cut sharply into the ground in the rightmost rim of the clearing, there was another tunnel. It was smaller than the channel at the top of the cavern had been, but still high enough to walk through without crouching. Url looked to Yori, who in his bewilderment merely shrugged and nodded uncertainly. But apparently this was good enough for Url, who stepped forwards into the mouth of the tunnel.

'*Url*!'

The voice echoed from somewhere far above them. Url stopped dead in his tracks, silent… It came again; louder and in several different tones:

'*Urrrrrrrrrrl*! … *Yorriiiii*!'

Still slightly dazed, it took Yori a few seconds to recognise that it was his Father and the others calling down to them.

'Down here!' Url bellowed back. But evidently the others couldn't hear him; frantic shouts of '*Urrrrrrrrrrl*!' and '*Yorriiiii*!' continuing to ring down around the clearing.

'I'll have to go get them,' Url grumbled, still staring longingly into the tunnel. He turned away after a few seconds, rubbing his eyes tenderly. 'I need to get out into more open ground so they can hear me. I'll be back soon,' he added, blinking and seeing the concern in Yori's face. 'Just sit here. Don't go anywhere!' And with that he was off, darting back the way they had come – or so Yori assumed, his memory feeling weak and languid – calling loudly for the others as he went.

Yori looked slowly around him, and as his gaze fell upon the tunnel he felt something strange, like a silent gust of wind swirling around his head and chest. It seemed to be trying to draw him in. For a moment he considered going – perhaps just taking a brief look inside – but with an effort he fought the urge, looking instead for a place to sit. As he did so a single, high-pitched cry echoed suddenly above him from the depths of the valley. Yori stopped, listening intently… but heard nothing else. Everywhere was as hard and jagged as the rest of the cavern had been up to now, but looking down he saw that in a small circle all around him the ground was perfectly smooth and soft. He could have sworn it hadn't been like that a moment ago, but he was in no mind to question it and he simply sat, carefully, still listening out over the towering ranks of crystal, trying to work out what it was that he had just heard. His eyes became heavy, tired. Sight was no use to him anyway: he let his vision blur; his eyelids drifting slowly, gently to a close…

That moment there came a tremendous crashing of footsteps beside him; several figures sprinting suddenly into the clearing.

'Yori!' cried his Mother, plainly relieved as she flung her arms around him. Over her shoulder Yori saw his Father, brother, and sister,

72

and then Abetta and finally Url appeared as well, all stumbling quickly and awkwardly in from between the two great spikes of crystal. Amongst intrigued glances around them they all looked exceptionally pleased to see Yori – though for Crick the annoyance at not having been the first to explore down into the cavern was still foremost in his mind.

'Sorry about that, my boy,' said Url with a high note of embarrassment.

'For what?' asked Yori. 'How did you…?'

'We… um, well, *I* –'

'We got lost,' said Abetta flatly, glaring sideways at Url.

'Yes – well, turns out that without you around –' he looked to Yori '– finding a way through this mess is a spot more difficult. But *we got here in the end…*' he added pointedly, glancing nervously towards Abetta.

'But… I was only waiting a few seconds…?' said Yori, uncertainly. 'How did –?'

'*Seconds*?' said his Mother.

'Son,' said his Father, kneeling beside him, 'we've been down here near three hours trying to find you.'

'But –'

'Wasted time which we won't get back standing around here!' said Url. 'Come on, up with you…' And together with Orlando he helped lift Yori onto what he suddenly found to be helplessly numb and unsteady legs. It took several minutes for him to recover enough of the feeling in the lower half of his body to allow an uncomfortable, wavering walk. When he was ready he nodded up to Url, still standing beside him; the old man supporting him firmly and kindly though doing a poor job of concealing his impatience.

'Crick should lead us down,' Yori whispered quietly.

'Hmm? Ah, yes, fine – Crick?' Crick looked over, 'Show us down, would you?' Crick didn't reveal it, but Yori saw the corner of his mouth twitch with the beginning of a proud grin. Yori smiled too. 'Everyone else close together,' said Url. 'In a line, one after each other.'

So with Crick at the front and Yori and Url bringing up the rear of the group, they stepped gingerly through the opening and into the tunnel, cutting down with what they now found to be a sudden steepness into the side of the clearing. After fifty feet or so it turned quickly to the right, and then continued to do so, though with the sharpness of the turn gradually easing, so that after a time they realised they were walking in a gentle, ever-widening spiral, deeper and deeper beneath the cavern, so far beneath the outside world that the very thought of it was as a dream.

They walked for ten minutes… twenty… thirty and quite probably far more, but once again Yori had soon lost all track of time. The surfaces around them were becoming even brighter and more intense, and unrelenting in their jaggedness, so that even though the tunnel was perhaps still the same size its walls and roof seemed now to be pressing in far tighter against them. Yori began to notice tiny holes no larger than a few inches across in the bottom of the wall to their right, through which came shards of an even more brilliant light soon complimented by thin wisps of an almost colourless vapour, imperceptible but for the hazy jewel-tinged blanket it created, covering the ground to about knee-height and churning slow and gracefully about their feet as they passed through. On still further they walked, utterly quiet, deeper… turning slowly, further on into the foundations of the world…

And then from nowhere the tunnel came to a sudden end before them; a narrow opening appearing to their right from which a glorious warmth spilled out in thick, wonderful waves of mist and light. Huddled close together and without a word, shielding their eyes against a strange brightness which struck straight to the very centre of Yori's heart, they stepped through…

Chapter Eight

The Heart

One by one they halted in the light, each straining to take in the at once simple and complex splendour of the scene before them. They had entered into a wide, almost impossibly high cave, capped with a distant domed crown which must nearly have touched the underside of the clearing in which a while ago they had been standing. The haze which had been spilling into the tunnel was here again, but thicker now, moving and tumbling as though blown gently by soft winds in numerous opposing directions all at once. Vast stumps and twisting spears of crystal rose sharp from the ground, and from the heights fell hundreds of long, shimmering strands, all at their tips curving inwards towards the centre of the cave where, raised high upon on a thick, sprawling dais of interlocking columns there sat a single, great gem.

Had the radiance of everything they had seen so far been condensed into a single entity, this was it. It stood the nearly the height of a man, shining with such easy majesty as to make it more than worthy of all the old Kings and Queens of history, with colours so clear and vivid that all memory of everything from deepest sunsets to bluest lakes seemed suddenly pale and pitiable in comparison. Thousands of perfect, tiny edges glittered wonderfully with every hue imaginable and countless more besides, so that to gaze into it was as though to see true colour for the first time. The haze rose up through the columns and swirled beneath it, but never touched it, folding away when it came within an inch or so to disappear into the expanse of the cave.

'What...?' Siu began, but her words trailed off almost pathetically as she stared with the others. For a long while nobody spoke a word.

Finally, slowly, Url stepped forward through the group. He was still supporting a wide-eyed Yori beside him; offering him into Siu's hands as he passed her and then continued, step by careful step towards the great gemstone. For a few seconds he was lost amongst a thick pool of haze which concealed a dip just before the platform, but as the ground rose he emerged into view once more. Six sets of anxious eyes upon him, he climbed carefully up the final few steps, stopping barely more than an arm's length from the wide, honeycombed platform, gazing up at it with eyes which sparkled clear and bright as the great jewel itself.

'Url...?' Orlando tried, but for a while all sight and sound were lost to the old man, save for that which shone above him. At length he turned slowly back to the family; tears welling, glistening in the corners of his eyes. With both hands he pointed, almost disbelievingly, back to the gem...

'The Heart... of Magic,' he said quietly, grinning nervously as the words left his mouth.

Yori gazed at the gem with a giddy smile similar to Url's, but the others each wore looks of stunned confusion. The very Heart itself? The jewel of myth and legend dating back before records began? Surely, it couldn't be. For certain this gem they had found was something... something great indeed. None would question that. But *the Heart*? The Heart was the stuff of tales, and of dreams; the inspiration for the queer adventures of old men. Not real. And yet... And yet to deny it so, stood now as they were before it, gazing into it as it gazed back through them, seemed somehow suddenly... impossible. For all the times each of them had through open word or mocking retort denied Url the truth of his belief, not one of them could find the strength of voice to deny it once more now.

'The...?' Aliya faltered.

'But what... How did it...?' stammered Orlando.

'It's wonderful, isn't it?' said Url. He stepped down through the haze and the deep sustained silence of the others, appearing before them once again.

'You've all heard the tales of the time before Magic?' he said, silhouetted oddly against the diamond glare behind him. Crick nodded uncertainly, but beyond that nobody moved or said a word. Of course they had heard the tales: many times, and most often from Url himself. But it was a long while since last they had truly paid him the attention he desired of them. And now with the wonder of his words seeming almost real behind him, there was not one amongst them who did not wish, and need, to hear them again…

'Many things were much the same as they are today,' Url continued, in tone and manner similar to those with which he had entertained Crick and Aliya and Yori through long evenings since the days they were born, though now with an intensity heavy enough to break for a moment the gem's hold over them, so that they could focus at least partly on his voice as he continued: 'People lived from the land; they watched the sun rise and fall; they made fire and they cooked with it; they drank from the streams; fashioned stone; used wood from the trees for building and burning; and did many other things just as we do now… But that was it. For the people of that age, the world around them was no more than what they could see of it, or do with it. Forests, lakes, the skies, birds, beasts: All of it was there – but in the minds of those people it all existed *separate* to them, as a wholly different type of existence.

But then,' he came a step closer, 'somehow, all these things began to take on a new life and new power. Our ancestors slowly began to realise that all the elements of the world around them, and even aspects of themselves, could be communicated with, nurtured – even controlled. Instead of just seeing things, or touching them, or doing them, they began to *feel* them as well. The *essence* of flame, of water, of air, and of light and earth and rock and all else besides was suddenly as real to people as the simple outer forms of these things which they had taken for granted since the beginning of time. And when sensed like this, people began slowly to realise how they could with practice *communicate* with and even *manipulate* these things in a way nobody had ever imagined possible: Fires could be made to burn brighter; water to change its course; light to bend and transform! And soon there were some who could feel the thoughts of others, or those of animals, or could perform physical feats of extraordinary skill!'

There was a happiness in him which had simply never been there before. The way he stood before them, so spirited in his talk of that which he had described a hundred times before, was truly wonderful to see… a relief in him no less than that of a drowning man kissed with the sudden breath of life. He was content, whole, in a way he had been searching for and dreaming of all his life. A way that he had begun to give up hope of ever finding. It made it almost difficult to pay attention to the bare facts of what he was saying. But listen the others did; eagerly, and to every word…

'Not all these gifts were attainable by everyone. In fact with rare exceptions people often found that there was only one aspect if any at all in which they would truly develop an affinity. For some reason, this new Magic seemed to seek out and link itself to only those characteristics and desires which held the strongest place in a person's soul. Those whose natural love was for the water,' he looked to Aliya, 'found that they could sense the waterways and the creatures that lived there. Those who craved adventure,' he looked to Crick, 'found that they may develop new skills to aid them.' He turned to Yori, smiling… 'And for some of those whose minds were naturally more open and compassionate, they found they could learn to hear the thoughts of those around them, and sense things which others could never dream to know.'

He paused a moment, breaking his eyes from Yori to glance back at the gem, as though to make certain it was still truly whole and real in front of him.

'The Magic didn't change who the person was, or what they enjoyed… it just let them experience those things on a deeper, wonderful level.' He smiled again, shaking his head gently, turning back to the family.

'Nobody knew why all of this was happening. Some of the greatest and most arrogant minds of that age said that it was because their generation had achieved an intellect far superior to that of their ancestors, and that we were being justly rewarded for our learning and wisdom. Some said that it was simply the world coming to life again after a long, peaceful slumber. And there were dozens of other ideas. There were even, spread thin across the world, a small number, a tiny band of believers, who thought that somewhere, somehow, a seed had been planted by the stars themselves, bringing us a hint of the wonder and Magic to which we had been ignorant for so long. Why, and in what form this seed – this *heart of Magic* – would have arrived, were mysteries they knew they would be foolish to even try and answer.

Or, rather, *most* of them thought so. A few, however, decided that if indeed there was a Heart, then truly it was something which deserved to be found, and cared for, and revered. They journeyed their whole lives, searching for it within, beneath, and at the very heights of each and every new land they came to. Most of them started here, in this part of the world, for it was here that the first signs of Magic had been experienced. And it was from this that the name *Heartlands* was given.

But after many fruitless generations of seeking, and a vast world around them to be explored, most of these men and women left to search elsewhere. They never found it… Right here,' he added quietly, '…beneath them…'

Url's gaze had drifted unconsciously back to the gem; his thoughts becoming lost and entwined within its magnificence. With enormous difficulty Orlando shook off his stupefied silence and tried to force a composure into his voice:

'But how do you *know* that this is it?' he asked; such measured practicality coming painfully to him as he stood in the gemstone's glare. 'It's clearly something extremely... impressive,' he added as Url turned sharply back to him. 'But... how can you know it's really the... well, what you say it is?'

Url considered it a moment, and then without a word he disappeared back through the haze, emerging again a few seconds later and stepping warily up towards the platform. He seemed almost more nervous than he had been the first time. He paused, studying the gem, and then, tentatively, he reached up a trembling hand towards it... The haze below him blew immediately into a frenzied whirlwind which tore deafeningly through the cave. Hot jets of blinding light shot out in all directions, and with it the air filled with a piercing scream which forced each of them onto their knees in agony. Then as quickly as it had started, everything vanished.

'*Url*!' screamed Abetta, 'What –'

'It's alright, it's alright,' said Url, getting to his feet with a rueful chuckle. 'We're fine... Heh... A little more severe than I'd expected! But, um, I think it helps to prove my point?' He dusted himself off, ensuring each of the others was standing and recovered before he continued: 'No mortal being can touch it.'

The first hints of excited glimmers were beginning to spread openly through the faces in front of him, though each still tightly tempered by confusion and the remnants of a lifetime's disbelief.

'So it didn't want you touching it...' said Abetta. 'Takes a great deal less than the source of all Magic for that to be the case!'

'Yori,' said Siu gently as Url scowled impatiently. 'What do you think? What can you... feel?'

The others turned eagerly towards a disorientated Yori, who though standing amongst them was clearly quite apart from any of their minds. His thoughts were elsewhere entirely.

'It's...' he began at length, 'like everything Url just said. It *does* feel like... a seed.' He blinked and looked to Url. 'But, one which will never run out of life. I always sense waves of Magic in other things, but this doesn't just have Magic *inside* it...' He paused, stepping forwards a half-pace from the others. 'It *is* Magic,' he said quietly. 'All of it. I – I can't describe it. But it *is* the Heart; it has to be. Even if I'd never heard the word before, that's what I'd call it.'

'Alright…' said Orlando, turning to face Url with waning but determined doubt. 'Say this really is the Heart… What are you – what are *we* going to do with it now that we've found it?'

'*What are we going to do with it?*' Url repeated, as though astonished by the question.

'Well, yes! Apart from to stand here and admire it, what is it that's driven you to search for it for so many years? What do you intend to *do* with it, Url?'

It felt like a question they should have asked before. But in all the times they had spoken of it, not one of them had thought to do so. Perhaps it was this which told above all else just how little faith they had held in the old man's dream. Now they came to it, the very idea of what would be possible with such a thing was overwhelming. But where they expected a great grin of amusement or twinkling of excitement from Url, they saw instead a sudden frown; a solemn stare with which he surveyed the others slowly in turn, returning finally to Orlando.

'You… you still don't understand at all, do you?' he asked, sighing wearily before coming slowly once again back down and through the haze to stand before them. 'When the Heart brought Magic into our world, it also, unintentionally I believe – brought something else. Something far worse. A darkness from beyond our world and our understanding, attracted through the stars to the Magic of the Heart like a terrible moth to the light of a distant flame.'

'The Black Wind,' whispered Crick.

'Quite. Or, rather, it brought the horror around which the Black Wind exists. The true Darkness itself; ever hidden, ever unknown, ever terrible.' He glanced to Yori and paused a moment, as though unwilling to speak the words in front of him.

'Sometime after the first Magic was found, the first breaths of the Wind appeared. They started small and isolated, hovering around the borders of our world like wolves around a flock, picking off the weak and unwary. But over the years these breaths grew and came together into one vast storm, engulfing horizons and destroying towns and cities and their peoples within as quick as sound. And all the time it looked inwards, in towards the light. In towards the Heart, seeking it, *craving* it. Don't you see…? The Heart is the key – the only key, beneath us this whole time – to ending the Black Wind! It is the one and only thing which can bring to us the peace our world has lived without for so long! The Heart is our *freedom*!'

'How?' asked Siu at once, leaving the others wide-eyed in their silence. After several seconds Orlando shook off his astonishment,

80

doing what he could to re-gather the scattered remains of his composure…

'*What are we supposed to do with it?*' he asked again, more forcefully.

'Umm… well in truth, *that* I'm… I suppose I'm not quite sure of…'

'You don't want to destroy it, do you?' asked Yori, with a sudden trace of fear.

'*Destroy* it? No! No, no, no… Apart from the fact that I don't even know if that would be *possible*, destroying the Heart would mean an end to all the Magic and light that it has given us… I would rather die than inflict such misery upon the world.'

'But surely that would be better than being overrun by the Wind?' asked Orlando.

'We're not destroying it!' There was a bite to Url's voice which the others had rarely heard from him before.

'What about telling the Council?' asked Crick, in part to break the tension.

'You are joking, boy…?' Url countered venomously, as the others each turned to face Crick with similar disbelief.

'I'm just saying – they want to get rid of the Black Wind as much as we do, and they've got people who know a lot more about it than us – and weapons, so…'

'You're right,' said Abetta, surprising the others. 'They do know more about it all than we do.' Her look hardened; her voice clear and quietly resolute: 'But that doesn't mean the Heart would be better off in their possession. There is a good reason why Url, your parents, and I have chosen to live so far from the City. The people there – at least, those who control it – cannot be trusted. They have been corrupted by endless long years of fear, and death, all of which have turned their minds slowly but inescapably away from all memory of peace and beauty. They no longer see the world for what it used to be, and for what it *could still be*…' She gave a small, sad frown. 'They have no concept of a better world beyond thoughts of victory and their own supremacy. They would use the Heart not to truly free us from darkness, but to make war upon it – whatever the terrible consequences for the rest of us. And they *would* be terrible. It would be a war the likes of which you can and should never begin to imagine: one to make even the great wars which have shaped our past ages seem like petty squabblings. And in the end, nothing would be left standing. Nothing. Even if the Black Wind was somehow crushed, and the Darkness defeated our world would still be destroyed. And if it *wasn't* beaten…'

81

'We don't tell the Council, then,' said Crick, turning uncomfortably from her distant glare.

'But if we're not destroying it,' said Aliya, 'and we're not telling anyone about it, then *what*? We just leave it here? Keep it secret...?

'No,' said Url. 'The Darkness is still growing, getting more powerful all the time... Soon it will be enough to overwhelm the defences of our lands, powerful as the Council thinks and hopes they are. We've lasted this long, but soon gates and Guardsmen won't be enough. They're already starting to get glimpses of it around the border.'

'I know,' said Crick, fear glinting like far-off flame in his eyes. He realised his mistake but too late; his Mother catching sight of the look before he could hide it.

'What do you mean, *you know*?' she asked.

'Umm...' Crick began, as Orlando let out a weary sigh, 'Nothing... I just meant – what Aliya said the other day... about what she heard the Guardsm–'

'No you didn't,' said Siu, studying him with the knowing gaze and assured distrust only a Mother could have. 'You've *seen* something, haven't you?

'No! I just –'

'You've been up to the border again! Haven't you?' It wasn't a question. 'Tell me!'

For an instant Crick struggled desperately to think of some acceptable response which stood at least a chance of passing for the truth, but as Siu's eyebrows rose in ominous unison he surrendered abruptly to his fate:

'Just once,' he said, almost truthfully.

The next few minutes were far from the most pleasant of his life, which looked for a while to be in danger of coming to an unnaturally quick end. Orlando fared little better, forced as he was to admit to his knowledge of Crick's last adventure through the ravine.

'This isn't getting us anywhere!' called Url into the commotion as his impatience finally got the better of his reluctance to interrupt Siu.

'Well it doesn't seem like there's anywhere else to go!' Siu snapped back angrily, turning suddenly from Crick. 'If we can't destroy it, can't show it to anyone, and can't keep it hidden, then what do you suggest we do? Use it ourselves? Defeat the Black Wind *by ourselves*?'

She had said it heatedly, clearly not expecting an answer. But Url was looking at her thoughtfully. And when he spoke, it was with words which none of the others were at all prepared for:

'Something like that, perhaps...'

Silence fell again through the spires and gently swirling mists of the cave. The haze moved lazily around their feet; each of them trying to establish how long it would be until Url came to his senses. Url seemed to have drifted into a deep contemplation of his own...

'Of course, we'd need their help once we got there...' he murmured, 'But, maybe...'

'Need whose help?' asked Siu.

'I can't think of any other way,' said Url, either not hearing or else ignoring her.

'*Whose* help, Url,' said Orlando.

'Don't even think it, Urlmaeus,' said Abetta, spurred suddenly by a mixture of resolve and fear which none of the others understood.

'Don't think what?' asked Siu, '*Url*! What is it you want to do? I thought you said you didn't know what we should do with it?'

'I said I wasn't sure,' said Url, breaking from his trance. 'And I'm not. Far from it. Maybe *once* it would have been possible, but now...? It would almost be foolish to try...' he added with a grave, agreeing look to Abetta. 'But as I say, I can't think of any other way... Can you?' A plea, carefully concealed but clear as day for the others to see, was contained within his words.

But Abetta could find no answer. She stared at him hard for a moment, but then like a wilting plant her strength seemed to wither and fade to nothing. She shrugged sadly.

'If you two don't tell us –' started Orlando, but Url silenced him with a heavy raise of his hand.

'When the Black Wind came,' he said, as though continuing from where he had stopped a few minutes earlier, though now with a thick air of solemnity about him, 'most people sought shelter in one of the three great Cities. Irraigion, the Capital; Iala, in the north; and here near the south... Immelus. The three great inhabitations of man, unconquered and unconquerable. Over time they swelled as the smaller, more distant villages fell, and their peoples fled. Defences were rebuilt and extended time and again, and new homes were constructed at an astounding rate, but even so it was barely enough to accommodate the vast numbers seeking shelter from outside.

And eventually the Wind grew strong and hungry enough that it began to threaten the Cities themselves, thinking the Heart to be in one of them. In each of the three the Councils debated long and heatedly about what should be done to protect themselves. And in each of the three, different paths were taken. In Irraigion, with its dozens of divided factions and interests, the arguing was so bitter and so prolonged that in the end no agreement or compromise could be found or made upon a single course. Even as the Black Wind crept across neighbouring hillsides their quarrels continued, and by the time they realised their foolishness, it was too late. Countless thousands died with barely a sword raised in their defence.

In Immelus, here, the path chosen was a cruel and misguided one; but it was, at least, a path. And one which has, though I take little pleasure in saying it, worked well enough to this day. Seeing the evil which the Darkness was bringing to the World, the people here grew to resent and distrust Magic. All Magic. They abandoned most of the skills and ideas into which they had started to explore over the years in favour of the simpler and better understood methods of our past. Walls and gates were built around the borders; men were heavily armed and harshly trained; the City's defences enlarged and improved in endless succession; and the Black Wind regarded as simply another approaching foe, such as we had seen many times in our past, and would no doubt see again for Ages to come.

But far away from us, in the great City upon the coasts of the open deepwaters of the North, they took quite the opposite approach. Their trust and their efforts were channelled instead utterly *into* Magic, not against it. The Council of Iala determined that if this Darkness was to be defeated, it could only be done through great Magics of their own. They too built defences... but defences of an entirely different kind. Where Immelus constructed huge walls of wood and stone, Iala laid out blockades of light and traps of Magic. Where the Guardsmen of Immelus wore thick armour and shields, the Paladins of Iala dressed in thin robes of whichever material best suited their particular Magic, imbued with spells and all manner of arcane skills. In place of the blades and hammers and arrows of the south, the defenders of the north wielded the elements themselves. And they... they had something else, as well.' He paused, retrieving his gaze from deep within the mist by his feet to look into the eyes of each of the others in turn.

'You see, while in most of the world the Heart was thought of by this time as myth, or forgotten about entirely, in Iala there were a good number who believed in it still – or at least, thought it possible enough to be worth planning for. So plan for it they did. They thought, and they studied, and they experimented; always learning what they could about how to harm the Black Wind. Of course with their relatively limited powers they could do little more than keep pushing it back when it reached too close, but through time they came to believe that if they could acquire the Heart, they could use its strength to do what they could not. And so, to harness the power of the Heart should it ever someday be found, they built the Torch.'

'The Torch…!' said Crick. 'I've heard of it! Natt spoke something about it once… An enormous building in the middle of the City, with a spire which reached a thousand feet taller than anything else…'

'Perhaps you're not as utterly uninformed as you would have us believe, boy,' said Url, with a weak smile and gentle nod of his head. 'Yes – the Tower of Elliad. It took near twenty years to build: each stone used in its construction first instilled with numerous kinds of the most powerful known Magics; more precious jewels and metals than most believed to exist in the world. And there, in a small room right at its peak, its faces open to north, south, east and west, they built a tall plinth, forged from the diamond-cut tips of a hundred strands of metal stretching all the way up from deep below the ground, rising and twisting through and around the whole Tower until they came at last together in the silent power of that room.

And after all that, they never found the treasure it was all designed to hold: the one thing that would make the Tower and the Torch complete, and unleash the Magic which could banish the Black Wind forever…'

'So you're saying,' Orlando began, slowly, 'that you want to get the Heart out of this cave…' he waited for Url to nod before continuing, 'take it across the border… travel, what, *hundreds* of miles…?'

'Several hundred, I believe, yes,' said Url quietly, nodding again.

'Travel *several hundreds of miles* with it through the Outerlands, and then use it in an ancient weapon the owners of which nobody in our realm has heard from for decades…?'

'Want…? *Want*? No. No, I don't *want* any of that. Unlike some of us –' he shot a quick glance at Crick, '– I value my life far too highly to *want* to risk it on any such journey. Unfortunately, however, the Black Wind seems recently not to be taking too accurate an account of my feelings. What I *want* has little to do with it: The unfortunate but rather simple truth of it is, we *must* do this.'

There was a brief moment of stunned silence; each looking to the other, or to the Heart, trying to stand firm against the sudden weight which had been cast down upon them. It seemed quite surreal that the Heart stood bright and magnificent as ever. Then altogether they erupted into a volley of questions and disagreements.

Only Abetta stayed quiet. Amongst the clamour she shared a subtle, fearful look with Url, which told him that she alone understood. She alone knew that he was right.

'– and besides,' sounded Siu's voice above the rest, 'we wouldn't last a day in the Outerlands! If the Black Wind really is getting as close as you say it is how do you expect to make it a single mile – let alone hundreds?'

'Well,' said Url, taking a deep breath, his face lifted slightly with a feeble optimism, 'on that point, in fact, the picture is perhaps not quite as bleak as it seems. As I said, the Heart is like a flame to the wings of the Black Wind. By moving it through the open we would, for sure, be attracting the Darkness to us… But I do not believe it would be able to actually *reach* us. As long as we stayed close to the Heart at all times, I think we would be safe.'

'You think…?'

'Yes. That is, safe from the Black Wind itself… We would have to reach Iala before the Darkness itself awakes and realises what we are doing. And there would, I admit, be other dangers along the way against which the Heart would not necessarily protect us.

'Will you please stop talking of how "*we*" are going to be doing all of this,' said Siu. 'Whatever happens, none of the children are going!'

There was an immediate cry of protest from Crick, but Yori had drifted back into his distant gaze towards the Heart. Aliya likewise was silent, though for her it was because she was simply unable to decide whether being forbidden to go was something about which to be frustrated or delighted.

'How would we even *move* the thing?' asked Orlando. 'I can't begin to guess how much it must weigh – and if we can't even touch it…?'

'I know,' sighed Url. 'And, well, I have no idea.'

'How would we find our way?' asked Crick, as if suddenly realising the scale of the task for which he had just a moment ago been thoroughly enthusiastic.

'We could take the Firstway, couldn't we?' asked Aliya.

'We could…' said Url, considering it. 'For much of the way, at least. But there would be times when we may have to abandon it and take a different route. And after this many years there may well also be parts of it which have fallen into decay or been lost altogether. I know well enough of the borderlands around us, but beyond that my knowledge is nearly as limited as most of yours. We must acquire a map, or at least something which will suffice as one.'

'But we've nothing of the sort!' said Orlando. 'And as far as I know at least, neither do any of those few we would call our friends.

The only records of parts of the world that far outside the Heartlands are held in –'

'I know,' Url interrupted.

'So you're saying one of us would have to go –'

'To the city.' He paused. 'I am afraid so, yes.' His eyes fell grimly upon Crick. 'And I can think of one amongst us who is perfectly suited for the task…'

Chapter Nine

The New Guardsman

The arguing, at first deep below the cool night air which skimmed quickly amongst the oaks of the Eigerhills, and then in no less passionate vein through the quite surreal journey home amongst lands unchanged yet somehow wholly different since last they had travelled through them, had gone on late into the evening, and then for several long days after that. Many bewildering hours were required simply for the matter to be retold and retold again, even before the truth and consequences of it all, if any there were, could begin to be judged. Not only on the first night did each of the family fall in turn into uneasy sleeps besieged by lingering questions and uncertainties which stood unwilling to be kept quiet until tomorrow. With the cavern and the great jewel it contained out of sight it was tempting at times to breathe easier for a moment, and imagine there was nothing to be done; that the responsibility was not theirs to shoulder. And then, responsibility for *what*? they soon and strongly came to ask themselves. From leaping as they had done in those first few minutes in the great chamber from witnessing a glorious gemstone, to somehow then transporting it so unspeakably far from where it now lay to do battle with the very source of the Darkness which plagued their world... It was a leap which in the calmer, quieter air of home was, if not quite wholly reversed, at least stepped briskly back from, and studied. And studied intently. But for all the arguments for and all the many more and seemingly greater arguments against the idea that they had found an object of such power as Url described, and that they should attempt to do with it anything like he had suggested, there was one thing which time and again would rise like a quiet shadowed statue above the bright figurines of logic and reason to hold sway and give hidden guidance to all considerations of its truth, and of what now was to be done... Their memory of it. For in one brief thought back to the sight and feeling of the gem as they had approached it could be wiped clean a full morning's worth of doubt. Though Yori may have felt it keenest, the stone had left its mark strongly upon each of them, though each was uncertain as to exactly how. Faith, as Url had held so tightly to for so many years, was not an easy thing to feel suddenly imposed within the selves of the others. It confused them; excited them; even angered them at times. But feel it they did. And after all that was spoken and argued, the inexorable truth was that nobody could think of an idea to better Url's. They had found the Heart, or something at least as close as made little difference to the planning of what to do with it. And whether they wished it or not, one or more of them now would be taking it to Iala, impossible as that sounded. Over everything that final thought stayed with each of them like an icy fall of rain.

Not that Crick in truth had made too valiant an attempt at coming up with any other form of plan. Rather, following the time and effort it had taken for Url's words to sink slowly in, Crick had come to the decision that this was for the present with only the merest shadow of doubt one of the finest things to have ever happened to him. Though his parents were still insistent that neither he, nor Yori, nor Aliya would ever be going on any such journey, the very thought and possibility of it made his skin bristle with an excitement which found its way down now to his heels as he pushed Railer on to fresh speed with a giddy energy.

He was riding once more to Fellgate. For the first time though, and with a new and somewhat disconcerting sense of honesty, he did so in the full knowledge if not agreement of his family. His parents and Grandmother had argued bitterly against it, but as Crick had finally managed to convince them, he was man enough now to decide this for himself. And as Url had repeated time and again, so long as Crick stuck firmly to the boundaries of his task, no harm should come to him.

There was a small part – though a small part only – of Crick which remained jealous of the others, working as they would now near every day around the Heart itself. Yet he knew too that the undertaking with which he had been entrusted was quite as hazardous and exciting, along with entirely essential if the journey north was to stand any real chance of success. Just as he began to contemplate the finer points of what it was that he was actually going to have to do, however, he looked up and around him for the first time in a long while, realising suddenly where he was…

A thin scattering of grey, sodden ash was still present from the agreeably large fires he had constructed with Natt and Leyon, many days ago now. The hurried but more than adequate campsite from where the three of them had launched their exploits into the hills didn't look to have seen any use at all since then. Ahead was the wooded hollow within which his Father had accosted them, and then there followed the short path up into the foothills. And beyond that, the Gate. Crick shook back his shoulders, attempting to construct the right composure into his frame. None of the rest of the plan mattered if he couldn't first convince the Guardsmen. For near-on the hundredth time he went over in full what he was going to say when he got there, his lips moving soundlessly as he rode. It was scarcely the most complicated of stories, much of it based in no small part on truth, or some distant measure of it. But the thought of actually attempting to speak to persuade those harsh and reliably untrusting men of it seemed to be pushing the words from his mind altogether.

The slightly pitiful air of concern he held about him, therefore, was real enough by the time Fellgate came into view, tall and dark ahead of him and suddenly more ominous than it had ever seemed before. He did what he could to mix in with it a trace of frustration, and then he vaulted from Railer and strode briskly up to the first of the Guardsman, a thick, heavily-armoured boulder of a man no less than three times the width of Crick, standing as still as the hills behind him a hundred feet out from the Gate. He leant upon the head of a giant ruby-encrusted battle-axe which rose from the ground to the summit of his mountainous shoulders, watching Crick carefully but with clear disinterest as he approached.

'You again!' the man roared before Crick could start. The voice emerged from somewhere deep within the bulk of his enormous frame, seeming to have grown in strength every inch of the way like air through a great horn. Whether it rung with laughter or irritation Crick found impossible to tell. 'Waddya want this time?'

'I… To be a Guardsman,' Crick replied with all the conviction he could muster, resisting the temptation to shield his ears. 'I –' he started, ready to relay the thorough list of reasons why he wished to leave his old life and help defend the great and glorious City of Immelus. But he wasn't given the chance:

'Ha! Knew we'd ged you somedime!' the Guardsman laughed. 'Go see sol... *solbug*,' he added, working to pronounce the word clearly, gesturing with a lazy swing of his elbow to the Gate behind him; colossal divisions of armour clattering heavily as he did so.

'I – err… thanks.' And with the Guardsman smiling stupidly to himself Crick stepped widely around him and made his way up to the Gate, trying frantically to work out which of the dozen or so figures ahead *solbug* was supposed to be…

Five men slouched either side of the towering wooden doors at the thickened points where the Gate merged harshly into the surrounding rocks; light brown leather beneath their dull mail; a cluster of long, silver lances strewn behind them, which they took up with muffled grumbles as Crick approached. A further three, wearing full gold plate and helms which curved intricately down the sides of their neck, chest and the black long-swords at their back, stood to attention in the centre where, for the first time that Crick had ever seen, the Gate was firmly shut. Two enormous wooden beams, each the width of a small tree, and several thick loops of chain were entwined across it, locking it tight.

And then, sheltered below a small, rocky overhang to the left of the Gate, Crick saw two others. A young man in extremely fine garments of glistening turquoise was talking loudly and animatedly, his wide jaw and important-looking features moving in a fashion that seemed quite unnatural. And beside him sat an even younger woman, possibly around Crick's age. She had a haunting mismatch of long, slick blonde hair and the deepest, blackest eyes Crick had ever seen, and in contrast to the brash oblivious nattering of the man beside her she was sitting silently, watching Crick as he approached. He couldn't help but stare back at her.

'First time this close to a girl, young Crick?'

Crick stopped dead in his tracks, realising he was but a few feet away from them, fighting suddenly to keep the confusion and concern from being displayed in his eyes. He studied the young man, frantically trying to work out how he knew his name.

'*I said* – is this the first time you've been near a girl, *boy*…?' the man repeated impatiently. His voice was that of the high and moneyed reaches of the City, but there was also a trace of hardness within it; a bite to his words which commanded attention. It was an intimidating combination.

'I – No – no, Sir. It's –'

'Then quit your staring, or I'll have your eyes.'

'Yes, Sir. Sorry…' Crick babbled, forcing himself with a curious and unsettling difficulty not to look anywhere near the girl. 'I've come –'

'To become a Guardsman,' he sighed. 'Yes, I know, I heard... Why?'

So Crick began. He spoke plainly but fervently of his boredom with life as it was; of his worries about the coming of the Black Wind. He explained passionately how he wanted now to do something more adventurous and more meaningful with his time than merely ride around his small corner of the Heartlands with his friends. He tried to repeat the story just as Url had instructed him, but under the heavy stare of the young man and the even greater weight of the soft, black eyes beside him which he continued to struggle not to notice, the words came out far quicker and more muddled than he intended. He delivered the main points across well enough, he thought, but as he neared the end of his speech he found himself surprisingly and worryingly breathless, still wondering above all how the young man could possibly know his name...

'Leisa's riding back in a few hours,' he said, pointing a large, beaten tankard which he had just snatched from the ground towards the girl beside him, before taking a large gulp from it. 'You'll go with her. They'll swear you in down there.'

'The City?' said Crick.

'Of course the City,' sneered the soft, stinging voice. 'Where else?'

'I –'

'Wait where you want.' He waved the tankard loosely away from the Gate. 'Just don't bother us while you do.'

Crick nodded, turning to find a place to sit, but as he stepped away the young man spoke again:

'When you get there, tell them Vice-Marshal Saulburg sent you. Crick nodded again. 'And if you're wondering how it is I know your name... It's because I make it a practice to know who it is who goes through my Gates. I've seen you many times, even if you've never noticed me. And for all your speed, boy – Yes, I've seen your movements, unnatural as they are...' One of the others in plain armour behind Crick spat heavily on the stone between them, but Crick had not the strength of will to turn to see which of them it was. 'And for all that,' the Vice-Marshal continued, 'you're one of the most unsubtle and unwatchful people I've ever laid eyes on. If you plan to do well as a Guardsman of these lands, or to survive as one at least, then one or both of those things will need to change. And change quickly.'

'I'll try to –' Crick began, but with a final dismissive flick of the tankard the Vice-Marshal had waved him away once more, returning the full of his rapt attention to the blonde-haired girl beside him. Crick turned, the glares of the Guardsmen unseen but heavy on his back as he stepped uncertainly away from the gate.

*

Three hours later and Crick was still waiting, sat hunched and restless upon the single patch of green ground he had been able to find amongst the floor of rock and dust. A fine drizzle, announced and accompanied still by long, faint rumblings of thunder echoing from somewhere behind the hills to the north, had appeared in the last half hour, and despite bright clouds from behind which the sun kept trying to burn its way through, there seemed no end to it. Crick folded his arms tighter about his knees, cursing himself for not bringing warmer clothing, staring jealously to where Vice-Marshal Saulburg and the girl, Leisa, were sitting, dry and warm beneath their sheltering roof of rock. The Vice-Marshal was relating another of an apparently endless supply of anecdotes, which judging by his own reaction to it must have been the most amusing yet. Leisa was sitting patiently as she had been since the moment Crick had first set eyes upon her, not saying a word as far as he had heard. She listened quietly and uninterestedly, occasionally going as far as to raise an eyebrow the merest fraction in response to a particularly shrewd display of wit from the Vice-Marshal. At all other times her shadowy eyes appeared open, but whether the mind within was awake or sleeping was difficult to tell. Whatever she was, however, she was at least dry.

But just as Crick was on the verge of paying notice to the pangs of pity he was feeling for himself, considering for a moment a retreat back down into the woods to wait out the weather, a glance at the other Guardsmen snapped him quickly from it: Perhaps they enjoyed the cooling rain, or perhaps with the passing of years they had merely grown accustomed to it, but in either case they seemed entirely unmoved, muttering and laughing quietly amongst themselves as they stood patiently in their places, their golds and greys now slick and shimmering amidst their black surrounds.

'On your feet, then,' called the Vice-Marshal finally, stretching as he stepped out into the rain, squinting into the sky, surveying the clouds with an almost condescending glare. The other Guardsmen fell silent at once, clattering rigidly to their places. Crick did his best to shake and wring the water from his sopping shirt as he got to his feet.

'You'll be at the City by nightfall,' the Vice-Marshal continued. 'If you –'

'*Nightfall*!' Crick interrupted, forgetting himself as the words worked their way quickly from his lips but slowly through his cold mind. 'The City's close to sixty miles away! How're we supposed to –'

'By riding swiftly.' He called back to Leisa: 'Don't let him slow you. If he does, leave him.'

Crick said nothing, but his stunned expression told clearly enough of his disbelief... Slow *her* down? It was the first time in his life that anyone had ever suggested the idea of him slowing anybody else down. The Vice-Marshal turned back to him, deliberately ignoring his astonishment...

'If you're lucky, you'll catch the Captain before he leaves. If not you'll have to wait until tomorrow. The Night-Watchman'll show you where you can sleep. You ready?' Crick nodded. 'Then get going. And mind you don't get her talking,' he added quietly with a somewhat perturbed glance over to the girl, being helped gently onto her horse by several eager Guardsmen, not that she seemed to require or have asked for it. 'You'll never shut her up...'

Before Crick was mounted Leisa had already made her way past him, trotting briskly down the path upon a stallion blacker even than Nightwind, without so much as a backward glance to Crick, the Vice-Marshal, or any of the other fawning Guardsmen. The Vice-Marshal himself had left and was talking to the men at the centre of the Gate, so with nothing else to do or wait for Crick simply turned and nudged Railer to catch up, nodding goodbye to the large Guardsman who was still standing as he had been all this time, unbothered and unyielding as a statue. The man gave a gentle tap of his helm with the blade of his axe as Crick passed, with a brief but honest grin which said *good luck*, and then he set his gaze once more down the slope.

For a short while as they descended the hill they rode in silence, slowly; Crick trying and failing to catch subtle glimpses of those black eyes, hidden now between thick veils of blonde which sprung gently back and forth.

'*What*?' she asked suddenly. Her voice was light, and soft; at odds to the brusqueness of the word. Crick's eyes darted away from her, back to nothing in particular in front of him.

'My name's Crick,' he said simply after a moment, at a loss for anything else.

'I know, you said earlier. And mine is Leisa, but that you know already as well. Not an altogether inspiring beginning to a conversation, is it?' She sighed, shaking her head irritably.

Crick turned slowly to face her again, finding her petulance more bewildering than offensive. He had a fleeting flash of respect for Vice-

Marshal Saulburg for remaining as talkative and buoyant as he had been for so long – though this passed as quickly as it had come.

'My humblest apologies, my lady...' he said, caught somewhere between a frown and a smile.

They continued for another few minutes in silence, but then from the corner of his eye Crick saw Leisa's blonde head fall forwards an inch, and her shoulders sink, as if all the strength had just been let out of her. She gave another quiet, weary sigh to complete the effect.

'Don't be...' she said. Crick looked to her questioningly. 'Don't be sorry.' She sat upright in her saddle. 'It's not your fault.'

'Tell me whose it is, and I'll see to it they change their ways...'

'My Father's, I suppose,' she said after a moment, ignoring what he had intended as a playful, gallant grin. She gazed sullenly into the distance. Crick was lost for a response, not having expected such honesty in the answer, if he had expected any answer at all. 'Or whoever it was who decided that in order for people like me to serve on the Council, we have to have spent time out here with idiots like *him.*'

'Saulburg?'

'Him, the others; they're all the same. They –'

'*Serve on the Council?*' Crick interrupted, suddenly aware of what she had said. 'You mean... you're to be a Councillor?'

'If your mind had but half the speed of your body....' She sighed again. 'Yes – I am,' she stated, a touch too plainly and deliberately for Crick's liking. 'But not until I've *proven my abilities in the field,*' she continued with a surprising venom to her voice which caught Crick off-guard. He studied her a while longer before speaking again:

'What abilities? And who's your Father? Is he on the Council?'

But Crick's sudden interest seemed to push further than Leisa was willing to go. In an instant she was sitting upright again above her saddle, her shoulders squarely back and head upright, staring dispassionately in front of her.

'The sooner I'm done out here the better,' she said quietly. 'It shouldn't take me long.'

'What won't?' Crick asked, but it was too late. He received nothing but silence. There was a strange new malice in those dark eyes which he didn't understand, and somehow didn't want to either. Without warning Leisa dug her heels suddenly and hard into the pitch dark flanks of her horse, setting it off at a pace the like of which Crick had never seen before. He fought hard to catch up, Railer resenting him the spurs but eager for the chase, and with their backs to the diminishing patch of bright cloud behind them they rode swiftly and wordlessly into the thin, stubborn rain.

*

Despite their speed, which somehow Leisa's mount seemed to maintain with ease, while Railer sweated heavily and laboured noisily beneath Crick, they only barely made it to the City by nightfall. Nonetheless, Crick was astonished at how far they had come in under a day's ride. They had crossed horizon after horizon through nearly a quarter the depth of the Heartlands; valleys, fields, rivers, lakes, woodlands, smallholdings and many other places in between passing in a swift, exhausting, rain-soaked blur. They had paused just three times, for a few seconds of breath, food and water, and to rest their horses, but at each Leisa had seemed impatient to set off again almost as soon as they had stopped. And all that time she had uttered not a single further word, despite Crick's several attempts. Altogether therefore when finally they circled south, around to the eastern tip of the bank of hills which crossed the north and western approaches to the City, and the first great towers rose up from the ground into view, Crick was filled with overwhelming relief, turning quickly to awe…

Twice before had he seen the City, on brief and secretive trips with Natt and Leyon into the hills which loomed large now on its far side. Each time they had ridden up into a narrow area of heathland which lined the crest of one of the tallest peaks, from where they could look down across almost half of the City in the distance below them. But never had he ventured further than that. Nor had he ever considered that he would actually ever do so. And never had he seen it from this direction before. The knowledge that he would soon be amongst those towers filled him now with renewed excitement, tainted with not a little apprehension.

Slowly the spires and upper levels of the vast and jagged sea of buildings appeared; high battlements and bridges slanting at all angles between them like the ladders of giants, and then beneath them all the colossal stoneworkings of what Crick knew was the first and outermost of many interlinking rows of walls. Men and women, children of all ages streamed into and out from the two wide, separate gateways towards which Leisa now led them: people of such odd and differing appearance and manner that it seemed quite impossible that they could all live here together. The distant helms and varying colours of countless Guardsmen were visible through small slits along the heights of the walls; the bulky frames of great armaments sitting proudly behind them. A procession of tall, armoured horses filed out from within the City, led by a single immense stallion which walked a clear foot taller than the rest. Dozens of men and women either side and within the gates called out fragments of news or the prices of wares which lay upon long stone tables behind them, neither of which Crick could hear well enough to understand. The noise… the bustle… the overpowering smells of brick and kicked-up dust amidst other curious, sharper scents… and the simple, astounding scale of it all from down at this level: None of it had Crick been at all prepared for.

And somewhere within that vast, sprawling mass of stone and metal, there would be a map. A map of the route from the Heartlands, north. All the way north. All the way to Iala. There had to be. If anywhere in the Heartlands, it would be here. All he had to do now, Crick recalled grimly as he entered into the sudden bleakness of the long, creeping shadows cast by the walls before him, was work out where that map was. And then find a way to steal it.

Chapter Ten

A Visitor in the Night

The sight of home struck always as a mixed blessing to Yori. On the one hand it meant at least one further night until he could be back again with the Heart, without the sight and feel of which the air felt cold and lifeless in comparison; Yori having felt the difference more powerfully with each passing visit to the Chamber. On the other hand, however, no matter the scale or splendour of greater attractions elsewhere, there could simply be no denying the comfort of good food and rest and one's own bed after a long day's work.

Eight days since they had found the Heart, they were still yet to resolve any of the most pressing challenges they would need to deal with before even beginning to contemplate a crossing of the Outerlands. Detaching the great gem from its enormous, tangled dais; removing it from the Chamber to the outside world; and finding or inventing some way of transporting it, hidden from view, once it was out, were all questions without easy answer. Or *any* answer, so far as any of the family could tell. For on the first two matters there had been all but no progress whatsoever. Each time any of the group reached closer in than an arm's length towards the Heart, the Chamber would erupt into a whirlwind of noise and light just as it had done when Url had first raised his hand towards it. And as for getting it out then to the surface – the task seemed almost impossible. There was perhaps a small chance of something being fashioned to help drag it slowly and with great difficulty up the twisting tunnel to the clearing in the valley above, but from there…?

Orlando had been somewhat more successful in his efforts at strengthening the family's cart so that it would bear the weight of the gem. The ageing contraption had been inherited from Abetta and Erik, Yori's Grandfather, who had died when Yori was four. Yori could recall only brief images of him – *feelings* rather than true memories. The cart made Yori think of him, though exactly why, he couldn't remember. It had languished patiently behind the stables for the past six years since Orlando had stopped making the journeys to the City to trade, and it was only barely large enough to hold the Heart, let alone any portion of the exceedingly sizeable mound of provisions they would need to take. And quite how they would disguise it from the eyes of inspecting Guardsmen, none of the family could say. But despite all this Orlando had set upon it enthusiastically, ripping out rotten beams and adding supports and new coverings wherever they would be needed. Dissected into pieces in the middle of the courtyard, it sat now as an emaciated skeleton of its former self, surrounded by varying strips of wood and stretches of canvas new, old, and older, and of all shape and size imaginable.

'Let's eat outside, tonight,' said Siu, smiling into the warm early evening as she dismounted and opened the gate, letting the others through into the courtyard. The day had been hot, humid, and completely still; thin layers of high cloud now being slowly flooded with intense reds and oranges from the sinking sun. The westward views from the hills around the cave had been spectacular all through the day, and for the second afternoon running they had been unable to tear Abetta away from them, leaving her there reluctantly, on condition that she return before the darkness was fully up.

Orlando nodded his agreement, glad as much for the interruption to the debate he had been having with Url since midway through the Eigerhills. For Url had been, and remained now, insistent that all members of the family should come with the Heart to Iala. This he said was both for the success of the journey and, in fact, for their own wellbeing as well. As dangerous as it may seem, he argued, there was in fact no safer place in the world to be than right beside the Heart. Whatever dangers they may face on the road north, they would surely be nothing compared to the perils of a small homestead on the verges of the Heartlands, with no Heart to seek shelter with should the creatures of the Black Wind finally make it through the borders. Unless those who stayed were going to move to the relative and short-term protection of the City, Url stated, they had no choice but to come.

Given the family's lack of understanding of what the gemstone truly was – of what powers it truly contained, and what protection it could perhaps indeed offer from the forces currently at bay beyond the Heartlands, it was difficult to find and express any form of clear and irrefutable reasoning with which to fault his logic. But as is the way with such choices, there was far more in play than the confines of logic allowed. It was instinct, rather, upon which Orlando was forming his judgement, so that for the moment at least he remained as plain as ever that it should be him and Url only who risked themselves beyond the borders. As straightforward as Url was trying to make it, the awkward truth was that to travel from here to Iala was a task so strewn with danger and – more hazardous still – unknowns, that the chance of it actually succeeding surely had to be exceptionally small. And if this was the case, he would far rather have his family back in their homelands making at least a stand against the Black Wind, than out in the middle of nowhere, alone, afraid, and utterly without hope of rescue.

Yori and Aliya meanwhile were more determined than ever that they should be allowed to go; their mother's response remaining a flat and unwavering *no*. But all three of them had quickly grown weary of the argument in the heat, leaving it to Url and Orlando to attempt, and fail, to settle the matter. Orlando too, however, had now long-since tired of the never-ending and inescapable circles of reasoning into which he was consistently being drawn, though Url remained as animated and eager as he had been several hours ago.

'Enough!' cried Siu despairingly as Url began once more to reiterate in different form a point he had made several times already. The others were so weary of the quarrel that they knew nothing of what he was actually saying; only that they were certain they had heard it before. '*Food* first. Then *peace*. And quiet. And rest…' she sighed longingly at the thought. '*Then*, if there's time, you two can go back to your bickering. Not for too long, though,' she added, kissing Orlando as he dismounted. I'd like my husband back at some point this evening…'

Yori's face contorted in a grimace of deepest disgust, doing all he could to turn his mind away from hers.

*

Half an hour later, and the Heart, the cave, Iala, and all other items of preoccupation were close to forgotten amidst a half dozen platters of ripe fruits, pies, and the substantial remains of a butterflied leg of salted lamb from the previous evening. All of it was imbued with an even more marvellously wholesome feel, eaten as it was under the wide, deep pink glow of the surrounding skies. Yori should have guessed that it wouldn't be allowed to last for long…

'We need to go deeper into the valley,' said Url, breaking the silence. Before Siu could say or do anything to stop him, Orlando had allowed himself to be drawn in once again:

'I told you –' he mumbled, swallowing with difficulty a far too large mouthful of lamb, '– I tried going with Aliya a few days ago: It's impossible. You can get maybe a hundred feet further from the clearing, but beyond that the crystals are just too big, too sharp, and too many! If you wait a while the smaller ones'll move to let you pass, but the others are completely unyielding. One of the others might be able to squeeze a bit further – Crick would probably be able to find some sort of way through, *if* he was here.'

Yori felt the wrench of his Mother's heart as clearly as if it had been his own. Crick was never far from her thoughts, but the sudden mention of him startled her even so. She got quickly to her feet, her lips pursed tight as she took her and Aliya's plates back into the house. Orlando held her arm briefly as she passed, watching her go before continuing:

'But even if *they* could find a way, there's no chance we would ever get the *Heart* through all that. None.'

'But we don't know what there is at the end of the valley…'

'*If* there's an end…' murmured Aliya distractedly, only barely conscious of the conversation as she lay back in her chair, her eyes closed to the deep orange of the sun which bathed her face and neck.

'Yes – well, I'm fairly certain there's one somewhere down there, and we *have* to find out what –'

'It makes no difference what's down there!' said Orlando.

'But until we *know* we can't –'

'Ah… finally,' said Siu, stepping back out through the doorway. 'She's back,' she added to Url's questioning glance, nodding down into the distance. From the west the hazy speck of a barely visible figure was riding towards them.

'Ah, good, yes…' Url muttered, flicking a cursory glance down through the fields. 'I'll go and have a look myself tomorrow,' he added, even before he had turned back to Orlando.

'What about the screeching?' asked Siu. 'I heard it again as we left.'

'As I've said, it's probably just the wind above.' He was as uncertain about that as the rest of them, but determined not to let it obscure matters further than they already were.

'And if it's not?' asked Aliya to his frustration. '*Anything* could have made its home down there…'

Yori watched his Grandmother approach as the others continued with their talk. Only barely had she kept to her word: Darkness was not far off; the half-hidden sun now shooting long, thin streaks of scarlet through the trailing cloud of dust kicked up by Chestnut. There seemed to be a great deal of dust… She had to be riding quickly…

'Something's wrong…'

The words had left his mouth even before he had thought them. It was something about the way she was riding… It wasn't just fast; it was purposeful. It was with… fear. In an instant he felt the air around him thicken.

'What is it?' asked Url quickly, jumping to his feet and stepping forwards, straining to see the approaching figure better.

'I don't…' Yori paused, closing his eyes… 'She's scared.'

'Scared? Scared of what? Is she hurt?'

'I don't know.'

'Wait…!' Aliya tried, but even as she spoke Orlando sped through them bareback above Nightwind, the only of the horses not yet stabled. Yori watched as his Father charged out with tight grip upon the speeding animal's mane through the gate and down into the fields. He met Abetta with a hurried greeting; the two of them speaking only briefly before riding quickly back up towards the home. Orlando reached them first.

'Get the horses ready!' he called as he approached. 'We need to leave.'

'What's wrong?' asked Aliya.

Fear and the opening scents of panic were beginning to engulf Yori's senses: partly his own, partly drawn like heat from a fire from everyone around him, and partly from the look on his Grandmother's face as she pushed an exhausted Chestnut up the rise towards them. Yori took Oden's reins as his Father darted quickly through the jumble of canvas and wood and disappeared inside.

'The cave –' Abetta gasped as she reached them 'He – found it! He's –'

'Who?' asked Url.'

'The Aulan…'

Yori saw Url's mouth twist angrily beneath petrified eyes. He could scarcely contain himself long enough to wait to hear what Abetta had to say.

'I saw him while I was on the ridge above the valley. He left his cabin about half an hour after you all left… went straight up the path

102

into the woods, towards the cave. I followed him – he went *straight* there; knew *exactly* where it was. He went in but I… I couldn't have followed without him hearing me… I didn't know what he'd do if he found me following him…' she added with a sorrowful look down to Url, who was holding the reins beside her.

To Yori's surprise as much as the others, however, Url simply reached up, held both Abetta's hands softly in his, and said, quite quietly, 'I'm glad you're alright… You did well.'

For a brief moment the air of alarm was replaced with one of quite surreal affection; a camaraderie so rarely revealed suddenly clear and strong between the two old adversaries, more honest by far than any of their usual wrangling. Yori glanced sideways to Aliya; Aliya to him; and then both to their Mother. All three of them stared silently at Url. Into the confusion Orlando came sprinting back through the front door fully-laden with saddles, straps, clothes, bags, and other items, but halting abruptly at the sudden silence in front of him.

'What's going on?' he demanded.

'Nothing,' said Url brusquely, returning to his former self quicker than it took him to turn and shake his head. 'Let's get going. You two…!' he barked at Yori and Aliya, pulling on the boots and cloak which he had left beside the door. 'Do something useful; help your Father.'

He disappeared into his cottage as Yori and the others readied the horses and changed swiftly back into their travelling clothes, and when he returned a minute later he was striding purposefully and angrily, his hunting bow hung loose around one shoulder and a quiver of thin, silver arrows tied tight around the other.

'Is that necessary?' asked Siu.

'Absolutely,' came Url's gruff reply, and with it he mounted and sped swiftly off leaving the others to catch him if they could; Crash coming within an inch of her name as she careered through the gate, neighing frantically beneath Url's frenzied calls of encouragement all the way down and into the dusk.

*

They reached the Eigerhills far quicker than ever they had before, but even this could not prevent the dark of night from enveloping them as they rode. Hardly a word had been spoken since they had left, adding greatly to the sense of unease as they made their way up the first slopes and into the utter quiet of the woods. When they reached the valley, Url looked briefly down towards the hut on the far side before leading them on, grunting something about the fact that no light

103

was coming from the windows. Without meaning to, Yori found himself nudging Cloud ever so slightly closer to Oden and his Father.

Even up here in the hills the night air was just as still and clammy as earlier in the day, making each step seem to crash thickly through the undergrowth. Even Yori's breath, quiet and slow as he was trying to make it, felt unnervingly loud. Url, however, seemed to be of a completely different mind, sacrificing stealth for speed as he pushed quickly on towards the cave.

Soon then they were rounding the enormous fallen tree-trunk which they had come to use as the mark for the turning into the clearing. The dark grey leaves thinned before them, and bending under the final low, sweeping, branch they saw the small hillock rise softly in the dark before them. Everything was silent, and to Yori's relief Url had finally decided to try to keep it this way, creeping low amongst the shadows until he had almost reached the far side. He looked warily around him for a moment, and then stood, carefully, still watching the entrance. He beckoned the others over to him. Leaving Cloud where he stood, Yori was the first to move...

He could feel it in Url's thoughts before he reached him, but this did little to dampen the rush of fear which washed through his chest and down to his fingertips as he stepped up to Url's side, seeing for himself the improvised and formerly camouflaged door of stone, moss, and leaves which Url placed each night over the entrance to the cave, now scattered across the ground several feet away, revealing the cold dark of the cave within.

'He's down there...' Url mouthed in a hoarse whisper, trying to peer into the gloom. After a moment's thought he drew his bow quietly from one side and an arrow from the other. 'Follow me. Don't make a sound. We go straight to the Chamber, fast as we can – he might not have made it there yet. When we see him – or he sees us – let me deal with him.'

'What do you mean, *deal with him*?' whispered Aliya. Yori was in little doubt.

'Urlmaeus, you don't use that thing unless it's to protect one of us...' said Abetta, giving a stern nod to the bow.

'He's *not* getting near the Heart!' said Url, forgetting for an instant his own call for silence.

'But what if he's already there?' asked Aliya.

'Then we... well, I don't know...'

'Why's he here at all?' asked Siu.

'How did he find out about it?' asked Orlando.

'I don't know – and I don't know,' said Url impatiently to each in turn, forcing himself with great difficulty to speak quietly. 'And right now, I don't care. Right now we just need to get down there and keep him away from the Heart.'

He slid his cloak quickly from his shoulders, moving to the opening of the cave. But before stepping through he turned back, eyeing them all severely…

'Not a word…' he said, turning and vanishing into the black.

They stepped lightly through the darkness of the cave, and down into the tunnel; Yori allowing himself the briefest of moments to bask in the warmth of the light which washed over him as they stepped through to the far side, making their way down towards the cavern. When they reached the opening they paused, looking out carefully over the edge, but there was nobody to be seen. As Yori studied the route ahead of them, however, a small impression in the crystal floor caught his eye, just beneath them.

'Look…' he whispered, pointing to the dip. And as the others saw it, they too realised that it could only be the remains of the Aulan's footprint. After the first trek through the cavern, they had found that where the crystal moved and flattened itself to allow a person to pass, it slowly reformed, over the course of a few hours, into its original shape. From the look of the mark, which was beginning to roughen and regain the former sharpness of its edges, with a slither of crystal around an inch tall growing from its centre, it seemed that it had probably been almost that long since he had been through.

Following the footprints took them a different, yet somehow slightly quicker route to the clearing before the final coiled tunnel, at which point Url motioned for Yori to stay back behind his parents. Every muscle in his legs and back aching from the effort of moving so quietly, Yori watched as Url started down the curving passageway, fitting an arrow softly into place, holding it half-drawn in front of him. Beside him, Yori saw his Grandmother watching Url and the bow uneasily, but she kept her silence. Fears were given all the time they needed to strengthen and multiply through the long walk down below the clearing, working their way ever deeper into Yori's mind as with an agonizing slowness they descended, step by step around the great spiral; the holes finally appearing to their right, filling the passage with narrow beams of light and swirls of haze. The opening appeared; Url pausing before it, his breathing heavy but silent. And before Siu could speak whatever words she was about to say he took a final deep breath and charged, bow first into the chamber…

'*Get away from it!*'

The sharp echoes of his voice crashed instantly back into the passageway; Yori recoiling from the shock of them. And he was not the only one. There was a distant, startled grunt... and then another shout of '*Away*!' from Url; Orlando dashing through the opening; Yori jumping around his Mother to follow, feeling the others enter close behind him...

For the briefest of moments the crouching silhouette of a tall, scrawny man was set in sharp relief against the glare of the Heart; Url still screaming at him from midway through the cave. But just as Yori halted, the man leapt down away from the platform and was lost within the thick haze below.

'Stop!' shouted Url again in vain. He drew the bowstring back tight into his cheek, aiming with quick, darting movements from side to side into the haze. Nothing re-emerged. A soft, almost inaudible whistling filled the cave. A subtle frown creased Yori's brow as he fought to ascertain whether it was a new noise, or simply the silence of the cave which he had never noticed before.

'Where's he gone?' asked Orlando, quietly. There were several confused, frightened responses all at once, the others each pointing anxiously into different points around the great platform which held the Heart.

'Quiet!' whispered Url above them all, holding out his arms, staring intently into the haze. 'This is the only way he can get out... You all stay here...' He stepped away from them, into the Chamber.

'Url...! Don't –' Siu whispered, but Url was completely deaf to her, focused only on the swirling vapour in front of him. Yori's heart beat faster still in his chest like a rising drum as Url made his way forwards, swinging his full-drawn bow from side to side with tense, nervous arms, straining to see into the moat of haze beneath him. He studied one spot... and another... finding nothing. Yori could feel the man down there, close yet distant; a curious presence... Just as Url was moving round to the left of the Heart there was a sudden eddy from within the haze on the far side. He turned, taking aim, but the instant he made his first step in that direction the haze beside him exploded in a violent squall of movement, a dark figure springing up towards him from the point that he had just turned away from. Before he could react the man had knocked him hard to the ground and now he charged, wild and tall, straight towards the opening. Yori froze at the sight and terrible, bestial sounds of the *thing* coming towards him, but suddenly he was flying backwards: his Father had taken hold of him, throwing him hard out of the way. The man was just feet away; Yori cowering backwards still further, terrified for his Father but too petrified to move, hoping desperately that the man would somehow pass silently through them…

A thick, sharp *crack* split the air. Something collapsed to the floor… and then nothing. Opening his eyes, Yori saw the man sprawled limp across the ground, his Father standing above him wielding a short, heavy stump of dark, polished wood, swollen and surrounded with a web of blunt ridges at one end. He held it aloft a moment longer, studying the unconscious form beneath him, before returning the cudgel to a concealed pocket in his cloak by his thigh. It was a long time since Yori had seen the weapon, and only the second time it had been used in anger, as far as he knew. It had been as effective as the last time: the figure was out cold, oblivious to the peculiar way his lanky, sinewy body had crumpled to the ground, which in some other distant time and place could easily have been comical. Siu stepped quickly forwards to kneel at Yori's side, supporting him, keeping a wary eye on the man as she did so.

'Well –' groaned Url, limping back towards them, grimacing and clasping his right shoulder, '– told you it would work…'

With a flurry of muttered curses Abetta stepped angrily around the man, inspecting Url's shoulder with considerably more force than was necessary.

'You're not broken,' she declared. 'More's the pity.' Url smiled at her. She did not smile back.

'He's coming round!' Aliya shouted suddenly, skipping back away from the man who groaned, raising a hand to the vicious, purple welt that was spreading quickly across the top of his left cheek and into his straggling hairline. Yori jumped to his feet and scuttled quickly to one side. The man started to push himself awkwardly up onto his elbow, but Url stepped forward, directing the hastily-restrung bow towards him while Orlando pulled the cudgel back out from his cloak. The man opened his eyes with a startled grunt, recoiling first from Orlando and then from Url in a swift scramble to get to his feet. Yori felt then saw his Father readying another strike…

'Wait!' he shouted; his Father halting inches before the wood made contact. Everyone else seemed to have stopped as well, looking with one eye to Yori while the other remained fixed carefully upon the man who was now cowering against the wall between them all.

He was terrified. Barefoot, trembling, and terrified beyond words. As he peered out from between his shielding arms, Yori felt the strikes of a broken, frantic tide of confusion and fear flowing in his gaze like dead leaves riding a bitter squall, each one of them streaked with a deep, horrible pain. There was no wickedness in him; no desire to hurt or get the better of them. In fact as far as Yori could tell, there was hardly any conscious thought at all… Just raw, overpowering emotion. Yori had never known another person like this.

'He's… just afraid,' said Yori, still staring hesitantly but directly into the man's eyes, shadowed as they were behind a veil of lank, black hair which fell untidily across his face. 'Move back,' he said to the others. His words came out as more an order than he had intended, though he made no effort to apologise or correct himself. In fact he continued: 'Let him have some space…'

After a moment the others did as he said; Url moving slowly around to block the opening again as he did so. Yori heard the gentle whistling once more as each of the family stared anxiously at the man, and he back at them.

'Can you… understand us?' asked Siu at length, her voice slow and quiet.

The man looked up at her, lowering his arms nervously. And after a moment he gave a weak, timid nod.

'Why are you here?' Url demanded. There was no answer.

'How did you find it?' asked Orlando. But again the man said nothing, his eyes now flicking constantly from one of the family to another.

'You know he can't talk,' said Abetta.

'Well we can't just let him go!' snapped Url. 'He knows too much… If he –'

But Url was wrong, and Yori suddenly found himself annoyed that the old man couldn't see it…

'He doesn't *know* anything!' Yori interrupted, with an anger that surprised him almost as much as it did everyone else. 'He doesn't know what it is, or how he found it, or how important it is… And even if he did he wouldn't tell anyone. *Look* at him!'

They did so, and finally it seemed to dawn on them – all except Url – that perhaps the confused, frightened mind in front of them might not be the threat they had assumed him to be. Whether he properly understood what Yori was saying or not, the man seemed to sense that he had an ally in Yori, giving what could have been a brief, nervous smile.

'We are in *his* part of the world…' said Siu. 'He could have just stumbled across the cave, even with the covering over it. And what else are we going to do?' she asked of Url. 'Unless you intend to keep him locked down here? Or…'

Url considered the *or* carefully for a moment, but a fierce look from Abetta snapped him from it:

'Alright, alright,' he muttered. He bent down to the man, his face a foot from his. 'But if you tell anyone what's down here…'

'He gets the idea, I'm sure,' said Siu, dismissively. She reached down and offered her hand tentatively, helping the man carefully to his feet, where he stood at least a foot and a half taller than her, even hunched over as he still was. 'You can go…' she said with a motherly smile.

The man glanced nervously to the opening – Url moving reluctantly out of the way – and then back to Siu, and to Yori.

'It's okay,' Yori prompted, motioning to the opening. Still looking at him, the man started to edge gently away.

'Wait –' said Orlando, reaching out towards the man's arm but stopping just short of touching him. The man shied away again but Orlando smiled and pulled back his hand. 'Maybe… maybe you can help us…?'

'*Help* us!' said Url, 'It's dangerous enough that he's been down here *once*! I won't have him coming down here every day. He's –'

A surge of anger welled up inside Yori…

'*You won't have him…?*' he said bitterly. 'What gives *you* the right to say who can and who can't come down here? The Heart is just as much his as it is yours!'

'The difference being that *I* know what needs to be done with it, while I doubt he even knows his own name! And whether or not we can make him understand, we still don't know whether he can be trusted!'

'He *can*!'

'You can't know that for certain.'

'I can know it far better than *you*!'

'That's enough!' shouted Orlando. And then, more quietly, he added: 'He used to live in the *Outerlands*…'

Yori had realised what his Father was saying before he had said it, but it took a few long seconds for Url's face to flash with understanding.

'Do you know how to get to Iala?' Orlando asked of the man. Url's face was suddenly alive with excitement again, though he showed none of it to the others. 'Do you know the quickest route to the Firstway from here?' Orlando tried again. 'Or Irraigion? Can you –'

'Slowly…' said Siu. 'He can't understand when you talk like that. Let me try…' She looked up at the man, speaking slowly and clearly: 'Home…?'

The man mouthed the word loosely back to her, but did nothing else.

'Home…' Siu persisted. '*Your home*… Where did you come from?'

The man stared at the ground for a moment, confused. Then with an uncertain gesture he pointed out through the opening and up the passageway.

'No – not your home above here. Your home *before* that. When you lived outside these Heartlands. With your family…?'

And at the last word the man's gaze lifted suddenly from the ground. He stared at Siu with dark, distant eyes; a sorrow of such intensity written across him that Yori felt even Url moved to the beginnings of pity.

'He remembers…' said Orlando, pleased with the progress. Yori, however, found it difficult to share the feeling, when one look at the man was enough to drain all happiness from him.

'Pass me some parchment,' said Url. 'And a pencil.'

Orlando took out the small rolls of parchment which he kept as ever wrapped around an old, short pencil in the inner breast pocket of his cloak, handing them to Url, who unfurled one of the pieces and spread it flat upon the smoothest section of the wall he could find beside him. The crystal rolled and sank slightly beneath his hand, but then was still. Near the bottom of the parchment Url marked a small circle, and then pointed to it.

'We – are – here…' he said. Then he drew the outline of a tiny cabin just to the left of the circle… 'Your home now… The valley – here…' He marked out several other features – the mountains in the north-east, the Maiyen at the northern border of the Heartlands, and Immelus to the right of the page, calling out the names clearly each time. Then he turned and pushed the pencil into the man's hand, folding his reluctant fingers around it, pulling him gently forward towards the wall.

'Now – *You*…?' he asked, with a broad sweep across the top half of the page. 'Family…?'

The man studied the parchment carefully, turning his head gently from side to side as he traced the outline of the cabin with the pencil, over and over again.

'Family?' Url repeated, slightly more forcefully.

The man blinked from his trance, mouthing the word again. Then, as they all watched silently, he moved the pencil carefully and slowly up to the line of the river to the north… and then across it. His quivering hand became completely still, and he paused a moment, taking in several slow breaths. Suddenly his fingers twitched, marking the parchment with a small line. And then, with a string of quick, tiny

110

scratches of the pencil, he began to draw. In the finest detail, covering every square inch of the page, he traced the paths of rivers, woodlands, lakes, hills, and even what seemed to be minute clusters of houses, working his way slowly up to the top of the parchment, filling in a wide swathe of the Outerlands with a geography that none of them had ever seen before. It was only when he reached the edge of the sheet, dropping it, holding out his hand to Url, that Yori realised that through all this, the man's eyes had been closed, screwed up tight in concentration. Url hurriedly took another piece of parchment from Orlando and put it against the wall in place of the first, and without pause the map continued to grow, in the same north-westerly direction as before, all the time with the same remarkable detail. And not once did the man open his eyes.

After a time he reached a point at which he drew a thick, nearly straight line into the north, but to Url's disappointment he left it almost immediately, turning west, still no more than a fifth of the way to where Yori expected Iala to be, far to the north. He reached the edge of the parchment and let it fall again to the ground as Url quickly placed another in front of him, and for several minutes the features continued to extend westward in various long, snaking paths. Then suddenly his eyes burst open, and he fell back away from the map with the same overwhelming surge of fear which had paralysed him before.

'What is it?' asked Url. 'Is this where you lived? Was this your home?'

But the man was no longer listening. Still staring, terrified at the map, he struggled awkwardly backwards and began to moan in a series of deep, guttural tones. Before Url could move to stop him he leapt to his feet and shot like an arrow out through the opening.

'Damn it!' cried Url with a fruitless grab for an arm as it disappeared before him. He darted as fast as he could across the jagged ground and out into the passageway, but it was too late. Only a thin trail of deep red spatters remained where the man's feet had been cut. Url returned, holding the shoulder which he had just wrenched once more.

'For a moment I really thought he was going to lead us all the way to Iala,' said Orlando with a sigh.

The others sighed too, though mostly from relief that the cave was their own once more. They cast their eyes about it more from instinct than because they truly feared anything would be damaged or missing. As they did so, Url bent down to pick up the final piece of parchment, holding all three of them out in front of him, staring hard and thoughtfully at the one in the middle. It took a few seconds, but slowly a cautious smile began to creep into the corners of his mouth…

'Actually,' he said quietly, still studying the second parchment. 'I think he almost has…'

Chapter Eleven

Black Wind Soup

The City seemed even more alive than usual today, if that was possible. Sitting beside a gently-playing water fountain in the shape of a strange, six-legged creature with thin, pointed horns and a ridge of spines across its back and sides, Crick gazed up to his left and right along the road. Wide enough with ease to accommodate ten or maybe more versions of the home Crick had known all his life joined end-to-end, with walkways and a great arched roof several hundred feet above him divided into great sections just far enough apart to allow in sufficient light to distinguish night from day, the sheer scale of it all, as noted instantly on his first arrival, was one of the many things which Crick was still yet to grow accustomed to. Hundreds of people were going busily about their lives, walking to and from the various towering buildings which lined the far side of the road in a solid, unbroken mass; while around and behind him they talked, laughed, ate and drank in one of the many taverns or smaller shops, which sat like the smaller but more boisterous siblings of their older brothers and sisters opposite them.

To the left the road extended further than Crick could see, like a great hallway of one of the race of giants Url had told him of so many years ago, while in the distance far to his right the surrounding cliff-like walls and archway opened out into the brightness of the Skycourt. Somewhere beyond the maze of alleyways, courtyards and residences behind him was the Garrison, and his room, though once again he had entirely forgotten the route back. For now, however, this didn't concern him. His attention was directed instead towards the crescent row of white stone steps in front of him, which led imposingly up and into the ornate, busy entranceway to the building on the opposite side of the road.

'Ah, Crick!' came a sudden loud, cheerful voice, breaking easily through the clamour of the crowd. Looking up to his right Crick saw the tall, muscular frame of Tarryn striding towards him.

Tarryn had joined on the same day as Crick. A rich, intolerably over-confident only-child of some important figures in the City, he was far from the type of person Crick ever would have thought to enjoy sharing a room with, let alone call a friend. But after just ten days he had, against every ounce of his better – or perhaps former – judgement, come to find him to be extremely amusing company. Moneyed and from the City he may be, but Tarryn, only two years older than Crick, had a sense of adventure and disregard for his own wellbeing which at times put even Crick to shame. For all his other faults, these qualities by themselves made him endlessly entertaining to be around, at least for Crick. Just now, however, Crick could have done without the interruption.

'Afternoon,' said Crick, trying to sound tired and unenthusiastic: both easy enough after the training they had struggled through today. Unfortunately, Tarryn's humour was as always in no way dependent upon or swayed by that of those around him. It was also incredibly – and often ruinously – infectious.

'Yes!' he said, beaming, taking a great sniff of the air for no apparent reason. 'Wonderful, isn't it? Have just been gracing the girls at the Wallow with my inimitable presence… Was on rather good form, if I dare say so! *Lovely* things, very amenable,' he added, grinning as much to the strangers around him, all forced into swerving around his bull-like frame.

'I'd be pretty *amenable* too if you paid me that much.'

'Ha! Yes, well, you never know – perhaps once I've made my way through the women here you'll get lucky! Until then, young Crick, I'm afraid you'll just have to wait.' He stopped, turning to look in the direction in which Crick was still staring. 'For the love of *wine*, Crick, tell me you're not considering going in… in *there*? You know how I feel about that place!'

'I thought I might just –'

'*Crick*! Dear, dear Crick – there are over a hundred different places of drink, debauchery , and other varying amusements in this City, and you have the nerve to tell me you're going to spend one of your last afternoons here in a… a *library*?' He whispered the word with apparent nausea. 'Are you unwell?'

'I'm fine. I –'

'Well then onwards!' Tarryn shouted, attracting the attention of several passers-by as he threw his arm around Crick, lifting him like a feather from the side of the fountain.

'No, really,' said Crick, trying to think of an excuse, struggling in vain against the quite unbelievable strength which had already made Tarryn one of the most feared competitors in the training yard. 'I've got to learn where all the Gates are around the Heartlands. You heard Saiak tell me that if I haven't memorised three-quarters of them by tomorrow I won't be allowed to leave with the squad next week.'

'Ah!' said Tarryn, dropping Crick heavily to the ground. 'Thwarted. Well, I suppose if thus the Captain has decreed it, then thus it must be! We don't want you missing out on our first little adventure, now, do we? I suppose you must do what you must do,' he added with a sigh and a dramatic bow made cumbersome by his bulk. 'Tis a shame though, to be sure… I fear I shall just have to find enough amusement for the both of us! Enjoy!' And with a further glance of utmost disgust at the grand wall of stone across the road he marched cheerily away into the throng of people outside the tavern behind them, leaving Crick more than a little relieved despite his well-feigned look of frustration.

'Oh…!' Tarryn called, disappearing amongst the crowd. 'A note came for you – I left it on your bed.'

'Thanks,' Crick called back quietly, eager to avoid any further conversation. 'I'll get it later.' But Tarryn was already out of sight. Crick shook himself back to concentration, turned once more to face the far side of the road, and wove his way towards it through the steady stream of people.

The Halls of Knowledge. *Library* was a term which didn't do it justice by half. Twenty-three sprawling levels of books, manuscripts, ancient scrolls, paintings, tapestries, statues, curious mechanical devices and instruments, and endless other such items arrayed through hundreds of separate halls, altogether forming virtually the entire sum of all learning, science, and art ever created. Or at least, that part of it which had been produced in the Heartlands, or else salvaged from outside them by those brave, foolish or desperate enough for coin to do so.

And somewhere, amongst it all, were the Map Halls.

A great many people were entering and leaving through the heavily-gilded doorway through which Crick now stepped, but the entrance hall inside was so vast that as he entered all around him seemed quite empty, and oddly quiet in the brief instants for which the doors remained shut. Dozens of wooden staircases, each suspended through thick, golden chains to rafters high above, curved delicately up to various levels of balconies; Crick trying to recall from his brief introduction to the City which one would take him most simply to the third level.

'And you're looking for…?' said a small, cheery woman who had appeared at his side as though from nowhere.

'Um, the Map Halls, pl–'

'Third floor, straight ahead, staircase five,' she said quickly with a thin, rigid smile. Before Crick could thank her she had turned away, and was greeting somebody else in similar fashion.

The staircase seemed surprisingly sturdy considering it drew no support at all from below, but nevertheless Crick felt a small pang of discomfort peering over the side as he neared the top. For all his adventurous attributes, a head for heights was a skill he had never quite mastered. It was none too soon, therefore, that he reached the top; the first Hall – *The Great City of Immelus, and Surrounding Lands* – directly ahead of him. To his left was a large golden plaque, embossed with a plan of this third level above many lines of fine, decorative writing, through which he had to read twice before he found what he was looking for…

The Outerlands and Beyond (Access Restricted) – Hall Forty-Seven. And after searching for a moment he found a small *47* – circled with a dark red ring, which for the most part was missing from the other numbers – in one of the largest-looking rooms of the level, on the far side of the first Hall in front of him, the front of which was open to the balcony and supported with a line of thick, golden pillars, decorated in spiralling lines of an ancient script which Crick felt he had seen somewhere before, though he didn't understand.

Brightly lit by dozens of enormous, low-hanging chandeliers of red and white candles, the *Immelus and Surrounding Lands* Hall contained numerous long rows of low wooden shelves and desks, most of which were occupied with people scribbling notes or sketches, or poring over various maps of differing sizes and colours. Every square foot of wall was covered in mapwork or diagrams of some sort, and to his left as Crick walked in a large huddle of young boys and girls were staring uninterestedly but politely up to a wide plan of some obscure part of the City which an elderly, softly-spoken man was describing in the slow, dull tones of a man who had regurgitated the words so many times before he no longer had to pay any thought to what he was saying. Further in were more desks, more shelves, and beyond them

116

clusters of large cabinets with glass lids, revealing all manner of items inside. Then Crick came to a tall, wide stone column, about ten feet tall, around which the outer walls of the City had been painted at the very bottom, with the surrounding lands painted above. He stared at it as he walked around it, slowly, intrigued; and then as he reached the other side he saw the man he was looking for…

Standing rigidly but glumly to attention, just before a small, solid door of dark green wood and curved metal, was a Guardsman who quite plainly did not want to be there. His name was Heuwan. After a great deal of quiet, subtle searching and enquiring, Crick had finally discovered that it was him who would be guarding the entrance to the *Outerlands* Hall for these few evenings. And Crick also knew – as did anyone else who had strayed within earshot of the lacklustre young man during dinner last night – that Heuwan would do almost anything to get out of it. He had a reputation wholly justified as an idler and a man who could rarely pass up the opportunity of a good night's drinking… Something which Crick was now relying upon.

'S'cuse me,' said Crick, as casually as he could as he approached the door.

'Hang on,' said Heuwan, holding out his hand sluggishly. 'Permission?'

'*Permission?*'

'Yes, *have you got permission*? If you've got it then let's see it… If not then you can't go through.' The words trailed glumly off his tongue.

'Oh, right… Sorry.'

Heuwan gave a brief grunt of goodbye, but Crick lingered for a moment, staring uninterestedly around him.

'Problem?' asked Heuwan.

'No… nothing really. Just bored.'

'*Bored*? Of course you're bloody bored – Look where you are…! Look who you're surrounded by…!' He swung a sombre glare around the silent, working figures of the Hall, engrossed as most of them were in manuscripts and great clumps of papers. 'Get out and enjoy the evening!' His attempts not to let his frustration break his smart posture were less than half-hearted.

'That's what I'm bored of, actually,' said Crick.

'Hmm?' mumbled Heuwan, seeming already to have forgotten Crick was standing beside him. 'What do you mean, *that's what you're bored of…?*'

'The City,' said Crick with a sigh. 'The noise. The people. Drunks everywhere, all shouting and laughing themselves stupid. Gets a bit… tiresome, after a while.'

'*A bit tiresome*! Are you simple, boy? It's called enjoyment! *Fun*! It's what I could, should and most certainly would be doing if I wasn't stuck in this dismal place all night.'

'Well *I* don't find it fun having ale and wine spilled all down me every few seconds!' said Crick, extravagantly patting several imaginary wet patches across his arms and shoulders. 'Or at least, I *think* most of it was ale and wine…' He screwed up his nose. 'He started putting all sorts of other stuff in there as I was leaving…'

'Who did?'

'Gerome – It's all his fault… him and his –'

'Gerome?' said Heuwan, suddenly wide-eyed and attentive. 'You mean, the master of Gerome's Tavern, up near the Skycourt?'

'Yeah, him. Him and his ridiculous, iniquitous, two foot tall pitchers of –'

'Black Wind Soup…' Heuwan interrupted; a far-off look in his eyes of such longing as even Crick hadn't expected. 'Drink of dreams…'

'Yes, well, not mine. Frankly –' Crick turned to look him straight in the eyes '– I reckon I'd rather be where you are tonight than out there amongst that lot.'

The change in Heuwan's face was quite remarkable; irritated weariness replaced in the blink of an eye with a look of such nervous, excited hope that Crick would have smiled had this moment not been so important. Instead he turned away, sighing once more into the Hall.

'Well, I hope you have a better night than I will,' he said with a cursory glance over his shoulder. And with that he started to make his way away from the door.

'*Wait*…!' came a hoarse whisper behind him.

Crick was forced again to hold back a smile, thankful to the gods for creating men as reliably predictable as Heuwan.

*

Several hours later, the Hall finally seemed to be emptying. Maps were being carefully stowed away into their cabinets, notes were being bundled together and leaving with their owners, and the Hall Warden was making his rounds, slowly tidying and politely *asking* those who were lingering whether they might like to consider making their way out soon.

Crick was watching all this from his position just in front of the small, thick, dark green door which he had been guarding since Heuwan had scarpered elatedly off towards whichever drink-house would have him first. He would be back to retake his place an hour or so before sunrise, just before he was due to be replaced – with the two Silvers he had gleefully promised Crick in return for swapping with him for the night. In the meantime he had left Crick with just two things: instructions that he was only to let people through to the *Outerlands* Hall who possessed signed permission from the Council, an example of which he had shown him; and a long, thin, heavy golden key.

Crick had only needed to use the latter a handful of times. Unlike many of the people in this Hall, the few important-looking men and women who came to visit the *Outerlands* Hall appeared always to be there with a clear and, more often than not, grim purpose, usually muting their conversations as they approached Crick, who would do his best to catch quick glimpses of the Hall beyond as he unlocked and opened the door to let them through. He had been unable to see much, however: just a blur of even longer rows of desks and huge bookcases before invariably the door was closed quickly against him.

Those people he let through to the *Outerlands* Hall tended to stay a considerable time, but now they too were beginning to leave as well. Without exception they passed him with barely the most fleeting of glances, as did the Hall Warden, who clearly assumed Crick to be the same Guardsman as earlier, with whom Crick fortunately had at least a passing resemblance, at least in his uniform. He waited, ready with the tale of how Heuwan had been taken ill and been forced to leave, but the excuse was never needed. By the time a middle-aged woman with an untidy knot of brown hair and the blue and gold streaked uniform of the Hall Wardens left the *Outerlands* Hall shortly later, locking the door behind her with a long gold key of her own and yawning a sleepy goodbye to Crick, he had not needed to speak or explain his presence there to anyone. And now, as the woman made her way around the large column in the centre of the Hall, disappearing between the pillars on the far side, Crick was finally alone; nothing but a locked door to which he had the key standing between him and his prize. Part of him knew that it would be better to wait for a safer moment – perhaps a time when he had, in fact, managed to secure permission to enter the Hall. But he knew too the importance of this map. Getting permission would take weeks, if he got it at all, and he was leaving for assessment at his first Gate in a few days. Were he not to take this opportunity the odds were he wouldn't get another for a long time. He couldn't take that risk.

He waited for what felt like at least another two hours, though in truth it was probably no more than a quarter of that. Then, peering this way and that, checking the silence of the Hall one last time, he took out the key slowly and quietly one more time, turned, and unlocked the door. The thick metal hinges creaked in a manner he hadn't noticed until now, and he opened it only a fraction before slipping quickly through and closing it softly behind him.

There was an altogether different feel to this Hall than there had been to the first. The desks and cabinets were generally larger, seeming older and better-crafted; the chandeliers were raised higher, casting a slightly weaker, yellow light; and there were many other small, decorative differences… but in truth it was none of these things which caused Crick to halt uncertainly. Rather, he realised with an deep sinking feeling in the pit of his stomach as he started to search anxiously around him, it was the fact that there was not a single useful map or diagram of any description to be seen. None at all. The dark plum walls were bare, but for occasional, repetitive plans of various parts of the Halls of Knowledge; there were no glass tops to the cabinets; and even the tomes which lined the bookshelves were locked behind thick strips of twisted iron bolted shut, as everything else in the Hall seemed also to be, with dull silver locks. All hope and expectation which Crick had foolishly allowed to build inside him since his success with Heuwan vanished instantly; the void filled with a cold, alarming feeling which squirmed quickly through his insides.

And as he made his way further through the sombre lines of ageing furniture, he saw nothing whatsoever to lift his spirits. Everything of any conceivable interest was concealed or locked firmly away. There were small, chiselled inscriptions on everything he passed, but they were coded in seemingly random combinations of numbers and letters which meant nothing at all to Crick. And even had he known where in this maze the right map was kept, there would be no way to get at it without making too much noise, and also leaving clear evidence that someone had been there. He tried his key against several of the locks, and with each was as unsuccessful as he expected. But as his mind and legs began to race through the Hall, his thoughts turning quickly to getting out before he was found, he caught a brief glimpse of a wide column, through a narrow gap between two more towering bookshelves as he passed beside them. He halted, stepping back to look between them… and at the end of the long walkway he saw, to his immeasurable relief, that he had been right. He sprinted through the

120

gap and in seconds was standing before it: fifteen feet wide at least, and reaching up all the way through the level of the chandeliers to the ceiling; similar to the first column he had seen in the previous Hall, except upon this was painted not the border of the City and the lands around it, but the border of the Heartlands themselves with, above and beyond it, what had surely to be the Outerlands. A thin wooden ladder, attached loosely to polished silver beams which ran around the circumference of the column, led up precariously all the way to the top, where the map seemed to shimmer and change depending on which angle it was viewed from. The lines of the map at eye-level were plain and imprecise, and as Crick walked slowly around it he found little detail except for the main boundary lines of specific areas. There were no names or descriptions at all. What there were hundreds of, however, were the same small combinations of silver letters and numbering that were on everything else around the Hall. If he could find the Firstway on the column, he thought, craning his neck to different heights and angles to study the detail, it would tell him where in the Hall to look. It was a start, at least...

After several more walks around the column Crick finally found his bearings, and he began with difficulty to trace his way left from the point he had taken to be Fellgate. He moved westward, along the border... and then up... and he was lost. The thin, painted lines had suddenly become jumbled and indecipherable, bearing no reference or link that Crick could establish to the area he had come from. He went back to Fellgate and started again: left... up... and lost once more. Twice further he tried, and twice more he found himself inexplicably losing his way as soon as his eyes left the line of the border, caught up amongst a blur of markings within which, whichever way Crick turned, had the feel of being lost inside a vast, unsolvable labyrinth. He had no idea what he was doing wrong, and no way of putting it right but to try yet again. He moved back and placed his finger firmly on Fellgate, trying to breathe new concentration into his wits...

A loud cough struck the back of his neck.

Crick nearly tripped over himself as he spun around, but all he saw was a blinding yellow glare from which he was forced to shield his eyes. He staggered backwards, striking his neck hard against the column and collapsing in a heap onto the floor.

'Another one...' said a quiet voice somewhere in front of him. As Crick squinted up the glare faded, revealing the stooped old man who Crick had seen lecturing the group of children several hours earlier. He lowered a small but dazzlingly bright lantern to his side, where it faded to a mellow glow. 'You lot never learn, do you...' he said wearily, in the same impassive near-whisper as before, making it impossible to know what he was going to do or say next.

'I – I'm sorry,' Crick stuttered, trying desperately to recall the quickest route out of here. 'I –'

'You have one chance and one only to tell me the truth… Why are you here?'

'I thought I heard someone in here – There was –'

'And you thought you might find them in the mapwheel, did you?' asked the old man, pointing an angry finger at the column, holding the lantern closer to Crick's face. Crick could feel the heat of it even above that of his own cheeks.

'No – No, I just thought I heard something over hear, so –'

'*Don't lie to me, boy!*' the old man screeched, suddenly seeming several feet taller and wider. Crick found himself struck dumb and immobile; none of his supposedly swift limbs reacting at all as the old man grumbled and shot a thin, wrinkled hand down towards him. With a sharp, wrenching pain Crick was lifted by the hair to his feet and dragged awkwardly out through the warren of cabinets and desks, out of the Hall, and through the small door into the next, all the while trying to work out what he was supposed to do… Run…?

The old man grumbled angrily to himself all the way through the Halls, ignoring Crick's squirming attempts at explaining himself; his vice-like grip of Crick's scalp such that the only way Crick could have got out of it would have been to physically overcome him. It would mean he would have no choice but to flee from the City – and from the map. But if he did nothing the outcome could be even worse… He had no idea what the punishment was for sneaking uninvited into somewhere he clearly shouldn't have been; would he be sent before the Council? Would they want to make an example of him? Crick was quite willing to take a beating or something similar if it meant staying within reach of the map, but what if they decided on something else? There were many, far worse things they could do to him. As he continued frantically to weigh his options, however, he found himself thrown suddenly head-first out through the pillars and into the wide, open balcony.

'If I see you here again,' the old man hissed, 'I'll have you flogged 'till there's none of you left. Understand?'

Crick nodded quickly, holding his breath as the old man stared angrily for a moment, and then, still grumbling, disappeared back inside the Hall.

His scalp felt like it was hanging by a thread of skin, his heart pounding painfully within his chest, but Crick scrambled to his feet with a relief which carried him swiftly down the suspended stairway and out from the Halls of Knowledge. A different but very similar woman to earlier bade him a quick, uninterested goodnight as he fled past, sighing a long, slow breath as the fresh night air struck his face.

But for a handful of unsteady Guardsmen winding their way drunkenly back from one tavern or another, the enormous street was deserted, and eerily quiet after the tumult of the day. The Guardsmen seemed to be drifting more or less towards the branch of the City which contained the Garrison, and having little better idea himself of which way to go from here, Crick decided to follow in their direction. He reached the far side of the street, grimacing ruefully as he looked back at the building behind him, recalling with a pang of irritation his smug optimism of earlier in the evening. He had survived more or less unscathed, at least. But the map now was a great deal further from his grasp. And he a great deal further from being able to return successful to his family.

*

The Guardsmen Crick had chosen to follow took hardly the most direct route back to the Garrison, though not for want of trying. By the time he finally reached his tiny room the sky was already beginning to turn from black to shades of deep purple; the sunrise squad – of which he was one – already beginning to stir in the corridors around him. Tarryn was absent from his bed – though after a night in the City it was generally more surprising to find Tarryn *in* his own bed than in someone else's. Crick sank wearily onto his own thin mattress, still struggling – though in vain – to work out how he was now to be able to get anywhere close to the map. But as he leant back there was a soft rustle beneath him… It was the letter Tarryn had mentioned. A simple *Crick*, underlined twice, was written on the front, in his Mother's writing.

Not trusting himself to stay awake were he to lay back again Crick sat resolutely upright, doing his best to blink away a giddy tiredness as he reopened the envelope which clearly had already fallen foul of the Eyrie: the small, hidden group within the City, nameless to all but the Council themselves, acting as their eyes, ears, and occasionally hidden hand in the night. Even before the words in front of him had formed meaning Crick found his Mother's scrawl to be strangely comforting…

Dearest Crick,

Hope you're well. We found Url at last – Don't know what route he was taking, but he seemed to think the path from our home was the Firstway! Aliya says your old map of the river has been really important and helpful, but I'm not too happy with her disappearing off all the time! It's essential that everyone helps take care of things around here – there's so much to do! There's still no sign of any heavy rains yet; between you and me I think the new shelter your Father has built for the horses is quite unnecessary! But I suppose he has never liked taking risks.

Anyway, hope everything's going well over there – we're all really proud of you.

Love from your family.

But Crick had barely skimmed the letter before reaching down to drag out from beneath the bed the trousers he had been wearing when he had first arrived in the City. He found the seam in the inner lining where his left hip would be, and carefully pulled at a piece of barely loose thread until it came slightly away. Digging in with his little finger, he caught hold of a tiny, crumpled piece of parchment; pulling it out and unfolding it to reveal several rows of almost illegibly small numbers written across it...

His name had been underlined twice, so reading from the second row he found he had to take – he squinted to check the piece of parchment – the fifth word first... *Found*... Then the – he checked again – twelfth... *route*. And on he went through the letter, taking the few words he needed and scribbling them beneath his Mother's writing with a piece of firestone from his pocket. His look changed first to one of excitement as he wrote... then exasperation... and finally a rather blank incredulity. He read the real letter to himself twice more, checking the words carefully, but the message remained the same...

Found route to Firstway – your map important but not essential – take no unnecessary risks.

Crick leant back and laughed. And promptly fell asleep.

Chapter Twelve

Scarlet and Sapphire

'This – is –'

The word had it come would have been *disgusting*, had Aliya not been forced to quickly suppress the relentless retching sensation which shot yet again from the pit of her stomach up into the middle of her throat. Overall it was rather an understatement to say that she was far from best pleased with the course the afternoon had taken. And Url's stupid grin was doing little to improve matters.

'I know,' he answered excitedly. 'But look…! It's working!'

And for all her revulsion, Aliya couldn't deny that he was right. Part of her even shared his excitement. A small part of her, at least. At that moment, however, she found it difficult to sing the praises of the Aulan – or simply Aulan, as they had come to name him, for lack of anything better – in the way that Url was doing repeatedly under his breath, as he worked his way slowly through another thick protrusion of crystal.

For though he had not intended it, it had been Aulan who had shown them the ghastly way of getting through these seemingly immovable structures, which thus far had blocked their path further down into the cavern. It was the specks of blood from his cut feet as he had fled the Chamber which had slowly turned a clear, silvery colour, before suddenly melting out across a perfect, wide circle around them, smoothing and removing large amounts of crystal which took almost a day to grow back into place. Url had immediately experimented with the effect again, pricking his finger with the tip of one of his arrows, watching giddily as again they saw, after a minute or so, a small pool of crystal melt away at the spot where his drop of blood had fallen. And now, at the furthest point down into the cavern that they had so far been able to reach, they were trying again, and on a far larger scale. And it was working.

Aliya hadn't been present for the kill, but the sight and smell of the bucketful of deep-scarlet buck's blood, beginning to congeal into thick, black strands whenever Url stopped stirring for more than a few seconds, was more than enough to prompt a fresh heave of her insides. She did her best to look away as Url scooped out another small handful, spraying it against the underside of an enormous overhang ahead of them; some of the blood spattering down onto the floor while the rest stuck grimly to its target. After another minute there was a brief silver shimmer of dispersing blood, a wide opening where the overhang had once been, and another, delighted squeak from Url.

Her Mother and Father were just behind, while Yori – fortunately – was standing in front of her, between her and Url, doing a wonderful job of absorbing most of the frequent splashes of blood which came their way. And in that line they were making their way slowly but surely through the passage which Url was creating, one stringy sprinkling of blood at a time. Somewhere far above them Abetta was keeping watch in the woods, as one of the family was always doing now, since Aulan's unexpected visit. She had been quite content not to be involved in this particular part of the endeavour.

Over the past few days they had caught brief glimpses of Aulan around his home in the valley above, and on one occasion he had crept up to within sight of the cave to watch as they were eating their lunch outside. There had again been an almost heartbreaking sadness in his eyes when he saw them, prompting Yori to suggest inviting him to help. But before they had been able to decide the matter he had scampered off into the trees, not to be seen again.

From the front came a mumble of confusion. Url had halted before the next blockage: a thick, spiralling shard of crystal three times as tall as himself, which twisted right to left across their path.

'Biggest piece so far,' said Url, examining anxiously around the edges of the shard. 'It'll take a lot of blood to move it all. We can't afford to waste too much if it's not going to lead us anywhere – there could be another one just as big on the other side. We *must* be getting somewhere by now…' he muttered, gazing up towards the far-off roof of the cavern, which continued undimmed as far as they could make out into the vastness beyond. 'But from the looks of it there's still quite a way to go. If we could just –'

'I'll go...' said Yori suddenly, and even as he spoke he had vanished beneath a tiny gap between the ground and the bottom of the crystal which Aliya hadn't noticed until now. Url was taken aback as well; unable to halt Yori and unable to do anything but stare open-mouthed and timidly at Siu and Orlando as they appeared.

'Where's he gone?' Siu demanded immediately, her eyes darting frantically around the Yoriless passage between her and Url.

'He – umm... Under there...' said Url, stepping to one side and gesturing nervously down to the small gap.

'*What*! You – *by himself...*? I thought you said you were going to –'

'I'm fine...' came a small, distant voice, echoing back to them above and beneath the crystal.

'Yori...?' called Siu, 'Are you okay? Where are you?' There was no answer. Orlando stepped forwards, shouting over the crystal:

'Yori? Son, where are you? How far through did you go?'

Again there was silence for a moment... then Yori's voice crept back to them again:

'I can hear something...' It was even quieter than before.

'What is it, lad?' asked Url, falling to his knees to call through the gap.

'It's... I think it's water – running water, like a stream...'

'Water...' he mumbled thoughtfully. 'Wait there – we'll be through soon! *Wait there!*' He jumped then to his feet, and without giving Aliya time to cover herself flung a thick armful of blood across the face of the crystal. And as Aliya wiped off the worst of that which had splashed back onto her face, arms and chest, Url and her parents waited, watching the crystal barrier impatiently, willing it to dissolve.

It took two further attempts before enough of the crystal had cleared, but finally they had cut through what had turned out to be the twenty feet or so to reach Yori. He was standing in a small crevice surrounded by crystals, little different to that they had been making their way through so far. But now, standing completely still and silent, they too could hear a faint trickling somewhere beyond them. Aliya threw Url a questioning glance, spotting the excited grin on his face.

'No idea...' said Url with typically disconcerting honesty. 'Definitely something, though, isn't it! Watch out...' he added, throwing a fistful of blood against the next wall.

On they went for perhaps half an hour; moving... waiting... moving again. And all the while as they continued the soft trickling turned slowly into a low, deep gurgle, as though of something far bigger than merely a stream. In place of the small, distant noise there had been at first, it seemed now to be all around them, making it more difficult with each twist of their self-created corridor to judge which way to go. Url guessed as best as he could, pausing every few minutes to listen. Whether Yori realised it or not, Siu had a tight grip of his collar as another sweeping section of crystal began to fade into the ground; each of them waiting anxiously…

A flash of black swept suddenly across the passage inches from their heads; Orlando springing forwards to pin Aliya and Yori to the ground beneath him as wings beat loud and quick into the air away from them. Url had whirled away from the creature, cursing as the bucket struck the ground, spilling most of what little remained of the blood.

'What is it?' asked Siu, huddled amongst the side of the passage with Abetta.

'It's fine,' said Url, torn between a distressed look down to the deep red puddle on the ground beside him and quick, nervous glances up around the edges of passage, 'I think it's gone…'

'I didn't ask how everything was, or where it's gone,' she answered, looking anxiously around her. 'I asked *what is it*?'

Url threw a subtle, enquiring glance to Yori, who returned with a wide-eyed shrug.

'Some kind of… bird, I suppose,' Url mumbled. Without waiting for Siu's reaction he scooped up the small amount of blood he could salvage from the ground, smearing it carefully over the soaring piece of smooth crystal in front of him. 'Get as much of it back into the bucket as you can,' he said desperately to Yori and Aliya. 'We still don't know how much further we've got to go. It *can't* be that far now…'

And finally, to their relief, it wasn't: Barely had Aliya and Yori finished scraping together the last of the blood into the bucket – Aliya taking the role of supervisor, staying at arm's length from what were now little more than strands of sticky, black sludge – when the smooth surface before them shone like liquid for a brief moment, and then began to melt away into the ground. Instead of leading them through into another channel of imprisoning outcrops, however, the sinking crystal at long last released them out into wonderful open space and a sudden, spectacular end to the valley…

Though they had been prevented from seeing it from within the passage, the roof above them now curved steeply down to merge with the ground several hundred feet ahead of them. And just in front that, visible between the soft crystal boulders which lined its banks, was the source of the noise they had been following: A wide, gently-flowing river of the deepest, clearest blue Aliya had ever seen. It appeared from somewhere amongst the wall of the cavern to their right, coursing slowly in front of them through to the other side. In all her years around the waterways of the Heartlands, Aliya had never seen anything like it: spectacular enough even from a distance, but the full extent of its beauty only truly becoming apparent as she walked wordlessly with the others up to its side, the crystal beginning to smooth and part more easily again beneath their feet. The water took on a mist-like quality, swirling and breaking in strange, peaceful patterns, while through it the crystal bed and sides of the river glistened with such clarity that at times it was difficult to tell whether there was any water there at all; silver mixing with sapphire to create a range of light, soothing hues which for a while put all thoughts of where and who she was from Aliya's mind.

'Where do you think it goes?' asked Siu after a minute to nobody in particular. Aliya blinked, seeing the others again, and then knelt down, peering inquisitively into the blueness beneath her.

'Careful!' whispered her Father, holding her by the shoulder. Though there was no clear reasoning for it, nobody questioned why he was whispering.

But somehow Aliya sensed that she had nothing to fear from the water. She bent closer, reaching a hand into it, and as she did so a breath of cool wind struck instantly through her body. She looked back to the others, but none of them seemed to have felt it. With both hands now she reached down into water, feeling the subtle touch of the wind again, and then she drew out a small handful from which there came a faint, clean aroma, like dew upon long grass just before sunrise. Without thinking she tipped her head back and drank.

'Aliya…!' she heard her Mother shout.

'Spit it out, girl!' said Url: but Aliya ignored them both. It was like drinking fresh morning air – so pure and crisp that she immediately bent down for another handful.

'Try it!' she encouraged to the others.

'Aliya!' her Mother tried again. 'We don't know where it's come from!'

Yori, however, had already decided to follow Aliya's advice, and was crouching next to her to take a sip from the handful she lifted up to him.

'Yori…' said Siu warningly, but just as Yori's lips touched the water there was another flurry of noise behind them; each of them dropping to the ground as black wings soared above them again, looping in a wide arc above the river, before landing on a tall piece of crystal overlooking the far bank.

A bird it was. But of a kind none of them had ever seen before. The size of a large owl, it wore a loose cloak of short, black feathers, interspersed with a dozen or so much longer and of a distant, dark blue which swept out gracefully from various points around its body, mirrored by an equally blue set of talons and a thin, arrow-straight beak which was almost as long as the rest of it. As it sat there, watching them calmly but suspiciously, it let out a sudden shrill cry, echoing loudly throughout the cavern.

'So that's what we've been hearing…' said Orlando, and as he spoke another bird plunged down from a hidden ledge somewhere high above the river, landing elegantly by the first. But no sooner had it touched the crystal than they both took to the air with a small hop, flying in winding circles above the newcomers into their realm, each giving another cry before soaring suddenly down like black darts into the river, from which to the astonishment of Aliya and the others they did not then emerge. They could be seen clear through the water, gliding with even greater ease than they had done above it, such that Aliya began to wonder whether these were at heart creatures of the air or of water… or perhaps of both?

For several minutes the – whatever they were – tumbled and weaved their way through the soft currents of the river. And then as quickly as they had flown down into it they flew sharply up and out into the air. With one last high-pitched call they swept away to the left of Aliya and the others, skimming the surface of the water until they disappeared between two steep overlapping banks of crystal which from this distance Aliya had taken to be one solid wall.

'Anyone got any better ideas?' Url asked, glancing eagerly to Aliya and the others in turn. Orlando looked across to the far side of the cavern, then upriver to his right, and behind him; finally turning back to Url with a shrug. 'Good,' said Url with a boyish grin. 'Follow me, then.'

The break through which the creatures had flown proved to be deceptively distant. As Aliya and the others scrambled slowly along the glistening riverbank there were several trips and muttered curses; the crystal stubbornly refusing to yield to their impatience. Url carried the bucket still by his side, though there was nothing left inside it now but for dark stains of dried, crusted blood.

When they reached the gap they found that it was cut like a slash from a great sword diagonally into the wall, wide enough for two of them, leaning at uncomfortable angles, to pass through at a time. The river disappeared from view beneath the ground as they made their way through the bright passage, reappearing beside them again as they emerged into the beginning of a winding tunnel perhaps a hundred feet wide – all but an arm's length of which was taken up by the water. The narrow ledge onto which Url led them seemed solid enough, but as they continued along the tunnel it began to rise steadily away from the water's edge, becoming narrower still, so that soon they found themselves clambering slow and awkwardly through the slim border of crystal nearly fifty feet up from the river.

'Umm, Url…?' Siu murmured uncertainly.

'I know,' said Url, with a similar note of concern in his voice. He stopped, studying the way ahead. It showed no sign of easing. 'I'll go on,' he said, frowning into the distance. 'You lot stay here.'

'I'll come,' said Yori.

'You won't,' said Siu and Orlando together.

'But I will,' added Orlando, stepping between Aliya and Yori and following behind Url. 'We'll be back in a few minutes,' he called quietly over his shoulder.

'Stay away from the edge,' said Siu, ushering Aliya and Yori awkwardly against the wall. They sat, carefully, the crystal beneath them obliging after a moment with small, curving seats around them. They watched Url and their Father crawling along the ledge, slowly but steadily higher, until eventually it turned sharply to the left and out of sight. Then they waited, silently above the low, constant whistling of the river, listening intently for the occasional muffled sounds of activity from in front of them. They heard the sharp outline of Url's curses more than once, interspersed with many sudden scrapes and clatterings of crystal; all gradually becoming fainter until, after a few minutes, they died altogether.

Aliya heard her Mother take her first proper breath since the others had left, and saw Yori staring up along the ledge, and was suddenly ashamed to realise that in the time since they had left she herself had not in fact been concerned about either Url or even her Father. Blinking her dry eyes hard, she realised that all this time, while she knew what Url and her Father were doing, she had been staring instead into the deep, swirling currents of the water below her, running far faster now in the narrowing tunnel than it had done when first they had found it. There was something entrancing about it; so much life and power, like a deep blue vein just beneath the skin of the world. She couldn't take her eyes off it. Beside her Yori now seemed equally enamoured with the crystal of the wall and ground around him, while their Mother alone was still staring anxiously along the tunnel to the point where the high ledge disappeared.

A sickening cry snapped through the silence about them:

'*Url*!'

While Aliya and Yori froze Siu had sprung up instantly, vaulting as quick as she could manage in the direction of her husband's distant, panicked voice.

'You two *stay here*!' she shouted as she left, and with another jolt of shame Aliya found herself quite willing to obey. She felt Yori's frightened, sympathetic glance as she watched her Mother scramble swiftly along the ledge, ignoring the cuts to her hands and forearms. But just as Siu reached the bend Orlando reappeared. Aliya caught only broken parts of the hurried conversation, but it was enough…

'Url's fallen in!' her Father confirmed a moment later, calling back to them.

Ignoring his Mother's command Yori dashed along the ledge, and this time Aliya followed. Their parents came back towards them, meeting them halfway.

'The ledge gets narrower the further you go…' panted Orlando. 'The wall started jutting out – Url tried to get past, but –' he looked back desperately behind him. 'It just gave way…'

'So let's go and help him!' shouted Yori.

'We can't – there's nothing we can do from there. The tunnel…' he added before they could ask. 'It ends just beyond where we got to. The river runs under the end wall – he tried to swim against it, but…' As he sunk to his knees the strength seemed to fade from his eyes, and he held his head in his hands. 'It was too strong. He – he just disappeared…'

The others watched him for a moment. Aliya fought desperately to think of something to suggest, her lips trying to form words which didn't come.

'There must be something –' Yori started.

'Aliya –' her Mother interrupted, '– quickly, down to the water – see if you can sense him in there.'

But by the time Aliya and the others had reached the point just before the short slanting passage into the main cavern, from where Aliya could reach down from the ledge into the water, she could sense nothing but the force and presence of the river itself. After half a minute she felt something moving towards her, her hopes raised for an instant, but a moment later another of the strange, dark birds soared quickly through the water from downriver, skimming light above the surface before diving back down and beneath the passage, through into the cavern.

'He might still be down there somewhere!' said Yori, distressed beyond comprehension or explanation. Only by shock and desperation were his tears being held back. But none of it felt real to Aliya. She expected to see Url clambering back down the ledge any moment. Still she watched and felt downriver...

'Someone's got to go in after him!' Yori tried again.

'Nobody's going in,' said Orlando, more calmly this time. He turned away, one hand upon his waist as the other grasped uncertainly at sweat-soaked clumps of his hair. In silence he gazed away from them back down the river, but Aliya had seen the look in his eyes already, and Yori hadn't needed to. Suddenly however he spoke again: 'We need the rope,' he said with a sudden, final surge of hope which startled and delighted even Yori. 'There's a chance he could have made it through to a pocket of air somewhere further on...' The suggestion and the hope it brought were forced, but necessary were Aliya and the others not simply to sink to the ground in despair. 'If we send down a line he'll see it – might be able to pull himself back...' There were many *could have*'s and *might*'s in the idea, both said and unsaid, but it was better by far than their current misery of inactivity.

'We'll be fine,' Siu prompted. 'Go...'

And without another word Orlando stepped quickly through them and away into the passage.

'Keep looking,' said Siu, and after a moment Aliya leant down once more, searching desperately for any sign of life along the river.

They had left the rope – foolishly, in hindsight – in the top cave, along with many of the other heavy tools which they had brought with them from home but not yet used. The wait for Orlando to reach it and return was terrible; minutes passing like long, silent hours as Yori and Siu looked continuously to Aliya for some sign of hope. But Aliya could find nothing. Over and over again she swept her mind through the river with all the power of thought she could gather, fighting to marshal the concentration she had found and held for a time with the waterfaeries; the calmness she had known just before she had sensed the Guardsmen crossing the bridge. But neither would come, and each new effort was as fruitless as the last. Url was nowhere. She could feel no life in the river beyond that from the water itself.

'He's taking too long...' Yori murmured; a silent anger taking hold of him, the last line of defence against his grief.

'It's a long way back up to the top,' said Siu, putting a softly trembling arm around him. A dreadful, resigned frown creased the top of her nose as she watched Aliya. She closed her eyes, resting her head upon Yori's.

'Url's going to be okay,' said Aliya firmly, with a soft smile to Yori. He gave a half-smile back, but Siu simply looked sorrowfully into the water, saying nothing.

Several more of the dark birds came and went in swift blue-black streaks from both directions; Aliya following those which went downriver, keeping track of them for many hundreds of feet until slowly they faded into the distance. As far as she could tell it was unbroken river all the way: If there was another tunnel or air-filled chamber down there somewhere, it was further or more obscure than she could see. Whether it was the peculiarity of the water or her own distractions which were limiting the strength and range of her senses, Aliya could not judge.

Yori's anger began to reveal itself in his sharp, shallow breathing. And in Aliya an aching bitterness was welling from the confusion of not knowing what to do or say… She felt helpless, pathetic in her attempts to find Url, but she could think of nothing else. She noticed her Mother glancing increasingly back towards the passage; concern beginning to grow now for her Father. But finally, as the unspoken tension was reaching an all but unbearable peak, the patter of his quick, muffled footsteps came towards them from the far side of the passage. Realising suddenly that in the past minutes her focus had drifted somehow from the water Aliya reached in a final time to check, following the current away from her, through the river. It was drained of all the endless beauty Aliya had seen in it before: its blue no longer glorious but rather a cold, miserable colour which Aliya wished never to see again. But see and follow it she did nonetheless, quickening as it rounded the furthermost bend she could sense…

'Lost something, my dear?'

Aliya very nearly collapsed straight into the water, barely halting herself as her Mother and Yori screamed with delight behind her. As she recovered her balance she turned, slowly, to see Yori hugging a damp, exhausted, and absurdly delighted Url – followed by a weary but reluctantly amused Orlando. She jumped up and joined the others, enveloping the old man entirely with hugs and furious questions.

'How – What happened?' asked Siu, embracing him above the spot from which Yori clung like a limpet.

After a moment Url chuckled, stepping gently forwards, giving a reassuring nod as he gestured Siu to one side. He placed his hands upon the shoulders of Aliya and Yori who stood, Aliya realised, less than a foot from the lip of the ledge. He stared at them both for a moment, grinning…

'You're going to enjoy this,' he said, and with a soft nudge he sent them both tumbling backwards into the water.

Chapter Thirteen

Child's Play

'Well, there's no denying it –' said Tarryn, grinning somewhat sympathetically as he studied the varying cuts and bruising being slowly revealed as Crick began awkwardly to unfasten and remove his armour. 'I think he came off the better!'

'*They* did,' Crick corrected him sullenly. Tarryn nodded, turning and chuckling to himself as he loosened the first of his own layers of mail. Crick saw again the old wounds across his broad back: deep, vivid scars which covered his skin from neck to waist like markings hastily inscribed upon an old, thick wooden desk. Crick too had several new wounds from today to add to his collection. With an impatient care he brushed the blood from the point above his waist within which the only partially dulled blades of the training grounds had found a gap through his armour.

It had been a long and painful day to rival even yesterday's. The burning in Crick's shoulders and arms as he attempted to lift his battered cuirass over his head seemed almost audible over the clattering and various conversations around him; each battered fibre of muscle screaming at him as though determined to remind him of his foolishness at thinking he had escaped so lightly. The afternoon following his wholly unsuccessful visit into the Outerlands Hall he had been told that rather than going to his first posting – which would have been Valegate, amongst a cleft in the mountains to the north-east – he would be spending another twenty days being retrained in the basics he had been put through already. This by itself may not have been too dreadful. Fortunate, even, given his pressing need to stay within the City anyway. The problem, however – and no small problem it was – was the fact that the rest of his squad, those at least who had passed these last ten days of basic instruction and testing, had been given the same orders, and also the reason behind them. The past few days had begun without fail with Crick being shunned, glared at, tripped or shunted on his way to breakfast; they had continued with wave after wave of all too real assault as Captain Saiak employed him gleefully for hours on end in place of the training dummy; and while everyone else dived eagerly into dinner and retired to their rooms or to the rare enjoyment of the City they were allowed, Crick's days had ended with late-afternoon guard-duty outside a small, insignificant building around the perimeter of the Skycourt.

Of course he could have thwarted some of the attacks – crossed the fine line into that speed he possessed born not from body but rather mind, and Magic. But that would have been to flaunt the very thing he knew he had to hide. Most already somehow knew, and the rest suspected, and that was surely a part of their disgust of him. And of the Captain's cruelty. But to reveal too openly his aptitude for that which they so despised and had been so well schooled and trained to distrust would be a step too far. If his time until now had been an ordeal, it would be little compared to the torment he would face were he to show himself plainly as a lover and practitioner of Magic.

Tarryn, meanwhile, quite content to continue in his enduring quest through each and every tavern and woman of the City, was the only recruit not to have taken an immediate and spectacular dislike to Crick. He went easier by far on him in training than he could have done, and was the only one ever to say anything to him not formed in some way around an order or an insult. The others had been quick to pick up on it, though, and were spiteful and unwavering in their attempts to punish it, attacking him with nearly the same vigour as they did Crick. Tarryn's size and ox-like strength allowed him to parry or simply stand firm against most of their blows, but there were some amongst their squad who were nearly as swift as Crick, and two who had plainly received instruction before now on the use of the many of the various weapons to which Captain Saiak was introducing them. Crick was relieved to see that Tarryn paid no mind whatsoever to any of his injuries, old or new, but it did little to lessen his budding guilt at what he was putting him through. Despite Tarryn's friendship, however, each new day was beginning to drag significantly more than the last. After so many years imagining what life in the City was like, the contrast between Crick's expectations and what he found himself immersed in now had snapped him almost unnoticed into a confusing daze, out of which it was becoming ever more difficult to extract himself. He was a new Guardsman, being trained within the Great City of Immelus: Terrible as that was to much of what he loved and believed in, it should also, he knew, be exciting. This was an adventure to rival any other he had. But Crick felt little of it. With each passing day he was taking in less and less of the training, seeing less and less of the differing faces, and enjoying less and less of the brilliant armours and savage weaponry and great structures around him. He was shutting himself off from it all. Only Tarryn, somehow, was able still to break through to him.

And while it may have given him the time he needed in the City to come up with another way of getting his hands on the map, that task itself was now even closer to impossible than it had been before. He had been forbidden from entering the Halls of Knowledge without permission and an escort approved by the Council, on punishment of a year in the dungeons with twenty lashes a day should he be caught again. It was a fate from which few returned. The Guardsman with whom Crick had traded places that evening had been sentenced to fifty full days in head-irons for leaving his post, and he had been replaced now with two older, stony-faced men with whom neither Crick nor anyone else stood any chance of bartering or fooling. And there was only one other place in the City, that Crick knew of, in which he was likely to find what he needed. With a stifled but unavoidable groan he put on his uniform, bent painfully to lace his boots round the line of thick, golden clasps, and stood to leave to go there.

'I'll see what I can bring back for you,' said Tarryn, slapping him on the back as he passed. The bright streak pain which shot through Crick's body was tempered only slightly by the kindness of Tarryn's intention.

Crick nodded his appreciation but left without a word, walking straight past the thick, wholesome smells drifting out from the food halls, and out of the Garrison. Despite his continued lack of understanding of this part of the City he had, at least, memorised the basic turns which would take him to most of the other important places, so that concentrating hard he was able to make his way gradually through the maze, street after long, twisting street, until once again the Halls of Knowledge loomed up tall in front of him. He glanced only briefly at the building, doing what he could with a tight hidden shake of his head to bar the memory of that night from returning to his thoughts, turning then to his right and stepping quickly along the long, soaring tunnel of a road. A distant bell played a series of high, quick notes, ending on a single deep tone that faded gradually into the noise of the City: a constant clamour which grew like an approaching wind before Crick. He passed between endless variants of walls, stairways, shops and square, glass-covered lanterns which hung atop tall posts of twisted black metal, seeing all, but noticing none in particular. The innumerable shades, materials and fashions of the different classes of the City were more difficult to ignore, strolling or pacing close around him as they were, but again he did his best. The noise ahead was rising to a crescendo; he wove between a group of charging children, screaming in some game of theirs as they darted towards and around him, and at last with a final pace he left shadow behind to emerge into the glorious, bright daylight of the Skycourt…

A vast, open ring, cutting sheer through the high surrounds of the City like a well carved deep into the ground, the Skycourt could almost have been a city in its own right. All manner of shops, homes, storehouses, taverns, and other more obscure buildings lined an outer rim which took an hour at least to walk around, all facing in and steeply down upon an enormous largely cobbled circle strewn with stalls, performers, gardens, sculptures, fountains, and more else besides than Crick had yet found time and energy to explore. And rising then from the centre of all of this, taller even than most of the enclosing City, the walls of the Sun Tower, snow-white with slivers of brilliant silver, shone down upon everything, reflecting the warmth of the sun to light all but the most remote, sheltered sections of the Skycourt with a clear, steady glow. Even on days when the sun was hidden, the Tower would still through some strange device gather whatever small light there may be found in the sky, amplifying it somehow and casting it down upon a never-ending swarm of activity below.

The Tower was used mostly as a housing for the less important – or else less public – aspects and meetings of the Council. While the Grand Chambers and other significant buildings were to be found in the City's centre, or along one of the main streets leading to it – none of which Crick had yet found cause or opportunity to visit, taking as they did nearly an hour to reach – the more mundane or sometimes secret running of the Council was done it was generally believed from the various rooms throughout the Tower here in the Skycourt. The Eyrie were rumoured to have their nest here, though those who said they knew this for certain were usually either fools or lying –playing a dangerous game with their lives either way. Amongst the many rules of the City, open talk of the Eyrie was a thing never tolerated, whether true or not.

Hundreds of tiny windows spiralled up into the dizzying heights of the Tower, visible between a thick, flowing lattice of silver beams which ran around the outside of the building, conducting the light from the sky in a strange and intricate way which had been explained briefly to Crick when he'd first entered the City, but which he hadn't understood then and certainly couldn't recall now. After studying it all at length, and surveying the Skycourt around it, it was towards the top of the Tower that Crick's gaze now drifted, and lingered... For up there in one of the highest levels, dedicated solely to the storage and study of items recovered from the Outerlands, looking down upon almost all of the rest of the City yet unseen and largely unnoticed themselves, were the Wilder Rooms.

And up to now, for good reason, Crick had barely even considered them. Apart from the half dozen Guardsmen set always around the single entrance at the base of the Tower which in the distance Crick could just about distinguish, the twenty-five or so throughout each of its endless levels, and the numerous traps, bolted entrances, and other hidden measures that were rumoured to exist, the punishment for entering the Tower without permission was – if the person was lucky – banishment. Not banishment from the Tower, nor even from the City, but banishment rather from the entirety of the Heartlands, naked and unarmed. It made attempting to steal something from the Halls of Knowledge feel pleasantly simple in comparison.

A sudden weight struck the back of Crick's shoulder: He stumbled forwards, the young man who had barged through him smiling bitterly as he ambled away. Two other men and one woman beside him were laughing, all dressed in the uniform of new Guardsmen, throwing Crick equally vicious glances of their own. With the exception of the man who had knocked into him – Jarrak – Crick couldn't remember their names, but he recognised them all as members of his squad.

'Having fun?' asked the woman, with grim disdain no less fierce than it had been several days ago. Crick thought better of attempting a retort, knowing that it would likely only serve to bring him more and greater injuries tomorrow. He held his tongue, watching them jealously as they disappeared down the steep cascade of steps into the Skycourt. He was growing more weary by the hour of life in the City, he thought again, looking once more to the top of the Sun Tower. Formerly a source of nervous excitement, a glorious prize to be claimed, the map was now a cursed weight around his aching shoulders. One way or another he had to find and retrieve it, quickly, and be done with this place.

*

140

By the time the clock tower a few buildings to his left chimed a slow, thoughtful nine, however, Crick was if anything even more convinced that getting into the Tower, up into the Wilder Rooms, finding and stealing the map, and escaping unnoticed were each – and certainly altogether – quite impossible. From what he could see of them, the Guardsmen at the entrance were unerringly strict and efficient, scrutinising each and every figure that approached them with polite, unwavering distrust. And they were only the first of many obstacles, none of which Crick had a good – or indeed, any – idea of how to overcome.

Unsurprisingly, whoever it was who was supposed to be relieving Crick did not arrive on time. His unpopularity seemed quickly to be spreading outside of his own squad, and he had been in little doubt all afternoon that he would be made to wait a while longer until he could leave. The thought of his bed, uncomfortable as it was, brought a tremendous weight to his eyes. He forced himself to study the various goings on around the darkening Skycourt in an increasingly futile struggle to remain alert.

Just in front of him a short, pot-bellied man, his hair reduced to a few long, grey wisps above his ears, was doing what he could to sell the last of what had earlier been a large and admittedly splendid selection of pottery, calling out to the crowds in the quick, unintelligible tongue understood only by fellow street-traders or those who knew them well. Beside him a woman was packing away her own stall, leisurely in her movements after a good day's trade, while around them dozens of empty tables and collapsed shades sat abandoned where others had already left. The great circle was emptying, but far from empty; many of the traders and buyers who were leaving being replaced by new men and women coming instead to enjoy the warm, sweet-smelling evening amongst the gardens, or sitting around the edges of the Skycourt to gaze lazily down across them. The busy clamour of the day was rolling slowly into the welcome calm of night, aided in no small part by the fact that all of the taverns here in this part of the City were off-limits to Guardsmen.

Although the sentries at the entrance to the Sun Tower had changed now, their temperaments certainly had not, and the Tower was as strongly secured as ever. Crick watched as one of the armoured figures bellowed heated rebukes at a group of young children who were clambering and playing amongst the lowest beams around the Tower, ten feet or so from the ground, but they simply moved away to another section to continue their games out of his sight. They darted amongst, hung from, and balanced upon the thin strands of silver with all the bravery and foolishness which came to children with such wonderful, natural ease. It lasted all of several short minutes, however, until one of them became firmly stuck, dangling upside-down with, as far as Crick could see, one of his legs caught in a join between two overlapping beams. The shouting from the Guardsman had been a pale whisper compared to the furious screaming of a woman who found the boy a moment later, which even Crick from where he stood was able to hear clearly. With the help of a passing couple she retrieved her son from the beams, marching him away with the tightest of grips around the back of his neck, continuing to berate him all the way through the circle and out through one of the many roads which led away on the far side. Crick smiled, not so much for the youngster's misfortune but for how much the boy reminded him of himself a few years ago. He looked back to where the other children were still playing, all laughing and climbing as though nothing had happened. The wilful forgetfulness of youth was a wonderful and dangerous thing, Crick remembered. Two of them now were struggling to reach the next set of beams, set seemingly a few inches further off than those they had conquered so far…

Crick's smile vanished. A jolt of something that may have been excitement flashed like fire through his veins as he looked up to the beams the children were reaching for… and then to the next… studying each new level slowly in turn until he came, at length, to the top of the Tower. He almost laughed aloud, frowning to himself at the very notion of what he was considering… Yet at the same time he couldn't help but take another look. He went through the route once more, carefully, in his mind. Images of the Outerlands Hall came back to him, and with them the memory of how even the most promising of plans could descend into chaos and failure in a single unanticipated instant. And *this* was hardly the most promising of plans. Surely, he thought to himself, his eyes at length reaching the top for the third time, *surely* it couldn't be that simple…?

'I said *you can go!*' barked a tired, blonde-haired, irritable-looking man who Crick suddenly realised was standing just by his right shoulder. 'Unless you want the night here too?'

Knowing that any form of greeting or communication would no doubt be entirely unproductive Crick simply nodded and strode off without a word, heading instinctively towards the Tower.

*

Read the grain like you read a book; it'll tell you all you need to know, and more… The lesson drifted slowly back into Crick's thoughts.

142

Despite his Father's efforts, Crick had never mastered the skill. For that matter, he had never truly mastered the patience to be able to read books themselves overly well, either. His Father would probably have a great deal to say about the history of the thick, dark beam which protruded through the ceiling above him, running from somewhere above his head across a short way to the far end of the small room. But no matter how long he stared, Crick could take no meaning from it. Perhaps, had he actually been concentrating, he may have been able to learn *something* from the wood – its age, or maybe with what type of tools it had so roughly been cut and worked. But his mind was on other matters…

Several hours since returning to his room, he was still now unable to tear his mind from the bright silver lattice of the Sun Tower. Inspecting it as closely as he had been able to without attracting attention to himself, he had failed to find anything of significance that he hadn't already seen before, and he was struggling so far without success to decide whether or not this was a good thing. One part of his mind – the part his parents had given him, and over which they still appeared to exert at least a distant semblance of control – was telling him, quietly and simply, that he had found nothing that would make the climb easy. Apart from being many hundreds of feet high, the beams also appeared to become increasingly outstretched as they neared the top. And there were few, if any, places to hide along the way. He would be visible to anyone who was keeping even half an eye upon the outside of the Tower. There would be no means of escape if he was seen. And then, even if by some miracle of fate he did make it to the top, it was impossible to be certain that there would be a way in. Compared to the windows on the lower levels, all of which were firmly shut, those near the top did look to be open in places – mostly important of all being the half dozen or so of those around the distant but distinctive level of the Wilder Rooms. But they could well be closed by the time Crick reached them, or else it could for all he knew have been merely a trick of the light. And above all, he thought once again, it was all just far too simple. With the importance of what was said to be held in those upper levels, and the security set permanently around the rest of the Tower, surely the Council of the great City of Immelus wouldn't have neglected to secure the outer surface of the Tower itself?

On the other hand, however, there was the other voice; the other part of his mind which was his and his alone. And as Crick lay there gazing absently into the wooden beam this other part was suggesting over and again that perhaps it was simply the case that nobody had ever thought of, or actually tried, climbing to the top. Certainly there were few that Crick could think of, but for himself, who would stand even a chance of making it. And even if there were others, the chances that anyone else would have had both the cause and the courage to attempt it were extremely slim. *Whether a thing's been done or tried before makes no scrap of difference to whether or not it's possible to do...* Crick doubted Url had had the towering lattice of the Sun Tower in mind when he'd given this particular jewel of wisdom. But that didn't mean he was wrong. It *was* extremely high, though...

He cast the fear aside again, taking another bite of the apple which Tarryn had left upon his bed, along with a wedge of yellow, tasteless cheese and a single sausage – a rather odd combination for a dinner which Crick appreciated and was growing increasingly fond of with each bite nonetheless – and re-read the crumpled letter which rested loose in his lap... *Take no unnecessary risks*... His Mother would most likely say that this fell firmly into that category. But if he couldn't get the map, then what? Despite the message, the truth as Url had made clear was that without some form of knowledge of the geography of the lands they would be journeying through which wasn't based in myth and guesswork, the passage to Iala would be even more exceptionally difficult than it already was. Not that this would prevent Url from trying. Knowing how to get to the Firstway was one thing, but getting from there to Iala with nothing else to help should they get lost, or need to take an alternative route... well that was something else entirely.

And there was a final reason why Crick knew, in his heart, that he would attempt the climb. It was the same reason he had spent all those many hours stealing out of the Heartlands as far as he dared; why throughout his life he had always been the first to investigate new places and new things, and why he had been delighted, initially at least, to come to the City at the first hint of Url's suggestion. It was the unquenchable sense of adventure which deep down he knew, one day, was likely to get him into irreparable trouble. Hopefully, however, that wouldn't be this day.

Suddenly the door burst open and Tarryn stumbled loudly through, cursing angrily at something on the ground behind him. Crick leant out from his bed, peering round the door, but if there was or had been anything there it was invisible to his eyes.

'Ah!' said Tarryn merrily, just about recovering himself. As he wheeled and looked up to Crick his eyes danced for a moment before coming to an awkward, blinking halt. '*Crick*!' he cried, ambling into the centre of the room. 'Crick, Crock, Crack... Ha! *Cruck*!' He bent

144

double with an instant's laughter, but by the time his nose was close to grazing the floor he seemed to have forgotten entirely the already obscure origin of his humour, straightening with a deep, confused breath. 'Good to see you. I – I brought you some more supper…' And bowing low he handed Crick with utmost delicacy a large, frosted bottle of dark, murky liquor from behind his back.

'I don't want to know where you –'

'I stole it from the smithy's alehouse!' Tarryn interrupted, pausing eyes closed for a moment before grinning like only a true drunkard could. 'Ha!'

'Thanks,' said Crick with his first true smile for days, folding the letter and placing it beneath his pillow. Not that there was much chance of Tarryn currently noticing it, let alone being able to read either of the messages it contained. 'Good night?' he asked, rather unnecessarily.

'Quite remarkable, actually – I met up with… What was her name…?'

It took Crick a few seconds to realise that the question was, in fact, aimed at him…

'Who?' he asked.

'That girl,' said Tarryn, crumpling into his bed; the boards complaining bitterly beneath him. 'In the – the…'

'The tavern?'

'Yes!'

'*Which* tavern?'

'I… I don't recall… Well?'

'Well *what*?'

'What was her name?'

'I haven't got a clue!'

'Ah… right. Shame…'

'Who else were you with?' Crick persevered. But the only further sound to be taken from Tarryn, after a few moments, was a low, deep snore.

Crick studied the bottle, running his finger slowly around the large, embossed *G* on its face, not even attempting to guess what was inside, and then placed it on the floor beside his bed. He lay back, but was still wide awake as he listened to the steadily increasing rumbling from the far side of the room. Tarryn would be dead to the world until dawn. And the Skycourt by now would be almost completely empty. It was still early enough for Crick to leave and be back before daybreak. He sat up, trying to think of a reason why he shouldn't go now… but nothing came. Nothing new, at least. Still he waited, half-hoping for a change of heart sprung from some sudden rush of common-sense. But still there came nothing. He wanted out of the City; he wanted the map. And if he was going to go at all, now was as good a time as any. So quietly – though with Tarryn's now thunderous snoring there was little need for it – Crick rose and began to dress. An image of home; of Natt and Leyon; of his family came suddenly all at once to his mind. He could be there within a day, if he forsook his task now and fled the City. Barely even would he be prevented from doing so, not yet a full-sworn rank of the Guardsmen as he was: a few harsh words and final strikes from the Captain were little to concern himself with next to the course he was about to take. Even as he left the room and crept through the black, silent corridors there was a large part of him which was torn. But as though the fresh air had wiped all uncertainty from him, a few short minutes later he found himself outside, scouting carefully around the training grounds upon which he was quite certain would still be found an ample stain of his own blood and sweat, and before he knew it he was sneaking swiftly through the smallest of the poorly-watched rear gates of the Garrison, running back towards the Skycourt.

Lanterns cast dim glows and pale, flickering shadows through the streets, as though urging Crick to even greater stealth through the unsettling silence. But now was not the time for that. Not yet. He could still, just barely, get away with being outside the Garrison at this time; there was no need to slink unseen through the whole of the City. The Skycourt, however, was a different matter, out of bounds as it was to all but a small number of people, of which Crick was far from one. And as the walls and arcing roof of the last road – the *Kyndrow*, as Crick had only today learned it was called – came to an end, revealing moonlit clouds beyond the soaring heights of the Sun Tower, Crick found it to be not nearly as empty as he had hoped for.

Looking carefully down across the circle, from just behind the corner of the building he had been guarding earlier, where another different Guardsman stood now in place of the blond-haired man who had replaced Crick, he saw the vague outlines of several Guardsmen patrolling slowly through the various sections of the courts, each lit in various places by gold lanterns hanging on assemblies of tall, thin wooden stakes. The six Guardsmen at the entrance to the Sun Tower had been reduced to three, but a fourth was patrolling in vigilant circles around the base. There were also, Crick noticed with a sinking feeling in the pit of his stomach, still a large number of windows lit from the inside with the flickering glows of fires or lamps, shining out onto some of the beams outside.

And there was another complication as well: one which he had known about all along but which he admitted to the forefront of his thoughts only now as he gazed up with some difficulty into the dizzying heights of the Tower. The truth was, whether or not this was something that *could* be done, the thought of actually doing it filled Crick with a distinct nausea. Having to be rescued from the Gargantree by Url, fewer years ago than he cared to admit, had been bad enough. And this was on a somewhat different scale altogether. There would be no Url to rescue him this time. The feeling of weakness angered Crick, bringing a cold, clinging sweat instantly to his back. And with it was released a sudden rush of anger at all that had happened in the past days. He thought of Captain Saiak, and all the others. He held the angry bruises just above his elbows and waist where the worst of the blows had struck. The thought of another day of that, and of them, and of not getting the map for Url, forced a heat and eagerness into his muscles which quite unbidden saw him standing upright, his shoulders back, looking busy but composed. The fear was still there, smouldering patiently just beneath the surface, but with a sniff of forced disdain he pushed it hard to one side, turning on his heels to his left and strolling casually around the corner of the building.

For though the Skycourt itself was forbidden to him at this time of night, it was an unspoken rule that Guardsmen were granted passage around the upper rim of the circle, so that they could move more quickly through the City without the considerable delay that would result from having to locate a different route around. The Guardsman stiffened to attention, shocked by Crick's sudden appearance, but when he realised who it was – or more to the point who it wasn't – he fell back into his slouch, ignoring Crick's nodded greeting.

He passed the clock tower, its vast ivory face ticking loudly above him, continuing around the narrow track beneath the other buildings, looking constantly inwards all the while for any sign of weakness in the Tower's defences. But there was little to raise his spirits: the Guardsmen maintained their patrols, the lanterns continued casting exposing spheres of light around them, and the Tower at the centre of it all remained still as high as ever. Fortunately, keeping to the shadows of the buildings beside him, Crick was certain that, so far at least, there was only one person who knew he was here… He looked back over his shoulder, spying the man he had passed a few minutes ago gazing uninterestedly across the Skycourt. He looked back ahead of him, and without changing his stride turned suddenly into a wide, unlit road with tall buildings either side which led away from the circle. Once he was through he jumped quickly into the shadows beside the wall, and froze.

Nerves found him once again as he waited in the dark. It wasn't yet too late to leave. Maybe he should wait for another time, or find a different way? He could be back in his bed in less than an hour, asleep if sleep by some chance would grant itself to him, free either way from all risk and terror of any of the many things which could happen to him if he continued. But then where would he be…? He shook his head, halting the debate before it could grow into confusing, unhelpful circles of doubt within him. He took a deep breath. He had a chance now. And he was going to take it.

With a slowness almost painful to sustain through his excitement, he leaned his head around the corner of the building. The first Guardsman was looking straight down into the circle. Crick did likewise – this time seeing the various gardens and monuments and empty stalls not for what they had been used for during the day, but for how they could help him tonight. He saw hiding places, and a maze of unlit tunnels, dozens of them, leading all the way through the divisions of the Skycourt up to the Tower if only he could just make it down to the first: a low but especially wide stone sculpture of a group of children sitting joyfully above a riverbank. The easy, unbridled glee of the children was at great odds with the swelling tide of fear and confusion within Crick as he studied them, but ignoring the irrational pang of anger this threatened to bring Crick looked quickly up to pick out the route which would lead him from there to the back of the Tower, going back and forth through it a number of times, changing his mind more than once… And then he turned to watch the first Guardsman again, and waited, his eyes darting down to the others as he crouched low to the ground, ready to spring silently out from his hiding place. One of them was crossing over the final part of his route, but none of them were facing him now. Suddenly he realised that the first Guardsman had turned away, stretching out his arms and back as he paced away from the circle, and so then without a second's pause Crick found himself scrambling silently across the path and down the steps, taking several at a time, sprinting to the sculptured riverbank and falling silently beside it. He held his breath… But there was no call or other noise to suggest that anyone had seen him. He peered around the platform of the sculpture, judging the distance to his next target. *One piece of the puzzle at a time*… Url's words, so often through the years arrogantly ignored or seemingly forgotten, now again sounding soft but clearly through Crick's suddenly open, eager mind. The way was clear, and looking back up behind him he saw that the upper Guardsman wasn't watching this unlit part of the circle. He dashed out quickly on all fours, keeping low to the ground until a few seconds later he was nestled between the two close, parallel rose bushes he had been aiming for.

148

Time seemed both to stand still and drag on forever as Crick continued to dive from one hiding place to the next, advancing slowly, carefully through the circle. Several times he was forced to stop and wait as a Guardsman came too close or looked in his direction, but keeping strictly to his plan he was able after twenty or more tortuous minutes to make it all the way to the back of the Tower, kneeling in the flickering shadow of a large, black metal boar, tusks longer than Crick was tall, less than thirty feet from the lowest set of beams. He paused a while, near-giddy from releasing the full power of his speed such as he had not done since arriving in the City.

From this angle, so close to the Tower, most of the upper levels were hidden from view. All Crick could see were the few dozen feet above him, and he had climbed far worse than them before. He could also see now that the beams were slightly thicker than they had appeared from afar: some a few inches wide, but others over a foot. Ideal for concealing himself behind. There was now just one Guardsman in the circle who was watching over this part of the Tower, along with the final, glistening figure who still patrolled steadily around its base, passing feet away from Crick, who had to mould himself quickly behind the front leg of the boar each time he came round, then move quickly back to avoid being seen by anyone else. Finally, just as the Guardsman patrolling around the Tower moved out of sight once more, the other turned and began to walk back around to the front. Crick bounded light as a bird from his hiding place, illuminated for a split second by the lantern on the far side as with three great strides and a final leap – made clumsier than he had intended by so much uncomfortable crouching and hiding – he was at last up and above the first beam. His brief smile of victory quickly vanished as he looked again up and around. He reached up to the next beam, pulling himself up again; able to climb four more levels before a long shadow started to creep around the bright base of the Tower beneath him. He halted, clinging tight to one of the vertical beams until the man had passed around the long, curving wall, and out of sight.

This was a fool's plan, without doubt. But... it was working. Slowly but surely the windows and beams came and went before him; the light, sand-coloured cobbles below soon merging into a single flat surface as the ground fell steadily away. Crick swung from side to side avoiding the rooms that were still lit, leaning out and looking up as he paused again to find that he was already over a third of the way up the Tower. Though how long it had taken him, he had no idea whatsoever. He caught his breath behind another thick, unlit beam, confident that few could ever see him up here even if they did have occasion to look.

What he could also see, however, as he had expected, was that the upper half of the Tower would be considerably more difficult to climb than the lower. The beams were barely within reach of one another, and there was also one level, four or so above where he was now, in which every window on this side was lit. He couldn't risk going round to the front of the Tower to look for one that wasn't, so there was no option but to check that nobody was near the window, and to get past it quickly.

Only as he started again did he realise how painfully his forearms and the lower part of his legs were beginning to ache; raw bruising and numerous reopening cuts now combining with the pain of the climb to make his limbs feel heavy and cumbersome as iron, so that for the first time he had to put real effort into reaching the next set of beams. By the time he had climbed the next few levels he was breathing hard; a steady torrent of sweat running down his brow and back. Crouching low upon the last beam before the light, he raised his head slowly, looking carefully through the window to see a small room lit by several many-wicked candles on low, wide bookcases all around the walls. Deep mounds of parchment littered every surface, with innumerable discarded quills and stamps lying above them. More to the point, however, there was nobody there. Relieved but grimacing with the feel of his palms and fingers being rubbed raw from clinging so tightly and constantly to the beam Crick stood and reached above him... A head appeared, feet away from his, just behind the window. He stumbled back, arms flailing wildly beside him but finding nothing. He was sinking quick through thin air, nothing beneath him but darkness and cobbles... but with a sudden sharp wrench of pain in the shin of his right leg he was pulled hard back into the Tower, crashing loudly against the beam. He hung there, not daring to move, seeing the City the wrong way up through the tops of some of the smaller buildings around the Skycourt; blood pumping to his head in heavy, painful waves.

He waited five seconds... ten... each of them long and terrible, and then with a great effort he lifted his head and looked above him: His leg had become trapped between the main beam and a smaller one just beneath it. An image of the boy who had been rescued by his Mother earlier in the day came back to him, caught exactly as Crick was now, the difference for Crick being that the ground was considerably further away, and the consequences were he to be caught considerably worse. And *his* Mother was unlikely to be rescuing him anytime soon. For a moment as he looked around him, scrabbling desperately for the beams above and just out of reach to his right, his confidence failed him completely: Even by his own, high standards, this was an absurd situation to have got himself into. A madness of his own foolish making. But still something prevented him from fleeing. Eventually he found a good hold of the lower of the two beams which were holding his leg.

Mercifully there had been no sound at all from inside the room. In the terrible seconds following the fall Crick had been waiting for a shout of surprise, or an alarm to be raised, but there had been nothing. Perhaps he had been wrong…? Perhaps it hadn't been a person after all? Even more carefully than before, putting the weight gingerly onto his right leg, he raised himself up, poking one eye up to the window… and this time keeping a firm hold on the beams as he saw the head once again, slumped sideways on a low, wooden desk. Standing a little higher, he saw that it was connected to the sleeping body of a man in the crimson robes of the Council, softly rising and falling as he slumbered. With no desire to study him any longer Crick moved silently around the beams to his left until he came to the next window, and after checking that the room inside was truly clear this time he continued to climb, doing his best to block out the past minutes from his mind but unable to shake off the knowledge that it could so easily have ended far worse. He had been lucky. More than lucky. And if there was one thing earned through a lifetime's trials that Crick knew about luck, it was that it rarely lasted.

After another few levels he could no longer even with the mightiest of his jumps reach the next beams directly; having instead to use the vertical beams to drag himself up across the ever-widening gaps. They were especially smooth and difficult to grip, making his progress slow and even more exhausting than before. He made the mistake of looking down for a brief moment, realising as if for the first time that he was several hundred feet up the Sun Tower… It was several minutes before he had gathered courage enough to continue again. But finally, every muscle and bone of his body screaming for respite, he pulled himself up level this time with a narrow opening in the Tower: a thin breach rather than a true window as the others so far had been, and lined with black slate around its outside to mark it out distinctly from the rest. It was, if Crick's rather unbalanced combination of knowledge and guesswork was to serve him well, an opening to the Wilder Rooms. It was unlit. And somehow amongst the surrounding windows of this section of the Tower, many though not all of which were closed, it was open.

There was nothing to bridge the gap from the beam on which Crick was standing to the opening, perhaps six feet away. But Crick was well past weary of going so slow and cautiously, and in desperate need of solid ground beneath his feet. He could see nothing of the insides of the unlit room, but dark and silent as it was he was certain there would be nobody there. Without surrendering any further time to thought he crouched low and sprang for good or ill towards the opening, grasping through to the brickwork on the far side and heaving himself swiftly through to tumble in a heap upon a hard, wooden floor. For the first time in what must have been hours he let his body ease; simply lying there for a few, deep breaths, smiling wearily. He had made it. *Now comes the easy part*, he thought stupidly for an instant before correcting himself: it was also supposed to have been the easy part once he had gained entrance to the Outerlands Hall.

At first he could see very little around him, but for the vague outlines of a large number of strangely-shaped objects, none of which he recognised. But as his eyes started slowly to adjust to the darkness, helped faintly by dim shafts of the soft grey of night from the window behind him and several others at some distance to his left and right, he saw that before him there were hundreds, maybe even thousands of other such items, stretching in all directions as far as he could see. He had entered it seemed into the lower level of a large, two-tiered room; several small sets of stairs with thick, decorative wooden banisters leading up to the next level. There was no particular order to the room – rather an exceptionally random scattering of tables, chests, shelves, plinths and cages, some hanging low from the ceiling, in or upon all of which was a selection of some of the most peculiar things Crick had ever seen...

Vials of swirling, gently-glowing mists of all colours glimmered silently upon the mounts or boxes which contained them. A row of long, thin fingers of metal with curved, forked ends, looking perhaps like the keys to some enormous manner of lock, were suspended from a line of thin, silver thread. Several tables, divided by long beams of silver, were covered in countless mismatched piles of unrecognisable coins, of all possible sizes and types. And as Crick moved slowly through the room, studying each and every item with renewed and growing curiosity, he bumped into a large, solid, twisted mass of bronze which came up to his waist, around and through which ran a thin series of cords of pristine emerald. The small number of ancient, intricately fashioned items of furniture which had been fitted amongst the sprawling array of oddities, along with the floor, walls, and ceiling, were all crafted from a similar type of old, rich wood, infusing the room with a warm, comforting smell despite the inexplicable danger into which Crick knew he had just thrown himself.

The steps bade a gentle warning murmur of good evening as he ascended to the next level, groaning with a voice which only the oldest of woods possessed. Crick wandered briefly what his parents would make of it; what stories they would glean. And it was only then, as he reached the topmost step, that Crick looked around him to see that there were not in fact just two levels, but many. What he had taken initially in the darkness to be a wall he could see now was merely a wide bookcase, behind which extended many further small staircases leading up, down, and across to countless other areas. It seemed that the Wilder Rooms were here in fact just one incredibly large room, spread out through these many separate but open levels and sections, seemingly spanning the entire diameter of the Tower. As Crick explored them, one after another, the objects he passed continued to baffle and intrigue him in equal measure... He found a small, silver bowl, above which water sprinkled gently down from midair as if from an invisible fountain. There was a cluster of miniature trees, each no larger than Crick's palm, which resembled perfectly a grove of oaks in late summer, though with tiny, bright red dots of some unknown fruit dangling from the tips of their branches. And there were more curious tools and instruments of various shape, size, and potential use than he could possibly count. There were so far, however, no maps of any kind that he could see.

He crossed a narrow archway of wood and rope, which ran back above one of the first sections he had come to, finding himself now amongst a collection of items which, though he still didn't understand what they were, had a distinctly more menacing sense about them. There was a line of cruel knives and other sharp, twisting blades and pokers, upon some of which Crick was certain he caught faint shades of long-dried blood. There was a dark orange sphere, the size of a head, like a small angry sun hovering two feet above the ground, from which hundreds of shimmering strands no wider than a spider's thread would appear for a few seconds at a time, reaching out to Crick as he passed. And at the very edge of the room, lying sideways upon the floor, there was a long column of mirrored glass which, when Crick stared into it, sent back his face hideously deformed – bone visible in places through yellow, leathery skin and bloodied, gaping wounds. He would have been pleased to leave this particular room, but just before he reached the next set of steps which led up to his left he halted...

In the open draw of a small, sturdy desk beside him, the spectacular jewelled face of a thick, black, oval brooch sparkled freely despite the fact that no light shone upon it. Crick gazed down at it a moment. Then, against all his better judgement – if any scope for further poor judgement remained given where he was and what he was already doing – he picked the ornament up. It had a warm, pleasantly heavy feel to it, and on the back were four small, inward-curving spikes around a circle of dull silver. Purposely thinking no more of the stupidity of the act he carried it onwards with him, examining and admiring it from different angles as he continued through the seemingly never-ending succession of rooms. He lost all count of the number of levels he had passed through, awed by the number and intrigued by the peculiarity of the tools and artefacts around him... The foot-tall likenesses of dozens of creatures, many of which felt familiar to Crick but none of which he could put a name to, stood guard around the edge of the largest section so far, hewn from every shade of metal and gemstone imaginable, their eyes as alive as any Crick had ever known. A semi-circle of black helms, and behind them two small, white and ruby-encrusted crowns sat above white, fractured skulls. And atop a broad, circular platform hundreds of brightly-painted plates, depicting Kings, Queens, open plains, blazing cities and great armies, seemed to illustrate some kind of story which Crick, to his frustration, had no time to interpret. But suddenly, quite unexpectedly, he came across the very things he had almost forgotten he was supposed to be searching for: Sprawling across a large arc of desks he saw mound, after mound, after mound, of maps.

His eyes by now were well used to the darkness, but even so it was difficult to make out the detail on some of them. Setting down the brooch beside him he studied each map in turn, fingering his way swiftly through them. Most were drawn upon fine, old parchment; others woven delicately into soft, silk-like cloth. There were even some which had been etched into thin plates of silver, bronze, or various other metals, their detail even without a good light still easily discernible. And through them all Crick searched for any sign of Iala, or the Firstway, or anything he recognised which would help him get his bearings. He prayed it would be easier than the accursed mapwheel.

After ten minutes he was still working uneasily through the first pile, fumbling as he tried awkwardly to force his hands into faster pace – and realising suddenly that he had no idea where the actual entrance to the Wilder Rooms was... The door, or doors, could be anywhere around him. But then looking down again he saw a tiny inscription: *Ellemeine*. He thanked the Stars for Url's lessons as a child as he recognised the word as a mountain far to the south of the Heartlands. And shortly after this he found another name: *Rahm*, one of the names formerly used for the impassable ice-desert of the South. He looked to the next map, and the next, letting the pile slip slowly back through his

154

fingers, stopping to study some of those he had already seen. Most were still indecipherable, but in a few he found marks and inscriptions which began to make sense. They were all maps of the south. And if that was the case, then perhaps...

He turned and crossed to the opposite desks, beginning again to search quickly and carefully through them. All those in the first pile were labelled with letters and symbols which he had never seen before, and in the second he likewise found nothing. More time was passing than he could afford, and halfway through the third pile he looked up to see a faint, dark blue beginning to creep through the windows in the distance all about him. Panic started to work its way into his fingers, his feet shuffling nervously on the spot, trying to persuade him to flee. Again he reached the bottom of the pile, and was about to release it to move on to the next when he spotted a small, but quite distinct, *IALA*. For a moment he was stunned, almost unable in his excitement to believe it. Carefully he withdrew the long, pearl-white sheet of cloth from the pile, holding it up before him... *IALA* was surrounded by many other marks and symbols, none of which he understood, but there was no doubting the word itself; a sketch of a city surrounding it, sitting just below the line of the coast, with unbroken seas to the north above. Amongst all the marks and words beneath it, a single line wove gently south to the bottom of the page, decorated with swirling marks and inscriptions to reach another, larger city: *IRRAIGION*. It was a map from the old Capital up to Iala. All he had to do now was find the rest of the way, from Irraigion down to the Heartlands. He set the map quickly to one side, moving to the next pile and studying the first parchment...

From the dim quiet somewhere below him there was a sudden scraping of metal and the *clunk* of an old, heavy door. Snatching up the map in one hand and the brooch automatically in the other Crick slid like a wolf to the railing to the right of the desks which formed the edge of the room, looking down through several levels of bridges and banisters to see, with a sickening turn of his chest, the far-off glow of a small, green candle being led into the room, carried by a woman who wore the robes of the Council.

Crick pulled his head back from the railing, standing for a second in desperate silence, trying to work out what to do. How could he have been this stupid... Below him he heard the bolstering yawn of someone who had clearly just awoken, and then the closing and locking of the door. The window was his only chance, and he had to do it quickly, before the woman had time to light too many of the lanterns and chandeliers. Keeping low to the wooden floor, stepping quick and light over the boards he began to retrace his steps out of the room and through the next, cursing himself for concentrating too much on the brooch during his search as he struggled to remember which way he had come. The woman was shuffling slowly about behind him, making the quiet beginnings to her day. Every few seconds another distant corner of the darkness would light up, slowly but surely eliminating the number of places left for Crick to hide. He crossed another walkway, looking back to see that the lights were still just about far enough away for him to make it to the window unseen, but as he turned to look for the next room he felt an icy pinprick in the side of his leg… He felt another, and then quickly several more, and as he looked down beside him he saw dozens of bright orange threads slithering ominously towards him: It was the sun-like sphere he had seen and avoided earlier, and he had walked straight into it. The orange orb at the centre began to pulse with quick shades of deep red with each new thread that burnt its way straight through his trousers and seared itself to his leg. He swiped at them, brushing them off, but as they tore from his skin the sphere exploded in a flash of brilliant white and a terrible, piercing screech. For a second Crick could neither see nor hear anything else, until with a quick, high-pitched snap like shattering glass the sphere and all the threads disintegrated into a puff of white dust, and were silent. Crick blinked hard, trying to regain his senses as the dust floated gently down to the floor around him. And as he looked up through it he saw, beside a lantern barely three rooms away, the woman staring straight at him: frightened and furious, still holding a taper to the newly-lit flame. All that happened next happened through such a fog of panic that Crick was and would forever be only barely aware of any of it…

He ran: swifter he was sure than any man or beast had ever dreamed to run before. All concerns of noise and secrecy were vanquished by pounding waves of fear which surged through every strand of muscle in his body; all bruising and pain forgotten entirely. He vaulted over desks and railings, flew like a tearing of the wind down steps and across walkways, hearing only vaguely the dim clatter of fallen objects everywhere around and behind him. He was at the window in seconds, but somehow, impossibly, the woman had got round in front of him, and she jumped angrily before him now to bar his way. He stumbled to a halt, but before he could decide which way to turn he felt the cloth of the map being torn from his hand.

'How *dare* you!' she shrieked, fighting to wrestle the map away from him, grabbing at his arms, her dagger-like elbows striking sharp at his face and chest. Crick could see only hazy outlines of her figure;

all detail lost and unimportant in the chaos. 'You'll – be –' Crick was blinded by fear and grasping, relentless hands. This couldn't be happening… Fighting with a member of the Council… The punishment… He had to get away. He reeled violently to one side, trying to throw her off; the world around him suddenly pausing as he watched her tumble, slowly it seemed, through the air…

If ever there had been a more terrible sound than the dull, heavy cracking of her skull, Crick would never have believed it. She struck the thick, patterned knuckles of a gold fist which curved around the corner of a large desk, crumpling in a pitiful heap to the floor, unmoving, gazing across the wooden boards to Crick's feet with shocked, unseeing eyes. For a moment Crick could do nothing but stand, horrified, simply watching as a stream of scarlet started to flow gently from the back of her light-brown hair. It spread in a smooth, red pool around the upper half of her body before merging eerily into her matching robes. Crick felt everything and nothing at once. Fear, so long a companion of his, and something he had thought he understood, was now suddenly given new and dreadful meaning. She was dead, he was certain of it. He had killed her. He had to go, quickly… But he didn't. He couldn't. He couldn't take his eyes off her. Somehow it seemed that if he did, if he left her like this, then she really would be… It made him light-headed just to think the word. He sank to his knees. Cold sweat crept across his body like an inescapable, unbearable sheen of guilt.

How he managed it, he didn't then and would never truly know, but somehow he found himself crawling through the window and, with map and brooch tucked firmly within his belt pockets, leaping for the beams. A part of him was climbing down from one level to the next, quietly avoiding the lit windows which were quickly becoming greater in number. But the rest of him still stood in that room, watching the lifeless body beneath of him. Even as he crossed the level where all the rooms were lit, reaching the point at which the beams started to become comfortably close together once again, he was still up in the dim, rich-smelling room, alone but for the shadow of what had, just seconds ago, been a woman.

A sudden clamour of bells rang out from the top of the Tower, bringing him quickly back to himself. He blinked and looked below: Guardsmen in the circle around him were sprinting towards the entrance to the Tower, from which a man could be heard shouting hurried orders amidst the drawing of long, heavy swords. They had found her…

He all but fell down the last few levels, and with nobody left watching the back of the Tower he jumped straight from the lowest beam, sprinting low through the circle and up the steps into the City. The sun was almost up: Someone by now would have noticed that he wasn't back in the Garrison. And after being caught in the Halls of Knowledge, few would believe it hadn't been him. If he stayed in the City it was the end of him. He knew what they did to those who attacked members of the Council. As for those who actually *killed* a Councillor. And though not perfect, he had a map...

He ran mindlessly through the City, passing several people who thought nothing more of him than yet another Guardsman late for duty after an evening's drink. The bells of the Sun Tower faded quickly behind him, but it wouldn't be long until the alarm was raised around the City. If the walls were secured and reinforced before he got there...

He veered off once again opposite the Halls of Knowledge into the maze of narrow paths. By fortune or sheer focus he remembered the turns, but this time when he reached the watergardens he circled round to the left of them, keeping the sights, sounds and smells of the rousing Garrison at a distance, sprinting where he could with all his speed all the way until finally he reached the long stretch of open, cobbled ground which separated the main of the City from the walls, the innermost of which were suddenly tall ahead of him. The gate was open but guarded by mighty halberds and blades in the hands of five broad Guardsmen, faceless beneath their all-covering helms; watched over by others above the wall or patrolling beside it. They were watching Crick even before he saw them. He couldn't turn back now.

Suddenly the quiet of the morning was shattered by the music he had dreaded: Great bells sang out all around him all at once, sounding an alarm through the City which Crick had been yet to hear himself. It was every bit as fierce and startling as he had been told. The Guardsmen stiffened immediately, halting in their pace, glancing quizzically to each other as Crick approached. They would be closing the outer gate...

'Halt there!' one of the silver statues bellowed. 'What business –'

'Captain Saiak!' Crick cried before the man could finish, forcing a crude impatience from his fear. It had been the first name to come to him. 'Where is he?' he demanded, still more furiously. He could only hope that the Captain hadn't risen early this morning.

'What's going on?' asked another of the Guardsmen, an old, gruff figure whose voice Crick recognised from the dinner halls, with tight wisps of silver hair and beard spewing from every join and gap in his helm 'The bells –'

'Of course they're playing! That's why I'm here! I need the Captain – *Now*!'

'He only left the walls a few hours ago,' said the first, lowering his halberd uncertainly. 'He'll be in his quarters, sure–'

'Don't you think I've tried that?' said Crick distractedly. He didn't have to invent his air of desperation as he pretended to scan through and around the gate, but trying instead to control and channel his terror into his act was no less difficult. 'We've searched the Garrison; he's not there.'

'But what's –'

'We don't have time for this! I need to find him: If you see him, tell him he's needed in the Skycourt!' He was already through their wavering blades and the gate before they answered, throwing hurried questions after him, but remaining where they were. One down...

The gates on this side of the City were all at different points along the walls, some half a mile apart; the walls themselves separated by a hundred feet or so of courtyards, storehouses, guard-towers and the like. Each gate was as well-guarded as the first, but with a constant whirl of movement Crick talked his way hurriedly through one after another, sprinting left or right between each new opening. Five gates... Six... Only at the seventh was he was truly challenged – stopped by a tall, dark-skinned Captain who for a time was unconvinced and unimpressed by Crick's babbling. But with exhausted desperation and a flurry of fast-talk of which Url himself would have been proud Crick contrived his way through again. Through the eighth wall... and finally through the ninth: only the very outer wall of the City now between him and open fields. And home. It was the newest and greatest of all the defences, with the most secure by far of all the gates, yet even so he breathed a half sigh of relief, disappearing into the sprawl of wood and stone to his left and finding after a few minutes the concealed narrow passageway that Tarryn had showed him, which meandered slyly through a gap between two of the buildings that backed onto the wall. He climbed through the thick mounds of fresh rubbish and discarded crates to reach a broken, half-boarded window near the back.

The inside of the building was as forgotten and buried in dust as he expected it to be; Crick leaping up the four short flights of stairs and bursting through an old wooden door which hung loose on only its top hinge, and out onto the open roof. He could hear confusion and orders being thrown violently about somewhere far to his right, but none of them seemed aimed yet in his direction. Compared to all he had been through tonight the climb across to the sliver of a break in the wall, within weeks to be completed into a fortified lookout, was straightforward, just as Tarryn had described, and in seconds he was through it and jumping out, falling awkwardly through the high drop onto thick mounds of gorse and dewy grass below, barely noticing what at other times would have been excruciating pain in his right shin and ankle as he rolled to his feet, pausing to look back at the City one final time. Briefly he thought he felt a shadow cross the hole in the wall above him, but looking up to it he could find nothing. And so with the sky brightening to pale blue around him he turned warily from the wall and fled into the long grass, barely able to breathe through terror and sheer disbelieving joy, checking the two small bulges in the base of his pockets as he ran, wide-eyed and exhausted into the dawn.

Chapter Fourteen

All the Things In Between

Amidst the distant snap and rolling of thunder and the gentle, dusty splashes on the stone around her, it was as if everything for miles around had just awakened, and was calling out to Aliya in a dappled chorus of clear, fresh voices. Birds, beasts, plants, trees, the very grass amongst them... all of it now almost as clear to some deep reach of her senses as the courtyard in which she was standing. That was why she alone was standing out here, in the rain. Light, thin spray, drifting slowly about her like something just barely more than heavy fog. And lots of it. Just the way Aliya liked it. She had felt through the rain before now, but never quite like this; never with such wonderful clarity.

Her Mother had insisted steadfastly that the family take the past few afternoons off from working on the Heart, partly since there was now little to do there before it was ready to leave, and partly because there was so much to be done at home. The horses and fields had all suffered, the former from overwork and the latter from lack of it; mounds of dust and dirt were beginning to pile steadily from room to room, left longer than they had ever been before; and across every spare inch of the kitchen stood large, half-filled sacks of dried foods and other provisions for the journey, for which there was still much to find or prepare.

After a good deal of discussion, and a great deal more argument which went back heatedly more than once to things already argued and thought to have been resolved following the finding of the Heart, it had finally been decided that it would be Url and Orlando who would take the Heart to Iala. And not one of the family was entirely happy about it. The arguing had stopped, for now, but Aliya knew it was only a matter of time until it started again. For the moment, however, she was quite content to be out here in the rain, feeling everything from the rocks to the few birds still fearless enough to brave the skies, across a wonderful little circle around the hill. The stormclouds spoke again, closer this time, as though they were making their slow, lumbering journey all the way here just to see and introduce themselves to her… Aliya smiled, wishing she knew how to answer them.

'Don't you think you've had enough for today, dear?' asked her Grandmother, speaking out through the door behind her. Aliya kept her eyes closed, waiting a moment…

'Could you ever have enough of your sunsets?' she asked. She heard the door close behind her, and then felt wet footsteps approaching.

'No,' said Abetta simply, squinting against the rain up into the rolling black and purple clouds above her as she stood beside Aliya. 'I certainly couldn't.'

There they both stood for a while in silence, enjoying the deep, wonderful character of this weather which most others would usually call *bad*. Aliya felt the fleeting outline of a rabbit or perhaps something similar darting into the open and disappearing again, and the shape of the hill around her down which some of the rain flowed; seeing the pools and streams which it flowed into, and the stones and trees it flowed around, or was caught by. It was like standing in the middle of an enormous canvas, an ever-changing painting being formed slowly around her. It almost rivalled a warm day on the banks of Lake Iris. Almost.

'Well, I think this old body's had about as much as it dares…' said Abetta after another minute or so. 'Don't be too long out here, my dear; I don't want you taken ill. It'll be more work for the rest of us around here with your Father and that old fool leaving.'

'I won't,' said Aliya, not quite truthfully; her eyes still closed as she watched her Grandmother walk back to the house. Just as the door opened there was another flicker of movement on the edge of Aliya's sight, somewhere down the eastern slopes, a mile or so from the house. It seemed… familiar…

'Crick!' she shouted delightedly, suddenly realising who it was.

'What? Where?' asked Abetta, halting half-in and half-out of the house. Aliya pointed excitedly through the courtyard.

'He's riding – he'll be here soon! Tell the oth–' But she stopped; her smile fading into the mounting strength of the rain.

162

'What's the matter?' asked Abetta. Still Aliya said nothing.
'What's the matter, dear,' her Grandmother tried again. 'What is it?'
'There's someone else.' She spoke the words so quietly she was surprised her Grandmother heard them.
'*Someone*...? Who?'
'I don't know, I've never seen them before. I... They're chasing him!'
Instantly the door swung shut, Abetta calling hurriedly to the others. In seconds they were all outside in the rain beside Aliya, each shouting frightened, hurried questions.
'*I don't know*!' said Aliya for the third time. 'But he's going to be here soon! He's just passed Snarl,' she added, referring to the large boulder in the altogether unnerving shape of a wolf's head which sat growling at any rare visitor who climbed the eastern path to the their home.
'Everyone inside, quickly!' said Orlando, ushering everyone except for Url back to the house. To Url he turned and whispered something, then he too came inside with the others, all gathering in the tiny sitting room just off the kitchen. Stepping through the doorway, separated from the rain, Aliya felt suddenly blinded. With water still streaming from her hair and clothes and pooling in the thick rugs she rushed to the window to try to recover some of her sight. She stretched to see across the dark courtyard and through the gap between the fence and Url's house, down the path which Crick would be riding up any second.
'What are you going to do?' she heard Yori ask as their Father disappeared into the tool-house from the back of the room, reappearing moments later carrying his cudgel. But Orlando ignored the question:
'Anything...?' he asked.
Aliya shook her head, but as she did so she saw the top window of Url's house swing open; the thin tip of an arrow poking through into the rain. Behind it Url and his bow stood focused on the courtyard. Yori clambered half onto Aliya's shoulder to get a better look outside. They waited; Aliya and Yori by the window, their Mother and Grandmother behind them, their Father in the kitchen beside them gripping the gudgel in one hand and the large brass handle of the front door in the other. Aliya was still staring ahead down the path when suddenly Url twisted round to his right to face the northern edge of the courtyard, snatching back the string of his bow and shouting something which became distorted through the rain.
'Now!' Aliya cried, though she couldn't see far enough to her left to see what Url had; and with a mighty heave her Father pulled open

the door and sprinted outside, Aliya and Yori following without pause despite their Mother's shouts of protest. There they saw Crick, drenched and mud-splattered in a strange combination of Guardsman's uniform and other clothes. He was already just inside the courtyard, reining the unfamiliar horse beneath him to a splashing halt. And riding hard into view around the corner behind him was another Guardsman.

'Quickly!' Orlando shouted, calling to Crick as he sprinted to meet him. Crick looked to his Father, and then around him.

Aliya was already studying the skies again; there was nobody else following them that she could feel. The Guardsman sped through the final length of the path and into the courtyard, bearing down upon Crick, but suddenly from above them all a tremendous '*Halt!*' crashed like thunder down upon the courtyard, shocking horse and rider; the white and light brown animal rearing up uncontrollably and slipping violently on the cobbles.

'Take one step closer and it'll be your last!' Url bellowed from his window as the Guardsman fought to stay mounted.

'Get back, son!' said Orlando, putting himself in front of Crick's horse.

But Crick sat fast, hands rested calmly if somewhat tired on his thighs; his look, Aliya realised, turned now to one of mixed amusement and irritation.

'Father – Tarryn,' he said slowly, gesturing from one to the other. He waited for the Guardsman to bring the still-panicked horse under control: It took several great slaps of encouragement across the creature's neck, but slowly it began to calm, contenting itself with a final flustered flick of its head. 'Tarryn –' Crick continued, '– my… ever-warm and welcoming Family.' He cast his hand across them all in turn, shaking his head at the various weapons and fearful, menacing looks aimed in Tarryn's direction; ending, with a long sigh, upon Url. 'They're all delighted to meet you.'

In the brief silence Tarryn's horse grew restless again, and rather than attempting to calm it he vaulted – surprisingly quickly for his size, which Aliya found herself rather struggling not to take notice of – landing with a great splash in his heavy armour as the animal snorted angrily, skidding again as it turned and cantered back out of the courtyard. Orlando lowered his hammer; relief outweighing his embarrassment tenfold.

'Delighted!' said Tarryn, straightening his jacket and offering his hand genially.

'Apologetic…' replied Orlando, shaking the hand firmly.

'We're not shooting him, then?' called Url down through the rain-swept courtyard, still aiming hesitantly but accurately towards the Guardsman.

'I don't think so,' answered Orlando. 'He's a friend of Crick's – I assume...?' Crick nodded. Url grunted with a none-too-subtle hint of disappointment, disappearing quickly from the window.

'Splendid to see you all, by the way!' said Crick, dismounting. He tried not to show it, but Aliya and the others all noticed a distracted fear beneath the small, wry laugh he gave. It did little to dampen their delight at seeing him, but they studied him anxiously nonetheless as he threw his arms gladly around his Father, his smile slowly fading as they stood there, silently, in the rain to which everyone but Aliya was now oblivious.

*

Half an hour later, the weather still pattering gently against the flanks of the house, each of the family and their new guest were more or less dry and warm, sat or perched around the kitchen, all having eaten their fill. Tarryn was the only exception, showing no sign of relenting as he made his way through a fourth slice of stale strawberry loaf.

'Sorry it's past its best,' said Siu, refilling his mug again with warmed wine.

'Nonsense!' said Tarryn through a gurgled mouthful, looking quite delighted with the situation. 'Just how I like it. If there's one thing you'll struggle to find in Immelus it's good, home-baked bread. Don't know why...'

'So how *did* he get involved in all this?' asked Url, nodding towards Tarryn, looking up briefly to Crick from the damp, slightly mud-stained section of pale cloth which was laid out carefully in front of him. He had been studying the map so intently since Crick had revealed it that Aliya had barely seen any of it, but she had at least spotted the small, intricate weaving of the word *Iala*. She was as excited as the others at the sight of it, and just as awed by Crick's account of how he had acquired it, though none of them could match the immeasurable glee in Url's eyes as he ran his finger delicately half an inch above the threads, mouthing the words to himself. The City, from what Crick had related to them, sounded terrible: The people there even more so. She didn't envy him his past days.

'Be polite!' said Abetta with a backhanded slap of his shoulder.

'Ouch! My apologies, good Sir,' Url offered to Tarryn. 'I was just wondering how it is that you came to be caught up in this – *our* – little affair?' He looked back to Abetta for approval – receiving none.

'Well,' Tarryn began, leaning back and swallowing the last of the cake, 'when I woke up and saw that young Crick here –' he gave a forceful slap to the small of Crick's back '– wasn't in our room, I took it upon myself to venture out for a quick search of the grounds for him. Didn't want him getting himself – or *my*self, I suppose – into any *more* trouble by being late for duty. And I – well, in truth I felt I could use a bit of fresh air myself… Must have overdone it a tad that night.' Crick gave a silent laugh. 'I was in one of the streets just outside the Garrison when I saw some gangly-looking thing shoot like a leaf in winter out over one of the crossings in the distance. Tried to follow – he was too damned quick for me of course. But from the direction he was headed I thought I knew where he was going. *Why*, I had no idea… Thought he'd probably just had enough. Not that I'd have blamed you,' he added to Crick with a nod. 'By the time I got to the house – there's other ways of getting to it, by the way,' he said with an amused smile to Crick's look of surprise. 'Avoids the guards altogether! Anyway…' He continued before Crick could voice his puzzled exasperation, 'by the time I got there he'd already jumped. Didn't have much choice but to follow him!'

'You could've just, *not* followed me…' said Crick, clearly not for the first time.

'Well that would have been frightfully dull of me, wouldn't it!'

'And when I heard him crashing along behind me, *I* didn't have much choice but to stop and wait for him,' said Crick. 'When he did catch up he saw the map and refused to leave and go back to the City without me telling him what I was up to.'

'Rather wouldn't let go of him, I'm afraid!' said Tarryn, laughing haughtily as he leant back, stretching his substantial belly. For a moment he seemed finally to have had enough to eat, but then his eyes turned once more to the strawberry loaf.

But above the map, Url wasn't laughing. And in truth neither were Aliya nor any of the others. They were all looking to Tarryn with polite concern – or in the case of Url, outright suspicion.

'And I also knew he'd be helpful,' said Crick, sensing their scepticism. 'He's stronger than all of us put together, and he knows more about the City and how the borders are guarded than we could ever hope to.'

'Good of you to say so,' said Tarryn, raising his mug to Crick.

166

'We can trust him,' Crick said pointedly. The room was silent as Tarryn drained his wine.

'Are you sure?' asked Siu. 'No offen–'

'None taken,' Tarryn interjected before she could finish, barely glancing up from his plate.

Crick nodded, smiling wearily as he watched Tarryn take it upon himself to refill his drink.

'Then we'll leave first thing tomorrow,' said Orlando, looking to Url, to cries of dismay from Aliya and Yori. Url nodded. 'You can help us get the Heart out of the cavern and loaded onto the cart, if you wish, and would be good enough to,' he continued to Tarryn, 'then if you ride hard you can be back in the City in another day or so. You'll just have to think of a reason why you had to leave for a few days. I don't know what punishment you'll face...?'

But Tarryn didn't answer. Instead he set his mug carefully down onto the table, looking with a sudden first hint of seriousness to Crick...

'You want to tell them, or shall I?'

'Tell us what?' snapped Url.

Crick was staring deep into the table. 'He won't be going back to the City,' he said in a long, slow breath.

'Why not?' asked Siu. 'If he's –'

'He's going to Iala,' Crick interrupted. He looked up nervously to everyone around him. 'And... so are all the rest of us.'

The silence then was long, and uncomfortable; unified indecision around the table as to whether to be briefly amused, or angry. But as Aliya studied her brother, she saw no trace of joking in him. And, little as she knew him, the other man seemed no less intent. He twirled his mug slowly within the frame of his large hand now, deep in thought.

'Why?' asked Siu through a dry throat after a while longer. She took a quick, deep draught of wine. Crick sighed once again before speaking:

'They're going to find out it was me who stole the map.'

'*What*?' Url shouted, forgetting the map as he stood quickly and leant over the table.

'How?' asked Orlando. 'I thought you said you were able to get in and out without anyone seeing you?'

'*Take no unnecessary risks!*' Url cried.

'I know!' said Crick. 'And I *was*,' he continued quickly to his Father. 'But I... I forgot about the letter. It's still there.'

'But that was coded – surely they can't learn anything from that...?'

'It *was* coded,' Crick conceded. 'Unt-' he shook his head... 'Until I wrote out the real version beneath it.' This time it was Url's turn to sigh, collapsing back into his chair and dropping his head into his fists. 'I forgot to throw it away... They'll search my room, and they'll find it. It won't take them long to work out where I live – most of the Guardsmen at Fellgate seemed to know.'

'*I told you...*' said Url. 'You should have *waited* a while after you'd stolen the map before coming back here, so you could get rid of any evidence like that and make sure they wouldn't link your disappearance to the map being stolen!'

'I know, it was the first thing you said to me earlier, remember?' Crick answered bitterly. He glared silently at Url for a moment, but then his gaze withered and broke. He sunk his eyes into the table once more. 'I just... I wanted to get the map back to you as soon as I could.'

'And once they've found this house,' said Tarryn, 'they won't stop watching it until Crick's caught. You won't be able to work on the Heart without them finding out, and there's less than no chance that you'll then be able to get it out of the Heartlands unseen. Either way, you'll never again be able to live here free and hidden from their sight, I'm afraid. Once within the Council's sight and thoughts, one doesn't get out.'

'Then it seems we don't have much choice...' said Siu with fearful realisation. 'We can't stay here.'

'No... No, you can't,' said Url. No smile came to him as he realised that in one way, at least, he was getting what he had wanted from the beginning. 'Looks like we'll all be going, then.'

For the next few minutes Aliya listened as questions and arguments were thrown quickly about her around the table, but in the end the decision was still the same. There was indeed little choice. They would all be leaving the Heartlands, and taking the Heart to Iala. The thought struck Aliya like ice.

'And might I suggest that we leave quickly?' said Tarryn.

'First thing tomorrow,' agreed Orlando.

'No –' said Tarryn, with a forcefulness and first real look of concern that Aliya had seen from him, '– I mean *quickly*. As in *tonight*... This very moment, in fact.'

'Now? But surely it'll take them at least a day or so to work out that Crick has the map, and then where he lives?'

'We're not ready!' said Siu. 'We've still not prepared enough food, and there's at least two more loads of supplies which need taking up to the cart...' The cart, at least, was finished, and had already been

168

taken up into the hills to ensure that it could survive the difficult terrain – a test in which it had performed admirably.

But Tarryn leant forward heavily onto the table, eyeing them all with a grimness which was clearly quite unnatural to him, yet at the same time disturbingly sincere...

'You all know that as far as running the Heartlands goes,' he began after a moment's thought, 'you have, at the bottom end of the scale,' he pointed with mocking pride to himself and Crick, 'the Guardsmen.' Each of the family was silent, waiting for him to continue. 'And you know, no doubt, that at the top, there's the Council, which controls *them*, and the *City*, and anything else they can reach in the Heartlands.' There were various nods and mutterings of agreement around the table. All apart from Crick. He was staring instead glumly into the air, seeming to have already heard these words before. 'And it's those things which you're worried about, isn't it?' Tarryn finished.

There was silence for a moment, before Siu spoke:

'Why? What *should* we be worried about?'

Tarryn looked almost pitifully at her...

'All the things in between. The things you *haven't* seen, and *don't* know about.' He took a deep breath. 'The Council doesn't just rely on Guardsmen for everything it needs done. It has countless other tools at its disposal, all of which deserve far more of your fear than *Guardsmen* do.'

'Tell them what you told me earlier,' Crick muttered, rubbing his eyes; the exhaustion of his escape finally breaking over him.

'Most people think that Immelus was *the City which rejected Magic* after the Black Wind came,' Tarryn continued without pause. 'Which it was. And, as far as most people are concerned, still is.' Url had pushed the map silently and unthinkingly forward away from him, so that he could lean further into the table, listening. 'But as hard as they tried, the various Councils over the years – and especially over the past few decades – came to realise that they simply couldn't survive without employing certain kinds of Magical defences against the Black Wind.' He paused, studying the reactions around the table, Aliya's included. The Council of Immelus... *using* Magic?

'And as they came to study Magic once again,' he continued, 'they also rediscovered that it could bring with it certain... *advantages*. Advantages which have little to do with defence,' he added bitterly. 'I've only ever heard whispers of them, but over a lifetime living in the City, with one parent in the Council and the other –'

'You have *what*?' exclaimed Siu.

'My Mother – she's in the Council.'

Even Crick looked shocked…

'I knew they were important, but I had no idea she was –'

'Well, anyway… The point is that after a lifetime of living like I've lived you come to hear a lot of things. Half of them have probably been drunken drivel; most of the rest lies. But if even a few of the stories I've heard are true, we need to get out of here, and now. None of you have any idea how much danger we're in if we stay, even for a few hours. None of you,' he repeated, looking to Crick. 'Once word reaches the border that we're trying to escape, and they start sending out people and… other things to block our way and track us down, we won't stand a chance.' It seemed for a brief moment that he was regretting his decision to follow Crick.

'If we're in so much danger,' said Url, 'then why did you *choose* to get yourself involved?' Crick's eyes flashed up to Url, but then moved across to Tarryn without a word. For a few seconds Tarryn looked as though he was struggling for an answer, but then, slowly, his grin returned…

'Because it's all rather exciting, isn't it?'

Url studied him hard for a moment, trying to work him out…

'I think I could start to like him,' he said at length to Abetta, breaking into an uncertain laugh.

'Doesn't say *much* for him, does it?' said Abetta flatly.

'But with his Mother on the Council…?' said Siu.

'The lad can't help who his parents are,' said Url.

'But surely they'll send everything they've got after him?'

'Crick said that once we're out of the Heartlands we should be safe enough with this *Heart* of yours…?' said Tarryn.

'*This Heart of ours*...?' Aliya echoed.

'He doesn't believe in it,' Yori confirmed.

'You d–' Siu started.

'I'm not saying it's not real enough,' Tarryn interrupted hastily, holding up his hands, 'in some form. I'm sure you've found something extremely impressive, in one way or another. Crick here certainly seems pretty convinced about it. But you have to understand…' For the first time since the others had met him he struggled to find the words, or perhaps the will, to continue…

'You can guess I'm sure how it is in the City,' he managed at last. 'I've been brought up amongst people who'd slay their entire families before admitting to belief or hope in things like *the Heart*! The only person I've ever spoken freely with about it all ended up nailed above one of the eastern Gates – I was only spared because of my parents. Since then I've never let myself think about it. I'm not saying I might not believe in it, deep down,' he said to Yori. 'Or at least that I'm not happy for others to. It's just going to take a lot before I can let myself think like that again. Just see me as an intrigued party coming along for the ride!' he finished with a poor but valiant attempt at a grin.

'We should be safe enough from anything the City will send after us, yes,' Url intervened, almost looking sorry for him. Tarryn seemed to have shrunk slightly into his chair; his thick wrappings of clothes and that armour he had declined to remove suddenly weighing him down as they had been unable to do before. 'If we can get enough distance between us and the Heartlands, we'll have the Black Wind itself between us and them... At least, we *should* do.'

'Precisely,' said Tarryn, straightening upright again. 'So all we have to do is get out of here soon, and success shall be ours!'

'That's not quite how I put it,' said Url, irritated by such careless talk of a journey through the Outerlands, even so pitifully half-joking as it was.

'Oh, close enough,' said Tarryn. But Url persevered:

'There'll still likely be dangers along the way which have nothing to do with the Black Wind, or the City. But... yes, we'll be safer, I feel, out there with the Heart than cornered here without it.' He looked around the table with a resolute glint in his eyes, daring anyone to disagree with him.

'Well, then, tonight it is, I suppose,' said Orlando, turning eagerly to the others for better suggestions. Despite their desperate longing for such a thing, neither Aliya nor anyone else could provide one. A quite surreal air seemed to have filled the room, at once stifling Aliya's breathing as she thought of the journey yet at the same time filling her lungs and limbs with the sudden buoyancy of terrified excitement.

'Come help with the horses,' her Father added, putting a hand on Yori's shoulder.

'At least you got the map,' Aliya said quietly to Crick as the others stood or stretched around the table. 'You were lucky the Wilder Rooms were empty.' She had been as fascinated as Url at Crick's description of them. But Crick, not meeting her eyes, did little more than mumble a distant form of acknowledgement. He left to go outside with Tarryn; Aliya watching him as he braced himself against the gust of wind and rain which swept into the room when Tarryn opened the door. On the far side of the table, she saw Yori studying him closely as well.

*

171

Despite the frenzied burst of speed with which they packed and readied themselves, by the time they were all assembled around the table again, draped in thick riding tunics, with the horses laden and waiting irritably in the courtyard, the skies outside had grown considerably blacker and colder. The storm seemed quite content in its place above and surrounding their hill; rain continuing to lash even more heavily now against the side of the house and doing nothing at all to diminish the pressing feeling that they were already being encircled.

'We ride to the hills,' said Url without ceremony once they were all silent. 'You,' he pointed to Orlando, 'take Yori and Aliya to the cart, and ride around to meet us where the river emerges. I'll go with the others and bring the Heart out to you.'

'As easy as that…!' said Siu, shaking her head, still as doubtful as the rest of them.

'No. But *possible*. And somewhat necessary, wouldn't you say?' He turned back to the others. 'Then we get the Heart loaded and head for… Esthmey Crossing, you say?' he asked, looking to Tarryn.

'It's not the closest,' said Tarryn, 'but of all the northern Gates it'll be the most lightly guarded. It's our best chance.'

'*Lightly guarded* it may be,' said Abetta, 'but even so, how do we get through?'

'I'm still working on that,' said Url.

'You're still…?'

'And then from there it's north-west to the Firstway, and then north, until Iala. Anyone have any questions?'

'Dozens,' said Siu. Url looked to her, pursing his lips kindly. 'But they can wait,' she sighed.

'Good. Then – shall we?' The room trembled with a flurry of rain as he drew open the door, gesturing out into the dim squall which was currently occupying the courtyard.

And it was only as Aliya neared the door, following behind Crick, that she realised with a sickening lurch of something within her chest that this was the last time she would see her home in what surely would be a long while. It had all happened so quickly… She stopped and turned to Url, who was still holding the door ajar; the only one left in the room apart from her. She found it difficult to mask the swell of fear and sadness which had been building inside her since they had agreed to leave. Of the three children, it had always been her who had struggled to talk openly and easily with Url, having little in common and spending barely any time alone with him. He had always been good to her, though. And seeing the look in her eyes now he closed the door to within an inch of its frame, wiped the rain from his eyes, and

172

paused. Unease and fear were too potent in his thoughts for him to manage a smile, but when he spoke his voice was at least quiet, and as kind as ever she had known it:

'Ride next to me when we leave. I'll tell you about some of the quite spectacular lakes and waterways we'll be finding along the way.' His chest lifted with a breath of hope at the thought.

And though she couldn't help but study more closely the small things around her which she had grown used to and come to ignore over the years – the creeping ivy and thick, ancient blackberry vines which led up to her window; the small flowers and sprawling gooseberry bushes which would likely be left to wilt and die in their long, white stone troughs along the walls; or the way the cobbles of the courtyard merged seamlessly into the foundations of Url's house – there was also a part of Aliya which smiled as she rode off beside Url, listening through the rain to splendid tales of the forgotten waters of the Outerlands, and then the vast, endless blue of the Deepwaters beyond. Never before, in all her life, had she thought that she may see for herself the great oceans of the north. She only wished that there was some way of avoiding all the things which lay in between.

*

They reached the Eigerhills in full dark. The rain had eased slightly but in its place the wind had strengthened, driving the remaining droplets into every smallest breech it could find or make in their clothing, such that while Aliya could no longer sense anything but vague outlines of the land around her she was at the same time wet, cold and uncomfortable despite her tightly-fastened cloak.

Url dismounted, followed silently by Aliya, Crick, and Yori. The decision of which of the horses to bring with them on the journey had been hurried and one of the most difficult of all, but it was done and there was no time left to discuss it now. Orlando waited upon the silent form of Oden, taking Crash's reins from Url; while Aliya took charge of Railer, watching as Crick helped Yori up onto the high back of Nightwind. These were the four who would go to Iala. The others – Chestnut now carrying Siu and Url; Tarryn's horse bearing him and Crick; and Abetta upon Jinta, an ancient mare of all shades of brown, well past the age of working but still willing and able to occasionally bear Abetta only – would all be sent back once they had reached the cave. Yori had been particularly loath to leave Cloud, but Url had insisted: food, water, and time all difficult enough to find or provide for four animals, let alone five. Those who were staying would be fending for themselves while the family were away, but they would have the shelter of the stables, and each of them knew the lands surrounding the hill well enough. Still, it was an unpleasant thought to be abandoning them like this. Aliya felt for Yori; quietly but immensely glad to have Nightwind coming with her. When everyone was ready the two groups shouted their soaked, windswept good-lucks, and with a quick nod to Url, Orlando led Aliya, Yori, and Crash to the left of the treeline; Url turning and continuing with the others to the cave.

The cart was hidden carefully amongst a small cleft in the side of a steep, rocky rise overgrown with thick tumbles of bramble and weeds, several miles along the path. Working slowly to avoid risking damage to the canvas, it took the three of them longer than they would have liked to disentangle it from its surroundings, even with Orlando's quiet, murmured efforts at manipulating the stubborn undergrowth. The brambles would sway slightly under his command, retracting away from his outstretched hand, but they obstinately refused to part completely, requiring a great deal of awkward tugging and cutting before finally their bulk could be peeled back like sheets of great, uncomfortable blanket over and behind the cart. But once they were finished, Aliya and the others were at last able to throw the supplies they had brought with them inside, climb in after them, loosen their cloaks, and catch their breath.

Her Father, Aliya noticed again, had done a remarkable job with the old, rickety mass of wood, wheels and fabrics which until even a few days ago had been unfit to carry anyone or anything, let alone a gemstone the size of her. The floorboards now were smooth and firm, and stronger by far than they had ever been before; the simple wood and leather seats were repaired, with those in the back moved to the edges to allow the Heart to fit, hopefully, into the centre; and the new, hardy, milk-white canvas which lined the sides and roof was clean, strong, and from what Aliya could tell as she inspected it, entirely rainproof. A thin set of wooden steps could be folded out from the back, while at the other end a small, curtained opening led through into the front compartment in which three people could sit beside each other, with reins for each of the four horses and two thick, heavy brake levers in front of the centre seat. The back section itself was large enough for perhaps a dozen people, but Orlando had included just four inward-facing seats, one in each corner; the rest of the space required for their supplies and, assuming the others could now get it out, the Heart.

It took a minute for Aliya, nearly asleep beside Yori in the relative warmth and comfort of the cart, to realise that her Father wasn't in there with them. She jumped up to the opening at the front and peered out through the curtain, and saw him struggling to attach the last of the horses to the crossbeam in the front right position of the four. She prodded Yori as she went past him, skipping lightly down the steps and round to the front to help with the awkward animal – Crick's Railer, naturally – who was wholly reluctant to allow himself to be fastened to the big, lumbering contraption behind him. Once finally they had calmed him enough to tie the last two thick leather straps which held him in place, the three of them climbed up into the front of the cart and set off, continuing slowly but now at least more or less dry around the edge of the Eigerhills.

After half an hour they turned west off the southward-running track, soon passing along the mouth of a wide valley whose sides curved dimly up and away to their right.

'Aulan's valley,' said Orlando, continuing carefully across the stream which ran out from within the hillsides – still little more than a shallow trickle here and no trouble, Orlando was pleased to see, for the cart. Had it been but a few hours later, the added rainwash from the surrounding hills would have meant this may not have been so easy. Aliya and Yori nodded uncertainly, pleased to have regained the bearings which in the dark and their weariness they had both lost some time ago. And beyond that it was another few long miles until they came to a deep, fast-flowing river; Orlando this time directing the horses to the flat bridge which crossed it, and then right, up alongside its far bank. The river started to twist jaggedly through the steepening hillside, lined with large boulders and divided by lengths of violent rapids which cast a cold, sweet-smelling spray into the air. At one point the front wheels of the cart became stuck in the loose, wet ground, but with Aliya at the reins and Yori and their Father working to free the wheels it didn't take long for them to be on their way again. Aliya was uncertain whether either of the others were, as she was, troubled by the fact that they had been halted in their tracks, albeit briefly, so early in the journey. But she said nothing of it.

With tired, heavy eyes they reached a further crest in the hillside from which, in the murky distance far above them, the high rocky peaks of the hill came into view. And in between, just a few hundred feet ahead of them, was the large, swirling pool they were aiming for. Formed where the underground river running through the cavern sprang finally into the open before rolling its way swiftly down the hill, the emergence pool glistened with a pale silver light; the moon, visible for the first time, peering briefly from between the dispersing clouds.

'It's clearing up…' said Orlando, cheerfully.

'Aren't you tired?' asked Aliya. Yori yawned again at the word.

'When you've raised three children, and when one of them's Crick, you learn to get through a night or two without too much sleep,' her Father answered with a smile.

They secured the cart a short way from the pool, and brought out the things they would need. Orlando placed a large clump of netting beside the water, beginning first to unfold and then with muttered curses to untangle it, while Aliya circled around the top of the pool with the ends of the two ropes that Yori was holding, tying them firmly around the base of the two largest boulders she could find.

'They're done!' she called back across to Yori, though with the rain now reduced to just a few occasional spits and the wind beginning to ease as well she was able to do so without shouting. The horses, she noticed, were becoming restless, stamping and throwing their heads in the air. Crash neighed fretfully, struggling for a moment against the frame of the cart. 'Throw me the w–' But just then as though something was tunnelling beneath her a gentle trembling struck the soles of Aliya's feet... She looked about her for its source, but suddenly the whole hillside seemed to erupt; a tremendous quaking lasting several seconds before fading slowly, almost peacefully into the night. It seemed to have come from the north-east; from the direction of the cavern. The three of them waited, motionless, looking apprehensively across the pool to one another. Orlando opened his mouth to speak but in place of his voice there came then an almighty crash of noise from the clear skies on the far side of the hill; a thunderous *boom* echoing down the hillsides towards and around them leaving Aliya staring, breathless, towards her Father as it faded again into the breeze. On all fours they waited anxiously again... but this time there was nothing more. The horses gave a final string of confused and startled snorts, and then they too fell quiet.

'What was it?' asked Yori quietly. But neither Aliya nor her Father answered him. Together they stared fearfully up into the waning shadow of the hills.

Chapter Fifteen

Esthmey Crossing

Out of the blinding flash of light and noise which had thrown him to his feet, Crick's consciousness slowly started coming back to him. Carefully, and while spitting out gritty mouthfuls of the diamond dust which had engulfed them, he sat up. He checked himself from head to toe, but nothing seemed broken or too badly damaged. Everything beyond the end of his arms was hidden amongst the strange, glittering fog the explosion had cast up into the Chamber. There was a muffled cough somewhere ahead of him...

'Ha... I think you – got it with that one, young Tarryn!' It was Url, his words broken and followed by a series of thick coughs and splutters, echoed in different voices around the Chamber.

'Is everyone alright?' Crick heard his Mother call.

'A few cuts, but I'll live,' he answered.

'Never better!' called Tarryn. He seemed somewhat amused.

'Mother...? Siu called into the haze. '*Mother*? Are you hurt?' The sounds of people struggling to their feet halted as each listened intently for Abetta, and there was a collective sigh of relief as her voice emerged, cutting angrily through the fog:

'When I find you, Urlmaeus...' Url's coughing stopped abruptly.

'Nobody move until this dust has settled,' called Siu.

So for the next few minutes they could do little but wait wherever they had landed, cleaning themselves off as best they could. Gradually the dust began to subside, floating gently down to the bottom of the chamber, and as it did so Crick saw four silvery heads appear around

177

him. And only then did they all realise that amongst them all, in the centre of the chamber, the Heart was no longer there. Url cried out, sprinting towards the great dais, disappearing immediately into the dust as he tripped over the uneven ground.

'Wait – until – the dust – has cleared…' Siu repeated wearily, but Url paid her little mind, jumping instead briskly to his feet and scrambling forwards again to the empty platform of interweaving strands of crystal which had previously held the Heart. But before anyone could say anything there came a solid *thud*, a brilliant flash of light, and a shriek of pain from Url, who collapsed once more out of sight… reappearing a second later several feet back smiling through a grimace…

'Found it!' he announced, grasping his hidden leg tenderly.

Crick and the others each made their own way, decidedly more carefully, down and then up into the middle of the chamber… and there it was, lying still and sideways on the ground before them, just visible through the clearing mist. Even on its side, however, it still reached close to Crick's waist.

'Right –' said Url, '– now we've just got to get it out of here and down to the river.'

'It's alright, it's not mine,' Tarryn said coolly to Siu, trying to wipe away the thick layer of blood which covered most of his chest and legs, onto which the dust was clinging and forming a thick, oddly-coloured paste. In their hurry to get going as swiftly as possible there hadn't been the time to hunt the animals whose blood would be required to extricate the gem from the Chamber, so Tarryn had suggested one of the horses he and Crick had stolen from the farmstead a few miles out from Immelus. Url had done the deed again with an arrow just below and back from the unfortunate animal's ear, storing all the blood which left of its own accord or could otherwise be drained into three large buckets. One such bucket had been left by the entrance to the chamber to clear the way out, the second had been used up almost entirely trying to remove the Heart from its surroundings, and the third Tarryn had been holding when the Heart finally gave way so spectacularly. Crick noticed a dull ringing in his right ear; he tried to shake it away, but it lingered irksomely in the background like the whispering of a nearby stream.

'Oh – right…' said Url, chuckling as he only now noticed the half crimson Tarryn. 'Yes, good – glad you're okay.' He turned to Crick. 'Go get the ropes, would you?'

But even simply looping the ropes around the Heart tight enough to allow them to drag it out proved no easy task. Though the rest of the

Chamber no longer swirled or reacted when anyone neared the Heart, the great gemstone itself was little less sensitive than it had earlier been to their presence. At first approach a thin rippling of colour could be seen to spread in gentle waves through the deep, near-hidden layers of the gem, and if anyone stepped within touching distance this wave would come quickly to the surface, the face closest to that person shining a fierce, daunting hue. And when, on occasion, Url or the others stumbled to within a foot or less of the Heart it would explode into life like the spark of a flint, repelling everyone around it with a sharp, unbearable snap of heat and light. They were forced therefore to cast the ends of the ropes around the various jagged edges from several paces away, tying most of the knots loose beforehand, so that it was nearly an hour before they had it secured well enough to begin.

By that time, however, a curious and unsettling change had begun to work its way into and through the surfaces of the Chamber around them. Yori had felt it first, and each of them had seen for themselves a few minutes later, as slowly but surely the crystal beneath, around, and above the dais started to lose its brightness, seeming in some places to melt and seep away through the ground like ice at the coming of Spring. The vast pillars were becoming shorter; the ground smoother and darker; the arching strands which hung down through the Chamber retracting into the upper reaches, now lost for the first time in a new, peculiar darkness. It had not been until now that Crick truly realised just how deep underground they were. The bright mist was also fading, no longer swirling around them but instead merely drifting languidly through their feet. It was as though someone was slowly turning down a lamp, threatening to transform the glorious Chamber into little more than an ordinary cave. And in all of this the only section which appeared to be unaffected was the platform itself upon which the Heart had sat: It stood in stark contrast to its surrounds as bright and regal as ever, though still easily outmatched by the Heart itself.

'Well,' said Url, returning through the opening into the Chamber from the spiralling tunnel beyond, 'it looks like it's happening all the way up into the cavern. Should make it easier to drag it out. Though if we're not quick, I fear we may have to do it in the dark...' he added, peering up into the heights and new shadows of the Chamber.

'Splendid,' said Siu under her breath.

'Come on, then, help me with these...' Tarryn called to Crick, holding out several frayed ends of rope. Just hours into the journey and already Crick was glad to have acquired Tarryn as part of the group. The softening ground, while making the going easier, did nothing to reduce the tremendous weight of the Heart, and it took every heave and

179

grunt of their combined strength to drag it finally from its place and tow it slowly out through the Chamber and up the long, winding tunnel.

When at last they reached the top, emerging into the narrow clearing, they were relieved to find that a similar transformation was taking place in the rest of the cavern as well. Relieved in that moment, but far from pleased, however. For there was also, unspoken amongst Crick and the others but quite loud and powerful enough in the feelings it stirred within them, a strange sense of loss for the wonder that was fading before their eyes. It was no small part of Crick that wished it could have stayed as it was, despite the difficulties this would have caused. To have been, in all likelihood, the only people along with Aulan ever to have witnessed this great jewel of the world prompted a sudden, bitter sadness which neither Crick nor any of the others found the strength or will to put into words.

They were afforded no time to linger and watch, however. There was only a short window of time within which the crystal beneath them was smooth enough to allow the Heart to be dragged across, but not yet disappeared so much so that the rocky, black, uneven ground below began to take its place. And Url, in between frantic sprints ahead with the remaining bucket, clearing the largest remaining spears of crystal from their path, was making quite sure that they kept up the pace. The cavern seemed far longer now than it had done before, enlarged still further by the fact that although the way ahead was clearing, the far end of the cavern was now hidden completely in darkness. Above them the agitated screeches and flurries of the strange water-birds echoed disconcertingly close. Url had described the creatures to him and Tarryn as they climbed the final paths to the cave – along with the rest of this rather absurd plan – but he had failed to mention how close to the ground they came. One swooped low out from the darkness, others following, all soaring side to side in turn across the cavern; their cries and the beatings of their wings – hundreds of them, it seemed – rising quickly into a whirling roar of noise which by the time the river could finally be heard somewhere ahead had surrounded them, stabbing at them from all sides and within inches of their heads. Even Tarryn was close to exhausted as the Heart was drawn the last few feet through a cut in the softening riverbank to the water's edge. Url was trying angrily but in vain to swat away the creatures above them, all of which avoided his blows with ease, plunging quickly into the water or around the Heart and screeching louder all the time.

'Let's just get this over with!' shouted Abetta over the din. 'We can re–' she ducked beneath the arcing tip of Url's knife, which made glancing contact with the flurry of feathers which had descended from the dark above her, sending the bird screeching into the water behind her. 'We can rest once we're outside!' she finished, getting to her feet with Tarryn's assistance, uncertain whether to thank Url or thump him. She decided on neither. Each of the group nodded their agreement, and with the Heart balanced precariously beside the water Url directed Crick, Siu, and Abetta to stand to its left holding half the ends of the ropes, while he stood with Tarryn and the rest of the ropes on the right.

'Ready?' he called, though the noise about them now was so overwhelming that Crick couldn't hear the word at all. But before Crick could respond Url already seemed to be counting down… '…Two…One…' And without pause he jumped forward into the river, as did Siu and Abetta, between whom Crick was caught and dragged in as well. The ice-cold water was suddenly soft and refreshing after the work of the past hours, and for the second before Url started once again to shout commands Crick felt oddly relaxed… even content. Then with a sharp *crack* the noise and splashing around him came suddenly back to him…

'Oh – sorry!' his Mother spluttered, having elbowed him on the back of his head in her attempt to stay afloat, kicking against the strength of the current while grasping the ropes which Crick had dropped.

Crick retook his share and looked to Url who, bobbing awkwardly a dozen feet away, gave an unheard shout at which all the ropes were pulled tight: the Heart wobbling, resisting for a moment… and then falling sideways with somehow just a small, neat *plop* into the water before them. And for some reason, against all logic and Crick's firm expectations, it did not sink straight to the bottom. Url had been right: the Heart floated gracefully just below the surface, flowing downriver with the current which Crick and the others now stopped fighting and allowed instead to carry them as well. With gentle tugs to left and right to stop the Heart colliding with the banks of the river, they drifted amidst the whirl of wings above and now around them as well down to the edge of the cavern. Suddenly Crick wished he had taken a better final look around him while he had had the chance; a wall looming suddenly tall in front of them beneath which the river disappeared. Despite Url's altogether inadequate instructions to him and Tarryn – *just breath normally* – Crick found himself taking and holding a deep breath as he was swept quickly beneath the water and through the tunnel…

'You won't be able to do that again next time!' said Url once they had surfaced on the other side, with a smile which even for him was irritatingly smug.

The passage here was yet to be affected in the way that the rest of the cavern had already been, glistening instead just as the others had described it. Even the water itself was now the clear, superbly vivid blue that Aliya had spoken of several times over. Crick, however, was also and acutely aware that the next and final part of the underground section of the river was coming up, just beyond the bend towards which they were moving, swiftly and with increasingly little control over the Heart. The water rolled and roared, frothing against the walls of the passage, turning back and forth within itself while maintaining its quick, onwards march, seeming intent on proving to Crick and the others how they were now wholly within its power.

'Just relax,' said Siu, seeing Crick attempting to take in as much air as he could.

'You can hold my hand if you want!' called Tarryn, sharing a gasping laugh with Url as he collided with the wall. Crick had a fitting, if not particularly witty response in mind, but before he could inform Tarryn of it they were rounding the bend: the end of the passage, a sheer face of rock and crystal surely two hundred feet high at least suddenly sweeping down ahead of them. Crick's eyes were fixed firmly upon the foaming water at the base of the wall, churning and spraying like soup in the mouth of a poorly-mannered giant before being swallowed and disappearing into the deep.

'They'll be waiting on the other side...' Url reminded them, shrieking amongst the excitement and noise of it all. 'Throw them the ropes then get out and help secure the Heart. Ha!' The end of the passage was upon them. 'Enjoy!' And the next second he, then the others, and finally Crick were dragged with a quick jerk into the foam, down beneath the surface... Crick held his breath for as long as he could, but pounded from all sides by the water and the others around him his lungs quickly began to burn. He searched desperately ahead for the end of the tunnel, seeing nothing but blue crystal walls continuing down indefinitely away from him. The idea of grinning as the others – even, annoyingly, Tarryn – were doing seemed insane, but finally he had no choice: He opened his mouth and with a great gasp breathed in... not water, and not air, but something in between. It tasted sweet and crisp, like ripe gooseberry juice, filling him with an energy and a sudden euphoric giddiness which made it difficult to pay attention to the ropes that were slowly slipping once again from his grip. He drifted lazily behind the Heart, the kaleidoscopic colours and patterns of the tunnel passing him by neither quickly nor slowly, and he found it something of a shame when suddenly he was swept up and out into the cool air of an evening he had for a moment entirely forgotten about.

'Grab hold!' someone was shouting.

'Catch!' called someone else.

'And someone do something about *him*!' Crick heard his Father shout. He felt a strong but briefly unsteady hand take hold of his shoulder.

'Come on, lad, bathtime's over!' said Url, treading water behind him. Crick snapped only partly from his gaze, swimming across awkwardly to help as a large net was cast out across the bobbing gem, ropes were thrown to the side, and with an enormous effort the Heart was dragged from the pond, squelching suddenly heavy once more onto the slippery bank, skidding a few feet before stopping, wedged deep into the mud. Crick collapsed to the ground beside the others, breathing hard; the thin, empty air feeling horribly dull and lifeless after the cavern and the power of the water. Url let out a quiet laugh…

'Easy as that…'

And once Orlando had ensured everyone was accounted for and unharmed, they simply sat or lay there silently for a time, recovering themselves. The rain had stopped; the solid mass of cloud broken now into dozens of weakening patches through which the pale blue of the hour before dawn could be seen tingeing the eastern skies. They were on a flat ridge a short way up a long, razor-peaked hill from where, looking down the slopes into the north-west, the first twisting part of their journey stretched out dimly into the lingering darkness of the horizon. Url, animated and oblivious to the numerous small cuts across his forearms and neck, explained to the eagerly awaiting Orlando, Aliya, and Yori what had happened in the Chamber…

'Did you know it was going to react like that?' asked Orlando once he had finished.

'There was always a chance of it happening, I suppose…' said Url.

'Well next time there's *a chance* of anything like that happening again,' said Siu, 'would you be so good as to warn us beforehand?'

'Ha… I'll, um, do my best,' said Url, with a sheepish grin. 'Yes. Now – let us see how this box on wheels of yours is going to hold up…'

It turned out that the cart held up extremely well. Even Orlando himself was quietly impressed with his work. The extra beams which he had fitted to the floor and axle may have made it slower, but they also gave it the strength it needed to bear the substantial weight of its passengers, their supplies, and now the Heart. The final lifting of the gem up into its place was considerably the most difficult element of the evening, until after a great deal of strain and mounting frustration it was discovered that with one of the thick, hessian mats used for covering the horses at night placed around the Heart, it could be pushed and pulled directly for short periods of time. Inside the mat it would glow and start to become hot, but as long as the contact was brief it would soon cool and fade again once the touch was removed.

So with Tarryn lifting from beneath, and the others each supporting him or pulling on ropes and makeshift handholds wherever they could find them, the Heart was scraped up from the mud, over the back of the cart, and placed and tied into position in the very centre, surrounded by the mass of seats, provisions and tools. To think that it would stay this way until the very north of the world... Url took the middle of the three front seats, with Orlando and Abetta either side of him, Tarryn upon Crash at the back-left of the four horses, and Crick and the others sitting around the Heart. And with dawn breaking behind them, lighting the topmost cliffs the same deep red of Tarryn's clothes, they set off carefully and silently down the slick grass; Crick appreciating for the first time the true scale of the journey that lay ahead of them. *Overwhelming* was a word he rarely admitted to recognise, but just now it was the only one he could think of.

*

When Crick next opened his eyes, a few tiny glints of sunlight were creeping through the tight threads of canvas above him. Looking back over his shoulder, he saw flat green fields lit bright beneath a clear blue sky, broken only by the deep tracks which the horses and wheels of the cart were making in the otherwise unspoilt grass. His Mother and Yori were asleep in their corners; Tarryn coiled as well as his bulk would allow amongst various sacks along the side of the cart, though Crick had no memory of him entering. Through the open curtain at the front his Grandmother was dozing quietly upon Url's shoulder, wrapped in a thin woollen blanket; the heads of Url and Orlando nodding drowsily along with the steady movement of the cart. From the opposite corner, behind the large hessian mound which was the Heart, Aliya yawned.

'Everyone okay back there?' asked Orlando, turning back. His lips made an effort at a smile, but his eyes and the rest of him seemed fast asleep. Aliya sat up, nodding groggily.

Before long everyone was awake, and Url pulled the horses to a stop. Crick tumbled out into the sun while Tarryn lowered the steps and walked down with the others, all stretching and shielding their eyes from the light.

'Get yourself some sleep,' Orlando murmured to Url, who was helping Abetta down from the front. 'You haven't rested since before yesterday.'

'Neither have you,' said Url blankly.

'We'll take the reins after lunch,' said Crick, nodding to Tarryn. He felt pleasantly refreshed, and with the prospect of reaching new lands which even *he* had never ventured to, the idea of leading the way thoroughly appealed to him. Url considered it a moment, grunted something which was probably an *alright*, and then lay down where he was by the wheel of the cart and fell instantly into sleep, curled tight half-buried amongst the thick grass.

'Let's get something to eat,' Orlando suggested.

'And then *you're* having some sleep as well,' said Siu.

'We shouldn't stay too long,' said Tarryn. 'Once we're well out of the Heartlands we can put up camp and rest, but until then we must keep moving.'

'I can sleep in the cart once we're on our way,' Orlando promised. Siu accepted it grudgingly, with a long kiss on his weary cheek.

While Url slept and snored, the others ate a small lunch out in the open field. To the west Crick could see the faint outline of the beginnings of a forest, but in every other direction green fields rolled gently into the distance. They had brought several large sacks full of dried fruits and meats; cheeses and thick butters wrapped tight in layers of giant dandelion leaf; a type of heavily-seeded bread which Abetta had baked, which was hard but tasted good and lasted, as far as anyone had ever been able to judge, indefinitely; a good selection of fruit cakes; the powdered remnants of the flowers of various berry bushes which could be used to flavour water or almost anything else that needed it; and many other small foodstuffs from which was provided a pleasant meal, despite being strictly rationed amongst them.

'How far have we come?' Crick asked his Father once he had satisfied the worst of his hunger.

'Not as far as I'd hoped. Seventeen, eighteen miles, maybe? It wasn't easy getting the cart safe down those first slopes with all the weight it's carrying. We managed to pick up some speed once we got onto this flat ground, though. If it stays more or less like this we should be at the Maiyen by mid-morning tomorrow.'

'And have we worked out how we're getting through the crossing?' asked Siu.

'Not quite,' Orlando sighed. 'I think he's hoping to charm his way through,' he added with a nod to Url. Abetta paused halfway through a bite of sunflower cake, glancing up dubiously. 'Obviously the plan's still got a few flaws…' Orlando agreed. 'We might –'

'Scavengers!' said Tarryn.

'Where?' asked Orlando, sitting up and scouring the horizon.

'No – *us*. *We* could pretend to be scavengers. They're one of the few types of people who're allowed to leave for the Outerlands in groups with carts full of equipment like this. We've enough tools in the back to make a show of it.'

'We don't have the permission,' said Orlando as though already having thought of and discarded the idea. 'And they'd still search us.'

'Well I can deal with the first problem. And as for –'

'How?'

'Parchment, quill, ink, water, piece of cloth, some red berries, maybe a piece of bark or two…' said Tarryn, listing them on his fingers. 'Any type will do – berries, that is. It won't be perfect, but it'll be good enough to fool whoever's guarding the Crossing, no doubt. And as for searching the cart…' He shrugged. 'Throw some dung inside the sack with it – claim it's a rare type of manure you're going to use to attract thorn-beetles, or something… *Anything*. They don't get paid enough to search deeper than that.'

'Dung…?' asked Aliya.

'Yes – yours, the horses'; either way it should do the job.'

'It seems a bit… simple, doesn't it?' said Siu as Aliya surveyed Tarryn disapprovingly.

'Well with a bit of thought I could perhaps come up with something more complex, if you'd prefer?' offered Tarryn. 'But this should work. Remember that as long as we reach the border before word of our – or rather, young Crick's – escape does, it shouldn't be too difficult to get through. Right now their minds are on what's trying to get *into* this place, not escape from it. We've just to hope and pray to any of the old Gods you can think of that it stays that way 'till we get there.'

'I suppose *you* managed it often enough in the past, didn't you?' Crick heard his Mother say with enduring umbrage in his direction. He kept his eyes focused on the horizon, taking another large mouthful of bread.

*

It was with a great swell of satisfaction that, half an hour later, Crick climbed the thin wooden rungs up into the seats at the front of the cart. He took the centre with Tarryn to his right, Aliya to his left, and an excited Yori leaning over his shoulder through the curtain.

After a second unsolicited tutorial from his Father concerning the workings of the cart, sleepy instructions from Url to keep riding northwest at a good speed, and a warning from Abetta not to make that speed *too* good, Crick shook the reins; Oden and the others starting obediently into a trot.

It was Ansmere Forest which they soon began to pass on their left, and Crick didn't need Tarryn's suggestion to stay well away from it. It was one of the largest forests in the Heartlands, well known for the rare and decidedly inhospitable spectre-wolves which roamed there, and a magnet for any self-respecting young adventurer. Unfortunately for Crick, Natt and Leyon they had been far *too* young and ill-prepared when they had attempted it, creeping little more than a mile before they were chased out screaming into the surrounding plains, deciding there and then never again to return. It stayed in the distance beside them for most of the afternoon, only fading away as the sun was beginning to fall through the western clouds, at which point Crick saw a line of low hills ahead, cutting across their path.

'Straight through the middle?' Crick asked of Url, who had just awoken and joined Yori through the curtain, looking refreshed and eager.

'Straight through the middle,' Url confirmed. 'We can find somewhere sheltered in there to set up for the night.'

So leaving the open fields behind, Crick led the cart through a thin vale between two of the hills whose sides rose gently away to east and west. From the eastern, a small stream wound down into the middle of the vale and then out to meet the family, and Crick followed it for a while until the point at which it turned to go up into the hill. A few hundred feet away it passed through a copse of tall, red maples with wide, sprawling branches, and with a nod from Url Crick pulled the horses gently towards them.

They ate well and rested beneath the low ceiling of gold and scarlet, and then by firelight Tarryn started work on the pass they would need to get through the Guardsmen. He began by staining the piece of parchment very slightly in places with soiled water from the side of the stream, drying it carefully beside the flames. He then wrote several lines in tall, curving script, before shaping a lump of bark and pressing it below the writing, through a piece of cloth which he had died a deep red; creating after a few attempts a pattern which bore a surprisingly accurate resemblance to the Mark of the Council – a wall of spears before a ring resembling the sun. He handed it up to Url, who read aloud, impressed:

'The Council of the Great City of Immelus has heard the words and seen the deeds and evidence of the holder of this Missive, and has decreed in accordance with all laws and principles of the Heartlands that they are to be allowed passage through the Gates and all other Crossings into and out of the realm, including the...' he trailed into silence, mouthing the rest of the words to himself.

'Simple, I know,' said Tarryn, leaning back with a satisfied grin, 'but like I said, it should do the job well enough. Now – if you'd all just sign your names around the mark, there...' He offered the quill to Url.

'*Our* names?' said Crick.

'Well, *your* names, *someone else's* name – it really doesn't make a great deal of difference. Do you think the Guardsman on a Crossing this far out from the City is going to know the real names of all the members of the Council? Just make it illegible enough and they won't be able to see the difference even if they are looking for it.'

'Ha!' Url laughed, shaking his head and signing his name in curving script proudly in the bottom corner of the parchment. All the others did likewise, and by the time the Missive reached Crick he was forced to admit that it did have a distinctly genuine feel to it – not that he had ever possessed a real version himself, he thought, remembering the Halls of Knowledge. If only he had had one of these, perhaps he wouldn't have had to... A blood red image of the Wilder Rooms appeared suddenly before him: her twisted, lifeless body, staring into him...

'Suitably impressed, I see?' asked Tarryn, snatching back the piece of parchment and examining it smugly once again.

'Yes, it's – well done.'

And while the others continued talking Crick made his excuses and left through the trees behind the cart. He found a quiet spot out of earshot beside a fallen, rotted trunk, crouched down with his head held firm between his hands, and as quietly as he could manage, was sick as he hadn't been for many years.

*

Url woke them well before sunrise the following day. The evening had stayed warm and clear, the dense trees providing more than adequate shelter from the breeze which blew softly down the slope around them, so they had all slept outside beneath the blankets they had brought – Siu fortunately having thought to add one extra when Tarryn had arrived. They made time for only the briefest of breakfasts and then packed quickly and quietly, so that even as Url led them off

188

back down the hill and then north through the rest of the vale, there was still no sign of the sun. They were soon out of the hills and back once again amongst flat, open land; little around them but an occasional patch of woodland or a lonely stream.

'Bit of a boring part of the world, this, isn't it...' said Crick, sitting beside Url.

'Never underestimate the virtues of boring, lad,' said Url. 'I'll admit, I've forgotten them enough in my time. But boring's *safe*... Boring lets you sleep at night, and set off again in the morning without a cold sweat down your back.' He shifted in his seat, straight-faced and lost for a moment in the depths of some distant memory. 'No... give it a few days, and you may well be thankful for a bit of *boring*.' Crick smiled, but the look which lingered upon Url's face told him that the old man was as serious as he'd ever been.

Url's guess from the previous day was proved more or less correct as, just before noon, a thin black line appeared on the horizon, snaking east to west through the far-off grasses like a great worm.

'It's the river...' Url called back to the others; Aliya's head popping immediately through the curtains. 'If I'm right,' – there was a snort of laughter from Abetta – 'we should be just a few miles up from the Crossing.'

'We'll start getting everything ready,' called Orlando.

A few seconds later an assorted range of groans and the sound of someone retching sounded from the back of the cart; Yori bursting through the curtain holding his nose tightly, bringing with him a thick, disgusting waft of warm air.

'He's put it in the sack with the Heart...' he said, still pinching his nose, no need to explain that he was talking of the heavy sackful of dung they had collected the previous night. 'It's made it all hot and – well...'

'I'd wager we won't be in for too much of a problem at the Crossing!' called Tarryn. 'Missive or no! They're not going to go anywhere near this bloody thing!'

'You sure?' asked Crick.

'Would *you*?'

'Good, good,' said Url, smiling. 'You lot just sit tight,' he added with a half-contented laugh. Abetta's hand appeared quickly through the curtain to clip him hard on the top of his cheek. The horses reacted to his unintended shake of the reins, juddering clumsily into a canter, still finding their bearings when it came to manoeuvring the cart at speed. Url released them to their own pace, and after another hundred feet they were speeding swiftly, if not particularly gracefully, through the bright grass.

It wasn't long before the worm on the horizon began to shimmer and take on its more water-like qualities. And when they reached the precipitous, dandelion-strewn banks of the river itself, Url paused to allow the others the brief opportunity to get out and breathe. But while they all recovered, inhaling great gasps of fresh air as far away from the cart as they could, Crick and Url stayed seated where they were.

'The Outerlands...' Url breathed.

Crick said nothing. In the immediate fear and excitement of the past few days, the true nature of their journey had become somewhat veiled. But now, standing at the border of the Heartlands, it was all suddenly real. He may have seen the Outerlands before, but never had he seen them like this... This time he knew he would be travelling not briefly but instead deep into them. Deep into the full history and mystery of it all. There would be no safe camp or home to return to this night; no quick escape back to Fellgate. The grass on the other side of the broad river was the same green as here; the sky the same light blue. To be looking both into and away from the Heartlands like this, it was difficult to identify any clear differences to speak of. Yet somehow, as he gazed ahead and focused for a while solely on the opposing bank, a sudden quiet came over Crick; a coldness. The far grasslands, the trees, and the undulating mounds of dandelions: all were the same, but in that instant they all seemed slightly darker, as though lit by a half-shrouded sun.

'I'm glad you're all coming along with me,' said Url, quietly. Crick blinked, returning to the cart. For the first time, he saw real apprehension in Url's eyes.

'I can't speak for the others,' said Crick, 'but did you ever honestly think you'd be able to stop me from coming?' It wasn't enough to bring a smile to Url's face, but it softened it, at least; deep, worried lines smoothing into the soft leather of the skin around his eyes and cheeks.

'Absolutely not,' he chuckled. For a while longer he was silent, gazing out across the river, but then with a slow, deep breath he raised himself up in his seat, arching his back in a great yawn. 'Anyway,' he said, slapping Crick on the back, 'we'll make it through alright.'

Crick studied the old man. There was a determined, even desperate hope in his eyes, behind the smile and indomitable spirit that Crick had always done his utmost to emulate.

'You do make it sound simple,' he said, quietly.

'That's because it is,' Url answered without a second's hesitation. He looked to Crick, still holding his shoulder. '*Everything's* simple in life, lad...' But as he turned back to the Outerlands he paused again, his smile fading. 'It just... takes a while to work out how, sometimes...'

His sigh trailed into the gentle whispering of the river. Crick waited, uncertain what to say to lift the air around them, suddenly thick and heavy. But just as he was about to try Url gave a final grip of his shoulder, smiling weakly and sitting eagerly upright in his seat once more.

'Let's get going!' he called back to the others.

'I think I'll ride one of the horses,' said Tarryn, stepping resolutely around the cart.

'No. We need to make everything look as normal as we can. Once we're through we'll get rid of the muck, and you can ride wherever you like.'

So after the others Tarryn made his way grimly back into the cart; Crick doing little to hide his smile.

'Oh, stop moaning!' Crick heard his Mother say amidst more of Tarryn's groans. Yori shot once more out through the curtain, gulping for air. 'Wait until you have children... *then* you'll know the meaning of a bad smell!'

'Right...' said Url, pulling out the Missive from his pocket and checking it. 'Everyone ready?' There was swift, unanimous agreement along with muttered curses from Tarryn, so wrapping the reins firmly around his wrists and with a final nod to Crick, Url wheeled the horses to their left and set off briskly above the edge of the river.

*

It took just under two hours, but suddenly the water turned sharply away to the north, running half a mile or so before circling back south and then west onto its former path. And there at the far end of the loop a wide, flat bridge crossed the water; a dozen or so Guardsmen – more than Crick had hoped for – sat quietly around the southern end. All wore different shades of armour, and amongst them were varying sizes and types of weaponry. The small selection of axes, hastily-fashioned spears, a hammer, Orlando's cudgel and Url's hunting bow would all be of little value here if it came to it. The Guardsmen spotted the cart at the same time as Crick and Url noticed them: there was no time for anything but a brief whisper of '*Quiet!*' into the back from Url, smiling indifferently and gazing far along the river and across the bridge with what presumably was supposed to pass for cheerfulness. Crick could see straight through it; he could do little but hope that the Guardsmen would be more easily fooled. The one of the Guardsmen shrouded in solid black plate, sitting just to the left of the bridge, stood and held out a firm, shadowed arm as they approached. Streaks of silver were revealed around his flanks: the honour marks of one who had seen combat, and proved himself well.

'What business do you have here?' he called when they were fifty feet out. Though the voice was unfamiliar the tone struck straight to Crick's chest, resurfacing freshly-buried images of the training yard and Captain Saiak and other moments from his brief time in the City. His side and shoulders and anger burned again with the thoughts. He wondered if he too would have gained that note of bitterness and arrogance were he to have stayed much longer.

'Scavengers,' said Url. He let the horses amble on, pulling them up just before the black figure, waving the Missive casually.

The Guardsman walked over to Crick's side and reached up across him to take the crumpled parchment, and even through the stench from behind him Crick could smell the bitter odour of what must have been several days of accumulated sweat. He did his best to pretend not to notice it. The Guardsman studied the Missive, and as he did so he gestured with a swing of his thin, black sword to two of the others to search the back of the cart. Crick's heart began to hammer quickly inside him, seeming to take up far more space within his chest than usual.

'Where're you headed?' asked the Guardsman, pawing at the Mark of the Council suspiciously with the thick, dark fingertip of his gauntlet.

'The Caern fields,' said Url. Tarryn had suggested them the previous night. 'We're trying to –'

'For the love of...!'

'What *is* that?' came the voices of the two other Guardsmen from behind the cart.

'What's the problem?' shouted the first, looking up from the Missive.

'It's... I don't know, Captain.'

A *Captain*? This far out from the City? Crick saw Url's hand clench nervously, though fortunately the Captain didn't seem to.

'Come have a see, Sir!' called the other. 'Or a *smell*!'

'Don't move,' said the Captain quietly, marching round to join the others. Several of the other Guardsmen by the bridge were getting to their feet; some curious, others warily picking up their arms. Crick and Url leant back through the curtain, and over the Heart they saw the

Captain and the other two staring, disgusted, at the large, near-steaming hessian sack in the middle of the cart.

'What is it?' the Captain asked quickly through the cart to Url. 'And who're they?' he said, pointing around at the others.

'*That*,' said Url, nodding to the Heart, trying to add a hint of impatience, 'is a year's worth of moth-muck. Thirty-one different ingredients, to be exact. Many of which, I'm afraid to say, I am not at liberty to divulge – secrets of the trade, you understand. But the odour to which I assume you are referring is quite simple: It is the finest collection of the rarest types of deer, wolf, boar, lycan and water-vole droppings you will likely find in the Heartlands. And all of it, as I was trying to tell you, to catch sabre-moths. Fifty Silvers apiece for the wigs alone in the City now! *Fifty*! Stars know what people want them for…?' Crick's heart leapt, though Url seemed not to have realised… 'They taste about as good as crusted dog's tail! And until you've mixed them with half a dozen other items they're no good for anything, really…' He frowned into the sudden, strained silence, apparently oblivious to its cause.

'*Stars know…*?' the Captain repeated after a moment, eyeing him distrustfully, almost nervously. The other two had taken a half-step back, scowling. One of them leant round to the bridge, and with a sharp jerk of his arm waved the others over.

'A figure of speech!' said Url, laughing. Tarryn and the others had averted their eyes from the Captain, struggling to disguise their fear.

'Not one we hear often,' said the Captain simply. 'Especially not from those to whom the Council is supposed to have granted permission.'

'And they say Guardsmen don't have a sense of humour!' said Url, laughing again and jabbing Crick in the ribs. But his feeble attempt brought nothing but hardening glares from the growing number of rough, unfriendly faces around them.

'And *they're* the ones who get to spread it out once we get there,' Url continued, grinning to the others. 'You can join us if you want?' he asked the Captain. 'We can always do with an extra –'

'Open it up.'

For a moment Url stammered to conjure a response… They were getting too close. Crick saw the old man's hand moving slowly to the reins.

'Believe me, friend, you don't want us to do that,' Url tried, forcing another laugh. But the Captain had lost the little patience he had: He raised his longsword, and covering his mouth and nose with his other arm thrust it straight towards the opening of the sack... But the instant blade touched hessian a thick, heavy hiss ripped through the air from the turn in the river behind them. Crick saw the thin blur of the bolt as it approached, and at the back of the cart Aliya did too, diving for the floor... But it wasn't meant for her: With a great crack and a shrill shriek of pain it struck the Captain just above his elbow, punching straight through the hard metal and lodging itself deep within his arm; the weight of it throwing him against the corner of the cart before he collapsed in muffled agony to the ground, his sword clattering to the floor of the cart. With another enraged scream of pain he looked back, as did Crick, just in time to see a distant figure darting away along the river.

'*Get him!*' the Captain bellowed to the rest of the Guardsmen, all sprinting forward already from their positions and converging upon the cart with swords, maces, and bows drawn and aimed fiercely towards the family.

'*Him!*' the Captain screamed in blind fury, kicking the nearest of his subordinates hard in the direction of the turn in the river. 'Get my horse!' he shouted to another, and once the stamping beast and a black lance which must have been fifteen feet long had been hurried to him he charged off amidst the others, leaving behind only one of the Guardsmen who had first examined the cart. 'Deal with them!' the Captain snapped back angrily as he disappeared.

The remaining Guardsman stared open-mouthed after the shrinking black sculpture; the Captain like pure, condensed night gliding through the air. Url looked sideways to the Guardsman, and after a long moment's silence and indecision he and the cart were waved distractedly onwards.

'I'd heard –' Tarryn began as Url shook the reins, but a quick look from Orlando silenced him.

By the time they reached the far side of the water, the Captain and all but the one of his Guardsmen left on the bridge were out of sight around the river. In time with the pacing of the horses Crick's heart began to calm to something closer to its normal rhythm, and slowly the great silence they had entered into started to make itself felt around the cart.

'*Superb*, Url,' said Crick.

'I'll leave the talking to you then next time, shall I?' spat Url, though it was clear the anger was mostly at himself.

'There've been reports of attacks from within the realm against some of the Gates,' Tarryn tried again, studying with an eager glint to his eye the dark sword the Captain had dropped. The bulk of the straight blade was dull, matted black, hatched with even blacker lines so thin as to be unnoticeable unless turned into the light; while the very outermost of the edges glistened a deep, powerful silver. 'The Council loves them, in a way. Attacks on their authority like that give it all the excuse it needs to extend and intensify its hold over anyone who doesn't live in the City. And over those who do. I'd always rather assumed they made most of them up, but... it seems I was mistaken?'

'Well, whoever it was, they have forever the honour of my thanks and friendship!' said Url.

'And the rest of ours,' said Orlando. 'Let's get some distance between us,' he added, still watching nervously through the back of the cart as the bridge began to fade through the lengthening grass. Crick guessed that he was not the only one expecting the final Guardsman at any moment to be coming to his senses and making chase towards the cart.

'Did none of you see who that was?' asked Siu suddenly; an impatience in her eyes telling that she had been waiting for someone else to realise it too. Crick and Url turned back to her, alarmed by the frightened quiver of confusion in her voice. But it was Yori instead who spoke:

'It was *Aulan...*'

But seeing nothing now behind them, Crick turned instead ahead, looking deep into the strange new grasslands and skies as finally the cart made its first cautious advance into the Outerlands.

Chapter Sixteen

The Black Crown

'I'm telling you –' Siu interrupted, more adamant still than she had been with any of her many prior attempts, '– I could see it in the way he ran off… It was *him*. It was Aulan.' She leant back heavily against the canvas, frowning as she pressed away the hair from her brow, remembering once more what she could of the blurred figure.

Url had pushed the horses hard for nearly an hour, and through each quick mile the talk had centred almost solely upon what had happened at the crossing, and whether or not it had been Aulan they had seen. They all kept saying the same things, the others; each asking the same questions or answering with the same futile muddle of uncertain fact and fragment of memory in reply, prompting the argument endlessly round in long, hazy circles. And for all their words, none of them were important. None of the others seemed to have realised, caught up as they were within the stifling web of their confusion, that they were now completely, horribly surrounded. Although, perhaps it was better this way; better they didn't know. Sitting in the front corner of the main section of the cart, wedged purposefully tight amongst a tall array of heavy sacks and tools, Yori had been taking no part in the discussion around him. In truth the effort of merely keeping open his eyes was becoming almost more than he could bear. His apparent drowsiness, as it must have seemed to the others, had nothing to do with tiredness, however. Far from it, in fact. Rather, he felt more awake and more alert now than he had ever been in any memory he could currently recall. And sitting there, silent as the tall grass which flanked each side of the cart brushing lightly against the canvas by their heads, he could feel it now: the terror; the very source of nightmare, unfathomable in its scale and power. And all around them, watching them…

It wasn't *evil*, in the way most people said it was. But it was something just as terrifying. More so, even. There was no *desire* to kill, as such; no *desire* to harm or cause suffering… These things simply seemed to be all it knew. It would consume the family, like night consumed day, not out of hate, or anger, or cruelty, but because for it there was simply no other way. Yori could feel it so clearly… terrible, all about him, clinging to the very horizon of the world like a thick fog, watchful and ever-patient. The sensation was of being plunged finally into the icy depths of a terrible lake he had been told stories of all his life. And it was everywhere. All around them, beyond the silent gulf of the Nothingness through which they were passing, to which the others in their excitement were still largely oblivious, and beyond even the Black Wind itself, it was watching them. Darkness, complete and undiluted, pure and perfect in its ancient, unwavering form and purpose. Yori could sense no crash of recognition from within that far-off night; no sudden realisation that they had the Heart. But somewhere far within its deep slumber it could sense something new about them, and what they carried. It knew they were different, somehow, to those few fools who had ventured out here before. It knew, and far beyond the calm that the others could see a vast and terrible storm was surging and wailing; the Black Wind roused once more to action like an orchestra given life and fresh purpose by a conductor distant and veiled as yet from sight. They had brought the Heart into the Outerlands like a flame into a great cave, and whatever the beast was that lurked within the darkness, they would never be free of it. The only thing keeping them alive was the light of the Heart itself, unseen yet brilliant, shielding them from the dark creatures which the others, had they been quiet enough, could probably have heard around them, hiding, waiting; but no match at all for the power of what lay beyond, should it ever find them.

But watching, and waiting, were all that power was doing. For now, at least. As though studying them, curious, trying to work out how and why they dared challenge it so, and what it was that they possessed. Yori wanted suddenly nothing but to lie down and fall into sleep, to be woken once the journey was over, to look perhaps up and around him and find himself amidst the great fortress of Magical protection which was Iala. But he also knew, as he sat curled up breathing quick, shallow breaths unnoticed by the others around him, that as long as this darkness surrounded them, sleep would be entirely unattainable. He could see nothing, hear nothing, think of nothing but the cold, terrible power which was watching them. His arm was shaking, or maybe it was being shaken…

'Yori?'

He blinked, and after a moment saw his Mother by his side. Everyone else was watching him too. At least the wailing of their pointless arguing had stopped.

'What's the matter?' asked Url from the front.

'It's Yori,' said Aliya. 'He's cold, and… frightened.' She said it with concern – pity, almost – but this only angered Yori more. How could they all be so blind? Yes, he was frightened. But they should be too.

'Can't you feel it?' he murmured. Slowly he felt the cart shudder to a stop, Url appearing through the curtain beside him. They were all silent now. Perhaps they would hear it… 'It's everywhere.' He tried then to explain it to them. He tried to describe what it was that was watching them. But it was no use. He could tell they didn't understand. How could they? They would never truly understand… Not until it was too late. By the time he had finished talking, the frowns and blank stares of confusion were deeper than ever across their faces, but they did at least seem quieter, more solemn than they had been before. Perhaps that was something.

'Can we get going, Url?' asked Siu, folding her arms tight before her as though against a sudden chill, though the day remained unchanged. Only now did Yori notice that the grass, tall and thick as it was, had no smell to it. None of the gentle, warm aroma which should have been filling the cart and their senses since the bridge. Around the mound of provisions Url was staring at him with deep concern, scowling briefly until, without another word, he turned back through the curtain, starting the horses off again through the plains.

And while it may simply have been the grimmer atmosphere in the cart which made them take notice, the others too now soon began to point out the subtle changes which had begun to transform the look and the feel of the land around them; none of them particularly grand or threatening in themselves, yet somehow put together seeming to form a new type of landscape which none of the group had seen before, mirroring far better than words ever could the fear setting in throughout the cart. Small, colourless bushes and tall trees set apart from anything else began to appear amongst the hardening grass, while ahead the ground rose and fell into the beginnings of a rolling series of hills. The clear skies were even clearer now, yet somehow the sun seemed to be struggling to reach through them, lighting everything with pallid, lifeless tones. And there were none of the sweet smells and sounds of this time of year which Yori and the others had always taken for granted. The world they had entered into now was that of a half-remembered dream, or distant memory; all that which should have been colourful and clear now drained of the very soul which gave it meaning and purpose.

But at least the others were noticing it all now. Whether in the front beside Url or in the back around the silent warmth of the Heart, they sat there, each as quiet as Yori, waiting and listening for something they couldn't hope to understand as the cart trundled onwards into the bright, dreary afternoon.

*

They didn't stop at all that day, spurred as they were by the desire to forge as much distance as they could between themselves and that which until so recently had forever been their home. Lunch was eaten on the move, providing a brief distraction from their surroundings, but with that exception there was little to cheer their spirits. The low hills turned soon into a long, tumbling horizon, which one moment would be stretched out in front of them for thirty miles or more and the next would be hidden from view behind another steep, green slope. When evening came it drew in quickly around them, forcing them to climb the last few miles to the top of the hill they were on in darkness, helped only vaguely by a weak, dull grey segment of moon. It was as warm as it had been the previous night, but nevertheless Crick and Tarryn slept just beside the cart, while Yori and the others slept inside. They knew in truth that it made no difference where they slept, as long as it was not too far away from the Heart, but having even a thin wall of canvas between them and the outside seemed to make the others feel slightly safer, and one by one they each drifted off into an uneasy sleep.

Yori, however, did not. He closed his eyes, but all through the night he listened to the silence around him, and felt the darkness beyond. It didn't sleep either. Several times he thought he heard a noise of some description in the distance, and through the darkest hours of the night he could have sworn there was something moving behind the cart, but whenever he sat up to look wearily outside the silvery grass and bushes were calm and undisturbed as ever.

*

Again it was Url who woke first; Yori more than a little relieved to finally have the company, though he had not the energy to make any show of it. The two of them clambered out of the back of the cart and up into the front seats, upon the centre of which Url unfolded the pieces of parchment onto which Aulan had drawn the maps.

'Now then...' he said, studying the one closest to Yori. His old, harsh voice was more comforting in that moment than any other Yori could imagine. 'If I'm right –'

'Ha!' mumbled Abetta from somewhere within the cart. There were several sleepy laughs and the sound of Tarryn stretching and yawning loudly down beside them.

'– there should be a small village a few miles ahead of us,' Url continued, looking out across the valley. 'The other side of that next hill. There won't have been anyone there for years, but we might find some tools or something else of use. We can exchange them for your Grandmother,' he added loudly, receiving a muttered string of curses in reply. 'It's on our route, anyway. We –'

'*Ah!*' It was Tarryn. Yori looked back around the side of the canvas to see the enormous Guardsman scrambling gracelessly to his feet amongst the grass, recovering himself instantly to brandish the long, dark blade of the Captain's sword at the underside of the cart. 'Get back!' he shouted. Yori tried to ask what was wrong but Tarryn's shouting had awoken Crick who, after recoiling first from the sword Tarryn was thrusting towards him then turned and with one look beneath the cart jumped to his feet and fell back to Tarryn's side.

'Get out of the cart!' Crick called to the others; Orlando leaping from the back while Yori jumped down from the front, running to Crick before turning and looking back beneath the cart.

'I said *get back*!' Tarryn bellowed once again, lunging forwards and swiping between the wheels where, just out of range, the quivering, confused face of a man was peering out from the shadow... It was Aulan's. Beside him lay a slim but solid wooden crossbow and an open leather satchel, from which the sharpened tips of several dozen thick bolts were poking. Tarryn swiped forwards again...

'Wait!' shouted Orlando. 'Aul– I mean, it's... it's you, isn't it?' he asked gently, peering beneath the cart.

'Hmm? You know the fellow?' asked Tarryn.

'Who is it?' asked Siu as she and Aliya came round to join Crick.

'Yes, yes, we know him...' said Orlando, waving Tarryn back.

'Oh – Right!' said Tarryn, 'Well... um, delighted to meet you!' He added, withdrawing the sword and replacing it instantly with an empty hand. But Aulan made no move towards it.

'It's Aulan!' Orlando said to the others.

'What are you doing here?' Url called, looking through from the other side. 'It *was* you at the crossing, wasn't it? Why were you there? Why did you help us?'

'*How* did he get here?' asked Crick. 'He can't have outrun the Captain and all the others, surely? And even if he did, I thought we were supposed to have the Black Wind around us now...?'

'We do,' said Yori quietly.

'Well then how did he get through?'

Nobody could answer that. Nor could they get any other answers out of Aulan, who with difficulty Siu managed eventually to coax out from beneath the cart. He stood there, shivering pathetically as questions were thrown back and forth around him; no better idea why he was there, as far as Yori could tell, than anyone else did.

'We're not sending him back,' said Siu, pre-empting Url only by a second.

Url halted, open-mouthed, looking from her to the others who, Yori was relieved to see, all appeared to agree.

'We've got enough food,' said Orlando.

'For what?' said Url. 'The next few days? Perhaps – but what do we do after th-'

'Looks like he hardly eats anything, anyway,' said Aliya.

Url was still uncertain. He studied the tall, dishevelled man for some time, in which he seemed to find little to allay his fears. But at length with a final look around the others he relented:

'You keep a close watch on him. If he starts acting strange –'

'Strang*er*,' added Tarryn, grinning and frowning indecisively as he tried to judge how well his banter would be received by the newcomer. But if it was received at all, Aulan made no show of it.

'Quite,' continued Url. 'Anything strange or dangerous by him, and he's gone, Black Wind or no.'

Siu nodded, already reaching out slowly, smiling, to Aulan, realising as she drew closer to him just how much taller he was than she. After a moment he took her hand, allowing her to lead him gently towards the back of the cart.

*

They set off shortly after breakfast, having failed to encourage Aulan to do any more than look distantly at the food they placed before him. It was only now that the others were all awake that Yori realised how exhausted he was. As he rested against his Mother in the back of the cart, gazing as Aulan was doing at the largest of the sacks directly in front of him, he thought he heard someone ask if he was alright, or if he'd slept well, but he couldn't find the energy to answer, or even to care who had said it. Aulan himself sat with knees tucked firmly up into his chin on the other side of Siu, childlike wholly in manner if not appearance.

'See if you can get him to draw some more maps!' called Url, suddenly realising that there may be advantages to be gleaned from the added company. But for the moment at least there was nothing to get out of Aulan except an occasional half-smile or brief blink of recognition at them or their surroundings. Whether he knew where they were headed or not, there was little doubt he intended to stay, for now at least.

The northern slope of the hill was steep and rocky, and though the trees were small in number their roots surged up through the soil like giant serpentine sculptures, twisting hundreds of feet out across the ground as though scouring desperately for water. Many were nearly two feet thick above the surface, forcing Url time and time again to cut an awkward, meandering path through to the bottom of the hill. Seeing that the next slope looked equally troublesome, they decided instead to travel around its long but clear western edge. The sun rose higher behind them, but it continued to cast down the same weak light, so that it was only with the first clopping steps of the two front horses, Oden and Railer, that they noticed the path: a narrow, uneven, poorly-cobbled track, all but hidden beneath grass which had grown up thick between its stones, curving gently to the right to lead them slowly around the hill. After a further mile or so they came to a low wooden sign emerging from the ground to their right; thick beams covered even thicker with moss and trailing weeds, and rotting heavily around its base. Url jumped down and wiped the sleeve of his forearm back and forth several times across the surface of the wood, reading aloud the name beneath:

'*Byllam.*' Yori felt a flicker of memory within him as he spoke it, though neither he nor Yori could place it.

And half a mile beyond that, the village itself appeared ahead of them. Or at least, the remains of what may once have been a village. For even from a distance, it was clear that well before the slow decay of time Byllam had suffered a violent end. Nothing had been left standing. The framework of some few buildings remained, but the rest were scattered unrecognisably across the ground. A splintered post marked the beginning of the village, adorned with large hinges that once had held a second, much larger sign reading *Byllam*, with an engraving of the surrounding hillsides around it, now lying in several torn pieces against the skeleton of what could have been a large village hall fifty feet further on. Along the indistinct main street into the community they were blocked time after time by large timbers and lumps of metals, while beneath them a constant crunching and crushing announced their arrival as they rode slowly over and through the possessions of the people who once had lived here.

'Where *are* all the people?' asked Aliya. In all the destruction there were no bodies, no bones; no sign of any remains at all.

'They'd have fled to the border and likely the City before it reached here,' said Url.

'Or tried to, and died along the way,' said Tarryn with an indifference born of his past, which he tried silently to blink away as he felt the brief looks given to him by the others – all apart from Url, who instead was nodding grimly. For a moment a deep pang of pity for Tarryn outweighed and helped mask Yori's fear of their surroundings; the hard-featured, soft-eyed man had been raised into a thing far removed from who he really was. Who he hoped perhaps he still could be.

'So… This is what the Black Wind does,' said Siu. Url gave a bitter sigh…

'Oh, it can do far worse than this, my dear,' he said. 'This is but the most basic sign of its work.'

It was only as they travelled further along the street, winding their way deeper into growing mounds of debris, that they started to realise that somehow everything seemed to have been blown inwards, straight towards the centre of the village. Yori was ashamed to think it, but as dreadful as it was he couldn't help but marvel at the precision of it all. No painter, sculptor, architect or any other could have done a better job with the symmetry of the destruction: homes, monuments, fencing and all the rest of the village lying in long, sprawling lines, all at exactly the same angle to each other as though great care had been taken to make the obliteration of this small, powerless place as total and perfect as possible, more of the same being revealed with each wary step of the horses...

Suddenly as they rounded another bend a cold hand plunged fiercely into Yori's chest. It filled him with a horror which in that instant he didn't understand and couldn't see. All that it told him, all that he knew, was that he didn't want to go any further. He didn't want to see whatever it was they were going to find there… but it was too late to stop them: He shut his eyes tight as Url let out a stifled, sickened cry from the front.

'What is it?' shouted Orlando. Yori felt his Father leaning quickly past him up to the curtain before making a disgusted, retching sound of the kind that few things had the power to prompt in him. He paused a moment; the others waiting as he turned slowly back to them with a look of revulsion that Yori could feel clear enough without looking. 'It's okay,' he murmured, having to force the words. 'It's… nothing that'll harm us now. It's just… poor bastards…' He took a deep breath and left out through the back of the cart.

Hesitantly Yori opened his eyes; his Grandmother leaning past him now, muttering to herself…

'…what all this fuss is ab–' But with a heavy tug she pulled the curtains fully open and was silenced, seeing with Yori the horror which rose high and dark above them beyond the front of the cart…

They had reached the centre of the village. Once perhaps a pretty, colourful square of spongy grass and the peaceful comings and goings of this quiet place, it was now… Yori couldn't take his eyes off it, yet at the same time still he fought desperately not to see. They knew now what had happened to all the people. Url had been wrong. They had never escaped…

Finally the wreckage came to an end. It was piled in tall heaps at each of the several entrances into the square, leaving the ground of the square itself unspoilt. But there, like a crown more monstrous than any of even the worst and most savage kings of old had worn, a hundred black, curving stakes rose sharp from the soil; some wood, some metal, most just a foot or so apart, spiralling high and higher still into the air. Thick, dark, shimmering droplets seeped down from the tips of each of the points like lines of frozen, jet-black rain. And amongst them, impaled like beasts through hunters' spears, were the bodies. Dozens upon dozens of them, hanging in contorted, awful poses, their screams still written loud across the mangled flesh which lingered terribly upon their faces. Clothes seemed to have been seared away in all but a few places from their bodies, leaving thick, crusted burns beneath. Bones, white and black and dusty yellow, were visible where great chunks of flesh had been ripped savagely away. Limbs which had been torn from bodies hung separately on neighbouring stakes like the charms of grotesque jewellery. There was a young man, maybe Crick's age, who had been folded backwards and skewered through chest and legs, facing down with such wretched grief as even Yori had never imagined. What looked perhaps like families, some still grasping each other's blackened, rigid hands, were piled one above the other upon the same spikes. Some had been stuck through the sockets of their eyes; others through gaping, squealing mouths; and at the very top there were some

204

for whom the stakes passed up through their middles so that they sat, their heads and limbs hung limp, watching the cart and the family below them now. The ground, Yori realised, wasn't unspoilt at all: What he had taken at first sight to be dark soil covering the square was in fact a single wide stain of blood.

'How –' Tarryn began, but even he was forced to clear his throat. 'Why hasn't it all rotted away?' he asked quietly. 'This must have happened years ago. How are the bodies still…' he trailed into silence.

'I think I'd rather not know,' said Url. It was a thing Yori could not remember the old man ever having said before.

'It's alright, you're safe with us…' Yori heard his Mother whispering. He turned to see Aulan still with arms held tight around his knees, now rocking gently back and forth, staring fretfully at the Heart. His brow glistened with a new sweat; his skin flushed and trembling.

'We have to go,' Yori called to the others, breathing hard with the effort of raising his voice above the horror of the scene.

'Well said,' his Grandmother agreed, holding him briefly by the knee as she pulled herself away from the curtain.

Url made no argument, and climbing back up into the front seats he began to turn the cart around. But amongst the rubble and the narrow street the task was a difficult one. Crick and Tarryn, sickened but awestruck at the scale and brutality of the torture in front of them, still hadn't left the mound at the entrance to the square.

'Let's go!' Url shouted; Crick stepping slowly back, still staring ahead of him, hopping onto the cart as it shuffled awkwardly from one side of the street to the other.

'Tarryn, please, get away from it!' Yori heard himself call. But Tarryn instead moved forwards, peering beneath one of the bodies. If Yori had had the strength to jump out and tackle him he would have done, but as it was he could do nothing to stop Tarryn's foot falling upon the first stone of the mound. For a moment there was no noise, no movement, nothing… But then suddenly Yori felt new eyes watching them. He looked up…

One of the heads at the very top of the crown had lifted slightly; a young girl staring down at them now from her terrible seat with blazing red eyes. Tarryn had seen it too: he fell back, the others one by one screaming or gasping, Aulan beginning to moan and rock faster and more violently as Url struggled furiously to turn the horses. He called angrily to Tarryn who jumped finally to his feet, turning and running straight at the side of the cart; more heads twisting and eyes opening from high amongst the spires, all gazing down towards Yori and the others as with a great grunt of effort Tarryn thundered into the back end of the cart, lifting it a clear half foot from the ground and over the brickwork behind which the wheels had been trapped, diving into the back as Url whipped the horses hard a final, desperate time. They watched as the crown disappeared behind them, bodies writhing now like worms upon the stakes, red eyes following them, imploring them to return. They were in so much pain, but from Yori and the others all strength and courage had been lost; all focus turned for those breathless moments towards keeping the silence absolute as the cart bounced quickly out along the road, Yori fighting in vain to wipe the image of their pleading faces from his mind.

Without a word they rode back the way they had come and then swiftly around the outskirts of the village, until they found the street and then the cobbled grass-strewn path which led out the other side; saddened almost more than anything else by the final large, cheerful *Byllam* sign they sped past, doing what they could not to look at it. Only when the half-buried cobbles ended, and the village was hidden completely behind them, did they stop; the others still breathing heavily, gathering themselves, talking quickly and quietly now about what they had just seen.

And again Yori took no part in it. In the corner of the cart he huddled once more, tight between two sacks, overcome with the sudden unbearable weight of knowing just how incomplete his perception of the threat around them had been. His first feelings of the Darkness, when he had crossed into the Outerlands, were not wrong, perhaps. But they had told him far from everything. Even if he couldn't explain it he still believed, somehow, that the Darkness itself had no real malice; no real anger, or emotion. But the beasts, and spirits, and whatever else it was that it had consumed and transformed into the tools of its awful work… they were something else entirely. They had carried out their Master's bidding with such delighted detail... They had been infused with such terrible rage, and hatred; such an unquenchable thirst – almost a *need* – for suffering and death. They hated, in a passion no word or thought could describe, all vestiges of hope, or freedom, or joy left in the world. And they would never stop, never, until either they were put still further beyond the death within which they now existed, or else they had created a safe passage of destruction and darkness across the world through which their Master could journey at will. They were, in the truest and most vivid sense of the word, evil. And they were everywhere.

Chapter Seventeen

A Step Too Far

'Urlmaeus, we don't have a choice – *Look* at him…' And with that Abetta pointed angrily towards Yori, lying curled in Siu's lap, his wide, milk-white eyes starting to become broken by thin, jagged streaks of scarlet. Url sighed, smiling kindly at Yori, who could manage nothing but a blank stare back at him.

'I know…' He swore beneath his breath, though far more with sheer frustration than any malice held towards Yori. 'I just wish it didn't have to cost us half a day.'

'We'd do it if it cost us ten times that, Url,' said Siu, simply and quietly, stroking Yori's fine, blonde hair.

'I know,' said Url, 'I know. Of course we would. And gladly.' He smiled again to Yori. 'We can set off whenever you're ready.' He paused, catching sight of Crick, Tarryn, and Aulan on the far side of the cart. 'What *are* they doing?'

'Teaching him to duel,' said Aliya, who was sitting on the grass in front of the cart. Over her left shoulder she had been listening to the conversation between her parents and Url, while over her right she had watched with quiet amusement as her brother and Tarryn struggled, not quite in vain, to instruct Aulan in the use of weapons other than his own crossbow. They had started, foolishly, with the Captain's sword, but having speedily come within inches of decapitation Tarryn had quickly replaced it with a long stick he had found nearby. Even with this, however, Tarryn still was not having a particularly pleasant time of it. For while he was attempting to explain the finer delicacies of swordplay to Aulan, Aulan himself was quite content to periodically strike out at random and with a startling speed towards various parts of Tarryn. Encouraged by Crick's endless and growing roars of laughter, Aulan was – though not quite in the way Tarryn had intended – becoming rather adept in the basic but surprisingly effective drills of lunging and sweeping. Considering the difficulty of what he was putting up with, from Aulan and no less from Crick, Tarryn was showing an exceedingly patient and good-humoured nature. It was a new side of him, wholly uncharacteristic of the typical Guardsman Aliya had expected on first sight of him, and to her dismay Aliya found that she couldn't help but admire it. Perhaps she wasn't even trying too hard not to... She quickly cast the thought aside.

Url was still watching out into the north-west, down what seemed to be the last of the current range of hills and along what would have been the fastest route to the Firstway. Aliya looked instead slightly to her right, towards the point at which it seemed they would now be stopping first: a cluster of trees and a stretch of marshy ground due north, within a valley between two of the final hills amongst which, according to Aulan's map, at least, there was a small lake: the only place they could see anywhere around them in which they were likely to find a small, bright yellow plant called the sunmallow.

For it was three full days now since Yori had last slept. He said barely a word any more, and when he did it was only with a terrible, gasping effort. He hadn't moved from Siu's side all day. And sunmallow root, also known as dreampetal by those who took it more frequently, or for rather more non-medicinal purposes, was by far the most effective thing Abetta could think of to help him sleep. It grew in damp, shaded spots beside small areas of open water, and the lake to their north was the most promising of all the sites they had come or been close to since they had left the Heartlands. Abetta was still in the back of the cart, rifling through several of her bags, cursing herself in her own indecipherable tongue for failing to remember to bring some with her.

'Don't worry about it, my dear,' Url called back as they all climbed into the cart. 'We'll all start misplacing all sorts of things once we reach your age.' This time he dodged Abetta's slap through the curtain. She cursed him again, going back without a second attempt to the bags.

Aliya rode in the front with Url this time, sitting to his left; her Father on Url's right. Turning Oden and the others ruefully away from the path they should have been taking, Url set off down the hill; Crick,

Tarryn and Aulan each piling in turn into the back, like the energetic little boy Yori should have been.

*

To everyone else's delight as much as Url's it took barely an hour to reach the beginning of the wet ground which separated them from the lake. The grass and mosses bubbled quietly under their feet as they climbed down from the cart to examine it, and in places there were small pools from which a wide variety of plants were growing. The strangest were the enormous lilies, nearly five feet wide and curled upwards slightly at the edges, with bright purple streaks running across their surface and matching flowers growing tall from their centre, casting a thin shadow down onto the base below like wonderfully delicate sun-dials. They were the first pleasant things to look at Aliya could remember since leaving the Heartlands, though why and how any sign of beauty should be permitted to thrive here and nowhere else were questions neither she nor any of the others could answer.

On the way down they had seen a track raised slightly above the deepest of the marsh, running from one of the hills to their right through to the trees on the far side. And when they found it, it turned out to be easily wide enough for the cart. Crick and Tarryn walked ahead to make sure the ground was stable enough, but there were few problems getting to the other side. With a snort of suspicion from Railer they reached the end of the marsh, passed beneath the low-hanging trees, and found themselves beside a small, cool lake. It was utterly silent. Certainly it was no Lake Iris, but to Aliya it was a pleasant and familiar enough distraction from the uncomfortable peculiarity of these Outerlands nonetheless.

Abetta set off at once to scour the muddy banks to their right; Siu going with her, leading an uninterested Yori by the hand. Aliya was about to join Url and her Father who had walked a short distance in the opposite direction, but before she did so she couldn't resist taking a swift feel of the water. She had noticed since they crossed the border that the few small streams and rivers they had come to felt, in striking contrast to everything else, even more alive than they ever had done before, despite the fact that so far she had failed to see a single creature living in or around them. And this lake was no different: Dipping her fingers gently into the clear, shallow water which rested motionless by the bank her mind surged suddenly outwards, every stone, plant, and tiny ripple of wind upon the glassy surface suddenly as much a part of her consciousness as her own thoughts.

209

'Anything over there?' Url called over Aliya's head to Abetta, who shook her head and started walking back. Aliya had almost forgotten that they couldn't move much more than fifty feet or so from the cart. It was Url's rule, born apparently of a great deal of thought and research. But though Aliya was certain, or at least as certain as her newfound faith in Url's knowledge of the matter would allow, that there were good reasons for it, it was nonetheless highly irritating.

'You three take the reins,' Url decreed to Crick, Tarryn and Aulan. 'Lead'em slowly round this way. We'll walk beside and keep looking.'

Brief as it had been, the walk had sapped what little remained of Yori's strength. He stumbled, suddenly unable to take another step; Siu carrying him back into the cart with a quiet breeze of whispered comfort in his ear while Aliya, her Father, Url and Abetta each made their way carefully along the side of the lake, stepping up and down through shallow potholes and mounds of plant-life, all searching for the small, bright yellow flower of the sunmallow. All the while Aliya struggled to retain her focus on the task; the still water of the lake seeming to call to her with beautiful, silent cries. She would have given almost anything to go for just a short, uninterrupted swim. Anything, she thought, snapping herself forcefully from her desires, apart from her brother's wellbeing. She ignored the lake now, keeping it beside but apart from her, continuing resolutely through the mud and tangled undergrowth which surrounded it.

After another ten minutes, however, it was, predictably, her Grandmother who caught sight of it first: a tiny dot of yellow twenty feet away, nestled low amongst a thin break in a thicket of holly. She nodded back to the others, and with Url helping she set to work on the surprisingly complicated task of finding and extracting the root. Url also cut from around the central flower itself several of the outer petals, which were said to have the opposite effect to the root, able to wake a person from even the deepest slumber, or else instil in someone already awake such energy and focus as to make any task pass by swift and effortlessly, at least until the effects of the flower wore off.

'Will one be enough?' asked Crick, pulling the horses up level with Abetta, sitting back and taking the moment to enjoy a thin piercing of sunlight which had found its way through the trees.

Abetta smiled through gritted teeth; her arms disappearing up to her elbows into the mud…

'The root from a whole plant like this will be enough to put Yori and the rest of us into sleep for the best part of five days…' she grimaced. 'If I can – just – Ah! There we go…' And up through the squelching mud she pulled a thin, brown, slimy length of root, the width and length of her arm.

'Rather Yori than me,' Crick muttered.

'It'll be perfectly... well, not pleasant, perhaps,' said Abetta with a slightly affronted scowl. 'But drinkable, at least – once it's been cleaned and prepared. I might slip some in with your dinner – calm that overactive tongue of yours...'

'Don't think she won't do it, lad,' said Url, frowning as he stored the petals in the inside of his cloak. 'Believe me.'

'If you hadn't...'

Quite without realising it, Aliya found that she had been gazing once more into the lake. It was only now, as her Grandmother's voice halted, that she paid any mind to the conversation. Or rather, the sudden lack of it. All the others had fallen silent... For a moment Aliya thought perhaps that they were still watching Abetta struggle with the root, but even that sound had stopped. She turned back from the lake, seeing her Father, then Crick, then the others, all wide-eyed and frozen, staring out beyond the front of the cart...

Onto the track barely twenty feet ahead of them an enormous, four-legged creature the like of which Aliya had never conceived was stepping slowly out through the trees. Taller than the horses by several heads, its sleek fur was a long, shimmering mat of gold tinted a deep emerald as it moved, covering all but the features of its face and the thick, foot-long claws which curved out and downwards from its paws, cutting deep into the mud. Its long, thick tail was forked at the tip into two tiny red barbs which sliced as a whip through the air, seeming almost to spark as they flicked gently from side to side. As it turned its colossal head to face them a ridge of long, black hair was revealed, sweeping down from the tip of its large, rounded nose to the middle of its back. And its face... The eyes and mouth were black and striking, and as it breathed its thick, fleshy lips curled inwards slightly with the great rush of air, exposing rows of thin, curving needles which matched its claws. Yet, somehow, it seemed almost... not human, but close. There was something about the way it looked at them, studied them as it came to a gentle halt in the middle of the track which gave it a curious air of intelligence, or understanding, beyond anything that Aliya or the others could comprehend. It waited, watching them, rooted like a boulder into the bank, seemingly as much a part of the ground as the mud and ferns which drifted carefully about its great, golden feet. Aliya couldn't take her eyes off it to look around her, but she knew for sure that all the others were as petrified as she was. None of them were armed, though even if they had been their weapons may as well have been the playthings of children for all the use they would have been against this… what was it? Aliya had never heard of such a beast – not even in any of the tales of the Outerlands that Crick had brought back with him from his adventures, or those that Url had heard during any of his.

'*Yori*! *No!*' Aliya heard her Mother whisper frantically from the back of the cart. As Yori burst instantly through the curtain Aliya braced herself for some reaction from the creature… But the being simply swung its eyes calmly across to Yori, who stared back, awestruck, more awake and alive than he had been in days.

'Everyone stay still…' Url murmured, rather pointlessly.

'*Don't* try anything…' Orlando added in a hoarse whisper to Crick and Tarryn.

And still the creature studied them, staring into each of them leisurely in turn, never moving more than its eyes and its slow, pendulous tail. In contrast to the slow, measured breathing of the beast Aliya could hear the short, frightened gasps of everyone around her, and was suddenly conscious of her own. The horses were stunned beyond fear, frozen in the sight of the first creature they had ever seen to be larger than them. A glint of sunlight flickered suddenly down from the trees across the deep black eyes, and for an instant they turned a familiar, pale white. Then, as calm and quietly as it had appeared, the creature turned with a final swing of its tail, stepped once towards the trees, and was gone.

Aliya shook her head as if waking from a dream. Nobody knew what to say. They stared at the spot where it had vanished without trace of sight or sound through the thick branches.

'Well, I'm… Um, I'm done here,' said Abetta quietly, still holding the root out before her. 'Shall we?' Url looked sideways to her, unable to find the words he was searching for. He simply nodded. Quickly and silently they scrambled out from the mud and back into the cart as Crick attempted to convince the horses to start moving. He spoke encouragingly to Railer, but it was Oden who finally broke from his fear, blowing and shaking his head gently at the others before turning under Crick's direction and trotting quickly with his three companions back for the trail through the marsh.

There were many things which Url in his many years had become good at, but not once in his life had he ever been, or pretended to be, a good passenger. Along with Aliya and the others he kept watch behind and beside them as they crossed the marsh, but as soon as they found firm ground once more around the base of the hill he called to Crick to stop, retaking his place at the reins and directing Aulan into the back.

'Okay – So what was that?' asked Tarryn. 'Anyone?'

Nobody even attempted an answer. Nor could any of them see where the creature had gone: The most newborn of wolf-pups would have struggled to hide amongst the openness of the marsh, let alone anything close to that size. Yet somehow it had vanished completely.

'Pass my bow through,' said Url.

'And the sword,' said Tarryn.

'And anything else that's got a sharp end…' said Crick.

'I fear that even you three noble warriors may struggle against it if it decides to be less friendly,' said Siu, but she passed the weapons through swiftly nonetheless.

Aliya peered out through the front of the cart as they rode on in silence, the others keeping watch from the back. All except Yori, who once again had collapsed into Siu's arms, his eyes brighter, wider, and more exhausted than ever.

*

Once they were well out of sight of the marsh and the lake, and back on their former track towards the Firstway, they stopped again; Abetta setting to work quickly on a fire to boil the sunmallow root into something more or less drinkable, having finished cleaning and dicing it since the lake. Aliya and the others, meanwhile, set to work instead on an eagerly-anticipated lunch.

'I suppose it might just not have been hungry…?' said Tarryn after a few minutes, through a large mouthful of fruitcake.

'Enough!' said Siu – not at what he was saying, but at what he was eating. 'You'll have finished it before we're a quarter of the way there!' She smiled beneath her frown as she pulled the rest of the cake from Tarryn's grasp; his deep, grey eyes watching it mournfully as it disappeared.

'*May just not have been hungry*…?' said Url derisively. 'Lad, creatures of the Black Wind don't just stop attacking because *they're not hungry*!'

'Well it's probably not a creature of the Black Wind, then, is it,' said Aliya.

Url looked at her, struggling for an answer…

'It has to – I mean, it can't *not* be a creature of the Black Wind. *Nothing* can live above ground like that out here without being part of it.'

'*We* are,' said Crick.

'We've got the Heart,' said Url.

'Maybe it's got something else?'

213

'Something else? There's only one Heart, lad.'

'How do you know? You're not *quite* old enough to have been there when Magic was introduced to the world...' Url threw a half-chewed lump of bread at him, realising the foolishness of such a waste even before Siu's scowl informed him of it. 'What if there's more?' Crick continued, dodging the attack. 'Or some other things which can protect against the Black Wind. Up in the Tower I saw desks full of –' He paused, staring deep into the grass in front of him.

'Full of what?' asked Url, but Crick was lost in thought.

'Just... different things...' he mumbled. 'Things that could have been anything – protection against the Black Wind, for all I know. Or for all *you* do.' He said nothing else. There was something wrong with him; something had happened in the City. But Aliya knew her brother well enough to know that he would never talk about it in front of everyone like this. Anything he tried this hard to bury within him would never be brought out by force or direct questioning. She would have to wait for a better time.

'It's almost ready, dear,' called Abetta. 'Stay there, I'll bring it over,' she added as Siu made to stand, Yori still held awkwardly in her arms.

'There are devices and Magics of the past which were rumoured to ward off the Black Wind,' Url said thoughtfully to Crick. 'But none that could shield a being forever. And none, that I have ever heard of, which were in the possession of a *creature* like that...'

'That was quick,' said Orlando, as Abetta carried over a small glass full of a thick, dark liquid which trembled oddly as she walked but was just slightly too viscous to spill over the sides.

'Doesn't want boiling for too long, sunmallow root,' said Abetta. 'It starts losing its effectiveness once it's in the water. Now –' She helped prop Yori up against Siu, who stroked his clammy forehead and kissed his hair. 'This won't taste particularly good,' she admitted with a kindly smile to Yori, 'but it'll do well for you.' Carefully she lifted the glass to his lips; Yori relenting after several weak groans of displeasure and taking a small, resigned sip. By the grimace which shook through his entire body it seemed fair to guess that the concoction tasted as bad as it looked, but Abetta and Siu persevered for several minutes, feeding and comforting him with slow, patient words and movements until finally the glass had been drained.

'Well done, son,' said Orlando, holding Yori's arm.

'It shouldn't take long,' said Abetta, wiping out the black residue from the bottom of the glass with the tip of her finger, and in a quick and practiced movement forcing it beneath Yori's tongue before he

214

realised what was happening. He gagged and tried to spit it out, alive with anger for a moment, but as quickly as he had sat up he collapsed back against Siu, his eyes drifting to a close, spitting in a feeble effort which dribbled down his chin. Kissing his matted hair again, Siu wiped it clean. He hadn't noticed any of them, standing close around him, their faces collapsed with anguished frowns, as they continued to be until Url hesitantly broke the silence:

'We should get going again,' he said, able this time to make it sound like suggestion rather than command as he smiled sadly to Siu, who nodded, still stroking Yori's cheeks. 'Sort the horses out,' Url added quietly with a pat of the back to Crick. They had let all four of the animals off their main attachments so that they could wander more or less freely for a while, though still tied by long ropes to the cart. Crick, Tarryn and Aulan began to gather and refasten them into position.

'How long will he sleep for?' asked Aliya.

'Impossible to tell…' said Abetta, with a long sigh. 'Maybe a day or two. I didn't give – I didn't give him much!' she repeated, having to shout the last few words above the complaining of one of the horses, which was refusing stubbornly to return into its place. Once again, Aliya saw, it was Railer who was causing the problem, stamping and neighing loudly, rearing away from Aulan's nervous efforts to calm him.

'What's the matter with you this time?' she asked impatiently, walking round to his front; Crick and Tarryn both occupied with Crash and Nightwind. But as she approached he reared up once more, this time breaking free of Aulan's grip, charging… Aliya felt a sudden weight against her, knocking her to the ground as the hoofs of the stupid animal thundered past, scarcely inches from her face.

'I – uh, thank you,' she breathed, winded but still conscious enough to blush at the figure staring down at her. He was quite handsome, close-up...

'Any time, my l–' Tarryn began, climbing to his feet and lifting Aliya easily and firmly to hers, but a sharp *crack* from behind him had caught the word in his throat: Railer had galloped the length of his rope; the bolt around which it had been tied sheering off and skipping quickly away across the ground behind the senseless creature. Before anyone could stop him Crick in a flash of movement had unfastened and mounted Crash and was speeding after him.

'Crick!'

'*No!*' shouted several voices at once.

'*Damn* that boy!' Aliya heard her Father growl.

In an instant Crick had almost drawn level with Railer, but they were getting too far away...

'Crick!' she called, as her brother came within a foot, reaching out...

But from a gorse thicket just ahead of him there came a piercing, awful shriek. Railer and Crash both stumbled to a halt without command, stamping nervously at the ground; Crick and everyone else staring breathlessly into the bushes... Url stepped forwards, bellowing angrily:

'*Get back here n–*'

A flurry of glinting edges several feet wide flew suddenly over the thicket, touching the ground lightly but not stopping; terrible snarls coming from a head of steel, its bright red eyes motionless amidst a dozen bent and twisted legs – if they could be called that – all sharpened into cruel, bloodthirsty ends, circling and flailing frantically around its body, carrying it like a raging squall of blades towards Crick.

'*A khaion*!' Tarryn screamed, aghast but drawing the sword from beside him and charging out towards Crick nonetheless. Railer had fled, but as Crick fought to turn Crash she tripped and buckled terrified beneath him, pinning his left leg to the ground with a great gasp of pain. Tarryn was sprinting fast but the beast got there first: Climbing over the horse it began to slash and bite savagely at Crick, who in his shock could do nothing but try and shield himself with his right arm. It wasn't enough; Aliya's stomach lurching as the sound of claw on bone and flesh sounded unbearably through the air followed instantly by Crick's dreadful screams. An arrow whistled suddenly past Aliya's ear but flew too long – but the thick bolt which followed it found its mark, hitting the beast's face with another piercing shriek. It looked up and charged again, crashing straight through the still-running Tarryn as too late he prepared to take a mighty downwards swing at it, bounding on towards the cart. Bolt followed arrow once more, each glancing hopelessly off the swirling blades. Url and Aulan reloaded as quick as their hands would work but the beast was all but upon them... But as it shrieked and leapt once more a streak of brilliant silver shot out through the curtains of the cart, striking it in a blinding flash from which nothing but a fine dust emerged, vanishing as it drifted slowly to the ground. For a heartbeat the skies around the group and the cart had been filled by a great scream of wind and confusion; the Heart blazed and snapped like lightning for a moment, and then all was silent.

'Crick!' screamed Siu, running off towards him without thinking.

'Go!' Url shouted to Orlando and Aliya. 'I'll bring the cart!'

From the corner of her eye Aliya saw Abetta leading the confused and frightened Aulan onto the cart; Url scooping Yori into his arms and carrying him into the front, snatching up the reins of the two remaining horses. With every racing step closer Aliya could see more of her brother, and more of the blood which covered him, lying motionless for a moment beneath a terrified, flailing Crash as she climbed awkwardly to her feet, her flank pierced in several places and matted a thick red. Tarryn joined them, clutching his chest, and with the cart coming up behind them they made the last few feet to Crick's side; Siu diving towards him but recoiling just short, afraid to touch him.

He seemed to have been cut everywhere but the leg which had been trapped; several deep, wet wounds flowing freely amongst what looked to be a thousand smaller, savage slashes. There was barely a patch on him which wasn't staining a deep crimson; clothing ripped and indistinguishable in places from the exposed pulp of his torn flesh. He writhed suddenly against the blades which were no longer there, overcome with shock, flinching as a brief, sickening scream found its way back from the beginnings of the chestnut-woodland into which Railer had disappeared. Had it not been for the distress in her brother's eyes, and also perhaps a slender admission of pity she felt in her own heart, Aliya would have smiled with bitter delight at the knowledge that it was the last they would see or hear of the stupid animal.

Chapter Eighteen

The Firstway

'Well, I'm afraid if you thought the sunmallow root looked bad…' said Abetta, bringing over a steaming tankard of a thin, dark green liquid, '…wait until you've tried this.' It took a great deal to bring such a grimace to her eyes, though she hid the look as soon as she realised Crick had seen it.

'Serves you right,' said Url to Crick's look of horror at the brew held up before him.

'Leave my poor boy alone,' said Siu, brushing Url aside and lifting Crick's reluctant head up into the bend of her arm. Crick scowled but drained the tankard in one, gasping for a moment afterwards.

'Quite – quite something…' he spluttered, attempting a grateful smile to his Grandmother. 'It would go down well at Gerome's,' he added to Tarryn.

'Ah! A shame I've none to enjoy myself, then!'

'Get yourself hurt like that and I'd be *delighted* to make you some,' said Abetta absently, studying Crick's reaction to the potion.

'Should we check his cuts again?' asked Aliya.

'He'll be alright until morning,' said Siu. 'Just don't move around too much,' she added to Crick, who acquiesced without argument, nodding and leaning back with a weary sigh.

'You know how lucky you are, don't you?' said Orlando, quiet and straight-faced.

'I know,' said Crick, scowling with the memory. 'But I *couldn't* just let Railer go… He didn't know what he was –'

'He wasn't worth risking your life for!' snapped Orlando. 'Next time just do what you're told!' The silence which spread through the others was instant and total; it wasn't often that Aliya heard her Father speak like this. 'I've let things go in the past that maybe I shouldn't have,' he continued, seeming to choose his words carefully despite his anger, 'but out here you can't keep acting like that! You're going to get yourself or one of the rest of us killed.'

Crick nodded, his frown settling after a few deep breaths into an accepting sorrow. Orlando looked down at him kindly; he opened his mouth again, but whichever words he had been considering never came. Instead he merely shook his head and strode wearily away to the back of the cart.

'He's just worried about you,' said Siu, quietly. 'We all were.'

'– *are*,' Abetta corrected. 'But at least that thing didn't hit anything important.'

'Um –' Crick pointed incredulously to his face, where the worst of the long slashes across his upper lip and cheek had only just stopped bleeding, and several other scabs and bruises had already formed.

'Like she said –' said Url, '– nothing important.'

Crick tried to throw a nearby stone at him but it fell limp from his hand as he was reminded fiercely of the number and depth of the gashes his right arm had taken, many of which were still weeping through the thick layers of bandaging his Grandmother had applied. His chest and the side of his ribs had fared little better.

'Yori, on the other hand…' sighed Url, looking back to the cart.

'I still can't work out what's wrong with him,' said Abetta. Her voice was quiet, and she fumbled nervously with the tankard that Crick had handed back to her. 'He… I *think* he's asleep. He *has* to be, with the sunmallow root. And he hasn't moved or said anything.' She looked anxiously to the back of the cart, into which Orlando was leaning, whispering to Yori. 'I just… don't know why his eyes keep opening like that… He looks so scared.' To see her as openly concerned as this was almost more frightening than any of the rest of the day's events.

'He saw the…' started Siu, looking to Tarryn.

'*Khaion*,' said Tarryn. 'Apparently they're seen quite often around the borders. They told us they were dangerous, but they never said they'd be anything like that.'

'Well I think Yori saw it attack Crick and charge towards the rest of us just as the sunmallow was putting him to sleep. It's as though his

219

body's dead to the world, but his mind just can't close down. He's terrified – in a half-sleep, unsure which way to go, or maybe how to get out of it. I – I don't know what to do...'

'Shouldn't we try bringing him round?' asked Aliya.

'The petals,' said Crick, nodding.

'I don't know if it would be that easy,' said Abetta. 'Or what harm it might do. I've never seen anyone like this before.'

'Just let him rest a while longer,' said Tarryn.

'But that's my point,' said Siu. 'I don't think he *is* resting. I think he's just...' she looked to Abetta, 'trapped.'

'If he hasn't come out of it by tomorrow evening, I'll try and wake him,' said Abetta. Tears were welling in Siu's eyes as she nodded, leaving one injured son to go and check on the other.

'Not one of our better days,' muttered Url, stretching out a crick in the side of his neck, shrugging as he looked around him. 'I don't think we'll be going any further this afternoon. Let's set up here; we can start early tomorrow.'

They had moved only a few miles from the field of the attack, just far enough so they were out of the grasses around which the clusters of trees and bushes of the type from which the khaion had pounced stood like dark, unknown hiding places for the creatures of the Black Wind. They rested now atop a small rise at the beginning of a wide, open stretch of heathland, from which they could see clearly for many miles around them across the sandy, gently-undulating ground; gorse and bracken growing thick and impassable in places, but the pale yellow tracks which twisted through them like an enormous, low maze meaning nothing could approach the rise without being seen. As the skies began to darken a fire was struck by Tarryn in a small depression in the ground just before the rise, and a late dinner produced; Aliya tending to Crick while Siu and Orlando kept silent, constant vigil over the comatose Yori.

For the first time since leaving the Heartlands, the meal was eaten in several different groups; Siu and Orlando staying in the back of the cart; Aliya and Tarryn sitting beside each other, helping Crick; Url leaning against the front wheel of the cart, poring over the next section of Aulan's maps, questioning Aulan beside him; while Aulan himself chewed slowly and absentmindedly on a tough strip of dried pork, seeming more at ease than any of the rest of them. Abetta had only a small slice of her seeded bread, before curling up beneath a blanket which Url threw to her and saying no more.

'I think Tarryn's got an eye for Aliya,' Orlando said quietly and seriously, wiping the beads of sweat from Yori's forehead.

'I think she's got two for him,' said Siu.

'Well I think I'll keep both *mine* on *him*.'

'I don't know – she could do worse,' said Siu, almost smiling as she let a drip of water fall gently from the cup to Yori's lips. 'The way he protected her like that – It was very… gallant.'

'I'll keep an eye on him…' Orlando repeated.

'No… *here*,' Url was saying outside, lifting the pencil which Aulan was holding and dropping it back lightly onto the line of the Firstway. 'Isn't there anything else you can remember about the road?' he asked with mounting frustration, brushing the clear space at the top of the parchment. 'Or anywhere else up this way?' But again Aulan's focus remained entirely on the selection of blackberries in his left hand; the right moving sightlessly across the map to trace around a series of hills he had already drawn several times over.

'Leave him be,' called Aliya as Url groaned again, massaging the bridge of his crinkled nose.

'Besides,' Tarryn was saying to Crick, polishing the edge of the sword already gleaming in the firelight, though spoilt slightly by a new and sizeable notch just above its middle, 'I'll expect the same degree of thoughtless self-sacrifice from *you* when it's my turn to get into something like that.'

'Which doubtless won't be long…?' enquired Aliya.

'Indeed. So you may want to keep your thanks to yourself for now, young Crick.'

'Well, thanks all the same,' said Crick. 'And you two,' he called to Url and Aulan. Url gave a quick nod before bending back over the maps; Aulan looked up after a swallow of blackberries, waving enthusiastically the crossbow which had remained proudly by his side all afternoon. The bolts, returned to full number following a thorough scouring of the field by Aulan after the khaion's attack, lay clean and freshly-sharpened beside him.

'You think we'll be attacked again?' asked Aliya.

'As long as your brother's around I'm quite sure of it, yes,' said Tarryn.

'I'll try and send them your way, next time,' said Crick, grimacing as he tried to sit up.

'Sure it's not broken?' asked Aliya, nodding to his leg. Just above the knee it was swollen and heavily bruised beneath the thick layer of sweet-smelling salve that Abetta had applied. Crick nodded back, a trace of uncertainty in his eyes.

'Saiak didn't quite get it right about khaions, did he...' Tarryn reflected. 'What was it he told us? *Just lunge at the middle of them... Strike 'em hard and they'll go down...!*'

'You were the one with the sword,' Crick muttered. 'Perhaps you should've just made better use of it?'

'*Perhaps* you're not quite as strong as you think you are...?' said Aliya to the Guardsman with a playful smile, taking care not to let Crick notice.

'And why exactly is it that *you've* inherited that sword, anyway?' asked Url, apparently having given up on the map.

'Because I'll be damned if I'm going to see it in *his* hands!' retorted Tarryn, slapping Crick's thigh gently with the end of the sword – though rather too firmly for Crick's comfort. 'Look at the job he made of turning a horse around! Once he's mastered that, *then* I'll consider letting him play with my new toy.'

Despite Crick's injuries, Yori's unknown sickness, and the fact that once they reached the Firstway they knew they would be without a map or anyone who knew the road until Irraigion, it was for this moment at least a quiet, peaceful evening. A fine, warm drizzle appeared once the sun had set like a soothing veil around them, freshening the air and making everything seem, somehow, far simpler. Not easy, certainly; but at least not as overwhelming as it had been a few hours ago. Aliya, standing for a long while with her face turned up into the rain, could sense nothing but the quiet of the heathland around them. Tarryn set up a shelter against the side of the cart, beneath which he, Orlando and Aulan were well protected; the others making their beds in the back. And lulled by the gentle dripping of the rain they each fell into welcome, easy sleeps, taking them through, uninterrupted, to the morning.

*

There was a clean, crisp bite to the air when they woke. They had not, as Url had intended, started early; Url now furious with himself for allowing them to sleep until nearly mid-morning. But even his curses as he marched gruffly around the cart ensuring everything was packed and ready to go did little to spoil the atmosphere. Crick, though far from mended, had regained a measure of his energy, stumbling or crawling around doing what little he could to help, though deciding without much consideration to allow the others to deal with the horses.

There were just two things which troubled the group as they set off after their late breakfast. The first, and most serious, was Yori. Still just as he had been since witnessing the khaion's attack, his body was

222

rigid, but with a fever and a look of terror in his eyes about which, along with the others, Abetta was becoming increasingly concerned. She kept a wet flannel pressed gently to his forehead and rubbed his chest in soft, circular movements, muttering in turns to herself and to him, rarely taking her eyes off him.

The other problem was the sandy ground, through which the horses, one fewer now than there should have been, soon began to struggle to drag the thin wheels of the cart. Still caught between a sadness for Crick and irritation at the difficulty Railer had put them in, the others made no comment. The rain had stopped before they woke, having hardened the sand in places into dark, firm tracks which made the going easier, but this rarely lasted more than a few feet before the wheels would begin to slip and sink once more. They made slow progress, creeping their way forwards through what turned out to be an extremely wide stretch of similar such terrain, often having to get down to dig out a wheel or clear some gorse from the underside of the cart. After nearly half the day was gone their surroundings looked virtually the same as they had done before they had started.

'Not to question your navigational competence,' said Tarryn, emerging through the curtain behind Url, 'which I'm quite sure is perfectly sound,' he nodded earnestly, 'but are you *absolutely* certain that we're not going round in circles?'

'That's the second time, lad,' said Url flatly. 'Didn't amuse me then, and doesn't amuse me now. Once more and I'll be finding a good use for that new sword of yours.' It may well have been a joke at Url's expense the first time he had mentioned it, but in truth this had been a rather more earnest enquiry; Tarryn nonetheless retreating wisely without another word.

The sun tracked slow above them as they forced a path due west for the remainder of the afternoon. Apart from several short breaks of necessity they stopped fully only once, by a small, sandy, muddy pond, so that Crick's dressings could be cleaned and changed as best they could. The two deepest cuts across his right forearm were still weeping, but Abetta's handiwork was holding, and no more blood had been lost. Many of the other injuries, especially the slash across his face, were still raw and painful, and the bruising especially around his thigh had become particularly striking. But on the whole, as everyone remained keen to remind him, Crick had been extremely lucky. Tarryn and Aliya took great pleasure in assisting Abetta's thorough cleaning of the wounds with twice-boiled water from the pond, followed by the application of a thick, off-white paste she concocted from a combination of several ingredients from her bags, mixed carefully together in a small bowlful of water; Crick receiving dispassionate glares of *serves you right* for every groan and squirm he let slip. It was only after another long ride, the sun sinking low ahead of them, that finally they saw the silhouette of the forest they had been aiming for, drawn from this distance like a straight and level line of pinpricks across the smooth, deep orange horizon.

'Want to try and get through tonight?' asked Orlando, sitting in the front beside Url. Url was already studying the map again.

'According to this,' he said, frowning at the crumpled parchment, 'it isn't that wide. But I think we've left it too late.' He squinted ahead of him, his face and the canvas behind him lit a bright red. 'I don't fancy getting stuck amongst a close forest like that at night, Heart or no.'

'I don't think the horses can make it much further, anyway,' said Aliya, leaning through the curtain. The three animals had endured an exhausting day in the sand, which barring a small number of exceptions had refused to relent in its awkwardness. Thick steam was rising into the cooling, early-evening air from their backs and necks; each tiny drop of moisture visible and shimmering vividly in the last of the heavy sunlight.

Talk turned once again, as it had several times throughout the day, to the magnificent creature which had emerged and vanished by the lake, as another evening's camp was set up amidst the heathland which everyone now was growing weary of. Without the rain the sand was loose and even more difficult than it had been, catching the wheels in hidden and deceptively thick drifts. It took Tarryn, Aulan and Aliya almost an hour to clear the front and underside of the cart of the mass of sharp, awkward bush which had built up slyly in each and every awkward nook of the wheels and axle since the morning.

'Were you *aiming* for this stuff?' called Tarryn from somewhere beneath the cart.

'For a big lad you certainly moan a lot about a little bit of work!' answered Url, lying back against a blanket he had placed upon a bank of sand, watching as Orlando carried Yori from the cart.

'Thought he could do with some air,' said Orlando quietly.

'Bring him here…' said Url, and as Orlando gently handed down his son, Url wrapped the edge of the blanket around him, leaning him gently in to his side.

'I'll try making some for him if you want…' said Abetta, seeing Siu looking towards her. 'But I still think it's best just to leave him be. He'll come out of it when he's ready; I don't want to force him.'

Siu was far from certain, but she nodded, and went back to holding together the dead bracken which they were using for tinder; Crick persevering stubbornly with the flints.

'Why is it,' he said, between grunts of effort with his uninjured hand, 'that of all the Magics we're supposed to enjoy a fondness for, *none* of us is any use when it comes to the making of fire?'

'You're just not doing it right…' said Aliya, leaving the last of the cart for Tarryn to clear, taking the flints from Crick and striking them hard together; a single, tiny spark flicking out and dying instantly into the air.

'Oh! No – you're right, that's much better, thanks,' said Crick, warming his hands against the awaiting mass of tinder.

'And there's nothing wrong with those flints, before you start finding excuses,' said Url. 'They've been serving me well for months. If there's no fire, it's nobody's fault but your own.'

'But why couldn't we have brought someone like – that old miner… The one who used to help us burning the fields each year…?'

'That *old* miner was *younger* than me, so watch you tongue. His name was Jerrikha.'

'Yeah, him – why couldn't we have found someone like that? He could conjure fire from nothing!'

'Not *nothing*.'

'Maybe not, but it was close enough…'

'Well either way *you* can't and neither can the rest of us. Just get on with those flints. Unless… My dear –' Abetta looked up suspiciously from her brief rest by the back of the cart, taking a deep breath… 'Watch the tinder a moment, would you?'

'Why?' she answered flatly, paying a brief glance to the bracken beneath Siu's hands.

'No – really *stare* at it…' said Url, holding his hand out to the tinder as though expecting a great inferno to burst forth from it any second. 'Give it one of your best *glares*… Go on…'

'If you weren't armouring yourself with a defenceless child, old man…'

'Yes! That's the one!' Url exclaimed, pointing to the ample scowl which Abetta was casting now towards him. 'Just aim it – a little – that way…'

Abetta couldn't help but release a smile as the others all laughed, though an hour later Url was certain that a sizeable portion of sand seemed to have made it's way into his serving of potato soup. Under Abetta's watchful eyes he smiled, and ate it anyway.

225

*

The next day began as early as Url had intended that the previous one should; Url setting the horses off at a quick pace, determined they should reach the forest and be out of the sand as soon as was possible. As the gloriously lit outlines of the treetops grew tall and wider, the horses also seemed to sense that easier ground lay ahead, battling well against the terrain as it rose and fell with increasing jaggedness across these last few miles. Just after mid-morning, reaching the top of yet another steep rise, the forest suddenly seemed to be upon them: A vast, unbroken wall of towering spruce, stretching as far as could be seen in either direction.

'Can you feel it?' said Siu, with gentle breaths of the air above her. Aliya looked across at her Mother questioningly.

'The forest...' said Orlando, in a slow, awed tone. 'It's so – I don't know what the word is...'

'I don't think there is one,' said Siu, her eyes now closed, her head swaying almost imperceptibly from side to side as she followed the dark green wall in either direction. 'It's... ancient. Enormous...'

'That it is,' said Url from the front. 'We're at the mid-point of a sand-timer: To the north and south it spreads out and keeps going well off these maps, but just here it looks to narrow to ten miles or so – maybe less.' He looked to Aulan for the confirmation he knew would never come, but Aulan didn't even give the enthusiastic smile which Url and the others were becoming accustomed to. He was huddled low in his seat, looking up anxiously into the trees ahead of them.

'What's wrong with him?' asked Orlando.

'No idea,' said Url. 'We'll be through there soon enough,' he added with a reassuring slap on the shoulder to Aulan, but still Aulan made no movement at all.

The ground began to level off, the gorse and bracken ended, and the sand, finally, started to become thinner and firmer, giving way to specks of green which emerged hesitantly in places like timid creatures at dawn, before growing in confidence and number as they approached the feet of the great trees, joining together into a single carpet of thick moss which disappeared out of sight into the darkened world of the forest. Url stopped the cart just short of the trees; the others each jumping out and craning their necks upwards to see the tops, or gazing along the perfectly straight line in both directions. All except Aulan, who stayed rooted to his seat, silent and unmoving.

'Not a bad one, as forests go...' said Url, admiring the scale of the scene.

'I've never felt anything like it,' said Orlando again, walking up to the first great trunk, around which ten people would have struggled to link arms, greeting a mighty root with a loud, deep slap. The ridges running up through the bark were close to wide and deep enough for his body to fit amongst.

'It all looks the same, though,' said Crick, looking up and down the line. 'Where are we supposed to enter?'

'Does it matter?' asked Url. 'Here's as good a place as any. Come on.'

As they passed beneath the dangling branches, their dense spines an assortment of dark green and silvery blue, a thick, black cloud seemed to sweep above the cart. Light and sound were suddenly reduced to their barest parts, creating a soft, pale world through which they travelled like visiting spirits of some distant plane, unheard along their new path of spongy, light green moss, apart from at the occasional snapping of a dead branch or cluster of needles beneath the wheels. It could have been darkest night or brightest day outside; in here it made no difference. It felt as though it had been this way since the creating of time; Siu, Orlando, and Aulan saying nothing as they rode onwards, the others talking in hushed whispers amongst themselves.

But altogether then they heard the cry: An unnatural, rising yowl which began to echo suddenly from the trees around them like the distorted voice of a young child, or many, wailing somewhere in the distance. Each breath was turned to ice in their lungs as the sounds grew louder for a moment... and then died away, like water sinking into the moss.

'It's just the wind toying with us,' said Url immediately. But there was little he could do to disguise the fact that he was as unnerved as the others. He nudged Oden and the others to a quicker pace. Aulan's eyes had shut tight, and he began to rock backwards and forwards in his seat just as he had done in Byllam, while in the back of the cart Yori's whole body started to tremble, his arms clenching wildly as though within his unconsciousness he was fighting to shield himself.

'As far as I can tell there's nothing in here but us,' said Siu, patting Yori's chest as much for her own comfort as for his. The captivated joy of minutes earlier had vanished completely from her voice.

'All the same,' said Url, 'keep still, and keep quiet. Abetta, get up front here... You've got the best eyes of all of us,' he added impatiently to her searching look. 'Come on – this isn't the time to be difficult...'

227

'I can show you difficult if you'd li–' Abetta started, allowing Url to help her crawl through the curtain, but suddenly the wailing started again, closer and more urgent this time: A child in terrible pain, screaming louder and higher until with a vicious snap it broke into a horrible, wild cackle which bounced heavily off the trees and against the cart. It began to fade, but then others joined it, all around the cart, each cry passing strength and new suffering on to the others. But from amongst them a sudden breath of warm air streamed out from the hessian surrounding the Heart, filling the closeness of the cart with a deep, constant tone, drowning out the worst of the noise of the forest. For a moment then there was silence.

'I suppose going back and around this place is out of the question?' asked Crick.

'Scared, are we?' said Tarryn, having to force his usually easy smile.

'Yes,' said Crick simply and quietly, still peering hesitantly out from the back of the cart. 'You?'

'I wouldn't be averse to getting through here as quickly as possible, I suppose,' said Tarryn, seeming relieved at the honesty. He flinched away from the canvas as another wail erupted behind him. The others may have laughed, had they not all jumped with a sickening leap of their stomachs too.

'Here, take him,' said Abetta, helping Aulan back through the curtain. 'He's terrified, poor thing.'

'Can you see anything through there?' asked Orlando, guiding the shaking Aulan to a spot at the side of the cart, covering his quivering legs with a blanket. It was becoming difficult to move or do anything now but sit and wait, so complete was the gloom around and above them. There were no breaks in the ceiling of the forest, no sign of light in front or behind them… just a deep, dull green which clung heavily to everything it touched.

'Nothing,' said Abetta.

'Just sit tight, we'll be through it soon,' said Url again.

Whether or not this really was the thinnest part of the forest, it seemed to go on for hour after tortuous hour as the wailing continued incessantly around them; the noises always the same, rising and falling in constant, tide-like rhythm, yet somehow impossible to ignore or to grow used to. They were so horribly lifelike… They couldn't have been caused by anything but the enraged weeping of young boys and girls – babies, to whom whatever was happening or had happened was too sickening to imagine. All the time the air around the Heart was becoming warmer and brighter; those in the back of the cart having to

228

shuffle further away from it, huddling close together in the corners, studying it warily.

The single comfort amongst this beautiful, wretched world was that although the moss was thick and soft, the ground beneath remained more or less firm and smooth. There were occasional low-hanging limbs beneath which Oden and Nightwind were required to bend slightly; Url attempting at first to hack away at them as they reached him, but finding when he did so that the wailing increased still further, deciding quickly instead to leave the others to brush softly over the top of the cart. Elsewhere there were other small dips and fallen branches, but nothing which blocked their path completely. The thought of having to stop and get out of the cart, even for a brief moment, filled each of them with nauseating dread, fixing them firmly into their uncomfortable places, unwilling to move for fear that it may somehow unbalance the cart or cause a wheel to twist beneath them. And like this they continued without another word through the forest.

*

'There's light up ahead...' said Abetta finally, and not a moment too soon. Time seemed to have halted altogether; not one of the others able to say how long it had been as they sat there, blinking and shaking their heads, trying to recover a sense of wakefulness, but utterly unable to remember what wakefulness felt like. Abetta spoke calmly, trying not to let her voice reveal her excitement, and likewise the others barely reacted at all apart from in their own thoughts and relieved sighs, fearing silently that any shout of joy or thought of success would serve only to anger the forest in some way. Excitement, happiness, and all other pleasant feelings clearly had no place here. Only Siu, after a moment's thought and silent study of the air about her, made any acknowledgment, nodding her agreement with a hopeful glimmer in her otherwise dulled eyes.

All the way to the very edge of the forest there were no changes in the surroundings; still not even the thinnest of breaks in the trees above them, no signs whatsoever that the gloom was coming to an end but for the rays of light from ahead, which even themselves seemed unwilling to enter. Finally, with no word or incident to mark their wonderful release, they simply rode on between the final boughs; the cries and the deep note within the cart ending as abruptly as if they had never been, the black cloud pulled swiftly back over the canvas as once again they found themselves beneath splendid sunlight. None of the group – except perhaps Abetta – even remembered that this was still the weak, imperfect sun of the Outerlands: To them it was, just now, the most wonderful, warming, early-afternoon they could imagine. They paused for a moment in the silence, near-blinded even through the roof of the cart, grinning mindlessly at the finest whites and yellows any of them had ever known, wishing never to go anywhere dark again.

'Well!' said Url, shuffling and straightening himself upright in his seat, studying the height of the sun. Though the very thought was absurd, it appeared that it couldn't have been more than an hour or two since they had been climbing out from the sand into the forest. 'Like I said, didn't take us long at all.' He gave a nervous laugh, unanswered by any of the others.

'We'll make the Firstway by tonight?' asked Orlando; the others too relieved to be out of the forest than to care what either of them were saying.

'Hmm? What?' asked Url as Abetta jabbed him gently in his side. She was nodding down the hill ahead of them.

'I said *so we'll make the Firstway by –*' Orlando repeated.

'Oh…' Url whispered to Abetta, smiling. And then into the back he called: 'Yes, yes I'm fairly certain we will…'

'How long?' asked Tarryn.

'Come and look yourself,' said Url.

'Don't worry, old man, we all trust your mapwork, really,' said Tarryn, with mock compassion. 'I just want –'

'I'm not talking about that,' said Url. He cleared his throat, folding his arms in front of him with a deep, relieved sigh. 'It looks like we're done using Aulan's maps.'

There was a moment's silence, and then in turn the heads of Tarryn, Aliya, and, leaning back awkwardly, Crick, appeared through the curtain.

'Is it the road?' called Siu impatiently after a few seconds in which none of them had said anything.

'Stop the cart,' said Aliya.

Url and Abetta clambered down as well as the others scrambled out from the back, sprinting around to join them.

'Unless I'm very much mistaken,' said Url, as they all came to a halt beside him, 'I think we might well have found the Firstway…'

The ground fell softly away for several miles in front of them. It was marked with steep, rocky rises to the left, but ahead the view was clear and unspoilt, all the way down to the bottom of the hill and into flat lands beyond. For another ten miles or so there were small patches of woodland, trails of long grass and bushes, and all the features typical of such a landscape. But then, beyond them, in a straight, grey track which cut abruptly through the green from north to south, everything was turned to stone. This was no mere *road*… It must have been a mile wide, at least. Hundreds of monuments, easily the size of the trees through which the party had just passed, lined the sides and were scattered throughout the centre; some clearly resembling people, but most others unrecognisable from so far away. Dozens of long, flat bridges and walkways cut along or diagonally across it, springing up and ending at seemingly random points, some simply stopping high in mid-air. As the distant clouds moved slowly above it sunlight and shadow swam in vast, curious patterns across the unbroken track, taking longer to reach from one side to the other than it did through neighbouring fields and hillsides.

'Did you know it would be this…' Orlando began, searching for the word.

'Big?' Url offered simply. 'I didn't know what we'd find. Thought it would be something special, though – didn't you?'

'I – well, yes, but… not like *this*…'

'Why not? It was built in a time before the Black Wind…' He turned to face the others, smiling at the thought. '*Before* everyone took shelter behind walls, and people swore their allegiances to one part of the world or another. It was before Councils, and Kings and Queens, and wars. These were years when the world was quiet, and peaceful. Somehow, somebody was able to bring everyone together for a shared cause…' He stepped forward and held out his arms admiringly towards the Firstway. 'And this was it. *This* is what can happen when tens of thousands of hands work *with* each other instead of against each other.' He put his own hands to his hips, and sighed. 'And that's why the world will never see wonders like this again. Not in my lifetime, at least. Or any of yours.'

'Well there was never much chance we were going to miss it, was there?' said Tarryn.

'So why was it so important we got a map?' asked Crick, his eyes flicking to Url with a sudden anger.

'Because without one it would've taken a lot longer to get here, and it would've been a lot more dangerous,' said Url. 'Same as it would be if we tried to get all the way up from Irraigion to Iala without one. Don't worry, lad; your hard work'll pay off, believe me.'

'I hope so…' Crick muttered under his breath, the first to turn and, hobbling awkwardly, make his way back into the cart.

As they reached the bottom of the hill the road disappeared from view, remaining hidden for the next hour. But slowly the dark tops of the monuments began to rise tall along the horizon, followed by the bridges… And finally the lighter grey of the road itself appeared: Great slabs of an odd type of stone, like smoothed granite, each twenty feet wide, joined together in perfect symmetry all the way across. The marble colossus of a woman half-bound in a strange, leathery armour carrying two thin, jewel-encrusted sceptres stood greeting them as they approached, and as they passed through her vast shadow they could see nothing now but stone into the distance. The bridges, which from the edge of the forest had appeared small at least compared to the road, now loomed tall and grand ahead, hundreds of feet high; some running towards them, others pointing away, and several in the middle of the road ignoring them altogether – though why any of them started and stopped where they did was still unclear.

The sound of hoof and wheel on hard, smooth stone brought a smile to all but Yori. Url led the horses a short way into the road, so that the silver-grey surrounded them on all sides, and then stopped to let the others out. A thin layer of dust and loose flakes of stone covered the surface, but neither footsteps nor the wheels of the cart made any mark upon it. When Orlando tried to pick up a tiny fleck, no larger than the pip of an apple, he found it to be startlingly heavy, almost fighting to stay close to the ground, requiring both his hands to lift. Altogether the scale and peculiarity of the road were remarkable, and for a time wholly engrossing; Tarryn the one to bring them back at length to their far less dramatic, though currently more pressing concern…

'Lunch, anyone…?'

Chapter Nineteen

Scarravers

Looking down upon the flailing, half-drowned figure of Tarryn in the water beneath him, Crick knew full well that a smile now would be of little assistance to the situation. Try as he did, however, it was clear that the look of sympathy he was attempting to force wasn't quite as convincing as he'd hoped for. Url's riotous roars of laughter in the background weren't helping.

'I dare you to laugh too…' Tarryn growled at him, wiping the water angrily from his face, which hovered now only barely above the level of the road.

'Wouldn't dream of it,' said Crick. 'Much obliged you found it for us.'

Tarryn said nothing as he dragged himself out from the water and back onto the road, pouring out the worst of the dark, slippery liquid from his boots. Another low rumbling filled the dark skies above, followed quickly by a sharp snap of lightning and a fresh gust of rain. Crick heard the wheels of the cart splashing through the wet stone behind him, and after a moment Oden came to a halt beside him.

'If you'd wanted a bath you could at least have waited until we stopped for lunch,' said Orlando, leaning back and grinning beside Url.

'No, I think he made the right choice,' said Aliya, smiling gleefully and frowning seriously as she leant through the curtain. 'His stench *was* getting rather overpowering.' Tarryn glared at her, wringing out his heavy shirt, but her continued smile seemed to break his misery: he laughed wearily, looking up into the thick, black clouds which had been following them all day.

'Well, you're not going to dry off out here,' said Url. 'And as you've quite amply demonstrated, we're not going to be able to cross this – whatever these things are. Let's head for that bird over there,' he said, pointing away towards the edge of the road, where the towering statue of a strange, grand bird of prey with vast, outstretched wings was perched upon an enormous, marble boulder. 'We can have something to eat; see if this rain'll leave us alone for a while.'

Shivering slightly though doing what he could not to show it, Tarryn climbed up into the free seat beside Url, taking care to soak Aliya as thoroughly as possible as he swung his dripping boots back into the cart, bringing in the putrid smell of sweet-smelling mud and long-drowned vegetation with them. Url led the horses off towards the daisy-strewn grass which lined the edge of the road; Crick following beside upon Crash. On the predominantly smooth stone of the road the cart had been moving easily and swiftly, only two horses needed at a time to pull it. So for the morning they had released each of the three in turn to walk more freely and rest; Crick and Aliya taking turns to ride it. Having been on the road a full day, neither Crick nor any of the others were any less awed by it. The endless statues of ever-changing people, beasts, plants, structures, and all manner of other objects and scenes were each carved with such persistently lifelike precision and care as to seem almost alive themselves, while above and between them the bridges continued to soar in all directions. On both sides of the road the ground was beginning to become rockier, sloping uphill away from them, gradually forming a wide valley through the base of which they were making good progress, though unable to see further than a mile or so to both east and west.

There had so far been just one significant complication to their journey since reaching the road. This came in the form of large, deep grooves which appeared occasionally without warning in the stone beneath them. Some were just less than a foot deep, while others could be over a dozen, but all were at least fifty feet long, cutting sheer across the road like the sharp, extended lines of a poorly-ploughed field. What could ever have made such marks in the seemingly indestructible stone had been a source of continuing debate, but what was certain was that getting the wheels of the cart stuck in any of them would mean at best a long delay, and at worst the end of the cart. And with the heavy rainfall which had started throughout the middle of the previous night, scattering the stone as far as could be seen with thousands of drifting pools, it was nearly impossible to be certain what would be a normal puddle and what would suddenly send the cart tumbling to a violent halt. Tarryn, therefore, had been given the unenviable job of walking ahead of the cart whenever a suspicious stretch of water was found, to ascertain whether or not it was safe to cross, using the wood-bound tip of his sword as he nudged warily at the ground ahead of him. It was a system which had worked well until now – the sword this time having failed to break the thin layer of rock which overhung a deep crevice, but the weight of Tarryn himself proving more than enough. Tarryn continued to glare into the thin mat of water as they rode beside it towards the grass, the groove only tapering to a shallow point once they had almost reached the shelter of the giant wings of the splendid, crowned eagle, each intricate feather of which, dipping down at the tips to just above the level of their heads, was nearly enough to shelter one of the horses.

As Crick pulled back his hood, he saw at the base of the eagle what appeared at first to be thick, twisting roots. On closer look, however, he realised that they were in fact a series of coiled, stone serpents, set in place of the eagle's talons, carved out of a far darker stone than the bird to which they were attached. They curved down and around the great boulder, their heads rising high above the ground, tongues hissing silently, faces alive with a fierce anger. The horses whinnied and refused to go anyway near the frozen, lurking creatures; Url having to turn the cart around so that they were facing away, back towards the road. Altogether the underside of the statue was more than wide enough to keep everyone dry, and with various groans and yawns Crick and the others stretched and prepared lunch beneath one of the wings while Tarryn changed into new clothes – most of which were a mixture of Crick's, Orlando's, and Url's, and all of which were far too small for him – in the back of the cart.

*

'Better?' asked Siu when Tarryn reappeared a while later. Tarryn nodded, flinging his sopping clothes over one of the snakes.

'I think it's Crick's turn to test the road after lunch, though,' he said, grimacing as he fought to loosen Crick's black wool and leather-lined trousers from around his waist. 'He doesn't seem too badly damaged to me,' he added, nodding to Crick. 'If he's got enough spirit in him to laugh at the misfortune of those he'd call his friends, I'm sure he's fit enough to –'

'Now that you mention it, actually...' said Crick, his words suddenly thick and painfully awkward through the dark red scab across his lip, frowning as he cradled his right arm.

'I think you might be right,' said Url to Tarryn. 'It was your own fault anyway,' he added to Crick. Crick turned back to work on the fire with Aulan; his grin disappearing however as he caught the brief look of lingering anger which passed across his Father's face.

'Couldn't it just be a mark they drew to show where the border is?' asked Aliya, ignoring the conversation around her and continuing instead with the discussion they had been having before Tarryn returned. 'It might not mean there's actually anything there...?' She was lying on her front, examining the unfolded cloth of the map Crick had stolen, squinting at the thick, red and gold semi-circle which surrounded Iala, running in a series of curled lines from coast to coast in a great southwards arc around the city.

'No,' said Url, with a sigh. 'Veya lines are only ever drawn where great barriers of some kind have been built. If I could only remember what form of barrier those colours represent...' He leaned over Aliya's shoulder again, staring with frustration at the map.

'How do you know about *Veya* lines, anyway?' asked Crick. 'I've never heard of them before.'

'Intelligence...' Url answered flatly. 'Knowledge... wisdom... A deal of reading over the years... An enquiring mind... Those sorts of things. Probably best you don't try your hand at any of it yourself, lad, you're injured enough as it is without straining your head as well.'

'We used to know a enture called Joyce,' said Abetta, carefully adding another handful of thinly-chopped carrots to the pot of water in front of her. 'He would appear –'

'*She* would appear...' interrupted Url, with a glance that said he knew his words were intended to annoy.

'Don't start that again,' said Abetta threateningly.

'He wasn't the most... *manly* of men,' Url whispered to Crick and the others, just loud enough for Abetta to hear. 'Especially for a enture.'

'You got on well enough with him!' said Abetta.

'Only because of that game he brought back with him,' said Url, slightly defensively. 'Remember...? With the coloured dice?'

'Remember...? *Remember*? How could I ever possibly *forget*! It's all you two did or spoke of for four days straight when he first taught you!'

'Five,' said Url, to nobody in particular. 'He loved it. Don't know why – he never won!'

'He'd appear every few months after some foolish adventure somewhere,' continued Abetta. 'We'd put him up in return for a bit of work around the house or the fields. It was before you were born, Crick, thank goodness. You were quite difficult enough without the influence of a enture around. Anyway, it was him who taught us most of what we know when it comes to maps and exploring.'

'What happened to him?' asked Aliya.

'He –'

'– went on another adventure,' Url interrupted. His smile had gone. 'Somewhere in the Long Plains. He hasn't come back yet.'

'Oh… Sorry,' said Aliya.

'Don't be,' said Url, grinning weakly. 'Chances are he's sat around the table of some other family losing more of his money to them, silly sod.'

'And I *do* remember him telling us something about Veya lines, once,' said Abetta. 'I think it's safe to say that there's something there. And whatever it is, it won't have been designed for warm welcomes.'

'Something to look forward to, then!' said Tarryn as the sparks of Crick's flint finally caught on the damp wood; Aulan applauding excitedly.

*

An hour later, with lunch finished and everyone sitting or lying quietly across the grass, the rain finally started to ease. The clouds showed no sign of breaking altogether, but they had at least lost the thickest of their darkness, turning instead a dull grey broken in places with streaks of white.

'I think this is as good as we're going to get for now,' said Orlando.

Without another word Crick and the others stood and stretched, and started to repack the cart. Siu watched miserably as Tarryn lifted the still motionless body of Yori from her lap. She had insisted that he be brought out for a while, but despite her hopes the fresh air had had no effect on him at all. He looked paler, weaker, and somehow more frightened than ever. And as Crick glimpsed the face of his little brother, before Tarryn handed him up to Orlando, he felt for the first time in a long while a sudden pang of fear, of the type and intensity which could only be felt for a loved one: the realm of feeling which dwelt always in the background but of which it often took some unexpected and terrible situation like this to be reminded. Crick found it uncomfortable, uncertain what to do with it; how to process such unfamiliar feelings for one with whom he was so familiar.

'He'll be alright,' said Aliya quietly, seeing the look in Crick's eyes. Crick nodded without looking at her and went to help Abetta cleaning the bowls and cutlery.

The now well-practiced routine of repacking and setting off took barely a few minutes; Crick, now on Nightwind, leading them out from beneath the great wing and into the fine drizzle which was sweeping in light waves across the road. Riding was sore and uncomfortable, especially across his ribs, but he was healed enough that it would do him no further damage, and he was quite content with discomfort if it meant escape from the tedium of riding endlessly in the cart. Veering around the water-filled groove they moved a hundred feet or so away from the rougher surface of the edge of the road, once again heading almost due north through the slowly-steepening valley.

*

'So all we know for sure,' Crick called back to Url a while later, 'is that if your memory hadn't forsaken you to the extent that it has over the years, we might know exactly what that line means?'

'I think young Tarryn was right, *boy*: You *are* starting to regain just a smidgen too much of your spirits. The next few puddles are yours for the taking.'

'I think that's going a bit easy on him,' said Aliya, appearing through the curtain. 'Maybe he should...'

'Maybe I should what?' said Crick, still keeping a watchful eye in front of him. He was in no doubt he would receive little sympathy and even less assistance, from Url and Tarryn at least, were he to make the same mistake that Tarryn had.

'What is it?' he heard Url say quietly. He turned back to see the cart rolling gently to a stop, Aliya gazing out blankly into the rain.

'What is it?' Url repeated a little more urgently. Aliya's eyes snapped into focus.

'There's something around us,' she said, frowning as she tried to feel through the rain.

'What –' Orlando began, but Aliya had already climbed through the curtain and over the seat next to Url, down to the road, so that she was standing between the cart and Crick. She gazed up, and around, turning in a slow circle until finally she halted, staring back the way they had come.

'What can you see?' asked Orlando, climbing out to join her.

'It feels like the whole road is moving...'

'Only behind us?' asked Tarryn.

'I – I think so... It's –'

'Well then might I suggest that *forwards* is perhaps the shrewd choice? And quickly?'

238

'I can't see anything,' said Crick, nudging Nightwind towards the back of the cart and passing Aliya, whose eyes were closed tight once more. The road was the same dull grey it had been all morning, and apart from the occasional swirling gusts of rain there was no sign of movement amongst any of the bridges or monuments as far as he could see.

'Neither can I,' said Abetta, scouring the distance.

'We'll keep going,' said Url, to an approving nod from Tarryn. 'Come sit up front with me,' he added to Aliya. 'It's probably nothing. But all the same, keep an eye out for anything. Or an ear… Or whatever it is you do…'

Url pushed the horses to a faster pace than before; Crick having to work hard to study the ground ahead of them as he trotted before the cart. They had only moved a short distance, however, when again Aliya's voice cut through the rain, louder and clearer than it had been before:

'There's something there…' she shouted, no uncertainty in her voice this time. She stood looking out to the close horizons on either side, and then again she jumped down from the cart, peering back down the unending grey length of the road. Crick could have sworn he felt the ground quiver gently beneath him. He searched the stone, and the statues, and the distant bridges, scanning each for anything unusual, but he could find nothing…

'There!' Abetta screamed suddenly from the cart. Crick clambered from Nightwind, gasping and clutching his chest and leg as he struck the ground, limping as well as he could round to see his Grandmother pointing back towards the base of a bridge which several minutes ago they had just passed within a few hundred feet of. The others too, including Url, were all leaning out following her gaze as she stared back to the bridge. It took several seconds, but then they all seemed to see it at once: a black, vicious-looking creature, its shape that of a grotesque ant or something similar, but closer in size to a wolf. As they stared at it, three thick, curved sets of pincers with glistening ends, almost longer than its body, unfolded from the scales which lined its back and sides to shudder menacingly out before its head.

'Fix Nightwind back onto the cart,' Abetta breathed. Her eyes were wide with panic.

'He may be ugly but he's only small,' said Tarryn, reaching back behind Siu and dragging his sword from the side of the cart. 'Leave him to –' But Url's hand shot out and pulled him briskly back despite the difference in their statures before Tarryn could jump down to the ground.

'*Crick*!' Abetta shouted 'The cart! *Now*!' Never before had Crick or any of the others heard her voice like that. He hobbled painfully to the front and pulled Nightwind to the cart.

'What is it?' he heard Aliya ask; Url jumping through the curtain and into his seat. 'Url?'

'Scarravers,' said Url, his whisper of a voice cracking as he spoke.

'*Scarravers*?' said Orlando. 'But there's only one of th–'

'No, there isn't. Where there's one there'll be… thousands…' Crick paused and looked up at him: he was terrified. A quiet, pleaded 'Hurry, boy,' was all he could manage.

There was a shout of protest from Siu as Orlando left the back of the cart, running round to help Crick tie the last of the fastenings beneath Nightwind.

'Get on!' Url shouted the moment the horse was secured, but as Crick pulled himself up to the nearside seat he paused again, distracted by a movement from the base of the bridge: Another glossy black shell was emerging through what Crick now realised was a tiny hole between two of the crumbling old stones, several feet from the ground. His shoulder was wrenched backwards as Url sat him forcefully in his seat while at the same time whipping the horses; the cart jerking forwards, splashing heavily through the water.

'What about the grooves?' asked Crick.

'No choice –' said Url, '– we have to get out of here. Keep yours eyes out for the beasts. *Not there*…' he added as Crick turned to look round and back behind the side of the cart, where suddenly almost a dozen more of the creatures had appeared out and down from the mound of stones and onto the road, and were scuttling suddenly with incredible speed towards them.

'Why not?' he asked.

'Look forwards – sideways – other places like the bridge where there might be entrance holes.'

'*Entrance holes*?'

'Entrance to what?' called Aliya.

'The nest,' Url answered flatly, his voice difficult to hear above the new rumbling of the cart. The wind and rain seemed suddenly to be biting harder around them. 'They'll have entrance holes all round the place – I think we've run right into the damned middle of it!'

'How do you –'

'Behind you!' said Orlando suddenly, pointing over Crick's shoulder to where, from the knee of a statue of a man wielding two heavy, golden axes several dozen feet from the ground another stream of the terrible creatures was emerging. Even before Crick could count

240

them they had doubled in number, and they too were now scurrying quickly towards the cart, close enough that Crick could see their glistening pincers crashing angrily together in front of them, each bite making a tiny, high-pitched *clink* which brought with it brief and distant memory of the hammer they had used in the tunnel.

'*My bow*! Url called through the curtain, but inside Aliya was saying something about seeing more of the creatures, and Url had to shout again before his bow was passed through.

'Take the reins,' he said to Crick, leaping up and over him with the sudden agility of fear while Crick slid into the centre seat. Orlando took the full quiver of arrows which followed the bow and passed it across to Url.

'Be ready with that sword!' Url shouted into the back, and then to Crick he added quietly: 'Faster! Give'em everything! If they get close enough to feel that sword we're done for.' Crick struck the horses hard; people and sacks and tools tumbling together behind him as the cart lurched forwards; the Heart for now staying firmly in its place.

'Someone else use the other bow!' Url shouted.

'I've got it!' Aliya called back, unable to veil her uncertainty. Training her in its use was one of the few things which had given Url cause to spend time with her growing up, some years ago now; she had attained a not unreasonable proficiency of sorts, though not once had she ever drawn back against anything living, let alone moving as quickly as these things were now.

'Don't waste the arrows; wait until they're further in. We'll never be able to get them all – just hit the ones that get too close.'

'There's – there's hundreds!' called Siu. Holding the reins in one hand Crick turned and peered back through the curtain, and between the heads of the others he saw that the road had turned a hideous, shimmering black: A swarm was chasing them, and even at the speed the horses were going they were only just outrunning the dark, writhing wave.

'*Crick*!' his Father screamed, grabbing his arm. Crick turned back just in time to see another black, squirming mass erupting from the top of a once-occupied plinth less than fifty feet ahead of them. He pulled the horses hard to the left, pushing them fast as they could bear, only then realising that the second set of scarravers had somehow gained on them, cutting off the road to the left. The gap between the two groups was barely a hundred feet, but with the first swarm behind them there was no other choice: Shouting the harshest of commands and striking the horses more fiercely than they had ever known the cart tore slick across the stone, Crick powerless to do anything other than hope that

241

one of the puddles they crossed would not turn suddenly into a deep gorge. The grass at the edge of the road had vanished in the confusion, the stone now around them on all sides while ahead the base of a bridge even taller than most sloped down to the ground towards them, its far end lost somewhere in the distance. Crick swung the reins to the right but before the horses could turn a single scarraver appeared as though from nowhere in front of them: Url's arrow caught it in the midst of its pincers to send it flying, screaming to one side, but the damage was done: the terrified horses kicked out and shot forwards, ignoring all Crick's screams of effort to redirect them.

'Hold tight!' he called into the back.

'Why?' called Tarryn. 'What's –' His face fell as he emerged through the curtain and saw the bridge approaching.

'We might be able to outrun them if they all follow us up here…' said Url, as unconfident as he was hopeful.

But suddenly there was no longer any choice: the cart shaking violently as the wheels bounced up from the smooth granite onto the rougher beginning of the bridge. At other times the ascent may have been gentle, but at this speed and with the sharp *click*ing of hundreds of pincers close behind it forced Crick's stomach into tight, squirming knots, and it was all he could do to keep his focus on the horses. He gripped the reins tightly, bouncing painfully from side to side in his seat, reminded one by one of his injuries, many still fresh and tearing against the sutures his Grandmother had put in place. Unable to bear the pain in his right arm he looped the reins around his left, feeling them digging into his skin with every new bounce and jerk of the cart. Crash was beginning to scream and thrash away from the sight of the scarravers, but Oden and Nightwind in front kept her in check and the cart moving forwards, higher away from the road.

'Just keep'em going,' said Url, disappearing through the curtain.

'We're losing them!' called Tarryn, 'Keep going!'

It was several minutes before they neared the highpoint of the bridge, by which time the scarravers were a good distance away; far enough at least that their terrible noise could no longer be heard. The walls on each side of the bridge were thick and nearly ten feet high but they provided little shelter from the wind and rain which tumbled and coiled quickly now over and about the cart.

'Good job…' said Url, patting and resting his hand gently on Crick's back. 'But don't let up until we're down and well clear of this place.

'I thought those things had been wiped out?' said Orlando, wiping his forehead.

'They were – in the Heartlands. Apparently that's not the case here.'

'What *are* they?' asked Aliya.

'They live in vast swarms underground,' said Url. 'They'll catch anything that moves and drag it back down for the colony to feed on.' His voice was quiet again, and as Crick looked back he saw him wrapping an arm tightly around Abetta, who was trembling, staring tearfully down to the floor of the cart. 'We've come across them before,' Url continued. 'Before the Council established groups to find and destroy all the nests in the Heartlands.'

'You never told us about that...?' said Siu.

'It's not generally a thing we ever wanted to talk or think of again. We lost...' But with a glance to Abetta he halted, simply watching her, his lips pursed lightly amidst clenched jaw and a distant, saddened look in his eyes which spoke of a grief old and yet too raw to allow into thought.

'Well, thanks to some positively wonderful driving by you, sir,' said Tarryn, sliding his sword to the side of the cart and reaching back to slap Crick vigorously on the back, 'I think –'

'*Gods!*' Orlando shouted, just as Crick saw it too: Riding up the last few feet of the sloping part of the bridge, they could see now that it ran straight and level ahead of them for half a mile or so – and then stopped. There was no barrier or smaller path running down the far side that Crick could see; the bridge simply ended, as if whoever had built it had suddenly grown weary of the task.

'Your choice of bridge, however...' said Tarryn, taking in a shallow breath. He took up the sword once again and turned.

'We were nowhere near the centre of the road...' Crick mumbled with desperate disbelief. 'I'm *sure* of it. This *can't* be one of the –'

'All of you, ready yourselves,' Url interrupted flatly, 'We're going to have to fight them off.' Siu tried to say something, but a switch seemed to have been flipped within Url, his voice quiet and trancelike as he spoke, low and steady yet somehow all the more powerful for it: 'Stay close around the cart; don't let them get amongst us. They're weak only between the joints. Don't think – just hit *hard*. Use whatever you need from the cart. When they get round behind us, try and push them back off the bridge. None of us realised either,' he added quickly to Crick, who was still looking dumbstruck at the approaching end of the bridge. 'It's done – forget it. Unwarranted self-pity won't help us now. It won't help *any of us*,' he added pointedly, gesturing briefly around the cart to fall finally upon Yori. Crick tore his eyes from the bridge to look to his little brother, and after a moment he gave a half-certain nod to Url, his focus returning.

'But why won't the Heart protect us?' Siu tried again. 'I thought – '

'These evils are nothing to do with the Black Wind. There's nothing *Magical* about them.' He had taken out the bandana from his inside pocket, and was hastily scrabbling back his hair from his face. When he spoke again it was through gritted teeth. 'They're just angry, *nasty* little things,' he growled bitterly. 'They can hide deep enough underground for years at a time, out of reach even of the Black Wind, apparently.'

'We're almost there,' called Orlando. Url appeared through the curtain.

'Pull us up just short of the edge,' he said to Crick. 'We need to be close enough to the end of the bridge that we can drive them off and not be entirely engulfed. It's our only chance.' He went back to the others, but his head poked out again a moment later: 'Not *too* close, mind…'

Crick's heart jumped suddenly into his throat as the view beyond the end of the bridge started to appear. The high walls had kept the road below hidden, and it was with a curious mixing of amazement and terror that he realised now just how high they had climbed. From beneath, the bridge had seemed tall, but from here it felt twice as high at least, closer to the clouds than to the long, grey strip of stone far below. The monuments which appeared one by one beneath them were little more than tiny playthings; the vast granite slabs which made up the road almost indistinguishable from each other amongst the endless grey patchwork that snaked gently until the horizon. Behind him, Crick heard weapons being hastily drawn, prepared and handed round. It sounded like Tarryn was trying to explain to Aulan – with swiftly mounting frustration – what was going on.

'He hasn't got a damned clue!' came Tarryn's exasperated voice. They were seconds from the edge.

'Just give him his crossbow and point at the things when they come!' said Siu.

'We're almost there!' called Crick, 'Hold ti–' But the horses lost their nerve or else came to their senses first: With a great crash in the back of the cart, Crick and his Father almost thrown from their seats, Oden and the others reared and skidded to a chaotic halt, snorting heavily and looking anxiously ahead of them to where, thirty feet away, the bridge fell away to nothing. A part of Crick had still hoped there would be something here – some small stairway that may have been concealed until now – anything… But there was nothing.

'Cover the horses,' said Orlando, throwing the hoods to Crick before climbing quickly into the back of the cart.

When Crick had finished he ran with what speed he could find to the back, avoiding his Grandmother who was running the other way. His Father and Tarryn were standing beside each other a few feet away holding axe and sword, while Aulan and Aliya were kneeling in the back of the cart, bow and crossbow already half-strung. Behind them his Mother was cradling Yori tightly in one arm, gripping one of Abetta's long, thin cooking knives with the other.

'I know you're still sore, lad,' said Url, reaching into the back of the cart, his bow draped tight over his shoulder, 'but we need you, too…' He handed Crick the small hand-axe which they had been using for splitting kindling. And even as Crick took it then the air was suddenly alive with a soft, high-pitched scratching which mixed eerily with the wind, through which after a few terrible seconds thousands of tiny metallic *clicks* could be discerned.

'It'll do the job,' said Url with an encouraging smile, seeing the disappointment with which Crick was studying the weapon. 'Strike fast. Don't think; don't stop moving. Now go stand by your Father: Don't leave his side, understand?' Crick nodded and did as he had been instructed.

'Ready up there?' Url shouted to the front of the cart.

'You just worry about *your* end!' Abetta shouted back.

'Keep them as still as you can – If they get out of control we're in trouble!'

'It pains me to tell you,' said Tarryn as he and Crick each turned to fix the old man with incredulous glares, the awful rattling growing quickly behind them, 'but I fear we're well beyond *trouble* just now.' Url made no reply, staring solemnly back between them.

'Turn round you *idiots*!' murmured Aliya.

Crick knew what it was he was about to see, but this did little to prepare him for it: The bridge below them had suddenly become a slick rippling mass of black shells and snapping pincers – thousands of them, covering every inch of ground and wall, appearing to devour the stone in a single dark wave as they scuttled quickly up towards the cart.

'But… How can we –' Crick started.

'*Don't think*,' said Url resolutely, pulling his bow from his shoulder with a deep breath and fitting an arrow to it slowly and precisely. 'Just keep hitting them. Don't stop. *Do not stop*. Stay beside each other.' He drew back the string, and after a moment Aliya did the same. Mercifully Aulan too now grasped the idea, readying and raising his crossbow likewise. Tarryn widened his stance, and Crick heard him take several slow, steadying breaths. The dark tide was almost upon them. Crick looked to his Father, who seemed about to say something…

'*Now!*' Cried Url; the instant twang of his bow followed by a crunch and a piercing shriek from amongst the vanguard of the blackness, and then by two more as Aliya's arrow and Aulan's bolt followed; the fallen creatures instantly overrun by the swarm behind them, which started now to converge down from the walls towards Crick, Orlando and Tarryn. Jet black eyes peered hungrily from between arched ridges of scale; pincers snapping, biting, ravenous… They were fifty feet away, almost gliding upon the wet stone; a new wind blowing the rain hard into Crick's eyes… Twenty feet – another arrow was loosed – ten feet…'

'*Arghh!*' And in a giant arc the silver haze of Tarryn's sword tore fiercely through the air a foot from the ground, sending five at least of the creatures flying backwards in a mismatched scattering of halves. Those behind were stunned, but only for a moment: The charge continued, Tarryn lunging out again, joined this time by Orlando. Crick darted forwards, striking one just behind its pincers; the small, sharp blade of the axe cleaving the shell in two, tearing out a greasy, black mass of insides. Another arrow flew from behind to Crick's left. Url shouted something but Crick was lost amongst a flurry of crashing blows and the strengthening *click*s around him. With just the single, small axe it took all of his speed, pushed fully despite the pain it brought him, to avoid being caught by the pincers which bit at him now from his left as well as in front of him. Tarryn's fury continued to sound encouragingly somewhere behind him; arrows and bolts finding their targets with wonderful speed, but as he let out a shout of enraged excitement his eyes raised briefly above the level at which he was fighting and he glimpsed the tumbling field of scarravers marching relentlessly towards them...

'There's too many!' he cried, hacking down to a set of pincers which snapped like a vice inches from his ankle.

'Just keep at it!' shouted his Father. 'If we can get –' He staggered as he lunged forwards but Tarryn was at his side instantly with another mighty sweep of his blade, tearing through the several scarravers which had sprung towards him. 'If we can kill enough of them,' Orlando continued breathlessly, 'they might give up…'

Crick had long since lost sight of Url, but he could imagine the old man's look of doubt at the words. Crick didn't believe them either, but there was nothing else to do: He jumped forwards, weaving side to side to reach his Father, swiping constantly at each dark form around him.

'*No!*' Url cried suddenly from behind, and only now did Crick realise that the scarravers were on all sides of them. He turned to see Aliya desperately restringing her bow: she wasn't fast enough, but Aulan's bolt ripped through two of the scarravers which were approaching the cart, sending them sliding as one quickly through those behind and all the way to the wall.

'We need to get back!' Crick shouted; his Father turning and looking back in horror towards the cart. Pincers flashed suddenly through the few feet of open ground and caught Orlando's thigh; his scream echoed by another as the great, raging form of Tarryn arrived to slash at the scarraver, disconnecting its body from the pincers which remained clasped tightly through Orlando's flesh.

'Go!' Tarryn shouted to Crick, seizing Orlando's arm and dragging him with them as Crick darted to and fro hacking a new path back to the cart. Crick had long since lost count of the number he had killed. He was covered in reeking, black blood and shattered pieces of shell, half-blinded by the howling gusts of rain which were whipping across the bridge, his shoulders ablaze with every dashing move he made. He held his left hand to his chest, trying to keep it out of reach of the pincers.

'Get out of there!' Orlando screamed. Several scarravers were climbing up the side of the cart, the tip of each leg in turn clawing heavily upon the canvas. Url jumped back, nearly throwing Siu and Yori through the curtain to the front of the cart. Aulan was so focused on the creatures that Aliya had to pull him back with her, and as Url followed them all out through the curtain the canvas tore, two scarravers falling through and gnashing wildly around them.

While Tarryn covered their retreat, Crick and Orlando forced a trail round to the side of the cart where Aliya and Aulan were standing, firing back towards them; bolts and arrows cracking through the air beside them, around their feet, and above their heads. When finally Crick reached them they formed a tight circle; Url standing on the seat above them, firing down the other side of the cart over Siu, Yori, and a struggling Abetta, who despite her best efforts could do no more to stop the panicked, rearing horses from slipping on the wet stone, beginning to inch the cart slowly forwards towards the edge of the bridge.

'I can't hold them much longer!' she called through the rain and drifts of sodden hair which covered her face, her voice strained with exhaustion.

'Get hold of them!' Url shouted down to Crick and the others. Tarryn made a grab for one of the horses, but a scarraver appeared beside him and he was forced to abandon the attempt to defend himself. Another came, and more, almost cutting him off from the circle, while all the time the cart jerked steadily forwards. Scarravers were slashing fiercely at the horses now; most crushed instantly beneath their hoofs but some finding their way through to the legs and flanks. Suddenly Crick heard his Mother's voice through the frenzy:

'There's something on the ground! *There*…!' And between swings of the axe ahead of him Crick looked across just long enough to see her pointing to the very edge of the bridge… but the horses blocked his view.

'What is it?' Orlando shouted.

'I – I can't see…' Siu called. 'A mark… sticking out from the bridge. I think –' But the clamour around them had grown to such a roar that the rest of her sentence was lost; the creatures climbing endlessly over each other, piled two or three high as they tore at any exposed part of the group. Crick could barely hear his own axe striking the shells, and couldn't make out any of what his Father was shouting, but he understood the meaning: Along with the others he started to hack his way towards the front of the cart; Tarryn sending wave after wave of the beasts tumbling over the edge with fuming strikes of blade and hilt and fist as they approached, scarravers now on one side, the flailing legs of the horses on another, and a drop to nothing but the road far below on the third. Orlando struck another scarraver between the eyes, knocking it back over the edge, where just below was revealed a single, square stone less than a foot wide jutting out from the end of the bridge, in the centre of which a soft depression in the vague form of a hand glistened like ice. Aliya screamed and fell back into the circle, her quiver empty, blood streaming down both forearms. Tarryn and Orlando closed together in front of her, both breathing hard; Orlando beginning to wither against the onslaught.

'Press the damn thing!' Url shouted from the cart. Oden and Nightwind were barely ten feet from the edge. 'Press it! Do something; *try anything*!'

'*Go!*' Crick shouted to Aliya, hurling her behind him and darting to his Father's right to intercept a scarraver which had leapt from a tall pile of broken bodies. The pincers were still firmly embedded in his Father's leg, onto which he could no longer bear to put any weight.

'I'm okay,' Orlando panted, unconvincingly. 'Do it!' he called to Aliya. '*Now!*' And with a fearful look in her eyes, Aliya reached and slammed her hand hard into the mark...

Nothing happened.

'Again!' Url screamed. And again Aliya struck the stone... And again nothing. The despair which until now had been held at bay by the fighting now came flooding into Crick's chest, mirrored in Url's eyes. They were everywhere, all around the cart, closing in like black fire, unstoppable.

'*Again!*' Orlando shouted desperately, crying out as another set of pincers found his leg, just below the first.

'Url!' cried Siu, stabbing at the snapping black blades which had appeared through the curtain beside her. Url plunged the metal tip of his bow down through the scarraver's head, lunging at another which had climbed up the far side of the cart. Crick swung at one in front of him, but as he did so a dazzling flash of light exploded from the end of the bridge with a piercingly clear ringing, like that of crystal being struck, stunning Crick, the others and the scarravers alike. Crick looked back...

Out from the very edge of the bridge a wide, circular disk of pale, almost transparent stone had appeared. It hovered, swaying gently for a moment and then settling, resting above nothing but the wind and air beneath it, glowing brightly. And it was only then that Crick noticed that in place of his sister it was Aulan who knelt before it now, open-mouthed as he drew back his hand slowly from the mark beneath him. Beside him amidst the former tumult Aliya was staring wide-eyed, confused and surprised as Crick – though neither could match the bewilderment and fear in Aulan's own eyes. It seemed he had no idea what was happening, or why he had done what he had. But whatever the cause of his action, its result was clear enough to see, and also to hear: For a brief moment there was almost silence; a peculiar stillness settling like the falling of a heavy fog upon the bridge...

But then the clicking resumed, the scarravers attacking again with renewed ferocity; clamour and chaos returning in an instant to the bridge.

'Get on it!' called Url. '*You want to stay here?*' he added as Crick and Tarryn looked nervously to each other and to the thin, translucent disk. Abetta released the horses, letting them edge blindly forwards past Aliya and Aulan and out over the edge of the bridge... The disk held firm, flashing bright red where the horses stepped but staying as solid as the stone of the bridge itself. Orlando pushed Crick backwards towards it, falling with him onto the brightly flickering mist. There was a grunt of anger or perhaps pain from Tarryn as Aliya jumped onto the disk alongside the front wheels of the cart, closely followed by Orlando and Aulan, and then finally Tarryn himself, still swinging ferociously as the rear of the cart passed into the circle.

'Now what?' called Crick.

'The mark!' Aliya shouted, diving past him to where the stone with the indented hand had turned around so that it was facing them still. Without question or pause she pulled Aulan with her and thrust his hand down once more, and immediately several rings of cold, red flame shot out around the disk; the rain fizzing into a thick cloud of scarlet steam as it struck them. As Aliya stood a scarraver jumped from the back of the cart, reaching her before Crick could, seizing her stomach and chest with all three sets of pincers. She fell back with a terrible shriek of pain but Crick caught her before she hit the flame; Tarryn severing the creature's neck so that it hung limp, still attached to Aliya.

'Check the cart for others!' said Url as dozens of scarravers snapped and screeched about them, trying desperately to reach them through the encircling wall of flame. But before they could do so the disk began to spin beneath the cart, detaching itself slowly from the bridge; steam rising and spitting into a dome and blocking off the maddened creatures entirely from view.

'What's hap–' Siu started, but with a brief jolt they were suddenly drifting quickly through the air and away from the bridge. Away, Crick realised with a short, painful gasp of relief, from the scarravers. The *click*s became quieter, the air seemed suddenly brighter, and together Crick and the others sank, exhausted to the ground – if ground it could be called. Nobody knew where they were going, or how this was happening, but for now at least they were safe. Then they remembered Aliya…

'I'm alright,' she said, grimacing as everyone but Orlando and Abetta rushed to her side. 'It was only a small one.' They all helped prise the pincers from her body; the blades somehow leaving only deep scratches and small puncture marks, but nothing worse. Orlando, however, had suffered far greater injury: the two sets of pincers both from far larger creatures, and his leg now matted heavily with blood. The lower set came off after a struggle, but the others were locked tight as a steel clasp. No strength or tool could be found to break them, even from Tarryn, and there was no way of pulling them off without tearing most of Orlando's leg away with them.

It was only now, still floating swiftly through the sky, that Crick noticed the dozens of ragged rips in his own clothes, and the thin, smeared scattering of blood trails beneath. Much of his Grandmother's stitching would have to be redone; the scarring would no doubt be rather unattractive. But for now this seemed unimportant. Everyone else had similar wounds. Tarryn was leaning heavily against the front wheel of the cart, bent double, his breathing quick and awkward, but as Crick went over to him the disk slowed, the rings of flame bursting one by one into thin trails of dark smoke. Gradually the disk slowed again, and then with a gentle shudder it stopped altogether; the steam and lines of smoke carried briskly away and fading into the wind. And to the group's delighted confusion they stood now high upon the southern edge of another bridge, wonderful in its emptiness and the quiet which filled the air about it, sloping almost immediately downwards to the road from the opposite side of the disk. Somewhere in the past few minutes the rain had stopped.

'How far have we come?' asked Aliya.

'Let's get down first,' said Siu. Crick eagerly agreed.

'How bad is it?' he asked, helping Tarryn to stand. Tarryn for a moment said nothing, holding one arm tight over his stomach as he leant on the sword and pulled himself up with the other, struggling all the while to reposition his overly-tight clothing back into place.

'It can wait until we're off this bloody bridge,' he grumbled.

Chapter Twenty

A Star Unveiled

The moment each of the group had clambered back into the cart Url untied the hoods from the still wary Oden, Crash and Nightwind and retook the reins; Abetta yielding them gratefully, her hands still deeply marked and trembling from the effort of controlling the animals.

'What just happened?' asked Aliya, using a small piece of torn canvas to wipe the worst of the blood from her front. Such was her puzzlement and exhaustion that her words came out angrily, though Crick knew it wasn't directed at any of them. Each of them were feeling the same. 'Url?'

'I – I've no idea...' Url answered without turning back through the curtain. 'I –'

'That was no ordinary bridge,' said Aliya flatly, aware of but ignoring the obviousness of the statement.

'Well this is no ordinary road,' said Orlando.

'But Url said that this was all built *before* Magic started appearing...?' said Crick. There came no answer.

'And correct me if I'm wrong,' Aliya persevered, 'but that seemed like some sort of Magic to me...'

'Perhaps these bridges were built sometime *after* the road?' Siu suggested.

'I don't think so,' said Url. 'They all seem to be connected to one another, somehow, and to the road itself. But...' He was leaning forwards, scowling into his hands; an air of such painful bewilderment about him that even Abetta was looking pitifully at the old man. 'They *can't* be...'

'Let me see,' Crick said quietly to Tarryn as Url continued. A pool of blood was welling in Tarryn's lap. He peeled back his arm from across his stomach, revealing a deep, long gash running down across the side of his ribs around to the front of his waist. He had been sliced almost from one side of his body to the other, with the shining tip of a pincer still lodged in one corner of the wound. Had he been as lean as Crick, the scarraver would probably have found its way to his innards.

'Tarryn!' Siu exclaimed, interrupting Url from his self-reproaching confusion. Orlando crossed around the Heart and knelt down beside Crick, casting several sacks aside and examining the injury for a moment before pressing the two folds of skin together as best he could. Tarryn grunted but made no complaint.

'Get us off this bridge to somewhere we can rest – quickly,' Orlando said in Url's direction. 'You'll be alright,' he said to Tarryn. 'It'll leave a good mark but I don't think anything important's been cut.' Tarryn nodded slowly; his eyes now pale and weary, struggling to focus.

'We need to get off the road –' said Siu, looking around at the dark red stains which covered everyone's clothes and the cart alike, '– find a stream, or lake; somewhere we can clean ourselves up.' She kissed Yori's forehead distractedly, staring wide-eyed around her. As Url nodded back through the open curtain Crick caught a brief glimpse of his red, tearful eyes. Abetta saw them too, sliding her arm through his, whispering something quietly to him. And so except for the easing wind, the cart was silent then as they rode down the steep, short bridge, back onto the smoother granite of the road. Crick had expected the cart to turn right to head back to grass, but instead they felt Url turn the horses left.

'I don't know how far *up* the road we've come,' Url called back. 'But we're on the western side of it now. Doesn't make much difference, I suppose.'

'How's he doing?' asked Abetta.

'We need to get him sewn up,' said Orlando, prising the pincer from Tarryn's side and examining it from ragged root to jagged, glistening tip; Crick equal parts impressed and concerned that Tarryn still showed little sign of discomfort.

'We're well into this valley now,' said Url. Crick and the others could all see for themselves through the gently-waving tears in the canvas, and Url knew it; the hesitation and disinterest in his words

253

revealing the fact that they were more a means to keep his mind busy and distracted than anything else. 'The sides here are rocky and steep,' he continued. 'There's bound to be a stream or pool amongst it all somewhere close.'

And, thankfully, there was: After turning north again and following the edge of the road for little over half an hour there was a murmur of relief from Url, and they left the stone. For a moment it was pleasantly familiar to be riding once more over grass, but after a few seconds the wheels began to bounce in sharp, heavy jolts over sporadic clusters of rough rocks; new groans coming from Crick no less than any of the others as each held gingerly their respective injuries. Soon, however, they heard fast-flowing water ahead of them, and with a long, quiet sigh Url finally stopped the cart. Crick helped Tarryn down from the back, gazing up and around at the new scenery into which they had been so curiously and fortunately propelled. The western wall of the valley rose high ahead of him; short, hard grass giving way to a solid bank of rock from which only a small number of thin, hardy trees were somehow growing, jutting valiantly out and upwards from their clawing, searching roots. Whatever distant ridgeline there may have been at the top of the valley wall was lost behind a veil of thin, waxy leaves and large outcrops of rock. The stream, comforting in its cheerful simplicity after the chaos of the scarravers, bounced quickly down through the rocks towards the road, but it never reached it: Just ahead of the horses it plunged suddenly into a deep well, disappearing out of sight; only the faintest sound of rushing water lending any clue as to its fate.

'It looks man-made,' said Orlando.

'Probably goes all the way under the road,' said Url.

They climbed a few dozen feet up the bank alongside the stream and found a small circle of flat ground, just large enough to accommodate them all. After several large rocks were moved to one side, and many other small stones thrown out, there was enough clear grass for everyone to sit and rest. The stream was neither wide nor particularly clear, but it was enough. Clothes, bodies, and the cart were scrubbed; wounds were cleaned and cared for; and beneath the uncertain skies they each found a moment, in their own time and manner, to pause at last and breathe freely, and do what they could to recover themselves.

*

After the best part of an hour the only things still in need of urgent attention were Orlando's leg, Tarryn's stomach, and the roof of the cart.

254

'If it starts raining again and we don't have proper shelter we'll *all* be in trouble,' Orlando said through gritted teeth. Crick was pulling carefully on one side of the pincers; Url and Aliya set firm against the other. 'Go on,' he continued, trying his best to muster a convincing smile for Siu, 'I'm alright.' Unwillingly, Siu stood and left to go back to the cart.

'Where's *he* off to?' asked Url, pointing up to Aulan, who was ambling slowly up the slope away from them, his head cocked a fraction to one side as though somehow more confused than he had been earlier. Despite long and extensive attempts by Siu and Url, Aulan had given no clue as to how and why he had done what he had upon the bridge, or even whether he remembered the events at all. '*Hey!*' Url called again. 'Aul–'

'Don't…' said Aliya, scowling. 'We shouldn't keep calling him that. He's one of us now.'

'You come up with something else then,' said Url irritably. 'But before you do, would you be so good as to fetch him before he brings a creature of the Black Wind down on us… *again*,' he added with a sideways glance at Crick.

'We need Tarryn's help with this,' gasped Orlando, brushing Crick's hand with unintended but unavoidable roughness away from the pincers. Having jogged up to Aulan Aliya now put a gentle arm around him, leading him back down towards the stream, from the bank of which he continued to gaze up wide-eyed into the heights of the valley.

'He'll be out a few hours,' said Abetta softly, leaning over Tarryn and opening his eyelids, peering beneath each in turn. 'And he'll be weak after that. More than weak. He won't be doing anything strenuous.' It was a command no less than a mere statement of the fact.

'How're we supposed to get these off, then?' asked Crick. Url was standing beside him, arms folded, thinking hard…

'Fire,' he said suddenly after a while, clicking his fingers in the frustration of not having remembered before. 'It's what we used to use in the Heartlands. Weakens the shell if you can get it hot enough. We need wood,' he added, nodding Crick up towards the low, spindly tree which overhung the stream a short distance away.

It took numerous maddening attempts to light the damp, semi-green wood, spilt by Crick with the same tool he had just used to tear apart the bodies of the scarravers, still stained and stinking with their shadowy blood. But the flames which licked up finally through his fingers came as wonderful relief after the dank persistence of the day's weather. While Aulan and Aliya helped Siu begin to piece and stitch the torn canvas back together in the cart, Url waited until the fire was going well before taking the hand-axe from Crick, wiping the worst of the debris from its blade upon his no less grubby trousers, and burying its end deep into the midst of the embers. Abetta meanwhile kept constant watch over Tarryn, whose snores came as a reassuring surprise. Crick, carefully and slowly adding small slithers of wood to keep the heat spread evenly between the stones of the makeshift fireplace, saw Url through the smoke standing a few feet away, gazing solemnly down into the flames. After a while he seemed to notice Crick looking at him, blinking quickly back from the depth of his thoughts.

'I… thought I understood most of the history of this place…' he murmured. His eyes hadn't left the fire. Crick scattered another small handful of twigs into the flames and sat up to study him properly. 'Most of the important bits, anyway. I thought I had a pretty good idea how Magic came to be – and when.' He raised his eyes to Crick. 'Turns out I must have it all wrong… *Every* account I've ever read – *every* tale I've ever heard told, of the old world, and the Firstway, and the beginnings of Magic, and the Heart… *All* of them have said that the Age of Magic began *after* the Age of the Kings. But… how?' He turned, staring past the cart, down the slope. 'How can *any* of them have been true, when that bridge, and that road, were built *with* Magic? The Firstway was built hundreds of years before the first recording of Magic in the world…' As he looked back to Crick there was such desperate confusion in him that Crick felt a deep pang of sorrow for the fact he had no answer to give. For half a moment he was glad that Yori was not awake; it was the pain of intense pity which Yori felt of others more keenly than anything, and struggled above all else to deal with.

'It's not your fault,' said Orlando. 'None of us expected you to know everything.'

'But how am I to believe now that I'm certain of *anything*?' Url replied. There was a desperation in his voice; he was asking again for an answer none of them could give.

'Well to be honest I never had much faith in you anyway…' Tarryn mumbled. He tried a laugh but broke off halfway through, clutching at his stomach; Abetta promptly pulling his hand away.

'Sleep well?' asked Crick. His mocking tone didn't seem to meet with his Grandmother's approval.

'You shouldn't be awake, yet,' she said, looking slightly put out that her estimation had been wrong. 'Back to sleep with you!'

'Or perhaps he can make himself useful now?' called Aliya, leaning out through a tear in the side of the cart. 'There's plenty to do!'

256

Tarryn smiled wearily and closed his eyes again; his slurred reply lost amidst the ebb of a long sigh.

'And if I'm wrong about all of that,' Url continued more forcefully, 'how do I know I'm right about any of the rest of our journey now?'

'It doesn't m–' started Orlando.

'I dragged you all into this! I... If anything happens to any of you it's *my* fault. Don't tell me you don't understand that – that you don't agree with me – I see it in your eyes. Look at Yori!' His voice nearly broke as he close to shouted the name, and he seemed unable to find the strength to fortify it. 'Look at your son! Look at what it's done to him already! The least I could've done was know what I was talking about before –'

'Oh, enough with your *wining*!' Abetta interrupted. Url shook with the power of his unspoken words but he fell silent nonetheless. 'We didn't have a choice: We *had* to leave the Heartlands, and we *had* to get that Heart up to Iala. Correct?' She didn't wait for a response. 'And get it to Iala we still must! That's all there is to it. Stop making it harder on yourself. It's... *boring*! And it's not doing you or the rest of us any good!' Her stern gaze broke as she looked up at him. 'Besides, I think that ought to be enough...' she added, nodding to the axe, the wooden end of which was beginning to steam near the blade. Crick pulled it hurriedly from the fire and dropped it on the ground beside him. Url was silent for a moment, but then he sighed, rubbing his eyes hard, and with a brisk shake of his head was able to regain from somewhere a portion of his usual spark. Gingerly he picked up the axe, kneeling down before Orlando and examining the pincers closely once more.

'Come and hold this end,' he said to Crick. 'And, if you'd be so kind...?' he added with a smile to Abetta, gesturing to the other side of the pincers. 'Not too tight.' And under his direction Crick and Abetta took gentle hold either side of Orlando's thigh; Aliya leaning out through the canvas again to watch. 'Pull as soon as I say so... Ready?' He lifted the axe high above Orlando's leg.

'Um – I –' Orlando stuttered nervously, sitting up straighter while ensuring his leg remained perfectly still, '– what exactly –' But before he could finish Url had plunged the axe down suddenly into the tangle of shell and sinew in the centre of the pincers; the hot metal slicing and singeing its way through several inches until it struck something solid. Url wrestled the blade from side to side as an awful, acrid smoke drifted up around them until after a few seconds there came a dull *click*.

'Now!' Url shouted; Crick and Abetta heaving on their respective ends, the pincers finally relenting and, with a stifled moan from Orlando, breaking free from his leg. Blobs of thick, black blood followed as the sharp, gleaming tips withdrew; Abetta there within moments, pushing Url and Crick aside and covering the wounds with handfuls of the same thick salve and clean cloth she had been using to treat Tarryn.

They journeyed no more that day, falling into uneasy sleeps as the sun sank early beyond the height of the wall beside them. In the silence, with no talk and no work to be done at least for the moment, the admission of just how afraid he had been upon the bridge fell down upon Crick like a cold shroud of shame. He was supposed to be the one of them who relished these things. He was supposed to be the one who found them exciting. He was supposed, always, to be brave. That was who he was. That was the part he played in the family. *They* all had their affinities for the elements, but it was *his* sense of adventure and *his* bravery which were supposed to be helping them through here. But he hadn't felt brave. He'd felt exactly as he had beyond Fellgate. Exactly as he had while being carried out flailing by the ear from the Halls of Knowledge. Exactly as he had at the top of the Sun Tower... Terrified. He could remember almost nothing of the bridge now – only a hot wave of fear which threatened to swallow him whole as he remembered the black, writhing wave around and above him, snapping furiously at him. A fear now swollen in these last hours by the confusion of knowing only that they knew so very little about the old world into which they had wandered, or about the curious gem, whether truly the Heart or not, within the dark, sleeping hessian over which he cast his eyes time and time again amongst the quiet of the cart. He hated that fear. Hated the way it found an opening into him whenever he was supposed to feel brave. He cursed himself for it, vowing never again to feel that weakness, but unable in his anger to do anything to halt the gentle trickling of the stream from transforming time and time again into the clicking of a thousand black and hungry pincers, waiting for him eagerly each time he drifted unwillingly into dream.

*

It took the sun an hour longer than was usual to reach them the following morning, having to climb as it did over the eastern heights of the valley beyond the road, the far edge of which from this elevation upon the western bank could just be discerned in the distance. All were grateful for the rest; even Url himself making no comment as he stretched noisily and crawled out from the simple shelter which he and Aliya had constructed against the side of the cart. Orlando, Yori, and Tarryn remained where they were while Crick and the others prepared breakfast and made ready to leave. A few prompt minutes later, climbing back out from the cart having collected the empty plates from his Father and Tarryn, Crick saw Aulan once again being led by Aliya back down towards the stream, agitated and reluctant, looking back with glances of confused intrigue towards the top of the hill.

'What's he looking for?' Crick called.

'He tried to leave last night as well,' Aliya answered, shrugging irritably.

'We're on our own bearings until Irraigion,' said Url. 'His maps,' he nodded to Aulan, 'don't go any further north than somewhere between where we met the scarravers and where we are now.'

'Which is where, exactly?' asked Siu.

'Further up the Firstway than we were,' said Url distractedly, still studying the maps as though hoping to find some as yet unnoticed new part of them which would lead on to Iala. 'I don't know!' he added in frustration, sensing the looks given him by Siu and Abetta. 'It's impossible to tell where we are in this valley. Unless you can see a nice helpful landmark that I've missed...?'

'I call it the butterfly,' said Abetta, dropping the cutlery she was wrapping and holding both hands crossed beneath her chin, both palms facing in towards her, in the old swear still used by people of her and Url's age. 'That any help to you?'

'Of course,' Url continued, ignoring her with a smile, 'if our young thief here had done his job properly, there wouldn't be a problem!'

Crick tried to smile, but the words had caught him off guard, taking him straight back to the Tower... that wretched face still staring up at him across these many miles as clearly as if he was still right there beside her. He blinked hard, but her silhouette remained, seared firm as iron into his thoughts.

'What's the matter with you, lad?' Url asked. ''Twas only a joke.'

'I know,' said Crick, brushing past him to avoid his stare. 'Nothing... I'm fine. These ready?' he asked of his Grandmother, snatching up the several small baskets of food and various other items around her and disappearing into the back of the cart before Url could voice whatever question or thought he had been about to put forward.

*

259

The road now was noticeably steeper than before. The gradient paled in comparison with the walls of the valley, which continued to soar on either side almost vertically into the air, but it was more than enough to add greatly to the horses' work, all three needed once again to pull the cart. Noticing the sweat beginning to shimmer across their backs, Crick once more put the argument to Url that they should be making use of the mysterious half-bridges to ease and quicken their journey. They had debated the point all morning. Whether because he believed it, or simply out of loyalty, Tarryn had agreed with Crick, though he still lacked the energy to make any real impact on the discussion. Abetta, Siu and Orlando meanwhile were utterly against the idea, arguing – in all fairness Crick knew, correctly – that they had no idea how the bridges worked, or where exactly each disk would take them, or whether after all this time they were still safe and in working order, or else once stepped onto would now perhaps fail and drop the group to their deaths. Url and Aliya were yet to make up their minds, but even had they decided in favour of Crick it was unlikely that any of them, including perhaps Crick himself, would have been willing to actually take to the bridges if it meant going so expressly against the pleas and demands of Siu, Orlando, and most particularly Abetta. The compromise, though not one which Crick had happily accepted, was that they would ride in a meandering line which took them close to the bridges, so that they would be within easy reach should they change their minds – or, to be more precise, though none of them spoke the thought, if they were attacked again. As he had expected, Crick's words fell once more upon deaf ears, the cart labouring slowly onwards to the left of the vast foundations of yet another bridge, this one whole and running further than any of the group could make out. Gloom and shadow were slowly replaced as they rode on by new warmth and light as the sun passed calmly above, turning cold greys to bright whites and silvers around them.

But somehow it wasn't just the cart which struggled: The day itself seemed to drag more slowly than usual. Barely a word was said; each of the group concerned for Tarryn, and for Orlando and finally still for Yori, or else quietly nursing their own niggling injuries while the hitherto inspiring grandeur of the rocky peaks, especially to their left, was surpassed now by a sense of the overshadowing confinement which they cast down upon the road. Crick gazed up longingly along the heights of the bridges as they passed, desperate to escape the depths of the valley even just for a few minutes, but he sensed that one more disagreement would snap the uneasy tension into argument. The thought came to him of how pleasant it often was to have Yori around in such times; even asleep, silent as he was, he seemed now somehow to exert a calming sway over the group, subduing if far from removing altogether any appetite for quarrel and tension. And so, occupying himself with vivid daydreams and imaginings of what Iala would be like, Crick simply let the splendid structures pass one by one beside him, forcing himself each time to hold his tongue.

*

It came as something of a surprise, therefore, when halfway through the warm, still, overcast afternoon, Url let out an excited shout, slapping Crick's thigh and waking him abruptly from his slumber.

'Look!' he said, pointing forwards along the road.

Crick rubbed his eyes, yawning, and seeing then on the horizon what at first he took to be simply another bridge. He was about to inform Url of the fact, but as his vision cleared and he looked more closely, he realised that it was in fact no such thing: Arching over the entire width of the road several miles away, marked with enormous, unrecognisable symbols visible even from this distance, and supported by dozens of thick, white pillars, it towered twice as high as anything else. Even the very tallest of the surrounding bridges and great monuments paled humbly beneath it. To the left of the great formation away from the road a small channel was appearing in the wall of the valley, behind which an enormous rocky peak rose to soar almost into the clouds.

'What is it?' asked Siu, pulling the curtains aside so the others could see.

'What do they mean?' asked Aliya, running her eyes across the symbols.

'I don't –' but Url was interrupted by a sudden scrambling behind him: he and Crick turning to see Aulan leaning awkwardly out from the back of the cart looking up towards the western side of the valley; Tarryn's outstretched hand gripping his belt, the only thing stopping him from tumbling out onto the road.

'I've got him…' said Abetta through gritted teeth, struggling to pull Aulan back so that Tarryn could release him. Tarryn gasped with relief, clutching his stomach, plainly fighting the urge to scream.

'What's the matter with him now?' asked Url angrily.

'It's the same as before,' said Aliya. 'He wants to get up into the side of the valley. Or beyond it. Maybe there's something up there he remembers?'

'Or maybe he just wants to get out of here for a while,' said Crick with a none too subtle hint of understanding.

261

Url sighed, rubbing his forehead wearily.

'You've opened it up again,' Abetta said quietly to Tarryn, lifting the bandaging from his stomach, beneath which Crick could see fresh blood beginning to flow. Aliya's arm was linked firmly around Aulan's.

'Look's like there's a trail leading up to that peak,' said Orlando, pointing over Crick's shoulder. Crick could barely make it out, but to the left of the enormous bridge of rock and symbols there did appear to be a small, twisting track which left the road, disappearing up into the cleft in the valley.

'Let's take it,' said Siu. 'We can't keep having him trying to escape like this,' she added to Url. 'It's going to end up killing one of us.'

'And if there's nothing there?' asked Url.

'Then there's nothing there. We've made good progress with the bridge; we can afford an hour or so.'

Url made no sign of acknowledgement save for a hidden grunt which could well have meant any manner of things. But after a few seconds he started to pull the horses gently to the left; Abetta all the while working patiently to once more make Tarryn's stomach whole.

There were no further clues as to the purpose or meaning of the colossal arch as they approached; Url's best guess being that it marked the border into the outlying lands of Irraigion, despite the fact that it was impossible to know how close they were to the City itself. It was now, for the first time, that Crick truly understood what it meant to be without a map in these lands. Url had been right: moving even a short distance without knowing what lay around and ahead of them brought an atmosphere so entirely changed to the cart that it seemed a different journey now altogether. The walls of the valley pressed closer still upon them; Crick's senses heightening to new levels as they moved away from what he had quickly come to consider the safety of the bridges, back to the side of the road. The end of the arch fell to meet them, built of the same, rough rock as that which lined the walls of the valley. Now that they were beside it, Crick and the others could see that it was at once both extremely solid and well-built, and also bewilderingly plain and austere. There were no railings or signs of a walkway above it, no decorations apart from the unknown symbols; just a vast mass of rock, built like a great grey rainbow into the distance. In the opposite direction from the road many tall, broad-leafed trees grew in the thin, winding cleft which broke the western wall of the valley, into which the small dirt track disappeared.

'Sure about this?' said Url.

'It's either that or we leave him here,' said Siu, nodding to Aulan. He was all but striking at Aliya and Orlando to get free of them and leave the cart. 'No…' she added even before Url had raised a questioning eyebrow. Url pursed his lips and set the horses off, away from the smoothness of the road to which they had all become accustomed and were now rather fond of, back onto the jolts and discomfort of a common dirt path.

Rather than clearing the rocks to allow for a path the track seemed to have simply been built around them. It twisted from one side of the channel to the other, rising gently at first but soon climbing steeply, pushing the horses closer to their limits with each carefully-placed step. The trees around them grew steadily taller and thicker, blocking their view in all directions. Several times they reached what must have been the very edge of the channel, at which the track would turn almost completely back on itself and run flat or even downhill for a time, before once again resuming its upwards course. In less than half an hour Crick had become thoroughly disorientated, unable to see back down to the road. And he wasn't the only one…

'We can't be lost,' said Url a little too convincingly. 'There's only one path up from the road to the peak, and there've been no turnings off it the whole way up.' But just then Crick saw through a gap in the trees to his right, beyond which the ground fell sharply away twenty feet or so. Beneath, another track was running parallel to them. Whether the same track they were on, or a different one entirely, it was impossible to tell. Url saw it too, signalling silently to Crick to keep quiet.

'Any chance of opening that curtain a tad more?' asked Tarryn. It's getting somewhat… warm in here. Crick tied the side of the curtain higher, and as he did so he felt on his cheek a waft of curious, stuffy air escaping from the back of the cart.

'I'm telling you,' said Aliya, 'it's definitely getting hotter.'

'What is?' asked Crick.

'The Heart.' Her hand was pressed lightly up to the sack in front of her. 'You were asleep earlier; I *said* it was getting warm.'

'I think she's right,' said Orlando, leaning forward and examining it himself, as though toasting his hands by a fire.

'Sure none of you are touching it?' asked Crick.

'Of course we're not,' answered Aliya.

'They're struggling…' Url mumbled. He was studying the horses; Nightwind and Crash beginning to slip on the loose dirt. The track itself was now running straight but steep ahead of them, and only Oden was managing to hold a firm footing, plodding slow but determined as hardened steel, keeping the others to an even speed. Crick was struck again by a pang of loss for Railer – he would have loved him to be here with them. He wasn't given long to mourn, though...

'Out you get,' said Url.

'Hmm?' Crick mumbled, taking a second to realise that Url was speaking to him.

'Need to be lighter – they won't make it otherwise. We can't be far off; we'll walk.'

Abetta climbed into the front, rubbing her wrists, the memory of the last time she had taken the reins clearly still fresh in her mind as Url passed her the heavy straps while Crick, Url, Siu, Aliya and a suddenly silent and impassive Aulan climbed out and walked alongside the cart. With the weight of the Heart still there it made little difference, but it was enough at least to keep the horses moving, marching steadily between the thick, overhanging branches. After a further mile the track widened, levelling off, the trees finally relenting in number and height and revealing beyond them then the tips of sheer grey cliffs, drawing steadily in and down towards a great overhang of rock perhaps a hundred feet high which sat directly across the track ahead of them. But just as Crick was contemplating the idea that the path had led them up into a dead-end, he glimpsed that at the base of the wall a low, narrow passageway had been created. Whether fashioned by hand or by time it was unclear, but either way it ran ahead for sixty feet or more before turning sharply to the left and into the cliffs.

'This pass wasn't designed for carts like this,' said Abetta, slowing the horses and frowning thoughtfully at the narrow gap.

'We'll go in front,' said Url.

But even with Crick and the others walking ahead the cart itself was only barely able to fit into the pass. At the bend ahead the walls narrowed again, the turn even tighter than it had appeared from a distance. If it didn't widen on the other side, there was more than a good chance the cart could become trapped.

'Any idea how far through it is?' asked Abetta, pulling the horses to a stop. Reluctantly Url halted likewise, casting a regretful look back to the cart.

'Shouldn't have given her the bloody reins,' he murmured to Crick. 'It won't be far,' he said so the others could hear, trying to gesture Abetta forwards. But she held firm…

'How do you know?' she responded flatly, almost before Url had got the words out, holding the reins in one hand as she crossed her arms. And as much as he admired Url, Crick couldn't help but agree with her. It would be foolish to keep going without knowing what the track did up ahead. He looked back to the turn: If it hadn't been for the attack by the khaion he would have run on to see what lay ahead of them, but as it was – feeling his Father's gaze blazing hot against the back of his head – he stayed obediently in his place. Fortunately, however, Url had no such qualms: with a deep breath he marched away down the track, unheeding of Abetta's angry calls for him to stop.

'That stup...' Orlando growled, disappearing from the curtain into the cart, back an instant later with the hand-axe Crick had used against the scarravers. He threw it to Crick, gesturing for him to catch up with Url. Crick sprinted forwards as fast as his injuries would allow, reaching Url's side just as he came to the turn. And looking around the track they both paused, silent for a moment, before turning to each other. Url wore an awed grin; Crick guessed it was not dissimilar to his own. For the cliffs, unyielding as they had appeared from before the entrance into the pass, in fact continued for barely more than an arm's length or two ahead of them, ending abruptly to bring the track out into an open, circular plateau, several hundred feet wide, covered with a low floor of thick, dark green grass.

'I think we'll make it through...!' Url called back. The cart jumped into life; Abetta's curses growing louder as she approached. And with the gasps of the others sounding in turn behind them, Crick and Url led the way through the end of the passage and out into bright, open air...

Quite how such thick grass was growing here, amidst the barren rock of the hills, Crick couldn't understand. But as his feet fell upon it, it was as though a weight had been lifted suddenly from his chest. He took a deep breath, closing his eyes for a moment, allowing himself a moment to enjoy the cool breeze which swept quick but comforting across the ground towards them. When he looked around him again he saw that the plateau onto which they had emerged was set against the steep cliffs behind them like a small green shelf upon an enormous wall of rock, the grass growing right up to the edges before falling away into the sky. It felt familiar, somehow... and after a moment's search Crick found the link through the distance of his thoughts, realising that it resembled an infinitely higher, grander version of the ledge beyond Fellgate upon which he had sat with Natt and Leyon; the ground distant and hazy, many miles below as he approached the western rim.

'That's far enough!' his Father called, being helped from the back of the cart by Siu and Aliya. Abetta had turned the cart to one side, reining the horses in close alongside the cliff.

265

'Did you realise we'd come this high?' Crick asked as Url came to join him. The others followed, peering anxiously though from afar over the edge as they approached. But before Url could answer they heard Aliya struggling in the middle of the plateau…

'I thought you *wanted* to come up here…?' she was saying, still holding Aulan's arm tightly. He was standing firm against her, unmoving, staring out beyond Crick and the others. The most peculiar look had swept into his eyes: not quite fear, nor excitement… Or perhaps an odd mixing of the two?

'Just let him stay there,' said Abetta.

'Keep hold of him, though,' said Url.

'Oh, I'll take him,' said Siu, noticing Aliya's look of frustration. 'There's not a great deal to see, anyway,' she added, walking back.

'I don't know about that…' Abetta murmured under her breath after a moment. Everyone turned to see her gazing out into the western skies; intrigued, confused.

'What can y–' Url started.

'I can't tell…' said Abetta. Her voice was soft, barely more than the murmur of the wind around her. 'There's… Can't you see?' She stepped forwards, Url taking gentle hold of her belt. She seemed not to notice him. 'The clouds…'

'What about them?' asked Url, looking from her to the dense ceiling of cloud, which appeared much as it had been all day. There was a sudden call from the cart:

'Um, anybody there…?' Tarryn's voice was loud and driven by an alertness unexpected of him considering his condition. 'If anyone's interested, this, ah… *thing* of yours is getting particularly warm now!'

Aulan was beginning to twist his arm away from Siu's, his eyes flicking back and forth between the western sky and the cart as he backed hastily towards the northern edge of the plateau. Siu was no match for him; Orlando hobbled back to help but before he reached them Abetta let out a startled gasp…

'Look!' she said. 'Don't tell me you can't see it…?'

And this time there was no doubting her: Many dozens of miles away, at a point where land and cloud had long since merged into a dull grey haze, there was movement. Not quick, nor distinct, but it was movement nonetheless. The cloud seemed to be turning, twisting around upon itself in a great circle like a slow, powerful whirlpool of the skies.

'Why is it doing that?' asked Aliya.

The continued struggling behind them reminded Orlando of what he had been moving to do, and still looking half out towards the

266

western horizon he went to hold Aulan's other arm, calming him just enough to stop him moving any closer to the edge. Crick joined his Grandmother close to edge of the grass; the swirling continuing, slowly in the distance.

'Is it getting brighter over there?' Crick asked, quietly. As the sky moved it seemed gradually to be casting out the dull greys, replacing them now with a curious range of lighter tones. The clouds, distant as they were, were separating and becoming more defined, making their movement all the more striking. Somehow the careful, measured nature of its movement gave it a menacing feel.

'I can see someth…' Abetta started, but her words trailed off as she stepped to the very edge of the rim. Crick darted forwards to put his hand around her shoulder, though again she took little care of it. '*What is that?*' she whispered to herself.

The wind had died to a hushed whisper; a sudden, absolute quiet blanketing the plateau. Even Aulan's struggling had stopped. Crick could feel his Grandmother pulling unconsciously away from him, as though drawn towards the clouds. Never had she stared at anything with such intensity. It was a look so removed from her usual composure that Crick found it almost as captivating as the clouds themselves… But like a beast awaking then her eyes flew suddenly open, and with a tremble that shook fully through her body she fell back heavily into Crick, barely time enough to gasp before a soft, shrill ringing descended around them, smothering all sound and air. It was everywhere, all at once, yet somehow Crick knew it was coming from the western skies within which the distant clouds, spinning faster, were billowing higher and higher above each other, separating themselves from the murky ground below, revealing… A mountain, perhaps? It had to be – yet it was so unlike any mountain Crick had ever seen or heard of that it seemed deserving of its own term. Its base, or what tiny fraction of it could be seen, was hidden within a vast crater, around which the lands were perfectly flat and featureless. But that which was visible above the ground consisted entirely of a translucent white rock, pale and dazzling, marked in places with vast scars of black which must surely have been thousands of feet high like the wounds of some great battle. As the clouds lifted higher still, circling ever-wider about it, great columns of near-vertical cliffs were revealed rising sheer from countless miles of jagged foothills below. The ringing grew louder, higher, as still more and more again of the mountain came into view. Crick put his hands to his ears but it did nothing to block out the noise, almost blinding in its shrillness. Beside him Aliya was shouting, but no sound came from her. The height of the mountain, far-off though it was, had grown level with where they were standing… then higher… and higher still it soared; fresh clusters of smooth, polished cliffs appearing with each passing second, incalculable in their number and their height, tapering slowly inwards until finally, barely discernable amongst the churning whites and greys of what surely had to be the roof of the world a single, great peak was revealed, blazing with a perfect, shimmering light. The ringing stopped. Hesitantly Crick unclasped his hands from his ears, realising for the first time that he was on his knees. He helped his Grandmother to her feet, and when she spoke her words were distant, quiet:

'That was –'

But suddenly they were falling again; knocked from their feet by an explosion of sound and light more forceful and pure than Crick had ever imagined. He struck the ground clutching at his arm and chest, managing barely to force open his eyes against the assault. Looking sideways across the ground he found his bearings just in time to see a thin streak of gold erupting from the summit of the mountain, piercing upwards into the skies for thousands of feet, and then turning, falling… Crick found himself unable to move as it grew brighter, and thicker… Through all the many miles between it was coming straight towards the plateau.

'Go!' Orlando shouted, his voice rough and harsh against the clarity of sound from the mountain. '*Get up! Move!*' he screamed again, and this time Crick found the strength to stand. But it was too late; somehow the light had almost reached them…

'Tarryn!' Crick screamed, '*Get ou–*'

But with a deafening roar, part ringing and part the cracking of a great whip, the jet of golden flame five feet thick tore like a magnificent spear of sunlight across the plateau between Crick and Abetta, pounding furiously into the side of the cart. Wood splintered like kindling, canvas bursting outwards in streaking shreds of flame as Tarryn was thrown from the back clutching a mass of clothes which Crick as he cowered could only hope desperately was Yori. Panic was everywhere; the cart only stationary in that instant because each of the horses were thrashing wildly in differing directions. Orlando was fighting to get to the rear of the flaming wreck to help the motionless Tarryn, but the force of the light knocked him back as soon as he had made it to his feet. Siu screamed for Yori; Crick looking around to the others, all helpless as he was. All except Aulan…

Standing upright and perfectly still, gazing inquisitively at the cart, Aulan instead seemed wholly unaffected by the force which had reduced each of the rest of them to shrinking low against the grass. The

others had noticed him too: Orlando just feet away, calling to him...
But there was no answer; no sign that he had heard at all. From the
corner of his eye Crick saw Aliya pointing to the cart, where amongst
the skeletal framework of the back section a ball of flame bright as the
sun was blazing; Crick's eyes scorched by a burst of white in the
instant before he turned away. It seemed to be feeding off the golden
light from the mountain, becoming brighter with every passing second.
It was all Crick could do to keep his eyes open at all; just able to make
out the outline of Aulan's face in the dazzling golden light. For a
moment he thought he saw a flicker of a smile... But when he blinked
and looked again the smile was gone, and in its place there was a look
of such horror – not mere fear or confusion as Crick and the others
were feeling, but true *horror*, as if somehow, suddenly, Aulan
understood what was happening. He looked quickly up and across to
the mountain, and back again to the cart, and then around at Crick and
the others; a clarity of consciousness in his eyes which had never been
there before. As easily as if there had been no flame, no light or noise
at all he ran to the cart, vaulting straight onto Nightwind and seizing
his and Oden's reins, heaving them sharply around in a tight circle
away from the wall and back towards the pass. The ringing was
building to a crescendo, the back of the cart shaking, disintegrating
further, but the base and frame stayed intact and in seconds the raging
sun was disappearing through the gap between the walls, the golden jet
following it until with a final, awesome screech of power the cart
turned the corner and vanished into the cliff, and was gone.

Crick took a breath and fought to find his feet, his senses dazed,
all idea of balance for a moment gone completely as he struggled to
take in everything that had happened. He didn't know what to do or
say first. He saw Tarryn stirring amongst thin lines of smouldering
canvas, and was running towards him before the battered corridors of
his mind were fully reformed...

'No!' Url bellowed as Crick reached the outline of smoking grass
which marked the cart's former position, spotting with a thankful
trembling of his heart a crumpled Yori tucked tight beneath Tarryn's
curled, shielding frame. Echoes of wood crashing against stone spilled
out from within the pass. 'The Heart...!' Url cried desperately. '*Stop
him*!'

Suddenly Crick realised: Jumping uneasily to his feet again he
sprinted in a single leap over Tarryn and towards the pass. If Aulan got
too far with the Heart their protection was gone. He tore across the
grass, all thoughts of his own pain leaving him as once more he felt
hard rock beneath his feet. He jumped nimbly round the turn and saw

the smoking cart rattling quickly away from him; the panicked horses slow through the pass but now beginning to pick up speed across the flat, open ground. With an almighty effort he bounded forwards, reaching the side of the cart; the back end bouncing up over a hidden root or rock knocking him sideways as he swung out blindly with his hand, ripping away a charred piece of the corner beam and hurling it forwards with all his strength… He heard a heavy *thud* as he fell, and then through the wheels he saw Aulan's body tumble to the ground. The horses reared and slowed, bringing the remnants of the cart to a stuttering halt behind them.

There was a scream from back beyond the pass – his Mother's, perhaps, or Aliya's. Fighting to force the air which had been knocked from him back into his lungs Crick climbed into the front seats, turning the reluctant horses, getting a brief glimpse of Aulan writhing in pain on the ground before whipping the animals forward. Careering through the passage he was about to call out to the others that he was coming, but as he rounded the turn his heart leapt suddenly to his throat: Oden coming within inches of his Mother, Yori in her arms. She was running, terrified, back into the pass; Aliya and Abetta beside her supporting Tarryn, with Orlando and Url behind them; Crick almost forgetting to halt the cart as he saw ahead what they were fleeing from...

A vast, brown mass, either one creature or many merged horribly together, was surging towards them, swamping the far quarter of the plateau. Its skin was like that of ragged, sweating leather; the stumps of a dozen twisted limbs striking mindlessly out from around several wide, snapping sets of teeth that gnashed short and crooked from amongst its centre. Its insides pulsed and writhed within it, its form shifting constantly from grotesque to terrifying; dark slime issuing from its base, rippling as it moved. The others ran to the back of the cart while Url jumped up to help Crick rein in the horses, controlling them fiercely as they fought with a madness to flee from the terrible being. Seeing the Heart – or sensing it, for there were no eyes amongst the monstrosity that Crick could find – it let out a low, gurgled wail, thrashing out angrily around it. The ground quaked at the impacts, but with Url by his side Crick held firm; the creature edging slowly backwards away from them. A faint ringing started again, but Crick didn't dare try to move the horses yet: He let the creature slink slowly back to the edge of the plateau, where it quietened, melting softly over the end of the grass and out of sight, leaving a dark, oily trail leading back towards the cliffs.

'Where is he?' asked Url immediately. 'Everyone on, now!' he added to the others. The clouds were swirling once more, growing brighter; Crick's mind swimming with the noise. He didn't know if he could bear it again... *'Where is he?'*

'I left him just beyond the pass,' Crick answered, grimacing at the pain rising swift behind his eyes. 'He was –'

But with a growl of anger Url seized Crick's half of the reins, readying the horses. With no canvas he could tell when the others were all on, crouched uncomfortably around the scorching Heart, the hessian having melted away into a slick of dark, molten brown across the boards. Without another word he turned the cart in a tight loop, slipping quickly between the walls.

Against Crick's expectation, and to his sudden fear, Aulan was still there. He was conscious, facing away from them as he knelt beside the track, unmoving but for a slow shaking of his head. Url stopped the cart just short of him, snatching up his bow as he jumped down to the ground, stringing an arrow as he approached and aiming firm at the centre of Aulan's neck.

'Url!'

'Wait!' cried several of the others at once.

'That's the last time!' Url roared, spitting the words in his fury. 'The last time I let you nearly kill the lot of us! You've been a danger to us ever since we left!'

'Url –' Crick tried, but the old man wasn't listening; his arms straining as he pulled the string tight into his shoulder.

'*Url...*' Aliya pleaded, 'he didn't do anyth... It's not his f–' But she broke off, silenced by a curious movement from Url's target...

Aulan was standing. Slowly, leaning heavily at first on his knees as he raised himself carefully up to his full height as he had never done before, he paused still facing away from them for what seemed a long while. But at length he turned hesitantly towards them, and as he did so Crick saw tears falling freely down his cheeks. He studied them each in turn, as though seeing them for the first time; his eyes coming to rest upon the quivering point of the arrow which Url, his arms weakening, still held out towards him. His lips parted, faltered, and then slowly, hindered at first by a gentle quivering, formed into words; the sound which came with them the most remarkable Crick had ever heard... the slow voice containing not one but many different tones, like the long, haunting chord of an organ, as though several persons were speaking as one. His throat was dry and coarse with long years of disuse, but still somehow the words themselves were clear as silk:

'I... remember myself...'

Chapter Twenty-One

An Outlander's Tale

Url's bow fell slack to his side. The old man himself was speechless as the others, each staring silently at the strange new figure standing before them almost as intently as he was staring back at them. There was a grandness and a dignity in his eyes, somehow. Though a grandness broken; cracked and wavering, as if on the cusp of sinking quickly back into the shadow within which it had lain dormant all these years. *But a grandness born from what?* the others each asked within the silence of their own thoughts, waiting for him to continue...

'Please...' his melodious voice, shifting from one to several other notes even within the space of the short word, faltered again as fear retook him. 'Please – may we leave this place?'

'What...' Url paused, shifting the bow awkwardly from one hand to the other. 'You can talk...?'

'The danger from the mountain is past. You are safe here, at least for now, I believe. Beyond its sight. And yet –' he glanced back to the pass, his chest trembling slightly with each deep breath, '– I can... still feel it... Please, let us leave and rejoin the road. I will explain once we are away from here. Away from it...' Only from the movement of his lips could the others read his whispered words. 'From *them*...'

Caught between a confusion of intrigue and distrust Url considered him angrily for a moment, but then with a soft flick of his bow he motioned for Aulan to get into the back of the cart. But as Aulan took a slow step forwards Url held out his arm...

'Get his crossbow,' he said, glancing to Crick. 'And any other weapons we've got in there. Keep them away from him.'

'I have no will to hurt you…' said Aulan softly. He seemed upset by the thought.

'Can you manage the horses again?' asked Url with a quick glance to Abetta, keeping one eye fixed firmly upon Aulan.

'Go easy on him,' Abetta whispered as Url helped her up into the front seats.

'Go *easy* on him…?' spat Url, incredulous. 'Up to now he couldn't *talk* – Now he *sings*! I don't trust him any more than I can –'

'Yes, alright, we know – You'd rather shoot him and be done with it. None of us understands him either… I'm just saying go easy on him until we've heard him out.'

Url grunted his acquiescence, motioning again for Aulan to climb into the cart. Once Aulan was seated in the front-right corner the others took their places along the opposite sides; Url kneeling beside Abetta and facing back through the few remaining tattered strands of curtain, his bow still strung and resting carefully in his lap. Crick, scowling away his abundance of various pains, cradled the Captain's sword unsheathed and ready by his side, running his finger back and forth along the edge of the blade, his eyes never leaving Aulan's.

The ride back down to the beginning of the track passed in uncomfortable silence; Aulan unwilling to speak, the others each as unsure as the next as to what to say or ask first. Siu held Yori once more in her lap; Tarryn, now with dark singes across the back of his head and down his left arm to add to his injuries, tended to by Aliya, who all the while did her utmost to pretend not to notice the brief glances which passed repeatedly between them. The sight of open ground through the dispersing trees, though pleasant enough in itself when it finally came, did nothing to quench the blaze of curiosity throughout the cart which grew with each fresh look at Aulan. Behind the softness of his eyes gusted a frenzy of thought and feeling which the others found almost frightening to watch for long. The skies above had cleared, and with a murmur from Url, Abetta pulled the horses to a halt in the shade of the last overhanging limbs before the long, flat grey of the road.

'Out,' Url commanded simply. Aulan waited, his hands still held loose and calm in his lap, until the others were all standing or sitting on the track around the back of the cart before stepping lightly out himself. His long limbs seemed suddenly far less ungainly than they had done up to now. With fearful, inquisitive eyes upon him from all sides he gazed back up towards the pass as if somehow, through the trees and rock which stood between, he could still see it clearly.

'Thank you,' he said quietly, distracting Url from whatever he had been about to say. 'I could not think – being so close to them…'

'*Them*?' asked Orlando.

'Who? Who are you talking about?' asked Url, suddenly agitated again, gripping his bow tightly, scouring the skyline around them. Aulan's eyes drifted softly over the trees and down to him, and then around at the others.

'You… have no idea, do you?' His lips quivered with something like sorrow. 'But then, why would you?' And then to himself he breathed: 'After all this time…' He sunk to his knees bent double as if suddenly overwhelmed and in great pain; clenched fists pressing deep into the hard dirt before him to keep him from collapsing altogether. Crick and the others glanced uncertainly amongst each other, waiting, until slowly Aulan sat back, folding his legs and taking a deep breath before opening his eyes and looking up to them all again. His features on the surface at least were unchanged. Yet somehow there was no doubting that the man they had known before now had been replaced. Whatever had happened up on the plateau was something apparently only Aulan would be able to explain. And Url was not the only one of the group growing restless.

'All your life you have sought the Heart,' Aulan began at once as though having heard the thought, turning from Crick to Url. Url stood as though carved from the very stone of the Firstway, his lips pursed tight together, one hand wedged firm into his hip while the other waited outstretched and resting upon his upturned bow. But after a moment he relented, giving the shallowest of nods.

'As, no doubt, many others of your time and those times now gone have done before you?'

Url hesitated again, but with curiosity now threatening to overwhelm his distrust he sighed, accepting the line of questioning…

'What of it?'

'No wonder. The tales they must have told…' And for a moment he drifted away again with the thoughts of those words, muttering quietly to himself; Crick and the others having to lean in a fraction to keep track of what he was saying. Even Url couldn't help himself. 'I didn't mean for any of this,' Aulan continued. 'I was trying to help… to show you!' His gaze lifted to meet theirs, pleading suddenly for forgiveness for a wrong they didn't understand.

'Show us what?' asked Aliya, her kind voice and kinder eyes unable to mask a fleeting irritation.

'*Magic!*' The single note was high and loud; a spark of gold flashing far within the depths of his eyes as he said the word. The others shared confused, uncomfortable looks between each other as he gazed sightlessly through them, entranced by the quiet melody of his own speech.

'My dear…' said Abetta, stepping towards him. Url put out a hand to stop her but she brushed it off impatiently. She took Aulan's large hands in hers, waiting the few seconds it took for him to realise she was there in front of him, speaking soft and simply once he was looking into her eyes: 'We don't understand what it is you're trying to tell us… Please, start from the beginning. Tell us –' she paused, uncertain herself where to ask him to begin, '– tell us who you are…?'

'I am… nobody, now,' came her reply. 'Nothing.' Abetta opened her mouth to speak again, but he continued: 'For so long, so many years, that has been all I have known.' He blinked, looking into Abetta's eyes like a frightened child. But suddenly there was an excitement to him also. 'But now I remember… I remember what I used to be! It was not always this way…' He leant carefully back against the end of the cart, withdrawing his hands from Abetta's, closing his eyes. 'The Magic you and your people know, and use,' he began, his voice at once drained and euphoric. 'And all the Magic there has ever been in the world…' He opened his eyes to Url. 'None of it started with the Heart.'

There was silence. Url was too stunned for words; his cheeks flushing a deep, veined scarlet with the anger of his own bewilderment. Who was this man to deny him a lifetime's belief? Every fibre of his strength seemed to be straining in the effort to stay silent, and calm, and to listen.

'Then, how…?' asked Abetta, quietly but before any of the others could voice their questions, ensnaring them in a deafening silence as they awaited Aulan's response.

'I don't know. We… we never knew. It was gifted to us, from somewhere beyond even our understanding. Why it came to us we never understood.'

'*We…?*' asked Siu.

'We were a quiet people. Unknown and all but hidden amongst the greater consciousness of the world. One of the many tribes of Azhera, long before the Unions were made, and cities began to rise. Thousands of years ago…'

'You… *Thousands of years ago…?*' Crick repeated, but Aulan seemed not to hear him.

'While most others occupied themselves with festivities, or feuding, or other such distractions, we stayed mostly to one side. We did all we could to not involve ourselves in the lives of others. We sought neither quarrel nor friendship, though often this itself cost us dear. Instead we merely considered ourselves, and our world; studying it, loving it. Living our lives as quiet as always we had done.

But one day, almost as one we felt a strange longing to go to the mountain – White Mountain, we had long ago named it, only the very topmost of which you saw just now. None of us could describe or explain it, but all of us knew it. We had ever lived in its shadow, foraging amongst its foothills, drinking from its waters… But beyond that our paths had always been blocked; barred by a great mist which would descend and confuse us, disorienting us, turning us around in our tracks even without our realising it. The truth of the mountain was ever one we thought would be hidden from us; one of the ancient truths of the world we had grown to believe could never be known by mortal minds. But now…' His head lifted a fraction as if to bask in the sun, and the fingers of one hand began to uncurl and stretch out and up into the air, reaching for the memory…

'When we went there again, a wonderful corridor through the mist was revealed to us. We knew not why. But it led us into the mountain itself.' He smiled, open-mouthed, but his voice when he spoke again at once rose and fell, becoming stronger and more frightened with every word… 'So we climbed. First down, and then up, ever up and around an infinite maze of sloping caves and hallways we climbed… Across black ravines which descended into the very soul of the world, and up stairways the width of rivers which seemed without end we climbed, and climbed still more… For days beyond count. We began to starve. Many of our number perished beside us even as we watched as we searched our way through. I can still see hear their groans, even now… But all control over ourselves was weakened with every step we took. We could think only of the mountain; think only of finding our way to its summit. We left them behind – our friends, our families, all who were too weak to continue. And we kept going, higher, further still into the darkness. And then we came to it…' His whole body was tensing, contracting, almost quivering with the thoughts; old memory being revealed afresh to him even as he revealed it to the others.

'It was a greatness none of us had ever imagined. There was… such… *power*!' His fists were raised unconsciously by his knees, clenched tight. 'A roofless hall, larger than any we had built or known, and open finally to the moons and stars whose light danced there upon us reflected countless thousand times amongst walls taller than the greatest trees… walls whose every surface from our feet to the skies above glistened with the brightness of…' He knelt, opening his eyes, turning to peer above the back of the cart.

'This *Heart* you prize so dearly… It was no more, or less, than a tiny fragment of those great walls.'

'What do you mean – *power*?' asked Tarryn. Beside him Url's posture had all but collapsed; the bow falling slack before him. 'What kind of power?'

'Magic! *Magic*, as you would call it! A life such as there had never been in the world… We were surrounded by it! The moment the light from those great walls struck our skin we felt ourselves *infused* with it. We understood nothing of what it was, but it… It felt not like something *new* that was being given to us… Rather it felt like something that had always *meant* to be a part of us. Something we had lost, or forgotten, perhaps. Or maybe just never been shown…? I – We could not explain…'

'But, then –' said Siu after a moment, '– how did the Heart get from there to the… I imagine they weren't called the Heartlands then?'

'No. As with most of the places of Azhera they were yet to be given names. The division and naming of the world into so many different things is a quite unnatural peculiarity of your kind, and one I am still unused to, I am afraid.' He sat back down against the cart, his eyes still wide with the scale of the surge of images flooding into him as he spoke…

'*I* brought it.' He breathed the words, studying the faces staring down at him; searching, waiting for their reactions. 'The Heart – *I brought it down*…' And when nobody spoke he continued:

'The mountain's hold over us stayed strong – *stronger*, even, now that we were a part of it. We stayed there, amongst the stars. Amongst their glory and their power. We ate nothing, drank nothing but the light of the walls. And we cared nothing of the loss of our old selves. For while our bodies withered, our minds grew with such wonderful ease and majesty as to make all else seem utterly unimportant. We did nothing, yet were always busy; simply… thinking. There seemed no end to the strange new knowledge and thoughts with which we were being filled. We never left…'

'How long were you there for?' asked Aliya.

'None of us knew. It made no difference. Time was a concern of the world we had left behind, no longer for us. We outlived the loved ones we had all but forgotten below. They searched for us for so long…' Only now did the others see that the whites of his unblinking eyes were taking on a multitude of other colours, pale and softly glazed beneath a thin frost of tears, blurring slowly about the vivid green at their centre like pools of rainbow water washing gently about small islands.

'We watched,' he continued, 'as the world passed out of the age we had known, and into another. From our watchtower over your world we sent out the first small fragments of the knowledge we were being gifted, intrigued to see how you would make use of it… You amused us with your fascination for everything from the most minor of what you named *spells* to the greatest of what you came to construct with your new powers…'

'The Firstway?' asked Url suddenly.

'One of many,' answered Aulan, nodding. 'And far from the greatest.'

What was left of Url's hard gaze broke slightly; the old man hurt rather than angered by the unintended slight on the creation he had for so long held to be the pinnacle of all achievement. The simple but overpowering idea of wonders greater than the Firstway occupied the minds of the others wholly until Aulan spoke again…

'We watched the coming together of the many lands of Azhera under a stream of new and different banners. We watched you make your peace, and your wars, just as had always been done, but now on far greater and more terrible scale. In truth, we cared for none of it. None of you could see how unimportant your interests and your squabbles were… None of you felt the Darkness approaching. As *we* did, long before it reached us.'

The mention of the Darkness brought a new attentiveness to the others. They stood motionless around him, desperate to hear more of this tale – uncertain though their belief in it may have been – but suddenly unwilling to make any sound or put forward any question that might throw its teller from his thoughts. The tones of his voice were filled suddenly with traces of a darker, colder chord…

'It took you so long to realise what was happening. And longer still to do anything about it – by which time you were almost destroyed. We saw it all, but… we did nothing. We *couldn't*… Our place was amongst the mountain. With the approaching of the Darkness we finally came to understand that *that* was why we had been allowed inside. *That* was why we had been granted the secrets held from us since the beginning of days: We were to protect the mountain, and guard its glorious summit – the gateway through which Magic could pass into this world.

The battles were terrible. The terrors your people witnessed were as nothing to what was thrown at us. It was onto *us* in our bright

278

fortress that the blackest parts of evil broke like raging, thunderous storms; horror given a new meaning unlike any there had been before. Devastating as it was for you, the destruction of your world was a mere distraction. It was *our* home which the Darkness sought to conquer above all else. There is no means of describing to you what we faced, in terms you could ever hope to understand.' He seemed to be fighting his way through a wall built of nightmare; the effort of sitting still and upright amongst them almost too much for him to bear.

'But high and alone within our enduring bastion of light we held out,' he persevered. 'Our defence was desperate, and weakening, but finally from the powers of the knowledge we had gained over time we found the strength to overcome our enemy. Under our assault the Darkness finally receded; its foremost tool of destruction, the cruelty you now call the Black Wind, ended with a final bitter rage... and all the appalling things it had brought with it were no more. We had won.' His drawn, impassive face and the sudden sagging of his tired, heavy shoulders were at odds with the words he was speaking softly into the dirt beneath him. 'We had won...' he repeated. Some of the others sat upon the path around him, waiting eagerly for him to continue, but they may just as well have not been there for all his glassy eyes could see.

'But something had changed within us. The Darkness had been beaten, but after suffering its onslaught for so long a deep and irremovable mark had been left upon us. We had become... angry, and frightened. Distrustful. Fearful that it could happen again. Afraid of losing what we had come to regard as *ours*. Never before had our tribe been known by a single name, as the others had been, but now in the likeness of a sect long-vanished in our people's past, we named ourselves the Vessels, keepers and guardians of the knowledge of the stars. We started to rebuild and strengthen the great barriers which had always separated our mountain from the outside, and we created others, and behind them all we withdrew still further into ourselves, into the never-ending stream of understanding of which, we knew, we had thus far glimpsed merely a fraction. No longer did we grant the world beneath us Magic, as once we had. We watched it... watched you... pass from one age to the next, and again we cared little for the changes this brought: so important to your realm, so meaningless to us. And in time, with the crumbling of old scripts and the withering of old minds, most of your peoples came to forget that Magic had ever existed at all. It was merely a myth; a curious anomaly in the history of the world, never perhaps even true. And certainly, so some came to believe, never to be seen again.'

'So this –' Crick started, leaning forwards, trying to absorb the meaning of the words, '– what we're in now... this is really the world's *second* age of Magic?' He looked from Aulan to Url, then around to the others. All were silent as the history of their world was being pulled down and rewritten before them.

'Do you think the City knows?' Siu asked of Url. 'The Council...? Do you think they know there was –'

'I've no idea,' said Url, running his fingers distractedly through his beard, his eyes flicking quickly over every part of Aulan, studying his loose, ragged clothes, the features of his face, as though to make certain he was not imagining all of this. Or as though in desperate effort to judge the truth of the man who was telling him such great and impossible things.

'I'd guess so,' said Tarryn quietly, grimly. 'Any knowledge that's ever been passed down to the main of the City and the rest of the Heartlands has been sieved and corrupted a hundred times over by the Council... Anything which may benefit them in some way, either then or sometime in the future, they hold back for themselves. There's so many centuries of history and secrets hidden within the City, they've probably forgotten half of it themselves... '

'I have no idea how many of your years passed,' Aulan continued, as eyes turned slowly back to him. 'All I know is that, one day, everything changed. Not within *us*... But within *me*. I know not why, but for the first time that I could remember I thought of myself as something separate, not just a part of... whatever it was that we had become. And at the same time – it felt like from the stars themselves – the feeling came to me that Magic wasn't *ours*... Not ours as we had come now to take and keep it. It had been *shown* to us, perhaps, and for lifetimes we had held it as our own. But in truth it belonged no more to us than it did to any of the peoples who lived down in the world we had long since forgotten. That was the point – the *purpose* of our being! Not to own and control it... But to *protect* it! For *them*! And I... I wanted to make it right... *I wanted to make it right*!' he said again, staring pitifully into Abetta's eyes. 'That's all I was trying to do...

The others, fewer in number after the war, and distracted by their own, *mighty* thoughts,' for a moment his voice had become sharp, and angry, 'failed to realise what I was doing, until it was too late... From the walls I took a tiny piece, no larger than my finger. And then back down through the mountain I ran, feeling more alive and lifeless with every step and leap I took. Suddenly I felt and remembered my own body again, knowing once more what it was to be hungry, and in pain. I heard their fury behind me... I could still feel their thoughts, but they

280

too could still feel mine: While I avoided one trap they would set
another ahead of me; when they barred my way I knew how to undo
their work or find a way around it. Their rage was unbounded. If it
were possible I felt more fear in those days than I had from the very
Darkness itself...' His words trailed meekly into the silence around
him; his arms and legs trembling as though longing desperately to
crawl tightly into a ball and hide, but being too afraid to move.

'But you made it out...?' Siu prompted, gently.

Aulan's frozen gaze snapped up to meet hers, and though he
didn't smile, the tension throughout his body did at least seem to ease.
He gave a barely noticeable nod.

'Once I was out of the mountain, they pursued me no further. But
I could still hear their call. They cried out for me – for *it*, but I couldn't
go back... *I couldn't*... not now.' It was clear that the years had done
little to ease whatever torment and doubt had filled him then. 'I started
to make my way back towards the fields I had once called my home, so
long ago. But the cries behind me grew. Their *anger*... The noise was
everywhere, so thick I could hardly see through it...

And then it stopped. *Everything* stopped... and after that I... I
knew no more...' He breathed deeply, instilled with a sudden calm. 'I
don't know what they did... I don't know what they did to me... All
my powers were gone. I felt so alone... naked... I could barely bring
myself to walk...'

'But, the Heart –' said Url, '– How did you get it all the way to
the Heartlands and down into that Chamber?'

'I... I don't know. Since that time my memories are those of a
dream... I know parts of what I have done, and where I have been...
But the details, and *how* and *why,* are questions I cannot answer. I
remember the first people I came to. I began, as I had intended, to
show them the Magic of the Heart – the Magic I could no longer use,
and which they by now had only heard of in legends of the time before
the coming of the Darkness. It was they who first called it the Heart. In
the confusion of my new world and my new self, I looked to them like
a newborn looks to the first faces to stare down upon him... *I loved
them...*' And as he spoke he came as close to growling as his voice
would allow, the anger returning suddenly to his words and face – and
this time it stayed, growing with each sharp breath, twisting his
features like the surface of deep water swelling and churning from the
heat of a great fire beneath; each hue of his eyes becoming suddenly
brighter and sharper. Though they didn't realise it, the others all
recoiled faintly from this new bitterness. When the voice came again

they felt each note and letter of it; its every inflection revealing even apart from the words themselves a new piece of his tale…

'But they betrayed me! They tried to take it as their own… They wanted not to *learn*, but merely to *use*… They had no interest in seeking an understanding of where this power came from, or what else it could teach us, as *we* had: they were concerned only with what they could *do* with it.' He lifted his head, pained with the effort of struggling through the thoughts. 'I didn't let them.'

'You…' Orlando started. 'What did you do?'

It took several long seconds for Aulan to speak…

'Some fell. Others escaped. Even I in my near-timeless life had never seen anything like it… Something had been brought out from within the Heart: A new power, one which had never revealed itself to us before. I know not where it came from, or why it appeared then as it did…'

'Where *what* came from?' asked Aliya. 'What happened to those people?'

'Perhaps *they* were still watching over me…' Aulan murmured, not listening. 'My former brothers and sisters… granted me one final wave of Magic with which to defend the Heart…'

'You killed –'

'I don't – I never meant to hurt them! I don't *know* what happened! All I had wanted was to show your world the power of the stars! I had expected you to admire it, to *treasure* it, to want to *understand* it. Not to try to *take* it as you did… so quickly, and with such little thought, or care…'

'So you –'

'What about the Black Wind?' Url interrupted; his outstretched hand silencing Aliya. The anger within Aulan vanished instantly, replaced with a look of overwhelming pain; the colour and brightness of his eyes fading slowly back to dull white. 'You said you defeated it…?' Url continued. 'From the mountain. But it –'

'It came back, yes.' He sighed, burying his head into his hands. 'I was wrong. *We* were wrong. The Darkness had not been defeated. Only repelled. The moment the spell which killed those people was cast I felt the distant horizons stir, and knew – though whether I realised it at the time, I am unsure – that that which had been hiding for so long would now return. If I had known it could ever appear again I would never have taken the Heart from the protection of the mountain. *Never*.' He looked up mournfully to the others. 'It is my fault the Black Wind returned to your time. The Darkness had always sought it, and will always do so. And with the Heart taken beyond the protection of the mountain, it could begin to feel for the first time how close it was to attaining it.'

'So why don't we just take it back…?' said Siu. 'Why can't we just take it back to the mountain? Rather than going all the way –'

'No…'

He had whispered the word, and as the breath fell from his lips his consciousness seemed to vanish with it into the air. Amidst the waiting gazes of the others he simply sat, unmoving, staring unfocused and distant into the trees beside Siu. Hesitantly and slowly she knelt, tilting her head to try to recapture his sight, but like looking through a thin mist he merely saw straight through her. Url, impatient but anxious, took a step forwards, waving the tip of his bow across Aulan's eye-line. He was about to speak, but the smallest flicker of Aulan's eyes forestalled him: The movement was fleeting and barely noticeable, but it caught the attention of all those around him nonetheless; followed at length by the gentlest crease of a frown and the subtlest hint of hurried, anxious thought hidden deep within the blankness of his appearance; each twitch of muscle and slow drifting of his eyes telling part of a story only Yori could possibly have understood. Siu reached out to him…

'No…' he said again, slightly firmer than before. Siu recoiled slightly, retracting her hand as he blinked hard. Finally his gaze returned to her, and with a breath he continued as he had been before. Url stepped back as he spoke, studying him with renewed uncertainty. 'In their eyes, the Heart is now no longer a part of them. Having spent so long in this world, they see it as spoiled, corrupted… a repulsive reminder of how their precious Magic would be misused and ruined were they ever to open themselves up to this world… Perhaps they are right… Beyond the pass just now I felt and you witnessed a small taste of their hatred and disgust for us and what we carry. They have never forgiven me, even after all this time. They will never accept the Heart back into the mountain. They would rather see it lost to the Darkness than be tainted by it themselves, so warped and closed has their mind become.'

'Then… what?' asked Orlando. 'Surely you must have a better idea than us of what should be done with it? Some way of protecting it from the Darkness?' Once more Aulan was shaking his head.

'As I said, my powers and memories are weak, or gone altogether. In that final bursting of Magic through the Heart my awareness was almost destroyed. And even were that not the case, it took the unity of all my people and the strength of the mountain itself to keep the

Darkness at bay once it began striking us with its full power… What use could I be by myself when that happens again?'

'The Black Wind has already brought most of our world to its knees,' said Orlando. 'How much more powerful can it become?' Aulan stared at him a moment, and then around to the others, as though unwilling to answer the question.

'Hear me clearly, now –' he said, sitting forwards, '– for above all else you *must* at least understand what it is you face. You judge the scale of the destruction of your world only by what you have seen yourselves – not by what is possible. Not by what has truly come before, unrecorded and unknown to you. All you have seen, or heard of; any rumour your people have ever whispered amongst each other – none of it compares to the truth of that which approaches us. What has hounded you up to now has been nothing more than the first gusts of the storm. The Darkness will never cease until it is pushed back once more, or until it has captured its prize. And with the Heart now fully revealed, as I fear, by our own unwitting actions, it will restrain itself no longer.'

'You mean –' Crick started, gazing up through the shadowy track towards the pass as the others each uttered similar reactions or gasps of horror, looking fearfully between each other and the Heart. But through them all Aulan spoke louder and more clearly still:

'It is coming… In all its power and fury it is coming now… It has felt the presence of the Heart. The mountain will never take it back, and if there is any other place it could be hidden or kept safe I do not know of it. No, I can think of nothing more hopeful than the course upon which you have already set out, bleak as it is. I know no more than you as to what they have built within the city of Magic since the second coming of the Darkness, but it would seem to be our best hope. Perhaps our only.'

The others looked uneasily around at each other again, each waiting for somebody else to speak to break the confused, sombre silence which filled the air. The sun by now was well into the west, and with Aulan's words still lingering over the rocky track the long shadows cast by the overhanging branches seemed somehow more menacing than before. The sky too, though still clear, felt dull, weaker than it should have been, reminding them all suddenly of where they were, and what lay around them.

'If your memories were destroyed as you say they were,' said Url, 'did you know what it was we were searching for in the cave? Did you remember the Heart was down there?'

'I... could feel that there was something important to me within the ground... But no, even when I saw the Heart again – I am sorry for frightening you as I did –' the others nodded their acceptance; Url grunting impatiently, '– even then I knew not what it was. Not fully. None of it was clear to me until just now. All I knew, all I have felt, all this time, was that I wanted desperately to be close to it.' Tears were returning to his eyes. 'I am... so sorry... for all of this. It is my fault... All of it...'

'But –'

'The rest can wait,' said Abetta. And with such sudden and welcome decisiveness was it said that even Url, still overwhelmed with the confusion of all they had just seen and been told, made no argument. He stood, staring distant and wide-eyed into the ground, his head shaking gently. 'Our plan, it seems, is still the same,' Abetta continued. 'We need to start thinking about setting up for the night, and I –' she folded her arms against their dreary surroundings. 'Well, I'd rather we moved on and found somewhere else.'

The others agreed silently, each kicking shallow clouds of lifeless dust into the air as they stood and stretched their legs, keen for the simple certainty, if nothing else, of getting back onto the road again.

'Does this mean you can help with the horses now?' asked Crick, with a valiant attempt at bringing some measure of cheer to the group. It seemed a long while since any of them had smiled easily.

'I believe so,' said Aulan, nodding gently; his voice once more serene and soft. But as he began to walk off with Crick towards the front of the cart – Url scowling deeply, watching him as he went – Aliya called to him:

'What's your name?'

The others fell silent again, surprised at themselves for not already having asked the question, and suddenly intrigued as to the answer...

'I... I cannot remember...' He tried to smile, but the sadness beneath pulled too heavily, and was clear for all to see. 'I suppose it means little, now...' The others started drifting back into their own thoughts and conversations, but as they did so the quiet tones of his voice sounded a final time: 'Although, if you do not mind...' he added softly, 'I am... not particularly fond of *Aulan*...'

Chapter Twenty-Two

Old Scars

'So you're saying that ever since the… explosion, or whatever it may have been, which protected the Heart from the people you met after your escape from White Mountain… In all the time since then, while the Heart's been underground in the chamber in which we found it, it has in truth been giving off only a mere fraction of the energy held within it…?'

After a full day of continuous and equally confused questioning, Url still showed no sign of relenting. In fairness, however, nobody seemed inclined to interrupt him. Rather, they had listened as intently as he for the answers, many of which had by now already been heard, but a good number of which still could not be understood. Aulan smiled briefly…

'Through the ages your people have invented new words beyond count,' he answered, his patience showing no sign of waning. On the contrary, in fact: After so many lost years in isolation he seemed now overwhelmed but quite delighted at the new challenges and minute delicacies of conversation – niceties which had, however, long-since worn thin upon Url. 'But as you have done so, your understanding of the oldest, simplest and most important *meanings* has been all but lost… No – even *fraction*, as you use it, implies far more than is the case. The word implies a piece, small though it may be, which can be held up and measured fairly against the whole. But that is not true here. Not true at all… For while the Heart has been hidden within the chamber in which you found it, it is false, or at least so vastly inaccurate as to be false enough for the sake of our talk, to say that it has been *giving off* any of its power at all. Rather, what have come from it – the base and aspirant Magics by which you have found yourself so enamoured all these years – have been nothing more than the lingering remains left over from the last time the Heart knew its true strength. The Magic known by your time is like –' he paused, thinking hard for a moment, seeming determined to make the comparison as linguistically accurate as possible, '– like the heat which lingers long after a great fire has died. It is a memory; the faintest... *aroma* of the past.' He smiled, proud at his use of the word. 'And nothing at all compared to what lies stored and waiting within. Although...' he paused, looking for a moment distantly ahead of him, remembering... 'No –' he continued at length, '– no, not *within*. Again you let your words mislead you. For nothing truly lies *within* the Heart. It is not a mere *container* of Magic. It is a *gateway*; an opening to the very stars themselves, through which their glorious power may be channelled...'

'But now,' Url broke in, giving a slight but swift shake of his head, resolutely ignoring the import of Aulan's digressions in his eagerness to extract those simple facts he was intent on pursuing, 'after what happened up on the pass, you think that whatever enchantment your people –'

'They are not *my* people. Not now. Not for many long years have they been *my people*...'

'Yes – fine, my apologies,' Url grimaced with a tense wave of his hand, 'but either way – you think that whatever guard they placed around the Heart has been broken now by that golden... light, or flame or whatever it was that came from the mountain?'

'It was neither light, nor flame.' Url gave an exasperated sigh, on the verge of conceding defeat. 'But... perhaps, yes. Can you not feel it? Can you not *feel* how much stronger it has become?'

Aliya made no reply, and on the surface at least was unmoved and unmoving as most of the others nodded around her. But within the excited expanse of her own thoughts she agreed wholeheartedly with the assertion. Ever since they had stopped to make camp the previous night she had felt something different, not directly from the Heart itself, but in the way she seemed suddenly to be even more highly sensitive to water than she usually was. When the cauldron her Grandmother had set above the fire had started to boil, she had heard and felt in vibrant detail every pop and murmur of the liquid. And as the steam drifted upwards into the evening air her thoughts had, for a brief moment, been pulled up in thin, meandering strands with it. When she had splashed her face this morning with a handful of their dwindling supply it was as though she was doing so for the first time, so clear and full of life did it feel. And now, somehow, as Nightwind and the others drew them steadily along through a dimly-lit noon upon the Firstway, she felt certain beyond doubt that they would be better off by far if they were to keep going up the road another mile or two, than they would be if they stopped at the small, dirty pool at the base of the valley wall to which Url was leading them now. There was far better water ahead of them… she could taste it.

'Can't we go on a bit further?' she asked.

'I've told you…' answered Url, looking back beneath the newly-fashioned opening into the back of the cart. It had been hastily sewn together using the few strands of canvas which had survived the inferno, together with a curious assortment of leathers, blankets, and even one of Orlando's large, old travelling cloaks which Tarryn had been particularly aggrieved to relinquish, being as it was the only item of clothing which bore even a passing resemblance to fitting him. 'This is the first water we've come to all day. For all we know, there might not be any more until Irraigion.'

'Wherever that may be…' said Orlando. The city, or any sign of it, was still notably absent from the northern horizon. There was nothing but the road.

'It'll be up ahead of us soon enough,' said Url testily.

'She seems pretty convinced…' said Siu, nodding to Aliya.

'And you know you won't hear the last of it if she ends up being right!' said Tarryn with one of the roguish smiles Aliya was still yet to find a way of effectively ignoring.

'Fine,' said Url, shaking his head. 'On your heads be it. We'll keep going. If we haven't found anything in half an hour I'm turning us around, and *you* lot can think of a way to make up the time we've lost – Something that *doesn't* involve risking ourselves on the bridges…' he added as Crick opened his mouth, no doubt to suggest just that.

It had barely been quarter of an hour, however, when altogether the others each began to hear signs of the water that Aliya had been so certain of: an enormous rushing which even Url after a brief feigning of deafness was forced to accept as being the sound of a great river up ahead of them, turning gradually into a heavy roar and soon after that into the unmistakable tumbling of water onto rock – though still all they could see was the road. And then quite suddenly they were upon it; the reason for there being no sign of it until now set vividly clear ahead of them...

For across a large, near-perfect ring perhaps a half mile wide and nearly as deep, the road seemed to have simply collapsed. The lip of an enormous crater, lined with odd arrangements of plant-life and twisted, broken stone, brought the horses to a halt. At the bottom, flowing from the eastern face to the west, a narrow but swift-flowing river was raging through a tight and twisting channel in a series of white, foaming rapids.

'Now *that's* more like it,' said Aliya with a smile.

'We might even be able to make it down there...' said Url, studying the sides which led down to the water. 'Over there...' He pointed a few hundred feet round to the left, where a series of the great slabs which made up the road were still more or less intact, leading in slanting, uneven steps down into the crater.

'They don't quite reach the river,' said Orlando.

'If we can make it down to that ledge,' said Url – Aliya didn't see where he was pointing, transfixed as she was by the power of the swirling water beneath her, 'we'll be within fifty feet... The Heart can protect us from that distance, can't it? Especially now?' He was looking beside him, to... They were still yet to think of a name for him; *Aulan* was no longer used out loud, but nothing else seemed to fit, and until it did *Aulan* was all Aliya could think of him as. Originally a term of general referral not commonly used with pleasant thought or intention, *Aulan* was also now simply a name – *the* name by which they knew him. It would have helped had he been able to give them any indication of what his true name may have been before, but as yet he had been unable to remember anything. The question when put to him once more earlier in the day had seemed to upset him, and had not been asked again.

'We should be safe there from the creatures of the Wind, yes. I believe so. Though may I suggest that at least one of us stays with the cart nonetheless while the others go down to the water...? The Heart will not protect us should the horses become frightened and try to flee.'

'*I'll* stay with them,' said Url, doing a poor job of hiding his lingering distrust.

'We'll take it in turns,' said Orlando, and with that everyone but Tarryn, Siu and Yori climbed out and walked alongside as Url led the horses carefully around the great, crumbling rim of the crater, pausing briefly at the edge before nudging Oden gently over the thick fracture which ran clean through the middle of one of the stones. Aliya could see the wiry muscles of the animals' legs straining to hold back the cart as it creaked and shook over the uneven surface: They made a good job of it, but Aliya and the others followed anxiously just behind and beside the cart nonetheless, prepared to steady it. Though as Url was keen to point out to them, quite what use they would prove to be against the weight of the cart and the load it carried if it decided to fall, would be interesting to see.

Fortunately, however, they were given no cause to find out. Several times the heavily-bruised cart – which Aliya in recent days had found herself developing a growing fondness and sympathy for – jolted over breaks in the stone, or skidded a few worrying inches, snapping Url quickly back to focus, but soon enough they had reached the flat, unbroken slab they had been aiming for: twenty feet wide, and just above the reach of the wet clouds of spray which billowed in thick, white drifts up from the river below, lending an occasional, glorious scent of freshness to the air which caught Aliya and the others by pleasant surprise as one by one they reached it. Beside the cart a thick bank of moss and small, violet flowers were growing against the rock; Siu sitting amongst them with Yori as Aliya and Crick helped Tarryn from the cart, placing him beside the others with a profound sigh of displeasure at the effort it had taken him to move.

'He stirred again, earlier,' said Siu, gazing down into Yori's closed eyes, stroking back the hair from his face. 'His arm… I felt it move.' Aliya was glad her Mother wasn't looking up at the rest of them: their pitying expressions would only have served to upset and anger her. But the truth was that nobody else had seen Yori move at all. Not once. Not for days.

Aliya had barely set Tarryn down and released his thick, log-like arm before she had turned and was clambering quickly down the rocks, most of which were wet and glinting in a suddenly bright midday sun. Somehow, Crick had made it down before her, greeting her with a large splashing of the cool water; *his* strength and spirits, at least, evidently almost returned to full working order, though whether or not this was wholly a good thing was debatable at best. But Aliya made no effort to wipe the water from her face. It felt wonderful… She waited, letting it trickle lightly down her cheeks and off the end of her nose, feeling every slow, smooth drip and each tiny, soft droplet which rested for a moment upon her lips, and then with a small skip she sprang down into the shallow pool in which Crick was standing. It was sheltered from the main strength of the river; quiet, and calm, yet still fresh and clear enough to drink: icy cold, and beautifully refreshing.

Everyone but Tarryn took their turn in the pool. Even Yori was brought down by Orlando so that he could be cleansed of the clamminess which engulfed him; his hot, red cheeks soothed, if only for a few minutes. Crick brought a bucketful up to Tarryn, before being sent promptly down again for several more by Abetta. Amongst it all, lying on the thick green carpet, sheltered from what little wind there was with warm sun high above and occasional murmurs of spray from below, Aliya closed her eyes. She could not have been far from sleep when next she heard her brother speak, panting slightly as he placed a final bucket of water beside Url, who was refilling the skins.

'So, tell me something…' he said, sitting next to Aulan, who was staring absentmindedly across the crater. 'You've lived for, what, *thousands* of years…?' Whether conscious or not, there was still a trace of disbelief in his voice as he said it; Aulan either not noticing or not caring, nodding gently either way after a moment. 'And the mountain,' Crick continued. 'White Mountain – your old home… It was… somewhere that none of the rest of the world could enter?' Aulan nodded again. 'You've got – you had – powers that our world could only dream of…?'

'Don't you start as well, boy,' said Url through a long yawn. 'Get to the point.'

'Alright then… Well, what does that make you…? What does that make your people?'

'They are not *my* –'

'Right, I know, but still… Does it make them – you – some kind of… *god*?'

None of the others had been speaking anyway, but somehow their silences suddenly seemed all the more intense. Aliya leant up quietly onto her elbow, looking from Aulan to Crick, unable to decide whether her brother's question was ridiculous, or perhaps strangely fascinating. The few, scattered souls whose belief still held in the innumerable gods of the First Days were even smaller in number, by far, than those who believed in the legends of the Heart; *the most backward and despicable kind of all believers*, as the Council held them to be, treating any they found who adhered to the old practices with a merciless intolerance which made their treatment of those who revered or practiced the simple Magics seem like the tender kiss of a summer's breeze. Neither Aliya nor any of the rest of the family, out of their own beliefs only slightly more than out of their fear of the Council, had ever gone so far in their defiance of the Council as to count themselves part of that way of life, and Aliya knew that Crick had only put forward the idea for the sake of argument. Yet the comparison, despite the discomfort it had brought, was an intriguing one… Certainly there were aspects of the legends which appeared to hold true in the case of Aulan, and the *Vessels* of White Mountain. Perhaps, Aliya realised, with a sudden and unexpected flicker of excitement, Aulan would be able to shed light on the truth, if any there was, behind the stories of the gods. But from Aulan himself there had been no reaction; his powerful, unfathomable eyes still fixed firmly ahead of him, across the spray.

'There aren't any spies of the Council out here!' Crick exclaimed with a hint of irritation, waving his arm petulantly through the air of unease which had fallen around their tiny corner of the crater. 'Not even the ears of the Eyrie can hear this far – I think we can speak freely! Besides –' he persevered after a moment, though half-heartedly, beginning to wither beneath the weight of the looks being given against him by the others, including a suddenly steely-eyed Tarryn, '– he had the *powers* of a god...'

'That's enough,' said Siu, looking anxiously to Aulan. 'I don't think –'

'Powers of a god...' Aulan muttered quietly. Siu fell silent; Url setting down the bucket and skins he was holding either side of him in a single quick, silent movement. There had been something strange in his voice. Something unsettling...

'*Powers of a god...*?' he said again, turning to Crick. 'A handful of spells, and you tell me I had the *powers of a god...*?

'I didn't –'

'How arrogant your kind are, *still*, after all this time, that you think of anything or anyone more powerful or wiser than yourselves as a god! In all these years, these passing ages of the world, have your superstitions truly changed so little? We were *ordinary people...*!' In a flash of movement he had gripped Crick's arm. Url was on his feet just as swiftly, stepping light and carefully back to the cart and reaching in to where, Aliya knew, his bow was kept. Abetta gave a small, quick shake of her head and he halted, his arm still halfway inside the canvas, studying Aulan.

'We were no more than you are, you *fool!*' Aulan continued. He had taken no amusement or interest from Crick's question... only somehow a deep, bitter anger. In a flash of memory Aliya was reminded of the fat leader's reaction to the youngest Guardsman of the group she had chased and tracked beyond the Talon, just before the Eigerhills; the warm, soft touch of the river lasting less than a heartbeat on her cheek... 'Do you not understand? *That* is why I desired to bring down what we had learned into this world... We were shown great things, and given great powers... But that did not make *us* any greater than that which we had left behind! *That* is what they could never understand... *That* is *why* I had to leave them! The power that came to us... the knowledge... *That* you can call the power of the gods! If you

292

want gods, look to the stars, and *beyond* them… Not to us. Not us… Not *them*… Not…'

His words collapsed meekly into a final ragged breath of anger; the fire which had roared into life in his eyes dying as swiftly as it had appeared. He released Crick's arm and sunk helplessly onto his side, fighting hard to keep his breathing slow. Beside the cart Url wore a deep, hard frown, withdrawing his arm away from the bow but standing firm where he was.

'Well that told *you* then, didn't it…?' said Tarryn. Where Aliya expected a grin or hint of amusement she saw only an earnest glare, not quite of outright disapproval, but close.

After a second Crick realised he was still holding aloft the arm that Aulan had taken hold of; breathlessly he lowered it slowly to his side, keeping a close watch on Aulan as he did so.

'Let's eat,' said Abetta. And somehow like an unexpected glint of sunlight through black skies the words broke the tension. No matter how often her Grandmother spoke them, Aliya always found them comforting, as though they were a type of some great Magic of which even Aulan, god or not, had never heard. Feeling the sun above her again, imperfect as ever in these lands but soothing enough for now, Aliya sunk back down into the moss, nestled half-buried within it, lulled towards sleep by the constant hum and spray of the river. Whatever truth there may have been to tell or know about the old gods would apparently have to wait – and there were many far worse places to wait in the Outerlands than here.

*

A small but nonetheless pleasing meal of boiled new potatoes and thin strips of dried pork, all sprinkled liberally with herbs from the pouch Siu kept for this purpose, now little under half-full, did much to return everyone, including Aulan, into fine spirits once again. Had only Yori been awake and well, the hour may well have been an enjoyable one. Instead the others watched as Abetta, humming quietly to herself as she worked, parted his lips a little to once more place tiny droplets of the strange paste she had been feeding him for the past few days beneath his tongue, waiting patiently for each to melt away before adding another. Orlando had to ask Siu several times before she would accept some food herself.

Crick, rested and restless, was busy brushing aside Aulan's unnervingly vigorous attempts at apology, doing his utmost to sustain the appearance of having been perfectly relaxed about the event; Aliya meanwhile sitting beside Tarryn, relieving him of his plate once he had finished the few leftover potatoes that Abetta – as was now the practice without question in the rare instances that leftover food was concerned – had given him.

'My thanks,' he said through a final mouthful, propping himself back up against the smooth, slanted piece of what had used to be road, down which he had slipped a foot or so throughout his unwavering attention to the meal. Meagre as the mealtimes felt to Aliya, it seemed that they couldn't have been much less than a Guardsman's rations in the City – the stretching of the clothes around Tarryn's chest showing little difference now to how it had been when they had set out. 'You know,' he continued with the grin and crease of brow which told Aliya she was supposed to be offended by whatever came next, 'you're not too bad at that – Might be a livelihood in it for you, once we're done with this little journey of ours…?'

'If you think I have any ideas of spending my days bringing you food and clearing up after –'

'I didn't say after *me*, particularly.'

'Oh – No, I know…' She resisted the urge to grimace, somehow finding it easier to smile back instead… 'I just meant –'

'Though now that you mention it, I suppose it's not the worst idea you've had…'

'I just…' but Aliya could feel the all-too-familiar sting of inquisitive eyes turning to hover upon her and Tarryn: Not for the first time did she wish that they didn't all have to be sat so close together. She had to change the subject… 'How's it feeling?' she asked rather pathetically, nodding to the bandaging across his stomach which, for the first time, was clean if perhaps slightly marked with sweat – unstained at least by the blood which until today had seemed intent on escaping at each new opportunity. Tarryn smiled for a brief moment at her discomfort, but then obliged:

'Not too bad at all. You've done a splendid job!' he added to Abetta, who was pretending no more or less than the others not to be listening. She glanced across and smiled briefly before going back to the pan she was scrubbing, now with noticeably more zeal than before. 'I think I'll be up and –' Tarryn began, but as Aliya looked at the bandaging a horrifying thought came suddenly to her mind:

'What about scarravers?' she interrupted loudly, turning to the others. They all fell silent, looking to her as though she had sworn. The word still had a horrible bite to it which none of them could ignore.

'What about them?' asked Url curtly.

'Well, we're not in the best of places down here, are we? If there's any around they could surround us without us knowing about it.'

'They hate water,' said Abetta. 'They get all the moisture they need from their prey. They'll keep well away from places like this. Water and fire...' she added quietly, staring deep into the pan.

'Water and fire,' echoed Url, watching her solemnly.

Aliya said nothing but was still uncertain as she looked above her, slowly around the great lip of the crater.

'We're safe enough down here,' said Url, holding Abetta by the shoulder as he passed behind her. 'Trust me.'

'Trust *you*...?' Abetta exclaimed, blinking back from her memories. 'Ha – well if *that* doesn't make the poor girl feel safer, I'm sure I've no idea what will!'

'Now, now, old woman,' said Url, grinning at the challenge, 'we've been getting on well enough these last few days; don't you go saying something you'll regret!'

'Urlmaeus, when it comes to you there's *plenty* I could say and *none* of it that I'd regret. You –'

Aliya left them to it, turning back to Tarryn.

'What was it like –' she asked, before he could get in the beginnings of another joke at her expense, '– growing up in Immelus?' She was surprised to see the smile disappear suddenly from his face. It was replaced an instant later, but this time with a far less convincing one.

'The City...? Big, busy; ale and women round every turn if you know where to look – Not that I partook of any such pursuits, of course.'

'Of course...'

'Apart from that, it was...' his shoulders dropped slightly as he struggled to find the words and maintain his cheerful demeanour, and in his eyes Aliya saw a brief unhappiness. It was another fleeting moment of honesty which, as far as Aliya could tell, he had as yet revealed only to her. She almost smiled at the thought.

'It must have been quite something, having parents in the Council?' she prompted. She had hoped to change the subject away from whatever darkened thought was troubling him – but instead she seemed to have struck right to the heart of it. His gaze fell beside him to the large clump of moss he was screwing up within his hand. It looked as though he was about to explain, but then with a quick, deep breath he changed his mind:

'It was lucky Crick got out of the Tower in time, when he got the map.' He leant back, releasing the moss and closing his eyes against the sun. 'Chances are he'd have run into my Mother, otherwise. I think she was supposed to be opening the Wilder Rooms that morning.'

'Oh… Well I'm sure Crick was glad to find out…? I suppose all he would have had to do was explain he was a friend of yours and he'd be –'

'That wouldn't do him much good,' Tarryn muttered. He gave a bitter laugh, more to himself than to Aliya. 'And I haven't mentioned it to him yet. Not that I'm purposely keeping it from him. I just…'

'Don't like talking about them…?' It seemed rather an obvious thing to say, but she was afraid to ask anything more direct. Tarryn gave a long, quiet sigh…

'They –'

'Well…' Url said loudly, standing and stretching, 'through sheer, unaided guesswork on my behalf,' he looked sideways at Aulan, who to everyone's disappointment had been unable to recall any of this part of the world, 'I reckon Irraigion's still a full day's ride away, at the very least. I'm getting bored of being somewhere I don't know anything about. Let's get going,' he finished, yawning; the well-practiced words flowing so naturally across his lips now that even though they were barely audible, each of the group knew clearly what he was saying almost before he had said it.

'Actually,' said Crick still lying on the thickest section of moss, arms behind his head, facing up to the sun, 'I'm afraid to say that after sheer, unaided consideration on *my* behalf, I've come to the decision that this crater here shall be my new home.'

'Oh!' said Orlando, 'Yes, well, good choice… Lovely spot you've got yourself. Not bothered about that *Black Wind* the old man keeps banging on about…?'

'As is the case with most important things in life, dear Father, I'll figure that out when it gets here,' said Crick with a confidence Aliya would have paid dearly to make her own – fake and forged by weariness and confusion though it may have been. 'Tarryn can stand guard. Once he's able to stand at all, of course…'

'I see. Well, until then, how about helping to repack the cart?'

'Couldn't possibly – far too full, I'm afr–' He spluttered the last of the sentence through the murky water his Grandmother had used for boiling the potatoes, currently being emptied upon him.

'This needs cleaning…' she said lightly when she had finished, handing him the empty pot and grinning like a child on the way back to the cart. 'And so do you,' she added with a rare, openly-shared smile between herself and Url. Crick looked around to the others, but to his consternation found nothing but approval and laughter. Without another word he stood, still wiping the cloudy water from his face, and made his way down to the river.

'Come on,' said Orlando, giving Abetta a congratulatory nod as he handed Aliya an assortment of plates. 'These need doing too.'

And after being under the sun for so long, Aliya found the water, if possible, to be even more wonderfully refreshing than it had the first time. She washed the plates and cooking equipment that she, her Father, Crick, and then Url brought down, and although she was well aware of the reasons why they needed to set off as soon as possible she found herself in no particular hurry to leave. She felt safe in the water. Protected. Perhaps the others felt it too…? She looked across to Url, but just then somewhere above her a flash of gold caught her eye… The plate she was holding dropped with a gentle splash into the water beneath her. She heard her Father ask her what was wrong, but in her shock she didn't dare speak or move, hearing gasps from the others around her as they turned, following her eyes back up the side of the crater…

Again the vast creature had appeared from nowhere. Its shroud of golden fur shimmered brilliant in the sunlight, broken by the few smooth drifts of black. Like one of the glistening statues of the Firstway it stood perfectly still, less than fifty feet above and to the left of the cart. Its keen dark eyes studied with a careful patience those of the group who had remained on that upper ledge, all of whom were oblivious to it. Perhaps it was simply because it was above them, or maybe because of the strange effect the sun had upon it, but it seemed even larger and more powerful here than it had done at the lake. There was a sudden splash beside Aliya as Url dropped the handful of plates he had just finished, leaping up through the rock…

'Url!' Orlando whispered hoarsely after him, but Url ignored him, continuing to climb.

A sudden low, deep rumbling stopped him dead in his tracks. The creature was looking down at them. It growled again, though growl perhaps was not the right word from something so majestic; still no sign of movement but for a gentle quivering of the fur around its throat. Aliya heard her Mother cry out in shock as she noticed it now, then each of the others as well. Siu dived for Yori but seemed frozen to the ground once she reached him; Tarryn crawling hastily backwards on his elbows until he was beside them. The creature looked from one group to the other, and then with a slow, lazy swing of its forked red tail it strode carefully off the edge of the rock it was standing upon, stepping grandly down towards the river; the ripples of emerald in its coat merging with though far more vivid than the moss around it. It picked its way with ease over the jagged ground, the tips of its long claws tapping lightly on the stone; pausing to gaze at Aliya and the others again once it drew level with them before stepping, gently, into the full strength of the river.

Aliya was surprised to find the fear she felt for herself and the others switching briefly to fear for the creature itself… but she quickly saw there was no need for it: The raging current was having almost no effect. The creature was standing as calmly as it had been on the rocks above them, utterly unconcerned about the flow which would have swept away any other being Aliya could think of in an instant. Even its fur, brighter and clearer now than it had been moments before, shimmering around its legs and those sections of its body which one by one became submerged, was doing little more than waving slowly through the water, floating peacefully as though against nothing more than a gentle breeze. It lowered its head to the foam, taking more in several great gulps than Aliya could drink in days, and then it raised itself up to its full height once more, growling another long, deep note against which the water in the pool around Aliya rippled excitedly. It took a slow, measured step towards them…

'Slowly,' said Url, quietly, starting to climb again back towards the cart. Orlando pushed Aliya and Crick after him and then followed himself; each of them turning back repeatedly to watch the creature as it made its way across to the pool and then stopped, still staring up at them.

The cart was almost ready by the time Aliya reached it; Crick helping Tarryn into the back while Url and Abetta took the front; the thick fog of barely-restrained haste adding intolerably to the tension. It was no small stroke of luck which had seen Url choose to face the horses up the slope and away now from the creature. Even as the last of the possessions were thrown inside he set them to a walk, each of the three unaware of the cause of the sudden air of alarm behind them; Aliya and most of the others walking beside once more.

'Where is it?' asked Crick.

Aliya looked back down to the pool again… but it was gone; no sign of gold, green or black save for that which grew from or lay upon the ground.

'Is it hiding?' asked Tarryn, leaning awkwardly out from the back of the cart.

'Point to *one* place down there where something that size could hide…!' called Url.

'Well where is it, then?' asked Siu, halting with Aliya and the others while the cart laboured slowly up the stone.

In truth, Aliya saw as she studied the interior of the crater beyond which they had ventured, most notably to either side of the raging channel at its centre, there were some places amongst the great fissures which had been made in the road which could possibly have given room for the being to hide. But despite this, and the logic of what Tarryn has asked, Aliya knew that it was no longer down there. *Hiding* somehow simply didn't seem to be a thing this creature would do. From them, or from anyone.

'If it wanted to hurt us it would have done it by now, surely,' said Aliya.

'Told you that himself, did he?' said Crick.

'Do you remember the first time we saw it?' asked Aliya, turning to Aulan. 'Do you –' and it was only now that she noticed the awed look on Aulan's face. 'Do you know what it is?'

'I – Yes...' he whispered, smiling nervously. 'I remember, vaguely, I think. And yes – I believe I do. It has been so long since I have seen him...'

'It'll have to wait,' said Orlando, ushering them away from the ledge. 'I think these poor things are going to need help getting back up here.'

Again they would have fared far better had there been four of them, Aliya thought angrily; but despite this they managed – with comparatively minor contributions from Aliya and the others – to reach the top. The breeze which struck them as they left the shelter of the crater was far colder than Aliya remembered.

'Any sign of it?' asked Url.

But still there was nothing. And even as they made their way around the side of the crater, looking directly as was possible out along the path of the river, it was as though the creature had never been there at all. Nobody spoke until they were safely upon the far rim, at first the river and then the crater itself beginning to disappear from view. Aliya sat up and strained her neck to see the last of it, saddened to watch it go.

'You were saying...?' said Crick, looking eagerly to Aulan.

'Alamos,' said Aulan. Aliya saw Url's head cock to one side, as though almost recalling the name. 'One of the ancient treasures of the natural world. He has lived since days long before even I was born, and reveals himself only rarely; the cruellest enemy of some, the humblest servant of others. I think he is still trying to work out which of the two he shall be to us...'

'But what about the Black Wind? How does he survive out here?'

'He can melt into and spring forth from the earth itself, as you have seen. And his strength is almost without equal. Even *we* never knew from where his powers came… He seemed, and still seems, to be possessed of a great vein of Magic to which we were yet to be introduced.'

'So what can we do to, well, make him *like* us?' asked Tarryn.

'Nothing. And it would be wise not to try. He will see straight through any deception or act. His eyes seek deeper than that. If he should appear again, and if he has decided against us, I beg you not to react. Make no move of resistance against him. It will be futile, and will only serve to anger him further. As far as he is concerned, I am afraid we must simply accept whatever fate has been chosen for us.'

'If you think I'm going to let that overgrown wolf take me down without me putting up a fight you're sorely wrong, my friend,' said Url, looking back with a combative grin to Abetta, who returned it with a disdainful shake of her head. Aulan seemed uncertain whether to be amused or aghast at Url's contempt for the creature.

'Maybe he's waiting for us to get rid of the old man before he comes and makes friends with us…?' Crick muttered to Tarryn.

'I say it's worth a try,' said Abetta, overhearing him.

'Hmm?' said Url, too engrossed in his own thoughts to have heard them. 'What? What is?'

'New type of soup I've been thinking of,' said Abetta absently. Url gave her a long, disbelieving scowl before turning his eyes back to the road.

*

'So what were you two talking about, anyway, back there?' asked Crick a while later, looking between Aliya and Tarryn. Aliya felt the eyes of her family turning one by one towards her; an uncomfortable heat rising swiftly through her neck and cheeks.

'Nothing much,' she answered, with what she presumed to be the greatest effort at cool indifference ever made.

'*Nothing*…?' said Url. It had been too much by far to hope that he could simply let this go. 'I couldn't quite make out what it was you were saying, but there were definitely words of some sort being spoken… Couldn't be *nothing*, now, could it?'

'My family, and Immelus,' said Tarryn as Aliya hesitated, not wanting to be the one to bring up the subjects. She gave him a brief, grateful smile for drawing the attention away from her. With a deep sigh, Tarryn continued: 'I never told you how close you were to meeting my Mother, did I?' he said to Crick.

'Your Mother? No… When?'

'In your little foray up the Sun Tower. It was probably her that discovered something had been stolen and raised the alarm – probably had to report to the High Councillors themselves. Though I suppose she would have enjoyed that,' he mumbled to himself, 'Any excuse…'

'What do you mean?' asked Crick. His whole body had suddenly become rigid. Aliya had expected him to be surprised, but not so shocked as he was. He was staring a hole in the floor of the cart between his feet, his shoulders imperceptibly hunched and tight, gripping one hand stiff in the other as though to brace himself from trembling. He seemed almost terrified. Aliya saw her Father, who was sitting beside him, eyeing him curiously, but Tarryn and the others appeared not to have noticed.

'She had first duty in the Wilder Rooms that morning,' Tarryn continued; Crick grimacing silently at the words, burying his eyes in his hand so the others wouldn't see. 'I *think* it was her, anyway.'

'It might have been someone else?' Crick asked, trying to mask his hope with lightness. 'Who?'

'Don't know his name, he –'

'*He…*' Crick sighed, pressing his hand hard against his forehead. 'So if it was a woman, it was… it was your…'

'Mother, yes,' said Tarryn, sitting up and noticing Crick's silent distress for the first time.

And finally it clicked within Aliya. She knew what must have happened; knew why Crick had seemed so upset whenever she had mentioned that night. For a moment she refused to believe the thought, but a look into her brother's eyes told him she was right… She felt as sick as he looked.

'Why?' Tarryn asked, studying him. 'Did you… Did you see her?'

'Stop the cart,' said Crick, leaping from the back before Url had had time to do so. The sound of his retching came as a surprise to the others, but not to Aliya. Orlando jumped out after him.

'What in the Darkness is the matter with him?' asked Url.

'Do you know what it is?' asked Siu. She must have seen the look in Aliya's eyes. Aliya simply shook her head; she didn't want to *think* what it was she was thinking, let alone say it. A moment later Crick appeared around the side of the cart, wiping vomit from the side of his chin; Orlando's concerned hand on his shoulder. He looked through the cart to Tarryn: a desperate, wretched look, ignoring Siu's questions.

'She *was* there, wasn't she?' Tarryn's voice was strangely flat. It took Crick a few seconds to speak…

301

'She… came in just when I'd found the map…'

'She saw you?'

Crick hesitated again, and then nodded, bringing gasps from Siu and Url.

'*What!*' Url shouted angrily.

'Why didn't you tell us?' Siu demanded.

'But the alarm wasn't raised…' said Tarryn, quietly. 'Not straight away. And you made it out…' It seemed to have dawned on him as well. For a few seconds everyone was silent.

'No…' said Siu, looking between the two of them. 'Crick… you –'

'Son, what happened up there?' asked Orlando; Crick still forcing himself to look straight through to Tarryn… or perhaps he just couldn't tear his eyes away.

'I'm so – I didn't know what to…' was all he could manage before he collapsed back onto the ground; Orlando easing him down.

'What happened to her?' asked Siu quickly. 'What did – what did you do?'

'I was just trying to get out!' Crick pleaded. 'I – she got in my way… tried to take the map… She was calling out for the Guardsmen! I couldn't – But, still, I wasn't trying to *hurt* her! I was just trying to get out!'

'Was she…' Orlando began nervously, looking between him and Tarryn. 'When you left her… Was she alive?'

Crick said nothing, but in his silence and the pain in his eyes was revealed the answer as plainly as if he had shouted it aloud. There was a shuffling behind Aliya: Tarryn had sat up, oblivious to Abetta's attempts to stop him. He scowled with pain but ignored it, sliding himself through the cart between Siu and the Heart, his gaze never wavering from Crick. When he reached the end he swung his legs out over the back. Aliya was just beside him, to his left, and by his right hand she saw the axe Crick had used against the scarravers.

'Stand up,' said Tarryn.

'Take it easy, lad,' said Url, disappearing from the curtain and stepping quickly round to the back of the cart.

'Tarryn, I know you're –' Orlando began.

'Stand up,' Tarryn repeated. 'You…' He gave a mighty, trembling sigh. 'You look ridiculous down there.'

Frowning fearfully up at him, and paying brief, miserable glances around to the others, Crick climbed slowly to his feet.

'Come here…'

Aliya didn't blame her brother for staying where he was. But Tarryn beckoned him forwards again impatiently; his eyes red and blinking back tears... but lacking the fury, the wildness Aliya had expected. Crick took several steps forward, stopping with a jolt just out of arm's reach as he spotted the axe.

'Ha,' Tarryn laughed quietly, appearing to notice the axe for the first time. 'Yes, I suppose by rights I should be doing what I can to cleave off certain parts of you...' He looked back to Crick, and then slowly reached out his hand. Crick stood frozen in place, eyes wide with shock. He watched Tarryn's hand suspiciously.

'I've only just mastered sitting up,' said Tarryn. 'Don't make me *walk* all the way over there.'

Carefully Crick took another, hesitant step, reaching out to take Tarryn's hand. Aliya wasn't the only one watching each and every subtle movement of the muscles of Tarryn's arm, but against all their fears he simply leaned forwards, sighed again, and gripped Crick's hand...

'It's over,' he said simply. 'Let it go.'

For several long, confusing seconds, nobody moved or made a sound.

'But... Why...?' asked Crick.

'I know you wouldn't have done anything you didn't have to do. She was in your way. You had to get out. I would have done the same.'

Not for the first time did Aliya wish desperately for a measure of Yori's skill at reading people... She studied Tarryn, trying to comprehend his reaction, but the eyes she had thought she was beginning to understand gave little away. All she could glean from them was a hint at the great pain which lay beneath; a pain which went well beyond the knowledge of what he had just been told. A pain of the type that must have taken a great many years to build. Standing small and nervous in Tarryn's shadow Crick had no greater insight either; his hand still held passively within Tarryn's, the rest of his body tensed and subtly angled like a frightened animal preparing to flee.

'But you're... you don't seem –'

'Upset? I...' His mouth held open for a moment, but he stopped himself from saying whatever he had been about to say. 'It's... rather a shock, yes. But, *upset*...?' He sniffed a sudden, indomitable breath, sitting upright. 'No. Can't say I am. Not really the right thing for a son to say, is it?' he added bitterly, seeing the look that Siu was giving him. He released Crick's hand, leaning back into the cart. 'Well, she wasn't exactly the finest of *Mothers*, either. Perfect match for my Father, though. Both intelligent; both from long lines of Councillors; both ambitious… Both hard and unfeeling enough not to let anything get in their way of or bring shame to the reputations they prized more than anything else. Even their son. *Especially* their son.

I could never work out what it was about me that frustrated them so much. I tried… For so many years I tried. But I couldn't be the perfect little Councillor-in-waiting they wanted me to be. I was always strong – *strong* was never a problem. But I was never *clever* enough, you see. Growing up I could beat all my friends when we fought, but I never won a single battle of wits against my parents. Eventually I gave up… but that only seemed to anger them more. You know those *old training wounds* on my back?' Crick nodded. 'Well, they're not. Not most of them, at least. They're the mark of failing to live up to the expectations of people like my parents. They didn't do it themselves, of course… Far too beneath them to discipline their own child… They left it to our stewards. Some of them went easy on me, pretended to strike me harder than they were. Some didn't… Either way, *she* would always be watching. Even when I was old and big enough to break the stewards in two, they forced me to take my beatings; threatened me with things far worse if I didn't go along with them. I hadn't spoken to either of them for more months than I can remember. Why do you think I was so keen to get out of that place? Just for your company…?'

Knowing he had no right in this moment to be the one who was upset, Crick made no reaction, but Aliya could tell that the words had stung. Tarryn had not been entirely serious, but it had not been far off.

'Listen, lad,' said Url. 'I'm sorry for your loss, truly, and I promise we can make time to remember her later – if you want, of course. But –'

'It's alright, we can go.'

'But,' Siu began, 'are you going to be okay? With…' She gestured anxiously to Crick, and as she did so the look which swept through her son was one of frightened, disappointed sadness that carried with it a silent weight which nearly struck him to the floor once more. Beside Aliya Tarryn gave a single, simple nod.

'Come on, you've held us up long enough already,' he said, trying to force an easiness into his voice, but in that moment suddenly unable to look at Crick any longer. With Siu's help he pushed himself back into the cart, this time allowing Abetta's hands to take a portion of his weight as he laid himself gently onto the boards, angrily brushing away the tears that had started to tumble across his cheeks. With her Father, Url, and finally Crick retaking their places throughout the cart, Aliya continued to study Tarryn across the end of the Heart which lay between them, realising she wished for nothing more than to be free to go and comfort him. And then into the afternoon they set off; Crash the only member of the party to dare break the silence, neighing quietly against Url's flick of the reins as she and the others continued their steady, northward march along the Firstway.

Chapter Twenty-Three

Fear's Grip

...There it was again... the fleeting breeze of a past life, still haunting the verges of thought; desperate, incessant – a quiet ember refusing to die like the others into the cold. Once more she was calling... Why wouldn't she leave him alone? Why couldn't they all just leave him here? Leave him alone... He didn't want to go back there; didn't want to leave... It was dark here, but darker by far out there, amongst that gathering storm, that endless night. He didn't want to go... *He wouldn't go...* They couldn't make him...

And so again he turned away from the stroke of her reaching thoughts; felt a cool wind brush thin and tender across his forehead. He ignored it as he had the other times, keeping it at bay, letting it pass without response... If he could just keep silent, keep still, keep away from them, then he wouldn't have to go back... It wasn't safe out there. They weren't safe. They thought they were – thought they were protected as long as they stayed close. Close to their great prize. But they had no idea what was coming... Nothing could stop it: day swallowed by a night from which no new day would come. They would suffer so unbearably... He couldn't let himself be taken like they would be. He wouldn't let it happen. The shadows here were terrifying, in this oblivion, this underworld deeper than deep, so far from the surface that all thought and sound and sight were one and nothing... But the darkness out there was far worse... What else could he do, where else could he hide, when the only place left for him to go was a nightmare more terrible even than that within which he was already caught…? He had to stay here… Just had to ignore them… Not let them pull him back…

There was a great consciousness ahead, in the distance across their path… One and many voices at the same time… Echoes of a deserted people; numbers and fury beyond count. Perhaps this was the place they had been talking about…

Time and time again had he drifted close to their world, sensing their progress, hearing them speak of days, and of nights, while in here time passed by and through him with no such measure: sleep and consciousness, life and death, sight and blindness all one and the same; a constant, unchanging as the rhythm of the deep black that surrounded him. But time and time again had he withdrawn from them… recoiled from the hope they carried, knowing it to be false; a trap; a wickedness so much worse than despair for the lie of it. At least despair was honest. At least despair told of what was to come. Hope lied… They would never understand that… not until it was too late, and the ghastly truth of it all broke upon them like the crashing of a great and terrible wave…

They… They were the ones who were trying to make him leave; trying to bring him out to share their appalling fate… He wouldn't let them… They wanted him back, but he wouldn't go to them… How could he choose that? *How* could he put himself willingly back amongst that? What madness would it be to *choose* to go back there…?

Maybe… maybe there was a part of him which wanted to be with them again. His… *family*…

No! *No*… he couldn't let himself think the word; couldn't let himself think like that… Couldn't let that part of him trick him into going back. Nothing was worth going back for… even them. The currents here were bleak, and cold. Suffocating… But through them at least nothing could reach him. Not even the Darkness could find him here. His body would burn and crumble with those of the others, but *he* would be safe here, hidden; an eternity of this emptiness far better a fate than a single moment of the agony which would bring the others screaming and flailing to their ends.

Something was blocking their way: the last barrier between them and the voices… or perhaps screams… Thousands… Each in different tones though all crying aloud the same tune… somewhere up ahead. Close. Not the very Darkness itself – that was still too far away. For now. But a small part of its wrath at least… the smallest demonstration of its power… its terror…

One of them had found a way through. The girl… *sister*… She was leading them over. Over the barrier from which they should have turned back; potent and pure, flowing swiftly before the voices; a mark to those who would read it to leave... to run... But instead they were excited, pleased...

Fools... Such *fools*! Even if they crossed the divide... even if they made it through the voices, and then through whatever else there was which lay beyond... none of it mattered. The Darkness had seen them. Seen them now for what they were, and for what they were doing. It knew what they carried. It knew. And after so long at bay the distant margins of the Outerlands – lands and skies and seas alike – were crashing in towards them now like the enfolding of the very borders of the world upon them, unstoppable and enraged, marshalled forth by the ancient hand of doom awakened... All of it would be here soon...

If only the golden blaze would come again... the power of the light... of the mountain... It had brought him back into this nightmare, roused him from the deep; perhaps it could take him from it too... Take him back to wherever it was that he had been before: asleep... unknowing... unafraid. He would do anything to be there again. Give anything... Sacrifice anything. Anything to be free of this torment. Anything to escape from here, without having to go back to *them* and what they would soon face...

They were nearly across. Struggling... arguing... but nearly across. Almost there. They couldn't hear it though... Still they couldn't hear the voices. They would, soon enough... They wouldn't be allowed to pass through... Perhaps *this* was where their journey would end... here... even before the Darkness itself claimed them. Maybe it would be better this way... Dreadful, but better than waiting for the Darkness. Anything was better than that...

The touch of wind blew light across his face again... It was her... her voice... She wouldn't stop... She would never stop. He knew it; felt it. They were never going to leave him here. They would try forever to bring him back to them. They would fight until their very ends to bring him back to them... And he loved them for it...

No! He wouldn't let them do this! He mustn't... He had to keep fighting...

But they were becoming too strong for him. He could feel the outline of their world around him now; figures and sounds moving somewhere above him, the surface of their existence pressing suddenly close about him... He was being drawn back into it... up... away from the gloomed shelter of his mind... Grey shadows of towering walls and great buildings spread high in all directions... Distant walkways silhouetted far-off against a sky whose brightness would soon be gone, overrun; streets speaking of the age and enormity of this place as they passed through them, one after another, slowly, deep into the sprawling realm of rock and timber, gemstone and metals which had once held so much life... All of it now silent and empty, abandoned, to *their* unseeing eyes and ears, at least...

The demonic choir whispered again: Excited, angry... hungry... More defined than before. Closer. It had sensed the coming of the others... They were hidden from it for now amongst the vastness of their surroundings... mice hiding in a great field of corn. But not for long...

None of this mattered, though... None of it was important... None of it – hope or fear, pain and joy and despair – none could get to him so long as he was here, here in this bleak sanctuary. It was so cold... So lonely. He was so afraid. Too frightened to move...

So many streets, and buildings, and carvings... no two the same... Thousands, around and above each other, using every space, creeping into and amongst themselves like the rigid trees and undergrowth of an ancient grey forest... the love and care which had crafted them long since disappeared, been destroyed, corrupted: transformed into something else.

Something echoed in distance; neither sight nor sound... Thousands of spirits – tens of thousands – all soaring and tumbling and gliding towards each other through the city... Above it, below, and through the streets too they came now from their nests, all seeking each other. The voices were drawing together. Then they would come...

Confusion shattered the thought... The others had come to a fresh halt in their road. The new face amongst them spoke with his many tongues again: The outlander; his shadowy thoughts still veiled behind whatever strange mask it was he wore. He was not yet revealed as he seemed to be. Many ways to go... choices...

The surroundings started moving again... They had chosen, and well: The song becoming quieter...

But from nowhere a gateway was suddenly beside them: One of them had seen it... His brother... It hadn't been there before... No... *Crick*! *No*...! The choir rose up in the distance; one and many... They knew the others were near... If he opened the trap...

Again the brush against his forehead... A hand this time; the fingers warm... soft... afraid... He fought not to recognise it, but the power of its tenderness was too strong... *Mother* – and with the word the tugging upon his heart made him cry out in fear and pain and sorrow into the dark... She was out there, her hair almost reaching down through the trembling, wrenching surface above him... They were all there... about to reveal themselves... He had to stop them!

No! *No*! He *mustn't*! Just stay still, silent, unseen… Don't let it see him…

They wouldn't realise what was happening until it was too late… If he didn't warn them…

A hand fell upon metal with a crash which tore through the air unnoticed by any of them… The choir stopped; listening, waiting. It was his brother… It was Crick: His fingers wrapping themselves light around the handle… slowly, but too fast… It was about to happen… He had to stop them… His family…

The surge of Darkness was there… coming… terrible…

He wouldn't let them die…

'Yori?'

His Mother… There was no time…

'He's moving!'

But Crick in his eagerness hadn't heard: his fingers tightening, turning… This was it… he couldn't let them! Even as the handle twisted in its place he was surging up through the darkness towards them into the dangling strands of his Mother's hair, erupting with a blinding blaze of terror into the daylight of their world…

'*Noooo*…!'

But it was too late: his scream as nothing to the choir's; the others finally hearing it too as an awful roar shook the walls around them, echoing back through the street they had entered… Their eyes, now finally filled with the fear which should have been there already, darted from the gateway to him as he collapsed towards the other side of the cart, his legs failing under his sudden weight… He breathed a shallow breath as he fell… He was back; he was with them. It had seen him… It would take him too… He gazed up into his Mother's eyes, all he could see as she leapt to take hold of him before he struck the boards; delighted, terrified, confused… the others all recoiling inwards from the distant screams which surged again through the city and the sky above. His brother's hand left the gate, its damage done… Yori tried to call out again but amongst a gasping sob of pain he managed barely a whisper…

'They're coming…'

And with that the haze around him cleared… The cart; his family; vast spears of marble crossing high above a silver, cobbled road… The small gate, wood crossed with beaten rails of simplest bronze, the dreadful trap they had sprung…

Still he looked into his Mother's eyes. They had won… He was back in their world. Their fate was his to share once more.

Chapter Twenty-Four

Retreat

'*They're coming!*' Yori screamed; such a frantic flaring of panic erupting from within him that for a moment all the others were stunned. The buildings around them trembled loudly for the second time. 'Nnnoooo!' he grimaced, struggling against Siu as she tried to calm him. 'No! We have to get out of here – *They're coming!*'

'There is someth–' but before Aulan could finish he collapsed to his knees, cowering suddenly from the gateway beside Crick, his head angling up into the skyline like a beast having gained the scent of a hunter. Through the endless jagged peaks of towers and walkways Aliya could see nothing, but she heard and felt it clear enough: a third time, and this time louder. 'We must leave,' Aulan managed to breathe as thin shards of stonework broke loose from the wall behind them, shattering as they struck the road. 'We must leave now.'

'Right – in…' said Url, lowering his shielding arm and brushing off the scattered fragments of stone which had flown up against him.

'Where're we going?' asked Crick, the last to jump into the back as the cart wheeled round.

'Back. To the river. Can you manage it again?' he added to Aliya.

'I –'

'It'll have to be faster than before…?'

Aliya gave a single, small nod. What else was she to do?

'We'll give you all the help we can,' said Url, striking the horses hard.

'This question is getting more than a little wearisome, I grant you,' said Tarryn as the cart bounced furiously over the cobbles, 'but what –'

'I don't know and don't care to find out,' said Url.

'It's the city,' said Yori. It was such a strange and wonderful thing to be hearing his voice again; Aliya wondered why then it also felt so terrible. Siu and Orlando were knelt before him, bracing themselves against the sides of the cart as they each held one of his hands; relieved smiles spoiled deeply by confusion and fear. 'The *people…*' Yori continued, forcing the words painfully through throat and lips unused to speech. 'The people who used to live here!' he shouted. 'It's them – They've seen us!'

'Hold on!'

Url's warning came just in time: Aliya held tight to the side of the cart as it turned sharp to the right sending tools, bags and persons flying to the other side. A small sack fell with a dull thud out from the back but Url ignored it. Watching it disappear from view, Aliya looked up from the road into the sprawl of the surrounding buildings… This wasn't right…

Somewhere amongst the howls behind them the sound of crashing stone signalled the collapse of some large structure… and again… followed by another swell of screams and a renewed quaking of the ground.

'This isn't the way we came!' Orlando called through to Url.

'Do you think I don't know that?' Url shouted back angrily. 'I – It's difficult to navigate through all this lot… The map doesn't give any detail for the city itself. *You* try memorising an hour's worth of turns while being chased back by...' he fell silent, uncertain how to finish.

'Alright, alright…' said Abetta, struggling to stand firm against the rattling of the cart. Orlando steadied her and helped her through to the front.

'What are you doing?' snapped Url.

'With any luck a better job than you!' she snapped back, falling into the seat beside him. She nodded curtly but acceptingly to the arm which came to steady her, but a second later she thrust it back towards Url and gave a sudden cry of 'There…!'

Url turned them quickly down the small, covered passageway she had pointed to on their left, sending Aliya and the others tumbling back again to the other side of the cart. The Heart quivered, threatened to roll, but after a moment's thought settled back into its place; only

Aulan's hands having reached out to steady it, the others looking on nervously.

'Please...' Yori murmured, looking up to the others. 'We have to go faster... Please – it's catching us...' He spoke quietly, but his whole body had begun to tremble, his breathing now quick and shallow as the frantic rattling of the wheels.

'Shhh... It's okay, son,' said Orlando, patting his chest gently, trying in his knowing ignorance to comfort him. 'It can't get to us as long as we're in here.'

Url turned back with a look of doubt etched upon his face, Aulan opening his mouth to speak, but with a raise of his hand Orlando silenced them both. Yori frowned but tried to smile, as unconvinced as the others, but pleased at least to hear the words.

Oden led them streaming out through the ragged end of the passageway as it opened into a wide, smooth courtyard, in the centre of which were the remains of three shallow pools surrounding what looked to have been a tall, spiralling water-fountain; the water long since replaced with browned moss and lines of thick, tangling vines. Wooden sculptures, now distorted with decay, sat around the edges of the courtyard in the doorways of small, comfortable-looking buildings. It must have been a lovely place, once; for a moment Aliya could picture without effort or difficulty people enjoying this quiet corner of Irraigion. Families. Children. The same people who apparently by Yori's curious sight were now gaining behind them, bringing down more and more of the city in great crashes which boomed through the passageway in the cart's wake, bringing a thunderous end to the short-lived quietness of the courtyard.

'Well...?' said Url.

'I've no idea,' said Abetta. Aliya looked out between them: there were four paths leading out of the courtyard ahead, all similar in their size and various decorations...

'Whichever takes us most easily south, surely?' said Tarryn, leaning round beside her.

'Good enough for me,' said Url, studying the sky for a moment. 'Either of those two...' He was pointing to the two leftmost paths.

Yori gave a quiet whimper, and an instant later the whole courtyard shook; the top of the fountain cracking and toppling sideways.

'Go!' shouted Crick as stone cascaded to the ground. With a frustrated grunt Url struck the horses off down the closest of the two paths; the cart bouncing back onto cobbles as the rest of the fountain collapsed heavily into itself.

'Are you sure this is going to work?' asked Crick, looking from Url to Aliya. Neither of them answered. It had been difficult enough crossing the river the first time, when they had been allowed all the time they needed. Aliya's mind was still weary from the effort it had taken to keep control of the water, and she still didn't truly understand how she had done it, or even *what* it was that she had done. It had been like Yori had always explained it: she had *seen* the water's Magic. She looked to her little brother, perhaps in hope of advice or merely for some look of understanding, but he was so scared... But the thought of doing it again, now, made her stomach turn. Even with the Heart, from which this new strength and power over the water seemed to be coming to her, she didn't know if she could be strong enough...

Through street after street they careered, the crashing and the voices growing ever-louder behind them like the approaching of a storm, once hidden, now suddenly released. Whichever way they turned, however hidden they felt in brief moments beneath the vast landscape of the city around them, they were never able to throw the pursuers off their trail for long. Walls shook, stone crumbled, streets clamoured down behind and around them; the frenzied anger of whatever it was that was chasing them growing time after time as it grew closer. The screams themselves had an almost physical quality, striking through to the very marrow of Aliya's bones, chilling her with their tireless rage. Even Oden was affected: his great presence now lessened by the fearfulness of the manner in which he threw out his head from side to side, fighting in vain to catch sight of the noises; his laboured breathing revealing his age truly for the first time since the beginning of the journey as he charged onwards with Crash and Nightwind through the city.

Walkways began to fracture and crumble from their centres almost directly above the cart, sending showers of greys and blacks tumbling thick through the skies, but finally the road led them out onto the edge of the open, mile-wide square which Aliya recognised from before. They were just a few hundred feet to the west of the road they had taken out from it a short while ago. Across on the far side of the vast number of stairways – some of which led up to grand, highly-decorated buildings, others which ran down into pits filled with what had looked earlier to be old shops and market stalls – Aliya knew that the edge of the city was just minutes away.

'We're almost there,' Siu whispered encouragingly in Yori's ear, hugging him tight to her but still unable to completely halt his trembling. He seemed to be slipping back into sleep, muttering inaudible cries of fear and warning to himself.

'Hurry, Url,' said Orlando.

Aliya expected an angry bark or some bitter response, but with a single brief look to Yori, Url simply sat taller in his seat and with a low growl struck the horses hard once more.

The surface here was mercifully flat – marble lined with wide strips of dark, polished wood that would almost have glinted had there been sun enough to shine upon it – so that for the first time Url was able to fully let Oden and the others go. They opened to a full gallop, Nightwind and Crash now taking the lead and surging forward against their harnesses, and in seconds the howling quietened: still there, but no longer on top of them. By the time they had reached the far side Aliya could no longer feel the rumbling around them. But she knew as well as the others that their peace was sure to be short-lived. To be able to hear amongst the silence their own, heavy breathing again was wonderful, but now they were back on the last few cobbled streets it would be gaining on them for sure. Aliya started to prepare herself...

The river... she could hear ... smell it: close now. She had to become part of it *now*; there wouldn't be time once they got there. With her eyes shut tight she reached out towards it... felt it... let it flow into and through her mind: deep, powerful, constant. Distant streaks of dark silvery-blue drifted far ahead of her, first in random flurries then slowly together into a single, wide trail from right to left... That was it... That was the river. She had found its power; its Magic. All she had to do now was stay with it... use it...

An explosion greater than any so far ripped suddenly through the air and brickwork to their left. Yori curled tighter into Siu's arms, murmuring something to himself which again none of the others could hear.

'It's almost around us!' shouted Crick. 'It's trying to cut us off!'

'No you don't...' Url growled, more furious than afraid. Aliya found the bitterness of it comforting. But suddenly she realised she had lost her link with the river. 'Here we go!' cried Url as around a final turn the tall, thin gates of the opening to the city, vast wooden trunks lined with rows of heavy brass studs, appeared. Aliya didn't join in with the terrified gasps of excitement around her: Rather she closed her mind to it as firmly as she could, seeking the river again...

And a minute later they were through the gates and back onto the large, familiar granite slabs of the Firstway over which they had already passed once this day. With her eyes still shut tight Aliya heard the difference rather than saw it. She was struggling to concentrate: The screams were close again: just inside the city walls, roaring out towards the gates. There were cries from the others with every building

315

that collapsed out of sight, one by one… It would be at the gates within moments…

'Everyone just do what you did last time,' said Url with a composure forced but effective enough for now. 'Crick – *Crick*…' He looked back and waited for Crick to turn away from the city, '– the ropes…' Crick nodded dumbly, looking immediately back to the gates. 'You help me out the front…?' Url said to Orlando and Siu. 'And you have the reins, my dear,' he added to Abetta. 'There it is…'

And Aliya had found it again too: When now she opened her eyes she saw the veins of Magic running through the wide strip of dark blue ahead of them like streaks of rippling silver splattered across a painting. She saw the vast, decayed remains of this northern side of the bridge which had somehow once spanned the river… And there, near-hidden amongst the sprawling shadows of those remains, tied up against the wooden pier, just as they had left it less than two hours ago, she saw the ancient, half-rotten barge which they had used to get across. Aliya felt a hand upon her shoulder… Her Father was talking to her:

'– be fine, just do what you did last time; let us do the hard work.' Either he didn't realise how difficult it had been for her the first time or he was merely trying to make her feel better. Either way he wasn't helping.

The cart veered left, off the road and down the grass embankment towards the river. They were nearly there. Aliya saw and heard everything around her but ignored it all; ignored everything but the river. This time she wouldn't let it go… she had to stay with it…

'Anyone else feel we're pushing our luck slightly using this thing *twice* in one day?' asked Tarryn, looking down through the front to the barge. In the panic it looked to be in an even greater state of disrepair than earlier; the long beams of its base and the low railings which lined the far edge held together seemingly by sheer stubbornness over anything else.

'I'm happy to turn around if you'd –'

'The gates!' screamed Crick.

Aliya couldn't help herself: Keeping her mind focused on the river but unable to resist the finger of terror scraping sharp down her neck she turned back to see…

It was as though a thick, black cloud was billowing out between the gates through which they had just passed. It spun and twisted, tumbling over itself, forming slowly into something almost solid upon the road just outside the city walls. As tall or maybe taller still than the buildings behind it, it started as Aliya and the others gazed dumbly upon it to take the shape of something like an upright beast, horned and

316

furious, coiling and raging against the sky, but before it was complete it let out a terrible, snapping roar, exploding into a rampant vapour once again and tumbling like water over a precipice fiercely down towards the river. Url was yet to let up the horses' pace: they sped magnificently over the last few hundred feet of flat ground, and it was only as they reached the first beams of the pier that Url reigned them in with a vicious tug of the straps. He turned and nodded to Orlando, disappearing from view as Aliya heard her Father, Mother, and then Crick exiting the back of the cart. She felt Tarryn watching her as she climbed past him into the front, asking her something. But she ignored him. She couldn't let her concentration waver now.

'You ready, dear?' her Grandmother asked softly as Aliya sat next to her. Aliya gave a blank nod, looking deep into the water ahead of her. The horses were being led onto the barge, confused and unwilling as they had been the first time; the pier creaking with the weight of the cart, the barge swaying with that of the horses. Aliya ignored it all: Her task was the water now... only the water... The others would have to deal with everything else.

Crick had already untied the first rope, and the instant the back wheels of the cart had rolled awkwardly onto the barge Url shouted for him to release the second.

'It's nearly here!' cried Crick, clawing frantically at the knot and leaping onto the barge even as the rope came away in his hands.

'Get up here, boy! Don't watch it!'

And with that they each worked furiously now on the wide, wooden wheel which turned the silver propellers on either side of the barge. Aliya felt the disturbance in the water; felt the barge begin to inch slowly away from the land. The ground was trembling behind her; stone being torn up from the road as the bestial cloud rolled across it; a great wind shrieking down through the grass; Yori's sobs turning to stifled screams... Away from the shelter of the pier Aliya suddenly felt the force of the river strike the side of the barge, pushing it downstream to their left... The others were fighting to keep control but again the current was too strong for them. The water trembled, frothed; the others each looking back in shock, shielding themselves as shadow fell around them: It was here. Aliya heard a quiet gasp from her Grandmother as together they plunged beneath the canvas – futile but in that instant all they could think to do... every muscle in Aliya's body tensed as finally the screams arrived like a gale of horror upon them...

317

'It...' Url's voice emerged hesitantly after a moment from the front of the barge, quiet and timid through the deep storm of wailing... 'They can't cross the water...!'

Slowly Aliya uncurled from beneath her Grandmother, not yet letting herself breathe freely again. Url was standing: the only one of the party, his hand on his waist in an effort at confidence, or perhaps simply to stop himself from shaking.

'Ha!' he laughed weakly, '*they can't cross*!'

In their cowering terrors the others at first shared little of his glee, but they recovered themselves enough to uncover their shielded eyes and look back to the bank...

Aliya had never seen or imagined anything like it. From within the cloud, at once quick and deathly slow, hundreds of emaciated, translucent figures were forming, men and women and children, raging forwards until they reached the water's edge from where they were clawing and snarling out at the barge; their crimson eyes filled with a desperate, burning anger. More and more of them came, furious and tormented, lining the bank scores deep for hundreds of feet in either direction. There was no end to them. Url's brief smile had vanished, and without a word he started work again on the wheel along with Crick, Orlando and Siu. Through the few seconds in which their concentration had faltered they had drifted nearly fifty feet downriver. Aulan vaulted past the front of the cart to help the others, and with the rising, thunderous volley of screams and howls behind them the barge started to creep forwards again; Aliya's head throbbing as she strained for a third time to regain her lost connection with the river.

'Ahh!' she screamed in frustration, 'I can't...' she jumped down onto the wooden floor, sodden with heavy splashes from over the upriver side of the barge. 'I can't concentrate from there!' she shouted back to Abetta.

'Aliya! What are you –' her Mother began as she ran past the agitated horses to the front and bent down towards the river, but as her hand plunged through the surface of the water everything around her was silenced: Her Mother; the others; the screams; all of it disappearing...

She was in the river. It was so easy now... as if suddenly its Magic had been lit up by a million waterfaeries. She thrust herself into it; took hold of it. She had to: the rapids were close, they had to reach the far bank quickly. And so alone now in the water, silent and cool, she let some of its strength pass... she couldn't possibly hope to control it all. But from every few strands of Magic which came towards her she chose one, and with a press of thought put herself in its way; tried to guide the slither of silver around to one side of her rather than allowing it straight into the barge. Sometimes she failed; the strand too strong or too quick for her. But again and again she was able to shield the barge from the current... It didn't turn to the right as she had hoped, but neither was it drifting downstream any longer. It was working: If she could just keep going...

But with every passing second the river seemed to be gaining in strength. They must have reached the middle, or close to it: At least, she hoped they had... The barge started to waver again as Aliya started missing strands she was aiming for... It was becoming too difficult; too strong. A piercing, pulsing pain shot through her mind behind her eyes... and again... Each new time she reached out again into the river it was as if somebody was hammering thin spines deeper into her skull: Suddenly she couldn't bear much more of it... She had lost all sense of time; all thoughts of where she was and why had disappeared. She was focused entirely on the river. Like a burning coal she felt the Heart behind her: warm, powerful. Whether she herself was still above the water or had long since fallen in she could no longer tell. She reached the next strand in time, deflecting it... then others... Several times she felt that she had almost turned them around completely, so that they were acting in the opposite direction, pushing or pulling the barge forwards; but she had no time to savour the moments. From side to side she glided time and again through the water, the barrier she was creating slowly becoming stronger, gathering to her will... Or perhaps the river was becoming weaker...? Someone was pulling at her shoulder, shaking her: She blinked, and with it lost her focus...

Her Father was standing above her. She couldn't hear what he was saying, but from the blurred corner of her eye something mud-covered and solid caught her attention. The southern pier. They were nearly there, well past the midpoint of the river now; the water in between glistening calm and clear, rippling low and gently before the barge. The screaming from the northern bank had died; now but a gentle tone amongst the breeze. The part of Aliya still linked to the river could feel its power easing, and as the barge slipped slowly into the stillness of the shallows she smiled weakly, thankful her job was done, feeling herself fading with the water, losing herself into it gladly once more as the strength of fear seeped piece by piece from whichever exhausted, ringing part of her mind it was that she had just used.

319

Chapter Twenty-Five

Fire without Flame

'*Crick*!' Url called again, impatient to make their escape complete. 'Pay attention – the ropes…'

Crick had been watching the last billowing plumes of the dark cloud as it disappeared back through the distant gates of the city; the screams which formed it still reaching back across the river until the last of it was out of sight. The silence which followed was wonderful, but a gentle bump as the barge met the pier reminded Crick of his role, and just as Url was about to call to him again he took the lengths of old, frayed rope which were being held out to him and jumped out to secure them.

'How is she?' asked Orlando, helping Siu lift Aliya into an awkward, sagging seated position, her head falling limp before her.

'She's exhausted herself,' said Url. 'She needs rest. Let's get her out.'

With the cart still swaying precariously above the water there was still work to do. The keenness of the horses – Crash in particular – to get back onto land was understandable, but problematic; the anxious animals stamping and straining continuously against their bindings. It took the combined efforts of everyone but Aliya, Tarryn and Yori, all of whom had been laid amongst the grass at the thick, twisting base of a large oak, to control the cart as it left the barge. Abetta let the horses out a few dozen feet into the trees, and then with a weary nod to Url she stopped; nobody saying a word as they collapsed onto the thick layer of twigs and leaves which covered the ground. For a long time, still gazing with cautious relief back upon the vast skyline of the old capital of Irraigion beyond the river, nobody moved or spoke a word.

*

It was night, or something oddly similar. Through the dark a girl dressed all in brilliant white stood suddenly at the end of a long, shadowed road, lit dimly from behind by a glow which turned the edges of her clothes and skin to silver, her brightness broken only by eyes of darkest black... She opened her mouth, raising her arms to the stars... but as her voiced carried up through the road it was deep, louder than it should have been... As night became day the beautiful figure faded, blurring into a swaying tangle of branches and leaves; another burst of Tarryn's laughter unclasping the last of Crick's desperate hold on the dream. The girl from Fellgate...

'And you do realise that we're going to have to get back over that river again...?' the former Guardsman was saying to nobody in particular. Through the trees above Crick the sky seemed much the same as before, and around him all the others were sitting just as they had been when his eyes had fallen closed; he couldn't have been gone more than a few minutes. 'Unless anyone fancies calling it a day here? We've got water, shelter...'

'Splendid neighbours!' said Crick, taking a deep breath and shaking his head to try to clear his mind, throwing a handful of twigs lazily in the direction of the city. Some of the others gave a tired, distracted chuckle, but from Tarryn there was no reply, his smile fading instantly. It was just as Crick had expected of him, but this made it no less disappointing. Over by Aliya and Yori, Crick noticed his Mother staring at him. She looked quickly away, but not before Crick had seen the discomforting look in her eyes... of sadness again, and confusion. The same look they had all had – sometimes hidden, often not – since the truth about what had happened in the Wilder Rooms had been revealed. They seemed to have forgotten, or perhaps had never realised, that excepting Tarryn, it was Crick in fact who had suffered the most from the revelation.

Back in the quandary of their present, the awkward and distinctly galling question of how best to yet again cross the river was put on hold for the remainder of the day. In the shelter of the small woodland which had grown to envelop the southern pier, with the boughs of surrounding oaks allowing through just the right amount of light and air, camp was set up, the horses cared for, and a meal prepared. Slowly but gradually Yori began to calm, and as Crick and the others started to

321

eat Aliya came round as well, yawning thickly; her condition no better or worse than was typical for her when she awoke.

'Well this makes a pleasant change!' said Siu, feeding Aliya steady mouthfuls of hot, pale yellow soup – Abetta had declined to say what was in it, Crick knowing only that they were running particularly low on most of the provisions that were usually used for such soups, and that he had certainly never tasted whatever this was before. 'All my children conscious and moving at the same time!' She looked across to Yori, lying with his head upon a dozing Url's lap, already smiling back at her.

'Yes,' grumbled Url. 'And why don't we try and keep it that way for a while, hmm?'

*

Crick had barely wiped the crust of sleep from his eyes the following morning before he was sent by his long-since wide-awake Grandmother to refill the skins. The cart was only a stone's throw from the river, but the trees in between blocked much of it from view, and it was only as Crick rounded the last of them, tripping groggily through its roots, that he noticed Url sitting within the dip of a small, grassy hollow by the water's edge. He was gazing intently upstream to the west, through the twisted remnants of the southern foot of the bridge, the map unwrapped and rolled carefully across his lap. Crick felt a fleeting sense of pride at seeing it open and being used like that, until he remembered again what it had cost to get it.

'What's the plan, then?' he asked, trying to distract himself from the thought. Url must have heard him coming: the old man barely reacting at all, paying Crick only the briefest of glances, as though in effort to ensure not a second more was wasted here than was needed.

'The barge.'

Crick stopped where he was, unsure whether or not it had been a joke. But as Url turned to look up at him, Crick saw the grim, determined glint in his eyes.

'There's no other crossing that I or your map know of for days in both directions,' Url sighed. 'And there's no saying that even when we get to them we won't find'em like this one...' He nodded to the divided skeleton of the bridge. 'We have to take it.'

Crick set down the skins and joined him by the water, the edge of the river playing just beyond his feet. The low, early light made the city stand out even more clearly against the pale blue behind; gilded walls and towers notched and stained with time and the violence that had befallen them but stretching proud nonetheless across most of the skyline, barring their way.

'Obviously we can't go that way,' Url continued, noticing where Crick was looking. 'Or that way,' he added, nodding down the river to his right '– unless you'd be so kind as to relocate those rather inconsiderately placed boulders and rapids down there…?'

'I would, but your nemesis has me doing other things just now… far too busy…'

'Ah… Well, it'll have to be *that* way then, won't it?' In the opposite direction the river continued more or less straight into the west for as far as Crick could see. Sprouting from the opposite bank were the beginnings of what in the distance grew to be a range of large, steep hills, flanking and disappearing away from the westernmost limits of the city.

'Told you we'd need it, didn't I?' said Url, tapping the map gently. 'We'll be off the road a few days, at least.'

'Hardly makes it worth it, though, does it,' said Crick, his grin lasting barely a second. He continued staring up into the distant hills, not wanting Url to see the sudden glaze which was threatening to break across his eyes.

'Doesn't it?' Url asked. 'I don't know about that. Listen –' he turned Crick's shoulder gently round to face him, '– Tarryn was right when he said you had to get out of there. If you hadn't, we'd all have suffered, and in time so would countless others. Nothing else is as important as getting this Heart to Iala. *Nothing*. You killed someone.' The words, stated so simply, felt like fiery steel through Crick's chest. Url saw but continued without pause: 'And Tarryn lost a Mother. And it's terrible. And you're both going to have to deal with it. So will everyone else. But you – listen to me –' he bent forward awkwardly to look Crick straight in the eye, '– You did what needed to be done. And sometimes what needs to be done can be an awful thing to do. It takes a brave person to see those things through. You did *well*, understand? I'm not saying it wouldn't have been lovely if she hadn't seen you. And I'm not saying you should go around happy and shouting about it. But neither should you be so upset by it. Between you and me, I fear there's going to be plenty more moments like that – choices that have to be made, and things that have to be done in moments not granted the freedom of long thought – before we're finished. I'll gladly pray to any god, King of old, or *Vessel* of White Mountain that you can name that whichever one of us it is who faces that moment has the courage you showed up in that tower.'

Crick could think of nothing to say. There was such a wild playing of emotions within him, each disagreeing and conflicting with the next, he had no idea which one to chose...

'*Brave*...' he muttered, shaking his head. There was that word again, like a creature stalking him, haunting him, challenging him. He hated it, and was unable to hide the fact from Url, whose shrewd eyes picked up immediately on the tension which rippled through his body. 'I didn't feel br–'

'*Feel*?' Url interrupted. '*Feel's* got nothing to do with it, lad. Brave isn't something you *feel*. It's something you *do*. What you did was brave. As far as I can tell, most of all you've ever *done* has been brave. Some of it *stupid*, mind... but mostly brave nonetheless. You should be proud of yourself, lad. Proud of who you are. *I* am...'

'Crick...?' His Mother's call drifted through the trees.

'Better get back to it,' said Url, turning back to the map.

Crick took the skins to the water in silence, watching Url as he studied the map and the river ahead of them. For all his reliance upon and insistence in his own beliefs and ways, even at the expense of his coming to be known as the arrogant, eccentric old man, there was also such genuine understanding in him. Such an astute, measured kindness. Perhaps he didn't even believe what he had said... Perhaps it had been merely a sermon with which to make Crick feel better and speed him on his way. Crick doubted it, but either way the words had done their work well. Before he left, Crick paused beside the hollow.

'Thanks...'

'Just saying it as it is,' said Url without looking up.

Crick still felt that a smile was beyond him, but he breathed a little easier at least as he walked back to the cart, feeling for the first time in a long while that the weight pressing down upon him since the Sun Tower had lifted, if only slightly. The face was still there... *Her* face... Tarryn's Mother. He could still see the blood. But it was distant now; calmed and faded behind a thin, but comforting wall of acceptance. When he returned to the others and Tarryn turned away from him this time he felt the sadness just as keenly as before, but the sharp wrench of distress, the bitter edge to the pain of his own shame, had gone.

*

Over breakfast Url told the others of his decision. Their agreement came with surprisingly swiftness; each seeming already to have assumed that they would be compelled to try the barge again. Certainly, nobody had any better suggestions. It was established that they would take the barge as far upstream as they could travel in the morning, keeping to the calm waters near the bank before crossing to the far side. The current would undoubtedly drag them back down a short way, but with fair fortune they should be so far along by that time that it wouldn't bring them anywhere close to the city or the rapids beyond. If they could find a particularly narrow, shallow, or slow-moving part of the river to cross, so much the better.

'We shouldn't need you to do anything,' Url said to Aliya.

'I feel fine now,' Aliya started quickly, looking disappointed. 'I'd like –'

'And after yesterday it would be far better if you didn't,' Abetta stated more plainly. Url nodded and continued before Aliya could argue:

'We're going to have to find a path through the hills to the north of the river, and make our way back round to the road.'

'How much does the map tell us about those hills?' asked Orlando.

'Not much – but enough, I think.'

'*Not much… But enough…* You *think…*' Abetta muttered slowly, smiling as she shook her head softly. 'Marvellous…'

'Quite,' said Url, waving her away like an irksome fly. 'By the looks of it, there should be a fairly steady climb through to the far side. There are some steep ridges leading down out of the northern slopes, but we should be able to find a way through them. At worst we'll just have to move along to the next ridge and try that. We'll find a way. And beyond that the ground seems clear and flat.' His confidence had grown even as he spoke; Crick finding himself infused by whatever unseen chest of optimism it was that the old man had just unlocked and delved into. But with the exception of Tarryn, the others didn't look to be sharing his renewed buoyancy.

'Besides –' Url continued, '– We get to see a bit more of the world… *Azhera*, didn't you call it?' he asked of Aulan.

'That was what the peoples of my time called it, yes. All land from east to west, north to south enclosed by the great deepwaters beyond. Azhera… From what I know, I do not think the word has been used for many centuries, now.'

'Well I like it!' said Url, rerolling the map tighter in his hands and tucking it carefully within his cloak. 'I think we should take it upon ourselves to be the ones to start bringing it back into use. And now that we're out here, I'll be glad to see as much of it as we can!'

Orlando carried a bewildered frown as he stood and took a slow, careful step towards him, peering deep into Url's eyes…

'*Crick…?*'

*

By late-morning, all remaining uncertainties put firmly aside beneath a warm haze of confidence, a good start had been made to Url's plan. The water along the edge of the river remained as calm as had been hoped for, and even with breaks every half-hour or so they had travelled a good few miles to the north-west; the city now hidden behind the first low, featureless strip of hills.

'Couldn't we cross here?' asked Tarryn. 'We're well away from the place.'

'Not well enough,' said Orlando. 'You saw how quickly that thing chased us down. Even here it could still reach us in minutes. And once we're over the other side we might not have a nice big stretch of water like this to hide behind.'

'We'd save a day's ride or more not having to go through these hills.'

'If you're that keen on the thing we can pay it a visit on our way back,' said Url. 'He's right, lad: Just because we can't see the city doesn't mean the city can't see us. We need to be further away before we risk it again.'

Tarryn pursed his lips and made no reply.

And as the hills began to loom taller and steeper ahead of them, Crick was not the only one to begin to share Tarryn's judgement, at least in part. From the beginning there had been little to distinguish the far bank of the river from the early slopes of the hills, but now with each slow turn of the propellers they were becoming entirely one and the same: the high hilltops, held together by a tumbling mat of thick grass, weeds and roots, dropping almost vertically into the water, all but impassable by climb, let alone traverse by cart. The deep green wall cast curious reflections on the water, creating barriers and swirls of movement where there were none, and turning everything to a dull turquoise, growing duller still as the wall grew taller and darker with each new stretch of the river.

An hour later, therefore, as the northern cliff parted either side of a wide, sandy cove, the river beginning to bend gently round to the south and the peaks of the green wall above long-since lost somewhere high amongst the clouds, there was agreement from all quarters that they had now come far enough. Half a mile further they landed the barge one final time to rest before making the crossing, and then, almost in silence, everyone took to their positions. There was little discussion, little debate; each knowing what they each had to do – Aliya insisting upon being by the water and helping as she had done

326

during the other crossings – so that with a simple nod from Url the barge set off quickly away from the southern bank.

And as it was, the crossing proved far less demanding than any of them had feared. Though the current at the heart of the river was still strong, the fact that they could afford to let it carry them back down to the cove, together with the efficiency with which they were now able to work and control the barge, meant that they reached the northern bank with time to spare, still several hundred feet before the point at which the cliffs parted. Aliya also proved herself both correct and remarkably helpful, somehow doing whatever it was she did to turn much of the current away from them, dizzy this time with exhilaration rather than exhaustion when finally the barge rose up with a soft murmur onto the soft, pale yellow sand which lined the inside of the cove.

'Just like that!' said Url, smiling broadly and looking back victoriously across the river.

'How about making this the last time we do that, for now…?' said Orlando.

'Not that it hasn't been fun, of course,' said Tarryn. 'But yes, I suppose three times *is* quite enough, for now.'

Tying the ropes around the tip of a large, jagged boulder a few feet from the water's edge, Crick could see through a scattering of thin trees all the way along the sheer, narrow valley into which they had entered. Another, taller hill formed an intimidating barrier to the north. Crick looked for signs of the valley continuing around to either side, less than enamoured with the idea of having to cross over it, but from this distance it was impossible to tell.

With each of the group keen to discover how their new route would treat them lunch was short and simple. Abetta's seeded bread was still no more or less fresh than it had been many days ago, but the sweet, cool water from just outside the cove went a way towards making up for it. The ground beyond the cove was covered with grass and clusters of tiny flowers growing in the shade of the trees – flowers which could perhaps have been white were it not for a thin sheen of dusty grey which clung about them like ancient mould – but it was also sandy and loose; the wheels of the cart sinking several inches rather than riding above it. Crick volunteered to get out and walk, happy to explore and to have a better view of the landscape around them, and knowing that if he didn't Url would before long be asking him to anyway. And soon enough all the others – except for Tarryn, who could still only manage an uncomfortable sitting in the front next to Url and Abetta – did likewise.

Even Yori was strong enough now to walk. Though naturally doing his best not to reveal it, Crick was delighted to have his little brother laughing and playing around him again. There were more smiles and laughter, and amongst them more words of encouragement, than there had been for a long time. And though the successful crossing of the river seemed to have put everyone into perhaps unjustifiably high spirits, Crick was certainly not going to be the one to remind them of their situation. He joined in with relish in the merriment, even succeeding in raising a smile or two from Aulan with the rather limited attempt at hide-and-seek he engaged in briefly with Yori and Aliya.

*

The valley was even longer than it had first appeared, and longer than Url had judged it from the map – assuming, as Aliya questioned more than once, that Url had interpreted the scenery correctly, and was, more to the point, looking at the right valley. But beneath them the ground grew no worse, and ahead the trees remained few enough for the cart to pass through without trouble. By the time they came to the single vast, steep scree-slope which curved around and above the north and eastern ends of the valley, there was still ample sun left in the sky, and it was decided without much deliberation to continue round to the west, where the valley rose steadily over firm, open ground into the main body of the hills. And after a further hour's slow march a shallow, sweeping pass came into sight up ahead, less than a mile away.

'Don't suppose you can tell us what we're going to find over there?' asked Tarryn, grimacing as he craned to see out through the cart; sighing with the frustration of not being able to walk with the others.

'Hills and woodlands, for about thirty miles. That's the best I can do. We're near the edge of the map here; it's… well… not really designed for people travelling *this* far off the road…' he added quietly.

Behind them the river disappeared now behind the western wall of the valley, while ahead the slope started to ease. With the smooth, green crests of the surrounding hilltops rising up like curious, grass-helmed giants on either side, the cart rolled slowly up the last few feet to the pass…

'Well, nobody can say you were wrong…' Tarryn muttered quietly as Oden, Nightwind and Crash halted without any need of command from Url. Crick and the others walked round to the front and looked out, silenced for a moment, but pleasantly surprised at just how accurate Url had been… Hills and woodlands, for about thirty miles. A great cluster of what seemed once to have been carefully-fashioned

328

copses rising and falling like the patterned waves of a frozen sea of green, all enclosed by a line of straight, light brown peaks to the north. With the exception of those final hills, none of it in between appeared to present too much of a challenge. There were very few steep rises that Crick could see; the woods dense but broken regularly by clear, wide trails, with a good number of streams and large lakes in between.

The quiet relief brought by the sight of this new terrain spurred them on with renewed vigour, down to the edge of the first clump of woodland. The tall spruces gazed down imperiously but with a sweet, welcoming scent upon them as they approached, murmuring quietly to each other about what surely were their first visitors in many long years. Siu and Orlando both began to explore the outer verge of the undergrowth; Siu sensing the presence of blackberries within while behind her Aliya could feel the coolness of a stream they had glimpsed from the pass. She seemed refreshed merely with the thought of it.

'We won't find anywhere better than here,' said Url, stretching and dropping the reins by his feet. Already passing sacks and foods wearily out to each other from the back of the cart, Crick and most of the others had themselves arrived at similar conclusions, but they obliged with muttered agreements nonetheless.

*

The following day started clear and bright; the chilled bite to the dawn air dispersing the moment the sun rose above the green of the eastern heights. A snaking route around the base of most of the hills, aided by the map, was not difficult to find, and in many places the ground was hard and flat, as though ancient paths were hidden somewhere beneath the years of earth, rock and grass. Indeed, this may well have been the case if the black, thread-thin marks woven into the map were anything to go by. Each area of woodland they came to was built of a slightly different assortment of trees, of all various differing types, all of which continued their gentle conversations as the group slipped quietly amongst them; Orlando listening intently, seeming occasionally to catch brief words or phrases, but unable or unwilling in his rapt concentration to share any of them with the others.

Shortly after lunch they passed the first of the lakes: a long cleft in the ground curling almost back on itself like a misshapen horseshoe, beside which they paused to swim and let the horses drink their fill. The ground on this western side sloped lightly down to the water; Url insisting that the horseless cart be secured before they left it. As the others were drying themselves off beneath the warm sun – Siu still trying with little sign of success to coax Aliya out from the water –

329

Crick went back up to untie it and make ready to leave, only to find the ropes lying in a tight, neat loop amongst the roots at the base of the tree he had tied them to. He stopped, confused…

'Did you untie this already?' he shouted back to Url.

'Of course not. Why?'

'I… Nothing – looking at the wrong rope…' Crick answered quickly, letting his words trail off, not wanting to reveal that he had forgotten to secure the cart.

But he *hadn't* forgotten; he was sure of it. Slowly he walked up to the tree… The loop was far neater than he or even Url usually made it. None of the others would have done it, except possibly… He looked up into the tree, frowning as he studied the branch he was certain he had tied the rope to: It had changed. It must have done – he would never have chosen a branch like that. But it was the only one; the next closest was several feet above him… It *had* to be that one… He picked up the rope, still staring hard at the branch as a gentle gust of wind blew through the trees, and suddenly in the brief chink of sunlight which found its way through the leaves a tiny turquoise gem glittered bright upon a small knot which jutted out from the top of the branch, fading the instant the upper limbs of the tree settled back into place. Crick reached out to it, but as his fingers touched what he had expected to be wood the gem shone again. The knot toppled, falling to the underside of the branch as Crick staggered backwards, barely suppressing a scream. The knot swung gently from side to side. He watched it for a moment, and then found that his head was tilting quite unconsciously round to one side, so that he was looking at the branch almost upside-down… He couldn't quite believe what he was seeing… For from the wood which connected the knot to the rest of the branch above it he could make out two short, stubby legs, and then two small arms, clasped loose around its wrinkled middle. The gem winked: It was an eye…

'Urrrrl! Guys! *Get over here!*'

'What? What's wrong?' Url was by his side in seconds, and apart from Aliya and Tarryn the others were close behind. Crick hadn't been able to move or take his eyes off the creature… whatever it was… its head still swinging contentedly below its tiny, plump body. Suddenly Url caught sight of it, and as he did so he let out a delighted laugh…

'A marmik! Look…!' he said, pulling Abetta forwards.

A marmik… of course… Crick suddenly felt rather foolish.

'A *marmik*?' said Abetta. 'I haven't seen one of those for – My goodness…' She stopped abruptly next to Url, her smile matching his as she saw it. 'Well he *is* a pretty one, isn't he?'

'You've heard of marmiks, Crick...?' said his Mother.

'I –'

'Big, brave, Crick...' mocked Aliya, appearing between them and kneeling before it. 'Afraid of a cute little thing like him... Or *her*...?' she added with a backwards glance to Url and Abetta. Url shrugged.

Crick of course *had* heard of marmiks before; of how they were supposed to be able to camouflage themselves against whichever type of surface they were born within. But never had he seen one, and certainly never had he expected to find one out here. Though now he thought about it, it did make sense: If anything could hide from the Black Wind for so long, it would likely be something like this. Its perfectly rounded eye flickered constantly between differing shades of blue and green as it moved; one of the rarest and most valuable of finds, eagerly and often cruelly sought by hunters, venturers and collectors for generations. They could live grand lives back in the Heartlands with a treasure like this...

'You stay away from him,' said Yori, scowling at Crick as he stepped past him. Crick stammered for something to say: He had barely thought it, and certainly had no intention of actually doing anything of the sort. He forced himself to remember how good it was to have his brother back amongst them.

Amidst the group the little creature's head had stopped moving. It let go of the branch and fell, instantly turning a bright silver from head to stubby feet, righting itself just before it hit the ground. After a moment's pause it waddled forwards, curling itself up into Yori's outstretched hands. Yori turned back with an enchanted smile, cradling the marmik. Siu and Orlando looked at each other for a moment.

'I suppose we can find room for him,' said Siu.

'As long as you're going to cope having him around?' said Url with a belittling pat of Crick's shoulder. Crick shrugged him off and went back to readying the horses.

*

The new companion quickly proved himself far more troublesome than his small stature and bumbling demeanour made him seem capable of, though none of the group, including Crick, could help but enjoy watching him. He seemed possessed of an unquenchable fascination for anything broken, untidy, or simply not in its proper place. And after so long on the road, and all the cart had been through, the little creature's work was endless. Clambering quickly around the cart across the laps and shoulders of Crick and the others, he spent much of the day straightening creased sections of the canvas, binding loose ropes into place or rolling them into small, neat loops, and moving items from one end to the other. The trouble with this, however, was that his idea of what counted as tidy, or in the right place, was frequently at great odds with what the others and, most particularly, Url, were used to. He arranged the sacks of food around the edge of the cart in order of size, rather than type; he attempted to tie together the ends of two ropes which would have sealed off the back entrance to the cart; and several times he tugged gently on the legs of Crick, Aliya, and Siu until they straightened them out in front of them. On the whole, though, his presence was welcome entertainment. He did little which couldn't be undone, much which was in some way at least helpful, and above all of this it was pleasing to have something to watch during the long silences as they continued through the once-intriguing, now increasingly monotonous landscape outside.

As the afternoon wore on a thick bank of dark, sullen stormcloud rolled in quickly from the south. With everything turned suddenly to night the sky broke in an explosion of light and deep, booming roars, drenching the hillsides with a near-inconceivable downpour from which Url was forced to seek shelter; the little silver marmik working furiously to keep the cart in good order beneath the steady pounding of the rain. To everyone's relief the weather moved quickly on through the hills, bringing out the sun less than an hour after it had disappeared, and for a short time everything from the treetops to the grass beneath them glistened and breathed tendrils of steam into the air, giving the hillsides a peculiar, dreamlike quality. But as the sun filled the land once again the last of the rain was soon burned away, returning everything to its former calm.

It was shortly after this – seven patches of woodland, as Crick had come to count the time – that Orlando, who had taken over from Url in the front, turned back into the cart…

'I can see the last of the hills. We're almost there.'

Crick stretched and followed Url out of the back.

'Where's our little friend?' asked Url as he passed Yori, who was curled up in the back corner. Yori pointed sleepily upwards: The little marmik was mirroring him, curled up in exactly the same position amongst the beams in the corner above.

The final ridgeline was just a few miles away, and Crick now was able to see most of the slopes leading up into it, along with the undulating line across them above which green faded gradually into a blend of dusty, sandy tones.

'We should get all the water we can while we're down here,' said Url.

'Let's try to cross today,' said Orlando, apparently anticipating what Url had been about to say.

'I think we'd be best off setting up down here,' said Url, sure enough. 'We can make an early start on it tomorrow.'

'I'd like to go today as well,' said Aliya. 'There's something about this place I don't like.'

It was only now she had said it, but suddenly Crick realised that he had begun to feel it too. It was something about being constantly enclosed like this, and perhaps also the almost eerie peacefulness of it all... It felt like wandering through an enormous burial trench. Not being able to see the world outside made everything feel slower; like they were wasting time they didn't have. Crick was surprised Url didn't feel the same.

'There's still plenty of the day left,' said Siu. 'We can make it to the top, at least. Then we'll know what's ahead of us tomorrow. It would be nice if we could see the road from up there.'

'We might...' said Url, taking out the map from his jacket pocket and unfolding it with Crick's help. 'It's a good way off... But we should be high enough up there, and there's nothing of note in between.' He sighed, looking up at the sun and then down to the slopes ahead of them. 'What do you think...?' he asked, looking back into the cart. Crick hadn't heard Yori getting out; the marmik perched softly upon his shoulder.

'I can't feel anything here,' said Yori after a moment. He looked unusually vacant. All day in fact he had been quiet, not at all like the day before. Aulan, too, had said barely a word.

'Exactly,' said Url. 'There's nothing in here but us. It's just your imaginations playing –'

'No...' Yori interrupted quietly. 'I mean, I can't feel *anything* here... *Nobody*. Not even any of you.'

For a few seconds nobody was sure what to say. Siu knelt before him, holding his hands.

'What do you mean, Yori? Why can't you feel us?'

'I don't know. It started after we crossed the river. You've all become... You seem far away. I can't see you any more...' His voice trailed off and his eyes drifted up to the silver creature on his shoulder, whose head had begun to swing from side to side once more. Save for its eye, the features of its face were little more than dim, shallow impressions, from which it was impossible to discern any form of thought or emotion, but somehow Crick felt that it was smiling.

333

'*He's* the only one I can feel, now,' Yori continued. 'And he's… different. Not like us. Not like anything I've felt before.'

Siu stood and backed away slightly from him, studying him and the marmik, trying to mask her fear.

'Well I think that decides it, then,' said Url, a grim look renewing the weary spark in his eyes.

'We'd be halfway up there by now if it wasn't for all this talking!' called Tarryn, leaning out from the back of the cart. It was the first time he had moved without much discomfort since the scarravers. It was good to see, and for a moment at least it distracted the others from Yori's words. In quiet murmur of conversation everyone climbed back into the cart; Crick leading the confused Yori by his free shoulder, the bright turquoise gem still bobbing in calm, constant rhythm the other side of him.

*

Rounding the eastern tip of the last of stretch of woodland, there was finally nothing left to go around: Up or back were now their only options. This time Tarryn all but demanded to be released to walk with the others, but still Abetta would hear nothing of it, keeping a firm eye on him from the front seat of the cart while Crick and the others walked beside, through the last of the grass and straggling undergrowth, up into the dull rock of the steadily steepening hillside. They had gone perhaps half a mile, just as dust was beginning to be thrown up by the horses and the wheels of the cart, when Crick heard Yori shout behind him:

'Hey! Where are you –'

The marmik, flashing a sudden bright silver, had leapt from his shoulder and was standing several feet back down the slope, its head darting between Yori and the woodlands below.

'I – I can't… We have to go *this* way…' said Yori, motioning up the hill. It seemed to understand: It stopped moving, gazing up at Yori and then briskly around at the others. Yori opened his mouth to speak again, but with a sudden, blinding flash of its eye the creature was gone. For a moment everyone stared at the ground, looking for some sign of where it had disappeared to… but there was nothing.

'I didn't know it could do *that*…' said Crick. Neither had any of the others.

'Well… he was fun while he was here,' said Url at length, uncertainly, patting Yori on the back and prompting him uphill. Yori said nothing, but as they walked he cast frequent glances back down the slope, gazing into the woodlands, as though in hope of finding a

334

tiny dot of silver amongst them. And though Crick couldn't explain it, he too found himself, for a few minutes at least, feeling an odd sense of loss for their little friend. A loose end of rope swung untidily against the top of the canvas of the cart, and for the first time in his life, Crick found it rather irritating. He would have moved to tie it back into place, had Aliya not got there first.

Several times the way ahead was blocked, either with loose stone or occasional columns of a new, reddish rock which nobody but Url had seen before, which stuck out from the ground like sharp burning spears cast sheer into the slope. At these junctions there was often little to choose between going left or right, and when there was the debate was usually settled with the simple but so far effective method of seeing which way Oden showed most interest in. There was only one point – as they found themselves caught within a narrow track in the side of a particularly steep section of slope, which turned out to be sealed at the end with a steep drop back through into the valley – at which they were forced to turn back and find a different way. But with that exception they continued slowly but steadily up through the wide, barren terrain, and with afternoon drawing to an end they finally approached the top. Crick, slapping thick clumps of dust from his boots and paying careful attention not to stray too far ahead, was the first to get there, and as he did so he looked suddenly down into a scene which all the threads and markings of his map had not done justice by half...

'It's...' he called without turning back to the others, lost for the right word. 'Incredible! Slightly, um, disconcerting...' he added, murmuring to himself. 'But, still...'

Somewhere to his left the sun had dipped low behind the ridgeline which continued far into the north-west, but it was still half an hour or so from setting altogether. The sky before them was empty, and endless, as though painted on a grander canvas than ever it had been before. And from the hidden western horizon, a light of vivid orange streamed back in wide, expanding shafts across a flat, boundless desert wilderness of sand and bright red rock thousands of feet below him, scorching every distant mile of sight, creating a blazing majesty of landscape Crick had never known; a deep, spectacular world of fire without flame.

'*That*, I did not expect,' said Url beside him. Together they surveyed the scene; Crick's attention lost amongst the sheer astonishment of it all, but Url apparently noticing something in particular, sighing deeply before whispering quietly to Crick: 'No road...'

'And no easy way down that I can see,' Crick murmured back once his eyes had adjusted to viewing the land in terms of paths and possible routes through to the other side. The slope beneath them was a forbidding mixture of sand and twisting alleyways of rock, some of which ended abruptly with high, impassable walls; some of which turned sharply to left or right and descended or rose into other, distant and unseen parts of the sprawling ridgeline; and the rest of which seemed to fall away suddenly into thin air.

'Maybe there's a path down through that…?' said Aliya, pointing to a long, wide crest a mile to their left which sloped down gradually, several hundred feet above the rest of the hillside, to meet the sands below.

'Perhaps,' said Url. 'But we can't get to it. According to the map there're cliffs just in front of it. Don't know how deep they are – but a cliff's a cliff: we'll never get the cart across.'

'What about water?' asked Siu.

'We've got enough to last us a good three days,' said Abetta. 'Four, if we're careful.'

'Even the horses?' asked Orlando. Abetta nodded.

'It shouldn't take us more than two,' said Url.

'Assuming we can find a way down here to start with…' said Aliya.

'Well, yes, that would be helpful.'

'Give me a couple more days and I'll *carry* the damn thing down!' called Tarryn. 'If that's acceptable with you, of course?' he added through the cart to Abetta.

'If we're still stuck here by then,' answered Abetta, 'you feel free.'

*

Having made camp fifty feet or so down from the dusty crest of the hill to avoid the strongest gusts of the new wind which blew across the peak from the south, the first attempt was made shortly after dawn the following day. It did not go well. By late morning, and following a tremendous effort from both the horses and all other members of the party, they had successfully managed to free the cart from the unexpectedly thick dune into which they had stumbled, only to bring it back more or less to where they had started.

'You – feel up to – carrying this – thing yet, lad?' asked Url through heavy panting. From the back of the cart Tarryn tried a smile, but he couldn't disguise his growing hatred of being carried

336

everywhere while the others did the work. Abetta wouldn't be able to restrain him in the cart much longer.

After some much-needed refreshment a different route was decided upon and the attempted descent began again; a path chosen now through a narrow break in the rocks to the west, across a wide stretch of loose but manageable sand and towards the ridge to which Aliya had pointed the previous day. As the ruby-sheened walls continued to block the way down, forcing them further sideways along the slope, Crick began to fear that they would soon have to turn back once more. And sure enough, a short time later the cliffs which Url had predicted appeared several hundred feet in front of them, forming a wide ravine which descended out of sight. There were no light-hearted quips, no jokes or even weary laughs this time; only quiet groans of frustration as they began to carefully manoeuvre the cart and the horses round in a tight circle to face back across the hillside. But suddenly Abetta called for them to stop: With her strong eyes and high vantage point from the front of the cart, she had seen a thin break in the wall below them, just before the cliff. Crick could have kissed her at that moment. And when they reached the spot, and found that it did indeed lead straight down alongside the top edge of the cliff, he actually did: the first such unrequested kiss his Grandmother had received from him in many a year.

From there the route was largely unproblematic. Several times the thick oak boards which had been used for crossing streams were required in order to get the cart over an area of deep sand, and on either side the walls of rock became so narrow at one point that Orlando was forced to dismantle part of the top of the cart so that it could squeeze through. But there were no more dead-ends, and nothing which barred their progress for more than a few minutes at a time. Though it was hard to believe, it had barely passed midday when Crick led the way triumphantly out from the confines of the hot, dusty corridor…

'I didn't know there could ever be this much sand in one place…' said Aliya, awestruck, as were Crick and all the others, by the simple, powerful vastness of what was spread out before them. Sand, light yellow with only an occasional tinge of red from this angle, as far as any of them could see.

'We hunted here…' said Aulan. His words were quiet, but they took the group by surprise nonetheless. They were his first in a long while. Since crossing the river he seemed to have been caught amongst his own thoughts; the joy of conversation he had relished since his awakening now lost, replaced instead with a cold detachment which had seen him eat and sleep away from Crick and the others, murmuring quietly to himself, almost angrily at times. But now as he looked out over the sands his eyes sparked with memory…

'This…' he paused again, stepping through into the beginnings of the dune. 'I think this was the furthest we ever travelled. We came to it from the west, not through here. The sands were home to… my memory fails me again… we prized it very dearly; a great creature, perhaps, or…' He frowned, trying to conjure forward the image, but said no more.

'I do so enjoy these encouraging little reminiscences he comes out with,' Url muttered. Abetta had slapped the side of his head almost before he had finished talking, but in front of them Aulan appeared not to have heard.

'Why can't I remember it all…?' Aulan was scowling west to east along the horizon, looking suddenly bitter and upset. 'I – *Why* can't I remember? I thought I had, but… there are still pieces missing! Pieces of me – who I used to be… I – I can't find them! I don't know how…'

Siu put a motherly arm across his back, looking to the others for suggestions. But nobody could find the right words. Slowly Aulan began to calm, wiping his eyes with the ragged sleeve of his shirt, looking down to Siu as he had done some time ago like a tall, lost child.

'I am sorry, again,' said Aulan. 'I didn't mean to… It is hard, not knowing everything about who you are. Especially when…' he turned and looked back to the cart. 'If it were not for me, none of you would have to be here. None of this would have happened.'

'Well it did; and we are,' said Url impatiently, climbing up into the front of the cart. 'If you want to feel better about it, get up here and try and help me pick a good way through this lot,' he added, pointing out into the sands and flicking the horses lightly with the reins at the same time. Siu gave him a look of disapproval as she ushered the silent Aulan up into the front seat; Url making a clear point of not noticing. Abetta took the other side while Crick and the others climbed awkwardly into the back, drawing the sides tight together to keep out as best they could the cloud of sand and dust which was thrown up as the cart started moving slowly into the sea of orange.

'So you know where you're going, then?' Crick called through to Url.

'North-east until we hit a big grey thing with a fair number of bridges running up and down it.'

Something about the way Aulan had acted or spoken seemed to have knocked Url into a sharp and thoroughly irritated frame of mind. Perhaps he had been reminded of his own feelings of guilt for bringing the rest of them on this journey. Perhaps not. But either way, as was

338

happening more and more as the journey continued, the mood of one spread like light from a flame instantly around to the others. They travelled in silence, the horses striding slowly through the sand which, mercifully, was just firm enough for Crick and the others not to have to get out and walk.

*

Waking came early, if sleep ever came at all, in the discomfort of travel through this strange, yellow land. Despite having sealed off each and every edge of curtain firmly, and countless times, there had been nothing any of the group could do throughout any of the long, hot and laboured miles they managed in the first day, or the longer, hotter miles of the second, to prevent a thick layer of fine dust from infiltrating the cart. Now at the beginning of the third it now coated everything and everyone; clothes, equipment, and bodies all a strange shade of dull orange; everything dirty and gritty to the touch. And with no water to spare for washing it all off, Crick was no less eager than any of the others to get through the sands as quickly as possible. Tarryn's snoring had also returned dramatically alongside his improving health, as though he was trying to make up for the past nights in which he had been mercifully quiet. None of this did anything at all to improve the group's declining spirits, and neither, as they started out into the rising sun, did the fact that still they were unable to see the road. According to Url they should have been less than half a day away; the map depicting that from the northern entrance to Irraigion it continued straight a short distance before beginning a chain of long, snaking turns – for what reason was unclear – and then straightening once more into the north. It was a western section of one of the loops which they should have been able to see by now. There was, however, a small rise a few miles ahead, part of a long series of dunes which tumbled away into the north-east, which despite being barely a few dozen feet high at its middle was enough in this eternally flat world to obscure the view ahead.

'I don't want to take us up,' said Url, pulling open the curtain slightly and bringing in a fresh cloud of discomfort as he poked his head through. Crick saw Aulan holding the reins, wide-eyed with concentration. 'Thought I'd let him have a go,' Url mumbled. 'After the other day, you know... Anyway –' he went on, frowning away Siu's approving grin, '– there's no point risking getting stuck up there. It'll only take us half an hour or so to get round it.'

'I was looking forward to seeing the road,' said Crick.

'You mean you were looking forward to finding out if it's there at all…' said Url. Crick shrugged. 'Well, if I'm honest so was I. The top of the rise isn't too far from where I can safely get us to: *You* can run up and have a look for yourself when we get there.'

'Url, I don't –' began Orlando, but Url had already gone, throwing shut the curtain.

For several minutes Crick listened patiently as his parents explained why he shouldn't leave the cart: all good reasons, undoubtedly; none of which had any impact on Crick. But in the end he didn't have to utter a single word. Quite without any input from him they seemed to talk themselves round to the idea of Crick taking perhaps a quick glance from the top of the rise, unable to disguise the fact that they were just as keen as Crick to find out whether they would be travelling along smooth road or through hot, dusty, wearisome sand this afternoon.

But with the others still talking, Crick, closest to the curtain, heard Url through the canvas, murmuring quietly:

'What in the…'

'You can have your fill once we get there,' Siu was saying to Tarryn, who had been grumbling unsubtly about the scarcity of food for the past two days. Crick tried to ignore them both…

'I'll take them now, lad,' Url added, presumably to Aulan. Crick leaned up to the curtain.

'Why is it d–' But as his Grandmother spoke there was a dull cracking beneath them. A moment later the left side of the cart sunk several feet into the sand; the back of Crick's head striking the corner beam as the others gasped and shouted behind him.

'What was –' Orlando began, but with a great splintering all about them they were suddenly falling. For a brief and endless second as everything plunged swiftly into darkness Crick felt the cart disappearing beneath him. He surrounded his head with his arms, bracing himself; someone beside him managing a short gasp… And with a terrible crunch he knew in the instant it took to shut tight his eyes that the cart was destroyed; all air thrust from his lungs as the small of his back hit something solid; bodies falling heavily across him as he tumbled into canvas, spinning sideways through it into shadow and down a hard, steep slope, coming finally to rest in a crumpled heap half-buried by cold sand, fighting for breath but not daring to move for fear of what might be broken; the only sound in the darkness the awful, choked screaming of one of the horses somewhere above him, loud and terrible amidst the silence of the others…

Chapter Twenty-Six

Divided

Through the break in the ground above light was falling at sharp angles into the darkness; shards of dull yellow through the fog of dust and fine sand, lightly skimming the hessian-covered Heart amongst the first scattered remnants of the cart but unwilling or unable to reach further down the slope to the others. The high, wailing note of Crash, and the dreadful sound of her broken legs flailing feebly against harness and loose sand continued as the only noises in this dark new place until Orlando's voice, sharp and frightened, cut like a slender arrow through the confusion:

'Is anyone hurt?' he asked roughly, forcing his voice above his own pains.

'I'm –' Yori spluttered on the words, '– I'm okay.'

'As am I,' said Aulan, quietly.

'Aliya? Crick?' called Orlando.

'I… think I'm fine…!' said Crick, with surprise which for an instant bordered on disbelief.

'Aliya?' called Siu.

'My shoulder…' Aliya spoke quietly, through firmly gritted teeth. Crick could see the outline of her motionless form a few feet away. 'I – *ahh*… I can't move it.'

'I'm coming,' said Orlando, hastily disentangling himself from a mass of wood and canvas. Crick began to dig his limbs gingerly from the sand, trying to twist himself round and up into a sitting position.

'Urlmaeus?' came Abetta's voice, further down than any of the others, hidden in the dark. There was no answer.

'Url?' Crick shouted. 'Url!'

'Tarryn?' called Siu.

'Fine…' answered Tarryn, though it was a similar *fine* to that which he had given after escaping the scarravers.

'*Url*…!' Crick called again, louder; and this time his voice came back to him a moment later… then again… a curious mixture of weak, muffled echoes with other, sharper ones amongst them.

'Where in the Darkness are we?' asked Tarryn.

'I think he's –' Crick started, but with a heavy grating of metal hundreds of feet below them torchlight spilled suddenly through a narrow gap, widening swiftly into the two sides of a low, broad doorway through which a dozen figures raced, all brandishing various lengths of blade and mace amongst the flames. The gold of the first of their torches lit up the base of the great hill of sand onto the summit of which the cart had fallen, revealing with it the twisted, unmoving body of Url, face-down, just feet from the bottom.

'*Url*!' screamed Crick, leaping out into the air and half-falling, half-flying down the slope until with a final bound he emerged from the shadow to Url's side, staring unarmed but defiant up at the approaching men who were now revealed to be wearing long, black tunics and simple, undecorated gauntlets and helms of dull grey steel. He heard his Mother's scream but made no retreat. He wouldn't leave him. But as the figures each caught sight of Url and Crick they hesitated…

'It's – They're *men*!' one of them exclaimed, peering closer; his rough voice trimmed by masked but unmistakable relief.

'*The seal*!' shouted another, his echoes merging with the remnants of the last. And then above them both a third came loudest of all:

'Get the crafters up here!' boomed the fierce bark of a man in full, crimson plate, standing motionless behind the others in the centre of the doorway. The thick, black scimitars which rested easily in each hand, curving out and back almost to rest upon his shoulders, looked as much a part of him as any of the rest of his body. As someone sprinted quickly away behind the doorway he turned back in towards the others: 'Take'em!'

'Crick, get back!' Siu cried again.

'There's others!' shouted another of the men.

'Spread out!' called the heavily-armed man. 'Up the sand! Find'em!' And then up into the darkness he bellowed: 'Show yourselves now without fight or you'll never see beyond this room!'

'Wait!' shouted Siu as one of the men came to within a few feet of Crick: Crick avoided his grasp, springing round behind him and relieving him of his sword along the way, but as he turned to raise it against the others a gauntlet clashed hard against the side of his cheek and he was thrown back into the sand; all thought, sound and vision swimming confusingly around him.

'*No!*' screamed Siu. 'We'll come! We'll come down! Please, just wait!'

'Then get down here,' said the figure in command. 'Do it now! How many are you? What were you trying to do? Why have you broken the seal?' The questions came like thick spits of rain in a storm... 'Where were you trying to go?'

There was a moment's pause as each of the group tried to make sense of the question...

'*Go?*' Tarryn repeated.

'Eight...' said Orlando, his arms raised as he walked quietly into the torchlight. Several men rushed to seize him. 'There's eight of us – some are hurt!' he continued awkwardly as his hands were bound behind his back. 'We're not here to take anything or do you any harm! We fell through from above –' And as he nodded up towards the dim rays of light and the splintered wreckage of the cart the men about him froze. The others, most of whom had started to fan out carefully up the slope, all halted, turning back, though still keeping watchful eyes out above them.

'You're from... you came from *outside*?' asked the man grasping one of Orlando's arms. He released his grip slightly, staring at him.

'Of course,' said Orlando. 'We're –'

'Shut him up!' roared the crimson commander, thrusting one of his curved blades angrily towards Orlando. 'And get the others down here! We need to seal the room!'

In seconds each of the group had either walked or been dragged roughly down the sand and out through the thick, black metal doorway into a small chamber, the rough rock walls of which were glazed a flickering succession of oranges in the torchlight. Crick had started to come round, but Url remained unconscious; Tarryn holding a hand across his stomach; Aliya gasping silently at the pain in her shoulder, holding her forearm delicately and at a curious angle in front of her. The others were each cut, bruised and afraid in various fashions and degrees, but they made no sound as they knelt, surrounded by the grim if somewhat bewildered faces of the armed men. The smoke of the many torches drifted up into small grooves in the roof, which joined together and disappeared into the rock above one of several open arches leading out of the room. As the last of the men passed through the doorway several others on either side pulled down at once upon thick wooden levers, and with a violent grinding the doors began to close, striking each other with a firm crunch with rang loudly against the walls; Url grimacing silently as the dying whimpers of Crash were sealed in away from him. In the centre of the crowded room the man grasping the two scimitars stood before the group, eyeing them carefully, waiting until all echoes had died away before he spoke...

'Any of you seen them before?' he demanded of the other men. Nobody answered. 'Neither have I...' He looked deep into the eyes of each of the group in turn, lingering upon Aulan, bending to open Url's lids, before finally releasing a long breath. He rested the tips of his blades softly on the ground beside him. 'And you have none of the shadow inside you...' he breathed. He no less than the others about him seemed awed by the statement.

'They're from outside!' shouted the same man that had said it before, near-stupid with excitement.

'Quiet!' ordered the man in charge as the others spoke hurriedly amongst each other, shouting out confused, excited questions. Most seemed to be addressing their leader as *Jericho*, or some brief variation of the name.

'Can you move yourselves, or do you need carrying?' he asked at length. In truth there was now little but the measured snap of efficiency in his voice, but Crick in his daze of fear and confusion was barred from seeing it that way:

'We can manage,' he spat, glaring at the men around him, some of whom chuckled openly as he raised himself uneasily from the ground, stumbling sideways into Tarryn. Tarryn pushed him back onto his feet, steadying him, though taking care not to look him in the eye.

'Good,' said Jericho, unbothered. 'Then follow me.'

He sheathed his blades either side of him and turned on the spot, striding out through the archway behind him. Several others followed, while the rest stood in a half-circle around the group, waiting for them to leave. With Aulan's help, Orlando lifted Url onto his shoulder, and with Abetta holding a handful of canvas to Tarryn's stomach, and Siu supporting Aliya, they started anxiously down the corridor the others had taken. It was only as they were nearly through the archway that each of them together suddenly realised they were leaving the Heart behind: It felt cold, and wrong. Terrifying... But with a hidden shake of her head Abetta silenced them all.

They walked on quietly through the close, jagged walls of rock. The low corridor sloped steeply downwards, curving slowly to the right, with many others leading off on either side. After several minutes they began to pass a series of high-ceilinged rooms from which men and women emerged asking hurried questions of Jericho. They could have been mistaken for people of the Heartlands had it not been for the highly polished beads of a strange black and white stone which sat delicately about their necks, and their dark blue and green clothing of some thick but almost silk-like material, which hung loose around them. Jericho ignored them all in turn even as their numbers swelled to a dozen or more, ordering the others to do the same, pushing onwards unswervingly down into the depths of the long, rocky warren.

Soon a group of six men and women came running breathlessly up the corridor towards them, wearing overalls of dull silver and bearing a vast and curious assortment of tools and materials. The oldest of them, a short man with a thick, unkempt beard which merged untidily into the top of his clothing, paused briefly before Jericho.

'*Fourteen*,' was all Jericho said, but evidently it was all the old man needed to hear, and he and the others hurried on past the group and away along the corridor.

There was no abrupt ending to the sides of rock beside and above them, as was typical for corridors. Instead, very gradually the walls and ceiling began to peel gently out and upwards, bringing the group seamlessly into a large, bowl-like cave, amongst the far side of which a vast, rectangular opening led through into another space, hidden for the moment in darkness. The loudest noises were still their own footsteps and the fluttering of the flames from the torches in front and behind as they were led around the edge, but slowly as they skirted the inside of the cave they began to hear the echoes of distant voices, hammerings, the whirring of strange devices, all gradually coming together and strengthening as though from some far-off town. An old flight of stairs chiselled thin and deep into the rock took them up the last few dozen feet to the lip of the cave, and there as they reached the final steps they found themselves halting, one by one, for a moment quite forgetting the armed men around them as they looked out through the wide opening…

They were staring out and down into an underground world, countless times larger even than the valley beneath the Eiger Hills, great as that had been. Far below them, as though crafted by the ancient passing of a nest of giant snakes, lay a great network of canyons, some long and sweeping, others narrow and twisting, through the centre of which an enormous, dark river lay like a black, half-coiled eel. Streams, hundreds of them, meandered like lengths of tight silver thread down the innumerable sheer walls to join with each other and merge into the river, or else form into small lakes set at intervals into varying heights of angular, rocky shelf. Treetops – *trees, here…* – were from such distance little more than vague green blurs, and the figures which walked amongst them no more than dark, slow-moving dots upon the ground. Tendrils of smoke drifted up from open fires and torches all across the floor and amongst the sides of the walls. And amongst it all, rising like the foundations of the world, stood vast pillars, thickest at their base but still the width of buildings by the time they disappeared into the black heights of the realm, hundreds of feet higher still than even the level of the cave in which the group were standing. The whole space was almost too big and too remarkable to behold all at once.

From the middle of the great river, perhaps half a mile ahead and to the right of the cave, a half-column shaped like a tall, extended goblet rose from the water, its serrated crown almost level with the cave. The base, tiny though it was against the scale of the river around it, was no less than two hundred feet wide where it emerged from the deep black currents. From the top, out of which light from what appeared to be hundreds of small, open windows was spilling, two long rope-bridges extended in nearly opposite directions: one spanning the divide between the column's head and a point a few hundred feet below where the group now stood; the other reaching out across to join with the point at which the other main wall which enclosed this remarkable realm curved round to the left and away into the distance, drawing the valleys and the river with it. None of the group could think of anything to say. There were no reactions, no questions, not even the briefest of exclamations of surprise or wonder from any of them, for none of them knew where to begin.

'You've never even heard of this place, have you?' asked Jericho, seeing the looks in their eyes as he turned back to them. The fierceness had gone from his voice – though it lingered still in his glare. 'Come on,' he added when none of them spoke.

He led them out of the cave and down a winding stairway set close against the wall. Through the interwoven blend of stone and wooden beams the floor of the valley could be seen many hundreds of feet below. In the wide, open shelf which appeared at the base of the stairs four men were standing expectantly; two armed with long pikes and two with short-swords and white, wooden batons; all in plate armour similar in shape to Jericho's, except black where his was blood-red. Behind them the rope-bridge dipped slightly out away from the end of the shelf, returning into sight just before it reached the top of the crowned column.

'We heard there was a –' began one of the guards, standing to attention as Jericho approached, but stopping as his eyes fell upon the group. 'Who're they?' he asked quickly. 'I… don't recognise them…'

'Let us pass, Kalise,' said Jericho, halting impatiently. 'I'm taking'em to Tholomus.' Though the guard was taller he cowered slightly under the weight of Jericho's stare, holding his ground only barely. Jericho seemed unwilling to have to force his way, but it was clear he would stand little of this delay.

'I need to know who they are…' the guard stated uncomfortably, the fingers of his gauntlets twisting uneasily by his sides. 'You *know* that… Are they – are they from *above*?'

'They are.' The other three guards stood straighter and closed up beside the first, whose eyes had widened with fear. 'There's no shadow in'em,' Jericho added.

'How can you –'

'I know *Darkness* when I see it!' Jericho shouted; impatience spilling suddenly into anger. 'They're clean. I don't know how they got here, but they're unarmed and no threat so long as I'm around. Now move aside while your doing so is still a matter of your choice.' He had made no move towards his scimitars, but somehow the blades seemed to swell and shimmer beside him. The guard lasted a further single, tense second before stepping to one side, the others around him following his lead without encouragement, and with a terse nod Jericho marched through them and onto the bridge, drawing Crick and the others in his wake. It was wide enough for five people to walk beside each other, somehow remaining as firm as if it were solid rock even as the group and the rest of the guards began to cross it. They could feel a multitude of enquiring eyes upon their backs as they walked, though these were quickly forgotten as more of the caverns came into view, vast and distant beneath them, twisting endlessly beside and through each other like some curious game of giants.

It was only as they neared the far side of the bridge that the heads and upper bodies of large gatherings of people started to distinguish themselves amongst the rock and firelight of the top of the column. The features of the column itself also began to take form: There seemed to be a dozen levels or more, each containing scores of different rooms, and around the very top thin cuts had been made into the rock like the battlements of a great tower, within which a ring of low, wide steps led up to a large building hewn flat from the rock. Thin stairways, cascading at irregular intervals around the sides of the column, connected each of the levels with wide, square ledges protruding from the points at which they joined together, upon which people now were congregating to watch Jericho and the group as they approached. Somehow message of their coming had spanned the crossing long before they had.

Elsewhere throughout the caverns, in addition to occasional clusters of what were plainly guards there were also men, women, and children of all ages. They wore simple but nonetheless fine clothing, and were all involved in varying degrees of talk, play or work. Some were cleaning or chiselling fine detail into the rock; others laughing or discussing things in small groups until they sensed the growing commotion around them. There was even one man, well into his final years, who was sitting quietly as the rock behind him on the edge of one of the lowest ledges… fishing. His short rod was held loose in front of him, and from it a thick line, visible even from the bridge, reached all the many hundreds of feet down into the river beneath him. A young girl, no older than five and cheerfully oblivious to the risk, was leaning out over the edge of the rock beside him, following the line as far as she could with her eyes. It had been quite impossible to believe at first, but as more and more such detail came into view it became clear that this was no mere temporary cluster of men; no mere garrison. This was a community. And a thriving one. These people truly had their own, strange and wonderful world down here. Unfortunately, the group were not as yet afforded the liberty to enjoy it…

'When the Arkon addresses you,' said Jericho sharply, turning back to them as they stepped off the bridge and onto hard rock again, 'you keep quiet and wait 'till he's done. You speak respectful to him. If not –' he nodded over the wall behind them, '– it's a long way down to the Black.'

They stepped towards the wide building above them through a throng of figures increasing swiftly in size and noise; all curious, most anxiously keeping their distance. Just as Jericho called out to the guards at the top the doors behind them were thrown open, and through them a true ox of a man strode quickly out and down the steps. He wore thick leather sandals and a tunic of dark blue and gold, no armour to be seen apart from that of his own powerful stature. He was tall, but not the tallest of men; broad-shouldered but not the broadest; but every lean inch of him rippled with a strength which even from a distance was intimidating; his hard jaw and heavy, black stubble seeming to have been carved from something altogether tougher than the rock itself. And even if none of this had been true, the gaze with which he surveyed the group as he came to a halt halfway down the steps marked him clearly as the leader of this place. The two full-armed and armoured guards who flanked him looked with all their might decidedly frail in comparison. For a moment there was silence. Everyone from the stairs to all quarters of the column and, it felt, the rest of the realm as well were suddenly still, waiting expectantly for the Arkon. He stood with fists planted firm upon his waist, and only after his eyes had been through the group twice over did he look then across to Jericho.

'They fell in through the fourteenth,' said Jericho immediately, taking a half-step forward.

'Is it being fixed?' His words were short and clear, snapping through the air in a manner that far louder voices struggled to do.

'Errin's group are working on it now. It –'

'Get two more up there,' the Arkon ordered to someone in the crowd, who darted instantly away. 'Have you checked them?' he asked of Jericho.

'I have. They're pure. I don't think they've ever heard of us before.'

'Is he dead?' he asked, nodding to Url.

'Not quite.'

'Mirrian!' the Arkon called out without waiting for further explanation, now watching Aliya, upon whom his gaze lingered for a moment. A few seconds later a fair-haired woman dressed all in white appeared, bending down to examine Url.

'You two…' she said to two men from the crowd. As they stepped forwards towards Url, Orlando's shoulders tightened, but the woman reached out and held his arm before he could make a move. 'He'll be well cared for,' she whispered with a kind smile containing a clear look of warning. Orlando stepped aside, frowning but allowing the men to carry Url away. The others looked helplessly from him to each other – the first time they had been separated from one of their number for longer than they could currently remember. The Arkon was studying them all again, scowling silently as agitated whisperings started amongst the crowd. When he spoke next, it was directly to the group:

'If I feel you are now or become at any point a threat to us, I will put an end that threat swiftly. I will do it myself. Do you understand my words?' They nodded. 'Bring them in,' he added, turning and climbing back up the steps. The two guards either side followed him; Jericho grunting for the group to do likewise.

As they reached the top, the open doors of the building revealed within a single great hall, the floor of which fell down away from the opening in a long cascade of steps, similar to those outside, before rising up again to a wide stone circle in the centre of the hall. In the middle of the circle sat a wide, round, stone table, with seats enough for at least fifty people. Flames licked gently against the insides of fireplaces around the outskirts of the room, while above the table a broad, dozen-tiered chandelier of a hundred candles glowed a bright yellow. A narrow walkway cut above the steps straight from the entranceway to the circle, and it was along this that the group followed the Arkon and his guards; Jericho and his men still surrounding them, the shouts and bustle outside cut off abruptly by the sudden slamming of the doors behind like a home shut tight against a storm. Though none of them realised it, all the family in that instant shared an image of the storm-beaten night Crick had returned from Immelus; the room they waited in now distinctly less comforting however than the small, familiar kitchen of their memories.

There was an opening in the far side of the table, and a narrow channel through the stone to an ornate, high-backed seat in the middle. The Arkon, only barely able to fit through, took his place upon it, and as he did so Jericho motioned impatiently for the group to take seats around the edge, facing silently in towards him.

'Where are you from, and what are you doing crossing these lands?' the Arkon demanded firmly before they were all in place. He received no answer. With the exception of Abetta, who remained stone-faced and unmoving, each of the group looked nervously amongst each other, uncertain what to say, or indeed whether they should say anything at all. The Arkon took a deep, slow breath.

'You can leave us,' he said to Jericho after several long seconds.

Jericho hid his reluctance well, shooting furious glances at those of his men who did not; curiosity for a brief instant threatening to outweigh obedience to their command. Only the Arkon's two personal guards remained, standing impassively either side of the table as Jericho and his men turned and left along the narrow walkway. The clusters of flame around the room flickered for a moment as the doors closed behind them; the group looking in all the time towards the Arkon, as he looked carefully out at them.

'I am Tholomus, Arkon of the Undervalleys,' he said in a deep, proud tone which rung for a moment amongst the chandelier above him. 'Perhaps you will give me your *names* now, at least?'

After a moment the group introduced themselves, one by one, all apart from Aulan, whose name was offered by Orlando.

'And your injured companion?'

'Url,' said Crick.

'He will indeed be well cared for; there is no need to fear for him. Now – is it true that you had not heard of us until now?' Though he revealed nothing openly of his thoughts, there was little doubting his shock and perhaps a sadness at their nods of agreement. He quickly cast the emotions aside and continued:

'Our people have lived here since night claimed the lands above. These valleys were long the secret of our ancestors, many hundreds of years ago, and when their homes were destroyed they sought shelter here. They never intended to stay, but as the Darkness lingered above, so they were forced to continue below. They built new homes, raised new families, and began here a new way of life, and over time we have come to create something from which I doubt most of us now would ever leave, even *if* the choice was ours to make.

But I tell you this because what we have here is fragile. There are many entrances into our world from above, and some even from below. And the Darkness is always testing them. We have the skills and means to hold it off, for now. But one mistake could destroy in moments all that which we have worked for. Alongside that, our food and water must be carefully controlled; our homes and bridges, waterways, and countless other structures and devices must be kept working; and there is more else besides than I could possibly explain to you now, even were I inclined to do so. I make no apologies for my abruptness, or that of any of my men. We are as we need to be; no more and no less.

That said,' he continued, leaning back into his chair, 'we are also a friendly people. Even I myself have been known to forge a smile on rare occasion,' – though he made no attempt at one now. 'You will find welcome and rest here, for as long as you need it.' He leant forward heavily onto his elbows, grave once more. 'But only once you have told me where you come from, what you were doing crossing the sands, and… how you managed to reach here through what lies beyond these walls. I – none of us – have never heard of such a thing. And also, perhaps,' he added, 'you may answer why a barrier great enough to keep the long night at bay should see fit to collapse under the mere weight of yourselves and your cart...' It was on this point that he seemed the most intent, studying each of the group afresh. 'Until you reveal your secrets, I cannot trust you. And if I cannot trust you...' Clearly he felt no need to finish the sentence, content the point had been made well enough already.

'We're taking the Heart to Iala,' said Yori suddenly, quiet but too quick for the others to stop him.

'Yori!' Siu exclaimed as Orlando dropped his head into his hands; Crick groaning, glaring at his brother.

'*Iala...*' whispered Tholomus, stunned. Had it not been for the escaped reactions of the others he may perhaps have believed Yori's words to be no more than the talk of a child, but as it was he studied them now with renewed intensity; the two guards standing open-mouthed, allowing themselves the briefest of glances across the table.

'Our knowledge of the overworld has grown dim through the years…' Tholomus continued. 'But… I thought the place was only myth?'

'We can trust him,' Yori uttered simply to the others. 'We need his help.'

'He sees more than most,' said Tholomus. 'And whether you believe in his judgement or not, he is right: As long as my keeping your secret does not threaten harm to my people, then keep it I shall, and I will help you as I can. You have my word. From anyone here that means a great deal, but from me – if I may make so bold to say so – it is especially so. Now – speak: Why are you journeying to Iala? And what is this *Heart* he speaks of?'

For some reason they all looked to Abetta for confirmation, though in truth they knew they now had little choice. There was no other means they could think of in that moment to explain in a fashion the Arkon would believe how they had survived through the Black Wind. And the simple, regrettable certainty was that they would now need tremendous help to get the Heart back above ground and onwards to Iala. It was Abetta herself who looked Tholomus in the eye, studying him as eagerly as he was still studying them.

'The Heart is something which many of our people have long sought after,' she began, carefully. And then, in a quiet voice which nonetheless commanded the attention of even those who were all too familiar with the story, she continued… She spoke of the Heart's power, of their finding of it in the Heartlands, and of their purpose in attempting to bring it to Iala. She explained the Heartlands themselves, and where amongst them the family lived, and she told of how they had managed to escape with the Heart through the border. Her descriptions of everything from the first ill-fated village they had come to, through to khaions, the Firstway, scarravers, Irraigion, and various events in between brought painful memories to many of the group, and a glint of awe to the eyes of the Arkon.

Excluded from the account, however, were all details concerning the beginnings of the Heart as the group had learned them, and how it had come to be in the Heartlands. Abetta gave instead only the base information the family had believed to be true when they had started on their journey. She referred to Aulan simply as a friend who had stumbled upon what they were doing, and had decided to come with them, just as she spoke of Tarryn. Aulan himself kept his head bowed quietly for most of the half hour which it took for Abetta to come finally to their attempt at crossing the sands, and their capture by Jericho, at which point Tholomus leant back slowly in his seat, silenced, drawing a long, steady breath as his fingers tapped distractedly upon the stone either side of him.

'And I thought *my* tale was a fine one...' he sighed eventually, leaning forwards again. It was impossible to tell whether more a grin or scowl lay within his gaze. Abetta and the others said nothing, waiting for his reaction.

'And the... *Heart*... It is still in the hall into which you fell?' he asked. Abetta nodded. 'There are people working around it as we speak – are they in any danger from it?'

'They'll find that it resists them if they get too close,' said Orlando. 'But apart from that it won't harm them.'

'I suppose you can offer me no proof of any of what you have told me?'

'Only that you have our word on it,' answered Orlando. 'And if *you* knew *us*, you would know that that means a great deal, also.'

Tholomus gazed in pensive silence for nearly a full minute, until finally, as though having to work its way through stone itself, a small, tentative grin broke across his hard face...

'Then that shall have to do,' he said, standing. 'For now, at least. I have no idea whether you are fools, heroes, or outright liars. But until I learn otherwise, I will grant you the benefit of my considerable doubt. I shall have your Heart brought into safekeeping here in the tower, and you will have all the respite and supplies you require until you are healed and ready to be on your way. And we shall see about building you a new means of transporting your treasure.' The two guards came to attention as he exited the back of the table, marching beside him again as he strode around to the others, gesturing for them to follow him back across the walkway. Each frowned to the other as they stood and fell into line behind him, certain it couldn't be this simple. A gust of conversation blew into the hall as he opened the heavy doors with an easy flick of his wrists, and he gave a quiet snort of laughter at the sight of the hundred or so people who were suddenly silenced, staring up at him.

'I swear we've dwelled so long down here the walls themselves have learned to talk...' he muttered quietly. Before he departed a solemn look fell again across his face, and he turned back to address the group a final time:

'Please understand... If my reaction to what you have told me seems, perhaps, less than you expected, it is only because I cannot afford it to be otherwise. You appear perhaps to be good people, and what you are saying may indeed be true. Or, it may not. You are far from the first to dream of an end to the Darkness. And it grieves me to tell you that you will not be the last. I cannot risk helping you any further than I have offered already. My concern is for these people, and them alone; *to the exclusion of all else…*' he added sharply, as Orlando opened his mouth to speak. 'You will be cared for, and entertained, and then you will be helped generously on your way… But of that moment then I will ensure that both you and your tale, if any of it should escape during your stay, are forgotten. As you can see, your being here has caused rumour and difficulty enough for me already: I counsel you strongly to do nothing to add to it. If you must say anything to anyone, as no doubt you will be warmly encouraged to do, say only for now that you are treasure seekers who have wandered too far from your home, and are trying to return. That will explain the Heart well enough.

I will make time to see you again shortly. For now you shall be taken to rooms which you may call your own while you are here, and I will arrange for you to be shown the valleys.' He nodded curtly to them all. 'It shall be… interesting, having you here. And pleasing to have you gone.' And with a brief nod he turned and disappeared down and around the steps; the crowd parting to let him through.

'Well, that didn't go too badly…' said Orlando, as for a brief moment they were left alone at the top of the steps, except for the guards of the hall who remained motionless by the doors. But before any of the others had answered, a tall, slim woman dressed in finer clothes than most of the others was approaching them from below, waving them down towards her. She introduced herself as *Elebet*, and with one look at Tarryn and Aliya, who despite their pain had made no complaint about their injuries so far, she led them quickly across the circle and down the first stairway she came to, deflecting the volley of questions which the emboldened crowd began to direct towards the group.

The view over and beyond the edge of the stone was remarkable, looking out as it did down the length of the wide river below until it swung eventually away to the right, through valleys and waterfalls and a multitude of small copses which had been hidden until now. There was little time to enjoy it, however: Two steep levels down they passed inwards through a narrow breach in the rock and into a tight, twisting corridor, passing several empty rooms until deep within the tower they came to a large, heavily polished wooden door. Behind it a surprisingly large sitting room with a ring of cushions amidst rugs of soft skins, decorated almost wall to wall with bright paintings and needleworks,

354

led off into several modest but comfortable bedrooms, and what looked to be two washrooms. No sooner had they collapsed onto the cushions than another woman entered, followed by a young boy and girl carrying an array of bandaging, herbs, ointments, and an assortment of other healing apparatus such as even Abetta herself could not help but admire. They set to work quietly on the various injuries around the group, and once Aliya's arm had been worked delicately – though nevertheless painfully – back into its place, and, finally, Tarryn's stomach cleaned and sewn up once again, they left, all without a word.

Elebet too then bid them farewell, telling that she would be back to bring them a dinner later in the afternoon, and commanding that for today at least they were to stay here in the tower and rest. There was no argument from any of the group. As the door closed gently behind her their silence continued; Crick gazing dazedly out and down through the long, thin opening which served as a window, beyond which the tall vertical faces of some of the valleys could be seen. The others meanwhile stretched or curled themselves tight amongst the cushions, and as they did so the shock and relief of the past hours struck them all in equal measure now; cold lumps sitting heavily in the tops of their chests which made constructive thought difficult, and constructive conversation all but impossible. Gradually all attempts at either were abandoned, sleep claiming them one by one; each still as uncertain as the next as to whether to call the room shelter, or prison.

Chapter Twenty-Seven

The Undervalleys

The Undervalleys, it quickly became apparent, were by a quite unfathomable scale even larger, more complex, and endlessly more intriguing than they had appeared at first sight. The tower and those valley walls surrounding it, though certainly the most populous and busy, was only a tiny fragment of the whole. The great river – referred to most commonly simply as the *Black* – continued in both directions for many miles amidst a winding maze of soaring walls, while to each side smaller ravines and networks of caves and tunnels forked away into regions so numerous and deep that even the people here in all their many generations had never fully explored them all. Trees, wispy-leaved, short-limbed and thick-trunked, drawing all they needed from the strangely bitter water, grew in small groves across the valley floors and sides, yielding occasionally a small, tough, orange fruit which was a large part of the diet. And beside the larger bodies of water there were small fields of thick, waxy grass and moss, and even patches of vivid red and white flowers, which also reached upwards in large swathes all the way up into the heights of the great columns which held this world together.

And amongst it all the people, under the leadership of a continuous succession of Arkons of which Tholomus was the latest and by most accounts one of the most widely respected, had learned to live in perfect balance, finding ways of attaining all the necessities, and many of the luxuries, which made their lives here so comfortable. Stairways and rope-bridges crossed in their hundreds like the threads of a frenzied spider between walls, across streams, and amongst the homes of clusters of families; the homes themselves built against, above, or into the rock at all conceivable angles and elevations. Waterwheels, some the size of great trees, others no larger than a man, turned slowly and constantly, funnelling water through an endless series of long, wooden aqueducts and pipes which spanned every quarter of the realm. Fishermen and women lined the banks of the Black, waiting patiently if apprehensively for bites of the large, extraordinarily strong eels which took the bait only rarely, but were enough if caught to feed several families at a sitting with enough left over for the following day's lunch. There were deep mines and open excavation pits, from whose depths a selection of ores and sometimes a curious jewel, similar to jet but with streaks of bright white, were extracted. And in several valleys, set aside for the Crafters and their work, all manner of things were mended, created, or stored; the Crafters themselves a common sight in their silver overalls and harassed expressions, moving swiftly from job to job anywhere and everywhere through the realm, and at all times of day – time measured, curiously, chiefly by the gentle changing of the red and white flowers which grew from the main columns, the petals of which would flourish, despite the apparent lack of sunlight, in the morning, and wilt into duller, smaller blossoms of pink when the world outside turned to night. It made a truly accurate time rather impossible to determine for much of the day, not that that was of great concern to most down here.

These and all other manner of wonders and oddities, however, did not mean that life in the Undervalleys was always easy. There was, as a rule, always something which was broken, or breaking. Arguments, though rare and usually short-lived, were difficult to avoid when encountering the same faces each day in such a conspicuously enclosed – if vast – environment. And the diet, though rich, was desperately unvaried. Such minor issues paled in comparison, however, with the difficulty, and danger, of what was known in most references as the *Breath*... For in this great event of the Undervalleys, which took place once every ten days, the lowermost openings out into the overworld had to be raised, in order that enormous bellows, hundreds of feet tall, could draw in new air while expelling the accumulated smoke and other unwanted vapours from distant openings on the opposite end of the Undervalleys. The Breath was the one moment in which nearly every inhabitant came together, requiring faultless timing and a great deal of cooperation and combined strength to operate the bellows, and absolute vigilance on the part of those unfortunate enough to be chosen – or brave enough to volunteer – to keep watch outside the gates. It was far from uncommon, as numerous tales and recollections held it, for creatures of the Darkness to show themselves at these moments. And though the openings were usually sealed in time, occasionally they were not. Nobody would speak further of these episodes, except to say that they had become more difficult to prevent in recent months.

With this exception, though, the people of the Undervalleys were content with their lot, and they quickly proved a cheerful folk to be around. The family, Tarryn, and Aulan were welcomed with forceful, friendly shakes of their right hands – the left held firm, open-palmed across the chest, as was the custom here – and once the swiftly-crafted account of their treasure-trading voyage seemed to be accepted they started slowly to join in with the various activities around them, thriving on – if also finding somewhat disconcerting for a time – the new and unexpected freedom of no longer having constantly to be attached to one another.

Having first received a brief tour of the main regions of the valleys, Orlando and Siu took great pleasure resting amongst the trees which, they said, felt more peaceful and in some ways powerful than any they had known before. Occasionally they would catch brief glimpses of Aliya as she swam and scrambled through the streams around them, muttering distractedly of how the current moved in a different, peculiar way down here. Abetta took a keen interest in the work of Ellein, the woman who had so efficiently nursed them when they had first arrived, speaking with her at length and sometimes accompanying her as she went adeptly about her duties. Url recovered quickly, and within the second day was almost back to his old self, but to the utter dismay and all-too familiar fear of the others he then with little further delay took it upon himself to expand any possible knowledge of the furthermost parts of the Undervalleys as best he could, venturing sometimes with a guide and more often without deep into any distant and as-yet unexplored cave, tunnel, or recess of any and every description. And as the agony of Tarryn's boredom quickly surpassed the pain of his now well-cared for injury he somehow made the acquaintance of a small group, all around the age of Url, whose afternoons and evenings, spent high in a small and isolated dwelling halfway up the towering face of one of the valley walls, far from anyone or anything else, comprised entirely of the creation, tasting, and whole-hearted admiration of a hazardously strong liquor, made from the orange *bailfruit*.

Aulan, frightened and hesitant at first, was after a time more than content to wander the walkways of the valleys, poking his head into each in turn, studying them, watching silently as the people went about their work and play. He said nothing to anyone, having agreed with the others that it would be far better to introduce him as a mute than to try and invent an excuse for his voice, or voices, but still he seemed to acquire several friends – or at least a small number of people who were happy to walk with him as he explored, explaining with a patience he found unnerving various sights to him as they came to them. It was the first time any of the group had seen him truly relaxed… happy, almost, but for the occasional, distant gazes into nothing he could still be found with when on his own.

Yori, despite all there was around him to see and do, was to be found almost every spare hour of each day upon the lowest square ledge of the underside of the crown of the central tower, sitting silently beside the old fisherman. He would wait, for hours at a time, as the pale, unmoving line reached down into the dark middle of the river, catching nothing but occasional, brief surges of current as the water eddied swiftly around the base of the stone which had been smoothed over time into the likeness of a great teardrop. When asked, all Yori would say was that the old man was *peaceful*. But seeing the good it was doing him, and relieved beyond words at the new stillness which came with each passing night to his sleep, Siu and Orlando were reluctant to question him further, or suggest too often that he might consider doing anything else with his time.

Crick, meanwhile, while partaking in an agreeable mixture of many of these pursuits, spent much of his first days simply being in any valley in which his parents were not, finding and creating a range of wonderfully convoluted and enjoyable methods of traversing from place to place without the use of any of the rope-bridges or walkways provided for the purpose. Overwhelmed by the number and intricacy of the rock-faces available for him to scale and descend he would often lose all track of time, so that one of the others would usually need to come looking for him when he failed to return for meals during the day. And it was on the morning of the fifth day, whilst working his way halfway across a high, knife-edge ridge which overlooked a narrow lake in the shape of a crescent moon, that again Crick heard from a distance somebody calling urgently to him from below. This time, however, he didn't recognise the voice… With one hand still required to balance himself above the rock he turned awkwardly, and saw beneath him a man standing impatiently upon a walkway halfway between Crick's wall and that of the adjacent valley. He wore the green and blue that was common amongst most of the people here, but there was something in the way he held himself, his long, thin back forced straight and tall, his hands linked precisely in front of him, which gave him a different and unwelcoming air to the others.

'What is it?' Crick called down. 'We've only just had breakfast! It can't be –' He stopped as the man grimaced at the clamour he was making; his shouting echoing back heavily from several directions. *Sorry*, he mouthed, climbing swift as he could down the ridge, hopping the last few feet onto the walkway.

'Sorry,' he said again. 'But it can't be lunch already, surely?'

'It is not,' the man stated haughtily, glaring at Crick down the full and spectacular length of his nose. It was rare for Crick to take such dislike to someone so quickly.

'Then…?' Crick prompted, brushing the dust from his clothes and doing his utmost to ignore the bright, sneering eyes.

'Follow me. The Arkon wishes to meet with you.'

'The…?' Crick paused, surprise and curiosity overcoming his antipathy for the man who had already turned and started to walk away. As Crick followed him briskly back through the valleys and up towards the tower he tried twice to ask why the Arkon wanted to see him, but each time he received no answer at all, and the two of them walked on in silence.

They entered the tower at one of the lower levels, passing several large, dimly-lit rooms inside which small groups of people were speaking quietly and intently amongst each other, before turning into a small hallway lined with low, simple stools on either side. At the far end, two guards stood before a tall, thin doorway, bordered with thick beams of the black and white gemstone – *moonslick*, as it had been named, in memory of one of the many treasures of the sky lost to the people of the valleys when their ancestors had made this place their home. Seeing Crick and his guide approach, the guards unlinked the dark metal chains which hung between them and opened the doors, ushering them through without a word. Beyond, a flight of tremendously high and awkward steps, lit by a row of dazzlingly bright chandeliers, led up to another identical doorway, and two identical guards who opened it again for them in identical fashion to the last. As the man stepped up between the guards, Crick still behind and several feet below him, he stopped suddenly, cleared his throat, and spoke clearly into the room:

'I've brought the boy.'

'Good, good – Bring him in, then.' It was the Arkon's voice, quick and impatient. The man glanced back to Crick and nodded earnestly into the room.

360

The candles in the stairway were so bright that it was only as Crick stepped away from them through the doors that he could see anything of the room inside. It was small, windowless, and undecorated but for large bookcases which ran around each of its five walls. A thick desk curved in a half-circle almost against the far wall facing towards the door, at which the Arkon was sitting. As Crick entered he was speaking to another man beside him, and after a moment Crick recognised him as the old Crafter who had led the first team up to the opening after the group had fallen through, though he couldn't remember his name…

'Will there be anything else, Arkon?' Crick's guide was standing so rigidly, and with such concentration, that Crick feared he might be about to strain himself. The Arkon seemed not to appreciate his over-eagerness either:

'How many times, Gliynen…?' he sighed. 'You know my name: *Use it*, please. There is no need of titles in here.'

'I thought… given the company…' he stumbled stiffly, gesturing to Crick.

'I'm sure the company won't take offence, and neither will I. So, if you please…?'

'Very well…' He cleared his throat with difficulty. 'Will there be anything else… Tholomus?' he finished grudgingly. Tholomus looked at him a moment longer before letting out another quiet, weary sigh...

'That's all for now,' he said, raising his hand to the door. Gliynen managed a final bitter glower at Crick as he turned and left; the guards closing the doors swiftly behind him.

'He takes his role… rather seriously,' said Tholomus, looking somewhat apologetically to Crick.

'Along with himself,' said the old Crafter. Tholomus let out a snort of laughter.

'Indeed. You remember Errin, don't you?' he asked of Crick. 'He's the poor sod who's had to repair the damage you lot did.'

Crick gave a small nod, suddenly anxious again as to why he had been brought here. But Tholomus gave another laugh…

'Relax, boy. You're not in any trouble. Not yet. Even if you do insist upon amusing yourself amongst the very places we've spent our entire lives building means of avoiding! I don't envy your parents, having to keep track of you! I swear, between you and… *Url*, I believe he is named?' Crick nodded again, '– between you and him, you must be responsible for half of all discoveries ever made in your homelands!'

'I – we do our best, I suppose,' said Crick, trying to sound light-hearted.

'Indeed…' And with that the Arkon's eyes flashed suddenly with intrigue, as though through Crick's words he had just recalled why it was he had brought him here. 'Indeed… Well, may I say, then, that your best –' he opened a draw beneath him as he spoke, and lifted out from within it something slightly smaller than his hand, wrapped loose amongst strips of grey cloth, '– is quite good enough, by any measure of the term.' He placed the bundle onto the desk before him, beginning carefully to peel back the layers of grey… And with a sudden shimmer of black Crick realised what it was:

'The brooch! I – I'd completely forgotten about it!'

He spoke the truth. Almost since the beginning of the journey had it lain unnoticed deep within one of the bags he had packed, wrapped up in such a way that none of the others were likely to find it. After much experimentation he had come to the conclusion that it was nothing but mere ornament, and for a long time he hadn't even thought about it. The way the Arkon and Errin were looking at him now, however, told him that in some way at least he must surely have been mistaken. They remained silent, waiting for him to continue. But Crick hesitated, looking to Errin…

'You can speak openly,' said Tholomus. 'I have told him everything.'

'*What*?' shouted Crick before he could stop himself. 'But you said –'

'I said I would keep your secrets so long as there was no threat to my people. With this, I feared there may be such a threat. Errin is one of my closest and longest serving advisors and friends, and apart from all else it was he who found it amongst your things. Now, tell me: Where did you get it?' His tone left no room for further argument.

'In the same place I found the map we told you about.'

'The *Wilder Rooms*, you called them? In your city – In Immelus?'

'Yes – it was in a desk just before the map. I didn't really mean to take it… I haven't told any of the others about it.' He looked from Tholomus to Errin and back again, and then finally to the brooch itself as curiosity began to well inside him. 'What is it?'

'You don't know?' Errin asked, seeming surprised and somewhat disbelieving.

'No,' Crick answered. Tholomus sat back into his chair, still watching him. 'I've no idea!'

'And the others – they know nothing of it? You are certain?'

'No – Yes! None of them have s-' But he was cut off by a knock upon one of the doors behind him. Tholomus ignored it, and Crick continued, '– like I told you, it's been hidden all the way.'

'If it meant so little to you that you haven't looked at it for such a time, then how is it also so important that you felt the need to hide it from the others?'

'I –' The question had thrown him; he had no good answer to it. 'I don't know,' he said flatly. Tholomus waited a moment before speaking:

'We shall find out,' he said, folding his arms and calling to the doors: 'Come!' The doors swung open immediately, and through them to Crick's great surprise stepped the old fisherman with whom Yori had been spending his days. He smiled airily to them all, giving a small, warm nod to Tholomus.

'Joseph, welcome. I am sorry it has been so long.'

'You have had far more important duties to keep you busy,' said the old man quietly, his voice like a slow drift of silk to the ears. 'And I am more than content in my days, and more than capable of looking after myself.' He smiled gently again.

'Still hunting Alyssis, I trust?'

'Alas, I fear the battle is no longer a fair one. I seem now to have stacked the odds too highly in my favour… For I have fished almost all the waters of our great realm: she must surely be running out of places to hide!'

'Ha! Indeed… Well, long may she elude you. I believe it's done you good to have something show you a taste of *dis*respect for once!' Joseph nodded. 'This young man here,' the Arkon continued, raising a hand to Crick, 'is Crick. He is one of our new guests.'

Crick smiled as politely as he could, but through his unease he was sure it made him look quite foolish. The old man for his part continued to smile back kindly.

'Crick –' said Tholomus, clearly and slowly. 'Have you told me all you know about this brooch?'

'Yes!' Crick answered quickly. 'There's noth–' but Tholomus' raised hand silenced him. 'Look at Joseph,' he commanded.

'*Look* at him…? What am I supposed to –'

'Just look at him, please.'

Crick did as he was instructed. The old man stared back at him, peering for only a brief second deep into his eyes… Or maybe it was longer… Suddenly Crick wasn't sure...

'He speaks truly,' Joseph said suddenly, breaking the spell, his placid grin widening as he looked back to Tholomus.

'I – Well, yes – exactly,' said Crick, surprised no less than he was relieved. This must be why Yori enjoyed his company so much. He had the same gift.

'Thank you, Joseph,' said Tholomus.

And with that the old man turned and left; the guards outside somehow knowing to open the doors before he reached them.

'I won't need it!' he called back as the doors closed. The corners of Tholomus' open mouth turned upwards into a smile…

'I was about to wish him good luck,' he said quietly to Errin. 'Well, young man,' he added, turning to Crick, 'it seems you have passed the strictest test I can think to put against you. I believe you. Hopefully, once we have explained to you what this is, you will understand why it is that I have had to question you like this.' He leant back into his chair, nodding to Errin. The old Crafter stepped thoughtfully forward around the side of the desk, sitting back upon it as he spoke:

'One of the few tales of the overworld we have managed to retain over the years,' he began, 'concerns a group who were known, in their time, as the Veil. Have you heard of them?' Crick shook his head, though in truth they did sound somewhat familiar. One of Url's tales, perhaps… 'Nobody ever knew the exact place of their origin, but we believe it was somewhere far within the easternmost reaches of our world. Some even speculated that they came from the coasts of the White Sea itself. At any rate, they were one of the first peoples to feel the coming of the Black Wind, and undoubtedly the quickest to learn from it. Through experiments too grim to talk of here –'

'Or elsewhere,' interjected the Arkon.

'Or elsewhere –' Errin agreed '– and by using a Magic only they themselves understood, they discovered, it is said, a means to ward off the Darkness, at least for short periods of time. It was this which allowed them to survive, and even prosper in a fashion and for a short time when the Black Wind grew stronger. Sealing their new power within various trinkets – *Mirrors*, they sold only to those who could afford them. Those who could not, they left to their fate. This brooch, I believe, is one of those forgotten treasures.'

It took several seconds for Crick to speak, and when he did his first words caught uncomfortably in his throat:

'You… think this can shield us from the Black Wind?'

'No. Only one of you. And only for a short time. If it even still works now at all. The power they created was great, but they could never discover how to make it permanent. Which is why all Mirrors were thought to have been used up by the time the Wind reached its peak. People purchased them, used them, and then found there were no more. It took such time and such exertion and such... *sacrifice*, to make each one, that the Veil soon hid themselves away, focusing their efforts solely upon the protection of their own dwindling number. This may not be the only remaining working Mirror, but it is surely one of a truly small number.'

'But – the Veil...' Crick said, looking from Errin to the Arkon. 'Are they still around? If they knew all this hundreds of years ago, maybe they've learned more since then...? Maybe they know how to –'

'Look around you, Crick,' said Tholomus. Errin was looking at him, frowning, almost sadly. 'Remember where we are... We have no better idea than you as to what happened to them. But as for what you say – I doubt it. If they had such knowledge, why does the Darkness appear only to be *growing* in its strength and ferocity? Anyway...' He unfolded his arms and gave a brief shrug. 'That is why I had you brought here. I am a busy man, and no doubt you have no small number of our valleys yet to scale, but I hope you can understand now why I had to know where you acquired it from. The people who crafted these things were cruel and dangerous, and those who possessed them often far worse.'

Crick nodded, but distractedly; his mind on a different matter...

'How does it work?'

'I thought it wouldn't be long until you asked,' said Tholomus with a smile, nodding again to Errin.

'The thorns on the back...' said Errin. 'When the Black Wind closes around you, and only then, press them to your skin. They will do the rest. I'm afraid I cannot tell you how long its effect will last... Perhaps only minutes, perhaps more.'

'Though of course,' said Tholomus, seeing Crick's excited grin and scowling deeply at it, 'you should hope and pray the moment never comes when you may find these things out for yourself.'

'*Myself*...' said Crick. 'So – you *will* let me keep it?'

'Of course,' said Tholomus. 'There is no doubting that it would come in useful here. But I am no thief.' He gave Crick a wry smile, wrapping the brooch once more within the cloth but placing it instead into the draw before him rather than into Crick's outstretched hand. 'Even if *you* are.'

'I should like to study it for a few days,' said Errin. 'But after that I will make certain it is returned to you.'

'Thank you,' said Crick, and when neither of the others spoke he continued, gesturing to the door: 'Um... shall I...?' Tholomus nodded, still studying Crick with a sure, piercing intrigue which in turn made Crick feel quite uncertain of himself. He turned to leave, the doors drifting apart with the first step he took towards them.

'But remember, young man,' the Arkon added with a heavy note of earnestness just as Crick stepped through the doorway, squinting against the corridor of dazzling light which descended steep beneath him, 'if you find anything down *here*, it belongs to me.'

*

The very idea of keeping another secret of such importance from the others was too much for Crick to contemplate. So that evening once all were back from their various pursuits, reunited in their quarters, he told of everything that had happened. With each swiftly-passing day their sitting room had accumulated new cushions of every possible colour, shape and size from well-wishers, new friends, and in particular from those seeking unsubtly to learn more of their journey. Sitting amongst or above the various mounds of pattern and material as he spoke, the others were as amazed and confused as Crick had been, with numerous questions he couldn't answer, many of which he wished he had had the sense to ask the Arkon or Errin when he had had the chance. Url in particular was incensed and troubled to learn that yet again there was another piece of the history of the Black Wind of such apparent importance of which he knew nothing, and he wondered long and openly into the evening as to how much more there was still to discover. But even though none of them fully understood it, and knew it could never protect them all, there was even so a distinct sense of triumph in the air as they left for bed, as though by finding this *Mirror* they had gained a small but much-needed victory over the Darkness. Crick, taking up his place again beside the long window, was struck by how pathetic and desperate this scrabbling grasp at success was, but he said nothing of the sort, watching once more as the Undervalleys beneath him fell gradually into their quiet, constant rhythm of the night. It was only as he closed his eyes and drifted slowly towards sleep, feeling as much as hearing the dull drone of the Black below, that he realised that, in truth, all the others had most likely been thinking the same.

*

The next morning broke slow and unassuming as those before. But following a few minutes' groggy slumber, finding himself leaning still against the window, Crick jumped swiftly to his feet, rubbing his

366

eyes and shaking his head, remembering suddenly that the day was due to be given over almost entirely to the Breath. Distant clusters of men and women were moving with distinct purpose below, and from amongst them came a range of new, far-off creaks and groans which had not sounded through the Undervalleys until now. And despite the exceptionally high expectations he had placed upon the event, spurred in no small part by Url's constant and enthusiastic speculations on the matter, it did not take Crick long to discover that the experience would be every bit as impressive and demanding as he had hoped for...

A walk and occasional scrambling of three hours or so took the group to one of the furthermost reaches of the Undervalleys, at which Crick watched from a distance along with the others as a hundred or so people, led at intervals by a selection of the oldest and usually most ill-humoured of the Crafters, operated the largest contraption he had ever imagined. A myriad of thick ropes, gears as large as a several men, and an unnerving rumbling of the walls around them led eventually to a vast, iron gate at the very end of the tunnel being raised inwards and upwards, whereupon a series of ten enormous bellows, fifty feet wide each and all somehow connected by long, trailing tubes of stripped bark and other materials, drew in great gulps of air from outside, sending it raging back up into the Undervalleys. At points to his amazement Crick caught brief glimpses of green undergrowth outside, blustering back and forth with the movement of the bellows, and amongst it he saw several of the dozen men and women who were looking out with keen eyes and restless legs for any sign of movement other than that caused by their comrades behind. The clamour, the rumbling, the frantic roaring of orders from wall to wall and up through the valleys all lasted most of the afternoon, until with a call from the Arkon himself who had come down from one of the several other locations in which similar activities were occurring, everything wound slowly down to silence. The bellows ceased, the whistling which Crick had started to become accustomed to grew fainter and died away into an eerie quiet, and slowly the great gate lowered, closed, and was locked with the careful raising of several thick stone beams amongst the curious, concealed activities of silent collections of dark, simply-dressed men and women, none of whom any of the family, Tarryn, or Aulan had seen before. Crick, not for the first time, asked a passing Crafter to explain the means and Magics used to secure the entrances, but again he was politely refused; the young, white-haired woman bustling quickly away from him muttering hurriedly about the amount of work there was still to do.

367

Crick might have been offended by her abruptness, had he not by now encountered similar attitudes to Magics of all forms throughout almost all the people of the Undervalleys. Magic here was a curious thing. It was a quiet, unspoken part of their way of life. It was used where required, but only in moderation, and never with anything other than a strict, determined indifference. It wasn't that the people feared it, or hated it. Rather they seemed almost upset by the thought and sight of it. Some used powers to work with the strength and speed of ten men in the mines and around the walkways, putting even Crick and Tarryn to shame; others with the merest touch could manipulate rock in such a way as Url spent many hours admiring, and many more trying in vain to emulate. A small number could throw thin threads of flame around the valleys, lighting the lanterns and torches from afar. And in nearly all other realms of life, from the waters of the Black and the streams which served it, to the darkness of the hidden heights of the realm, and everything physical, psychological, and elemental in between, there were men or women, boys or girls to be found who could feel and make use of Magic in one form or another. And as in the Heartlands, there seemed to be no clear reason for why some could employ Magic while others could not. All of it was fascinating for Crick and the others, but to their initial bemusement none of these people spoke or seemed to take any pride in what they did. If there was any means or chance by which all Magic might be cast out of the world, the lands above and below returned to how they had been long before, Crick was certain they would take it without question, and it filled him and the others with a strange, nagging sense of unease as they spoke with and came to know a wider selection of the population with each passing day.

This aside, however, there was nothing but a growing familiarity, a homeliness, to be found in the valleys. As Tholomus started to make his way back now from the gate, flanked as always by his two expressionless guards, he must have seen the look of mixed intrigue and longing on Crick and Tarryn's faces: Pausing to come and speak with them, he told them that next time the Breath took place, they could help. It seemed a trifle of a thing – a Father offering his children the chance at pretending to help him at his work. Yet somehow too, whether despite or because of this, it felt rather wonderful. Perhaps this was what a life unpursued and unharassed felt like... A life Crick had all but forgotten.

*

368

As the Arkon had promised, and before long insisted upon, work also began quickly on a new means of transport for the family and their load. Only Oden and Nightwind now were left, Crash having been put out of her misery by the Crafters who had come to her first, finding her two hind legs broken and tangled horribly amongst the wreckage of the front of the cart. For the first day after his consciousness had returned to him Url had been inconsolable, and since then he had refused to speak of it, saying only that the family themselves had been lucky not to have been more badly damaged in the fall. Oden and Nightwind meanwhile had been brought through the Undervalleys to the shock and amusement of all who witnessed them pass; the first such animals they had seen in many lifetimes. Whatever the group drew behind them now would need to be light enough to be managed by the two of them alone, and with that in mind Orlando set to work on a design with a full team, eight-strong, of Crafters put at his disposal by Tholomus.

Crick helped where he could, but in the days which followed he found himself drawn increasingly into the work and pastimes of a particular group of young men and women with whom he was becoming unexpectedly close to. Perhaps born of the enclosed nature of their lives here, or perhaps from the fact that they were the first new friends he had made in what felt like a lifetime, but whatever the reason he found himself rising early in the mornings to find them, and looking forward to seeing them again in the evenings. Occasionally, amongst adventures of his own, he came also to accompany them on whichever job they had been tasked with for that day: usually somewhat dull or difficult to them, but almost always providing a good many hours' interest and enjoyment for Crick. He harvested bailfruit; he fished; he helped repair or construct new sections of walkway; and to his greatest satisfaction he took a small but fascinating role operating the bellows during the following Breath. And on several occasions, to his Mother's lasting disapproval, he was allowed to follow alongside a section of guards as they patrolled the openings around the upper regions into which the group had fallen through, discovering as he did so that theirs had been merely the fourteenth of seventy-three such breaks in the sands above, though this number was constantly changing with each new storm which ravaged this part of the overworld from time to time.

And Crick was far from the only one who was continuing to enjoy themselves here. It was rare, as the days passed, that any of them would return to their housing in the tower, usually late in the evening, without some new tale with which to amuse the others well into the early hours of the following day. Tarryn's, perhaps, became rather similar and predictable after a while, but even they in their own way were nonetheless entertaining. For a people so cut off from the world for such time, the men and women of the Undervalleys could barely have provided a more generous welcome, and Crick with mounting difficulty did all he could to put firmly to one side his consciousness of the fact that he was being drawn quickly into this way of life. Instead he tried as best he could simply to experience it, and enjoy it, and to let himself rest, and smile – common luxuries he had been without for too long.

*

It was both quite suddenly and all too soon, therefore, that the time came, twenty-two full days since their arrival, when the final echoes of hammerings sounded out from within the hollow in which the new cart had been built. All the group were now better healed and fed than they had been since starting on the journey; new tools, weapons, and provisions had been set aside for them along with those that had been salvaged and mended from the fall; and all of a sudden there was little else but comfort keeping them here any longer. They had no good answers to the question, frequently repeated, of why they had to leave so soon, enquired of them by almost all those they had met. But they had little choice. They had lingered plenty long enough as it was. At dinner that evening, taken in another of the several great halls on the fifth highest level of the Tower, as had been the case for most of their time here, they could each feel that something had changed in the way Tholomus greeted them. As others finished he asked the group to stay behind, and, not one for the giving of subtle hints, once everyone else had left he asked directly:

'Is there anything else you need before you leave?'

There was no trace of unkindness in his voice, but it was clear where the conversation was designed to end. And with a gentle sigh and a smile, Url replied in a similar tone:

'You've been extremely good to us. We have all we need, and more besides. If you'd be kind enough to help us through to somewhere we can get the cart out onto open ground again, we shall say our goodbyes tomorrow.'

Though he had known they would be leaving soon, something deep within Crick sank at hearing that it would be the following day, complaining angrily that he had only begun to scratch the surface of such a fascinating way of life. He tried to ignore it, just as he tried to ignore Tarryn and Aliya's poorly-concealed smirks at the way Url had spoken... Over many mealtimes and other more jovial conversations

370

Url had come to form a great respect for the Arkon, admiring his blunt but high-spirited manner, speaking to him with a reverence which, as far as anyone knew, he had never shown anyone – with the exception perhaps of Abetta on her more intimidating days.

'I shall meet you by the cart after breakfast,' the Arkon said plainly with a small nod, striding past them and out of the hall. And with that the weight of realisation seemed suddenly to settle heavy upon the others too... They were leaving.

*

By mid-morning of the following day the group, their possessions, the cart, the horses and the amongst it all the Heart had all been escorted, carried or dragged down to the end of the valley in which they had first watched the Breath; Errin dropping a small package into the lower pocket of Crick's cloak as they walked, with a swiftness and subtlety Crick had somehow come to expect of him, though he had never seen it displayed until now.

And it was now as he approached the gate that Crick saw just how wonderful a job his Father and the team of Crafters had done. The new cart was quite remarkable. Amidst a welcome air of familiarity it was also in many ways unquestionably a great improvement upon its predecessor ; slightly smaller than the old one, but with every inch of space and material designed and joined together with such skill that there somehow seemed to be more room than there had been before. There were two seats at the front, rather than three, with reins and harnesses built individually for Oden and Nightwind. A tight, shallow, slightly domed covering, made largely from the old canvas, covered both the front and back sections, and in the back itself a small hollow had been created in the floor within which the Heart was securely set. There were high, narrow chests around the sides, inside which everything had been stored neatly away, and six spaces in between where the insides of the cart curved outwards slightly for the group to lean comfortably back into. An entirely new axle and wheels had been fashioned, partly using the wood of the trees which grew here, and occasionally with a hard, light metal which was difficult to extract and more difficult still to work, but of which Tholomus had allowed as much as was needed to be used. Supporting some of the corners and joints, and forming the dome over which the canvas was stretched, were thin strips of moonslick, which though few in number and small in size gave the new cart a distinct feel of the Undervalleys. Every inch of it was so smooth, precise, and wonderfully put together, each join and piece of material singing with the quiet voice of the realm, that there was even a part of Crick, small but welcome, which was suddenly looking forward to journeying within it.

Standing small amongst the great bellows, with faces peering down from all sides, the end of the valley was more crowded by far than it had been during even the busiest of the Breaths. Though they had said their goodbyes to many of them already, a vast number of people had arrived after breakfast to help the group; all standing to one side now as the Arkon stepped forwards...

'You are welcome back here anytime,' he boomed, to warm calls of agreement from amongst the crowd. Crick found it strange, and somewhat saddening, to realise that of all of them it was only Errin, Joseph, and the Arkon who knew truly why they had been here, and what they were setting out now to do. Or at least to attempt. The thought brought an unexpected and unwanted squirming clawing its way back into the pit of his stomach; a discomfort he had come close to forgetting.

'How will we get back in?' asked Aliya.

'Oh, I have every confidence you'll find a way,' Tholomus said with a smile.

'Just wait by the openings,' whispered Errin, who was waiting beside the cart.

'Rather that than crashing through them again, please,' said Tholomus, nodding.

'Is there anything we can bring you if we return?' asked Orlando. *When* we return, Crick hoped silently. 'Anything from the overworld you can't get in here?'

The question caught Tholomus by surprise, and he looked around him for suggestions... There were calls from some sections of the crowd for various fruits and other foods of which the people had read about but never tasted; and from others for some of the weapons and tools which the group had brought with them, which were not truly needed down here but had been sources of great interest – the bows in particular. There were eager requests for maps and scripts and tomes or any other such writings and information about a world above long-since fallen into legend. Then, from somewhere amongst the back of the crowd, high upon the main beam of one of the bellows, a distant voice shouted:

'*Grapewater*!'

'Ah, yes!' said Tholomus through the laughter and cheers which had followed the word, turning back to them with a grin he had only seldom revealed until now. 'Of course – Do your people know of grapewater?' He searched through the group hopefully...

'He means wine,' said Tarryn with a knowing nod. 'I've already promised some to my fellow associates here…' he added as everyone turned to look at him. 'Apparently in several of the scripts they have of the days before they lived down here, there's mention of the delicious and heartening qualities of *grapewater* – must have been what they called it back then.'

'Ha! Wine!' laughed Url. 'Yes, I'm sure we can do something about that.'

'Splendid!' said Tholomus. 'That settles it, then: When you've… completed your task,' he put in awkwardly, 'and managed to come into the possession of some *wine*, we shall look forward to seeing you back here.' And on his command then the great network of ropes began to strain once more; the gate sliding slowly and loudly back towards them. A gust of cool, fresh air rolled in, bringing the sweet scent of new rain, silencing each and every figure around the cart in a brief moment of quiet pleasure.

'Remember…' said Errin as Crick and the others clambered for the first time into the cart, Url and Abetta taking the front seats, 'this opening is many miles north-west of the one you fell through. Further up along that map of yours than you'd expect. From my reckoning it looks like you'll need to travel east of north-east for a day at least before you reach your road.'

'I wish we could tell you at least what the terrain will be like between here and there,' said Tholomus.

'So do I,' laughed Url. 'But no matter…' He slapped the frame of the cart behind him, smiling at the pleasant, solid echo it brought from the surrounding walls. 'With this new beast of burden I'm sure we'll find a way. You all ready?' he asked into the back; nervous, almost giddy with a manic excitement in his eyes Crick couldn't understand.

Crick waved goodbye to those he recognised amongst the crowd, the others doing likewise, as once again Url started the horses with a gentle flick of the reins. So much had happened in the past days, but as the cart started to roll slowly out through the gate, smooth and silent, it was as if nothing had changed at all. Cheers and delighted calls of *grapewater*! Followed them out onto a carpet of thick grass, staying loud and clear for a short time until becoming muffled by the branches and undergrowth of the thick forest into which Url began to lead them. A vast cliff of vine-strewn rock was visible for a few short seconds above and around the gate behind them before being hidden behind the trees; the gate lowering slowly back into place, silencing the voices with a final, heavy thud. And suddenly, almost surprisingly, the group were on their own again. For a moment nobody seemed sure how to break the silence they hadn't felt for a long time…

'I suppose it's too late to ask whether any of them wouldn't mind going instead…?' asked Tarryn, cradling tenderly in his lap the extraordinarily large, wooden cask of bailfruit liquor he'd been gifted by his new, yet now old and distant, friends.

From around the cart he received several smiles and half-laughs of acknowledgement, but no spoken reply. From Crick and the others speech felt in that moment tremendously difficult; the final thudding of the gate still echoing in their minds, seeming to have drawn the air harshly from their lungs.

Chapter Twenty-Eight

The Forest-Ward

Had the new cart been any wider or less nimble it would have struggled through the closeness of the forest. As it was, and to a none too hidden measure of Orlando's pride, Url was able with only minimal delays to keep to a reasonable speed for most of the afteroon, bearing as close to east of north-east as was possible amongst the dense undergrowth. For a long while nobody had anything to say. Crick hated the silence, so different to his past days in the Undervalleys; soon quite literally jumping at any opportunity to clear the scrub ahead, or untangle the canvas from a knot of trailing bramble, of which there were many. And it was as he returned to his place following one such clearing of the cart that Crick noticed the fine, glittering dust which lay around the base of the Heart, between the gem and the rim of the hollow in which it sat.

'It's been producing that since we arrived,' said Orlando.

'Tholomus mentioned it to me,' said Url, nodding. 'It was probably doing it before – we just didn't notice.'

'What is it?' asked Aliya.

'Well, if we left it alone for a few hundred years or more, it would likely end up as something similar to the Chamber we found it in.'

'Errin said that it seems to stay bright for a few hours –' said Orlando '– half a day, perhaps. Then it fades and disappears altogether. Then more appears.'

'It doesn't like being out in the open and moved around like this,' said Url. 'It needs somewhere silent and still to keep its form.'

375

'But – again –' said Aliya, '– what is it?'

'The Heart doesn't look to be wearing down at all,' said Crick. The edges now, even in the dim green light through which they travelled, were still just as sharp and pristine as they had always been. The fall through into the Undervalleys, and all it had endured since then, had put not even the slightest of marks upon it.

'It won't,' said Url, and then to Aliya he added: 'It's not actually dust from the Heart itself: It's what the Heart does to the air around it. Turns it into... Magic, I suppose...'

It was difficult to judge from Crick's map – in the Arkon's possession until today – exactly where they had emerged into the forest. But from what little they could see of the ground around them, Url guessed they were at least twenty miles from the north-eastern edge, and then another ten or so from the road. Gradually a routine developed in which they would move for a few minutes, then stop to clear the way ahead, not wanting to risk damage to the cart so early. Crick soon decided simply to stay out and walk; Tarryn, Aliya, and Yori soon joining him. They kept a steady but for the moment unhurried pace, hacking easily away at the greenery with the several moonslick-edged machetes Errin had provided for the purpose – or in Tarryn's case, his sword. Whatever rains had been here recently had stopped now, but tiny droplets still clung to every surface, spraying Crick and the others as they worked, refreshing rather than frustrating them in the increasingly still, humid air. And the horses, restless after so long in the Undervalleys, seemed to relish working again, Oden especially; each stepping lightly but with the sure strength of well-rested muscles through the bushes. It was difficult to tell whether they missed the presence of their fallen comrades as much as the family did; for now at least they showed little sign of it, caught up as were the others in the intrigue of this new place. The sands of the desert, so apparently infinite at the point the cart had fallen through, seemed a world away now; none of the group able to explain just how they had not merely come to the end of, but seemingly left that scorched and barren land so far behind. Great as the Undervalleys had been, their few miles alone surely could not account for such a distance of travel. It was a question which remained unanswered, lingering in the sweet, close air of the forest.

*

'How come they didn't sense the Heart?' asked Crick, halting suddenly as he realised that while they may not have told anyone but Errin, Joseph and the Arkon of their purpose, there were still many who should surely have sensed the power of the Heart. He couldn't understand why he hadn't considered the matter before. Perhaps he was thinking more clearly, more cautiously, now they were back amongst the uncertainty of their journey. It felt hard and unpleasant after the ease and openness of life in the Undervalleys.

'They did,' answered his Father. 'Some of them, anyway. Mostly those who were working with me, so close to it every day.

'There were others, too,' said Url. 'It's part of the reason Tholomus wanted us gone. He told me there were some amongst the people who were beginning to realise there was something more about us than what they'd been told. Not just those with Yori's sensitivity; all different types of Magic were starting to become stronger. Fireworkers were burning themselves with new and greater flames they couldn't control; those like Yori were learning things about others they'd never known before, and had no right to; tools and machines were being ruined by hands too strong to work them properly… It was happening all throughout the realm. It was slow, but down there even *slow* is often too fast. Some people were getting excited, others scared, and some others just plain confused. But the simple fact is that to them, new and different mean bad and dangerous, and Tholomus didn't want it spoken of. Made everyone who reported or saw such things swear to silence. And he was probably right – You can't say he's done anything other than a good job of keeping them all safe so far. Naturally you lot were far too busy to notice any of it,' he added to Crick, in front of whom a great tangle of slick, trailing vines, each the thickness of his arm, hung down from the branch above. 'He made sure word was spread that it was something to do with the seal breaking when we fell through, and that after being in the overworld for so long we were bound to bring in a bit of Magic with us. Think the idea held… but it wouldn't have much longer. We couldn't have –'

But as Crick drew back his arm to swipe at the vines their dangling tips flicked suddenly up from the ground towards him, shuddering as they tried to wrap themselves around his blade. He screamed, recoiling clumsily back towards the cart…

'What happened?' called Orlando.

'The vines!' said Crick, standing perfectly still. 'They tried to… They *moved*!' But they were doing no such thing now… They had drifted back down into their place, hanging limp and unthreatening as they had been before.

'Just the wind,' mumbled Url, slowing the horses but not stopping them.

'*What* wind?' asked Crick, still holding the blade aloft. From the corner of his eye he saw Url gazing about him, giving the impression of an uninterested shrug.

'A branch falling somewhere above, then.'

'*What branch*?' Crick whispered angrily. 'And if it was, why was it only the tips of the vines that… I'm telling you, they tried to *hit me*!'

'They…' Tarryn froze; his eyes shooting open in sudden realisation… '*Nobody move*!' he whispered hoarsely.

'What exactly does it look like we're doing…?' asked Aliya quietly, watching wide-eyed as the leaves of a thick, low bush seemed to be waving at her. Crick saw them too… and then other parts of the greenery around him, much of which had begun to stir, swaying or gliding slowly through the trees all about them.

'Tarryn… What's going on?' asked Url as the cart halted.

'Um… yes, completely forgot… Ha – sorry…!'

'Forgot wh–' started Abetta, interrupted by a thick, gnarled bough which had dipped down from the canopy above her, hovering inches from her face.

'Someone told me the stories about it,' said Tarryn. 'Thought they were joking... Not even sure *they* knew whether they believed in it or not! It's –'

'A forest-ward!' said Siu, jumping down from the back of the cart with a smile Crick couldn't quite believe. 'Why didn't you tell us there was one of these out here?'

'Well, it was a long night, you see: lots of things discussed, ideas put forth and received, and so on, and I –'

'You were drunk,' said Aliya, managing to frown briefly while keeping careful watch over the mass of small creepers which had begun to dance around her.

'I… Yes, slightly.'

'It's wonderful…' said Siu, walking slowly beside a low holly bush, trailing her hand inches away from it; the leaves turning in to face her as she passed.

'Put those down,' said Orlando quickly, gesturing to the blades Crick and the others were still wielding. 'It's inquisitive, but it won't harm us. Not as long as we don't threaten it.'

'You've seen one before?' asked Crick. The wet moss around his feet was unfurling, growing, creeping slowly up the back of his leg.

'Never,' said Orlando. 'But my Grandfather found a whole woodland of them once, somewhere in the very south of the Heartlands. It'll let us pass… Won't you?' He addressed the dangling limbs above him directly almost as if speaking to a child; Crick managing a weak laugh beneath his scowl of disbelief. But as he did so there was a quiet rustling of leaves all around them. The cold moss which had started to circle up around Crick's knee sank back into the ground, and in front of the cart the vines and branches parted gently into a high, green arch, revealing for the first time a clear trail through the forest.

Crick watched his parents move for a while amongst their surroundings, whispering gentle words and rhymes, some of which in places took him instantly back to his earliest years, although he couldn't remember the detail of any of them in particular. At length he and the others each climbed cautiously back into the cart, and with the greatest of care Url moved the horses on through the opening. As he did so, dozens of bushes, branches, weeds, vines, grasses and flowers of all types seemed to uproot or detach themselves from their surroundings, sprinkling the cart in a steady cascade of cool rain, meandering slowly along behind and around them. Whether one single, separate being or rather a strange, ancient consciousness rolling through the forest, drifting into and through each tree and patch of undergrowth in turn, Crick couldn't tell, and for a long while he could extract no answer at all from his parents.

'So it's… just… going to follow us, then…?' Aliya attempted, quietly. But with their heads still stuck firmly out from the back of the cart, gazing excitedly around them, their parents seemed entirely unaware that she was there.

Crick sat back into the smooth curve in the side of the cart behind him, gazing at the Heart, his bemused smile matching his sister's, happy enough for the moment that this being, whatever it was, did not appear to mean them any harm. It was a simple thing, but now they had left the protection of the Undervalleys it was one which once more, he knew, could no longer be taken for granted.

Chapter Twenty-Nine

Hollycrown

The steady swell of their talking and their laughing… the sudden bursting of the air within the cart as they called time and again to each other across and around the Heart, their attention and amusement still held, no less now than earlier, by the various tumblings and surges of the branches and greenery of the forest beside and above them… They were all so noisy. Not that they could help it, of course. This was the only means they knew of how to speak with each other. Yori missed the old fisherman; in all their hours together, neither of them had ever so much as had to speak aloud their name.

Yori continued to watch and listen with only the vaguest of detached interest as the others discussed their time in the Undervalleys, interrupting themselves occasionally to point out various new movements of the entity which was following them still as they passed uncertainly through the forest. But even this small part of their conversation, close by as it was, he was seeing through a haze; a bright, shimmering mist, of which the others could see nothing but the effects which it was having upon themselves. Aliya, apparently, had been the first to notice it, using it to help them cross the river into Irraigion – and then back again shortly thereafter. But now the others seemed to be sensing it as well; finding now that they were reunited and close once more to its power that their particular affinities for the world around them were growing keener, slowly and surely, than ever they had been before…

The forest, its greens no greener, its inhabitants no taller, all unchanged in any of their countless shapes and sizes, felt nonetheless different to Yori's parents; alive and understandable in a way they had only known or believed possible in dream, as though each restless shrub, each eager segment of limb, leaf and root were now no more or less than children granted after all these ages of the world their first true power of thought, learning to express themselves for the first time, speaking confused babblings to each other which as yet made little sense to the ears of man. His Grandmother, squinting this way and that from the front of the cart, could be heard muttering to herself as she gazed through the forest, taking new detail from all those things she had seen so many times before throughout her life, while beside her Url made little attempt to prompt her into talk or one of their much-loved arguments, intrigued and distracted as he was by the soft ground beneath them, wandering quietly and mistakenly whether it was the new cart or perhaps something new about himself which was causing him to feel it all more clearly, neither of which were true. Aliya to her delight was finding she could turn and channel almost to her will the tiny droplets of moisture which fell down and pooled amongst the sides of the cart, playing them around and against each other like the dancing of the waterfaeries she had almost forgotten, until with a final plop they came together and were, for now at least, too heavy for her, plunging down and off the edge of the canvas out of her control. And between them all, Crick's leaps now took him half-inches further in his enduring sense of self-imposed duty to be everywhere and see everything at once, his slick movements somehow slicker still than before, like those of a snake with newfound poise writhing swiftly about its prey, watching from beyond the gulf which persisted between them as Tarryn marvelled proudly at the renewed surge of strength in every muscle of his frame, beginning almost to break things clean in two rather than unfasten them, the Captain's sword taken up once more and feeling all but weightless within his palm. Even Aulan, whose thoughts and moods after all these days Yori still had found no good way of judging or predicting, being at once spirited and bitterly reclused within the same slow breath, was now suddenly aware of a part of his past he had thought to be lost; the tall stranger only barely less a stranger now after all this time, intent and focused entirely on some hidden importance as the cart swayed gently over roots and undergrowth, slowly away from all thought of the Undervalleys.

But amongst them all, alone and suddenly lonely again within his own thoughts, it was only Yori who could see why; only him who could see how these and other, greater though thus far unnoticed changes amongst and around them were all coming to be. For since he had returned to this world, many days ago in the wreckage of the old capital, he had been aware that the power being given off by the Heart was growing. Whatever had happened up beyond the mountain pass, while he had been asleep, had brought a great change to the gem… unlocked perhaps the beginnings of its true power. It was not fully released… not yet… But it was close; like the clearing of an ancient throat before a great, forgotten note could be bellowed anew into the world. He had tried, perhaps from fear and the bewilderment of his long sleep, to ignore it all at first. But after so long sealed away out of sight in the Undervalleys, it was still happening. And it was stronger now than ever. Even in the tower, within whose many thick tombs of rock it had been locked during their stay, Yori had felt it. He had mentioned it to the others, who of course amongst their distractions had taken great fleeting interest in what he said, just as they did again now, now that they were all finally beginning to feel it for themselves. But it wasn't the same… None of them could *see* it, like he could. None of them would ever see beyond the size and shape and simple colours of the gem which lay amongst them. He wished as so often in his life he had wished that for just an instant someone else could be there to share his world… He longed for the quiet, steady presence of the old fisherman beside him again.

Soon it became impossible to tell whether they were following or being followed by the forest-ward and the tall, ever-shifting archway it provided, not that they had ever truly known to begin with. It travelled with them through the afternoon, and when the first rain came again that evening it weaved a wonderful shelter around them, keeping them and the cart perfectly dry through the night. Beneath its grand lattice of branches and shrubs Yori could tell, somehow, that they were indeed as protected as the others all felt they were. Nothing but the full weight of the Darkness itself could have penetrated it. Even the energy of the Heart struggled to break out, dancing light but constant amongst the dark green dome of foliage in a perfect, beautifully random series of sparks and glistening swathes of wet, silvery light which only Yori could see, keeping him amused and comforted long after the others had all fallen into sleep.

*

Had they known how close they had come to the edge of the forest, Url would probably have pushed them on further that night. For they had been going barely two hours after breakfast when quite suddenly the final trees to make up the drifting archway swayed and parted, releasing the cart into clear, open ground which rolled away into a quiet landscape of gentle greens and light brown rises, to a distant horizon still tinged a dull yellow from the early sun. As Url led Oden and Nightwind out to graze their fill on the dewy grass, Siu, Orlando, Yori and Aulan paused to say goodbye to their latest companion. Yori wondered what had become of the little silver marmik.

All the others would have liked perhaps to stay a while longer with the forest-ward, but Yori felt his Mother in particular loath to leave it. As she stood gazing up amongst its rafters a small, blue petal drifted down through the leaves above her, hovering a second above the ground before landing softly at her feet. *Not fallen*, she somehow knew, but rather dropped to her with a definite if for the moment unclear sense of purpose from the being. And as she picked it up she spoke of being able to feel the flow of the forest; a cool and pleasant curiousness which stayed with both her and Orlando as they started off, once again, in Url's best estimation of the direction of the road.

*

They must have been further north or west than Url or even Errin had supposed, but finally as afternoon was drifting vaguely into evening Oden and Nightwind brought the cart around the side of a wide, featureless slope, and through a gap in the hills the grey and white stone of the Firstway was suddenly visible ahead. From this angle and distance it was but a mere thin track cutting beneath the horizon, but it was no less magnificent for it.

'We may well have taken the long way,' Url sighed, 'but we made it.'

'Any other surprises we're likely to come across between here and Iala?' asked a wholly straight-faced Abetta. 'Any hidden peoples, creatures… cities that come alive, or the like…?'

'Now they'd hardly be surprises if I told you about them *now*, would they?' said Url, leaning across and nudging her gently with his shoulder. She liked the touch… even if as ever she did her all to show otherwise.

'If we could avoid *scarravers* as far as possible, that would be splendid,' said Tarryn, far more frightened of the thought than his easy grin suggested. There was still sadness in him, too. Such sadness. And an angry confusion. He found it no less difficult now than before Irraigion to look Crick in the eye. None of the others, amused rather than concerned as they should have been by his antics, had realised that that was why he had spent so much of his time in the Undervalleys raging quietly through each and every bottle and tankard he could lay his hands on. For all his size and strength and otherwise unsubtle manners, he hid this side of himself well.

The bridges and statues grew taller now: all changed, but all much the same as they had been before Irraigion. The only real difference was in the stone itself, which was more cracked and marked than it had been so far, as if telling of far longer or more intense assaults by the Black Wind. There was no sign of the wind itself just now, however, nor any of its creatures. And that was good enough for the others. They celebrated as the cart crossed the pebbled threshold into the road, eager to make up for lost time.

But Yori stayed silent. He knew that he was not the only thing who could sense the new power of the Heart. After losing clear sight of them in the Undervalleys the Darkness was speeding towards them again now… hungry. The fact that there was no sign or sense of any dark creatures nearby was poor cause for celebration. The beasts had merely fled before the terrible coming of their master. They would see few such creatures now, if any; little sign of Darkness but the Darkness itself as it descended upon them. If the Torch didn't work…

He abandoned his thoughts before they could form into fears, speaking nothing of them to the others. Certainly this had been, and seemed still to be, their desire; the rest of the journey and what lay beyond having been referred to only briefly if at all, never lingered upon for longer than was strictly needed as days passed to nights in wilful, blissful ignorance of the matter, buried with the false calm and confidence of what they had believed to be safety beneath the sands. And his knowledge now would bring them nothing but the pain and anguish he was fighting so dearly to keep to himself. Blind as they were, it was only the occasional hopeful, uplifting voices of their minds which were keeping him from sinking into the dusk of his fears. If they fell to despair too, he knew he would be able to bear it little longer; the cold of sleep already calling to him again, inviting a return to the shelter of the nothingness he knew so well. Url was keeping to a good speed, and fear and arguments would do little to help. So curled sideways within the shallow seat his Father and the Crafters had provided, Yori pretended to doze as the cart rolled onwards, hoping beyond all hope that they would reach Iala before the Darkness reached them, seeing the fate which approached from afar, but so far as he could tell, utterly powerless to prevent it. It was all he could do.

The only distraction to all this, though far from a pleasant one, was Aulan, his thoughts and feelings still masked behind a barrier which Yori couldn't overcome, no matter how hard he tried. There was nothing in any recent word or action of his to give Yori real cause to distrust him, but not being able to understand him as Yori understood each other person he had ever known was greatly discomforting. There was far more taking place inside him than his calm, silent facade gave away. Not being able to see it was nearly as frightening as the coming storm.

*

With the exception of a series of first several, then dozens, then what must have been hundreds of oddly-shaped, crystal clear lakes of pristine emerald, through all of which the Firstway somehow found a nearly straight line, and from which Url was able to at last gain some near-confident form of bearing, there was little with which to tell the next days apart. They made quick and constant progress, pausing for meals only briefly, if at all; rising early and pushing on until the last of the light had gone. Yori was relieved that the spirits of the others remained high, even though he struggled painfully to join with them himself. Nearing the end of the fourth morning on the road, talk had turned again to Iala, which Url now believed to be less than ten days away. The sky above was clearing and bright after a morning of showers, but across the stone ahead thick flurries of rain were still making their way back from the cloudbank which was inching slowly away into the north-east. An early lunch, made comforting and sweet-smelling by the last, plump morsels of bailfruit, was being taken in the cart; Crick and Yori in the front, keeping the horses to a slow walk beside each other. The labour of the journey was plain upon Nightwind, whose legs and hind quarters rippled with newfound strength and leanness. While still no match for the matured, hard-earned enormity of his Father, his great height made him almost equal now in grandeur.

'...I know – but what if the Black Wind *has* taken it?' asked Aliya, breaking from her proud gaze at the animal. 'If there's nobody left there who knows how to work the Torch, how can you be so sure that *we'll* be able to figure it out?'

'I told you,' said Url wearily. 'And we've been over this a hundred times... Everything I've ever heard about it has said that all the Torch needs is the Heart. We shouldn't have to *do* anything.'

'Ah,' said Tarryn. 'So all we need do now is discover some means of bringing what you *know* and what actually ends up happening on this journey of ours closer in line with each other...' His tone and meaning were playful, but the words struck a nerve within Url nonetheless:

'If you'd like to take the lead the rest of the way, I'd be delighted!'

'And what if there's another spirit-ogre like the one in Irraigion?' asked Aliya.

'*Spirit-ogre…*' Url repeated with a jaded laugh, shaking his head disapprovingly. 'I'm all for naming things as I see them, but that's just –'

'If it's good enough for their centuries-old texts,' said Crick, referring to the passages he had been shown by his associates in the Undervalleys, which documented the creation of the first known entity long before Irraigion was believed to have been taken, 'then it's good enough for us.'

'Either way, there's nothing to worry about,' said Siu. '*I* was told that all the spirit-ogres this far north are actually quite delightful. Url…?'

Url paused a moment, scowling irritably at her, and then to Aliya he grumbled:

'There won't be any in Iala. The one in Irraigion – and others, as I'm sure your newly-knowledgeable brother here can tell us – was only formed because the people there waited until it was too late before putting up a fight. At the very least, we know that Iala was preparing her defences long before we lost contact. There won't be one of those things there.'

'Then what will there be?' asked Aliya.

'Whatever it is I'll send you out to greet it first!' snapped Url. Under the weight of their mockery, gentle as it was meant, his patience was beginning to wane. Yori was about to say something to change the subject, as so often he did unnoticed by the others in such moments, when Crick elbowed him gently…

'What's that?' he asked. 'Up there…?' He was pointing across to a tall, solitary hill on the eastern side of the road, maybe five miles ahead.

'It's a hill, son,' said Orlando, who had overheard and was eyeing Crick with mock concern. But Yori had seen what it was about the apparently simple hill which had caught Crick's attention: Nestled around its top, in what at first appeared to be a simple ring of trees or thick bush, something more definite had been crafted. From such distance it was impossible to tell what it was, but nothing natural grew with such precision. All the others were looking through the front now; Url drawing out the map hastily from the small, moonslick-encrusted chest behind him.

'There's nothing shown on here,' he said, frowning as he surveyed the cloth.

'Shall I take us closer?' asked Crick.

'No,' said Url in time with several of the others. 'Keep to this side. We can get a better idea of what it is once we come level with it.'

To Url and Yori's relief all conversation was put on hold as Crick prompted the horses faster along the road; the canvas on the right side of the cart raised and fastened to the top by Tarryn so that he and the others could see the hill clearly. There was unquestionably something there... And as they came closer to it, Yori began to *feel* it as well: The air seemed warmer, thicker somehow; though not in a stifling or unpleasant way. It felt... safe. But it was Aulan who realised first:

'A Haven!' he cried; the tones of his voice lighter and more joyful than they had been since well before Irraigion.

The others let out replies of confusion or disbelief, but Yori smiled: Aulan was right. Yori had never seen the Haven built, relatively recently, in the Heartlands, and had never before thought to feel one this close, but he knew that this was one of them, as clearly as if whoever had built it had inscribed it into the very air around it.

'But they were only built in cities...?' said Siu.

'Apparently not,' said Abetta after a moment, seeing the look in Yori's eyes.

Crick was looking to Url, who shrugged. Crick took this for a *yes*; Oden and Nightwind turning obligingly towards the hill.

By the time they reached the far side of the road, Abetta was able to tell that much of the green ring which grew tall around the top of the hill, sealing off the summit now from view, consisted of large, thick bushes of holly. There was no path leading up from the road, but neither was there anything to greatly hinder the cart; the slope gradual and smooth, with little but occasional clusters of wilted dandelions upon the ground. None of the others said anything to stop Crick as he took the cart off the road and up towards the ring of holly, which seemed to grow taller with each minute they approached – whether in truth or simply in their minds Yori couldn't tell.

Either way, by the time they reached it the holly towered high over the cart: deep green masking endless tangles of thick, black roots within; all quite impossible to move or even see through. A thin band of flat ground encircled it, around which Crick began to move them, searching for an entrance. It took all of half an hour, but finally at the north-easternmost tip of the ring, they found it: a break in the holly barely more than a foot wide, the inside and far end of which were hidden in deep shadow.

'Is it safe to leave the cart here?' asked Orlando.

'I shall stay with it,' said Aulan.

Url tried, but still now was unable to hide his distrust...

'Thank you,' he said, shaking his head, '– I'd rather stay myself.'

'No,' said Abetta flatly, taking Tarryn's hand as she climbed down from the cart. 'Urlmaeus, you're coming with us. You have to start trusting him! Thank you –' she added to Aulan as Url attempted a reply, '– that would be good of you. We won't be long.' She gestured irritably for Url to get out: He followed, but spent a good several minutes tying each of the reins tight around numerous thick roots before he was ready, for all the good that might do; Yori and the others peering hard through the breech in the holly, but for all their desire seeing nothing more than a foot or so in front of them.

'We won't be long,' Url repeated finally and firmly to Aulan. And then reluctantly he followed the others, Yori in front, into the gap, and along the narrow tunnel through the close walls of green and brown.

The blades and points of the holly dug sharp into Yori's legs and arms, even through his clothes; but though they ripped viciously at cloth and leather they made no mark or damage at all upon his skin, causing nothing but the faintest itching. It was all over so quickly – not more than twenty paces through – but as he stepped out into blinding brightness it seemed suddenly like many hours had passed; his whole body tired, the sun somehow having doubled in strength... He stopped, shielding his eyes; Crick falling into the back of him as he too was disorientated by the light. In turn the others all emerged one by one behind, each squinting and reaching around for themselves and their bearings, and it was only when Url came through last of all that the light dimmed suddenly to the long-forgotten brightness of a normal, midday sun which Yori had begun to think he had only ever imagined, its enveloping warmth a joy he hadn't known or thought to see again since leaving the Heartlands... But before he or the others could put voice to their surprise, all stunned to a stumbling clumsiness by their entrance into this sudden stronghold of light here in the very midst of the Outerlands, they were halted by a disturbance on the ground almost beneath their feet; a long line of tiny, bright silver flowers growing and curving around the opening, all twisting and breaking up as Yori watched into a multitude of different segments, until slowly amongst the grass the simple words were formed:

Here is built Hollycrown, True Haven of the North.
For All Who Need It.

And looking above them, up towards the summit onto which the sun was casting a warm, golden blush, everything was suddenly revealed; at once perhaps the most beautiful and distressing scene Yori had ever beheld... For from all along the great ring of holly behind them, thousands of thick columns of root snaked inwards, above the ground, towards the top of the hill. Along the way they met and split apart, or rose above each other, twisting at points to form hundreds of small, hollow shelters. And where they all met, at the very top some half a mile away, they rose into an enormous dome, deep red with the dots of millions of berries amongst the few bright green leaves which shone in the sunlight. And everywhere, across the ground, in the shelters, and leading up to the dome, there were bones. Whole skeletons wiped a clean, dull yellow with the passing of what must have been hundreds of years. There were thousands of them...

'I thought these places were supposed to be safe?' whispered Siu, backing towards the opening. She tried to draw Yori back with her, but he stood firm.

'They were,' said Url.

'It is,' Yori corrected them. He felt the others turn to look at him, and was surprised they couldn't see it for themselves... The way their bodies were laid out; loved ones beside each other, the bones of children lying gently amongst those of their parents... 'They all died peacefully.'

'*Peacefully...*?' echoed Crick; the shrillness of his incredulity tearing through the blessed calm of the place, and annoying Yori. 'They still *died*! Peaceful or not, it's not a good sign, is it?'

Yori loved his brother, but the manner in which Crick so often saw only the surface of things like this dismayed him greatly.

'*Time* killed them,' he said, gazing up towards the dome. 'Nothing else. They were safe here... As close to happy as they could have been...'

'There don't seem to be any signs of injury on them,' Abetta confirmed, stepping carefully above one of the roots, crouching to study several skeletons which lay curled up against it.

'Could we see inside, first?' Yori asked of his Mother, who had been about to suggest that they leave. She considered him a moment, before nodding.

'Stay with me, though,' she said.

So picking their way lightly through bone and root they made their way past the shelters, inside each of which were the remains of dozens more, all laid carefully beside each other.

'They must have created the Haven,' said Url, 'but then not had enough supplies to outlast the Wind.'

'That's why –' said Aliya, '– I *thought* – they were all only built in or close to the great cities… where there was already water and food enough for years. Why build one here?'

'Some of the cities with the first Havens became too full,' said Tarryn. 'People were turned away. Even some of those who'd lived in the cities all their lives were thrown out. What do you expect will happen to the citizens of our great and noble *Immelus* if the time comes and it gets too crowded? This must be one of the small sanctuaries built by some of those who were forced to leave.'

'How do you know all that?' asked Crick. 'I wouldn't have thought you'd have been taught anything of *Havens*?'

'We weren't,' said Tarryn. 'But some of the scripts are still there for those who wish to read them.'

'*There*… The *Halls of Knowledge*?' Crick asked, eyebrows raised, looking at Tarryn intently… '*You –*'

'I may have wandered into them from time to time as a child,' Tarryn murmured, almost smiling as he glanced back at Crick. 'Accidentally, of course. And before other pursuits made themselves apparent to me.'

'*For all who need it…*' said Url quietly. 'If nothing else, they created a place where they could live out their last days in peace.'

'A not unworthy goal…' sighed Abetta, hovering for a moment above the curled-up remains of an infant, which lay amongst two full-grown figures like a crumbled star held tight within two facing, crescent moons.

'I've never seen these before…' said Aliya, pointing to the black-stemmed flowers of snow-white petals which were starting to appear as they neared the crest of the hill, growing from beneath many of the remains.

'Mournblossom…' breathed Orlando. There was as much sadness in his voice as there was in the word itself. 'One grows –'

'Where ten people have fallen,' Siu finished, just as quietly. Yori looked up across the last few hundred feet of the slope, through which the ground levelled off before the dome, and saw a whole field of the flowers laid out ahead of him. He was afraid to guess how many must have died here. Perhaps Crick had been right after all… Peaceful, safe or not, this was suddenly not a place in which he wished to linger much longer.

Small gaps between the upturned roots which formed the sides of the dome led into a dark maze, into and through which Url led them for several minutes. It became tighter and darker; only the weakest of light making its way down to them, roots crossing from all angles and at all heights. But just as their thoughts began to turn to going back, Crick, who had taken the lead, let out a gasp from somewhere ahead of them…

'What is it?' called Url.

'Come see for yourself!' answered Crick, his enchanted voice dying thin and quiet into the curves and hollows of their surrounds.

Though it was difficult to know exactly where they were within the dome, there was little doubt when they stumbled shortly upon Crick that they had found what must have been the central and most important room of this strange place; wide and long, little higher than their heads where they stood and rising only softly into the middle, and altogether every bit as eerie as the rest. The arching roof let through none but the thinnest shafts of sunlight, falling all at different angles onto a floor in which little but the occasional root or pile of bones broke through a thick, perfect layer of mournblossom, barely indistinguishable in the shadow from a heavy blanket of new-fallen snow. Broad, root-formed partitions divided the utterly silent hall into several different sections; the warped shapes of what may once beneath have been furniture causing odd swells in the carpet of white, while in places the rusted ends of tools, weapons, and tall ornaments not yet entirely buried by the growing flowers showed dull and idle…

But into the calm there came suddenly a great squall, a frenzied consciousness Yori felt a split second before seeing its owner spring beast-like from high amongst the deep furrows of the long wall to their right, leaping away from them, growling through the screams and shouts of shock from the others whom Yori had been too slow to warn, fading quicker than a heartbeat between a dim break in the far end of the room, all somehow without disturbing a single white petal beneath him, the snow merely swaying gently in his wake.

'Out!' Url had already shouted… '*Go!*' he screamed again, leading the way himself; Crick already having vanished into the darkness by the time Yori and the others had fled back out of the room and into the murky maze of roots.

'Crick, don't you go out there by yourself!' called Siu.

'I'm… see… omes out!' was all that could be gleaned from his reply.

They struggled through the roots with little idea whether they were following the same path as before; Crick too far away to hear or be heard; Url grunting frantic curses as he barged hurriedly through the roots, calling quickly upon to Tarryn to take the lead… But finally black became brown, brown becoming lighter shade by shade until with a gasp of crisp air and sunlight they were outside again, Crick a few dozen feet away, looking round hurriedly to each side of the dome…

'It hasn't come round,' he said breathlessly.

'What was it?' asked Aliya.

'I don't know,' said Url. 'It moved as a wolf, but –'

'What is it, son?' Yori heard his Father ask of him.

'It was a *man*,' said Yori quietly. To him it had been plain to see; only now did he realise that the others had little idea.

'A *man*…?' said Aliya.

'It can't be,' said Url. Not up here – There's nothing to live on…'

'Unless…' Siu's eyes were filled with quiet terror as she studied Yori. 'Are you sure the Haven still has strength against the Black Wind?' Yori nodded.

'There's no Darkness here,' he said. 'He's just a man, like us.'

'All the same, probably time enough for us to leave,' said Url. 'Come on.'

'But if *he's* surviving here, maybe there's others?' said Aliya as they began to make their way back through the field.

'Which is why we're leaving,' said Url.

'No – I mean, maybe they're trapped here…? Maybe they need our help?'

Yori was upset that he hadn't had the thought himself, but he had felt no such feelings from the man: All he had felt was fear; overwhelming fear of Yori and the others.

'We're full enough as it is,' said Url. 'We can't –'

'There!' cried Orlando… and reeling round Yori saw the figure leaping over the ground around the dome towards them, howling furiously: naked, filthy, his long, ragged hair trailing thick about him; as wild a man as was possible to imagine… but a man.

'We won't make it to the entrance,' said Crick.

'Anybody bring a weapon?' asked Url. Nobody answered.

'Close up – tight together,' snapped Tarryn, and no sooner had he said the words than it was done; Yori pressed tight into the middle of the group. Through a gap between the chests of Tarryn and his Father he saw the man closing the last fifty feet towards them. Tarryn's muscles tensed; each of the group breathing in a single great breath as the grunting drew loud and closer in swift, raging bounds… and then continued past them. For a few seconds nobody moved or made a sound, but then slowly they broke apart, so that Yori could see…

The man was still and silent, crouched low to the ground, thirty feet from them. And as he looked more closely, Yori realised that below the man were the remains of two bodies, still covered in patches with loose, merged fragments of flesh and clothing.

'Stars above...' whispered Url.

'They can't have been dead more than a few years...!' said Abetta.

'I think –' began Siu, '– It looks like he's guarding them.'

He was. Beneath his thick, tangled mane of once-blonde hair, his eyes burned with the fear and courage of protection over a loved one... his family...

'His parents,' Yori murmured quietly.

Still none of them moved. They watched him, as he watched them; his breathing gradually slowing, his growling finally ceasing. After a while longer he sat back onto the ground, little more flesh on him than there was left on his parents, and with loving, clumsy fingers he started gently to stroke the bones beneath him.

'He's grown up here,' said Siu, blinking away the coming of tears.

'Look – he's eating the berries...' said Aliya.

'I thought they were poisonous?' said Crick.

'They are,' said Abetta. 'Extremely. His body must have adapted... learned to cope with them.'

'What about water?' asked Crick.

'I – I don't know... Maybe he gets enough from the dew, or the berries...? I can't think of anything else.'

'But how did his *parents* get here?' asked Aliya. 'Where did they come from?'

'How did they make it here so recently?' asked Tarryn. 'There are no villages or cities for days, and they surely hadn't the protection we have...?' The question itself was difficult enough; the fact that they would likely never find an answer even more painful.

'What are we going to do?' asked Siu, silencing the others for a moment.

'We're not taking him with us,' said Url, reluctant and briefly overcome by a flood of guilt, but defiant nonetheless.

'We can't just leave him here!'

'Why not? He's safer in here than any of us are out there.'

'But he –'

'He won't come,' Yori interrupted. 'He won't leave them.'

For ten minutes in near-silence they watched as he picked from the hundreds of berries around him. He seemed to be exceptionally selective about which ones he took, pausing to study and often smell them individually in turn. Occasionally he would stop altogether to pat with utmost care the bones beneath him, grunting quietly to them, keeping one eye always upon the group. It was only as he shuffled slightly to one side that Yori saw that for every few berries he was extracting from the holly he was choosing what looked to be the biggest or brightest of them, cleaning them as best he could, and placing them then carefully into the exposed, gaping jaws of each of his parents in turn, pressing them down softly with thumb and forefinger into the pools of dark mulch which lay within.

'We've spent long enough here,' said Url finally.

'It's not his fault you're afraid...' Yori answered distractedly.

'We're leaving. If he truly won't leave them, we have no more business here.' And with that he set off down the slope, not wanting to acknowledge what Yori had said.

Siu opened her mouth to argue, desperate not to leave... But she could find nothing else to say. She was the last to move as Yori and the others started walking slowly across towards the channel through the tall bushes; the man tensing again as they passed slowly around him. He gave Siu a final, lingering look as she left, with eyes that once perhaps had known happiness. Even the others could tell that it tore horribly at her heart. Yori could sense their surprise that he himself was not more affected. But in truth he felt no real sadness from the man... He had lived this way for so long, he simply knew nothing else. *Simply knew nothing else...* He recalled dimly thinking something similar about the Darkness itself, a long time ago now.

Once they were gathered by the entrance, stepping delicately through the silver words which curved still upon the grass, Url led them through without pause; each of them gazing up to the Haven, feeling the warmth and wonder of true light upon their skin one last time before they left, knowing they would not feel it again until Iala. The holly this time let them pass untouched, soft and relenting against their bodies and clothes; time through the dark corridor passing in the few short seconds it should have taken earlier. But before he reached the end, Yori heard Aulan's voices speaking from beyond the bushes:

'He was here, again.'

'Here? Who?' asked Url; Crick having to push him out of the way as he stopped in his tracks, blocking the passage.

'Alamos.'

'*Al–* When?' asked Crick as Url and everyone else looked one by one down the slopes, scanning the wide, open ground. The air was suddenly stale and dry again in Yori's throat. The others, doing what little they could to hide the fact from themselves and each other, all tasted the disheartening change too.

394

'You should guess by now that he is *no longer* here,' said Aulan. 'He *was* here. I saw him just as you all left. He watched you go in, then disappeared.'

'Why didn't you call us back?' Url shouted angrily, paying quick glances to the reins, ensuring there had been no tampering with the knots he had tied. To his frustration he found nothing.

'I did,' said Aulan, calmly. 'I called for you. Quite loudly. Many times. The bushes must have barred my voice. The Heart is undamaged,' he added as Url strode quickly round to the back of the cart. 'And still there...'

Url mumbled the essentials of an unpleasant retort to himself, climbing into the spare front seat and snatching the reins. Why he always felt the need to show his fear as anger like this, Yori could never understand. But it made Url feel better, at least. Safer. And that was good enough.

'May I ask –' said Aulan, '– What was it like?'

Url ignored the question, starting Oden and Nightwind back down towards the road the moment everyone had climbed into the back of the cart. But in the old man's silence, Crick leant through and began to explain all that had just happened. Yori watched the excited glimmer in Aulan's eyes for only a moment before a dark, heavy feeling tugged at his chest from behind. He wished desperately not to turn to see his Mother so upset, but as ever he had no choice... She was staring back up towards the towering ring of holly, seeing it now only as a prison. Long after they were back on the road, and it had disappeared from view, she said nothing. With the pitiable image of the naked, muddy man staying vivid in the minds of the others as well, they too became quiet, absorbed in their own, sad thoughts; those thoughts given all the time they needed to mature and fester through the long, grey, uninterrupted quiet of the road. For such a wonderful monument of hope, and all its initial fiery splendour, the Haven had inspired little but gloom throughout the group; a dark cloud in the otherwise clear and lifeless sky, which stayed with them well into the remainder of the day.

Chapter Thirty

Reflections of Home

'Now just how *exactly* are you doing that?'

But as Tarryn spoke the tiny, glistening fountain which Aliya had formed from the water before her collapsed in upon itself, dispersing in a series of small ripples which lapped gently against her legs.

'Well I'm *not* doing it any more, now, am I?' she answered, trying to force a frown, soaking him with a torrent from little more than the deftest flick of her fingers as he sat on the bank beside Yori; even the water which had initially been sent straying towards her brother somehow swerving slightly with a gentle swaying of Aliya's head and finding its target. 'And to answer your question,' she continued, staring bewildered but pleased at the thin mist which lingered for a second in the air, showing the curving path her water had taken, 'I don't know. I just was.'

'Well do it again, then!' said Tarryn through the damp sleeve he was using in vain attempt to dry his face. 'Except this time put some effort into the endeavour... Make it *bigger*...'

Pretending to ignore him, but with every intention of creating another which was tall enough to truly soak him with, Aliya concentrated once again on the water in front of her, trying to think it into form as she had been doing before.

There had been no intention of stopping this early in the afternoon, but the shimmering waters of the narrow lake, set right against and partly into a worn, cracked section of the western edge of the road, had been too much to resist. The crumbling stone merged almost seamlessly into the rocks and tall boulders which surrounded the water; a dozen towering redwoods and an enormous, sheer scree-slope on the far side sheltering the lake from much of the day's sun, while scattered green and purple butterfly bushes – though regrettably here containing none of the dancing creatures which gave them their name – let through a constant flow of air, altogether keeping the water to an icy cool even at this time of day. Her Grandmother had insisted on boiling it thoroughly before it was drunk, but Aliya amidst her games had been unable to resist skimming a handful or three from the surface, studying as she did so the elaborate facade of the ruins perched precariously upon what little flat ground there was left of the far bank, built from and now half-buried by the encroaching rubble of the slope behind. There had been several varied assertions on first sight as to the building's original purpose – perhaps the foundations of a guard-tower to watch over the road, or a storehouse to keep passing armies and nobles fed and cared for. Or perhaps, as Url had proposed, an entrance to one of the lost great mines which would have supplied materials and jewels for the powerful cities to north and south. Or perhaps simply a home... Aliya had put forward the idea almost unwillingly against the charm and intrigue of the others, but as she sat there watching it she could picture its inhabitants so clearly, stepping out each morning straight into the lake, never having to venture too far from it. She would have enjoyed living here.

Leaning back against the nearby cart, or lying outstretched upon the thin, dusty grass in front of it, the others were talking still of Hollycrown. Rarely did Aliya fail to be shocked at just how quickly a thing difficult or upsetting could lose or be stripped of its bitterness simply with the placing of a day or more's ride in between. It didn't always work, of course – many parts of this expedition alone could well attest to that. But it seemed to have done so here. Even her Mother now was able to talk of the orphaned, feral man without having to try too hard to hold back tears. She and Url appeared to have arrived at the agreement that once their journey with the Heart was complete, they would return to see if they could help him; both of them, along with the others, apparently content to pass swiftly over the complexity of the first part of their plan.

'Send some of that over here!'

It took Aliya a few seconds to realise Url was speaking to her... Her focus wavered, collapsed: more ripples from what had been the budding swell of water before her now washing soft and cold against her shins. Her thoughts had been so immersed in the lake that she hadn't actually seen what she had formed, but Yori's grin and Tarryn's raised eyebrows told her that *something* had happened, at least.

'Go get it yourself, you lazy –' Abetta started, and judging by Url's yelp she must have made contact with whatever she had thrown.

'I'm not thirsty,' said Url, lying back again. 'Just wanted to see if she could.'

'What about you, my dear Abetta?' asked Tarryn. Url nearly choked on his chuckle. 'You still haven't told us exactly what it is you're feeling from the Heart...?'

'It certainly hasn't done anything to improve her temper,' mumbled Url, just loud enough for her to hear, keeping one wary eye open.

'Only small changes, my young, *well-mannered* admirer,' said Abetta, this time throwing only the words in Url's direction. 'All of which are difficult to explain. It's as if... if I look closely, there seem to be new colours forming that I've never been able to see before. Colours which no person or painting has ever described, coming from all manner of things. The ground, these trees here... even the sky itself... They're all different. Not brighter, just...' she paused, lost amongst the high, red limbs of the trees. 'And they don't need *daylight* to be seen, either,' she continued at length. 'They're just the same whether its night or day.'

'So you can... see in the dark?' Tarryn prompted, trying to make sense of it. Yori too was listening attentively; Aliya abandoning another attempt at the water to watch her Grandmother instead. There was no smile or mark of fascination upon her; none of the excitement which Aliya felt towards her growing fluency with the water, or the others felt to their various aptitudes.

'Almost, I think. Yes.'

'Ha! You might come in useful after all!' said Url, but his voice fell upon unhearing ears.

'Though, in the past few days,' she spoke quietly, looking down into her enfolded hands, 'I seem also to have acquired the capacity for... something else entirely.' She frowned a deep grimace. 'Something I have only heard of once before...' She looked up anxiously to Url, who was leaning up onto his elbow, waiting quietly for her to continue. With a deep breath she unclasped her hands, slowly raising one of them up in front of her...

'*Whoa*!' Url had recoiled before any of the others realised; but then they must have seen it too, each flinching with shocked shouts of confusion or, in Crick's case, wholly unrestrained amusement.

'What is it?' asked Aliya, still unable to see what all the excitement was about. But as her Grandmother turned her hand round slowly towards the lake, she saw well enough: The little finger was missing. Gone, completely, as though she had never been born with one. 'Wha... *How...?*'

'I don't quite know...' Abetta looked to her hand, and the finger reappeared instantly.

'Can you do it to anything else?' asked Url, kneeling before her, examining the hand.

'Only parts of my own body,' said Abetta. 'And nothing much bigger than that.'

'Try your nose!' said Tarryn. Aliya was more than a little distressed to see him wearing exactly the same grin as Crick.

'Leave her alone,' said Siu, still rolling the sapphire petal which the forest-ward had dropped to her carefully between her fingers. 'Unless...' she looked sideways to Abetta, 'I mean – can you...?' Abetta looked back at her for a moment, took a deep breath, and...

Crick almost collapsed with laughter. Everyone else was caught somewhere between his reaction and that of Abetta's... For she took no pleasure in what she had done.

'Why aren't you more excited about this?' asked Tarryn, leaning forward and squinting hard at the flat, dark impression at the centre of Abetta's face, until suddenly with a blink of her eyes the nose was there again.

'She's just worrying over nothing,' said Url, sitting next to her, elbowing her gently. 'Aren't you?'

But still looking almost fearfully at her own hand, Abetta said nothing. At length Url began to explain for her:

'Unless any of you know any different,' he sighed, 'there's only ever been one other person with the power to hide things from sight like that.

'The ghost of Grendleweir!' said Crick. 'I remember – you used to tell me about her when I was younger!'

'Did he, now...' said Siu, glaring at Url.

'I also told you to keep your spirited mouth locked shut about that,' said Url.

'Perhaps you ought to let the rest of us in...?' Orlando suggested.

'Surely you've heard of her?' asked Tarryn. It's one of the first scarestories I was ever told! One of many my parents' servants entertained me with...'

'And a scarestory is all it is,' said Url. 'She was supposed to have been a –'

'*Supposed to have been*...?' Crick interrupted. 'You told me she was *real*! You said she was still around!'

'Yes, well, I say a lot of things. Never let the truth get in the way of a good tale, lad – you know that. Slows it down.' With Crick looking outraged, he continued: 'She was *supposed* to have been, originally, in her less, well, *ghostly* days, the last surviving heir to one of the great families of the province of Grendleweir, about five days' ride beyond the south of the Heartlands. They said she –'

'*They*...?' asked Orlando.

'Yes! *They – people – stories*... Do you want to hear this or not?' Orlando pursed his lips, and motioned for Url to continue...

'They said she learned, somehow, how to shape the way people saw things. She could hide them, or change their appearance, or do any number of other things with them. All of which was fine – if peculiar – until her brother died: killed under the wheels of one of the farm carts the people there used to bring trade into the Heartlands and elsewhere. She was barely out of her youth, childless, and he was the last of her blood. She inherited the house and lands, mile upon mile of them, and for years nobody saw or heard any sign of her.

Most came to assume she'd died. But then, when *accidents* started happening throughout the villages close to where she lived, the people started blaming her. A young girl was killed, stepping out onto a stair which was no longer there, and so in their rage a great crowd broke through the gates into the woman's lands, looking for her. But when they reached the rise on which the house was supposed to be... they found nothing.

They hunted her for months. Dozens more were killed, and most of the rest fled, before finally those that were left cornered her in an alleyway between two enormous barns. But she'd led them into a trap. She brought down every brick and timber of the walls, killing herself along with all of them. And in the moment before she died, it's said she cast a cloak around the entire province, villages and all. Nobody's been able to find it since.'

'And she was real enough,' said Abetta, seeing the looks in the eyes of most of the others.

'You don't know that,' said Url. 'And even if she was, what's that got to do with you? I mean, granted, you're already a step ahead in the *old*, slightly *senile* stakes –'

'Though in that respect neither of them hold a candle to you, of course,' said Tarryn.

'I'd start sleeping with that sword between your sheets if I were you.'

'He does already,' said Aliya. As one the others each turned to face her: it was a moment before she realised what she'd said... 'No –' she tried, '– I mean, I didn't mean it like *that*... Obviously I don't *know* what he sleeps with under his –' She could feel her cheeks flushing furiously: giving up on the idea of talking herself out of it she turned instead angrily back to the water, paying serious consideration to diving straight in and seeing if she could reach the bottom.

'Well, true or not, it should prove another useful talent to have,' said Crick. 'If we're ever to find our way back through the border into the Heartlands.'

The others were taken aback... An unspoken understanding seemed to have been born recently that the task ahead was quite difficult enough without talk of what they were supposed to do afterwards. Whether he was breaking this on purpose or out of carelessness, Aliya couldn't tell.

'What will they have done to our home?' asked Yori.

Aliya saw her parents look to each other – only briefly, as if that would hide it from Yori – neither knowing what to say.

'Decorated it with gold and packed it with wine!' said Tarryn, quite convincingly. 'We're going to be welcomed back as heroes, Yori – once they realise what we've done!'

Heroes – perhaps. Murderers... certainly, thought Aliya, and she could tell Crick was thinking the same. Still she couldn't help but be angry with him about it. Surely there must have been some other way of escaping the Tower and the city...? Everything would have been so much simpler now.

'And if not,' said Orlando, 'I'm sure there'll be plenty other places that'll welcome us.'

Maybe here, Aliya thought, looking longingly again across to the ruins.

'Will it happen straight away?' asked Crick. 'The Heart – the Torch... will they work straight away, or will it take time for the Wind to be pushed back?'

'I wish I could tell you,' said Url, sighing, stabbing the ground with the blunted end of his knife.

'So do the rest of us,' grumbled Tarryn.

'And I suppose you can't tell us what will happen to the Heart, either?' asked Crick again.

'It won't be harmed, will it?' asked Yori.

'Nothing can harm the Heart,' said Aulan from inside the cart. Aliya had almost forgotten he was here, sitting by himself, as he had been insisting upon with increasing diligence in recent days.

'Nothing…' He may have said more, but his mumbled words were lost through the canvas.

'I suppose that answers that, then,' said Url.

Aliya focused again on the water, creating several further small, delicate fountains in slow succession, each rising an inch or so higher than the last from the tranquil surface. Amidst her almost childlike excitement she was vaguely aware of Crick talking behind her…

'…and once we're done, can we get our own horses for the ride back?' It still pained him to talk of riding any other but Railer, but he made little show of it. 'The cart's comfortable enough,' he continued, 'but I've done –'

'What's wrong…?' her Father's voice cut suddenly across Crick.

'Oh! Whoa –' Url shouted. 'What's the matter with her?' The fountain collapsed, splashing against Aliya, and she turned to see the others all jumping to their feet in alarm… All except her Mother. Beside the cart, sitting just as she had been, perfectly still but for her outstretched, trembling hand, Siu's eyes were rolled back far into her head, dark red where they should have been white…

'Her hand!' shouted Abetta, hurrying towards it. 'The petal!'

Aliya saw it, held tight between her Mother's thumb and forefinger, its blue quickly giving way to the deepening red of her eyes. Orlando reached to take it from her, but as he knelt it burst suddenly into flame, engulfing her hand in a violent, twisting ball of fire…

'Aliya!' Url shouted, but Aliya was already reaching for the empty bucket beside her. With Url calling out again behind her she swiped it down towards the water, but even before it touched the surface she looked to find it somehow fully filled. After an instant's confusion she held it up to a waiting Crick who took it and in the blink of an eye was at the cart, and as he set it down Url and Orlando thrust Siu's blazing hand into it, smothering the fire with a sickening hissing and spitting. A puff of steam tainted with the sour reek of burned flesh rolled up from the bucket, and with an agonising effort Siu gulped desperately for air for several long seconds before finally catching a shallow breath. Orlando laid her writhing to the ground, breathing hard and unable to form the words she was gasping for, but through the confusion the sharp snap of Abetta's voice called loud and clear for her to be taken to the lake's edge, where the wounded hand and forearm, already red and blistering, could be better tended to.

Aliya could do little but wait as her Grandmother worked with all the skill and swiftness her long years of practice had granted her. Behind them the charred remains of the petal lay at the lip of the overturned bucket, still smouldering until Url approached and stamped a furious boot down upon it; Siu screaming one short note as it hissed and died, startling them all, before collapsing helplessly into the water and the bed of supporting hands around her. When her Mother opened her eyes again, Aliya saw that they had returned almost to normal.

'Look at me, dear...' said Abetta quietly. Aliya knelt down to take her Mother's other hand. 'Look at me...' Abetta said again. 'Look at me...' – repeating the words softly until finally a focus came to Siu's eyes. She blinked, looking up at them all, landing upon Orlando as she tried to force voice through her unwilling throat...

'It's alright,' he said softly. 'Don't try to spe–'

'*They're chasing us!*' she shrieked, no louder than a whisper but every bit as terrible and piercing as a scream. And as she spoke her breathing became short and sharp again, her focus fading; Abetta doing all she could to calm her.

'Chasing us?' Crick repeated.

'*Who?*' asked Url with a harsh snap to his voice more directly and forcefully aimed at Siu than he had intended.

But Abetta would allow no questions and no further talk from Siu. It was several minutes until, with a gentle squeeze of her hand, Aliya saw her Mother open her eyes again, and give a weary nod.

'I'm alright,' she said, trying to sit up. Orlando helped her, kneeling into the water behind her so that she leant back exhausted against him.

'Try and keep it submerged,' said Abetta. Siu grimaced, biting her lower lip hard as she looked down at her hand, which was beginning to turn a pale, waxy white in places beneath the water.

'My dear,' said Url, kneeling down in front of her, 'I know you're in pain, I'm sorry, but we need to know – We *need* to,' he added forcefully to Abetta, but she seemed to agree already. '...What happened? What did you see?'

'They were burning it...' said Siu with wavering voice, tears coming to her eyes.

'Burning... The forest?' asked Orlando, looking instantly back to the black, crumpled remains of the petal.

'Its guardian,' said Tarryn. 'The forest-ward.'

'I could see flames...' Siu whimpered, shuddering violently, almost convulsing at the memory. 'Flames from the fire they had made of me! Reflected all about me in their armour. Such pain... They had arrows of fire and men who seemed to turn the air ablaze from nothing... So many of them! They were *killing* me!'

'You saw through its eyes?'

'*Who* were?' Url demanded.

A deathly silence boomed around the lake as they waited for the answer; Aliya desperate not to believe what fear was telling her...

'Guardsmen... From the Heartlands. From Immelus...' And with that she was lost again, shutting her eyes tight against the pain.

Each of the group reacted differently, but all with the same look of terror in their eyes. Aliya watched as though from a dream, waiting for her Mother to say something to wake her from it. But when Siu spoke again the dream became darker still... and was made suddenly real...

'There were rows of Guardsmen in front, all in chain and leather; swords or bows borne by most... Lances were being thrust into me... Spectre-wolves held back on long chains –' Crick stood and took a sharp breath, '– howling and biting and tearing at me... Then behind there were others – so many of them! I couldn't see who they were, or what they carried, but most were heavily armoured... great twisted helms amongst them... and all wore the colours of Immelus. *Everything was flame*!' Her eyes became wide and red again with the words, her breathing laboured: Orlando tried to calm her, but she continued... 'And there were others even behind them... They carried no weapons, but I was more afraid of them than any of the rest... Their *eyes*...' She looked horrified, almost disgusted as she remembered them...

'Okay, okay...' said Orlando, wetting her glistening brow and cheeks with a sprinkling of water from beside him. 'It's okay... you're here, you're with us.'

'It sounds like an entire pack!' said Tarryn.

'But why?' asked Crick, apparently already having come to the same conclusion. 'They wouldn't send one of those all this way, surely – even for... for what I did...' He looked anxiously to Tarryn.

'No...' Tarryn answered, raising his eyes to the cart, from the back of which Aulan was peering nervously. 'They wouldn't.'

Url rose slowly to his feet, staring deep into the lake, frozen with horror...

'They know we've got the Heart.'

'What!' cried Orlando.

'The Heart...?' said Crick. 'How? *How* can they know?'

'No... no...' Aulan was mumbling, still watching from the back of the cart, rocking quickly back and forth, '...no... we can't let them...'

'I don't know,' said Url. 'They ca–'

'And how can they have got this far *without* the Heart?' asked Aliya.

'It's impossible!' shouted Crick. '*We've* only just made it through as it is! They *can't* have… Are you sure that's what you saw?' he asked of Siu. She gave only a petrified nod.

'But – that doesn't necessarily prove they're real…?' said Aliya, clinging to a hope she knew was seconds from forsaking her. 'Maybe it was just an image? A kind of dream?'

'…We mustn't let them near it…' Aulan continued, '…we *mustn't…*!'

'She wasn't thinking,' said Yori.

'We have to go… *Now!*'

'What do you mean?' Orlando shouted to Yori over Aulan's screaming.

'She wasn't thinking,' Yori repeated. 'When her hand was on fire… She wasn't *thinking* of anything. She was just *seeing*.'

'And what she described couldn't be much closer to one of the Council's hunter-packs,' said Tarryn. It was the first time Aliya had seen him truly afraid, she realised. At other times, even with the scarravers, or in Irraigion, there had always been at least a spark of anger or excitement in his eyes, concealed for a time perhaps, but still there… but not now. Now there was little but fear. For several seconds only Aulan moved or made a sound, swaying with arms clenched tight around his legs, his eyes darting to each of them in turn; scared and confused as he had been so long ago. Everyone was waiting for someone else to make the move…

'Pack up the cart,' said Url, glancing to Aliya and the others as he held Siu by the shoulder, smiling kindly to her for a moment before striding quickly up towards the bank. 'We're leaving.'

Something turned within Aliya's chest; all feeling disappearing in a flash from her limbs… She had heard the simple words so many times before, and with the greatest of efforts Url had spoken them little different now to how he always did. But never, in all the words and screams of terror that Aliya could remember, had she ever heard anything so frightening.

Chapter Thirty-One

A Kiss for a Kill

The heavy shade of dread through which each of the group now scrabbled desperately to make ready to go brought memories of the storm-swept night they had left their home come screeching back to Crick's mind. Several times as he helped lift his Mother into the back of the cart he could have sworn he was standing in the small, cobbled courtyard, surrounded by the aging walls of his own home… But blinking, they vanished, replaced once more with the lake, the fibrous trunks of the redwoods, and the wide, grey slabs of the Firstway. In barely a minute the horses were moving again; Abetta wrapping Siu's hand in a damp weed which she had snatched from the lake.

'It'll have to do for now,' she said, frowning displeased at her hurried work before placing Siu's hand into the bucket in front of her. 'I know, I know…' she whispered as Siu flinched away; her hand held firm by Abetta.

'How've they followed us through the Undervalleys?' asked Aliya. 'Surely Tholomus wouldn't grant them passage?'

'How could they have found them in the first place?' Crick asked. 'We did it by pure luck!'

'Or lack of it,' said Tarryn.

'Perhaps they've just come straight up the Firstway…?' said Orlando.

'Through Irraigion?' asked Crick.

'If they can make it through the Outerlands without the Heart to protect them, there's no saying they don't have protection to get them through the city, too.'

'Protection enough against that *thing*?'

'They *must've* come through the Undervalleys –' said Url from the front, '– else they wouldn't have met with the forest-ward.'

'And *that* certainly wouldn't have let them through,' said Orlando.

'It didn't,' said Siu. 'It was putting up such a fight... But they were so many. And so powerful... Most of them weren't even needed: they were just standing, watching... laughing...'

'And if they haven't just been using the Firstway,' said Url, 'it means they know more than just where we're headed to... It means they know exactly which route we've taken. They're tracking us.'

'But how?' said Crick. 'Across the river; through the sands... you can't track through that...!'

'Not by any means *you* know,' said Tarryn.

'They're following the Heart,' said Yori.

Url turned back with a strange, solemn dullness in his eyes, suddenly seeming older, more tired... 'You think Yori's the only one who can feel the way he does?' he asked of Crick.

'Well, no –' Crick answered, '– but I didn't know there were those who could track the Heart from such a distance...?'

'One thing, amongst many, that I hoped your brief time in the city would show you,' he sighed, drained by and struggling at the effort of having to state it outright, 'is that they have things and people there far beyond anything you understand. Anything you could *ever* understand.'

'Did *you* know they'd be able to do this?' asked Orlando.

'I... I *knew* nothing of the sort,' said Url. 'But I guessed – And so should all the rest of you,' he added, staring back at them all defiantly. He turned away from them, striking Oden and Nightwind to faster pace with a sharpness of whip they hadn't felt since Irraigion. 'I never thought they'd leave the Heartlands.'

'Looks like you underestimated them just as much as any of us did, then,' said Crick. Url sighed again, composing himself silently before answering...

'Indeed I did.' His voice was bitter; his shoulders trembling not with fear but with anger. Anger at himself. Crick knew it would do no good to force the issue any further. There was no point now.

'We'll struggle to outrun them in this,' said Tarryn with the calm a lifetime's training had brought him. Crick admired it, feeling almost embarrassed for the way he and the rest of the family had reacted, until with a jolt like a sudden clap of lightning he remembered what it was that hunted them now; no place for embarrassment amongst such fear.

'We don't have much choice,' said Orlando. 'If they can sense the Heart, there's nowhere we can hide. Running is all we've got.'

Crick saw Yori look to the Heart, lying calm and warm as ever between them all, with a thoughtful frown, as though not quite agreeing with what his Father had said.

'The boy…' said Aulan, apparently having seen it too. 'He knows… He knows a way…'

Everyone looked quickly to Yori, but he was shaking his head…

'I don't,' he started earnestly. 'I only… I thought there might be something, but…'

'Tell us,' prompted Siu, rubbing his shoulder gently with her good hand.

'It's just that, I can *see* what it is that they're tracking. I thought that maybe because I can see it, there might be some way that I can stop *them* from seeing it…'

'Don't try anything like that,' said Siu.

'He might have to,' said Url. 'You know I'm right,' he added, turning back. 'And so is Tarryn: They're only a few days behind, and they'll be moving far quicker than we can hope to. I can't see any other option for now but running, but… well, neither can I see any way that running's going to work. If we can't find a way of slowing them down, or covering our tracks, they'll take us well before Iala.'

Siu hugged Yori to her, kissing the top of his head. The others sat staring at each other, struck dumb in their uncertainty. What else was there? If they ran, they'd be caught; if they hid, they'd be found; and if they made a stand they wouldn't last a minute. *Slow them down… cover our tracks…* It was all they could hope to do.

'Pass me the map,' said Crick. His Father took the carefully rolled cloth from the chest behind him, passing it over the Heart. Crick felt the warmth from the gem beneath his arm as he took it. He spread the map carefully across his lap and began to trace their route from the lake to Iala; somewhere there had to be a way…

'Shift, then,' said Tarryn, shuffling round so that he was facing Crick, drawing the map softly down onto the boards between them. As he leant forwards to study it he glanced up – the contact only brief, but containing within it a quick nod which told that for the moment at least, all was forgotten. Their eyes then fell together to the map, and quietly, earnestly, and with every ounce of conviction expected of two freshly-trained Guardsmen, they began to examine the way ahead.

*

Had it not been for the need to rest and water the horses, close to exhausted now of the new strength their rest in the Undervalleys had provided, Url would likely have kept pushing through the night. As it was, they stopped for little over four hours; Orlando keeping watch behind them, for all the good it might do. Everything was changed: the skies, the road, their thoughts, even the cart and themselves – all silent and darkened now by the knowledge of their pursuit. Crick closed his eyes but found no rest whatsoever. And from the constant muffled rustling of cloaks and sheets around him, and the notable lack of any snoring, he could tell that most of the others were faring the same.

In place of sleepy yawns therefore there were thankful sighs when at last they started moving again. Still fully dressed, Crick rose and stretched beneath the clear, black sky, moonless but with an array of stars which quite made up for it; taking the front seat at Url's request. The air was bitterly cold, but to Crick at least it felt good: the fresh, sharp bite taking a small but welcome fraction of his attention away from the Pack behind.

Hunter Packs… He had been pleased not to discuss them further with the others when Tarryn had first mentioned them. How much the rest of the family knew, beyond that which they had heard in tales and warnings, he wasn't certain. Though in truth, most of what was said in those tales was real enough; if anything perhaps not going far enough, which considering the infinite and seemingly incredible accounts played out by talesmiths and drunkards throughout the Heartlands, was fair measure of their true horror. Crick had heard frequent mention of them in the garrison, and twice had men and women been pointed out to him by those few awed members of his squad, including Tarryn, who would sink as low as to speak to him at all. Both times the figures had been walking through the city with a wholly different bearing to any of those around them; unassuming in their dress and initial appearance, yet somehow also quiet, colder. And always by themselves. Along with these mostly highly trained of Guardsmen, the Packs comprised many others with abilities never seen, it was said, by any but those they trained with, or those they killed. Some were even reported to wield Magics. All manner of the most terrible and powerful of beasts were under their command, bred and trained in hidden, secret shelters of the Heartlands, and even when all together they could move as quick and silent as the wolves which had inspired their creation. Few of the Council's myriad weapons and tools of control were as ruthless and successful as this. Once a Pack picked up the scent of its prey, it never lost it. Never.

'I hope it does this time…' said Yori quietly. He was sitting in the front beside Crick, who had been staring wide-eyed along the starlit road; his gaze drifting idly between the bridges and monuments, all now bigger and more ancient in the thin, grey light.

'Sorry,' said Crick, patting the back of Yori's hair. 'I didn't mean for you to hear.'

'None of you ever do…' said Yori, and then with an attempt at a smile: 'Don't be sorry. It's not your fault. You can't help it any more than I can.'

Crick studied his little brother… With each passing day he felt he was understanding another small part of him, yet it was quite clear that even now after all they had been through he was still a long way from knowing his depth and intricacies altogether. He wondered if he ever would.

'If you could turn your feelings off,' he said, 'but then could never turn them on again… would you?'

Yori looked up into the sky, almost smiling for a moment…

'I don't know.'

'When you've done your turn up here,' whispered Tarryn, appearing at Crick's other side with a furtiveness quite awkward and unnatural for him, 'we need to talk.' And without waiting for Crick's response he continued on to check the horses.

'He thinks he's found a way…' said Yori. Crick watched Tarryn's hands fumbling distractedly with the reins; Tarryn silent, grim, unresponsive for a moment as Url called to him from behind the cart. If he had found a way, it wasn't one he enjoyed the thought of.

*

Sure enough, when Url took back the reins shortly after sunrise Tarryn motioned for Crick to sit between him and the unfurled map in the back of the cart, both of them facing back down the road. Immediately tracing two fingers up along the route ahead, and speaking a few murmured words the others couldn't hear, Crick quickly realised what it was that he was thinking…

There was a final lake, perhaps sixty miles ahead; the last of the long, speckled series through which they had been moving. It was far larger than all the rest, and the only significant obstacle around which the Firstway had to veer before reaching the Veya line – still as much a mystery as it had been at the beginning of the journey – and then finally Iala, turning westward and keeping close to the lake's edge for the most part, while to the east a short range of hills looked down upon the water. And it was just before that lake that Tarryn's fingers divided. The first, symbolising the cart and all the others, continued round the road to the west. The second – him and Crick – meanwhile, went instead in the opposite direction, round to the east, and then up into the hills. He wanted to try to lure the Pack away from the Heart...

'...using us as bait?' Crick finished the thought out loud, though keeping to the barest whisper. Tarryn nodded, leaning back. 'But... how're we supposed to get them to follow us?' Crick asked, shielding his voice from the rest of the cart and picking the first from an immeasurable list of questions. 'They're tracking the *Heart* – they'll never go for us instead.'

'Yori,' was all Tarryn mouthed back.

'But he doesn't know if he can –'

'He'll have to try.'

Crick considered the map again... Even *if* Yori could somehow hide some of the Heart's radiance from the Pack, the plan was still an impossible one...

'What about the tracks?'

'We'll take one of the horses. Oden. The cart'll run fine along the road with just Nightwind. We can fashion something to tie behind us to make it look like wheel marks, and we'll be going across ground where they'll be clear enough for the Pack to notice. The others can keep to the stone and hard ground; they won't form much in the way of tracks, and any they do should be easy enough to cover.'

'But –' Crick started, louder than he had meant to; only now realising the main flaw in the plan, '– what about the Wind? If we're away from the Heart for –'

'You've got your brooch.'

'And you?'

'The dust,' said Tarryn after a moment.

'The... You can't be serious...? That won't hold off –'

'Yori seems to think it might.'

Crick looked behind him, into the rim around the Heart. The thin layer of dust glittered back at him, just as it had done since leaving the Undervalleys. Beyond it he saw that Yori was watching them intently.

'He can hear us, can't he?'

'Probably not every word,' said Tarryn. 'But I think he gets the gist of it.'

Yori gave a small nod.

411

'I asked him earlier about the dust,' Tarryn continued, 'and he said that until it fades it's got almost as much power as the Heart itself.'

'*Until it fades*… So you'll be protected for –'

'Half a day, maybe. Maybe more.'

'Maybe less?'

Tarryn shrugged.

'And you can't see that this is a bad idea…?'

'I can see plainly that it's a terrible idea,' said Tarryn, sounding more than a little like Url once had, grinning just as he had used to when about to go into duel against Captain Saiak or any of the rest of the squad. 'Arguably my worst since electing to join you on this little quest. Let's hear yours…'

Crick struggled briefly for a response, but with a gentle shrug he gave up, glancing between Tarryn, Yori and the map with a silent shake of his head. The sheer audacity of it all brought a short-lived grin to his face, but then like the weight of a wave following calm water the truth of the plan crashed against him… He knew what this was likely to bring for one or both of them. The fire in Tarryn's eyes told that he knew it too.

'Let's see if anyone comes up with anything better before we get there,' Crick breathed, grim-faced and hopeful. 'If not, we'll tell them then.'

*

But through both that day and the next there were few other suggestions, and certainly none which stood any chance of success. There was talk of Abetta disguising them all, and of Aliya somehow keeping them hidden beneath the water; but neither of them were yet up to such feats, even with the potency of their powers appearing to increase almost by the hour. Orlando suggested shedding all weight from the cart; tools, food and all. But though this was done to an extent it had little effect with the Heart and themselves still weighing them down. So despite all that had been said concerning the futility of running, it seemed so far to have become their only plan. Crick caught Tarryn's eye occasionally as mile followed mile; what little talk there was around them focused solely on what lay ahead or followed behind. Words of poems and tales of the old Battles were brought to Crick's mind: those parts where warriors stood waiting to charge… Crick felt like one of them now, waiting to make his move, trying frantically as he sat in his silence to trade his fear for fierce courage. It was, after all, what he was supposed to be good at. *Fear isn't something you feel…*

Url's words came back to him as he folded the map again, having once more found nothing new within it, caring little now for its soft cloth and delicate workings as he forced it roughly into the inside of his cloak... *It's something you do.* But those words though he tried to hold to and take comfort from them sounded thin and hollow now. All those poems and tales told little Crick remembered that explained the painful, pitiful wrenching of his insides as the group laboured onwards in what felt now to be a painful slowness, ever-further along the road.

By afternoon of the third day of the pursuit – or at least what was now known to be a pursuit – the tension in the cart was stifling, rising breath by breath into a thick, heavy fog which smothered all act and thought, almost every instant of which in both cases was devoted to largely ineffective attempts at quickening their pace, or to continued and futile discussion of what they were facing, and how best to face or avoid it. The air outside had become damp and chilled but the sides of the canvas were rolled up anyway, not that this brought any but the briefest feeling of relief. They would be at the final lake within hours. Tarryn looked across again, impatient, but Crick shook his head and looked away, scowling into the Heart. He would leave it as long as he could.

*

'The road turns up ahead...'

Having waited what felt like an eternity for the words, Crick took a shallow gasp nonetheless when finally Url spoke them back into the cart.

'We'll stop for water,' Url continued, rubbing away the tiredness he had permitted briefly to encroach into the corners of his eyes. 'Try and make it round to the northern side before tomorrow.'

Still Crick said nothing.

It was only when eventually they came to a halt upon the eastern bank of the road, the Firstway curving away to the left and along the distant edge of the enormous lake, that Crick finally, uneasily, brought himself to speak:

'Wait...' he said as the others stretched, starting to bring down buckets and skins quickly from the cart; Aliya already by the water's edge, gazing into it. His voice echoed strangely off the delicate marble scales of an enormous water creature – part spear-toothed fish and part something else entirely – which was rising from a point a hundred feet or so into the water, looming out high over the edge of the road, unsupported by anything but the point at which its tail met the water. Tarryn stood by Crick's side. His voice must have been even quieter

413

than he had imagined, for none of the others seemed to have heard him... 'Wait,' he said again, louder. Heads turned and lifted to watch him. 'We need to...' In all the time he'd had, he could at least have thought of a good way of starting what he had to say...

'We've found a way to slow them,' Tarryn put in impatiently.

'How?' asked Url sharply, his eyes snapping to them as he helped Siu down to the road. Without another word the others each halted whatever they were doing, coming quickly if uncertainly to stand in an arc before Crick and Tarryn.

'You're not going to like it!' said Crick, trying to smile. But the others stood silent and straight-faced, waiting...

'We're going to draw them off,' said Tarryn.

'*What*?' said Siu.

'How?' asked Url.

'And who's *we*?' asked Aliya.

'Me and Tarryn,' said Crick.

After a second's confusion a volley of questions and argument struck the two of them like wildfire. But with a deep breath, and doing what he could to speak above them all, Crick began to go through the plan, which he had been repeating and trying to refine in his mind all day. They were silenced almost immediately, listening doubtfully as he spoke... They had all the misgivings that Crick had had, and more. He could see it in their eyes. But somehow, with the help of several shrewd and timely inputs from Tarryn, the plan had almost seemed to make sense. As he finished they stood there wordless, at least for a moment...

'But if they catch you...?' said Siu.

'We'll be taken back and locked up,' Tarryn lied. 'And you can come beseech the Council for our swift release when you're done with the Heart.'

'What if they split?' asked Aliya. 'If they send some after you and the rest after us, we could all be caught anyway.'

'They won't,' said Tarryn. 'One of the strengths of a Pack is also its only weakness: It never breaks up. They'll either all follow you, or all follow us.'

'We're so close now,' said Orlando – Crick sighing as his Father continued, '– we *must* be able to make it, surely? We've been on the move almost constantly; they –'

'So have they,' said Url, frowning; his thoughtful eyes meeting Crick's. He agreed with the plan, even if he hated it.

'And they're faster than we are,' said Yori quietly. 'I can feel them now...' he added, looking back down the road. 'But I –' he turned to Crick, '– I still don't know if I can do it...'

'Just do what you can,' said Tarryn. 'Even if you can't hide the Heart from them altogether, you might just do enough to confuse them. We'll have the dust around us, so they should feel that, and together with the trail we'll make I'd be surprised if they didn't choose to follow us. Just do what you can.'

'We should make it look like we've tried to cover our tracks,' said Crick, thinking out loud.

'But been too hurried to make a good job of it,' Tarryn finished, nodding.

'We are wasting time we do not have...' said Aulan, his voices almost unified in a set of soft, frightened notes. Crick and the others tried to ignore him, though the fact they knew he was right made it difficult.

'What'll you do if the bridge isn't there any more?' asked Url, referring to the crossing marked on the map which spanned the divide between two of the highest hilltops of the range, above a thin river which flowed into the easternmost tip of the lake. His tone had changed in the past minutes to blend with that of Crick and Tarryn's: someone discussing a plan rather than discouraging it. Crick saw the others notice it too.

'We'll leave whatever it is we're dragging,' said Tarryn, 'and make our own way across. Hopefully old Oden will be able to make it with us; if not...' Each of them, Crick, Tarryn and Aulan included, turned to look at Oden. The thought of leaving him for the Pack was... unthinkable. Over the course of the journey Tarryn had acquired almost as much a fondness for him as all the rest of them, and he spoke now with distinct anguish, and somewhat apologetically, as he continued: 'Well if not we'll just go the rest of the way on foot. It's only fifteen miles or so to the road from there.'

'And how long do we wait for you once we're on the other side?' asked Orlando.

'You don't,' said Crick.

After a moment his Mother began to speak, but there was no time for any more of this...

'We've talked enough!' said Crick, not quite shouting. 'If we leave it any longer it won't work – We need time to get ready, and more of it to get some distance between us...'

'I was only going to say,' said Siu, hurt beneath her reproachful stare, 'that you two better make it round in time.' Her gaze swung several times between the two of them. 'Because if you don't, after they're through with you, it'll be my turn…'

It was Url who broke the silence, in which somehow it seemed to have been agreed that, absurd as it was, they were going to go through with the plan…

'Someone come give me a hand; we've got work to do.'

'I'm sure one of us mentioned that already,' Tarryn murmured as he left to help.

Crick started to go too, but before he had taken a step he found himself being drawn into a tight hug by his Mother.

'You *look after yourself…*' she whispered quietly.

'He'll be alright,' said Orlando, holding Crick for a moment by the side of his head and giving a resigned nod as he left for the cart. Crick was trapped in his Mother's embrace until Aliya spoke up, sounding deeply offended:

'Why can't I go?'

Crick used the moment to escape; listening from a safe distance as his Mother forbade with great eloquence any further talk of that or any other new ideas.

*

At most other times and places Orlando would have been distressed to see his work so significantly spoiled, but now beneath the curious rippling shade of the stone creature above them Crick watched his Father work with a zeal unmatched by any of the others as much of the exterior of the cart was dismantled swiftly before him. The moonslick proved as difficult as Crick had expected to break apart, but with everyone working on it the white and black beams were quickly wrested from their joints and laid in pieces amongst a swathe of other materials on the ground. A simple frame was hammered and tied into form, equal in length and breadth to the axles of the cart. Thin curves of metal, ripped from the narrow beams which formed the main dome over the cart, were secured to the underside of each corner; bags laden with any and every last spare piece of equipment and morsel of food placed and fastened above them. Then, dragged with a hint of past familiarity by Oden through the grass, there was a grand murmur of relief from various points between the road and the lake as the impressions it created were seen to be not wholly dissimilar to those of the cart itself. Not as neat, nor as deep, but close enough. Hopefully.

'Leave the dust 'till the last minute,' said Abetta.

'Yori, how are you feeling?' asked Url, brusquely but not unkindly, glancing up briefly from his third checking of the frame's

416

fastenings. By this, of course, he had meant to ask how confident Yori was feeling about being able to shield the Heart; a question more important than any other, and as yet a question still worryingly unanswered. But sitting by himself, just in front of the cart, looking further back down the road than any of their eyes could ever see, Yori wasn't listening. Aulan was watching him from the edge of the lake, holding Oden and Nightwind as they drank.

'Yori?' asked Crick, but still Yori didn't respond. The way he was staring, motionless and open-mouthed, his arms tucked tight between his knees, made it feel as though the Pack would be seen creeping through the horizon any moment. Crick's eyes started playing cruel games with him, toying with the distant dust-clouds, creating tiny, dark figures which would surge forward from the grey-blue expanse before melting seamlessly into the road, or the bridges – of which, according to the map at least, there were no more from the far side of the lake to the city. They should have used them while they'd had the chance; perhaps that was how the Pack had made such good ground...

But there was no time to linger on such regrets. The thought of setting off into the hills terrified him, but the idea of staying here any longer was far worse. He left Yori to himself and went back to wrapping up the brooch. It was the third time he'd taken it from his riding cloak since the Undervalleys... He didn't know what it was he was checking for; perhaps just seeing it was comfort enough. He watched the dark, swirling mists of its face again for a brief second, before Url called him over.

'We're not going to get it any better than this,' he said, sighing, rubbing his forehead frantically as he ran his eyes back and forth across the contraption, trying to find a further means of improving it. 'You sure you're going to be able to keep up all the way?'

'There's hardly much choice,' said Crick, patting Oden's flank. 'With this behind him he'll only take one of us; and moons bless him but I don't think Tarryn's up to being the one running alongside. It'll be good to feel myself moving again, anyway...' He thought back to the last times he had truly run; truly moved like only he could: the mountain pass chasing Aulan... escaping through Immelus... fleeing from the gorge with Natt and Leyon. Terrifying as they had all been, he couldn't help but notice the tinge of exhilaration, the great surge of spirit which ran through the memory of each of them. He wondered how they would compare to this if ever he had the opportunity to look back upon it. 'It'll make it feel like we're putting some real distance between us and them.'

417

Url's hands finally slowed, and then fell loose onto the ropes before him. He looked up at Crick with deep, sad eyes, trying to find the words…

'I'm sorry, lad. For all this.'

'Don't st–'

'You know if there was any other way I could think of…'

'I know.'

'And – come here…'

Crick stepped carefully over the corner of the frame; Url clambering to his feet, placing his hand upon Crick's shoulder, looking hard into his eyes…

'Listen to me, lad. Tarryn's a good man. He's done well for us, and for you. I like him. I do…' He paused, pursing his lips before continuing… 'But if that dust wears off before you reach us, you don't do anything stupid and Crick-like, understand? You use that brooch *yourself*. You put it on *yourself*, and you *get back to us*,' he jabbed a finger hard into Crick's chest with each word; it hurt but in the urgency of the moment Crick made no show of it. 'It doesn't matter what it takes. You get back to us…'

'Url, I –'

'You promise me that,' he almost spat the words through gritted teeth, gripping Crick's shoulder tight with his strong, bony fingers, 'or I'll go myself in your place; old man or not…'

'The dust'll stay good,' said Crick. What else could he say…? He had barely paid any mind to what he would do if that moment came. The thought made him want to retch. 'We'll have more than enough time to get back round to the road. You just make sure you get to us.'

'That I will.' He pulled Crick to him by the back of the neck, hugging him briefly, releasing him with a smile. 'Let's get these two prettied, then!' he called to the others as he strode back to the cart.

Removing the dust from around the Heart proved more difficult by far than they had presumed. As if each grain was attached by some invisible band it slipped back stubbornly and repeatedly through their fingers, requiring several pairs of hands working carefully at the same point to free a tiny pinchful at a time. And once freed, it stuck to whoever or whatever it touched in much the same way. It took nearly an hour, but with a final stroke by Siu across the back of Tarryn's hand both he and Crick were covered, head to toe, skin and clothing, in a fine, shimmering layer, gleaming as they walked beneath the sun. Had the occasion not been so daunting, Crick would have laughed out loud at the sight of Tarryn: big, brave, and bold… and sparkling like a finest Princess of old.

418

'You look…' Aliya began, pausing at the glares from Crick and Tarryn. All the others were standing around her; even Yori and Aulan having left their various reveries to study the two new faeries in their midst.

'Splendid!' said Abetta, managing a laugh. Siu didn't share it; she didn't seem to notice the dust at all.

'Off with you, then,' said Url. 'Make good speed, and don't –'

'*Make good speed*, you say,' said Tarryn, turning to Crick with a disappointed frown. 'Well that is a shame; I was hoping we might take it slow… maybe do a spot of fishing for dinner?'

'– and don't stop for anything.' Url finished. 'If you have to leave the horse,' he added, looking straight at Crick, 'you do so.' Crick nodded, knowing what Url had really meant, and still refusing absolutely to consider the idea.

'Are you going to be able to cover your tracks well enough?' asked Tarryn.

'We'll be fine,' said Orlando. 'Just worry about yourselves.'

'*That* shouldn't prove too difficult,' Tarryn chuckled.

Altogether each of the group started moving towards each other, hugging without touching, and saying their *good lucks* and *goodbyes*. But amongst them all Url stood fast where he was…

'No, no, no…' he interrupted, clapping his hands loudly above the talk. 'We're not doing this… We're *not*…' He turned to Crick and Tarryn, gesturing firmly to the hills behind them. 'We'll see you two soon. Let's go,' he added simply, waving the others quickly back into the cart.

'Umm…' Tarryn mumbled, looking suddenly deeply uncomfortable. 'I –' he looked to Crick, then to the others, straightening himself upright. And then with a deep breath he strode quickly over to the cart… 'Ah – Pardon me,' he said awkwardly, gesturing Url aside and reaching Aliya, who stood wide-eyed and stunned as he held each of her arms gently within his great hands, smiled a nervous smile, and kissed her, lightly, on her cheek.

Nobody said a word as he turned and walked back, resolutely ignoring each and every stare and smile, leaving Aliya to turn a steadily strengthening shade of scarlet, unable to take her eyes off him, oblivious to the single speck of Heart-dust which had been left beside her lips. Tarryn must have seen the look upon Crick's face, for as he passed him he slowed, frowning; a half apologetic, half defiant look in his eyes…

'Let's, um, call it even, shall we?' he mumbled flatly. And with a single long stride he swept around the would-be cart and mounted

Oden without pause, waiting impatiently and with only the briefest of backwards glances for Crick to join him.

Chapter Thirty-Two

An Alchemist's Secret

It was strange, seeing the sunset dancing through the water like this… Aliya hadn't been prepared for it. As she ascended, emerging cautiously from the dark, she paused, stunned for a moment by the curious blending of reds and oranges skipping slowly amongst each other, their brightness dimmed somewhat but their beauty only magnified, as though viewed through a lens of diamond, while below her the dark shadows of the lake's depths stood oblivious to it all, content as ever in their gloom. A sudden urge to race onwards to the surface for breath almost overcame her… but she fought it. There was no need… she wasn't really here… She repeated the thought over and over, still gazing up into the quivering lights. She had to stay calm, stay focused… The others needed to know…

With a flick of her mind Aliya turned away and slid quickly towards the southern bank; the rays of gold and green flowing alongside her, carrying her, it seemed; the water rushing past her, into and through her, cool and soft… mud and rocks beginning to rise up towards her… It had to be here somewhere… She darted left and right through weeds and stones, past boulders half-lost above the surface; much longer now and she would have to leave…

But suddenly there it was, appearing through the blue ahead: the thick, stone tail built into the lake's floor, and beyond it the shadow of the creature above, stretching out far beyond the edge of the water. Aliya let herself drift gently up to it, resting beside it for a moment… She could feel nothing, hear nothing…

But then she realised she had nothing to fear from them – if they were there at all. They wouldn't see *her*, for *she* wasn't truly there… Even so, it was slowly and quietly that she moved around the mass of old, rough stone…

A long snout, black and scarred, was arcing down from a creature unseen, lapping at the water ahead of her. But she was too small and it too busy to notice her. Others were joining it, biting and gnashing for their space. Then studded hoofs and long, slender legs approached, wrapped heavy with silvers and blacks, all crashing into the water. Aliya's world rumbled and roared, all sight and sound restricted for a moment to a few short murky feet around her. She waited for it to clear; nervous, impatient… They didn't have this time to waste…

But it hadn't been wasted.

Her Grandmother had been right. They were here. As the water cleared, the light brown clouds sinking slowly back into their familiar ancient bed of silt, figures became suddenly and dreadfully whole along the bank; others behind… and then still more. More than could be counted. Aliya tried to make out their detail, but at first could see little beyond simple outlines of shape, size, and colour… Spears stood proud into the air; the shadows of all manner of other weaponry hanging upon the backs or beside the legs of those who moved back and forth along the bank. Some of the figures glinted as if on fire, while a warm, waxy glow coated the dark leathers of others.

But amongst them all, near-hidden on first sight, there was a small group, perhaps four-strong, which the sun seemed entirely unable to touch. Aliya found herself drifting towards them before she realised what she was doing; she halted, not ten feet from the thirsting wolves and horses still quenching themselves in front of her. She didn't breathe, didn't move; barely shifting her eyes as she watched the group…

They were far smaller than the others. Frail-looking, like wisps of grass standing small amongst hardened trees. The cloaks which covered them were dull and ragged, unmoving upon their slim, hunched shoulders as they huddled close, facing in towards each other, heads bowed. They could perhaps have been mere children asleep on their feet were it not for the stolen, curious glances and wide berth given them time and again by the others. Not one of the larger men or women ever came within twenty feet of them; none spoke to them; none would dare to look openly for long.

There was still so much that Aliya couldn't see. The others were waiting for her… Carefully she let herself rise to the surface…

And as she broke through into open air the sharp throb of their noise struck her hard; strong and constant; none of it gentle or pleasant, as though these were terms they had never been taught or allowed to consider. Arguments, shouts, grunts filled every inch of the air around the stretch of grass between lake and road where Aliya and the others had stopped and divided earlier. Weapons leaned up against each other in small pyramids upon the ground, most unrecognised by Aliya but all unmistakable in their deadly purpose; men and women sitting restlessly about them, eating, talking. Beyond them lean, snarling wolves of silver and darkest black, and men alike were studying the ground... sniffing, touching it, some with heads and hands pressed down close upon it; all looking back and forth to east and west. Two in full, silver plate were flanking another in scarlet robes, the antlered horns of their helms thick and fierce above them; all three watching the others work... arms now folded, now pointing impatiently... all angry...

Suddenly beyond them all a new terror flashed briefly into view. It was hidden for a moment by two men crossing along the bank, but then there again. It was... Aliya had never seen its like before... Surrounded by ten men all with oval shields taller than themselves and long, cruel lances pointing inwards, there stood the most enormous travesty of a man imaginable. He... *it*... growled a constant, dull note as it lumbered slowly along the road, standing four clear feet above anything else; muscle and sinew bulging from every rippling part of its hideous form, stretching black, leathery skin tight across its body. Patches of coarse hair grew dark along its arms and legs and across its chest. It gave a vicious snort at the points of steel which came too close... disappearing as it was led carefully behind a large cluster of wary Guardsmen.

At length a shout rose high above all the others. Immediately snouts were dragged back from the water, hoofs rearing and stamping away out of sight, weapons taken up and made one again with their owners; the din dying to quiet mumblings amidst the sharp clattering of armours. Helms were re-borne, eyes and mouths all set to fixed, hungry glares and snarls, and with a single final call the Pack moved off in silent unison, suddenly for all their former clamour and brutality now undeniably whole and perfect too...

And away from the road. It had worked – the figures moving now away from the water and off across the eastern border of the stone... and then beyond, into grass and mud and thicket... towards the hills. But through a panic of confusion and fear Aliya's joy was tempered as though by icy rain. Amidst the dispersing and swiftly-disappearing Pack the beast was visible once more. It howled and thrashed violently

423

upon the ground, flailing out a black trunk of an arm against the lance that had dared move it on…

'Ah…!' A hard voice but clear; Aliya feeling its bite above her rather than hearing it… In her unthinking silence she had drifted right to the water's edge…

'What is it?' came another.

'Dunno… Ugly thing. Dinner…'

Aliya turned, saw the glistening tip of an arrow…

And with a great snap across her neck she blinked, and was back to herself.

'It's them,' she gasped before any of the others had spoke, unclasping her hand from behind her head and the wound she had expected to be there. 'The Pack – I think they're –' she shook away what she could of her dizziness '– they're following Crick and Tarryn.' She sank back onto the road, exhausted.

'How many?' asked Url as soon as her head touched stone. 'And how strong?'

'Are you okay, dear?' asked her Grandmother, peering deep into her eyes. After a moment Aliya nodded, and not wanting to give the swirling, glistening memories time to fade she began quickly to tell of all she had seen…

Her Mother nodded long and grimly at the numbers and weapons she recalled; the others listening silently, struck dumb and frozen to their places around her, grimacing at the description of the beast… But it was then as she remembered almost as an afterthought the small, cloaked figures huddled close against each other that both Url and Aulan suddenly recoiled as one in horror of her words…

'*Four*, you say?' asked Aulan the instant she had finished describing them. Aliya nodded, and as she did so Url collapsed to his knees, sinking his head into his hands.

'Why?' she asked.

'Who are they?' asked Orlando.

'All facing inwards, unmoving?' continued Aulan. Aliya nodded again. 'You are certain?'

'Yes!' answered Aliya, a swelling irritation lending strength enough to push herself to her feet. Aulan gazed at her a moment longer, and then with glazed eyes he turned slowly away.

'Url…?' asked Siu.

'They can't be…' Abetta whispered. But when Url's eyes lifted to hers, it was as though the last small vestiges of hope drained from them even as the others watched…

424

'What else could they be?' he answered quietly. The shrug he gave was almost peaceful.

'*Stalkers*?' said Abetta quietly, as though still not believing it. The word brought with it a sickening strike to the very pit of Aliya's stomach, though she couldn't comprehend or picture clearly its meaning. She heard both her parents stifle a gasp. Url simply nodded.

'I'll explain once we're moving,' he said before any new questions could be raised. And with a distant gaze as forlorn as Aulan's he stood, letting his legs carry him swift and instinctively to the front of the cart.

They had stopped just before the crest of a long, smooth rise in the Firstway, several miles beyond the pointed north-western tip of the lake, beside a stream which ran parallel to the road before cascading down the steep stretch of rocky ground to meet the water. Through the distance Abetta's ever-watchful eyes had detected the vaguest hint of movement upon the southern bank of the lake, where they had earlier stopped, and though it had seemed impossible that the Pack could have gained on them so already it had been suggested and at length agreed that Aliya would try her luck through the stream, to see if she might discover what was down there. Jumping back into the cart as Url roused Nightwind from his brief respite, Aliya couldn't for all the thought she was giving it decide whether she was pleased or not to have found out. Amidst it all she felt a nagging sorrow towards whichever curious and hitherto long-hidden creature it had been which she had taken control over and led, presumably, to its demise. But it was as nothing to what she felt for herself and the others. Whatever these latest evils were, they seemed close to breaking the last of Url's resolve. He pushed the cart on, as fast now as Nightwind alone could manage, but for a mile at least he said nothing, his shoulders suddenly heavy and tired in a fashion Aliya had never seen before. There was little fight left in him. It was as frightening as the thought of the Pack itself. At length Siu leant forward to him, impatient as Aliya and the others for answers, but as she opened her mouth to ask for them she hesitated, seeing the ghastly manner in which he sat – slunk low in his seat, shaking his head and scowling desperately to himself all the while. She turned away, addressing Abetta instead...

'They haven't existed for a hundred years...?'

It was only with those words that Aliya realised her Mother knew something, at least, about what the figures were. And looking beside her, Aliya saw a similar look in her Father as well. There was confusion in them also; they knew far from everything – but it was only to Aliya and Yori that the term *stalkers* had held no meaning at all.

Even Yori, however, now seemed to be gaining a small understanding, slowly gathering thoughts and images from the minds of the others like a parched shrub drawing faint hints of water from its surroundings.

'So we thought,' Abetta sighed, glancing to Aliya... For a moment a cold pang of guilt crept up within Aliya's chest for what she had told them. A foolish feeling, but one she couldn't help. But then with a quiet smile her Grandmother added: 'We're lucky you were able to warn us.'

'They're a wickedness I thought and hoped to have left behind long ago...' said Aulan, seeing the anger of confusion in Aliya's eyes. 'Though, it is unfair to call them so. It is not their fault...'

After a moment Aliya shrugged impatiently, and Aulan continued:

'They were born of the studies of an alchemist to one of your great Kings, long ago. His name eludes me.'

'Raiyuun,' Url grumbled impassively from the front. 'King Atholis.'

'Indeed...' said Aulan, with the wide, distant eyes of memory. 'Raiyuun. We knew about him, even high in our mountain home. In the King's grace he worked for many of his young years; healing, killing, creating as he was instructed. But in his later life, with the first coming of the Darkness, he became disillusioned with his labours, and he left to seek out, as so many others did before and after, a way of fighting back against the Black Wind.

He never wrote of his methods, nor spoke them to any but the ancient beasts he kept as his own and his guardians. So nobody knew the means by which he created, after many years of toil, four potions. *All different*, he would later say, *but all linked by a common strand...* When he was finished, he took them to four villages in turn, disguised as a simple traveller. And there into the waters of each village he emptied one of the four vials he carried hidden amongst his clothes. Then he retired, and watched, and waited... For many months, the people were all unaffected. There were no signs at all that whatever he had thought to have created had worked. Whether this was his design or not, nobody knew.

But then, in one of the communities, a child was born. And it was a child unlike anything the people there had ever seen. Its skin was that of old parchment; thin, and frail, through which veins and muscle pulsed clear and bright beneath. In place of eyes were smooth, empty sockets; soft lumps of flesh for its nose and ears. Fingers and toes were fused together, hanging limp at the end of each useless limb. And from its birth to the day, not long after, that it was cast into the depths of a

426

far-off lake, it wailed a constant, quiet note from the sharp ridges of its blackened gums, bringing a terrible sickness to all those who heard it.

The parents were cast out of the village, and the child never mentioned... But then it happened again. In that village and the others, newborns, one after another, spilled forth with the same, dreadful features. Raiyuun returned, taking a child from each village and presenting them to the King who, he hoped, would see what had been achieved, and help him produce enough of the potions to help defend against the Black Wind... But when the King saw for himself what the four children were capable of when brought together, he had Raiyuun imprisoned, out of sight and sound of any other man; taking the four children and all the others from the villages, and using them for his own ends. For although Raiyuun had not found a way to vanquish the Darkness, he seemed to have created a means of confusing it... When the offspring of the four potions came together, they were able, somehow, to turn the Black Wind in circles upon itself.'

'They could control it?' asked Aliya, incredulous.

'No. But they could make it so that for a small area around them, it could at least not fully control itself. And it was not only the Darkness: *People*, too, they could render senseless with their screams; feeling their presence without sight or sound, crippling from afar any their master ordered who strayed too close.'

'Who was their master?' asked Yori.

'Whoever it was who first stood amongst all four of them at the same time. Foolishly, and to the detriment of thousands and perhaps the very history of our world, Raiyuun had granted that first honour to the King. With the four around him, that person had only to focus his thoughts upon another being for it to collapse into madness. It was said that the screams were worse than any torture: Any who suffered them, even for a moment, were forever haunted.'

As an image of the Pack came fresh to Aliya's mind she heard her Mother whisper Crick's name desperately across the strengthening dark of the lake. They would be at full speed now, closing in upon them: her brother, and her... well, not *her* anything, yet – but almost... Her thoughts raced to find a way to help them; some way of sending help through stream and lake... But she knew there was nothing. They were on their own. There was nothing Aliya and the others could do but wait.

'What happened to them?' asked Yori.

'The King took all the newborns from the four villages, until there were no more. He put them under his control, or that of his closest allies, and for a time he ruled with absolute dominion, conquering all

427

those around him. But the *stalkers* led shortened lives, and Raiyuun, despite all the years of torture he endured, often at the hands of his own creations, never gave up the secret of how he had created the potions, except to say again and again that they were all connected in some way. When the last of the stalkers died, the power upon which the King had come so heavily to rely was gone. Within the year his enemies had retaken their lands and their peoples, and annihilated every trace of him and his. The stalkers became a terrible page in the history of that part of the world, rarely mentioned. And over time they were forgotten.'

'Almost forgotten,' said Url. 'It seems the Council has long had other ideas.'

'How can something like that have been forgotten by *anyone*?' asked Siu.

'One thing which never ceased to astonish us,' said Aulan, looking pitifully at her, 'as we watched you pass the burden of existence from generation to the next, was the way in which your kind was able to cast aside uncomfortable parts of yourselves and your past as though they had never existed. Whether or not this is right or wrong was not for us to say. It is simply… how you are.'

'So this is how they've been moving through the Outerlands…' said Orlando.

'I believe so. The Darkness of course is still infinitely more powerful than they are. But they are merely able to ensure that, for the time being, that strength is not used against themselves.'

The cart was moving faster now that they had crossed unnoticed beyond the highpoint of the rise, but the Pack felt closer than ever. The lake was hidden, as were the distant hills into which Crick and Tarryn were struggling, oblivious to what it was that chased them. The air in the cart, already close and stifling from the growing warmth of the Heart, was thick now with fear and guilt.

'It changes nothing,' said Url, suddenly finding new strength from some hidden reserve only he had been aware of. 'Crick and Tarryn'll delay them in the hills. We'll meet the boys on the road, and be in Iala before the Pack has found their way out again.'

His voice weighed heavy with hope rather than belief, but if nothing else it shook Aliya and the others powerfully back to the task at hand. They were so close now: one last effort and they would reach Iala. And so with her heart still lost for now to the two lonely figures riding and running beyond the lake, Aliya focused on one deep, hot, frightened gulp of air after another, trying to remember how long it had been since she had breathed an easy breath, wondering how long it would be until she could do so once more. Behind her the night was deepening.

Chapter Thirty-Three

A Chase into the Stars

'Are you tiring?' asked Tarryn, close to breathless himself despite being the one of them being borne aloft by Oden.

'No,' answered Crick, as yet still truthfully, straining to see through the dense veil of firs to his left while jogging beside them. 'I just don't like losing sight of the lake like this.'

'It's but a mile or two away; we're fine. And the bridge can't be more than five or six ahead of us. What are you hoping to see through there, anyway? Even your Grandmother's eyes couldn't reach through that shadow.'

'I don't know… Thought perhaps I might get a glimpse of something. This ground isn't meant for this type of movement,' he added, pausing to look back at the deep tracks the frame was carving into the damp, soft earth, broken every now and then by roots like drifts of granite from the trees either side of them. The long, tight channel through which they were moving was bordered along each flank with the ruins of once-great walls, now little more than waist high and all but overgrown with innumerable mosses and plant life. The trees came right up to the stones but then stopped abruptly, even their topmost limbs seeming unwilling to lean across the walls in the gentle breeze; the roots alone daring to make their slow, surreptitious voyages beneath the stone and across the track.

'And what were you going to do if I *did* say I was tiring, anyway?' Crick asked, running again to catch up.

'Tell you to stop whining about it, naturally,' said Tarryn. He was staring up through the channel ahead of them, soft blue and grey in the starlight: It ran straight as a spear through the two woodlands on either side, flat for another half a mile, beyond which the walls and trees looked to end and the ground to begin a long, steady climb up into a smooth hilltop shrouded wholly by the night.

'You think it's up the top there?' asked Crick. 'The bridge?'

'We'll find out soon enough.' His answers were becoming short and distant again; what little hint of cheer there was clearly being forced through unwilling lips, and never reaching his eyes at all. With the others around it had been easier to begin to speak with him again; to try to begin the mending of that bridge which had been so dramatically brought down. But with just the two of them here the awkwardness was more intense and more consuming than ever. Crick detested it; he felt within him the rising of a new nausea to rival even that born of the terror which was spurring them onwards now. Tarryn seemed to sense that he was about to say something, for before Crick could speak he cleared his throat and began to talk distantly of some arbitrary occurrence from their time in the city. Crick laughed and joined in with the memory, his words as irrelevant and forgettable as Tarryn's.

Finally with the ending of the trees and the beginning of the long ascent the frame began to bury itself more deeply still into the ground, so that they were moving slow enough to warrant Tarryn dismounting and jogging beside with Crick. He panted heavily with the effort but kept a good pace; neither of them speaking as they climbed higher towards what they now could see to be a wide, tree-covered ridge – firs again, tall but widely scattered so that even with their lowermost long, reaching limbs there still looked to be space enough to fit through without trouble. More than once the frame became stuck fast in the ground, needing one or both of them to heave it out; poor, valiant Oden all the while asking for no encouragement, but Crick giving him plenty nonetheless. At times the frame had to be fully carried or dragged up sections of the slope. It was hard work, but not constant; Crick's sweat-soaked shirt turning instantly cold and sticking uncomfortably to his skin in those moments where he had little to do but walk. Tarryn kept himself busy on the far side of the frame, only ever looking to it or the ground ahead, responding briefly or not at all to the few and weakening attempts at conversation Crick continued to make.

It must have taken all of two hours, but finally the thin, gentle crunching of an eternity's fallen needles beneath their feet marked the beginning of the upper woodland. There was no bridge and no sign of

431

the river, but to their relief the flat ground through the trees was broken only occasionally by the smallest of undulations; the frame slipping smooth as water over them, above the moss and the silvered, rustling litter of the trees. Tarryn retook his place upon Oden; horse and rider complementing each other with their reflected size and silences in a way Crick was surprised not to have noticed before now. And for the first few minutes they moved through a peculiar air of calm; the silence growing to be almost as complete as that of the terrible forest through which they had journeyed just before reaching the Firstway. Crick's mind worked unceasingly to cast out and forget the screams they had heard back then, so long ago now, but with little else about him to take their place the voices came back time and time again to his thoughts, all about him...

Suddenly over his shoulder Crick saw Tarryn's head jerk up; his upper body spinning round in the saddle to look back the way they had come...

'Did you hear it?' he asked quietly, staring intently back through the branches.

'They can't be this close yet, surely?' said Crick as he halted, falling back behind the cart and listening through the night... Nothing. But the look on Tarryn's face said different...

'Get rid of some of that weight,' he said quickly, nodding to the four large, mismatched nests of sacks, ropes and tools tied above each corner of the frame. As he spoke his other hand was feeling for the saddle below his knee: the sword remained undrawn, but his fingers rested gently around its hilt as he swayed uncomfortably above Oden.

'What did you he–'

'Do it now!' Tarryn interjected in harsh whisper.

Crick thought better of arguing, and as the frame began to slide faster over the ground he danced all the while about it, unfastening bags and loosing knots and casting out various items from within.

The soft, high tone of a river ahead shortly thereafter sounded for a brief while as a whistling beacon of relief, but as it grew into a heavy rumbling Crick realised it would also mask all sound of the approaching Pack behind. Oden was put to full speed, slipping and struggling at times in the loose ground but persevering with wonderful effort, as though having sensed the need for new swiftness. Frustration began to well within Crick; the woodland stretching out far longer than he had hoped, the sound of the river rising again and again to new levels but always seeming to be just as far away... Several times they were convinced they were about to come to it, only to pass around yet one more set of trees and glimpse the silver woodland continuing far into the distance ahead of them. Each of Crick's senses were strained to breaking as he ran alongside Tarryn, keeping watch in front and behind, above and beneath him, slipping between branches as nimbly as the breeze itself.

Finally, with a great shout of delight from Tarryn, the trees came to an abrupt end. With a weary snort Oden nudged his way out through the last few long, trailing limbs, and slipping beside him just as the sharp spines snapped back into place Crick suddenly found himself looking out across a high, wide gorge. A great cliff sank out of sight almost at his feet; Crick searched for the bottom but was forced to lean out uncomfortably beyond the edge before he found it... Far beneath them, crashing and foaming between the walls, a powerful current was raging right to left sending a scream of noise and fine, cold mist back up through the gorge to where Crick and Tarryn each stood transfixed for a brief moment against the looming silence of the night.

'There...' said Tarryn, pointing to his right where, several hundred feet upriver, a long, thin silhouette, dipping slightly in the middle, crossed from one side of the gorge to the other. Tarryn dismounted, and he and Crick held each side of Oden's reins, leading him carefully along the thin section of clear ground before the edge of the cliff. As they came closer the bridge took on its simple, ancient form and a range of muted, silvery colours in the starlight.

'It's not wide enough for the frame,' said Crick, noticing that Tarryn was already giving a long, quiet sigh.

It didn't look strong, either. How old it was, neither of them wished to guess. When they reached it they studied quietly its frayed ropes and rotten, damaged or in places missing boards. At this point of the gorge the far northern side was slightly higher, and upon it the trees and dense undergrowth grew right up to the edge, thick and black within; every foot of the cliff-top unyielding apart from in a small, sheltered circle around the distant stack of crumbling stonework onto which the end of the bridge was attached.

'We'd never get it down there, anyway,' said Tarryn, surveying the forest which stood opposite them.

'So... do we go back?' asked Crick, as much to himself as to Tarryn. 'Find another way through?'

'I fear we've no longer the time. There are no other crossings for many miles – that was the point, remember?'

Crick turned from the bridge to the trees behind, and then back again... Tarryn was dismounting.

'What shall we do with him?' asked Crick, rubbing the long, firm underside of Oden's jaw. Foolishly as he spoke he glanced over the edge of the cliff; the river below so distant that all definition was lost from here. A thin line of grey, tumultuous slithering was all Crick could discern. If they fell through there would be plenty of time to think whatever final thoughts might come to them; Crick wondered briefly what those thoughts would be…

'Keep him tied here,' said Tarryn. 'He can't make it across this…' he nodded to the bridge. 'And we might need him again if we have to come back. They'll get him whether we tie him up or let him go,' he added, slightly impatient as he caught sight of the reluctance in Crick's eyes. The idea of losing another of the horses like this made Crick feel ill with sadness. 'Go!' Tarryn snapped. 'I'll follow.'

Refusing to say goodbye to Oden just yet, Crick passed his hand gently over the side of his cloak just below his breast, feeling the small, heavy brooch still wrapped inside. Then, staring resolutely ahead, he took a slow, careful step onto the first board… It creaked slightly, bearing its first weight for many years… but it held firm. With one foot Crick bounced softly upon it, the other still safe upon the grass, and then slowly, gripping the two main ropes tight either side of him, he started to cross. Several times he had to step clear above open air, doing what he could to not let his gaze drift down to the tumbling waters below, knowing that of all moments this was no time to let his fears get the better of him. One board held strong until he lifted his trailing foot, cracking suddenly like kindling into splinters beneath him; strands of rope coming away rough in his hands as his grasp tightened vice-like around them. The bridge began to sway – only gently, but still far more so than was comfortable – as Tarryn started behind him, cursing under his breath. The last few steps were steeper than they had looked from the beginning, but Crick ignored the aching in his thighs and forearms, stepping one measured foot after the other, holding his breath high in his lungs until at last he felt the glorious press of firm ground beneath him again. As he walked on through the short, cracked walkway of stone, however, no smile came to him…

'Well?' called Tarryn gruffly, still struggling on the bridge. 'How is it?'

'It's…' Crick didn't know what to say. Or at least, he didn't know how to say it. Before him, the impenetrable forest which he had imagined from the far side of the gorge may once have been here… but no longer. 'We'll…' his throat dried and the words faltered and died before he could finish.

'*What?*'

'We'll manage,' he called back, weakly, finding it an effort to raise his voice. *How* would they manage? *He* possibly could scramble down and then scale the far side – but Tarryn...?

'*Manage*?' puffed Tarryn, heaving himself awkwardly up the last few feet of bridge. 'What do you mean, *we'll manage*? We don't have much of a...' he paused, stepping up beside Crick, and seeing it now too, '...choice,' he breathed. For a moment neither of them spoke...

'Landslide?' asked Tarryn with disconcerting calm, as if enquiring about no more than a type of tree or the subtle intricacies of a rock they were passing.

'I don't know,' said Crick. 'It doesn't seem to have *slid* anywhere... It's more like the ground's just... swallowed it.'

The rift was almost as deep as the gorge they had just crossed, and wider by far. From Crick and Tarryn it sloped steeply down, littered with boulders and fallen trees; slick tumbles of shrubs and tangling roots jutting out at curious angles amongst each other. But the other side, through which Crick and Tarryn's gaze raked back and forth, up and down, was never less than vertical; harsh, thin overhangs of loose soil and rock spiking sharply from irregular points along the wall like the teeth of a great saw.

'Well,' sighed Tarryn, 'either way, it'll take me hours to get up.'

'There might be a way around it,' said Crick. Tarryn studied the trees either side of them, unconvinced.

'I'll meet you back here,' he said, darting off to the right. Crick took it as his cue to go left, sprinting through the trees with both the gorge and this newest setback visible either side of him. But within seconds he was brought to a halt: the rift curving round in front of him from his right, breaking through into the gorge. How he hadn't seen the opening earlier, he couldn't understand.

And when he reached the bridge again, Tarryn was already there waiting for him.

'Almost ran straight into the bloody thing,' Tarryn said with a bleak laugh.

'There's no way round?'

Tarryn shook his head, staring at Crick. And in that look Crick knew what he was about to say...

'You –'

'I'm not going on without you,' Crick interrupted plainly.

'I'll follow behind,' said Tarryn; but Crick was still shaking his head.

'I'm not going on without you. We either both go back –'

'It's too late for that.'

435

'Then we both go forward. Together. We'll cut the bridge; it'll buy us the time we need.' He knew what Url would say to him now, but he cast the words aside. He wouldn't leave Tarryn. He wouldn't go on ahead. After all he'd done to him already, he *couldn't*...

'You're as stubborn as they come, young Crick.'

'Being around you has that effect.'

Tarryn sighed, gazing across the rift...

'Fine,' he said at last. 'Your way it is. Find us a route down.'

'Where are you –' Crick shouted as Tarryn turned, hopping light as his bulk would allow onto the bridge.

'My sword!' Tarryn called back. 'Fear not, you can carry it for the climb! Hurry – Find a way.'

But everywhere was much the same. Looking out over the edge of the rift, Crick saw to his left a route down which they could scramble without too much difficulty... There were obstacles, many of them, around or over which they would have to clamber; but nothing insurmountable. But beyond that, no matter how hard he looked and how desperately he wished it to be different, the wall was sheer all the way along. Cutting the bridge would delay the Pack for another few hours or so, perhaps, but for Tarryn to reach the top was going to take almost all of that, if it could be done at all. The others could be gone by the time they reached the road... Or, worse, they might wait, and be unable to outrun the Pack for the last stretch before Iala...

Through the steady roar of the river behind him the thin, clean sound of a sword being drawn caught Crick's attention. He didn't know what it was that made him turn back: perhaps the slow, careful way the blade seemed to have been withdrawn from its makeshift scabbard; perhaps the fact that no sign or sound of movement upon the bridge followed it. All other noise seemed suddenly to have vanished into the night sky, abandoning Crick with a terrible leap of his heart. He sprung to the edge of the gorge...

Below, standing calm as the trees, motionless in the far mouth of the bridge, Tarryn was staring back up towards him. The Captain's sword hung loose but carefully by his side.

'Tarryn...' said Crick, working every muscle of his chest and throat in an effort to sound composed and commanding. 'Don't you –'

'I won't have you slowed on my account!' Tarryn called back. For a moment they looked at each other...

Crick made a leap for the bridge, but as his first step landed upon it he caught the brief shimmer of falling steel: The dark blade of the sword slashed clean and swift through thick rope and the wood beneath, sending one half of the bridge collapsing and lurching sideways into

436

the air. Crick reeled back, turning, grasping for the ground as his legs fell away beneath him. He clutched a sharp handful of soil, root and rock, digging each nail and finger hard into whatever small hold they could find, and as he dragged himself up and to his feet he grimaced angrily, screaming bitter, desperate curses back across the gorge. One rope still remained… Tarryn could still make it back across…

'I'd never hear the end of it,' said Tarryn, ignoring him. He raised the sword again, Crick screaming with all the breath in his lungs for him not to do it, but with another great swing the final rope was split. It fell, slowly it seemed, with what remained of the bridge; wood, rope, and the last of Crick's hope crashing into the wall below him with a clamour he didn't hear. He sank to his knees, still watching Tarryn as he fought to stop his sharp breaths turning into hard, angry sobs.

'I'm long-past bored of all this running, anyway,' said Tarryn, apparently unmoved. 'It's just not me. If I'm to be taken, whether by Darkness or Pack, I won't have it happen while I'm pissing around halfway up a wall of dirt. It's about time I went and did what I'm good at.'

'*We could have made it!*'

'Not with me slowing you down. You know that. Don't take it too personally,' he chuckled sadly. 'It's not just *you* I'm doing it for. You've all been more a family to me than I ever thought I'd have. Say –' he hesitated at the words, but continued, keeping his eyes firm and level, his voice as soft as the raging torrent below would allow: 'Say goodbye to her for me. To all of them…'

Crick's mind was blank. He could think of nothing to say. Even if he had, he doubted he would have had the strength to say it. His hands stayed clenched tight above the cold soil as Tarryn untied Oden from the stone which had for so long held the bridge, mounting and calming him with a firm pat of his thick neck. Once the horse was still he wrapped the reins tight around his wrist, holding the sword loose beside him in his other hand. He looked a final time to Crick… It was difficult to be certain in the pale light, but it seemed at last as though the harshness of his gaze had broken, the distance held between the two of them in that moment lessened, and he smiled; the gentle twinkling of the fading dust on his skin finding its way briefly to his eyes.

'I wish I had spoken more with you over the past days,' he said. 'For that, I am sorry. Truly. You've been a good friend, Crick. As much and more a comrade to me in Immelus as I was to you, whether you realised it or not. You… You did what you had to in the Tower… Let it go.'

And with that and a sharp heave of the reins Oden rose up and charged like a rolling of thunder away from the gorge, forcing a path through the close limbs of silver, the sword held high and alive above Tarryn with the unleashing of his rage, the last of them to be seen as they vanished amongst the deep shadows of the trees, each bellowing loud and fierce as the other into the sudden igniting of the night.

And amidst the starlit silence which followed Crick sank lower still and cowered to the ground, suddenly afraid.

Chapter Thirty-Four

The Veya Line

'They're not there, are they...?'

Yori could hear his sister put forward the question, but he did all he could not to feel it. Just as he was trying to ignore the thoughts and feeling of all the others around him. He knew they wouldn't find Crick and Tarryn waiting for them where the road swept north again up ahead, and he knew what that would do to them all... The failure of such desperate hope as this, from so many of those he loved all at once, was one of the most savage kinds of misery Yori knew. If he let himself feel it now, what little control he had over the Heart would be shattered in an instant. He fortified himself with the bitter knowledge that there was nothing he could do for Tarryn and his brother. The only way he could help any of them now was to keep as much of the Heart away from the Pack as he could. He doubted it was doing much good, though. The Heart was so strong. It seemed still to be growing, like a flower steadily blossoming. Why, precisely, and into what, he didn't know. But he knew nonetheless that they had only barely seen the beginning of it.

And when his Grandmother answered, sure enough the storm of their despair raged around the cart, strengthened by each of them in turn... all except the one he couldn't see. The Outlander; still just as much so to Yori as he had been at the very beginning of the journey. But he couldn't think about him now. He mustn't think of any of it...

Not understanding the Pack, or knowing where exactly it was, made the already painful task of preventing it from seeing the Heart that much more difficult. And apart from all else, Yori didn't truly understand what it was that he was doing now, or how he was doing it… All he knew in his confusion was that he was putting a part of himself, that deep region of his mind which until now he had used only to study things, between the Heart and those who sought it. But how long he could maintain his effort, he didn't know. The energy was seeping around him, through him, no matter how hard he tried to hold it back, like water escaping through his fingers. He could feel it wearing away at him, as though the bodily shell which kept even him separated from the Heart was being slowly removed. He was terrified and fascinated at the thought of what would happen were it to be taken away altogether.

'We're not leaving without them,' said Siu. '*We're not!*' she shouted again when nobody answered, so shattering the quiet of the gentle onwards rumbling of the cart that even Yori turned his head to watch her.

'It's still early,' said Url. 'Let's wait until we get there; they might have turned up by then. Or they might be there already, hiding.'

Aliya looked quietly to Yori; he gave only a small shake of his head.

There had been no more bridges since the lake. And now, as the road began its long, arcing turn northwards, all the other monuments which had so far been scattered across it were removed as well, leaving just the statues which lined the borders in the distance either side. It was also slightly narrower: not by much, but enough so that both verges could be seen at once from where Url stopped the cart in the middle of the road. If Crick and Tarryn were anywhere close, or were making their way down through the hillsides and fields behind and to their right now, from the north-east of the lake, the cart would stand out clearly for them against the road. Then again, as Url's mind repeated over and over as they waited, so it would to the Pack, also.

All eyes but Yori's were stuck fast to the horizon behind them, scouring the brown, rolling lands for any hint of movement. But nothing came. Every minute stretched for hours; the movements of what few high clouds there were filling lifetimes as they crossed slow and unnoticed through the skies.

*

Yet somehow through it all mid-morning came sooner than any of them had imagined.

'The dust will have faded by now,' said Url, almost unheard from the front, his head still buried in his hands.

440

'There's still the brooch,' said Orlando.

'For one of them.' He spoke with the pain of one who spoke because he had to, though all he wished was to sink from the cart and sleep and weep beside it.

'And *one* of them is more than enough to wait a while longer for!' shouted Siu.

'We can't stay here any longer,' said Url with desperate patience.

'We're not moving!'

'My dear Siu, you have to think of the others now! Think of Yori and Aliya!'

'Don't you *dare* tell me to think of my own children, you old *fool*!' Siu screamed, shrugging off Orlando's hand on her arm. 'I *am* thinking of them – Of *all* of them! All I've ever done is think of them! I *won't* leave them! Any of them!'

The cart was silenced for a moment; Siu leaning slowly this time into the arm that Orlando offered her again, trembling slightly. At length it was Abetta who broke the impasse, reaching forward and taking Siu's hand in her own...

'We have to go,' she said; her voice quiet and kind as ever it had been, breaking slightly. Her tears mirrored Siu's as she looked into her daughter's eyes. 'He's got the brooch, and he's as fast as they come – he may still reach us. And if he does we'll be of no help to him if we let that Pack get too close.'

'But – what about...' Aliya was unwilling to say Tarryn's name in place of her brother's, but the others all recognised her thoughts. None of them held it against her. Siu held out her arms and Aliya crawled into them, shutting her eyes tight. Over her head, through the cart, Siu looked again to Url; deep, terrible lines creasing her brow as she gave amidst a scowl of disagreement a single, reluctant nod.

'You know I've never thought of you as anything but a wonderful Mother,' said Url, smiling sadly as he turned back into his seat and took up the reins. 'Keep hope – they're strong lads.' But there was little left within him but despair as he sighed a long, miserable breath, releasing Nightwind with a weak shaking of his wrists. As the cart moved off, Yori was the only one amongst them without tears. He couldn't afford tears... he couldn't let himself break... not yet.

*

From time to time Yori allowed himself the briefest of glances at the road around them as they moved. It was strange, being not merely the only thing moving, as they had long-since grown used to, but now the only thing at all upon the endless, smooth stretch of stone. The

441

statues on either side all faced inwards, no less varied and wonderful than all those countless others which had passed before, and all adding to the feeling that the group were being closely watched as they crossed this final length of the Firstway, soon to discover the meaning of the Veya line that had worried them for so long.

Within hours the landscape had been reduced around them to ground so flat and featureless as to be almost crushing in its vast, unbroken simplicity. Even the sands above the Undervalleys had at least offered dunes to keep the mind occupied; here there was no such variation, the last of the straggling grass giving way to uninterrupted fields of rock and dust with only the occasional, living skeletons of thin, peculiar trees breaking the otherwise dry and desolate expanse, standing frail and alone in the distance, their rambling webs of roots spreading hundreds of feet in all directions, searching desperately for water amongst the arid, light brown ground. The vague shadow of a long, unwavering stretch of mountains kept distant company far to the east, soon the only reminder that there was perhaps a world beyond this silent, barren emptiness.

The map showed the Veya line to be within half a day's quick ride, but after several hours there was still no sight of anything ahead. The heat of the full sun beat down thick upon the road; the horizon fluid and hazy as they pushed ever-on towards it, hearts and minds divided constantly as to whether they hoped to see anything moving behind them or not. None of them had yet given up all hope on Crick. Tarryn, however... Yori could think of no way he could have survived. The dust by now would be gone and, strong though he was, he had none of Crick's speed.

The bleak emptiness of the lands around them; the thoughts of Crick, and Tarryn, and the Pack behind, and then of the Veya line and finally Iala ahead; and maybe with all that also the fact that after so long together there was simply little else left to say, meant that conversation was sporadic and, when it did occur, limited to its barest parts. There were murmurs of discomfort in the heat, despite the sides of the cart being tied up; there were requests for water to be passed around; occasional enquiries of how close they should now be to the Veya line, changing quickly to confusion as to why they were still yet to see it. And amongst it all there were the sighs or stifled sobs, coming as a ghastly shock to Yori each time, increasing in number and sadness as they travelled further without Crick's arrival.

And still Yori kept his mind firm before the Heart: a wall around which the Heart's strength was seeping, and against which it was battering, constantly; wearing violently away at the foundations of

442

Yori's will, loosening them, weakening them... He didn't know how much longer he could continue...

*

'What is that...?' he heard his Father ask a long while later. Yori wondered whether he himself had been asleep...

'It can't... It can't be the deepwater already,' Url answered hesitantly amidst the gentle uncurling of the map, now heavily creased and stained a dull yellow. 'We've still got –'

'It's not water,' said Aliya.

'No...' said Abetta. 'No, it's not... I think it's just a dip in the land.'

'It'll have to be quite some dip: It stretches for miles – look...'

'I know; my eyes see further and clearer than yours, remember... That's what it is, I'm certain of it.'

Yori set their talk aside again.

But whatever it was they had seen, it came upon them far sooner than he had expected... It felt like barely minutes had passed before he heard and felt their exclamations of surprise around him; all thoughts switching for a moment suddenly to what lay ahead rather than behind. Carefully, making sure to leave a part of himself standing always against the Heart, Yori opened his eyes and craned his neck to see between Url and Abetta...

A *dip in the land*... Unlike Url, Abetta was rarely one for embellishment; but even by her standards it had been an understatement of astonishing scale. Half a mile ahead, the whole world seemed to end in a sudden shelf: cliffs sinking out of sight for as far as the eye could see to west and east, while through them, like a river having worn its way surely down through a hillside, the Firstway plunged steep down countless thousands of feet to new lands far below. And there, several miles further on, it came to an end. And what an end it was...

Neither Yori nor any of the others felt the need to ask if it was the Veya line: Its sheer size spoke of that clear enough itself. Above a wide chasm rent through the ground like an enormous, curving scar, hundreds of black pillars, each nearly as high as where the road was now, leaned out from the far side to dangle great gemstones halfway across the divide, each glinting a different, glorious colour in the sun. Where the road came to an end at its centre, a bridge took over; the single crossing point, narrower perhaps than the road but still two hundred feet or more wide, arching high from the southern side into the north. At its peak it widened further still into a large disk, crowned with dozens of tall golden spires arcing first out and then in towards each other, supported beneath by a vast stone column which disappeared into the depths of the chasm. From somewhere within the circle, shards of light and strange shadows were flicking softly through the spires, falling upon and merging curiously with the white and black stone of which the bridge was built. What it all meant, Yori could not begin to imagine. But in all its remarkable scale and power there could be little doubting it had been intended to keep things out.

'Anything moving down there?' asked Url, turning his head slightly to Abetta while keeping his eyes fixed hard upon the bridge. Abetta looked a while longer: she was reluctant to have to give the *no* which hung at her lips, but there was little else for her to say.

'Were you expecting to see them here?' asked Orlando. 'People from Iala?'

'I thought, perhaps...' Url was discomforted, afraid... 'I just thought that if this was their first defence against the Black Wind, maybe they'd be here, watching out for it...' His back stiffened in his seat and he shook the reins. 'No matter. Likely they built it so there was no need for them to always be around.'

'Do you know how it works?' asked Aliya, speaking to Aulan.

'I have never seen such a thing before,' said Aulan. He had not uttered a word since the lake. 'I am unsure whether it existed in my time... Rumour spoke of the great defences of this place, but never of such a creation. It is... quite beautiful, is it not?'

'I'll tell you once it's let us through,' Url grumbled.

'I can't see *anything* beyond it...' said Orlando. Url turned back to him with a frown that said he shared his confusion and concern. 'It's only, what, fifteen miles from here to the city itself? Twenty?'

'Something like that, yes.'

'Well surely there should be some sign of life down there? Buildings, roads, farms... *Something*...?'

The others all looked again, finding nothing. Siu was keeping watch behind them once more, willing Crick to her. Yori felt eyes turning to him, wondering...

'I can't feel anything,' he answered, quick and toneless, before they could ask. He was only barely managing to keep his link with the Heart as it was, without their distracting him. But it was true enough: He could feel no more than their eyes could see beyond the chasm. It was the great gemstones which lined the sky above it... all linked... all connected to the bridge... They were so powerful...

The gradient of the road was such that everyone had to brace themselves against a part of the cart; the Heart staying firm in its place,

444

but anything else not tied fast or stored away doing its utmost to roll or fall to the front. Even so, the astonishing difference in elevation between the two planes meant that it was nearly an hour before Yori, eyes closed, began to feel the ground levelling out beneath them. The air had become thicker here… heavier. Amidst a bitter grit of sand and dust, Yori could taste it. Perhaps in all this time on the road they hadn't truly realised just how high they had come. With all the varying sections and colours of the incredible structure now a thousand feet or so above them, they approached the wide, imposing foot of the great bridge in silence. Only now did the bones of thousands of creatures become visible ahead along the edge of this side of the chasm, arrayed so that they were all facing in towards the road. Some were little more than dust amongst dust; others far more recent. Wolves and other common beasts were clear and plenty, some little different to those Yori had seen a dozen times before. But they paled in comparison to those which lay between, to a great many of which even Url or Aulan could not begin to put a name. Great tusks, horns and claws still held their points; wings, some several times the width of the cart, were folded up into the air or stretched flat upon the ground around beings which would once have stood high and longer than a home; and in some places there were the thick, mottled remains of what looked to have been enormous, ridged shells, taller than a man and longer than twenty. And all, from bridge and road right round the edge of the chasm as far as could be seen, were black. Not darkened by age, nor stained by burning or the passing of a storm or plague; but black from within. Creatures of the Darkness.

What substance the bridge was made of was difficult to tell. It wasn't stone, as they had first thought… It had the grain and smell of wood, but it shone with the hardness of newly-worked metal, almost like moonslick; black and white each casting back oddly different reflections of the cart as Url brought it to a stop. In front of them, above the entrance to the bridge, a thick arch became emblazoned suddenly with thin lettering of fire, bursting into life as they gazed up towards it. Aulan climbed out through the side of the cart, studying the symbols…

'Can you read them?' asked Url.

'I… It has been a long time since I have looked upon such language…' He smiled, casting his eyes slowly over each mark in turn.

Url had little patience for this, but he waited silently. When Aulan spoke again his voices were each loud and clear, the words slipping softly from one to the next…

445

'Light from the dark, find shelter within: Our home, flame eternal through the night.'

'Flame eternal...' whispered Aliya, looking to Url. 'Didn't you say that that was one of the terms people used to use for the city?'

Url was nodding, almost smiling; but he stopped as he saw Siu's face.

'I'm sorry,' he said, gently. 'We... have to go on.'

Siu neither smiled nor shook her head; her brow crumbling with pain and the effort of not falling to tears again. They had made it through the Outerlands; across this bridge and their journey would be close to complete. But for all the suffering they had endured to get here, there was no happiness now. Crick and Tarryn gone, and the Pack biting closer than ever at their heels. Yori wanted it all to be over. He wanted to be home.

'We should t–' but as Orlando spoke Url jumped to his feet, looking anxiously about the cart.

'Did you feel that?' he asked. 'The ground...!' he added, jumping down to the road and pressing his hands to it, listening intently... As he opened his mouth to speak again a quiet tremor flashed suddenly through the stone beneath them. They all looked quickly back to where the road disappeared up between the cliffs, hidden in shadow.

'Get in,' said Abetta, waving Url back to his seat.

'Can you see someth–'

'Yes! Go!' she shouted, taking hold of Url's arm. *'Quickly...'*

As soon as the cart began to move the road quaked again, stronger than before.

'What is it?' asked Siu. 'Is it... Could it be him?'

Abetta squinted into the distance, and as she did so Yori cast his mind back along the road... The distance was great: never had he felt anything from so far away. But he tried nonetheless; the Heart beating like a gale against his back, always searching for a way through, finding it again and again.

'No,' said Abetta finally, just as Yori began to feel the same. 'I don't think so...' The rattling of the wheels covered Siu's quiet sobbing. 'It can't be,' Abetta continued. 'It's too big. But...'

'What?' Url snapped at her.

'I don't think it's the Pack, either...'

Something powerful nudged at the edge of Yori's mind... He had felt it before... He could feel it bounding down towards them; such speed and power. And there was something else as well: smaller, quieter, but...

'Wait!' Yori shouted as the cart streaked onto the first stone of the bridge. He felt again, to be sure... But it was... It was him! 'Crick!' he called, jumping awkwardly from the cart before his Father could stop him. '*Crick!*' He was alive... The others were all out of the cart as well now; delight still caged within their confusion. Yori knew he should explain, but for a moment as he called to his brother he was too excited to do so...

'It's Alamos!' Abetta exclaimed suddenly.

'Alamos?' shouted Url, still securing the wheels of the cart.

'He's brought Crick with him!' said Yori.

'Is he hurt?' asked Siu. Yori couldn't answer... It was difficult to know from here. He waited, silent with the others,

'Are we sure he's friendly?' asked Orlando as a great, golden-green figure came tearing into sight, leaping in enormous bounds down towards them.

'It's too late to change our minds now,' said Url.

'He's got Crick,' said Siu flatly. 'We're not going anywhere.'

'Where *is* Crick?' asked Aliya. 'I thought you said –'

'He's there,' said Yori. There was no doubting it now; it was Crick.

Suddenly Abetta gasped, her eyes wide with shock...

'What is it?' asked Siu. 'What can you see?'

'Be strong, dear,' said Abetta quietly.

'What can you see?' Siu shouted. Abetta couldn't bring herself to speak, but seconds later they all saw it for themselves: Between the great, dark jaws of Alamos, teeth bared like rows of perfect, pearl-white blades, Crick's body hung like a ragged doll, marked with thin scatterings of red, shaking as the creature sped like lightning across the flat ground.

'Put it down,' said Aulan urgently, drawing Yori's attention to Url behind him, hastily stringing his bow.

'Shut your mouth,' Url grunted.

Green and gold were within seconds of them... Url raised the bow between Orlando and Yori, but then with a deafening roar that nearly shook them from their feet Alamos came to a skidding halt just before the start of the bridge, not fifty feet away. Tall and magnificent he stared at them, breathing heavily and with difficulty through Crick, whose head and legs dangled down either side of the jaws...

A wonderful, familiar voice broke the silence:

'Why do you always greet my friends like this...?' asked Crick, raising his head and scowling at Url.

'Crick!' Siu screamed joyfully, running forwards. But Orlando caught her arm, holding her back.

'Are you alright?' called Url.

Crick nodded, smiling at them sideways. He turned to look back into the deep, wide eyes behind him...

'I, um... I think I can manage from here...' he said awkwardly.

The creature lowered its head carefully to the ground; its mouth opening with the soft, high ringing of sharp blades. Crick lifted himself carefully up and out through the teeth and stood before them, bruised and bloodied, but whole. He held out his arms...

'It's okay –' he said when none of them moved, '– he saved me.'

Yori was first amongst the others to reach him; hugs and kisses and warm greetings lasting only a few seconds...

'Tarryn...?' asked Orlando.

Crick's smile withered and broke, and he gave a small shake of his head. But from behind him a deep, booming voice broke suddenly through the air:

'Young warrior and old met their ends well,' said Alamos.

'Oh! Yes –' said Crick amongst the gasps of the others, '– and, um, he can do that...'

'You... You speak our language?' asked Url. He was studied intently by the deep eyes for a long while; neither Yori nor any of the others wanting to break the silence, all still clutching to the same part of Crick, waiting...

'In fact,' said Alamos finally, 'it is you who speak mine.' Yori felt a rumbling through his chest as well as beneath his feet as the words came like a warm breeze; his clothes ruffling gently around him. 'Of all the many changes I have seen of your race, that is one mistake you have ever continued to make... But, either way: yes, I speak it.'

Each of the group stared up into his large, black eyes for a moment, puzzled as they were amazed and entranced. Aliya took a small step forward...

'He... he died?' she asked in a quiet, timid voice. She didn't want the answer – none of them did – but she had to have it...

But it was to Yori that the eyes turned next:

'There is no need for that, any longer,' said Alamos.

'How do you –' Yori started.

'I see more than most. Even you. I can see what it is you are trying to do. It is brave for one so young to attempt so much. But they are too close now. And you are doing more harm to yourself than you realise.'

Yori looked to Url, who, after a few seconds, gave a hesitant nod. And like releasing a long-held breath Yori let down the wall, feeling the Heart's energy flowing smooth and freely past him once more. He felt light, almost dizzy with relief.

'You know what it is we carry?' asked Url.

'He knows everything,' said Crick. 'Doesn't seem to care too much, though…'

'I have long-since learned not to involve myself in your quabbling,' said Alamos.

'What do you call *this*, then?' said Url, nodding to Crick.

'Not that we're not extremely grateful,' said Siu, jabbing him in the ribs.

'I help you not for what you are doing,' said Alamos. 'But for what you are.'

'Which is…?' asked Url. The creature considered them a moment before answering…

'Hope. A hope and a brightness in these dark lands and times such as I have not seen for an age.'

'How did he die?' asked Aliya, angrily.

'We got to the bridge,' Crick answered quickly, seeing how desperately she needed to know. 'But the ground on the other side was almost impassable. It would have taken him hours to climb. He…' his eyes grew wide and sad, staring unfocused ahead of him, unable to meet Aliya's. 'He went back… cut the bridge.' A lump of hot, furious pride came to Aliya's throat; she bit her lip, shaking her head angrily, walking a few steps away from the others. She wanted nothing more than to be by herself. 'He didn't want to slow me down…' Crick finished, frowning bitterly as he spoke the words.

'It was the choice he made to protect you all which proved finally to me that you were deserving of help,' said Alamos. 'That, and your admittance to Hollycrown. Many have asked for my assistance over the years, but rarely have I granted it. Desperate pleas mean nothing if issued as so often they are from cruel or unworthy souls. Not to my ancient mind, at least. You are all very different, though. It has been… so long since I have seen such kindness. He fought on until his last breath, as did the one who bore him.'

'Oden…' Orlando sighed, squatting low to the ground, resting his elbows heavily upon his knees. Siu held her hand gently on the back of his neck.

'They took many with them,' Alamos continued. 'Not for a single moment did he falter. Not once did he seek mercy or escape. And all because he would risk no harm to you...' He seemed lost in thought for a moment, murmuring quietly to himself... 'Wonderful...'

'What happened to *you*, then?' asked Siu, still clutching Crick's hand. Yori doubted she would ever let it go again.

'I made it over,' said Crick. 'But not quickly enough. There must have been another bridge, or some other crossing: They were upon me before I was out of the hills. I couldn't understand how they were so fast... I could hear them; there was this... *screaming*...' For a moment his focus wavered. He swayed backwards but regained himself as Siu and the others sprang to support him. 'They were so close...' he continued before they could ask. 'They almost had me surrounded. The dust was beginning to fade and fall, too... There were other things trying to reach me...' He opened his shirt, and with a deep pulse of black the brooch was revealed, stuck fast to the middle of his chest.

'Is it painful?' asked Orlando, examining it with the others. Crick shook his head, running his finger around the edges of the ornament, beneath which his skin was pulled tight.

'Awkward, though,' he said. 'Don't know when it's going to come off... or how.'

'Seems to have done the job, though,' said Url.

Crick shrugged, still caught in the fear of his thoughts...

'Then he just appeared...' he nodded to Alamos. 'Right beside me, out of the trees. He told me I had to trust him, picked me up, and fled.'

'Unfortunately your bodies are... not designed for the means by which I usually travel. I make no apologies for your wounds,' he said to Crick, 'but I trust there are none too severe. I was as gentle as my speed and your need allowed.' Before the beginning of the journey Crick's injuries may have brought great concern from himself and the others, but compared to the clawing of a khaion or the bite of a scarraver the few thin scratches across his arms and legs, bloodied as they were, now looked decidedly unimpressive.

'I know,' said Crick, nodding gratefully. 'Thank you.'

'You must go now,' said Alamos; the black ridge of his spine bristling suddenly. 'They are close. I may not cross through here like you, but they can. Move quietly: The Chasm's defences lie not only in its Magic... There are ancient beasts asleep within its walls, put there to bar the way of those not taken by Darkness yet still unwelcome to the city. I shall wake them once you are safely through so that they may delay your enemies, but you would do well not to do so yourself. They will care little for what you carry: only for your flesh and your bones. I shall see you again: Where you go, it is likely that you shall need my help still further, and I wish you to have it. There is another

450

way into the city: the way the Darkness learned to use. I will find you once you have p–'

'The Darkness...' Url breathed.

'No!' cried several of the others.

'You didn't tell me that!' Crick shouted, just as horrified as any of them...

'I could not give an answer without first the question,' Alamos answered calmly.

'It found a way in?' asked Url, raising his hand to Crick. 'The Darkness...?'

'I had assumed you knew...' said Alamos. And then without pause or thought he added: 'Iala is destroyed.'

It was as though in the instant of the three words what little air there had been was torn suddenly up from the road. There was no sound, no thought; nothing but the slow passing of one second to the next amidst the numbed silence which descended like a cold, smothering fog around the foot of the bridge. Yori felt the others stagger, even though in their horror they didn't move a muscle. Iala destroyed...

'When?' asked Url. His voice was quiet, crushed. 'What happened?'

'Are there any left?' asked Siu.

'I have not seen, myself, what has become of it and its people,' said Alamos. 'I have not ventured there since the Darkness claimed it. I sense the pain of the city from here, and have no desire to be any closer to it than I need to. It fell just twenty years ago.'

'But this –' Url turned to cast a weary hand along the bridge and the chasm beneath, '– whatever it is... It still works?'

'As powerfully as when the stones were first strung,' said Alamos, nodding slowly. 'They thought the waters would protect them from the north; as indeed they did for many years. But the Darkness learned to overcome them. I am sorry... Iala was great indeed. But I fear you walk now into no more than its empty shell.' He stretched his hind legs out behind him; his tail snapping back and forth impatiently...

'Goodbye. It will take time for me to find my way into the city: You are by yourselves until then. Your quest is yours to see to its end, and I cannot say whether that end will be well. But you have won my favour. I shall do what I can to protect you until it is decided.'

With slow, careful steps he moved away from them, and then as though curling up for sleep his body twisted round upon itself, sinking to the ground... but not stopping when it reached it. The stone of the road became loose and fluid, merging with the gold above, drawing Alamos down into it, and in seconds he was gone.

'*Cannot say whether our quest will end well...*' said Url with a dismal laugh, still watching the ground where Alamos had disappeared, which had already hardened back into stone. 'I think he already has.'

'We don't know what state the city's in,' said Abetta. 'The Torch... The Torch may still work.'

'And whether it does or not,' said Siu, 'we can't stay here.'

Url seemed spent of all emotion, saying nothing as he turned and walked back dazed towards the cart. After further hugs Crick was finally released, but he held Aliya back with him, speaking briefly with her while Yori and the others retook their places. His words did little to halt her tears, but it gave them at least a thin casing of happiness as she returned.

Yori watched his own, changing reflection in the blacks and whites of the thick wall which lined the edges of the bridge as the cart rolled slowly up towards the towering, golden spires. The light and shadows streaming out from amongst them became more intense as they approached, hiding whatever lay inside from view. No matter how vast the bridge had appeared from the side, it was far greater still now they were upon it: For ten minutes none of them spoke, each watching the openings which started to appear along the walls, above which glimmered shallow engravings of various different creatures, white where the stone was black, black where it was white... including several times amongst them the wide, cruel pincers of a scarraver. When finally they reached the spires the cart halted in front of them like a wounded ant before a grove of sweeping, barkless trees. Url turned, giving a truly helpless shrug; Yori and the others doing little but shrugging or nodding back. So squinting through the deep streak of shadow ahead of them, Url set Nightwind forwards, striding blind between two enormous trunks of gold...

A ringing, higher and louder than any Yori had ever known, assaulted them before they could see what they had walked into. Yori could feel something above them gazing down, studying them; light and dark dancing against his closed eyes, disorientating him... But in a sudden flash all of it was gone: the noise, the light, all ending like the popping of a bubble, leaving them feeling none the worse. All the others must have felt what Yori had, or something close to it, for blinking and rubbing their eyes they each climbed out from the cart, looking up into the heights of the strange, silent chamber they found themselves within. A stone of jet, slightly larger even than the Heart, was floating just below the point where the tips of the spires met,

452

unsupported by anything but air above or below. Into the soft, golden light around it, each of its many faces cast a beam of bright white light or, in some cases, deep, black shadow. Yori knew as well as the others that they needed to leave, but he couldn't resist staying just a little longer... There was something quite wonderful about the stone; its smooth, dull edges not glistening like others gems, but the Magic which lay within more powerful than any he had ever felt, save for the Heart itself.

'*Yori*!' he heard his Father whispering. When he turned he saw several of the others gesturing for him to get back into the cart, already seated themselves.

Having made whatever brief and splendid trial it had been designed to carry out, the chamber ignored them now as they crossed cautiously through; Nightwind's hoofs and the wheels causing only the briefest of disturbances amongst the thin, golden mist which covered the ground. Yori was still staring back, trying to keep sight of the chamber as it became hidden once more by light and shadow between the trunks of gold, when suddenly he was engulfed by several things all at once; a painful tide sweeping thick across him through which he had to fight to keep himself afloat. The echoes of hundreds – thousands of voices, long-since silenced, drifted all about him, wailing of their terrible ends. And at the same time he felt the others in the cart around him: shocked, frightened themselves; looking down and out upon a scene which somehow had been hidden to them from the far side of the bridge. Yori almost knew what he would see before he turned...

The destruction was absolute, and everywhere. Iala had been a great city indeed, for its outskirts to have extended so far... But no longer. Across the lands below them now stretched a patchwork of ruin which once had been home to so many. It was almost as his Father had said it should be: buildings, roads, farms and countless other signs of the life that had been here... Except now only their outlines remained: an unending labyrinth of simple foundations of rock and wood upon the ground scattered far into the distance, supporting nothing but sand and air. How long and violently the Black Wind must have raged here, trapped like a great squall within the very defences that had been built to keep it at bay. How terrible their suffering must have been. Nothing could have survived this...

Chapter Thirty-Five

Iala

Even the sand was paler, heavier than any that had come before. As they passed down from the end of the bridge it crumbled pitifully before the wheels of the cart, neither tumbling away nor sticking to them, as if still afraid or unable to make anything close to movement. Everything was the same: rubble, the occasional shred of bone, and all else that would be expected of the outer border of a great city strewn chaotically across the flat, off-white ground, quieter despite the openness than the deepest of tombs, and just as lifeless. The pathways and roads, so broken and heavily specked with wreckage, were a poor guide into the city; Url, wide-eyed and silent, simply following instead whatever clear trail he could find which took them still further north.

But amongst it all there was still a sliver of relief, feeble as it was, which fuelled the flame nearly extinguished in Crick's heart as he watched silently from the back of the cart. They hadn't blamed him. Even Aliya, upset as she was, didn't seem to be holding Tarryn's death against him. He knew there was nothing else he could have done. It had been Tarryn's choice, not his. And yet... When all was said and done, there could be no denying what had happened. In the dark of the hills he had left Tarryn behind. With every passing mile inside the jaws of Alamos his fear had grown as to how the others would greet him. But seeing their smiles, however brief, and feeling his Mother's hand still now upon his shoulder, he knew there was no bitterness or anger there towards him. They were as delighted to see him as he had been to see them, if that was possible. The Pack had been so close... Tall shadows and the awful grunting of the beast they sent ahead to cut him off pressed painfully against the back of his eyes... the *screaming*...

'Crick?' his Mother asked again, turning his chin gently towards her. For a second he struggled for words. 'You're shaking...'

'They've got something terrible with them,' he said. 'And they were so many -there must be hundreds...'

'We know,' said Orlando.

'We saw,' said Siu. 'When they reached the lake,' she added, nodding to Aliya.

Crick listened intently as Aliya described what she had seen through the water, and how; her words matching perfectly with what he had heard behind and around him. If it hadn't been for Alamos...

After several miles the ruins began slowly to grow taller and more dense around them; one of every dozen or so buildings still half-intact between their obliterated neighbours. Unlike the total defeat of the outlying parts of the city, here there were signs at least of struggle; walls and doors fortified from the inside, with strange armours draping the bodies of those whose remains could be seen to lie within; while soon the black bones of creatures of the Darkness began to litter the ground as well, struck down in the death throes of the doomed city.

'Why aren't there any weapons?' asked Crick, having seen few but the most basic of hammers, axes, and other tools.

'They relied on Magic, remember,' said Url. 'They had no desire for the weapons we take for granted in our part of the world. I don't know – perhaps they were wrong...' He spoke quietly, saddened by the thought. 'Perhaps blades and arrows and all our other tools of war would have helped them – at least to survive a while longer.'

'Url...' said Orlando, quietly. When Url turned back the toll of the last days was marked clear upon his face. Crick looked around to the others, all of whom had a similar, grubby weariness about them. He was certain he looked worse. 'What are we doing?' his Father asked, reluctantly. Url turned back into his place, as though having expected and been prepared to counter the question. 'Where are we going, now? If everything's destroyed, we –'

'Until I see the Tower of Elliad in pieces before me, our course is the same,' said Url; forcefully, but grasping subtly for Abetta's hand as he spoke. She gave it to him, looking across with the kind eyes the others knew she forever held for him in such moments – however well-hidden they in other times and places might be.

Just then a great shrieking soared through the sky above them.

'It's from the bridge!' said Aliya.

'Alamos must have awakened the beasts which lie beneath it,' said Url. 'Let's hope whatever terrors there are can hold off the Pack a while longer.'

'But even if they do,' said Siu, '– what then? How can we keep outrunning them now?'

'We could hide our tracks again?' Yori suggested. 'Loop round and get back to the bridge?'

'How did you do that, by the way?' asked Crick, realising suddenly that he knew nothing of *their* flight round the lake.

Before any of the others could answer Url had pulled Nightwind to a stop, stepping down from his seat and placing the palm of his right hand flat to the ground, wriggling his fingers gently to bury them in the sand. He closed his eyes tight in concentration, and the next second Crick felt a quiet trembling beneath him. He looked to the others, all unmoved and impatient, while around the cart the sand was quivering softly, dancing to an unheard tune… then stopping the moment Url opened his eyes. When Url withdrew his hand, its mark was the only one within several dozen feet: All others, down to the smallest of ripples and including the trails just made behind the cart, had been smoothed entirely away.

'He found he could do it just after you left,' said Aliya.

'It worked on the road?' asked Crick. Aliya nodded.

'We could have done just as good a job with a brush and some careful riding,' said Abetta, apparently not for the first time. 'But I grant you,' she added with a cautious smile, 'this way did have a certain charm.'

'It won't work again, anyway,' said Url, retaking the reins. 'They'll have all routes back to the bridge blocked off.

'What about…' Aliya paused, shrugging meekly as everyone looked to her. 'We could take a ship…?'

Crick's first impulse was to laugh… Most of the others seemed to feel the same. But neither he nor any of them made a sound. Where else was there for them to go?

'We could get ourselves round to the other side of the chasm,' said Url, considering it out loud. 'If we set sail before the Pack reaches us, it'll take them days to realise what we've done. Longer, maybe. It could work…' he murmured to Abetta.

'What if they're all destroyed?' asked Yori.

'This place will have had ships by the thousand,' said Url. 'Traders and ferryers; venturers and warboats; and all manner of others. There has to be one left amongst them.'

456

'The Tower, first,' said Abetta. 'Then we can see what the Wind's left for us.'

Url was still deep in thought as he nodded, slackening the reins; Nightwind's guess of the best way through the city as good as any of theirs.

It wasn't long until the skyline ahead was filled with the shapes of still more and larger buildings, all beginning to take a warm glaze from the westering sun. The haggard remains of great statues stood tall amongst and above them like disfigured watchmen watching silently over the destruction.

'Where should we head for?' asked Siu.

'Straight down the middle,' said Url. 'Unless anyone has a better suggestion...?' It was one of the few times in Crick's life in which he felt Url was truly asking for help with the question he had posed. He had no idea of the answer; and little strength left with which to try and find it. 'Can either of you two feel anything?' he asked, looking between Yori and Aulan. Both had been subdued since passing over the bridge; Aulan especially so. Aulan shook his head, but Yori stared blankly back, fear etched suddenly across his face.

'Son?' asked Orlando, rubbing the back of Yori's neck. Yori blinked and turned to him...

'It's almost here...'

'We're safe from it with the Heart,' said Url.

'No,' said Yori simply. 'We're not. *It's* almost here...'

Url sighed, apparently well aware what Yori was talking about, but stripped bare of the energy required to consider it now atop everything else. To the surprise of Crick and the others Yori took no notice of him, continuing in his quiet, guarded voice:

'*The Darkness*... From both sides of us. I can feel it... It's bigger than the skies, and deeper than the seas. It doesn't matter whether we outrun the Pack or not...'

'Yori,' Siu tried.

'We can't beat it,' Yori continued simply through her.

'Shut up, boy!' Url screamed, scowling with pain and regret as soon as the words had left his mouth.

'Url!' Siu admonished him. Url was bent nearly double with exhaustion as he tried to answer...

'I know... I'm sorry. I'm sorry, lad,' he said, trying to look Yori in the eye. 'I just...' he held his head in his hands. 'I can't do this any more... If the Tower's destroyed... I can't – I'm sorry...'

457

Crick looked uncomfortably across to his Father, unsure what any of them should say. Fortunately, there was one at least amongst the group whose nerve still held…

'Get in the back, then,' snapped Abetta. She thrust out a hand for the reins. 'I'll take over.' Url studied her a moment, taking a deep, slow breath as if to inhale new life and new fight into his body, perhaps not yet too old and too weary for one more refusal of surrender.

'Damned if I'm going to let you drive us though here,' he sighed, managing a quiet, mirthless laugh.

'Get on with it, then,' said Abetta, looking irritably away and resting her hands in her lap.

And with that Url raised his tired bones up into the seat once more, prompting Nightwind forwards.

'I'm sorry,' he said again, turning to Yori.

'I know,' Yori answered, still staring vacantly into the Heart in front of him.

*

Quite apart from the fact that it lay now in ruins, the city up close could still barely have been any more different to either Irraigion or Immelus. Walking alongside the cart with the others, but for Url and Abetta who remained beside each other in the front, Crick found himself – aided by the constant and thorough throb of his imagination – looking around into the first and only city he had ever been able to picture himself living in. The streets had been wide, and open, with clusters of benches running through their middles, facing in towards each other. There had been trees and plants of all types and sizes, planted with the wonderful measured unpredictability of a garden left to itself for several years, some of which had found new life since the fall of the city, growing again hesitantly through the destruction. Buildings, though numerous and grand in their own way, would have had none of the towering height and overbearing feel of their likenesses in the other cities. And above all this, pervading each new mound and swathe of rubble that was arrived at, damaged and broken but not yet dead, was the sense that Iala had been built to be enjoyed. This was – had been – no mere container of a society; no simple, soulless tool from where a people could be ruled. All about Crick's feet were the remnants of stonework and curiously fashioned metal, decorated with lines and engravings with no other purpose than for decoration itself. This, thought Crick, as he led the way through a narrow break between the debris, had been how cities were supposed to be.

458

But through it all fear still played constantly within their minds: the sounds of crumbling rock and other distant echoes bringing sudden leaps to the hearts of each of them, including Crick. Not knowing how the Pack would fare at the bridge, and still with nothing resembling the great Tower in any direction, or any clue as to how to find it, they had little time to indulge in the joy of their imaginings of how the city once had been; trudging aimlessly onwards as the skies began to fade around them. The long, jagged shadows made it hard to navigate the cart through the rubble, and harder still to stay focused on the task at hand.

The trail led them through at length into another wide, open track running north through the city, which widened still further before long into an enormous square, sentinelled at each of its four corners by the heavily-wounded statues of two men and two women, their knees near-twice the roof of the cart. The thick marble rods they had once held aloft into the centre, the ends of which were painted rich, dark greens and blues, now formed a wide, splintered cross above the shattered cobbles of the courtyard.

'Their faces...' Crick whispered, seeing that the features of each had been slashed cruelly away.

'Why did it do that to them?' asked Aliya.

'So that they may not see to protect the city,' answered Aulan, lagging behind the others. He spoke quietly, as if to himself alone, making his words difficult to hear. Yori watched him for a moment with a curious, fearful gaze before stepping to Crick's side, walking quietly alongside him; no answer to Crick's questioning eyes as they made their way around the cross and onwards down the long, straight road.

*

'We must be nearing the coast soon, surely,' said Crick, rubbing the red, tender skin around his brooch. The brooch itself still shone a dim, swirling black within his shirt. Yori seemed not to have heard, but as Crick opened his mouth to speak again he heard the cart come to an abrupt halt behind him. He turned to see Url sat forwards in his seat, studying the scene around them.

'This isn't right...' he murmured.

'You don't say...' Crick whispered under his breath. He shrugged his look of confusion back to the cart.

'*The stone*,' said Url, hearing but ignoring the sarcasm. 'Look at how it's stacked...'

Crick looked, but saw nothing. Where they had come to within this impossible maze of grey he could no longer say; only the dipping sun and Url's word having kept him convinced all the long while he had been walking that they were still heading north. Rubble lined the sides of the road around them; slightly closer now, perhaps, but otherwise no different from all that which had come before. The others likewise were looking aimlessly about, bewildered by Url's sudden reservation.

'It's been *built* like that,' said Url. He gestured to the blocks as if pointing to the obvious. 'And *recently*... Look – there's no sand above it... no smaller stones or dust or anything else you find in ruins like this. These walls have been put here on purpose, *after* the city was destroyed.'

'Survivors?' asked Orlando.

'A trap?' asked Crick, seeing the fear in Url's eyes. *Tarryn would have thought so, too*, his mind called to him, unexpected and painful.

'We should find a different route in,' said Url, reaching for the reins.

'I can manage quite well enough,' said Abetta.

'Surely if there are people still here, we *want* to be found by them...?' asked Siu. Url thought a moment before answering; a deep scowl lining his face...

'I don't like it,' he said, shaking his head. 'If they're here, I want to find them on *our* terms, not theirs.'

'Url, we –' Orlando started, but Url spoke above him:

'Let's go – Turn us,' he added quickly to Abetta.

'But this looks to be the quickest way through,' said Siu as Abetta started to pull Nightwind round upon himself. 'We don't have t– '

In a sudden rush of leather and tumbling stone the ruins exploded into life around them: Shouts came from all sides, loud and urgent as figures beyond count sprang up and out from the rocks, throwing off the thick, brown cloaks which had concealed them and closing swiftly in upon the family... Crick moved with a speed beyond even his understanding, snatching Yori up beneath his arms and flying back with him towards the cart, trying to remember where the nearest weapon had been stowed. The others moved slower but all were doing the same, each converging in upon the cart, but just as they were about to reach it a soft, terrible noise stopped them all like ice in their tracks: the quick puncturing of skin and flesh. As he looked up, Crick saw the thin trail of black smoke which had passed through his Grandmother's neck and on through the cart, and from the corner of his eye he saw too the thin, outstretched hand from which it had been cast. Several of the others screamed but Crick was frozen; watching, numbed, as Abetta slumped forwards from her seat. Url caught her, calling desperately to

460

her even as he fell with her to the ground. The men and women were close around them now, taking hold of each of them in turn, but still Crick couldn't move. All he could hear were Url's frantic pleas. Siu surged forwards again towards the cart, but Orlando caught her in time to halt the dozen hands which had raised in her direction. She fought for a moment, beating violently at his arms, but he gripped her only tighter to him. Crick felt his wrists and shoulders being secured either side; their captors coming to a halt in a tight circle around them and the cart. All eyes were upon Abetta, and upon Url who knelt above her, ripping off his shirt and pressing it hard against the small, open wounds; blood pulsing dark and swift through his fingers. She was trying to speak…

Your – hand… she mouthed at last.

Url shook his head fiercely; his trembling hands still working quickly at her neck.

'Your hand, Urlmaeus,' Abetta gasped, gagging through the blood; Crick's stomach turning at the noise. Her quiet voice carried horribly through the silence.

'There was no need, Yanna,' said one of the men in the same deep, rolling accent of the others.

'They were about to flee,' answered the hard, cold voice of the woman who had cast the spell. 'She was turning the animal.' There was none but perhaps the faintest trace of remorse.

One hand still tight around her neck, Url reached down with the other and clasped both of Abetta's. They looked quietly at each other. And with that look the silence about them grew, and in that moment it seemed they spoke a lifetime's unspoken thoughts and regrets. And then as his tears fell heavy onto her cheeks Url bent down, and pressed his lips softly to hers.

There was nothing any of them could have done for her. But not being able to be beside her, to comfort her as she shuddered and gasped her final breaths, was an agony Crick had never known. In seconds her life's blood was drained, saturating the ground so that even above the sand it formed a ghastly pool around her and Url, binding the two of them in their last moments together. She was still looking deep into his eyes as the spark left her own, and as it did so a wail of such rage erupted from within Url that even the woman who had cast the fatal curse was taken aback by the savagery of its pain. His chest suddenly empty, his heart missing a piece he had never thought could leave, Crick gazed down upon the lifeless form of his Grandmother. The hurt was beyond understanding; never had Crick's eyes left the motionless body, yet now as he looked on he waited expectantly for something different, some movement or sign that the terrible joke of the past minutes had ended. But no movement was made, and no sign came. There was nothing. She lay silent and still in the dusk upon the sandy road of Iala; Mother and carer to them all, now forever beyond the healing she had given them so often.

Chapter Thirty-Six

Seek Always the Stars

'Search them – quickly,' came a voice which had not yet spoken; sharp and commanding. And afraid. They were all afraid, even as much as the family themselves. At least, as afraid as the others had been a few moments ago... Now above all else it was pain which governed their minds. Pain as pure as fire, and heavier than steel; the grey-blue sky growing suddenly darker still as Yori cowered helplessly against his Mother's wailing, feeling distantly but caring nothing of the hands patting and gripping at his chest and legs. He could hardly breathe for the grief around him.

'Owin!' The rising cry came from somewhere behind the cart... 'See this!'

The thin, square-jawed man who had given the first order strode through the rest, eyeing each of the family in turn as he passed. Shouts and excited murmurings were coming from those already behind the cart, looking in, but when he reached it his face remained unchanged, giving nothing away. Even Yori struggled to understand his thoughts.

'Too heavy to move now,' he said. 'Take anything small; anything useful.' He gestured the others up into the cart. 'We must leave.'

'Why couldn't you have just killed the damned horse!' Url screamed as he was dragged to his feet. He turned his head, struggling to keep the woman in his sight. 'You didn't have to hurt her! Aghhh!' he thrashed viciously against the men who held him, screaming through his teeth. '*You didn't –*'

'It is done,' said the man in charge, striding round to the front of the cart, from inside which came the clattering of upturned chests and items being thrown hastily about. He passed Url without a second glance, climbing back over the line of rocks which bordered the road. 'Bring them!' he shouted back over his shoulder. 'Leave the woman. Kill the animal.'

'*No!*' screamed Url and Siu together. Aliya would have sunk to her knees had it not been for the men holding up her arms behind her back; no strength of heart left with which to issue the desperate plea for Nightwind.

'We're not leaving her here!' shouted Url, fighting again against the arms which bound him, oblivious to the sharp ripping and grazing of his skin. 'I'd rather you –'

'Enough!' called Owin, turning back and raising his hand impatiently. 'As he wishes – bring her, quickly. Kill the other.'

An arm pushed hard against Yori's back, prompting him towards the side of the road. As he stepped forwards he saw a hand being raised slowly towards Nightwind.

'Wait,' said another new voice, deeper and softer than most of the others. From its place a man with sallow cheeks and a patchy, unkempt beard of bronze stepped out to stay the hand. 'Let us not kill another of theirs. Allow them to end the life of their own, as we have always done.'

'Still you live in the past, Benamin,' said the man whose forefinger still stretched ominously between Nightwind's eyes. 'Very well…' he sighed, lowering his hand and looking around him at the items being brought out from the cart. His eyes fell upon Aulan's crossbow. He took it from the woman who carried it, examining it clumsily in front of him. 'This is a weapon?' he asked of Url. Url nodded. 'Use it, quickly.' He held out the bow, keeping hold of it a moment longer as Url reached for it… 'Do not try it against us. We are faster and more powerful. You will die as she did.'

'I need a bolt,' said Url with quiet disgust.

Nightwind. The last of the fated four who had brought them so far, and worked so bravely for them. But with Abetta still lying bloodied and unmoving in his shadow it was impossible in that moment to pay him the mind he deserved of them, and not one of them now had the strength to object to his killing. Aliya collapsed into a silent sob, her hands still bound and held high behind her, pleading quietly for none of this to be true. Resting the tip of the bow upon the ground and drawing back its tight string with shaking, weary arms, Url took the single bolt which was handed to him, and as it clicked into place a dozen hands raised to him at once, fingers held carefully at differing angles, all apart from the forefingers, each of which pointed firmly at Url's head or chest.

'Do it now,' said the woman who had slain Abetta. 'Or *we* shall.'

Standing not two feet from Nightwind, Url lifted the bow into his shoulder and raised the end above him to aim a few inches below the unsuspecting creature's ear.

'Sorry, lad,' he whispered... and with a thick twang the bolt passed clean through the back of Nightwind's head, felling him instantly.

No sooner had Nightwind shuddered and collapsed than everything started moving again; the family pushed quickly away from the cart and over the rocks, deeper into the city. But the long walk Yori expected ended abruptly after less than a minute, as they came to a thick stone doorway being held open at a strange angle above the rubble around it, dropping steeply down into the ground. Still dazed with the grief of the others around him Yori stepped distantly through the opening, treading carefully down a short, near-vertical stairway, supported as he moved by the roughened hand of a woman who stood below. It was pitch black, the others following behind; curious, frightened faces peering in towards them from the edge of the weak globe of light which sunk down from above. Abetta's limp body dripped dark specks of blood onto those beneath her as it was passed down, and then with the last of the men and women the doorway swung inwards with a great crash, making the darkness complete. For a few seconds there was silence...

'It is safe,' spoke Owin through the black. Immediately sparks glittered into life and grew into flame from several places at once, revealing a small, low hall; its tilted roof barely high enough at this end to stand upright beneath; its sides collapsed and strewn across the floor with the fallen, broken rock of surrounding buildings packed tight in their place. Their captors seemed more numerous now, within this small space. Sixty at least, all staring silently at Yori and the others as they were brought into the middle of the hall and commanded to sit. Siu cradled the head of her Mother in her lap; Aliya beside and Orlando behind her, holding and supporting her as Owin stepped forwards towards them. Figures stood or sat on the thin, irregular balconies of rock all around them, waiting...

'You came through the Darkness,' said Owin; a deep frown ingrained within his glare, unchanging as he spoke and thought.

'Not the welcome we'd hoped for,' Url growled. His eyes burned brighter than any of the flames around them.

465

'How?' asked Owin, ignoring him.

'There was no need to kill her.'

'How?' asked Owin again.

'I should have struck you down when I had the chance.'

'Answer me!' Owin screamed, and from the flinches of those around him Yori knew it was an anger rarely revealed.

'My only relief,' said Url – Suddenly beside him Yori felt a change within his Father… he was about to reveal the Heart – 'is that soon enough you'll share her f–.'

'We came to trade,' Yori spluttered, interrupting just as his Father opened his mouth to do the same. He felt the confusion of the others but continued, hoping desperately they would keep their silence. This was not like the Undervalleys, much as it felt the same to them… This Owin was no Tholomus; these people neither kind nor welcoming. They could not be trusted with knowledge of the Heart.

'We came to trade,' Yori repeated, realising that his voice had been dry and cracked the first time, the interruption coming out more as an incoherent splutter than the words he had intended. 'The gem you saw in our cart…' he continued as Owin's eyes lingered angrily upon Url. 'We couldn't trust our own people not to take it from us without payment, but we knew of the honesty and riches of the people of Iala. We set out here for the rewards we deserve from the treasure we've hunted for so long. We had no idea the city was destroyed.' He sat back, taking a deep, hidden breath. In that instant it had been all he could think of.

'Why does the boy speak for you?' asked Owin.

'He speaks as well and true as any of us,' said Orlando, his eyes flicking curiously across Yori as he looked to Owin.

Owin scowled still deeper, thinking for a long while…

'A good tale,' he said finally, his eyes switching to Yori. 'But something about it feels false. I do not believe it.'

'Believe it or not, it's all we can tell you,' said Url.

'Who are *your own people*?' asked a woman standing tall behind Owin. 'Where are you from?'

'We live in the shadow of Immelus, city of the south,' said Orlando.

'*Immelus*…?' said Owin, his rigidly-folded arms slackening with shock. His surprise was echoed from all quarters of the ruined hall. 'Of the south?' he repeated, looking again to Url. Url nodded. 'If you had said Harrem, or Kolysis, or one of the other northern cities – even perhaps the old capital – I may have believed you. But Immelus?' He strode quickly to within an arm's reach of Url, staring at him with all the venom of a great serpent. 'Do you take us for fools?'

Url this time was calm as he returned the glare; neither hostile nor afraid...

'How long did your people lock themselves away within their lands before your home was destroyed?' he asked. There was no answer. 'How many years have you lived in ignorance of what has befallen the world around you? Irraigion is home to nought but Darkness, now.' Quiet gasps swirled around the hall, but none loud enough to interrupt him. 'It fell to the Black Wind long ago. So have all the other places you speak of. Immelus and Iala were the last two to stand. We are no friends of the Council which rules our homelands,' he said, quite honestly. 'But we hoped to find some here. I am sorry we were mistaken. Truly – more sorry than you can imagine.'

Around the hall all faces turned to Owin, eager for his reaction to help them form their own. Owin turned and paced slowly, looking to the tall woman behind him for some silent council.

'How?' he asked, turning back. 'I ask again, and for the last time. Tell how you reached us through the Darkness...?'

'My son,' said Orlando, placing his hand on Crick's shoulder. He had realised Yori's distrust of Owin and the others, even if he still feared for the Heart, lying open as it was to any who might come upon it now. Yori tried to sense the Pack, to find out where they were, but he could feel nothing. 'He wears a Mirror of the people of the Veil,' Orlando continued.

Crick parted the top of his shirt, bringing mutterings from those in front of him. Those who could not see his front leaned or moved round to get a clearer look. They were impressed, but not shocked: They had seen such a thing many times before.

'A pretty trinket,' said Owin. 'Though not one I would expect such distant and lowly hands to possess...'

'*Lowly*?' said Crick, disgusted by the word, covering his chest again.

'It has been in my family longer than I can remember,' said Orlando, silencing Crick with a grip of his shoulder. 'I cannot tell you how it came to us, any more than I understand how it works.' Owin and several others gave a derisive snort as he spoke. 'But it got us here,' Orlando finished.

'Why him?' Owin asked, nodding to Crick.

'He's the fastest and strongest amongst us. We thought his strength would enhance that of the Mirror's.'

'They call *us* ignorant,' spat a man sitting behind them.

467

'Tell of your journey here,' said Owin.

And so without pause, and leaving out all matters relating to the Heart, and Aulan, and Alamos, Orlando began to describe all that they had been through. He took care to include as much detail as possible, weaving quick and plausible tales around the many parts he was forced to change, never hesitating or contradicting himself, speaking for nearly half an hour before he came with a quiet sigh of relief to the crossing of the chasm into Iala. Many times Yori felt the others around him growing restless, fearful of what was becoming of the Heart, and each time he quieted them instantly with a look unseen by the eyes that studied them – even unnoticed by the family themselves. All the time Abetta lay between them, held or watched over tenderly.

When Orlando had finished Owin made no reply, turning instead into the crowd behind him, speaking with them hurriedly and quietly. Their talk was difficult to follow word for word: their accents strong and their words quick and reduced to the fewest possible, like a body held up by none but its few main bones. But to Yori their meaning was clear enough: They didn't trust what they had been told. They had the eyes of those who had gone through too much. Yori doubted they would ever trust again; he almost felt a pity for them… but seeing his Grandmother's body in front of him again all pity was quickly gone. Siu was still stroking her hair; the others around her still weeping, or not far from it. Yori couldn't bring himself to hate the Heart, but he wished desperately in that moment that they had never found it. The thought was clear in Url's mind, too.

'This is all you have to say?' asked Owin at length.

'It's all there is,' answered Orlando, resting his head gently upon Siu's.

'They'll be getting worried, Owin,' said a woman who so far had remained apart from the discussion. Owin looked to her, and then back to the family, sighing as he came to his decision:

'We cannot stay here the night. Bring them.' And with that he signalled for the stone doorway to be raised.

The night now was close to full-dark, the air cold and still as Owin led the way through the city. Their twisting trail was lit by flames which burned like torches about the upturned hands of the same people who had illuminated the hall, the fire as much a part of them as their own skin. Owin insisted that Abetta be carried by one of his men – a tall, broad-shouldered youth with the faintest attempt at a beard – so that they could move quickly over and between the ruins. Thankfully, none of the others argued; Orlando lifting the body delicately into the thick arms which were held out for her. The young man took her as gently as she was given, unable to meet Orlando's eyes as he did so.

The others positioned themselves carefully around Yori, shooting confused and anxious looks towards him as they set off along a winding path deep into the tallest and most densely built part of the city they had yet come to. *Why had they not told of the Heart...? Cold and cruel as most of them were, these people were surely the only hope... The Pack... The Pack would be here soon... They would find it... There wasn't time for this...!* All these and more were thrown at Yori... He tried to whisper quietly to them each in turn, but it was difficult to do so without being heard or seen. And in any case he could think of little to say. Everything they thought and feared was true. Yet also he knew that placing the Heart in the hands of Owin and his people would be as harmful and futile as giving it to the Pack, or else leaving it for the Darkness itself to claim. They had to find another way...

'Where are you taking us?' Crick asked.

'Back to our – children and elders,' said the plump, balding man beside him, wheezing as he struggled to keep up. 'Those too slow or too weak – to risk bringing – out into the city like this. *What?*' he asked sharply, noticing the look Crick was giving him. Orlando tried to intervene:

'How many are th–'

'Enough talk!' said Owin suddenly, halting and turning back to Crick. 'You use your mouth when your ears and eyes are all that matter now. Keep quiet or another of you dies.' There was no falseness in him: he was committed absolutely to each word. He waited for Crick to give a small, indignant nod before setting off once more.

Twenty long minutes passed in silence, Yori still trying quietly to convince the others of the need to hold their tongues, when from ahead of him Url gave an uncontrolled shout of shock, bringing the whole party to a stop. And only as Yori looked up before him now did he realise that beyond a long stretch of open ground, just to the left of the trail, something new and wholly different broke the monotony of the ruin. Cast smooth and almost shimmering against the harsh angles of the surrounding rubble, the thick, star-shaped base of what once had been a vast tower stood clear above the rest of the city. Stone and metals entwined in high, sweeping patterns, arcing in and then up like the beginnings of a great, jagged candlestick, even its remains now rose several hundred feet or more into the moonlit sky; its top three-quarters lying scattered in a long, crumpled line above the ruins beyond. They had come to it at last...

'You know what this was?' asked Owin.

'We...' Url fought hard through his pain to find the right words, gazing open-mouthed up towards the slanted, crumbling top of what little remained of the tower. All he had dreamed, for so long... in pieces now before him. 'The Tower of Elliad, I believe,' he said with the air of an interested visitor to the city. 'Something to do with fighting the Darkness, wasn't it?'

Owin gave a grim laugh, kicking away a piece of wood before him as he left the trail and strode towards the Tower; those around him doing likewise. With hurried glances of fear and sadness passing between them, Yori and the others followed, all energy spent, their legs unwilling to carry them further.

'It was their *only* hope of defeating it,' said Owin, '– towards the end.'

'*Their*...?' asked Orlando.

'The Council. And those who followed them. Fools to a man...'

As the flames were brought closer in around them, tall symbols became visible at head-height through the dust and sand which covered the outward-sloping part of the base; symbols of the same type as had greeted them so warmly before the bridge. Yori longed for Aulan to keep his silence, but no sooner had he thought it than Aulan's quiet, tuneful voice played against the Tower like notes through an organ:

'*Seek always the stars...*'

'He speaks the old tongue...?' said Owin, as all those who had ignored Aulan thus far considered him now. Aulan's eyes had not moved from the Tower...

'*For only then shall you find them,*' he finished.

'He's always spoken like that,' said Url, dismissing it as casually as could be made to look convincing. 'Just as he's always been fond of books and tales of distant places. I'd wager he could tell you more about the history of your city than you know yourselves. Not that that should prove difficult.'

Owin studied them both a moment. He didn't believe or have time for any part of Url's words, but with a deep breath he accepted them, for now.

'I'd listen to none of it,' was all he said in reply, and as he did so he spat viciously at the Tower. 'Long may their bodies feel the cold of the night for their trust in this accursed thing.'

Some of the others shifted uncomfortably at the words, but none objected aloud. Whatever conflict there had been amongst the city, these men and women were still consumed with its bitterness.

'What h–' Url started, but Owin halted him:

470

'Questions and answers can both wait for tomorrow. Come – we are close.'

Yori couldn't help but feel for him again. For all of them. They had no idea what was about to strike what little remained of their home. There would be no tomorrow for these people. And with the Tower destroyed, if Yori and the others could not escape tonight with the Heart and find a way to conceal it utterly from the Darkness, they too would be sharing that fate.

They were close indeed: the Tower was still well within view behind them as they ascended shortly thereafter into the soaring ruins of what must once have been a truly magnificent building. Colours were reduced only to different shades of silver beneath the night, but they were many and striking nonetheless; pillars and stonework shining dim but somehow beautiful beneath the debris which covered them. Before they reached the top, however, they came suddenly into a small hollow, no more than a hundred feet wide, from the outskirts of which dozens of faces were peering nervously out from half-opened doorways in the rock, lit dimly from within.

'You should all be inside!' Owin growled; not as angry as he made out. But as soon as he spoke the doorways were flung open, children running out hurriedly into the arms of their parents. Not all those around Yori were greeted in this manner, however: Owin was only one among many who marched soberly through into the middle of the hollow, talking between themselves, still missing terribly the loved ones who were no longer here to welcome them back.

After the children came others: old, infirm, or otherwise unable to move quickly through the rocks, as the thick-bellied man – who was panting furiously after the climb – had said. Then, from an opening into the northern face of rubble thirty feet above them which overlooked the city far to the south, a small, hunched figure stepped out. From the clothes and what Yori could sense, it seemed to be a woman, but beyond that it was difficult to tell. Her face and hairless scalp were twisted and scarred as if by flame; one of her gloved hands resting upon the shoulder of a young girl who stood beside her, the other tucked tight into the pocket of her cloak, as if to stop it hanging loose. The hollow was quieting; all faces turned in once more to the family as those who had captured them whispered quickly to the others. An old, frail voice from above silenced all of them instantly:

'Who are they?' the woman asked simply. The skin had hardened tight around her eyes, making it difficult to know who she was looking at, or even if she could see at all.

471

Owin answered her, explaining all that had happened. Yori could feel the revulsion of the others amongst his own as the killing of Abetta was passed over as mere introduction; Owin nodding to her body without any trace of compassion. The old woman listened quietly, waiting until he had finished before responding with a quick volley of questions concerning details of the account with which she was still uncertain. Her words were few and concise, even more so than Owin's; each chosen carefully as though to conserve what little energy she had. Finally she seemed satisfied with what had happened – though far from convinced of the family's tale.

'You are sure they are unarmed?' she asked.

'Certain,' said Owin.

She bowed her head and thought a moment longer; the young girl beside her staggering slightly under her weight, so that another, slightly older, came to take her place.

'We shall send their dead to the stars in the morning. After, I shall talk with them. For tonight, keep them in a dwelling without anything they can use for weapons.'

'They can stay with me,' said a man behind Yori. He had spoken before… 'There is room enough for all of them, just about,' said the bearded, untidy man who had asked for Url to be allowed to kill Nightwind. He stepped a short pace forwards into the hollow, speaking louder than he enjoyed… 'And there are no weapons of any kind, Driska, as you well know.'

Yori felt murmurings around him, as though there were those who felt uneasy about the suggestion. But tiredness seemed to be getting the better of the old woman…

'So be it,' she said, turning back to her doorway. 'Keep a strong watch over his door,' she added with a brief glance to Owin, and with that the stone slammed shut behind her.

The talk which her presence had restrained swelled instantly once more around the ruins; Yori and the others turning quickly to the man behind them, who nodded for them to follow him away through the crowd. Ignoring each glare and muted muttering thrown towards him he led the family beyond the eastern lip of the hollow and down to a wide, overhanging ledge upon which a thick but narrow metal frame was being held open by a woman of similar age. She frowned uncertainly as they approached but accepted the man's brief kiss, stepping back from the doorway to allow each of them through in turn.

The room which had been constructed within was something close to square in shape, with the exception of one corner in which the floor and roof turned in to meet and merge with each other. Large, ripped

472

tapestries and rugs of gold and crimson covered the bare rock of the walls, lit softly by the warm glow of half a dozen thick candles, beneath each of which pooled deep, undulating mounds of fallen wax. Furniture was limited to cushions and a low, semi-circular table which fitted snug into the wall to their left, but there were enough books, charcoaled sketches, and tiny, wooden figurines to make the room feel quite full, especially once Yori and the others were all inside. A low, uneven archway led through to an unlit corridor beyond. Url began to speak, but as he did so the door closed shut with a loud grating behind them, the man interrupting immediately and with a sudden urgency, fighting to keep his hoarse whisper of a voice low and calm:

'Bless and curse you, wonderers from the south, whoever you may be! You should never have brought it here!'

Chapter Thirty-Seven

A Friend amongst Foes

'I'm sorry –' he continued hurriedly through the stunned silence of Yori and the others, striding swift through the room as he cast off his cloak. 'I understand why you did – or at least I presume I do… but…' he sighed, throwing the cloak into the darkened room beyond. He turned to the woman still standing by the doorway: three thin plaits linked gently above the rest of her soft, brown hair; her eyes as perfectly blue as any Yori had known, unspoiled even as she shot a series of anxious frowns around the room… 'Ellie –' he continued, '– they've brought the Earthstar!'

She stared back at him a moment; stunned at first, even amused. But then on seeing the solemn look in his eyes, she seemed finally to realise he was serious.

'The Earth… But… *How*? How could you tell? Owin said nothing of –'

'He doesn't know! None of them do! He saw it, they all did, but–'

'Did *you*?' she interrupted. 'Did you see?'

A trembling smile lifted his eyes and the wisps of beard around his cheeks as he looked through the room to her…

'It was wonderful,' he said, softly. And for a moment that was all he could say. 'A gemstone, as we expected. Smaller than the Euclas Stones,' he held out his hands with difficulty to the width of the Heart, 'but with such… It was all that the scripts tell of, and more…'

'The *Earthstar*?' asked Url.

'My apologies, again,' said the man, kicking parchments quickly from beneath his feet and gesturing keenly for them to sit where they could around the room.

'Please,' the woman said to Orlando as he bent down with Abetta. 'She may lie in greater comfort through here...' She led him through into the corridor, carrying a taper lit from the desk beside her, bringing several lanterns to life as she stepped through to reveal a smaller but even more richly decorated room. A single low, wide bed occupied most of the space; its head, and that of Abetta's, hidden from view around the wall.

'She was your Mother?' the man asked of Siu. Siu nodded; fresh tears not far from her eyes. 'I am sorry. It was a cowardly act. It was Yanna,' he added as the woman returned; both of them visibly revolted at the name.

Yori and the others took seats in a wavering circle in front of the cushions, and as Orlando returned the man spoke again:

'I am Benamin. Ellienne...' he added, draping his arm softly around the woman as she sat beside him, '– my wife.'

'Ellie,' she said, smiling.

'Please –' said Url, holding out his hand. 'Thank you – but there is no time for this... Don't think us rude, but if you know anything of why we are here, we need you to speak it now!'

But Benamin far from took it as rudeness; rather he seemed to appreciate Url's desire for straight talk, even if he was yet to understand it.

'The Earthstar?' Url asked again.

'You may call it something else,' said Benamin. 'The *Godstear*...? The *Heart*...? The Heart...' he repeated, seeing the recognition in their eyes. 'All are one and the same. You sought the Torch of our city, did you not?'

Yori and the others looked to each other, uncertain.

'How do *you* recognise it but not the others?' asked Orlando after a moment.

'We may all have been the few who survived the death of our city,' said Ellie, 'but that does not mean we are all alike. I would hope that I too would have recognised the Earthstar for what it was; but I can say for certain that my husband would. As for the others...'

'Once the city began to fall,' said Benamin, 'the minds of our people were lost to madness.'

'Not all,' said Ellie.

'Indeed, not all... but most. Instead of fighting back as one, a feud broke out between those whose faith remained in the Torch, and those

475

who believed that it had been our efforts spent in search of the… the *Heart* which had weakened us. We had the Council on our side, and indeed the truth; but they had numbers – great numbers. And such *anger*… They were victorious, if by what has happened here you could ever imagine to call it that. But by that time the city and its people were all but gone. The few of us who were left built new homes into and beneath the ruins of the old, in which we linger to this day.'

'But why can't they recognise the Heart?' asked Url, trying at least in part to conceal the impatience of his ignorance.

'Because for them the main of their lives has been spent in pursuit only of the crudest and most unimportant aspects of Magic – though they of course would argue otherwise. They have lost the wisdom our city was founded upon; forgotten the beliefs within which our ancestors grew and thrived. Magic without such framework is a poor and terrible thing. They care and understand nothing now of it now but for the spells and curses and damage they can wield with it. You were right not to trust us,' he said, looking grimly to Yori.

'You understand what he can see?' asked Siu.

'He has a mind like so many I have known in my time…' He sighed, his gaze half-falling to the floor between them all. 'I was a teacher. My charges were those newly-taken from their Mother's breast. I would talk with them; educate them; help their minds attune to the world around them, sensing the very things your son does. You have the thoughts and talent of so many of those who were first presented to me,' he said, smiling as he looked up to Yori. 'A natural gift, yet to be nurtured to its potential by proper instruction.' A hint of former pride tinged the last of his words.

Siu was about to reply, but instead it was Crick who leaned forward and spoke:

'Can he be trusted or not?' he asked of Yori.

'Crick!' said Siu.

'Mind your tongue, boy,' said Url, though it was clear he agreed with the putting of the question. But Crick paid no attention to either of them. Yori looked once more to Benamin and Ellie, and then turned back to Crick with a small, but certain nod.

'There are more following us,' Crick said quickly, turning to Benamin, shrugging impatiently to the others. Benamin was silent a moment, looking fearfully to each of them…

'*Following* you?' he asked.

'Pursuing us,' said Url. 'They've done so all the way from Immelus, though we didn't know it until recently. A Pack sent by the Council of our city, to capture the Heart.'

Benamin murmured something under his breath. 'I sensed a great fear within you,' he said aloud, 'but I could not see that. Perhaps it is because you are so foreign to me; or it may be that amongst such company as Owin and his like, my mind has grown weak… Are they strong? How many are they?'

Frightened, uncertain glances were passed one to the next around the group. But from them Benamin seemed to take all he needed to know, nodding slowly as he drew out of the silence some measure of their thoughts, or in some cases memories.

'We don't know for certain their numbers,' Url said at length. 'But they are strong. And they are many. Far more so than us, at least.'

'Where are they now?' asked Ellie, putting a hand on Benamin's forearm.

'We heard a noise of what could have been battle from the bridge when we were maybe five miles past it,' said Url.

'*Battle*?' asked Benamin. 'They woke the Guardians?'

'I believe they were awoken, yes,' said Url. 'But it was not the Pack themselves who did so; nor us. We had help, from a creature we know now as Alamos.'

'*Alamos*!' exclaimed both Benamin and Ellie together.

'So he is named here, also,' said Ellie, excitedly, '– but… but only in poems and the oldest of tales…! Surely you do not mean Alamos *himself*?' Her eyes glistened with wonder; a remarkable relief from the fear and hurt of the past days, if only briefly.

Swiftly Url described their various encounters, and the appearance and manner of Alamos; Ellie and Benamin listening with rapt attention to each new word, their eyes filled with all the awe of children seeing legends come to life before them.

'He said he would try to make his way into the city to find us,' Url finished.

'But for all we know the Pack could be through already!' said Crick. 'We have to get back to it now!'

'No,' said Benamin, raising a hand to steady Crick's fear. 'Without a watch being kept over the bridge itself, knowledge of the struggle would not reach us for a time. But if the Guardians were to fall, and the bridge to be crossed in anger, we would know of that, even here, I assure you. The Heart will not have been taken yet.'

'You're certain?' asked Crick.

'Beyond doubt,' said Benamin.

That the Heart had not yet been claimed was wonderful to hear, but unlike the others the news barely touched the surface of Yori's spirits…

'But…' he began, quietly, 'it's not just the Pack which seeks the Heart tonight.' He looked around at the others with wide, frightened eyes he could do little to hide any longer. Instantly they were drawn back from their fleeting respite, a cruelty for which he felt the creeping of a pang of guilt despite the knowledge that what he knew needed to be told. The eyes of Benamin and Ellie were darting quickly around them all, searching for an explanation…

'The Darkness,' Url continued, when he saw that Yori could not. 'The Darkness is coming for it.'

'The shadow beings have always sought it,' said Benamin. 'Surely you know that from your journey…? They would have been all around you – though unable to come too close. It was the Heart which protected you, was it not?' Url nodded. 'I thought it looked too weak to be able to protect you all,' Benamin continued, nodding to Crick's chest. But Url was shaking his head…

'You misunderstand,' he said, looking straight into Benamin's eyes, taking a careful breath before speaking his next words clearly:

'What you talk of, our people call the Black Wind. But that is not what we fear now.' He gestured to Yori… 'What he speaks of is that which lies behind the Black Wind, giving the shadow its malice and its strength. We talk of the evil which cannot be stopped.'

'The…' Benamin hesitated… 'You mean… the Opus itself?'

'Yes!' said Url, recognising the term. 'Yes – I've read that name used for it. The Opus… By his reckoning,' he nodded again to Yori, 'it will be here within the day.'

Benamin was stunned to a motionless silence. A faint frown was all he could manage for a time as he studied Yori, hoping suddenly for this to be some tale which now had been pushed too far. Hoping – but seeing in Yori that it was not.

'But… how do you know this?' asked Ellie, truly frightened for the first time, though still unable to understand it all. 'And why now? We have been free of the Opus since our world last fell to it – *hundreds* of years ago…? Why does it come now?'

Rubbing his dark, tired eyes, Url took them back to the true beginnings of their journey, telling of all the many things which as yet had been left unsaid. He spoke of his finding of the Heart, so long ago now; and of their befriending of Aulan, and his secret which had been revealed in the mountain pass. He described – in terms too simple for Yori's liking, but adequate enough to make the point – the manner in which the Heart had been revealed to the Darkness by the mountain's golden flame, and the steady swelling of its power since then. As the story was told one of the candles behind them flickered its last light

478

and died, casting that small corner of the room into shadow; nobody moving to replace it as a thin, black tendril of smoke drifted up and disappeared against the stone. And through it all Yori could feel the Heart, even from here, as though he were closer now to it than he had ever been before…

And finally Url told of Yori himself: of what he was capable of; of how he had fared during the journey; and lastly of what he saw approaching them now…

'I trust the power of his awareness far more than that of my own eyes and ears,' he said. 'We all do. If he says the Darkness will be upon us by tomorrow…' he looked despondently to Yori, 'then so it shall.'

For several long, slow breaths the room was silent. At last the time had come when they could speak open and clearly again about what was to be done. But now that time was here, it was all but impossible to know where to start…

'I… I can feel nothing of it…' said Benamin, straining silently to reach out across the city. His mind was far from weak, but it had suffered such hurt… Yori could see the scars hewn upon his consciousness as clearly as any of the many wounds the family carried with them now. Benamin could see little further than the ruin around him.

'Why do you call it the *Opus*?' asked Crick. Url and Benamin together both opened their mouths to speak; Url gesturing for Benamin to continue…

'One of the many legends of our people – one of the few which has survived the trials of time, at least – tells that all evil in the world was created in the last and greatest song of Ariel, one of the forgotten gods beyond the seas, whose heart for some reason turned against the boredom of the peaceful days in which the ancient world existed. After an age of ages spent singing of the wonders of the world, Ariel cast the words of this new song into the skies, speaking aloud all the thrilling, terrible things she had dreamed over the years. But the stars heard… and down to the world they sent as punishment everything that Ariel had desired.' His eyes flicked briefly around at the crumbled wreckage which was his home.

'There is little need to tell the rest. As it is today, so it was then no more than a tale with which to amuse and instruct and frighten children. But the idea has stayed through the generations. Ariel's Opus will forever be how we think of it. I had…' he almost laughed, 'I had never expected to hear it for myself…' He trailed into silence, but Ellie took up his place:

'If you had simply left the Heart where it was...'

'The Darkness would still have found it,' said Url, so defensively that even to the others it was plain that ever since he had first discussed it with Aulan the thought had never truly left his side. 'It would have taken longer, perhaps, but the outcome would have been the same. What we did was –'

'What I would have done also, in your place,' said Ellie, raising her hand. 'Please – I do not seek to blame you for any of this... only to understand. Revealing the Heart, and bringing it here as you have done: on both counts were you wrong.' The words struck like an axe heavily through the chests not only of Url but of all those who sat about him. 'But on both also you cannot be said to have chosen unwisely. With the knowledge you had, and more importantly with that which you did not, no mind could have elected a more honourable course.'

'It matters not why or how any of this has happened,' said Benamin. 'Nor whether you chose well or poorly. We must decide what to do with it now.'

'Is there no way of rebuilding the power of the Torch?' asked Crick.

'Only –' Benamin started, but a sudden tapping on the metal door froze them all in their place. Nobody spoke; Benamin and Ellie turning to each other uneasily. The tapping came again, quicker and louder. Benamin stood and crossed slowly through the room, drawing himself up to full height and doing his best to brush off his dishevelled, anxious look. Mustering an air of calm, he reached up and unlocked the door, gently pushing it open...

'If they ask –' panted an excited, grey-haired man, slightly older than Benamin, barging his way sideways through the door as quick as a serious limp on his right leg would allow, with several enormous rugs, cushions, and other such things tucked tight beneath each arm, '– I came to give them these...' He stood before them all as Benamin, visibly relieved, closed and locked tight the door behind him.

'Is it true?' the man asked urgently, his gaze snapping first to Ellie and then back to Benamin, striking the latter twice with outstretched elbows as he wheeled inelegantly back and forth. 'Maria told me – Is it true? Did they bring the Earthstar?' His eyes were wide, his breath held as he waited for the answer; his array of possessions quite forgotten beneath his arms.

'I had hoped perhaps that she might see it too,' said Benamin, smiling weakly.

'Then – It is? It is true? The *Earthstar*? And *here*, in the city?'

480

'It is.'

Rugs and all were strewn wide across the room as the newcomer raised his hands to his head and turned again on the spot as if in a daze, struggling to keep the clamour of his celebrations from passing beyond the door. As he reached out joyfully to Url, however, Benamin took hold of his arms and lowered them. The man picked up on the sadness in his eyes instantly:

'What is it?' he asked, glancing quickly to each of them. Benamin gestured to the space between Ellie and Siu, waiting until he was seated before, with a swiftness of language which Yori had never before thought possible even amongst these people, at times missing out whole words or parts of sentences which by rights should have been there, he explained all that had been discussed. Like a child flicking through a storybook the man's animated features flickered constantly from one emotion to the next, but it was upon stunned dismay that they came finally to rest.

'This is Ibriam,' said Benamin to the others once he was finished, leaving him to absorb all that he had just been told. 'Friends do not come any older or dearer. Beyond him, his daughter, and my Ellie, there are no others left in the city whom I would trust.'

It was Siu then who introduced the family one by one, realising that they were yet to do so even to Benamin and Ellie. When she had finished, Ibriam turned back to Benamin...

'She said you felt it even before they were seen?'

'I did,' said Benamin. 'But not long before. Sometime after they crossed the Divide, I believe.'

'And the others knew nothing? Even when they saw it? They felt *nothing*?' He was astonished, scarcely believing it possible. Benamin shook his head, almost sadly. 'Truly they have lost the ways of our Fathers,' Ibriam sighed.

'If he can help us,' said Url, 'then that's wonderful – thank you,' he added genuinely to Ibriam, who nodded eagerly, '– but we need to focus on tonight. What are we going to do?'

'To answer your question –' said Benamin, turning back to Crick as if there had been no interruption, '– To rebuild the Torch would take numbers such as we no longer have, knowledge which has largely been lost, tools which if they survived at all are buried deep beneath the city, and time far beyond the few hours you say we have left. No – it cannot be done.'

'Taking it below would be futile,' said Ibriam, thinking aloud.

'We have found ways through to some of the vaults and other deep places of the city,' Ellie explained. 'We could seal the Earthstar beneath many hundreds of feet of stone and ruin, but...'

'It wouldn't stop the Darkness reaching it, eventually,' Url agreed.

From a deep refuge of Yori's mind the tangled greens and browns of Hollycrown appeared suddenly in front of him...

'What happened to the city's Haven?' he asked – aloud, apparently, for the three new faces each turned to him; quiet rage and sadness laid bare beneath them all.

'It was destroyed during the fighting,' said Benamin. 'The woman with whom Owin spoke when you were brought here... Driska... It was she who cast its final wound.' His eyes still shone towards Yori, but in that moment they looked straight through him, seeing nothing but memories.

'Let us not talk of it now,' said Ellie, grasping his hand. 'Besides, it is doubtful even the Haven would have stood against the Opus for long.'

Something flashed through Ibriam's mind: a sudden hope...

'Black Isle...' he murmured, looking from Benamin to Ellie. 'Black Isle!' he said again, more definitely.

'What is that?' asked Orlando. 'Where?'

'It is overrun,' said Benamin, thoughtfully, still looking to Ibriam.

'With beings which would flee before the Earthstar, or surely die in its presence...!' said Ibriam.

'It is too far,' said Ellie.

'Not if we set out now! It would be a near thing, yes – but –'

'Benamin!' Orlando called out above them.

'Before the time of my Father's Father,' said Benamin, barely pausing for breath as he turned to him, 'a dark island grew from the depths of the waters twelve miles or so to the north-east of the city. It was formed of a black stone which had never been seen before, rolling like a violent tide strangely back and forth upon itself, with rough skin like that of a great sponge, though setting hard and sharp as a blade. It was like black, boiling water, suddenly frozen.'

'And the beasts were completely blinded by it!' said Ibriam, cutting to the point.

'Blinded?' asked Url.

'As though a mirror had been placed before them,' said Benamin. 'Much like the effect of the one you wear,' he added to Crick. 'Only small pieces could be brought back to the city at a time, so heavy was the rock; and while they aided those who needed to leave the protection of the city, they could still be overcome by numbers or an especially powerful creature of the shadow. It was clear that should the Opus ever come again, these few shields by themselves would be of no use.

And so, in place of bringing the rock back to the city, a great bastion was built upon and into the island itself. Many thousands of feet deep, with space enough for all the city and more, and food enough to keep them alive for many years. If the Opus came again, it was to there that the people would have fled.'

'Why didn't you speak of this first?' asked Url; agitated, excited; new hope spawning inside him.

'Because I have paid it no mind for longer than I can remember. This is the first time I have heard mention of it for perhaps twenty years. I say it is where they *would* have fled, because for all my lifetime it has been overrun with beasts of the shadow.'

'How?' asked Crick. 'How did they get there? You said they couldn't –'

'None of us knew. It made no sense. *How* they found it was as much a mystery as how they crossed over to it, and why they went at all… The men and women who returned from sailing close to the isle spoke of thousands of the beasts walking senseless above the rock; blind, but still far too many and too powerful to allow any of us to set foot there. When the shadow came, we could not through any means we had at our calling to reach the island we had hoped for so long to rely upon.'

'But with the Heart…' said Url, his eyes by a great measure more alive than they had been in days.

'It may be possible, yes,' said Benamin.

'It *shall* be,' said Ibriam slapping him on the back.

'It shall *not*!' said Ellie sharply. 'I take no pleasure from saying it – but indeed I say again it is *too far*, and the task of getting the Earthstar to the opening at the centre of the isle once we get there too great! If what the boy says is true, we *cannot* make it in time!'

'But what else is there?' asked Ibriam.

'I can't think there's any better way,' said Url, turning to Yori with eyes that longed for some different answer to a question already asked. But casting his mind outwards, listening to the wild tempest at the borders of his thoughts, Yori knew he couldn't give him what he sought…

'It will be here before the next sun,' he said, doing all he could to speak the words without feeling them.

'Well we need to going now then, don't we!' said Ibriam, clambering to his feet impatiently, doing what he could to keep concealed his irritation at the awkwardness of his movements.

'The others…' said Benamin.

'If any see us, we shall simply have to fight or outrun them. What choice do we have?'

'*Outrun them*?' said Siu. 'How are we supposed to do that, dragging the cart behind us?'

'Will that even be possible?' asked Crick. 'The cart –' he added, looking between Url and Orlando, '– Can we move it ourselves?'

'Five of us should be enough,' said Orlando. 'We managed it with four in the Undervalleys. It won't be fast, though.'

'How far is it to the ship?' asked Url. 'I assume there *is* a ship that will bear us?'

'There is,' said Benamin. Only a handful remain, and of them there are two I can think of which are strong enough, and with decks suited for driving the cart onto.'

'The Aurora and the Yinsis?' asked Ibriam. Benamin nodded.

'There *is* another way!' Ellie exclaimed, suddenly realising… 'The Divide!'

'The defences around the city,' said Benamin, turning to Url.

'You want to *cast it in*?' asked Ibriam, incredulous. 'It would still be found – and in the meantime we would all be –'

'Of course not,' Ellie interrupted irritably, leaning forwards and speaking clearly: 'But there is a part of the divide we built with much the same materials and Magics as Black Isle…'

'The Chamber of Trials!' said Benamin, his eyes flashing with intrigue at the idea.

'The golden chamber at the centre of the bridge,' Ellie explained to the others.

Ibriam was playing with the thought too, but he was unconvinced…

'We would never outlast the Opus in there.'

'We could take food enough for months,' said Ellie. 'And perhaps find a way to get more… Even if everything fell around us, the Earthstar would stand, surely?'

'It may do,' said Benamin.

'We would have to get it out and hide it amongst the outskirts of the city before your pursuers have crossed the bridge and sealed off the southern routes,' said Ellie. 'And I do not say we would survive even after that… But even if we did perish within the Chamber, the

Earthstar at least would still be safe, I think. And it is better by far than racing to a place we have no hope of reaching!' she finished to Ibriam.

'You don't *know* that,' said Ibriam.

'I have made the crossing twice myself!' said Ellie. 'My own eyes have seen –'

'As have mine!' shouted Ibriam.

'Quiet!' Benamin grimaced. 'If they hear us now all hope is over before it has begun.'

'Whatever we try,' said Aliya, 'how can we get through the others? She said for a guard to be put around us – surely that will be here now? We can't get away without them seeing…'

'And we have no weapons,' said Crick.

'What good would they be?' asked Siu. 'You saw what she did – the woman who…' She couldn't bring herself to finish the sentence.

'What *was* that?' Url asked, looking to Benamin.

'The wound she cast against you in the road? It was one of countless such abuses of Magic our people learned to harness. There are many far worse than that. You are right,' he said to Siu. 'Forcing our way through the others would… not be easy…'

And for the first time in what felt like an age, nobody spoke, and there was silence amongst them. Perhaps, after such hurried discussion as there had been, a simple break in the talk was no more than that; a mere pausing for breath and with it a chance to take in all that had been said, so disorientatingly quickly had so many great things been spoken. Of all those gathered within the small, candlelit room, not one of them was certain of the scale of all they had just heard, or even of their belief in all or any of it, so swiftly had so many great things been assumed and, now, apparently agreed upon. Perhaps the silence had come as an unbidden collective attempt to make sense of it all. Or perhaps it was simply because none knew what to say, or where it was they were supposed to go from here. Or perhaps, Yori thought, looking around at the others as each waited for the next, nobody wanting to be the one to break the welcome spell of calm, it was because it was only now that, as one, they each understood that the deaths of Tarryn and Abetta, terrible as they were, may perhaps not be the last.

'We know not a small amount of Magic between us, too,' said Ibriam finally, looking to Benamin with a strange sadness Yori didn't understand.

'We swore –' Benamin started.

'I know too well the oaths we made,' Ibriam interrupted. 'And I know too well what it would mean for us to break them now. But if it means the others may live to protect the Earthstar…'

'Something troubles you...?' asked Ellie. It was a moment before the others realised she was talking to Siu.

'I just...' Siu started uncertainly, trying to find within her better words to use... 'Is the idea of telling the others really that unthinkable? I mean, if we explain to them what it is that's about to befall us, and make them see that they have little choice but to help us, surely –'

'I like the idea of going against them even less than you,' said Benamin. 'I know what they are capable of, in their hearts as well as in their Magics. But alas you ascribe them a sense of logic they no longer possess. They seek nothing but vengeance. And while the stubbornness of one angry mind is great, that of many together is almost unconquerable: If we were to tell them that a power greater than any they had ever known was in their midst, they would see only its use as a weapon. They would fight until their last breaths to wield it against their enemies. They would perish as they raged, and then the Earthstar would be taken. No – they must not learn of it.'

'If that's the case,' said Siu, 'they won't stand a chance, whatever *we* do. We're sentencing them all to death.' She looked sorrowfully to Benamin as the others each took in deep breaths, appearing to understand this for the first time themselves. 'I know you have no love for them... but –'

'It is the end they have crafted for themselves,' said Benamin sharply. 'I will not tell them.' It was only as he said it now that Yori realised that the bitterness which raged within Owin and the others was just as present within Benamin too. It was simply better hidden. Neither Yori nor any of the others objected either, however.

'Stars!' Url shouted suddenly, raising clenched fists tight into his eyes. 'I'm a fool!' he said through his arms.

'Well, I –' Crick began, but Url ignored him completely:

'We *do* have a weapon! A small one, but...' And amidst the confusion of the others he reached quickly to the long, slim pocket on the outside of his trousers, just above his ankle. 'I can hear her cursing me even now!' he muttered to himself as he untied the fastening below his knee, reaching in with thumb and forefinger, and drawing out... nothing but his own fingers.

'It's... your hand,' Orlando suggested. And indeed it was, curled almost into a fist as Url held it out in front of them.

'Is there a parchment you no longer need?' Url asked quickly of Benamin, who despite a look of utmost scepticism reached back for the closest sketch behind him, quickly setting it down and choosing another, and passing it across to Url. Aliya seemed to have guessed what was happening, and from Url's thoughts Yori too could see...

486

Even in her dying moments, she had been thinking of them… Url instructed Crick to hold the parchment flat in front of him, and then, with a sad grin, he moved his fist in straight line, five inches or so below it, watching as the parchment tore smoothly in two before the stunned gazes of the others.

'She placed it in my hand as she took her last breath,' said Url, looking to Siu.

'One of her skinning knives?' asked Orlando.

'I believe so,' said Url, nodding sadly. 'It was right there in my hand as they searched the rest of me. With everything that's happened, I completely forgot about it.'

They all watched for a moment as Crick set a piece of the torn parchment down half a foot above Url's fist, where it curved gently around the invisible point of the blade. 'It's not quite all we need,' said Ibriam, smiling as he reached out to trace a finger up along the handle and blade. 'But it's far better than –'

A shiver ran suddenly up Yori's spine… All the others felt it too: each gasping or jumping to their feet as around the room the figurines danced and tumbled to the floor with a shallow trembling of the rock.

'What is it?' asked Url, seeing the surge of fear passing between Benamin, Ellie and Ibriam.

But without a word Benamin had vaulted to the door; distant, panicked calls filling the room as he heaved it open. Ibriam limped after him; Yori watching through his Father's legs as the two of them climbed twenty feet or so through the rubble before turning back to look over the dwelling and out across the city. When neither of them spoke, Ellie rushed to join them, instructing Yori and the others to remain inside, but when she reached them she too was silenced. Briefly through the darkness Yori thought he saw a glint of strange, green light reflected in their eyes. Or was it blue... then red too amongst them... The rumbling came again and with it Url made to push his way through the others to the door, but Orlando halted him as Benamin and Ellie came skipping hurriedly through the stone back down towards them, the others all parting to let them through…

'The Euclas Stones are burning!' Benamin whispered breathlessly.

'The bridge,' Ellie explained, still standing wide-eyed in the doorway. 'Its defences are falling…'

Chapter Thirty-Eight

Hidden Dawn

'It is decided, then,' said Benamin, returning from the far room with his cloak. 'We have no other choice – we cannot reach the Chamber now.'

'Black Isle...' Ellie breathed. A terrible dread flashed in the depths of her eyes.

Ibriam was still standing beyond the door, his head darting to and fro as he peered quickly up and around the ruins. Whatever guard had been stationed to watch over Benamin's home was still nowhere to be seen. He turned back to the others...

'We must go now!' he whispered; only the vaguest outline of his words reaching the room through the rumbling and shouting above.

'Ready yourselves,' said Benamin, fastening his cloak hurriedly about him. Ellie was doing likewise. The crunching of wooden figurines and the tearing of parchments were added to the confusion beneath Aliya and the others as they scrambled to their feet, none of them knowing what they should do. They had little *to* get ready. Without the cart, and their possessions, and amongst it all the Heart, they were simply themselves.

'I must bring Maria,' said Ibriam, his head appearing suddenly through the doorway. Benamin looked at him a moment, chewing thoughtfully on the inside of his lip, before giving a reluctant nod.

'Meet us along the east path to the harbours. And be quick – we cannot wait for you once we get there.'

But just as Ibriam turned to leave, Aliya saw through the doorway half a dozen figures suddenly revealed in a flash of dark green at the lip of the hollow, looking down towards the home. Her gasp alerted the others, but before any of them could speak or react Owin's voice crashed loud and heavy down the stone:

'Why are you here, Ibriam?' Those either side of him spread further out as they followed him down, cutting off any exit. Amongst them, on the far left as Aliya looked, was the woman who had killed her Grandmother, a hungry grin faintly twisting the lines of her mouth and eyes like those of a wolf in hunt.

'I brought blankets for our –'

'What do you know of this?' Owin barked, throwing Ibriam aside as he reached him and addressing Url through the doorway.

'They are more afraid than we are,' said Benamin, stepping between them. 'They know nothing of –'

'Do not tell me this is chance!' shouted Owin, and with a furious growl he struck Benamin back and lunged in towards Url, pinning him to the wall by the neck with a thick, scarred forearm. 'That the bridge should be awakened for the first time in years within the day of your arrival is no mere *chance*! What follows you?'

Only one of Url's hands grasped at Owin's arm: his right, unnoticed to most of the others, was clenched tight by his side, still gripping Abetta's hidden blade. A swift raise and Owin would be dead in an instant, but there would still be no way out through the others. More were arriving from the hollow, confused and frightened, silenced now as they saw through the doorway.

'*What follows you?*' Owin screamed again...

But like a soft breeze into the storm came Ellie's hand, reaching out to Owin, landing light as fresh silk upon the bulk of his shoulder. She didn't flinch as he whirled to strike whoever it was that had dared touch him; his fist halting inches from her cheek.

'We are wasting time,' she said, looking calmly into his eyes.

'They are all alight!' came a panicked cry from above. 'The bridge is crossed!'

'We must take up positions quickly,' said Benamin. 'We must find whatever this evil is which has breached our city before it finds us.'

Owin's glare lingered a second more with Ellie, before with a final thrust at Url's neck he stepped back to the doorway.

'*You* will come with us,' he said through Url's choking, jabbing a finger hard into Benamin's chest. 'The rest of you will stay here.' He took hold of the fronts of two of the men behind him as he turned.

'They do not leave,' he growled, dragging them either side of him and into the doorway. 'Out of my way, *cripple*!' he shouted, sending Ibriam once more to the ground.

Benamin pulled Ellie to him, whispering something into her ear as he kissed her.

'*Now*!' Owin called, and unwillingly Ellie released her husband, standing quiet and impassive as she watched him leave.

Both of Owin's men remained inside. One was tall and fair-skinned; the other, eyeing the family warily, slightly shorter with thick, dirty brown hair. Only as he reached out to close the door did Aliya see that upon each of the latter's hands only his forefingers remained; the other digits appearing to have been torn untidily away at the knuckles. Huddled close together opposite them, just in front of the archway into the back room, Aliya and the others listened as voices rose and shouting echoed once again outside, then slowly grew fainter, and finally was gone altogether. The rumbling too had stopped, and in its place a series of sharp, nervous breaths remained as the only sounds in the darkened room; all but two of the larger candles having been put out during the confrontation.

'There is no need to look at them so, Tommus,' said Ellie, addressing the shorter of the two. 'What do you expect them to do, unarmed and unempowered as they are? Sit...' she added calmly to the family. 'It will be a long while before we hear news.' Several of them shot long, questioning looks at her, but again she simply gestured to the scattered cushions.

'Um – no, don't!' shouted the taller of the men, uncertainly. 'You are all to stay where you –'

'They will be far less concern to you if they are seated and comfortable,' said Ellie. 'You are welcome to join us too, of course...? I have some merryweed ready to brew, if you would like?'

'Just keep yourselves away from the door, and from us,' said Tommus, loosening his cloak and resting heavily against the frame of the doorway, shaking his head impatiently at his partner's look of protest.

'May I at least make some for ourselves, then?' asked Ellie.

'You have what you need in here?' asked Tommus, stifling a yawn and rubbing his eyes. Ellie nodded, and after a moment's consideration he waved a weary hand for her to continue.

Lifting out a thin, oval stone from the wall beside her, Ellie took from the small cavity beyond a selection of tiny, silver goblets, two sweet-smelling wooden containers, and several rods and long chains of bronze. She passed them to Aliya and Crick, telling them to set the

490

items in the middle of the room amongst the others. And then, bringing a final large, bronze pot, she sat cross-legged before them and began the assembly of a curious instrument, just over a foot in height, into the centre of which she hung the pot. A thick, sweet smell escaped into the room as she opened the two containers, taking a pinch from each and sprinkling the fine dusts – one green, the other a greyish black – into the container. From the floor itself a soft, blue flame smouldered into life, engulfing the apparatus but emitting no heat that Aliya could feel; and though none of them had seen Ellie add any water, there came after a minute the sounds and steam of some boiling liquid from within. And all the time as she worked, none of them spoke. Tommus, running the tip of one forefinger distractedly over the raw, bare knuckles of his other hand, gazed distracted and anxiously at the wall ahead of him, but beside him the other man was watching Ellie, absorbed in the smooth, quiet way she moved despite the heavy scowl of distrust in which his unpleasantly pale, lifeless face seemed permanently set.

From the pot Ellie poured at length a drop of steaming, dark green liquid into each of the goblets, loading them carefully onto a circular silver tray, and kneeling to offer them round to each of the family in turn. Aliya took hers with an uncertain smile; her eyes watering as she took in a breath of the thick, sweet vapour, so that she almost didn't notice the way in which Ellie, her back turned to the door, had hesitated briefly before Url. Desperately trying to portray what she could of her thoughts through her eyes, she looked first down to Url's clenched hand, and then nodded faintly to the tray in front of her. It took Url a moment to realise, and another to agree, but with a second frantic nod from Ellie he reached up finally with both hands, watching the two guards over her shoulder, releasing the knife soft and quickly onto the tray as he took one of the remaining goblets.

'Are you sure you won't have one?' Ellie asked, turning cheerfully to the door once Siu had taken a drink. 'We have a spare…?' She stood, taking a sip of one the final two goblets. Aliya saw Url shuffling quietly, almost kneeling, as if trying to prepare to spring forwards. Crick, with far greater chance of success, was doing likewise.

Tommus took no notice of Ellie, but the eyes of the other followed the goblet in her hand, a sudden thirst coming to his lips…

'To keep you quiet,' he mumbled, waving her over. Crick was leaning up onto his fingers, his breath held, ready… But as Ellie approached the men there was a sudden hammering on the door…

'What?' shouted Tommus. 'Who is it?'

491

Ellie paused, then took another small step towards them, her hand moving slowly across the tray, hovering above the knife...

'It's a ranckworm!' came Ibriam's voice from outside. 'We're all needed down in the city!'

'A *ranckworm*?' Tommus exclaimed, reaching for the handle. 'How could one of those –' But through the thin chink he had opened in the doorway shot a streak of flame, thin and quick as an arrow, striking him hard in the chest. Embers pounced wildly in all directions as the taller man reeled back, and before he could regain his senses Ellie lunged at him, arm outstretched towards his chest. The tray clattered to the floor, not quite covering the sound of the long blade between the top of his ribs. Bubbles of blood spilled from his mouth as he stood for a moment, stunned; another flame flying at once through the entrance to strike the writhing Tommus straight between the eyes. Ellie withdrew the knife, and like trees felled by opposing storms both men collapsed heavily together into the same spot, just before the doorway. A heartbeat later Ibriam was there, panting, staring down at them.

'Thank you!' breathed Url, climbing to his feet with the others, staring quietly as the taller man convulsed before releasing a long, rattling breath. It felt strange to Aliya to take such relief and even pleasure from a thing so sickening; fear and with it now this small measure of revenge apparently making for a potent and disconcerting blend. Tommus had been dead before he fell. Ellie still was standing above him, disgusted by the sheen of blood which had burst across her hand and arm. Without seeing what she was reaching for, Siu took the knife gently and awkwardly from her, comforting her.

'I did nothing but talk,' said Ibriam. And he stepped to one side, inviting into the room from behind him a girl with long, auburn hair, and robes which would have matched had it not been for the thin layer of dust and dirt ingrained upon them.

'No-one else was struck, were they?' she asked excitedly before any of them could greet or thank her. Her eyes shone bright as stars, for a moment taking little notice of the two bodies strewn at her feet. 'It has been more than a long while since my skills were tested like that... I *told* you!' she added, turning back to Ibriam.

'My daughter, Maria,' said Ibriam. 'Twenty-three years of defiance; twenty-three years learning the Magics the others use so freely, against my will... all justified, I fear, in a few seconds. You did well,' he added, nodding sadly to his daughter.

'You've explained it all to her?' asked Orlando.

'We must leave,' said Ellie flatly, suddenly shrugging off Siu's attempts to help and struggling alone though in vain to wipe the scarlet from her skin.

'I know far from all,' said Maria quickly. 'Even with the swiftness of talk between my Father and me there is still a great deal as-yet unsaid. But I know enough to know that the rest must wait. Black Isle...' she breathed to herself, sobered and lost for a moment in the thought. Ibriam put an arm across her shoulders.

'There is no time for her!' Ellie added angrily, already half out the door as she caught sight of Orlando disappearing into the other room.

'We must!' said Siu. 'I can't –'

'She will slow us. For the sake of those of us who are left, we must leave her!'

Orlando returned with Abetta draped across his arms, pausing in the silence...

'I can take her,' said Crick. 'I'll still be faster than...' he paused, looking awkwardly to Ibriam.

'And *I* can be faster than you imagine, when my mind is set on it!' said Ibriam, taking his weight off his good leg and standing straight and tall, looking defiant though not harshly down at Crick. Again there was silence; each looking to the others for a decision...

'We *must not* slow for her,' said Ellie.

'We won't,' said Crick. Ellie stared at him a moment longer, then nodded, leading Ibriam and Maria hurriedly through the door.

But their flight halted almost before it had begun: No sooner had Aliya stepped up through the entrance and around to the right of the home, beyond which Maria was guiding the way into the night down another thin trail through the rubble, than she ran hard into the back of her Father. He had stopped dead in his tracks, and was gazing open-mouthed across the city.

'The Euclas Stones,' said Ibriam, as Aliya herself looked out...

Through the heavy black of the sky, in a great arc which skimmed the very edges of the horizon ahead and either side of them, dozens of distant flames were burning, each a different colour but all with the same, magnificent intensity. Though in size they were little more than large stars in the distance, Aliya was certain she could feel their many-hued warmth even from here.

'The gemstones that were set above the Divide?' asked Url.

'*And all alight,*' Ellie reminded them impatiently before Ibriam could answer. 'Come... Explain on the way if you must.'

The trail continued in something close to a straight line, down and away from the eastern bank of the ruins. But once they reached the low-ground Maria veered right, picking up a new route which by Aliya's reckoning had to be taking them back more or less parallel to the main road into the city, somewhere along which, with luck, the cart would still be waiting.

'The Stones have not burned for nearly seven years,' whispered Ibriam as they crept light and quick as they could through the passage, all eyes and ears strained for movement or voices around them. 'They are quite a sight, are they not?' The effort of moving so swiftly, limping awkwardly through the rocks as he was, was already becoming too much for him. Though he tried, he couldn't hide the pain in his voice.

'And it was before I was born that they were last *all* aflame like this!' said Maria excitedly. 'A pack of thunderhounds – near-twelve foot tall each!'

'Only one was as large as she says,' said Ibriam. 'And of them all, only that and two others made it through the Divide. Though even then it still took us two full days to bring them down.'

'A pack it was then,' said Url, 'and a pack it is now. And I fear this one will prove the worse. Is there no way of knowing how they fare against your people?'

'None except in Magics beyond any of us,' said Maria.

'With luck,' said Ibriam, 'they will have been met further out, towards the bridge.'

'And *without* it?' asked Crick. With the exception of Url's glare, there was no reply.

'If I had been allowed to *practice* my skills more as a child...' said Maria under her breath.

'Your mind would have become as darkened as theirs!' said Ibriam. 'Useful as your talent has been –'

'And may still be...' Url interjected.

'Indeed. But even so I make no apologies for –'

'Quiet yourselves!' whispered Ellie. 'We are nearing the road.'

It was not the main road which Ellie spoke of, but another:

'The east path,' Maria announced softly as they came to it, crouching silently amongst the stone. It was not a true road like the other – rather a long, curving track which had been cleared roughly through the rubble, running away to their left, north-east, towards the coast.

'It will take us to the East Harbours once we have the Earthstar,' said Ellie, standing to peer around them. 'The only of the three great dockyards of the city not to have been completely destroyed. Will your cart make it through here?'

494

'So long as it doesn't get any narrower,' said Orlando.

'Are we going to take the road the rest of the way to the cart?' asked Url. 'It's taking too long moving alongside it like this!'

'There may be watchers there,' said Ellie, shaking her head. 'Such as those who first caught sight of you.'

'Then they'll see us when we come back with the cart anyway!' said Crick.

'*That* we can do little about,' said Ellie. 'And at least by then we shall already have the Earthstar. We cannot afford to be seen before then.'

'I can manage fine,' said Ibriam, shuffling uncomfortably onto his good leg as eyes began to turn towards him.

'Can *you*?' Aliya whispered to Crick, whose brow was beginning to glisten with the effort of the all too dead weight he carried. Seeing her body draped so awkwardly above him was terrible to behold, almost for a second drawing Aliya's mind away from their flight. She was uncertain which was worse. She looked away from her Grandmother, casting out the horror of one to focus on the terror of the other; the both together too much too bear.

'I'm fine,' he nodded, heaving the sagging body back up onto his shoulder as they set off again across the path and on into another winding trail through the remains of what seemed now to be homes and monuments, some of which angled above them or jutted out in front of them. Briefly Aliya was reminded again of the crystal-strewn cavern through which they had first had to drag the Heart... The memory was painful, bringing to mind sudden images of her Grandmother and the quietness of home, and she tried again to cast it aside. But try as she did, she couldn't rid herself of it completely; the thoughts adding weight and darkness to the already darkened parts of her mind, drawing out fears which until now had been kept carefully hidden behind a shield of nervous excitement. Though the pace was slower as the group crept silently forwards her heart was racing faster within her; an icy sweat creeping up and around her neck. Suddenly, beneath the cold, black night, she was truly afraid.

Through the shadows to their right brief glimpses of the road came and went, but each time to Aliya they felt further away. The silence itself, so strained and essential, became after a while a growing curse; a terrible ally without which they would not survive, hovering unbearably about them, daring them to break it. Seconds turned agonisingly into minutes; minutes to what must have been hours, for it felt like an eternity before Maria crouched finally to a halt once more, looking left and right through another thin break in the rubble.

Somehow, unnoticed to Aliya, they had circled around in a long arc to the right. They waited now at a narrow opening into the central road, through which only one of them could move or look at once. Ellie waited for Maria to turn back before asking what she could see...

'It's still there,' Maria whispered, pointing to their right, north along the road. 'The cart. Two hundred feet, perhaps. There is nobody around it that I can see.'

'We wouldn't see them, whether they are there or not,' said Ibriam.

Each looked to the other as they paused before the opening, not now because there was any question of what was to be done, but simply to gather the strength and courage to do it. Aliya tried, hopelessly, to calm her breathing; she looked to her Grandmother's body, realising she was lucky still to be doing so at all, but the thought only brought a quicker, more uncomfortable thumping to the inside of her chest.

'When we get there, we loose Nightwind and get moving,' whispered Url. Aliya's heart sunk again at the name, as though having long-since been cast out into dark water and reaching its murky depths, her spirit was now being trampled steadily into the mud of the bed itself. 'Nobody speaks,' Url continued, oblivious as he needed to be to her distress. 'Whatever happens, we don't stop. *Whatever happens...*' he repeated, looking to them each individually until they nodded their assent. 'You put her inside,' he said to Crick, 'and then come up front with me. The rest of you get round the sides and back. Yori, you... *Yori!*'

Aliya nudged Yori beside her, wrenching him back from wherever his thoughts had begun to take him.

'We need you to feel out around us as we go,' said Url. 'See if you...' but Yori was looking instead to Ellie, studying her...

'Yori!' Url tried again angrily.

'We can't make it, can we...?' said Yori. Amongst them all he was neither sad nor afraid; a hint of an accepting smile touching his lips. But almost before it had appeared Url's hand had reached to him, taking firm but gentle hold across his cheeks, turning his head so that he met Url's eyes. Even now there was no flinch of surprise, no emotion at all on his face. His eyes were suddenly glazed, but still Url tried to reach through to him:

'We need you to try and tell us if there's anyone around,' he said clearly, releasing Yori.

'He couldn't tell last time,' said Aliya.

'I said he needs to *try*!' said Url impatiently. 'That's all I'm asking of him!'

'If we sit here any longer we are dooming ourselves,' Ibriam growled. He squeezed and gave a firm pat to the outside of his right knee. 'On with it: let us get this thing done.' And between Ellie and his daughter he half-ran, half-fell through the opening, stumbling quickly away into the road and out of sight. Maria was tight on his heels; Ellie following her. Url was next, his hands gripping clumps of the twisted stone either side of him, but as his muscles readied to heave him out into the open he turned back to Aliya and the others...

'This is it. It's not... how I thought it would turn out...' He hesitated, refusing to look at Abetta but clearly unable to think of anything else. Then he drew a sharp breath, steeling himself angrily against his grief... 'But we're almost there. We're nearly done. Nobody stops – nobody goes back...' And with a silent grunt of effort he was gone.

Her Mother... Yori... Aulan... then Aliya herself was through, sprinting low along the road; the cart little more than shadow upon shadow ahead of her. She heard Crick and her Father behind but didn't dare turn to see them for fear of stumbling on the stones which lurked like hidden fiends across the ground, waiting to trip any who strayed too close. The darkness played with the edges of her vision but she refused to be drawn into the confusion of it, keeping her eyes focused always on the cart. Their footsteps, quiet as they were, seemed to echo terribly off the rocks; Aliya wondering desperately how far back along the road the sounds were travelling. Others were already working on the front of the cart when she reached it, and she turned instead to help Crick load their Grandmother hastily into the back. A part of her knew she should be disgusted by the sound made as the body tumbled unceremoniously onto the boards, but in the silent frenzy in which she and the others were moving and working she had little time to notice it.

The Heart was still there. It glistened, calm and soft as ever as Aliya watched it a moment; a thick layer of dust around it covering the items which had been thrown about within the cart. And it was hot: not the warm glow that had been there for most of their journey, but a thick, stifling heat, surrounding the Heart in a tight bubble, singeing Aliya's hand as she reached in towards it.

Grunts of frustration and the sound of a blade through leather came from the front as Aliya took a position at the right corner of the back of the cart; Aulan to her left, his eyes darting fearfully all about them. As Aliya turned away from him she saw Yori a few feet from her, looking back silently down the road.

'*Get him in the cart*!' called Url through gritted teeth, noticing Yori as he lifted one of the sets of reins, wrapping the thick, heavy straps over his shoulder. The others were returning from the front, finding strong beams around the cart on which to push. 'We can't afford to keep making sure he's with us all the time!'

'Yori…' Aliya whispered. '*Yori!*'

But he didn't move. His head cocked sideways a fraction, as that of an owl picking up a distant sound…

'They've heard us,' he said softly.

The others halted where they were; listening, watching between him and the road.

'They've heard us,' Yori said again, making no effort this time to lower his voice, which weak though it was had the feel of thunder about them in the silence. Still he made no sign of movement. Aliya reached out to him; Url cursing the delay…

'They've seen us,' said Yori…

But the instant Aliya's hand closed upon his arm the night came suddenly alive in an explosion of brightest blue all around them. From the western side of the road, half a mile back, a brilliant flare had been sent into the sky, bursting in a shower of sapphire sparks which drifted gently back down towards the rubble.

'Watchers!' Ibriam exclaimed.

'Aliya!' Url shouted.

'The others will have seen the signal,' said Ibriam as Aliya dragged Yori from his feet. Aulan took him from her, swinging him in a swift, single movement into the cart beside Abetta.

'Now!' Url shouted. 'Everyone – *Now*!'

And from all around the cart at once came a series of creaks and groans; the wheels labouring reluctantly into life once more.

'This is too early!' Aliya heard Ibriam say on the far side. 'We cannot outrun them from here!'

'What choice do we have?' asked Ellie angrily.

'Shut your mouths and quicken your legs!' said Url, straining with the effort. Aliya did what she could, but beside Aulan she felt weak and unhelpful. He was pushing with such brute force as she had never seen before; a sudden aggression making him almost a match for…

She wished Tarryn were here. His strength and his smile she longed for in equal measure.

'How many will have seen us?' asked Orlando. Just in front of Aliya, Yori was kneeling beside their Grandmother, gazing back between Aliya's head and Aulan.

'I cannot say,' said Ibriam. 'Owin's plans have always –'

'Two,' said Maria. 'Most like it's Krab and Riiku – I'm certain it was one of Riiku's signals, and where there's one there's usually the other of them. But that's not to say there's not others nearby.'

Despite its slow start the cart had begun to pick up speed, Aliya needing almost to run in an awkward fashion as it rattled loudly through the road, checked but never halted by the loose stone and other debris that was too small to see, or upon which they came too quickly to steer around. The mountain of ruin from which they had earlier fled now loomed tall again ahead of them; distant flames flickering amongst the rubble around the hollow halfway up, noticed by all of them but mentioned by none. All Aliya's thought and effort was channelled into the single beam upon which she pushed, trusting in those at the front to steer them well. She stumbled on a thick crack in the road, grasping the cart to regain her footing, but as she looked up again Yori was lunging towards her: He struck her shoulder and head with both hands, throwing her sideways, and as she fell into Aulan a streak of red cracked through the air from behind them, missing the corner of the cart by inches.

'Is anyone hurt?' called Url amidst the screams of shock. Immediately the cart began to lose speed.

'Don't stop!' shouted Ellie.

'We're fi–' But as Aliya spoke another flame swept forwards from the black behind her, striking the road twenty feet back, exploding in a shower of embers and flame which scattered violently across the stone about her feet.

'Go!' Maria shouted. 'I'll do what I can to delay them!'

'No!' called Ibriam, but as the cart rolled forwards Maria was revealed on the far side, standing tall and brave as one of the statues which had lined the Firstway; a ball of flame growing into life from the palm of her outstretched hand.

'Ibriam!' shouted Ellie, as with a sudden twist of Maria's arm the flame was released, screeching through the air with the snap of sudden wind, lighting the sides of the road a golden red as it disappeared into the distance.

'Do not wait for us!' called Ibriam as he ran back to Maria, around whom another flame was already burning. Through Ellie's curses a strange crackling pierced the air, growing louder and then vanishing as a bolt of blue lightning tore above the cart. Another followed it, this time straight and level, two feet from the ground... Ibriam was still yet to reach Maria, but as she flung herself to the road he thrust out with both hands and an almighty effort into the air above her: the lightning turned from its course at the last moment by a silver pulse which came forth from his palms like an expanding shield, billowing out an arm's length in front of them before melting like smoke into the air.

'Is everyone alright back there?' called Url.

'They won't last by themselves!' said Aliya.

'Are any of you hurt or not?' asked Ellie angrily.

'We're fine,' said Orlando.

'Then keep moving – we're almost at the turn.'

Jets of blue and red tore time and again through the air behind them; some still coming close to the cart but most now crashing into the left of the road against the rubble of which Ibriam and Maria had taken shelter, firing back flame and waves of silver of their own. The cart began to veer to the right, staying close to the high wall of black, twisted metal which edged the road, and soon Ibriam and Maria were lost from view.

'What Ibriam did back there…' said Siu, breathlessly. They were all fighting hard for air; Aliya's thighs and shoulders burning with the effort.

'Do not assume because we have spoken of our dislike for the way our people have come to use Magic, that we do not know any ourselves,' said Ellie.

'Is Ibriam's knowledge more powerful than that of the others?' asked Url.

'No. But between him and Maria, they should be able to hold out long enough.'

'Long enough for *us*…' said Aliya bitterly.

'Which is all that matters!' said Url.

'They knew the cost of their decision,' said Ellie.

Being spoken to as though she didn't understand the importance of their task angered Aliya, but the lack of compassion or regret in their voices appalled her. How could they accept the fates of the others so easily? If it came to it, was her own life to be sacrificed with such little thought? For a brief moment she hated the Heart and what it had brought them; she fought to halt herself from screaming aloud into the night, pushing instead ever-harder and more angrily against the cart.

'There!' called Crick before Aliya could put voice to her thoughts. She looked up to see Yori lying across Abetta, his eyes closed, frowning deeply into his arms.

'The turn?' asked Ellie. A wheezing grunt of a reply from Url told them it was.

Ahead of her Aliya felt the front veering gently to the left, but then without warning it turned sharp to the right. The abrupt change slowed the cart, needing another great heave to get it moving again, but Url's exhausted call for renewed effort as they left the road and passed through into the new trail was cut short as from somewhere ahead came the sudden clattering of tumbling rocks, growing quickly closer.

'Do not stop!' Url growled.

'We have nothing left to defend with!' said Orlando.

'Then we'll go straight through them!'

'I shall do what I can,' said Ellie.

'*Crick*!' Siu screamed.

'Boy, get back here!' shouted Url.

'I can get round behind them!' Crick called back, his voice already distant. But suddenly to their left the ruins trembled; stone dislodged and sent rattling down towards the cart. There was no time and no place to seek cover; Aliya looking up helplessly as the cart rolled away from her, her heart frozen, trying to form meaning from the shadows but unable to do so until something large moved above her...

'Al–' she tried, breath coming to her in shallow gasps, '*Alamos*! It's Alamos!'

She sunk to the ground as she heard the cart come to a stop ahead, Crick sprinting back towards them. There were panted sighs of relief all around her, but it took a few seconds before any of them could find the strength to speak...

'If the others don't finish us off,' said Url, leaning back against the cart and clutching at his chest, 'I think that might just do it...'

'You took your time...!' said Crick, almost smiling as he arrived.

'You are being followed,' said Alamos simply. His deep, solemn voice was at great odds to Url's laugh which followed it:

'You don't say...!' he muttered.

'Please –' said Siu, '– our friends, behind us. They need help!'

'No!' said Url, grimacing with the pain of getting to his feet again. 'Now that he's here we should keep him with us! He can move the cart far quicker than –'

'We can do that well enough ourselves!' said Siu. 'And if he can rescue the others we stand a better chance of getting through!'

'He –'

'Your load is your own to carry,' said Alamos, silencing them. Url opened his mouth in frustration, but held his tongue. 'There are none in front of you that I saw,' Alamos continued. 'But if behind you there are those you call your friends, and they are in need of help, then help them I shall.' He cast his big eyes down to Siu...

'Back along the road –' she said after a moment, pointing behind them. 'A mile – maybe two…'

And with a low, deep rumbling of the stone around them Alamos sprang at once above the cart, clear across the trail; great slabs of rubble crumbling and crashing beneath him as he bounded away without another word.

'That wasn't the right choice,' said Url, already at the front of the cart and wrapping the reins around him again. 'We should have kept him with u–'

'*Kept* him?' Yori hissed suddenly from the cart, with a fury and disgust which took Url by surprise. 'Like a *dog* to be told to sit and fetch and carry for you? You have no idea what –'

'Either way,' Ellie interrupted, shaking herself from an awed silence, 'it is a choice which is made. *Alamos*…' she murmured softly beneath her breath, lost again for a moment before she blinked and returned to them… 'Is everyone –'

'Wait –' Siu interrupted, '– what about Benamin?'

'He would not want us to waste time thinking of him.'

'But when the others learn of our flight, what will he –'

'I know not what he will do, or what will become of him,' said Ellie, her voice breaking as she spoke. 'None of it changes what *we* must do now! Are you *ready*?'

'On three!' shouted Url; Aliya bracing herself once more against the cart… '…two… Now!'

The ground was no rougher than before, but with aching limbs they struggled this time to force life back into the cart, suffering further with each frequent twist in the trail. Quite how Nightwind and the others had kept up such effort for so long, and over such difficult terrain as they had passed through, Aliya couldn't comprehend. *Nightwind*…

'If Owin and the Pack keep each other occupied long enough we should have a clear run at the harbours, shouldn't we…?' asked Crick.

'Stop jinxing our fate and pull, damn you…' Url grumbled.

'Take comfort from your hope if you can,' said Ellie. 'But they won't; not now they know we're moving. Owin will send some after us, if not all.'

'When they see Alamos with us…' said Orlando.

'*If* he returns,' said Ellie.

'I'm not entrusting too much of my faith in him,' said Url. 'Powerful – certainly; but quite how his mind works I've no idea…'

'He appeared to have little interest in the Earthstar,' Ellie agreed.

'We mean more to him than you all realise…' said Yori, so quietly that only Aliya and Aulan could have heard. 'Far more than he means to you, anyway…'

'The others don't know he comes to help them!' said Siu. 'If they hear something approaching them –'

'Neither of them are fools,' said Ellie. 'They will not attack without first distinguishing friend from foe. See now – we come to the crossing we made earlier…'

They passed without slowing between the familiar breaks in the rubble either side of the trail. Briefly amongst their own clattering Aliya thought she discerned a call from the hollow above, but if there had been such a sound there were none which followed – whether for good or ill, Aliya had not the strength nor will to attempt to decide.

The others too kept their silences until they were well past the crossing, and even then spoke only loud enough to be heard above the cart, for all the good it would do. For a mile, maybe more, every step of which was agony in mind as much as body, Aliya pushed blindly on into heightening ruins; the streak of open sky above her taking on a deep blue in place of the black, though not enough to lend any real light to their surroundings. No relief could be taken from the lack of sound or movement around them, however. Aliya found a part of herself wishing desperately for a far-off cry or some sign of battle, so that for a moment at least she might take comfort from the belief that the threat lay there alone, not waiting in the shadows just beside or ahead of them, amongst the trail which seemed without end.

*

'There will be open ground ahead of us for perhaps half a mile,' said Ellie finally as the trail jerked once more to the left, running now straight for as far as Aliya could see. 'Beyond, there is a line of buildings. There is no way of getting the cart through: we must take it to the right of them, and then back round into the harbours. The Yinsis is closer; it will be on the first pier to our right as we go down alongside the sea wall. Do as I say when we reach it: there is much to do to get it moving, and all must be done in time.'

'Is everyone alright back there?' called Url. 'We're almost done! Keep moving!'

'They're behind us…' said Yori.

'What?' shouted Url. 'What did he –'

'There's someone behind us!' Aliya called. 'Who is it?' she asked of Yori as Url shouted the same. 'Yori?' But he would say no more.

'*Who?*' Url called again.

503

'No time,' said Ellie. 'Concentrate – we are here – to the right...
Now!'

And for an instant all consciousness of the chase was thrown from
Aliya. She was transfixed, lost, even as somewhere her body still
laboured and fought against pain and exhaustion; engulfed by a deep,
fresh smell drawn in upon one of her great gasps for breath, filling
every part of her, swelling inside her lungs like a thick, rich mist.
Never had she felt anything so powerful, so timeless, and so full of life;
the Magic within it almost whole and touchable. In all the times she
had heard or read of the salt-air of the deepwaters; in all the tales Url
had told in quiet moments between the two of them throughout their
journey; in not one of them had she been told of the feeling they stirred
within a person's heart when met, as now, for the first time. A
sweetness and a bitterness played in wild harmony amidst the cold of
the night, speaking of the ending of the world upon these shores and
the beginning now of that which lay beyond, singing loudly to a deeply
hidden part of Aliya which had never before heard song. It puzzled and
dismayed her to think that she had somehow lived without it for so
long...

But like a cloud blown away upon a winter's wind her dreaming
ended and she was running and pushing once more, every part of her
aching, fear clinging to her throat and chest like a blanket of ice...

The buildings Ellie had spoken of were hidden beyond the cart.
All Aliya could see as she emerged from the trail were borders of ruin
behind her curving back and away to left and right, and in front
nothing but wide, open ground stretching into a dark, foggy distance.
The ground itself was hard, smooth stone, crunching beneath them as
though covered by a thin layer of sand or dried salt blown in upon the
air.

'Daybreak is close!' panted Ellie as they tore across the stone.
Yori had curled himself up within Abetta's lifeless embrace, his eyes
shut tight.

'It has been so for the past hour!' said Url. 'Something hinders it!'

'It's not here yet,' said Crick; the force of his words all but spent.
'We still have time...'

Aliya could think of nothing to say. Words of encouragement
suddenly seemed a waste of breath; all thought and effort turning
instead to the cart. They were so close...

At length tall buildings began to appear from the gloom to their
left: rock and the trunks of old trees, all cracked and twisted and fallen
in chaotically amongst each other. There were gaps through the rubble
all along the long line, but none large or clear enough for the cart.

Never had so short a distance been so far; each step like that of nightmare taking them forward inch by mere tortuous inch no matter how hard they struggled to quicken their pace.

'*It's them*!' cried Orlando.

Aliya turned, still gripping the beam in front of her, and saw Ibriam and Maria several hundred feet behind, sprinting frantically through the opening from the pathway, heading straight towards the buildings rather than following the line of the cart.

'We will meet them on the far side,' called Ellie. 'We are almost at the end,' she added to Aliya. 'Everyone – hard to the left... N–'

But with a blow quicker and stronger than any she had ever known, Aliya's right leg was thrown back suddenly beneath her. She tumbled with a cry of pain to the ground, almost tasting the metallic bitterness of the sting which sprang like wildfire from her thigh up and through to the rest of her body. She heard the others calling out, and someone running back to her...

'*The Pack*!' cried Url. Terror beyond all that of the night so far filled the air as he spoke the word; Aliya fighting to lift her face from the cold ground. 'Ahead!'

Aliya heard her Mother calling her name as she approached, and felt Aulan's big arms suddenly around her, lifting her.

'Wait!' Siu shouted.

'No time,' said Aulan, as close to gruffly as his voices would allow; Aliya already bouncing heavily upon his shoulder as he sprinted back with her towards the cart. The sound of metal striking and scraping quickly along the stone was suddenly all about them.

'Keep low!' Url shouted.

The cart was still moving as Aliya was thrown down beside her Grandmother; a jolt of pain screaming sharp through her leg once more. Only now as she looked did she see the long, thin, scarlet bolt, near-two feet long, which had passed clean through, just beside the bone.

'Is she okay?' asked Orlando.

'Her leg,' said Siu. 'She can't walk, but –' A shriek took her last words; Aliya's heart leaping to her throat...

'*Siu*!' cried Url.

'It missed...' came Siu's weak voice. Aliya saw her Mother briefly as she fell back behind the cart, Ellie helping her to her feet; both of them doing all they could to catch up to the front.

'How close are they?' asked Aliya. Amongst the panic there was no answer, but as the cart began to turn to the left and she leaned painfully from the back, she saw for herself...

Not a mile away, streaming fast around the easternmost ruins of the city, all the figures she had seen thus far only through other eyes were now real and whole before her own. Whatever order there had been amongst the Pack broke now, or at least seemed to break, as it gained sight of the cart: dim leathers and metals racing forwards with terrible speed. Some between them were stationary, raising the sharp outlines of great bows into the air; while from behind tall figures lumbered, slower but no less frightening. And then in the wake of them all Aliya saw those she feared greatest: the most magnificent of all the armours, mounted upon steeds which were suddenly released, charging wildly round the flanks of the others. A wicked howling rose into the sky from somewhere within the city, followed by others; the many sounds all coming together after a moment into a single, long note which raked at the very borders of Aliya's heart, threatening to take the last of her courage.

To the other side of the cart Ibriam and Maria had drawn almost level, aiming for one of the tight passages through the rubble. A mass of stone hid them suddenly from sight as the cart passed around the end of the easternmost building of the range, but before the view behind was gone altogether a flash of movement caught Aliya's eye...

'It's Owin!' she shouted. 'And the others!' They were pouring through the opening, following Ibriam's path towards the buildings far quicker than he or Maria could hope to move, as desperately as they were trying.

Stone turned to planks of smooth, thick wood beneath them; the Pack coming into view once more as the cart lurched left again, round the crumbled corner of the building and into the harbours. Through the rear of the cart Aliya was staring straight at them now: the towering, armoured horses at the front, closing the open ground with every quick breath she took. Bolts continued to rain down around the cart like specks of strengthening rain, one striking the beam above Aliya's head with a heavy thud, another landing just short of the cart, fizzing wildly beside Aulan's ankle. Aulan paid it no thought; all there was of his mind now lost entirely to his efforts, every part of him driving ever forwards with strength outmatching all the others combined while the tiny, curled figure of Yori trembled helplessly before him, clinging to Abetta's arms.

'Where's Alamos?' Crick called.

'Others went round to the west!' came Ibriam's voice calling loud from the distance ahead of them. 'I think he went to cut them off... *Alamos*! It was truly him!' 'We're not going to m–' Aliya tried, but others were shouting above her. Gritting her teeth against the pain and shielding herself from the raging heat of the Heart she crawled through to the front, looking out between Crick and Url onto a low, thick stone wall. Through the bases of great silver pillars which had once stood above it, the topmasts of an enormous vessel several hundred feet away rose tall and grey above all else. From the left, Maria was sprinting towards them from the ruined buildings; her Father labouring behind her.

'The Yinsis?' called Url, turning back to Ellie with a face so lined with dirt and exhaustion that those seemed to be all it was built of. Ellie made an effort at a reply, but all she could manage was a thick, rattling breath of acknowledgement. Aliya glanced quickly back through the cart...

'They're too close!' she shouted to Url. He reeled back, apparently not having noticed her there until now. 'The riders! We're –'

'We can't move this thing any quicker!' Crick spat angrily.

'Just keep your head down!' said Url. 'Look after your brother!'

Even through her fear the dismissal angered her more than she dared express. Being a hindrance rather than a help in this of all moments was too terrible for words.

Ibriam and Maria joined them a second later: Maria pulling at the front with Crick; Ibriam, wheezing furiously, pushing beside Aulan; both heavily singed across face and neck. A pool of blood was welling around and beneath Aliya's leg, still dripping steadily from the spot where the bolt had exited the inside of her thigh.

'*Alamos!*' panted Ibriam again, a smile somehow breaking across the weariness of his face. 'He was incredible!'

'We'll need him again,' said Aliya, nodding back to the Pack. Ibriam didn't turn: instead he looked to her, his smile fading as quickly as it had come.

The front of the cart tilted suddenly away from them; Aliya bracing herself against the corner as they plunged steeply down towards the level of the ships. Flame soared an arm's length above them as the cart picked up speed down the slope; a fountain of crimson sparks raining back upon those at the front from an explosion a few dozen feet further on. The sudden crashing of waves beyond the sea walls was added now to the confusion, and after a moment Aliya all at once saw and smelt and felt the rushing of the water itself: rolling, glowing in the dull light from the east, which was becoming marked with wide blots of pink. But as she looked up into the east itself, Aliya despite all that was happening about her paused, struggling to understand the horizon... Above, and to the north, the sky was as would be expected of it in the minutes before dawn. But in a thick strip between the eastern sea and the sky, curving curiously all the way round to the south, everything was black. A dark, impenetrable ridge of black, as though the stirring sun had forgotten this day to light that part of the sky, or else a thin arm was being held up before a painting...

The sea wall was close on their right as the cart tumbled swiftly over the wooden ground, almost faster than the others could keep up, but up between the thick, silver pillars behind them Aliya saw the first of the riders crashing along the upper level, seconds from the turn. Ibriam saw the look in her eyes, staggering as he turned to look round for himself. He sighed as he turned back to her, scowling at the Heart...

'Say nothing...' he growled quietly, and with a final great push at the cart he turned away again, halting but an instant before limping fast as he could manage back up the slope. Even if Aliya had been able to think of something to say, some way of thanking him, he was already too far back. And never could any words of hers be any match for the greatness of what he did now. He stood no chance against them, the tips of their jagged helms appearing briefly before the rest of their clattering, raging forms. Aulan ignored him, still working frantically at the back of the cart as a wide, horned mass of armour appeared swiftly through the others, bearing down upon Ibriam; the dull tip of a lance being lowered smoothly to chest-height...

'No!' screamed Maria suddenly. '*Father*! *No!*'

'No!' shouted Ellie, catching hold of her as she left the cart. 'He is gone!' Amidst their struggling Aliya saw a swirl of bright silver forming around Ibriam. 'He would not wish you to die with him!'

And with a crack like the snapping of a great tree the silver fog around Ibriam was sent soaring from his arms, throwing the riders, less than twenty feet from him, hard from their horses; the animals themselves rearing and tumbling likewise to the ground. Still Ibriam ran forwards to meet their fury; a haze of silver mists swirling above and all about him. As he disappeared beyond the top of the slope Maria gave a final cry, screaming and weeping and pounding the side of the cart as she returned to Crick's side.

An enormous pier struck out into the sea to the right, the first of several in long rows behind it. The Yinsis was the only ship, moored halfway along, tall and grand as any Aliya had seen painted or had described to her. The ground levelled; the cart swerving right, towards the pier... But from far behind and above them, beyond the bend in the wall, a jet of flame streaked suddenly down across the water. It was thick; slower than the others but somehow all the more remarkable and terrible for it. Aliya lost sight of the sweeping column of fire as it passed beyond the canvas of the cart, but as she leant through the front her eyes found it again, watching desperately as it crashed into and through the helpless flank of the Yinsis. Even as a great ball of flame and splintered wood rose high into the air another streak was fired from the wall, and others of all sizes and speeds on either side. One by one they struck the ship, none missing their target, setting each and every plank and sail of it ablaze, felling masts like kindling and ripping great holes across deck and bow.

But above all this it was Ellie's reaction which caught Aliya's thoughts; the sudden focused rage with which she seemed infused briefly blocking all else from Aliya's mind. As the others cried out and cursed and weakened their effort, Ellie screamed fiercely for them to turn the cart to their left.

'The Aurora!' she cried. 'She is our last hope!'

Through the depths of what had once been the main bulk of the ancient harbours they ran and pushed desperately now; great flames rising high and loud from the Yinsis behind. More structures than could be counted had once stood here: fewer than in the main of the city, but with no easy path amongst them. The cart turned this way and that, Ellie calling frantic directions all the time, while to their left the sound and spray of the sea roared up with each swell of the water like the beating of some great drum through a vast, square opening in the ground, surrounded by a fence of tangled, wooden beams through which there was a sudden wave of movement... Just as Aliya realised what it was a whip of blue lightning flew towards them, striking the fence; a long section of the beams exploding in a shower of sapphire rain.

'They'll cut us off!' shouted Crick.

More lightning came, followed by streaks of the black upon black which had killed Abetta. Aliya couldn't find Owin amongst them but his voice, wild and enraged, echoed down amongst the ruins from the foot of the line of crumbled buildings which formed the far border of the harbours like a high line of rough, rocky hills in the distance. There were at least twenty others with him, all running and leaping down the slope towards the far side of the square, all aiming to meet and block the cart at the corner. There was nothing Aliya could do... The others, gasping and moaning and all but crying out with the effort could go no faster.

A tremendous flash of silver and the high screams of several men came from the distance behind them, but even as the echoes bounced upon the twisted fragments of walls which littered the ground a great roar shook the air ahead: By the time Aliya had turned to look, Alamos was almost upon them, leaping through the last of a series of colossal, fallen pillars. He veered away to meet Owin's men, and as he did so Benamin slid down from his back. He tumbled but picked himself up instantly and without pause was running behind the raging, snarling mass of gold, green and darkest black before Ellie's cry could stop him, sending pulses of thick grey light towards the stunned figures. He glanced only briefly to the cart, waving them on furiously towards another, smaller pier which was appearing before them now a few hundred feet away. Before any of them could stop her, Ellie too was gone, sprinting towards him. The roaring of Alamos and the short-lived screams of those he met first drowned all attempts to call her back, but they heard the last of her reply:

'– Maria! She knows what to do… Do not stop! *Do not* –' She fell sideways to the ground to avoid a crackling spit of lightning, and was lost from view amongst a shattered line of fence.

The Pack were through in force into the harbours now, streaming either side of the wide, open square. Those who took the southern edge became caught in the furious battle between Owin's men and Benamin, Ellie and Alamos; flame and snarls and violent streaks of air and lightning striking out in all directions, rending the skies, shattering stone and wood and all else about them.

A small, final dip took the cart down towards the water, beneath a great stone archway, still whole, built above and between the thick, high walls either side which spanned the entrance to the pier.

'Keep going!' called Maria; the wheels rattling heavily above the thinner beams of the pier, only barely wide enough for the cart. 'It's at – the very end!' Only fear was driving them on now; all strength and energy utterly drained from their bodies.

'*Url*!' Crick shouted.

'Get the Heart on board!' Url answered. He had dropped the reins and come to a halt amidst the archway, his hands spread wide and pressed gently against one side of the walls. Beyond him the Pack were closing: blades and armour and teeth all flashing bright beneath the piercing light of the flames shot through from behind.

A dozen sailboats were tied against the many platforms built out from either side of the pier, but ahead the Aurora appeared: white boards, golden mast and fastened, scarlet sails all sharp and bright despite the curious, lingering gloom; smaller than the Yinsis, still a blazing beacon in the distance to the right, but unlike the others here consisting of a wide, open deck and a flat wooden bridge leading onto it. Suddenly the ground quaked, and from behind them there was a sharp, deep cracking...

'He's brought it down!' cried Orlando...

Aliya turned to see Url sprinting towards them, long hair clinging wet across his face; the archway behind him crumbling from a narrow break at its centre, collapsing in after a second's silence across the entrance to the pier.

'Straight onto it!' Maria ordered. They were a hundred feet from the ship. 'Two of you get the moorings; the rest with me!'

'The dark...' Crick shouted suddenly, no breath left within him to complete the word, pausing a moment before trying again... 'The Darkness! It's...' his voice trailed off. Aliya looked across into the east...

No longer was it a thin line of shadow behind which the horizon was hidden: Before the dawn now stood a great void; a cliff of darkness, reaching from the waves to the clouds and beyond; the very sea itself being cast aside by its power. All pain had gone from Aliya's leg. It was warm, numb, even as she crawled back to Yori's side...

'Yori,' she tried, shaking him; gentle as her desperation allowed. 'Yori... please... *please!*' she begged through desperate tears. 'You need to wake up!' The others were screaming out to Url... 'Yori! You need to hide us! It's here – it's coming! You need to hide us from the Darkness! Please! *Yori!*'

With a sudden crashing they were on the ship. Aliya crawled quickly from the back, watching hopelessly as the others sprinted around her. Ropes were untied, pulled and thrown about the deck; parts of the ship creaking into life... But slowly... too slowly... None of it was going to work: They would never catch a wind quick enough to escape. A flicker of light shone from Yori's eyes: He was awake, staring at her...

'*Url!*' her Father screamed...

At first when Aliya looked the pier seemed empty... but then she saw him: face down, pierced head to toe by a dozen bolts swaying in ghastly rhythm as he squirmed. A cluster of men were standing above the wreckage of the arch, raining fire and bolt towards the boat, striking many of the vessels in between; and then through them came at last the horror Aliya had seen from the lake: Strength and savageness surging from within every rippling muscle of its terrible frame, the beast was unleashed, charging towards them; great wolves leaping through the rubble behind it, howling again as their cruel eyes fixed hungrily upon Url and the boat.

'No!' Crick cried... 'Damn the stars! *Url! No!*'

Maria barked at the others to follow her… But Aliya had seen and heard enough. She knew not what she hoped to achieve, or even what she was doing; but she knew she had to be close to it…

'Hide us!' she begged a final, hopeless time of Yori, and then in blind fury and terror she forced herself, half-crawling, to the far side of the ship.

'Crick!' Maria shouted angrily through the chaos: He was still gazing along the pier, but he was looking now above Url's body…

'It's her…' he whispered, almost to himself.

'*Crick*!' Maria called again, but above her voice there came another sound, a ringing, soft and quiet at first but rising quickly as Aliya listened for it into an awful wail, a sharp scream which seemed to sweep along the pier and envelop the ship in a hot, stifling cocoon. It grew again, and then upon it was added another note, and another; four of them soon screeching terribly through the air, so that within seconds all the group but Aulan were halted or slowed from their work, grimacing against the heavy throb of pain, confused and terrified. Aliya reeled backwards as with a howl of anger her Father swept past her, his arm and hand clasped tight around both ears, dragging Crick away into the riggings which Maria through her agony was still trying to work. Through the blinding, crippling piercing of the screams only the smallest sliver of Aliya's mind was left to her, but it was enough; remembering her course she stumbled sideways, away from the cart, ignoring all else around her as she fought to find the far side of the ship. Neither she nor any of the others knew or realised until she was up above the railings: They screamed to her, but the waves beneath called her all the stronger, drawing her into them… For a second she stared out into the silent deepwaters, and then through noise and misery and fear she fell, weightless for a wonderful instant until with a cold slap she struck the water… gasping, salt burning her eyes and the back of her throat as she thrashed to find the surface. She caught the bolt with her sleeve, wrenching it within her leg, and in her scream was all the pain and terror of the evening… of the whole journey… She tried to find the Magic in the water; tried to control it as she had done before… but all that came were screams – hers, the others; they were all the same now. She needed the water: her life and those of all she loved who still remained were somehow balanced upon it… But in the chaos all thought and control were gone. She could do nothing. Alamos howled a drawn and terrible note amidst a dozen sickening snarls; wood cracking somewhere along the pier. He was dead, or close to it… They all were. The blood red of one of the sails was finally released, falling swiftly into place, but too late… no wind would find them in time... And then in the distance she saw it: another cliff of darkness, or perhaps the far edge of the same, coming this time from the west. She could see them both now, either side of her... They were ten miles out perhaps, quicker than anything she had ever known, bearing down upon the city like the very walls of the world collapsing in upon them. Black Isle would be gone for sure. A rope was cast down beside her, someone calling for her to take it, but as she did so a speck of light appeared from beneath the boat, deep below her... Aliya let the rope run through her hand as another came, and another: clear, bright blue amongst the murk of the sea. Memory flashed within her, the specks becoming brighter and quicker, and with a rapturous sob she knew suddenly what they were...

Waterfaeries burst out through the surface all about her, flitting dazzlingly through her hair and arms. She could feel them probing around her injured leg; their gentle touches causing no pain. Then, as quickly as they had appeared, they vanished back down into the water, gliding out into the sea in all directions. Aliya lost the rope altogether; no breath left within her with which to call after the lights as they disappeared... The ringing wails returned, the cries and flashes of the fight above were with her again as she floated, cold and alone in the water; tears and screaming blinding her, choking her...

But as she cleared and opened her eyes everything beneath her was suddenly alight: Where each one had disappeared a hundred came back now; a perfect shoal of light soaring up through the black towards her, faster all the time, until with the prickling touch of ice wind beneath her Aliya was lifted out from the sea upon a wave of brilliant blue, cast down into her Father's reaching arms, collapsing with him to the deck as the whole ship groaned and twisted violently about them. The tangles of light were everywhere, spinning wildly through the air, filling the sails, taking and deflecting the bolts and flames and streaks of light and darkness which were being rained down upon them from all along the pier and the gaps in the great grey walls behind. Her breathing was quick, but it was as though no air was coming to Aliya's lungs; her vision swimming and fading before her... Yori was kneeling within the cart, his eyes thrown wide and alive with shock; an outstretched hand pressed firm against the Heart, blazing and spitting against the insides of the canvas. Her Father gave a terrible scream, and with the sound her body became utterly weightless, her eyes rolling back irresistibly into the perfect calm of oblivion, seeing nothing but the most perfect blue... Whatever would be now, she gave herself unto without fight. She could do no more...

Chapter Thirty-Nine

Whispers of a Forgotten World

Darkness fell upon the city like a great flood from east and west; shadow upon shadow, form upon monstrous form all coming somehow together into a single being, a sweeping black mountain writhing and crashing amongst itself through sea and furthest sky, maddened by the vanishing of the Heart, swallowing the land in pure tempest unbounded. No thoughts came from it – no reason or emotion; but yet the ancient consciousness which lay buried and protected deep within was there, powerful and filled with single, undiluted purpose as it had been all those many years ago. Beaches, walls, ruins and all else within disappeared beneath the colossal surge of its foundations; distant screams merging with the howling winds which preceded the black cliffs like the very essence of rage unleashed before its master: men, women and beasts, each halted from their fighting just long enough to see their ends approaching; and amongst them all the ghastly wailing of the four – paralysing, terrible beyond words even from so far away, now swallowed with the rest.

But whatever the boy had done, it was working...

Sailing on a wind of azure light, the ship was hidden from that which sought it, drifting slow but unseen into the great uncharted waters of the north, surely the only place left in the world which would now remain free. The black flood would take an age to drain from the land... The world they knew was gone... Azhera was taken once more...

Inconsolable was their grief for the ones they had lost. None of them spoke, even to ask what was to become of them now. They gasped and wept where they had fallen; drenched and bloodied and bruised, barely strength enough left to crawl to each other, or to their dead. Their trust and fate was given wholly now to the myriad water creatures which bore and helped conceal them amongst the waves.

What was to become of them now... A thought so vast and frightening they barely dared contemplate. But in truth, it was simple, whether they accepted it or not: They had left the world behind – but they would find in time a new world now, somewhere beyond the seas. And they would start again. The Heart was still whole, and free, and hidden... That was all that mattered.

If they had only known how desperately the others wanted it back; his former family, awakened now from the slumber forced upon them in the Mountain by his taking of the Heart. They had been so close to retaking it, up on the high plateau, so many days and long miles ago... If they had only surrendered it then, given it back to the Mountain, perhaps none of this would have had to happen; perhaps from that stronghold of light the Darkness would have been held at bay once more...

But the Mountain had not deserved it. Not even now, after all these years, did they deserve the treasure he had stolen – no, not stolen... freed from them. They were not its rightful keepers. Though perhaps they had come to it first, they were never meant to also be the last. The world still had the right to know of Magic; and the Mountain, righteous as they believed themselves to be, would still do all they could to conceal it. It had not been his fault that it had ended so terribly the first time he had tried... not his fault the simple minds of the simple, stupid fools he had come across had not appreciated it as they should have... Perhaps now he could find a people who did... A people of a new world who would love the Heart as he did; who would learn to use it to bring to the world the glory of the Magic that the Mountain still would hold as their own; to sing the eversong of the stars as always it was meant to be heard, not censored and sullied as befit the wishes of those others.

And if not... then perhaps the other had been right in his talk... Power of a god. Yes... If others wouldn't listen by choice, then perhaps they could be made to by force... Or maybe... no, maybe that was still too perilous. He shouldn't risk that happening again... He wouldn't...

He could take the power for himself...

Yes! Yes – he would take the power for himself... He would take the Heart as his own, drawing from it all knowledge and power and

Magic he could... Then he would show them. Then they would see. It was for their own good, whether they would know it or not... Power of a god... None and nothing could take it from him then; and with it he could tell the story as it was meant to be told...

Perhaps these few who had survived with him now would continue still to believe what he had told them; believe that the Mountain no longer hungered for the Heart... Truly a foolish tale. But a tale they had accepted so far, to their eternal misfortune. Perhaps they wouldn't. Either way, he would not risk their getting in his way... Neither White Mountain nor these few frightened souls would he ever let claim the Heart. These mortal creatures and those others now dead had served their purpose, and well enough. But their childlike, artless minds were becoming too attached to it. Not their fault, perhaps... but dangerous nonetheless. Too dangerous. The one amongst them especially; the one who saw further and deeper than most... If he or any of them realised what he planned, they would do all they could to stop him. And he would not let that happen. He would wait until it was safe to do so, of course; but when that moment came...

A gust of wind rippled the torn, melted covering of the cart... The boy was watching...

*

Yori turned from Aulan's gaze, staring down upon the weeping, charred remains of his ruined hand... He had heard everything. Tears welled in his eyes, but he was too afraid to blink them away.

The Heart was hidden; Aulan was right about that. Yori remembered nothing of what he had done; nothing since they had reached the ship... All he knew now was that he was joined to the Heart in such a way that without thought or effort he could conceal it, while about him the minds of the others were clearer and closer than they had ever been. Even Aulan, so long a mystery, was finally revealed to him now, and amongst his plotting he could feel the change in the Heart as well as Yori...

For as though having found new Spring after a long and frozen Winter, the Heart was suddenly full-bloomed; fiercer and more powerful than ever, stirring now with the first murmurings of a strength of Magic not known to the world for so many hundreds of years. Yori could feel himself and all else changing; feel eager strands of new Magics emerging, released at last from their glorious prison, working their way swiftly into the cart, the ship, the others like the great roots of a tree reborn. He recalled the Magics he had witnessed in the city; seeing and hearing and feeling again the skills and powers the people of Iala had possessed. And he thought of all the Magic he had ever known; every marvel ever learned, or used, or created or seen by himself, his family, even the great City and the Council themselves… All of it – each skill, each spell and each long-held secret – all would pale as nothing against what was to come. Everything would be changed by this new power. New beings would be given life; others returned from the darkened existence within which they had been trapped since last the Heart had allowed this much of the power of the stars to flow into the world. The walls of the dam were finally thrown open. Great things and small; wonders and terrors alike; the origins of legends and dreams beyond imagining would all once more roam freely through the seas and skies and lands, if any there were which remained unclaimed by the black flood. Yori could sense the beginnings of their presence alongside his own, though for the moment at least they were little more than ideas; seeds ready at last to erupt into being. It was a rare thing indeed, to be present for and conscious of the sudden turning of the world from one long age to the next; but that indeed was what had just been witnessed, Yori was certain of it… The veil around the Heart had ended: The scale and intricacies of what would be possible now, now that its true power was finally unlocked, he could barely imagine. All that had been shadow would finally be made bright. The first true age of Magic had begun.

But there was one thing which Aulan did not know; one thing he couldn't see… The Heart would never be his alone to control. Amidst his excitement and his plotting he was blind to the fact that while the Heart seemed whole, perfect as ever, there was in truth a part of it, deep within, which had been split open. Through some strange blending of Yori's powers and the closeness of the Darkness, unknown and unknowable in the ancientness of its Magic, the Heart was torn open now to the world in such a way as it had never been before. And the only thing standing between the power which spilled forth from it, and the rest of the world, was Yori. Frightened, wounded, distraught as he was, it was Yori's grip alone on the Heart which was containing it: not a true veil like the last – but a thin cloak, perhaps, held aloft and strong by some deep, aching part of Yori's mind, unable to keep the torrent of Magic from leaving the Heart, but powerful enough to stop it reaching any further than the cloud of waterfaeries around them; the fluttering creatures pulsing with fresh intensity like a cloud of perfect, blue diamonds as they too sensed the new greatness in their midst. With Yori alive, he knew somehow that this cloak would remain as long as he chose it to. Without him, there would be no boundary to the reaches of the Heart. But never would it be to Aulan alone that the power of the stars would pass.

An immense, distant crashing reached Yori through the soft whistling of the wings about him: the last of the city, perhaps – or the last shattered defence of the doomed lives within. Already the various greys and dull yellows of the shore were low and dim upon the horizon, such was the speed with which the ship was being cast softly through the sea. Several thin pillars of smoke, and another far wider and darker which had to be the Yinsis… a screech of red and golden flame, and a final great bursting of silver… then all was gone. Between sea and sky there was now only black. Yori wondered whether he would ever set foot on firm ground again.

Aliya's weeping brought him back to the ship; she had awoken, her sobs all the more heartbreaking for their gentleness, her grief and that of the others shrouded only partly by their horror and disbelief. Yori made no effort to raise himself from drowning in the tide of their pain, knowing without doubt that it would be in vain. Crick was beside her; the bolt he had drawn from their Mother's chest lying loose and terrible across his lap. It had been one of the last to make it to the ship before the waterfaeries had shielded them – but one or ten, it made no difference: It had struck straight to the heart. Only barely had she had time to utter her love for them all before she fell. Their Father was behind them, trembling hands pressed gently to their backs, comforting and being comforted in his silence. He tried to speak; tried to find the words with which to make sense of all that had happened, and what would happen now. But nothing would come. Nothing but a gasp of pain he wished so desperately to hide from the others, but in the rawness of his misery could do nothing to prevent. And there on the deck beyond the end of the cart lay Maria, her fingers still gripping tight around the rope on which she had been working, watching sideways, back towards the vanished shore, mourning her own loss.

The six of them it was, drifting silently into the smoothing surface of the deepwaters of the north; Yori feeling none of the bright, clear dawn revealed to them now behind the Darkness, through the glittering specks of blue which surrounded the golds and scarlets of the ship. His face was set, his one good arm linked tight and still around his knees, but inside he raged and wept with such a storm as even the Darkness itself could not compare, cursing all and everything that had brought them through this path, crying out for the loved ones and homelands he knew he would never see again. His eyes were heavy and reluctant, burning suddenly as he raised them slowly through the tear in the cart…

Blazing with the sudden, cold light of a hundred frozen flames, each a different, icy hue against the cloud of blue behind, the silent gaze of Aulan was still upon him.

* * *

www.ingramcontent.com/pod-product-compliance
Lightning Source LLC
Chambersburg PA
CBHW071337020726
47502CB00001B/125